PEANUTS & EGGCUPS

Sara Mendes da Costa

London | New York

Published by Clink Street Publishing 2016

Copyright © 2016

First edition.

ISBN: 978-1-911110-50-7

For those who guide me
I thank you with all my heart

Acknowledgements

I want to thank the following people for their love, guidance, support, generosity of spirit and encouraging belief throughout this creative journey. Be it large or small, you have all played a significant part during this fundamental time in my life and I will be eternally grateful to each of you.

Richard (Riedy) Riedel – For being such a huge and important part of the journey & for your advice, encouragement, belief and friendship.

Sabrina Blair – For your unwavering enthusiasm and conviction. Let's face it…this is your book.

Derek Price – for making that all-important introduction…and for giving me the heads up!

John Edgeler – for pointing me in just the right direction.

Annette Crossland – A for Authors – for your tremendous love of and belief in this book – and me – and for giving me faith.

Bill Goodall – A for Authors – for your significant help and support through this process, your encouraging feedback and your amazing editing skills.

Gareth Howard, Kate Appleton and Hayley Radford at Clink Street and Authoright for your friendly and effective support and guidance and your first class, professional services and results.

Tash Willmore – Culpepper & Co – for your incredible, beautiful design skills and your heart-warming, sunny disposition.

James Alexander – for your patience, amazing illustrative skills and brilliant humour!

Emma Walton – Clearheaded Communications – for all your wonderful help and advice throughout this journey.

White Glove for your amazing service.

AnnA Rushton – for seeing something in me I wasn't sure was there.

Martine Delamere – for foreseeing the future!

Marianne Craig – for helping me believe and create my path.

The late great Rex Baker – my inspiration for Mr H - for giving me such great material and always making me smile.

Annie Eddison – for being the most fabulous and supportive best friend throughout my journey (and always) and of course for being my Catherine.

Tina Pile – for giving me huge hope…and telling me off when Peanuts & Eggcups kept you up too late!

Lou McGregor-Temple – for your reassuring belief and for sharing the fact you couldn't put this book down.

Alison Bell – for being my oldest, dearest friend in what will be a lifelong friendship and showing me that relationships like Maggie & Catherine's are not only possible…but cherished.

Carolyn Brice/Loder for laughing so hard at one part of the book, I realised I might actually have something here.

Madeleine Lee – for our wonderful times together discussing and dreaming about all things book!

My parents, Reg and Meg Mendes da Costa for always correcting my grammar, for encouraging me to read as a child…and then to write.

My siblings, Sue Nicholls and Simon Mendes da Costa for being brilliant fellow writers with whom I can discuss this insular yet amazingly rewarding creative process.

Jeanne Ayling – for keeping me balanced, in tune, aware and alert and for your treasured love.

My cherished friends and family spirit side – you know why. Thank god for you all.

And finally for my darling Michael for your wonderful patience, humour, support, your constant belief in me …and of course your love.

You're all awesome…and I love you XXX

So, my story started nine months ago with an invitation which had the power to change my life… and not necessarily in a good way.

I was trying to ignore it but my best friend Catherine was having none of it.

'Open it Maggie! Or I'll email everyone at your work and tell them you snogged that guy in your office in the men's toilets at your Christmas party.'

'I didn't!'

'Yes you did, you told me. In fact, scrub that, I'll tell them you had sex.'

I ripped open the envelope, scowling. Best friend indeed.

You have been cordially invited to get completely shedded
in the company of your old friends… and enemies!…
at the Tillmouth Academy school reunion.

Ours wasn't a huge school so a leaving year had been named, and anyone from the fourth year (our year at the time), fifth and sixth years had been invited to come along for the night of a lifetime.

That was all well and good, in principle, but the fact that I was due to walk smack bang into Luke Henderson, love of my life since the age of ten, who had broken my heart (totally) and my hymen (just as effectively) on the same night over ten years previously, before buggering off to university without a word and then moving to Sweden, never to be seen again, had fuelled not only my hatred for him but also my, until then, unknown fear of school reunions.

However, you know, sometimes things happen for a reason.

If you'd have asked me nine months ago whether I believed in fate I'd have answered, only the village one where still, to this day, I clutch my sides giggling helplessly about a particularly hilarious incident involving my mother (not so hilarious for her, it has to be said), a pint of scrumpy and a large drunk dairy cow but, if you asked me now? Well, that might well be a different matter.

Chapter One

It was the morning after the night before and I woke up knowing that the semi- drunken state I was still in from the previous evening would grow into a monster hangover.

Self-loathing ensued. How could I have got so wrecked! (That's a rhetorical question by the way – I knew fine well how) The problem was, today of all days I needed a clear head. Midnight was the decision deadline and soon enough everyone would be on at me to make up my mind about the reunion.

My thoughts went to the previous evening and I groaned mournfully. I decided that in order to alleviate the guilt I would completely blame Pip for making me drink so much. OK, he hadn't forced it down my throat but he hadn't stopped me either; and he knew the pressure I was under! I also blamed the off-licence for being so conveniently on my way home from work to my Clapham flat. I know I could have avoided it but I'd had this overwhelming urge to just 'pop in'. Just to see. It had looked very warm and inviting, almost Christmassy with its fuzzy orange lighting; and the special offers in the window had seemed particularly special. Besides, I'd rationalised as I picked up a couple of 'Buy one get the second half price' bottles of red, I'd need something just in case anyone popped in unannounced (When does that ever happen, Maggie?). And a glass of red wine a day is supposed to be good for you isn't it? I mean *isn't* it?

I'd decided I could just sip a glass, slowly, with the healthy food I'd picked up from the deli for the first day of my detox. It was, in fact, the fourth 'first day' of my detox in the last fortnight and what with the red wine there might be more to come. But, I was going to do my best. I'd also bought some heavy duty ayurvedic tea which, and I had this on good authority, would strip the lining of even the most abused stomach.

Fair enough, the large chocolate bar hadn't been part of the plan but, it was *dark* chocolate and isn't dark chocolate meant to mirror the hormones released when you have sex? Seeing I was currently living in Sex-Drought-

3

Central at number one No-Men-Parade, it was undoubtedly the right purchase to make.

Charlie, the slightly weird, overtly tattooed and alarmingly-pierced guy who ran the offie – sniggeringly labelled by my friends as 'The thinking woman's armpit' – had observed me with what looked like respect, even admiration as it was my fourth visit in a week. He had his pinkie poking inside one of his tunnel earrings and was pulling thoughtfully on it – which made me feel a little queasy if truth be told – and his bloodshot eyes smiled knowingly, as if we were both members of the same clandestine alcoholic association. He actually looked like he might give me a congratulatory thwump on my back any minute.

At one thirty in the morning, I'd had to cover one eye to see my way to the bathroom.

The evening hadn't exactly gone according to plan.

Pip, my adorable, loveable, gay neighbour from the flat downstairs, had accidentally locked himself out of his flat. Not 'the most reliable gay in the village' at the best of times. When I'd walked up the stairs, Pip had been sitting on the floor in our shared hallway outside his front door, merrily eating a Twix and grinning at me in between mouthfuls.

Of course when Pip explained what had happened, it seemed only right that he should come up to my flat while he waited for his boyfriend Andrew, the sensible one, to return home and rescue him. And seeing as I had bought the wine, it seemed only polite to open it and share it with him; he was my neighbour and it was a neighbourly thing to do. And of course, I couldn't really ration Pip so, when we finished the first glass, I poured him another and then, understandably, as *he* drank a second one, it seemed only polite that *I* keep him company and anyway I was now sure it was two glasses, and not one, that the body needed. And then of course when the first bottle was gone it seemed only polite, once again, to open the second bottle. I didn't want him to think I was stingy after all. And besides, by that time, I had decided that it was actually two *bottles* of red that were good for you. Yes *that* was it, I'd remembered at last. And when Andrew scurried in from his office job in the city to collect Pip, it was only right that Pip should pop down to the offie to get another couple of bottles so that Andrew could catch up and we could carry on and I could achieve my red wine optimum daily dose. I would have gone myself, but even through my cloud of alcohol, I really didn't think I could face Charlie, his suggestive pinkie tunnel gestures and knowing looks again.

And then, for some unexplained reason, it had seemed like an excellent idea to play Twister and to drink Tequila shots – courtesy of Andrew – at the same time. Quite difficult when, in my case, my arms were either side of Pip's leg, my face was practically up his bottom and one leg was suspended in mid-air with a plastic daffodil in my sock. Andrew's idea not mine; pah, sensible indeed. Andrew on the other hand was prancing about the front room with a pair of my knickers on his head! My *knickers!!* And not even a good pair! (That might have made things marginally more acceptable) Goodness only knows where he had found them. I really, *really* hoped it hadn't been in the dirty washing pile on the floor of the kitchen.

So that's why I had a hangover. Red wine was bad enough on its own, but was seemingly lethal when mixed with tequila, and not very much food, on account of the fact that by the time we decided we were hungry the pizza place was shut so we only ate cold chicken and salad for one. Whose idea was it to detox anyway?

In the guilt-ridden warmth of my bed, I groaned again as the landline started ringing. I expected calls today but, still, it was very early. I slid out of bed and clutching my stomach I wobbled out of my room to the phone's unexplained position in the middle of the small landing floor. My head spun unhelpfully as I bent over and answered it. There was dark chocolate all over the mouthpiece and to top it all it was my mother calling. Great! Now don't get me wrong, I love my mother, but mixing her with a hangover is one hell of a major owy!

Barbara Parsons: "Mum".

Mum is that nosy, but charming neighbour who always has her ear to other people's walls and her eye behind the twitching net curtains. A great believer in delivering cakes when new people move into the area, she has no scruples about inviting herself in to get their life story, before they've so much as unpacked a teapot.

'Do you know what day it is on Friday?' she began, without so much as a 'hello'.

'Er, Friday?'

'Don't be flippant, Maggie.'

'Mum, it's very early, is something wrong?'

'I'll tell you what's wrong shall I? Friday is your Uncle Henry's birthday.'

'And…?'

'And your father's only gone and invited the lazy so and so to stay for a long weekend. As if I haven't got enough on my plate.'

'Like what?' I sighed, regretting picking up the phone.

'Like Bridge.'

'You don't play Bridge!'

'Yes but I'm thinking about learning. Anyway, there are my coffee mornings, I was contemplating holding one of them on Friday. Ooh... *and...*' she gushed proudly, 'the WI have asked me to do a talk on clothes and makeup for the over six...um fifties'

Oh Lord.

'When?'

'July,' she said defensively, '...but I'll need to prepare!'

'Mum, that's months away, surely you can cater for Uncle Henry for a couple of nights; he is Dad's brother.' I clutched myself protectively and sat down on the three stairs that led down to my little hallway.

'I've been frantically trying to get things moved out of the way so his big fat bottom doesn't knock them over when he walks past.'

'He's not that big, Mum. OK he is but it's not his fault; he's got a thyroid problem.'

'So he *says*,' she scoffed. 'He's bound to break the bed again. He did last time.'

'No, Mum, if I remember, you hadn't fixed the single beds together properly to make them into a double and Uncle Henry fell through the gap in the middle and on to the floor.'

Mum sniggered.

'He was like a beached whale caught in that sheet.'

'How did he get up?' I asked, a vague, fuzzy, memory forming.

'He didn't, not for ages anyway. We found him the next morning fast asleep on the floor between the two beds. We had to ask the man doing the double glazing to help him up. I gave him a bottle of your father's malt as a thank you and said I'd circulate his credentials to the Neighbourhood Watch.'

'Anyway,' she went on, 'I don't know if I told you, but Mrs Banbury swore that their line was being tapped.'

'*What?*' My insides were groaning now.

'She said it was something to do with their oldest, Trevor. Nice boy, very tall, you'd like him.'

'Mum...' I threatened.

'Well anyway, he had one of these radio thingies, you know the ones they have on those big lorries to talk to each other about the latest Yorkie bars and the like.'

Why oh why had I answered the phone?

'Oh, what are they called again? People who use them call police cars cigarettes, and villains, band…, um, Band-Aids I think it is. There was a film about them: SD, SB…?'

'CB?' I offered.

'Yes! CB radio!' she cried.

Suddenly I clicked.

'Mum,' I managed a chuckle, 'you mean Smokey and the Bandit, not cigarettes and Band-Aids. Remember? That old seventies film you liked we used to do that dance to the theme tune when I was little. You fancied Bert Reynolds, him with the hair?'

'You told me it was a toupee!'

'That was the point, Mum. Look never mind what's all this got to do with Mrs Banbury's son Trevor?' I could feel my hangover from hell starting to kick in properly; any vestiges of 'I'm still a bit drunk from last night' were seeping away and leaving room for toxins, gremlins and anxious thoughts of self-loathing. I would never drink again.

'Well,' she lowered her voice conspiratorially and I inadvertently leant into the phone, 'Mrs Banbury swears that the police thought he was up to some illicit drug dealing or something because of him always being on the CB radio and talking in all this code business. Of course he wasn't, he's *such* a nice boy; very tall…'

'Yes, yes, I know that. You've said that already.'

'Have I really? Do you know what, I'm sure it's these hormone pills I've been taking. In fact Mrs Bartholomew was saying…'

'MUM! For goodness sake, Mrs Banbury…?'

'Yes of course, sorry darling… anyway, she swears she saw the Smokey people watching their house in the middle of the night. And every time she picked up the phone, it made a funny clicking sound. So, that just goes to show, you never can be too careful. Even this conversation could be being tapped.'

'Oh Mum', I managed an affectionate giggle, 'what are you like?

'What do you mean?'

'Have you been doing any drugs recently?'

'Well, like I said there are these hormone…'

'No, not them, anything illegal?'

'Maggie! What do you take me for? I don't do anything like that!'

'And no one would think that you might?'

'Of course not! This is a very respectable neighbourhood!'

'Well, in that case, unless you've been stealing from the church fund or have accidentally stumbled across the latest FBI intelligence codes, I think the phone line is safe. Don't you?'

I heard her sigh.

'I suppose so but, still, you never know.' She sounded almost disappointed. 'Anyway,' I tried to seem gracious amidst a strange hot cold sweat thing which

had just crawled across my skin in a toxic wave, 'it's lovely to hear from you but are you just calling to tell me about Uncle Henry and the perils of phone tapping?'

'No, I'm not.'

'Ri-i-ight.' I remained patient. 'So…?'

'This reunion of yours…'

Here we go.

'I assume you'll be dropping in to visit your parents? You remember us? The mother who gave birth to you without drugs and with hardly a murmur and a father who lovingly worked his whole life just so he could put you through a private education?'

One of the problems with going to the reunion was that it was in Tillmouth where my three closest friends and I grew up… and where Mum and Dad still live, still in our old house and I really didn't want to have to drop in the next day with a hangover – not that I'd decided to go you understand… or would ever drink again.

'OK Mum, I get the message but I don't even know if I'm going. Anyway, it hasn't been that long; I saw you a couple of weeks ago.'

'By accident!' she cried. 'Bumping into us in John Lewis certainly doesn't count.'

She had a point.

'I'll make it up to you, Mum, promise.'

Glancing at the clock and realising I was now running late, I finally managed to end the call with promises to get in touch as soon as I'd made my decision; and if I did go but didn't have time for (couldn't face) dropping in, I'd see them at Mr Henderson's birthday party.

My hangover was throbbing through me with a vengeance now and my mind went, unhelpfully, to Luke. I thought about meeting him again after so long and a flash of panic shot through me. I remembered the day Catherine and I had checked the acceptance page on the school website. I'd scanned down the list of acceptees, unsure whether I wanted to see his name or not. I pretended to myself I didn't and also loudly to Catherine – 'God I really hope that arse Luke isn't going!' And then *bam* there it was. *Luke Henderson, sixth year* – accepted. Hell. Gorgeous godlike Luke: six foot of stunning, blue-eyed, long, lean, muscly, hunk. At least he had been when I'd last seen him over ten years previously. He'd been the love of my life and then totally *destroyed* my life.

Would he even recognise me? That's if I went of course.

I pulled a face in the bathroom mirror as I applied mascara with a shaky hand. My otherwise brown eyes were looking distinctly red and my hair was mimicking an overgrown bush. My dark curls had taken on an alarming life of their own and, despite copious amounts of hair serum, it was like I was trying to convince the world that bad 'perms' had come back into fashion.

As I walked along the road, my coat pulled around me against the chilly spring morning, my mobile rang from my bag and I raised my eyes to the sky. Which one would it be now? I fished the phone out and saw it was Catherine.

Picture a five foot four, somewhat dumpy, twenty-seven-year-old virgin, with little round specs, breasts the size of balloons, a heart of gold and the ability to get excited about the smallest things. That's my best mate Catherine.

If she had been a dog, she would have been a chubby little Golden Retriever puppy that strains at the lead and is prone to wetting itself when excited, a fact not that far from the truth actually. A lover and avid follower of anything 'alternative', I was surprised she'd stuck it out as an NHS nurse for so long. Besides that, I couldn't believe they had actually found a uniform to span the circumference of her breasts!

'Morning! Guess what?' she bubbled, excitedly.

'Cat, I'm late for work and I've got the hangover from hell. I really can't talk now.'

'No but you have to listen. This is important,' she said.

This was her third attempt in two days to convince me to go to the school reunion.

'There's no getting out of it now.'

'Go on then.'

'It's fate,' she announced, proudly.

'What is?'

'The reunion, it's in the stars!' she enthused, as if it would cement all decisions on the spot. 'At the very time of the reunion, you're destined to meet a man! It must be a sign, Mags. We have to go or we could be tempting fate! Oh Mags, think of it. It could be him!'

'Him who?!'

I put my hand up to my clammy forehead to check for signs of a convenient temperature to give me a reason to turn back and avoid going to work. There were none.

'"The one" of course! The man of your dreams, your destiny. And I'm going to meet someone special too unless I am already in a relationship, in which case it will get stronger around that time,' she quoted.

'*Please* can we talk about this later, Cat? My head's too woolly to concentrate and I'm going to be so late for work.'

'Promise me you'll decide at work then.'

'I'll try.'

'You can't try! You either do or you don't. There's no in-between, it's impossible,' she said, no doubt citing from her ultimate personal power trilogy *You CAN Build Rome in a Day*.

'OK, OK I'll decide at work. Ring me tonight. Just let me go before I throw up all

over the phone!'

'Fab! You see, the thing is, Mercury, planet of communication, is...'

'Cat!'

'Sorry, sorry, sorry, I'll call you tonight.'

I wondered idly if Catherine had any weird and wonderful visualisations I could use to nuke my suffering, or one of her herbal tinctures that smelled like poo and tasted like rotten vegetables.

As I walked past the butchers, a rather hunky butcher's lad came out of the doorway with a broom and started sweeping water out over the pavement and into the drain having washed the shop floor. I thought I recognised him from the previous Friday night down the pub but he'd not had a shirt on then, so it was difficult to tell. Also, I had an awful feeling he had been on the end of one of my loud drunken 'BAAAAAs' which tend to come out my mouth when I'm drunk (I'm rather proud of my sheep impression) so I hurried on quickly. He, however, gave me a whistle and when I eventually turned back to surreptitiously grin at him, allowing of course a suitable gap so as not to seem too vain, he'd called his mate out and for some reason they seemed to be laughing and pointing at me. Oh no! I'd been right. I would never *ever* drink again.

It was almost twenty past nine by the time I got to work. My boss, Justin, was going to murder me. I got the usual feeling of dread, as I leant on and pushed open one of the heavy glass doors with its big brass handle. I nodded a brief hello to Old Sam the doorman who was sitting reading the paper as usual and, as I whooshed past him, I tried not to breathe in and wondered whether I should mail an anonymous note about his BO.

I quickly climbed the wide spiralling stairs up to the second floor, following the signs saying 'CapiTel' (known to the staff as 'CrapiTel'), London's crème de la crème of telemarketing'.

Thankfully, I wasn't one of those poor unfortunate people who spent all their time on the phone. I had been, when I first joined, but I was doomed from the start. On my first day, I had been close to tears by the time I went on my eleven o'clock break, having had the phone slammed down on me four times. I stuck with it as long as I could but after a while I applied for a job in the sales and marketing department as a trainee account executive; amazingly I got it and after a while made the grade to drop the 'trainee'. It wasn't a particularly challenging role. Lots of office based administration but a small amount of client-facing stuff, which I loved. It may have been pretty boring work most of the time but, I had to admit, it was safe and, right now, safe was good.

I walked gingerly into the main, hi-tech, open-plan office and headed past the hive of activity; row after row of voices chattering and selling. It was like walking through a beehive and constantly being stung. I focussed intently on the floor as I passed through to the next glass-partitioned office, my office, which seemed miles away. I hoped that, by looking down, no one would really notice me. I had already had two doctors' appointments and a mysterious appointment at the hospital, which I 'couldn't really talk about', in the last three weeks.

No such luck.

'Parsons!' A voice boomed down from the second office up ahead, causing people all around me to stop what they were doing.

Justin. *Dracula's cousin*, according to Craig, one of the business development guys.

Justin was a slimy snake. All snidey and slick and in true snakelike fashion, he was always happy to slither up the backsides of senior management at head office, when the need arose.

'This is the third bloody time in a month you have been late. Perhaps you'd like to share your excuse with the whole office.'

Arse.

Justin was about as cold and calculating as they come. There are no two ways about it. Tall and very slim, with dark slicked-back hair, a sleezy stance, and the most piercing steel grey eyes I had ever seen.

He leant against the doorway between the two offices, his chic grey Armani suit mocking my humble Top Shop bargain coat.

'Well?'

'Sorry, Justin, my um mother rang just as I was leaving; family crisis,' I lied, finally reaching him face to face.

'Your mother needs to get herself a bloody watch then doesn't she? Maybe then she'd know not to ring you when you are supposed to be in here at nine o'clock in the bloody morning!'

'Sorry, Justin, I'll tell her.' I squeezed past him, feeling both embarrassed and annoyed at him bringing my mum into things, even if I had started it.

'Make damned sure it doesn't happen again, Parsons, or you and I will be having serious words.' I was aware of him disappearing into his office.

I could feel my face reddening and tears mounting, painfully aware of all the sets of eyes watching me.

Heading for my desk, feeling mortified, I passed Justin's PA Mandy, filing her long pink nails, and sitting on the edge of her desk outside his office, emanating smugness.

Her bleached blond and perfectly groomed puffed-up hair made mine look like it had been let loose on the moors all night. Her skirt was doing an impression of a belt and her boobs appeared to be battling for promotion to the neck area.

She stared at me as I went by, giving me one of her condescending 'I'm better than you, and Justin and I think you're so pathetic' looks, which I reciprocated with a 'yeah, well we all know why, cos you're shagging him' looks back.

Darling Mandy, once friend and confidant to the rest of us, had flipped sides when Justin had flipped her on her backside over the desk one evening. Craig had spied all when he had nipped back in to retrieve his forgotten jacket. From then on, it was 'us and them'. Mandy was consorting with the enemy.

Bill, the admin manager, and Craig were both in and sitting at their computers at our little island of four desks with just Maureen missing. She was probably doing the morning tea run. Her big flowery handbag and shawl were on her chair.

We were in the smaller of the two bright, modern, offices, along with the other admin, business development and marketing staff. It was much quieter than the main one, which was a godsend that morning.

The sun shone in through the large clear windows and on to my desk showing up a layer of dust on my computer screen. Like PC, like flat I thought ruefully.

Once I was settled in, I checked my emails. I was in luck, one from Jenny.

Jenny Henderson, gang member number three and Luke's very beautiful, raven haired, younger sister, was my token petite friend. Not a habit I often make, choosing friends that make me feel like King Kong's sister by comparison. But Jenny was an exception seeing as we had grown up together and she was really very lovely. Actually that was a bit of a lie. She was a sharp-tongued, feisty little hooligan the majority of the time but I still loved her.

She'd emailed a very funny story, currently redoing the rounds, which ended up with a positively obscene photo of a strapping, incredibly well-endowed, naked hunk, leaning against a tree. There was a naked woman sitting at his feet with a big contented cat smile on her face and his penis was level with her nose. I stared wide eyed at the Adonis. His penis was the size of my forearm! And it was flaccid! What would it be like erect?

Jenny had added her comments:

Have you met my new boyfriend, his name's Dick Long and I have fallen in love with him for his caring nature and love of animals. Oh, and his ability to lift me up in the air without using his hands!

Men suck, only not in the right way! What ya up to Magsie and when are you going to decide about the R? Need an answer asap lady, call me soonest.

Think have got cystitis – shit, how???

Men are arseholes, women far better at PR.

Email back. J X

I emailed back:

Does Dick Long have a brother?? If so, give him my number!

Agree, men arseholes, especially bosses. Still not decided on R yet, need more time. Have a good day and drink plenty water and cranberry juice. No antibiotics, Catherine would do her nut!

Mags xxx

Five minutes later the phone rang at my desk, catching me off guard.

'What do you mean "still not decided"?' Jenny barked. 'Err, hell-o-o… deadline tonight.'

'How's your cystitis?' I asked.

'Don't change the subject.'

'Like I said, I haven't made up my mind yet.'

'What's your bloody problem, girl? We'll all be there to hold your hand. I'm gonna go dressed to the nines and show those halfwit blokes that women can wipe the floor with them in business.'

Jenny saw herself as a woman in a bastards' world and thought that by dressing tough and acting tough she'd show her superiority to the male population. I personally didn't think she needed to prove anything. By all accounts she was a first-class businesswoman; known worldwide, she was a PR whizz in the travel industry having worked herself to the bone up through the ranks to the top end of a well-known and well-respected public relations company. Jenny was likely to achieve more by her twenty-eighth birthday than I would in a lifetime. But she was still never completely sure of herself. Her mum, Amelia Henderson, had died in a car crash when she and her brothers had been very young and Jenny had always seemed to have a dreadful insecurity around being rejected and abandoned. I'd wondered many times if this was the root of her issues.

'Look, Jen, I know you mean well but just give me the rest of the day to decide, OK?'

She tutted. 'It had better be a yes. Oh and remember Dad's seventieth is coming up.

You've got to come to that or he'll never forgive you.'

What she really meant was *she'd* never forgive me.

14

'That's a definite, I promise,' I said.

'Good,' she said.

'Good,' I said back.

'Good.' She seemed to want the driving seat.

'Bye then,' I said bravely ending the conversation.

'Bye, later right?' she said starting it up again.

'Later,' I replied, but she'd hung up.

I replaced the receiver once again taking in the alarming photo of the three-legged porn star on my screen. Unfortunately, Justin chose that moment to come up behind me, casting a snakelike shadow across my computer.

'If you're not careful, you and I are going to fall out big time, young lady. Now, you can stop emailing your boyfriend and get these files in order, then my office pronto. I'll give you fifteen minutes,' Justin said aggressively, throwing a load of files on my desk.

'OK. Sorry, Justin, no problem.' I tried desperately to close Jenny's email but it seemed to have locked my computer up and my screensaver was now a twelve-inch penis.

Craig piped up beside me, singing tauntingly in his chirpy cockney accent. You know those annoying little dogs that follow you around sniffing you and then start humping your leg? Meet Craig. He had never, yet, tried to hump my leg, but after the drunken snog in the toilet cubicle at the Christmas party (yes that was him) he'd never stopped hinting at it, only not my leg of course. *I would never ever, ever, drink again.*

'Maggie's gonna get bollocked,' he sang. 'Flipping heck, you look rough.' He peered over the small partition between our desks.

'Shut up, Craig.'

'Emailing your boyfriend eh?'

Chance would be a fine thing!

'Shut up, Craig.'

He shrugged his shiny suited shoulders and carried on playing 'Patience' on his computer.

'I didn't know you had a boyfriend anyway,' he said, slightly sulkily.

Maureen, the wages clerk, arrived from the direction of the kitchen. Her chubby face was slightly sweaty from the hustle and bustle of the tea run. Maureen had a tendency to be a bit of a gossip; a big heart and an even bigger nose, metaphorically speaking.

Despite her being at least twenty years older than me, Maureen and I were close and I tended to confide in her, although sometimes I wasn't always entirely sure how secure my secrets were.

As sweet as she was, one of her unfortunate tendencies was that she collected fluffy creatures and stuck them onto her computer. Every office has a Maureen. They sat there along with two little furry toy kittens, given to her by her best friend Marjory, for being a 'good egg', and a photo of Marjory's son, Maureen's godson, Godfrey.

Maureen was currently going through a stage of having a strange affinity to anything Scottish. Scottish shortbread, men in kilts, haggis, re-runs of *Take The High Road*, even one of our Scottish clients. You name it she was into it. Even though the closest she had ever come to going there was a day trip to Gretna Green with a coach party the previous New Year. She and Marjory had come back armed with Highland fudge (from Gretna Green?), Highland honey (hmmm…) and an array of fluffy creatures with tartan sashes to add to the collection.

'Morning, Maggie; thought you might fancy a cuppa.' Maureen beamed at me, passing me a strong tea with two sugars, my usual morning necessity. Then, after taking a good look at me, she surreptitiously passed me some aspirin from the depths of her handbag. I smiled gratefully.

'So, have you made your mind up yet?' she asked eagerly, settling herself down at her desk and taking her hairbrush out of her bag to brush her 'rather too long for her age' hair. I had confided in Maureen when the invitation had arrived.

I tutted. 'No, not yet.'

Taking a large mouthful of hot tea I swallowed painfully.

'I really don't know what to do for the best,' I admitted.

'Oh but you have to go, Maggie, I'm dying to know how it all turns out. You never know, your Luke could still be the man of your dreams and two childhood sweethearts could end up falling in love all over again; please go,' she pleaded.

'Maybe *he* won't go,' I suggested. 'Besides he's not *my* Luke.'

'I thought you saw his name on a list somewhere.'

'I did. It was on the website. But it could just be a ploy to get people to sign up, you know like they did for the first Band Aid concert.'

'Did they?' she asked, surprised.

'So I heard. Something to do with Bob Geldof convincing bands that other bands had already booked, when they hadn't. Just so the new bands he was pitching would book and then he could convince the original ones to book after all, if you see what I mean; something like that anyway.' My head began pounding.

Maureen looked very confused and I wondered if I'd got my facts right. Sir Bob had always been a bit of a hero of mine.

'Well I'm sure they wouldn't do that for something as important as your school reunion,' she said seriously. 'Anyway, why don't you ask your friend… Julie? Didn't you say they were related?'

'Jenny. She's his sister.'

'There you go then, a perfect spy.'

I shrugged, trying to appear busy hoping she'd change the subject.

'Oh Maggie, go on. Why not?' she asked.

'Why not what?'

'Ask her!'

'Maybe; I'll think about it. I've just got to get this stuff sorted for Justin.'

Craig, having obviously eavesdropped, stuck his head over the partition again.

'She's hiding something, Mo'.' He narrowed his eyes.

Suddenly Maureen, Craig and even Bill, were all staring at me. I blushed heavily.

'Go away all of you!' I shooed.

'Spill!' Craig fired a paper bullet at me through a makeshift peashooter.

'Ouch!'

I frowned and began foraging around for food in my desk drawer, finding a half eaten donut from the previous morning.

'Look, I just don't feel comfy talking to Jenny about Luke, that's all.'

'Why?' They all choroused.

'Oh for goodness sake, she doesn't really know how things were back then, OK?'

I took a bite from the donut and jam oozed out, spilling onto my lap; typical. Craig

looked like he'd just completed a Rubik's Cube.

'I get it! Your bezzy mate doesn't know you shagged her brother, right?'

'Be quiet, Craig.' Maureen passed me a tissue so I could wipe off the spilt jam. After a moment, she put her hand caringly on my arm.

'Is that it though?' she asked.

I tutted.

'Do you think she'd mind?' Bill sat opposite with his trademark green cardigan, and glasses halfway down his nose, sucking away on a Werther's Original from the customary packet on his desk.

I had asked myself the very same question time after time. I felt, at some stage, the whole Luke thing would have to come out and I would be forced to come clean with my petite friend. I didn't relish the idea of that at all. For someone so small, she had rather a large fiery temper.

'What gives with this Luke bloke anyway?' Craig asked dismissively. 'Bet I could show him a thing or two.'

'Craig, it's a girl thing.' Maureen explained. 'It's a very special bond between a girl and the boy she lost her virginity to.'

'Maureen!' I cried, swivelling around quickly to see who else might have heard.

'Ahhh lost your cherry to him did ya? No wonder you're in such a two and eight,' Craig said, knowingly.

Maureen misted over. 'Did you absolutely adore him, Maggie?'

'I guess.'

'What does he look like?'

'I don't know! I haven't seen him for ten years. He's been living in Sweden for the past eight.'

'So, what was he like back then?'

'Kind of a young Brad Pitt I suppose, only better; much better,' I said miserably.

I was immediately transported back to my youth and visions of the young Luke flooded my mind. I got quite breathless just thinking about him, but then reminded myself of how it had ended; bastard.

'Well if he was that scrummy, I don't think you have a choice,' Maureen said, 'and if you don't go, I will!'

'You never know, he might have lost his looks,' Bill suggested.

'Yes, or he might have got even more gorgeous and come along with some stunning girlfriend and then I'd feel sick all evening and not be able to enjoy myself,' I said anxiously.

A voice boomed behind me.

'Maggie! I'm waiting!'

Justin stood tapping his watch in my direction so I left my desk and followed him into his office.

At least we were back on first name terms.

Once inside, I closed the door quietly behind me and sat down ready for a bollocking. About how I'd been late three times, my work was suffering, I looked a mess and my taste in boyfriends was making all the men in the office feel inferior. But it wasn't that at all.

'I have some unfortunate news about Greenwich Finance,' he said curtly.

Greenwich were our main client at the time and to a certain extent my responsibility.

'We won't be working with them anymore.'

'But why?' I was shocked.

'They've found a more suitable company elsewhere,' he spoke without meeting my eye.

'But that's ridiculous. We were doing so well for them and the sales manager said...'

'They're taking their business elsewhere and that's all you need to concern yourself with.'

'But we...'

He faced me. 'Leave it, Maggie!' he snapped then continued more calmly. 'Now, I would appreciate it if you would use your discretion when discussing the matter outside the company, understand?'

'Yes... OK,' I said quietly 'Well I'm very sorry to hear it.' And I was. I'd really enjoyed working with Greenwich. My contacts were a great laugh and I'd even got to take them out to lunch a few times. Justin dealt with the powers that be though, the two main partners.

They were a husband and wife team, Alexander (the Scottish one who Maureen was currently into) and Sandra. They were always on the phone, especially Sandra who seemed to run the show. She was a bit aloof, but really professional and very together. I rather looked up to her if truth be known.

'What shall I do with all the outstanding stuff?' I asked.

'Just tidy up loose ends and don't make any contact with them. Come to me when you're done. If any of them ring, particularly... well any of them, put them through to me immediately OK? Close the door on your way out please, Maggie.'

And that was that, I had been dismissed. I stood up and started to walk to the door but Justin 'ahemmed' to get my attention.

'For goodness sake Maggie, sort yourself out before you do anything else!'

He motioned his eyes downwards and I followed his gaze.

Oh noooo, how embarrassing. How utterly, *utterly* embarrassing! With a flash, I now realised why the lads at the butchers had been laughing and pointing at me! I had only gone and left yesterday's knickers inside my tights and there they were, halfway down my calf for the entire world to see. Great! Could the day get any worse?

Having come back from the toilets to extract my knickers my phone rang again. I turned to check if Justin was watching but, thankfully, his office was empty.

This time it was Pauline; final gang member.

Pauline: vegetarian goal defence and definite 'phone a friend'.

The only one of us married, she lived out in the country with her husband Terry. She'd probably have been up since the crack of dawn, walking the dog and feeding the horses. Pauline was an avid march goer and supporter of anything green. A staunch Green Party member and, whenever a motorway was being carved into a landscape, she'd be the naked one chained to the tree.

'I've had Jenny on the phone,' she said.

'So have I.'

'She's instructed me to convince you to go the reunion.'

'I only spoke to her a little while ago! I told her I'd let her know tonight.'

'I know but, you know Jenny, she wants it all sorted the way she wants it to happen.

She doesn't take "nos" and "laters" very well.'

'I just need a bit more time. Besides, I'm far too hungover to think about drinking all night at the school reunion.'

'Want to talk about the real reasons you're not committing?'

Pauline had always been direct.

'Listen', she went on, 'I know you've got your stuff to deal with and, don't worry, I don't want all the gory details, but the past is the past and this is a good time to put it behind you once and for all. It's been much too long since we all got together. We used to be so close. It'll be a laugh and, besides, I for one need this. I haven't been out properly for ages. I always seem to be forced to stay in and look after the place while Terry's at work until all hours, so please say you'll think about it really hard, Maggie.'

I agreed, feeling a bit guilty as we said our goodbyes.

We used to call ourselves 'the gang', although, really, Catherine and I had been best friends and so had Jenny and Pauline. And we spent as much time in twos as we did in a four. It was true, we'd always been close especially at school, but these days I hardly saw Jenny and Pauline. Life had taken us all off in different directions, especially this last couple of years. Jenny spent most of her time globetrotting or, if not, working all the hours she could and as Pauline was married, I didn't feel as comfortable just calling her up anymore. Besides, I dreaded talking to her husband Terry. I wasn't particularly fond of him and I always seemed to trip over my words whenever we spoke. It *had* been ages though. Perhaps Pauline was right. Maybe it was time to put things behind me; time to get the gang together, for old times' sake.

Despite my earlier resolve though, after work I trudged home with my indecision still intact. All day I'd been toying with the idea that Luke would be taller and broader and more gorgeous than ever and would turn up to the reunion arm in arm with Scarlett Johansson. I was attempting to give the lovely Scarlett acne but it simply wasn't working.

It had turned overcast and grey, and the rain was coming down gently. I felt strangely calm and cleansed walking along, despite my hair turning even more afro on contact with the first drop. It was as if the rain was finally beginning to wash away my hangover. It was a relief to get the day over; in fact, it was a relief to get most days over where work was concerned. I was in the wrong type of job really. Generally, I felt much better if I was on the move. I loved getting out and about and doing things, and quite frankly, working at a desk most days did my head in. It was only my workmates and the client-facing stuff that kept me going. I guess I stuck it out of comfort. All in all, my job was boring and unfulfilling and I really needed to change it, soon anyway. As soon as I had discovered a cure for slight laziness, apathy and perhaps mild alcoholism, which tended to promote the former two.

As I finally placed my key in my front door, I heard the landline start to ring. Honestly, I'd be glad when this day was over.

I took my time getting in thinking that if I went slowly enough, the call would go to answer phone. But it seemed I'd left it on 'answer only' so it didn't. Considering the amount of rings I suspected it would be Catherine.

It was, again.

'So, how was your day?' she asked brightly down the receiver.

'You mean have I decided whether I'm coming or not?'

'Well, yes actually. Have you?'

'No,' I replied.

'Right, I'm coming over. I'll be there in twenty minutes.'

'But…'

'No buts, I'm on my way. I'm hanging up OK?'

There was a pause.

'I said I'm hanging up…'

The threat was a little empty but I conceded wearily.

'All right, but I've still got a bit of a hangover so don't give me a hard time.'

I began to tidy up the remains of the previous night. I spied the mournful pile of dirty laundry still in its position on the floor of the kitchen. I had placed it there the previous morning so I would have to wash it or keep tripping over it all night. That had really worked hadn't it.

And where had the knickers gone from last night's Twister experience? They weren't in the pile. They weren't down the sofa or anywhere in the lounge. They had disappeared! I tried hard to focus on the previous evening in the hope that I might suddenly remember but it wasn't to be. Perhaps it was best to not know? It was a bit worrying if I thought about it. I'd never been entirely convinced about Andrew. I knew he professed his allegiance to the gay community but I had my suspicions. He spoke with the vigour and insistence of someone who was hiding something. My knickers?

Having washed up, I was just about to start hoovering when the doorbell conveniently interrupted.

I buzzed Catherine up and she arrived several minutes later, huffing and puffing her way into the room carrying a suspicious looking carrier bag.

'When are they going to fix the flipping lift?' she moaned, mopping her forehead and cleavage with a tissue and taking off her glasses to give them a wipe.

'How long is a piece of string?' I said noncommittally leading the way into the lounge.

'So, come on, where exactly are you on the reunion then?' she asked, plonking herself down in my armchair clutching the carrier bag which made a loud clinking sound as she did so.

'Ouch!'

She pulled out the corkscrew from beneath her backside and put it on the table.

'I guess you could say I'm going round and round on a rather bumpy playground roundabout, which is making me feel sick,' I replied, taking my usual place on the sofa and grabbing my Snoopy cushion for protection.

'Luke?'

'No.'

'Don't give me that. How long have I known you?' she asked.

'Too long,' I admitted.

'Exactly, so we need to sort this out once and for all and you need to put the past behind you.'

'You sound like Pauline.'

'Do I?' she answered innocently, looking more than a little guilty.

She put down the carrier bag, which clinked again. My suspicions were correct; two bottles of red wine and a large packet of jelly babies for good measure. And, despite my genuine protestations, she ordered me to fetch two glasses, opened one of the bottles with the handy corkscrew and poured me out a glass, which I drank obediently, feeling the vestiges of my hangover finally draining away.

They were both right of course; I knew they were. I had to put the past behind me, but it hurt – a lot. Going back into the past where Luke was concerned was very, very, painful.

Luke was Jenny's older brother. She had two brothers, Luke, and then Tony, who was a year younger than us. Luke had been my one and only true love. He had, quite literally, taken my breath away. I'd utterly worshipped the ground he walked on, and I'd been absolutely blown away when he'd finally asked me out. I'd just finished my fifth year at Tillmouth Academy, and he'd returned from his first year at a university in London. It had been a year where I'd pined for him having secretly been in love with him since I was ten. And now, it was really happening. I was finally going out with Luke Henderson.

It had been the summer holidays and Jenny and Pauline had been away at some summer camp on the Isle of Wight. We had weeks of long, dry, sunny days; blisteringly hot and dusty. But all I had really noticed were my feelings; out of control feelings. Darting one way then the other; overtaking everything. Like nothing I'd ever experienced before. I couldn't eat or sleep or concentrate. Luke was on my mind all the time.

We were both quite shy together and our dates were full of surreptitious glances and grins. We didn't do much; nothing particularly adventurous, just the cinema, maybe the local cafe, or long, lazy walks together talking and laughing and eventually kissing. We'd got on so well, it was like we'd known each other all our lives. I mean we practically had, but it felt so different now. We'd connected. It was like he was feeling and thinking what I was feeling and thinking and we'd end up saying the same things and finishing each other's sentences.

Then, after just three weeks and half a bottle of wine each, we lost our virginity to each other down by the river in Tillmouth; two kids, fumbling about on a picnic rug with a cheap bottle of wine and a condom. Hardly the perfect romantic picture but to me it was; I was in love.

We had lain there together under the stars and held each other. It was wonderful. I wanted to stay with Luke forever, just being together like that; no one else, just us.

But that didn't happen. Things changed. I had no idea why, but they did. One minute we were lying there happy and content and the next, well the next, it was like I was with a whole new person. I was the same but Luke was different.

I remember him sitting up and, quick as a flash, something wasn't right. I'd been lying there watching him and admiring his lovely smooth strong back when I felt the change. It was subtle, but definitely there. I saw his back tense and he looked at his watch, and then that was it. The moment was over, the magic was gone and my life had been altered, in that one brief switch. It was like… well, like he'd got what he wanted and that was enough. He made some excuse about having to get home. Sure he was polite; Luke was always polite. Friendly, polite, funny, intelligent, all of those things, but now he was just polite. I remember it like it was yesterday. He'd seemed in such a hurry to get home. He even started to pull the rug up while I was still lying on it. It was horrid. I thought I must have done something really wrong.

It had been one of the most important moments of my life and I could feel it slipping away from me. I could feel Luke slipping away from me. One minute I'd been a virgin and then, the next, I wasn't. I was a woman but I sure as hell hadn't felt like one.

Luke had been leaving to go back to London a couple of days later and although I didn't know it at the time, that evening would be the last time I'd see him. Certainly for the next ten years.

We'd said goodbye at my parents' gate but he was still acting very weirdly. Things felt so strained. I'd started to say something but ended up getting my words all muddled up. I so wanted him to make firm arrangements to see me again but all he did was promise to write. I willed myself to believe things were OK and that he hadn't suddenly gone off me after having sex with me. I desperately wanted to believe that he loved me like I loved him.

And then he was gone and I was left at the gate. I crept quietly into the house and up to my room. Mum called out and asked if I was OK and if I wanted any supper but I shouted down that I was fine and was having an early night. I needed to be by myself. I felt very alone; more alone than I can ever remember. I had just gone through something that, right then, I didn't feel able to discuss with anyone. Not even Catherine. I'll never forget that feeling.

In the quiet seclusion of my room I was still tingling from the whole experience. I was probably a bit in shock. I had no idea if I'd been any good at sex. Whether Luke had really enjoyed it as he'd said he had. I had no benchmark after all. I wished fervently that we had ended with more of a definite plan to meet up again but, for some reason, it didn't seem that Luke was committing to anything definite. I felt sad at this. In fact, I felt sad overall.

After lying there in the dark for a few hours turning the events of the evening over in my head, I decided to sleep on it and to talk it all over with Catherine in the morning. I felt weird about telling her but I couldn't not. She'd known I was meeting Luke so would be dying to know how it had gone. I felt guiltily thankful that Jenny and Pauline were away. At least I wouldn't have to face them, particularly Jenny. I couldn't even tell her I'd been seeing her brother let alone share with her what had just happened. I just couldn't. It seemed wrong and I wasn't sure she would approve.

Still, if nothing else, I knew Catherine and I would munch our way through a couple of bars of Galaxy and find something to make things all right. Something to make me feel it had all been OK.

Catherine had been shocked, excited, jealous, intrigued, all sorts of things really. We'd done our usual dissection of events and I'd shared most of the experience with her. She'd oohed and ahhed at the nice bits and we'd roared at the funny bits and, it being my first time, there were funny bits.

But there had been something in her expression as she'd listened to my story. Something in the way she'd watched me as I talked. Like she was worried about how I really felt underneath.

I think she must have realised how shell-shocked I was because after a while she looked me straight in the eyes and then reached over and gave me a big hug.

Suddenly I began to cry. I cried and I cried until I was sobbing. It had hit me. Bang, all of a sudden. I was no longer a virgin. I no longer had the safety of innocence. The safety of not knowing, not needing to know what sex was all about. All I was left with was this feeling of incompleteness, and maybe some guilt although I didn't know why. I just wanted Luke. I thought about how lovely, how... *right*, it would have been if he had been there to share things with me. To talk to, to laugh with and to make plans with. But he wasn't. He had gone. He had left me.

Eventually, I'd stopped crying and we'd talked properly about how I really felt. Catherine advised me on how to play it cool and how quickly to respond when Luke wrote to me. She was being kind. I knew she was.

And for a few bearable weeks, I allowed myself to dream that I really was going to see Luke again and start up a relationship with him, travelling to meet him at university in London, and doing what couples do when they are in love. When they have made love together for the first time.

But as the weeks turned into months and the months grew in number, I knew that Luke had no intention of getting back in touch with me. Catherine was lovely about the whole thing and tried to make excuses for him and think of reasons for what had happened. Saying I wasn't to blame myself. I couldn't have known. He probably had too much studying to do. Or maybe he'd forgotten my address? But I knew, as you do when it happens to you, he wasn't going write or phone or come and see me or invite me over. Luke was living his life in the big city, with loads of other girls flocking round him, no doubt. I had obviously misread things. To Luke I was probably just an immature kid and he had simply been after one thing. Although I hoped he had liked me, even a little.

I let the dreaming continue for weeks, then months, and then even years, but he never got back in touch. He never came back from university, not even for the holidays, and I had left Tillmouth to work in London myself by the time he returned home to live there again. After a while, he moved to Sweden where he'd been ever since.

So, that was Luke. That was what happened and that was why things felt so hard to deal with. It was painful, unfinished business.

Catherine and I sat in my lounge in near silence with our wine, twisting and turning our glasses, sipping quietly.

We'd talked about the past and she had tried her best to be supportive and encouraging but after a while she seemed to sense it was best to leave me with my thoughts.

I sat analysing how things had been then and how differently I felt about things now. It was a fine line. I got myself into such a state I felt a migraine coming on. It was probably just the hangover returning but I chose to label it a migraine.

Then, I felt empty. I had temporarily managed to clear my mind of analysis. Thinking had momentarily ceased and I was left in a void.

Suddenly, though, with a flash of decisiveness, I knew. The opportunity of seeing Luke again was simply too much of a pull to avoid. I had to find out why things had turned out like that. Why he had left me. What I'd done.

'OK I'll come,' I said, proudly, smiling at my best friend, knowing how she'd react.

'Yaaaaay! Oh brill! I knew you would, I just knew it. Well actually there was a point where I wondered, but only for a moment.' Catherine got up, unsteadily, from where we were now sitting on the floor and began to dance round the room spilling red wine as she twirled.

'Careful, that's a twenty pound Ikea rug,' I admonished, in mock crossness.

'Sorry!' she said grinning from ear to ear and not looking particularly sorry.

Later on, when Catherine had left and I was clearing up, my computer bleeped out an alert to me. I had a new email – from Jenny.

I imagined her still working away, dedicated as ever to proving her worth in the world.

The email didn't say much, just 'Maggie, see attached'.

I clicked on the attachment that simply read in big letters;

'WELL??????'

I emailed back.

'YES!!!!!'

The wheels were in motion.

As if with a sixth sense, my mother phoned again the following morning.

'You're going then,' she blurted.

'How did you find out!?'

'I can't believe I had to hear it second hand.'

'I only decided last night Mum!'

It seemed my *friends* had been two steps ahead of me all the time.

'Never mind that,' she continued, 'it occurred to me, are you going *with* anyone?'

'Meaning?'

'You know, *with*, with. You see if you are, and if you *do* decide you can spare us a moment on the way back, I'd like to be prepared you know.'

'No, Mum, I'm not going *with*, with, anyone. And I really don't think I'll be popping in, not this time. Sorry.'

'You never know though; you might meet a nice young man at the reunion. Maybe someone special, even your future husband,' she suggested hopefully.

'Has Catherine been talking to you?'

'Horoscopes are not to be knocked you know, Maggie. Mrs Cook swears by them. She and her husband met at Bingo on a night where her horoscope had said she'd meet someone special. Of course it wasn't all plain sailing.'

'Oh?' I hated myself for being even the tiniest bit interested.

'Oh yes. They nearly came to blows on a bogus calling of 'house'. Not a pleasant sight by all accounts.'

'Who is Mrs Cook anyway?'

'Mrs Blatchington-Forster's daily, up at the big house. Lovely woman, so much to say about life.'

The goings on in the Blatchington-Forster's house, no doubt.

'It's worth considering, Maggie, that you might meet a nice rich man who's made his fortune in some wonderful company and who can look after you without you having to lift a finger.'

Mum's dream had always had a rather unhelpful habit of filtering into my life.

'Yes, Mum, you never know. I'll be sure to let you know when I do and, of course, we'll name our first born daughter in your honour.'

'Ooh that would be ni…. Oh, you're doing that awful sarcasm thing again aren't you.

Honestly, Maggie, you get more and more like your father every day.'

Chapter Two

The Friday afternoon before the Saturday night reunion, Catherine and I were round at her flat trying to get her packed. We'd taken the afternoon off for preparation purposes and she was coming round to spend the night at my place.

I loved Catherine's flat. It was warm and homely and smelt of incense sticks and candles, which were dotted around all over the place. Ornate mirrors and chunky photo frames containing prints of her family, friends and in particular her two nieces, adorned the walls, along with pictures in crazy felt tips that they had drawn for her.

The flat was on the third floor of a large Victorian house with high ceilings and sash windows. There were open fireplaces in her bedroom and in the lounge and her furniture was big and squashy. Her favourite chair was next to the lounge fireplace, with a big Indian throw slung over it, and her pile of reference books (her bibles as she called them) were stacked up beside one of the arms, covering various alternative 'ologies' and self-help topics. The ring left from her Cedric the Pig mug was clearly apparent on the weathered, chunky wooden coffee table and the worn, embroidered footstool had permanent imprints of where she rested her feet after her long shifts.

We were in Catherine's bedroom and I was sitting on her patchwork-quilted bed, which was so high up I could swing my legs without touching the floor. I felt like a kid every time I sat on it.

Unfortunately, I was currently witnessing world war three break out because Catherine was in a complete flap. Despite her E plan, F Plan, Weight Watchers, boiled egg and grapefruit diet, Atkins, Shmatkins and anything but thatkins diets she'd been on for the last year, she'd put on weight. In itself, no major deal you could argue but, when you consider that all outfit plans for the reunion had revolved around last year's favourite red party dress, which was now a complete 'no no', things weren't too favourable on the style front.

'What on earth am I going to wear?' she wailed. 'Oh why didn't I try it on sooner?'

'What about something else?' I suggested.

'There *is* nothing else!' She thumbed frantically through her wardrobe, flinging her sequinned Christmas dress on the bed in disgust. 'This is soooo out of fashion.' Another dress followed and landed beside me. 'My little black number no longer black, more like mud grey. Oh God, I wouldn't be seen dead in this.' Another out-of-favour outfit sailed on to the pile.

I pulled what I hoped was a helpful face.

'It's all right for you' she said accusingly, 'you're already sorted. You're going to look fantastic in that dress you bought, all legs and bum and sex and... stuff.'

What could I say? I rather hoped she was right. I'd gone out and blown a whole load of money I didn't have on a stunning little black number. Short, sparkly and clingy in all the right places. Luke wouldn't know what had hit him. Not that he was the reason for buying it, you understand.

'It's no good,' she declared, 'we have to go shopping.'

Catherine plonked herself down on her chair and started putting on her shoes.

'But we haven't got time!' I cried. 'You've got your haircut booked in just over half an hour. That could take ages, and what if they run late? Besides you'll ruin your hair if we rush around all over the place!'

'I don't care. It's a life or death decision. Loads of shops open late; we'll have enough time I know we will. I don't want to be the only one looking like an old trollop in a too tight dress, especially in front of all those beautiful, successful people.'

I went to protest that she couldn't possibly know they would be beautiful or successful but then realised I'd gone through exactly the same thought process before buying my own dress.

'Oh damn; this has ruined everything.' She stood up and began pacing the room frantically. 'Why can't I be more organised? Where's my rescue remedy?'

I passed her the little bottle from her bedside table and sighed. Catherine glanced worriedly at her watch and I softened.

'OK you win. We can whizz round when you've had your hair done but it doesn't give us long. We'll have to hurry.'

She sat back down on the bed, tipped her head back and placed several droplets of remedy on her tongue before taking three deep breaths.

'What if I don't find anything?' she asked fretfully.

'You will and if you don't then mud grey will be making a big comeback tomorrow night.' I giggled.

Catherine didn't giggle back.

Cutz the hair salon, was heaving with women desperate for a quick jooj for their Friday nights out. The glitzy Lavender Hill salon was alive with the hubbub of blow drying, hair washing and chattering, as people swapped small talk and chattered nervously throughout their transformations. Funky music was being pumped out of the speakers and coffee cups and wine glasses clinked as excitement built and tension turned to relief as each client was sprayed and pumped one by one.

I'd never seen it so busy; staff were running about all over the place. One of the juniors was frantically trying to sweep up the hair, which was landing again as soon as she had.

Cutz was *the* place to go and a treat that Catherine and I insisted was worth its weight in gold. I didn't come very often though. I found it too depressing that I could leave the salon feeling like a million dollars with my new sleek blow dry and, within an hour, my curls had bounced themselves back in 'afroness' with a new found gusto.

We sat down in the waiting area on a very low black beanbag sofa with giant armrests and huge squashy cushions.

'I don't know if I'll make it out of this chair alive!' Catherine said worriedly, trying to pull herself up to sit forward on the edge.

The salon was decked out in black, white and chrome, with the odd purple neon light here and there for good measure. The floor was brilliant white and very slippery it seemed as, much to our amusement, yet another turban-headed woman skidded her way to the cutting chairs.

Catherine was soon whisked off to the washbasins and I was left, quite happy to relax, flicking through magazines and drinking coffee while she was being beautified. She'd tried for a Saturday morning appointment but it was another case of having left things to the last minute, so she was stuck with a lucky cancellation on the Friday and would have to restyle it the following evening.

There followed a flurry of water and towel turbans and scissors and snipping and spraying. I watched while rejuvenation happened around me.

As I sat people-watching, my attention fell on a curly haired woman having her hair done with ceramic straighteners. I'd been aware of them of course but never believed they'd actually work on me. Soon though, my eyes were out on stalks and I was mesmerised. All traces of kink and curl had totally disappeared. They were amazing! I *had* to have some. My life, and my unruly, mad bush of dark hair, depended on it. My credit card began to twitch in my pocket.

One hour later Catherine emerged. Her hair looked great. A couple of inches had been chopped off the back leaving it longer at the front and blow-dried into a very chic French bob. She had tucked it behind one ear.

'Do you like it?' she asked eagerly.

'I love it!'

She was clearly very pleased and kept glancing in the mirror behind the till and tossing her head in a 'just stepped out of the salon' type way.

'Joe Riggs is going to fall madly in love with me, I just know it,' she said rather too seriously. An old school heart-throb, and the first boy she'd ever kissed, she had emailed Joe not long ago through Facebook and he'd sent her one back saying he was looking forward to seeing her again at the reunion. Her hopes had gone straight through the ceiling. I rather think she was hoping for a rematch.

'I've just paid over a hundred pounds for some hair straighteners!' I confessed, feeling sickly excited and resisting the urge to whip them out right there and then and give myself the once over.

Once outside, Catherine knew exactly where she wanted to go.

'I refuse to buy anything without a designer label. Who knows who will be there tomorrow and I, for one, am not going to be slagged off by anyone for dressing like an old blob.'

So we headed for Chic – London, the trendiest designer store in Northcote Road. As we entered a couple of bustling assistants looked down their snooty beak-like noses at us, while a third eyed us suspiciously from behind the till. But Catherine was too focussed to care. I cursed the fact that on the rare occasions I ventured into a designer store, I always seemed to look like a refugee.

I followed behind Catherine as she hurried round the store like a mad woman picking up and putting back; picking back up and adding to the pile on my arm (yes, my arm), as the assistants followed closely behind us tidying up the rails and tisking loudly.

Then we were shown to changing room number two, carefully pointed out by assistant number one who insisted that Catherine put a chiffon scarf over her head when trying on the clothes. I wondered how it would make a difference as it was only about a foot long and six inches wide. I tied it round Catherine's neck and she nearly choked to death before she'd even started. But we managed to get it in place by wrapping it loosely round her necklace.

There then followed a wild frenzy of trying on and taking off, which constituted me standing outside the changing room while Catherine, getting hotter and hotter with each outfit change, thrust clothes at me and grabbed clothes from me and kept sending me off to get different sizes, colours and styles. I was sure I had half the shop over my arm at one stage.

The woman in the next cubicle came out and patted me kindly on the arm.

'Don't worry,' she smiled sympathetically, 'I'm sure your friend will find something soon.'

I *wasn't* so sure. Time was tight and things weren't getting any easier.

'Catherine,' I said tentatively to the blue curtain.

Silence.

'Catherine?' I said again, feeling a bit of an idiot.

I heard a muffled sniffle and, sensing movement had stopped in the cubicle, I poked my head in, only to see Catherine in the corner, clothes everywhere, crying quietly and rocking gently. *Houston, we have a problem.*

'Oh God, Maggie, what am I going to do?' she sobbed 'It's all going to be ruined. I'll never find anything now.'

'Hey don't worry, we'll find you something,' I comforted, offering my hand, which she took for me to pull her up. Unfortunately, she was heavier than I'd anticipated and she pulled me back down again and we both ended up in a heap on the floor, which started us off giggling helplessly. At least it had cheered Catherine up.

I led her out and apologised to the assistants that she had received some bad news on her mobile and did they mind retrieving all the clothes in the cubicle. I wondered whether the giggling had sounded anything like crying. It probably hadn't.

It was only when we were halfway down the street, that I realised Catherine still had on her chiffon scarf! Oh well, only the dress, earrings, make-up and shoes to go then!

Catherine began to look very forlorn again. The clock was really against us now.

I tried to think of a solution but couldn't.

What happened next had even me convinced it was 'meant to be'. If I hadn't been there and witnessed it for myself, I wouldn't have believed it.

A guy came past, handing out little red leaflets. I almost ignored him but something made me stick my hand out and accept one. I glanced down at it, reading it half-heartedly, Catherine peering over my shoulder with vague interest.

'PARK AVENUE'

Fabulous New Boutique!
Three floors brimming with high-class fashions, designer labels & end-of-lines.
All shapes and sizes catered for. Knock down prices! Huge selection!
10% discount on presentation of this leaflet.
270 Lavender Hill, Clapham.

Catherine and I exchanged amazed expressions, both checked our watches at the same time and then without a word started running back in the direction of Lavender Hill.

'It's a sign!' Catherine called out breathlessly to me as we raced up Northcote Road past a blur of trendy shops, bars and restaurants, both very red in the face. We cut through some of the more residential roads and finally made it back onto Lavender Hill and finally to Park Avenue.

On arrival, the boutique certainly looked the part but there was a notice in the window apologising that it had to shut early, due to unforeseen circumstances.

'Oh no! It's an omen,' Catherine cried.

She was near to tears again. But we had precisely twenty-five minutes, the place was packed with choice, and we were going to find something for her if it killed me!

Thirty items later, with my arms considerably more muscly than pre shopping trip, a fraught assistant, a tired storeroom girl and a very hot and bothered Catherine all looked decidedly dishevelled in the changing rooms. But at last, Catherine had found what she was searching for. A satin purple dress, which made her skin look pearly white and Botticellian and her boobs appear even more enormous than usual. It was sleeveless with little straps and a heart-shaped neckline. It was gathered in at the front to give an obscene amount of cleavage and snug fitting on the body, with a flowing length and slight bias train. To finish it off, Catherine positioned the shimmering, delicately crocheted shawl around her shoulders.

'It's fantastic!' I exclaimed. 'You look amazing!' Despite the red puffy cheeks, the mascara tear-stained face and a 'hair do' that was now really more of a 'hair don't', she did look lovely. If nothing else, she would cause a stir parading the twins around with her the following night. I could see Catherine making a lot of friends at the reunion.

'I do rather, don't I,' she agreed modestly.

Having stopped for a well-deserved drink, it was getting dusky by the time we reached the car and the streetlights pinged on above us as Catherine started the engine. The roads were quite clear and there was an air of calm about us at last. Catherine glanced at me as she drove.

'Thanks, Mags… for being there for me in my hour of need.'

'All part of the service.'

'As a proper thank you, you could always have the scarf I accidentally stole from Chic, if you like?'

'Thanks, I'll pass,' I said, wiping the windscreen with it.

Chapter Three

I woke early, quickly remembering and panicking about what day it was. I'd had my usual fear-induced dream of being naked in a public place. This time I'd been in the hotel bar at the reunion and everyone had been laughing and pointing at me, chanting 'speech, speech'!

I got out of bed and slid into my slippers. Snuggling into my towelling robe, I headed to the kitchen for some orange juice.

Catherine was still fast asleep on the sofa-bed in the lounge, so I quietly pulled the door to so as not to wake her.

I sat down at my little square kitchen table by the window, which overlooked roofs and chimneys of the buildings below. I lived in a tall old Georgian building, separated into flats. I gazed out at the hazy blue early morning sky, the sun filtering through the chimneys and onto my face. It was a lovely view, tranquil and high above all the stresses of the streets below. But sitting there I felt far from tranquil. Fear was mounting up inside the pit of my stomach; only a few hours until I saw Luke for the first time in over ten years. What would he say? How would he react? How would I react? Would he look the same? What on earth would we talk about? That's if we did talk. The whole thing could turn out to be just plain awful. Right then, sitting in my pyjamas, I felt vulnerable and completely unsure about the whole thing. I wondered if it was too late to change my mind.

Why, after all these years, did he have the power to make me feel like this?

Catherine had reprimanded me when I'd said that to her.

'Luke's not *making* you feel like anything. The only person who can *make* you feel anything is you! You're the only one who can control your feelings,' she'd cited.

That may well have been true, but I still hadn't figured a way to stop falling about like a rag doll at the mere mention of Luke's name.

It was unrealistic really. It had been years. Time had moved on. My life had moved on and so had his. But it was like all my feelings for him were just under the surface. They may have been in a secret place, which I didn't access very often, but the door to that place was so easy to open, it might as well have been permanently ajar. The mention of his name, the smell of his brand of aftershave or just a sighting of someone who looked remotely like him and whoosh, the door opened and the feelings came flooding out. Ten years might as well have been ten minutes.

Perhaps I was worrying over nothing. He probably wouldn't even remember me.

Pah! Who was I kidding? Of course he'd remember me, and it would be embarrassing for both of us. I suppose I'd known I would have to face it someday, and it seemed this was the day.

Then, of course, there was me. The me I was about to show to everyone. The me who hadn't achieved all that much, who hadn't gone to university and hadn't got a degree, who hadn't studied to be a doctor, a lawyer, a scientist or anything like that. I knew for a fact that a lot of people turning up later would have. Oh yes, they would have achieved a great deal more than I had. Tillmouth Academy had been that sort of school. I tried to convince myself it didn't matter but, deep down, it did. I had an OK job I supposed; I'd had worse, but the long and the short of it was I felt like I was selling myself short. As much as I knew I could be a tad lazy at times, and I did generally prefer socialising to working, I actually felt the job was a bit beneath me; inauthentic. Every day I went to work, I was getting deeper and deeper into this quagmire of a job that I didn't like and that didn't like me. Being in the company of nice people made it worse, because the nicer they were and the more fun we had as a team, the less likely I was to leave. It was becoming more and more difficult to leave my comfort zone and I was feeling a distinct lack of respect for myself.

I couldn't remember the last time I had pushed myself, taken a chance on something; felt the fear and done it anyway. If I didn't confront things and make some changes, everything would remain the same; stagnantly, boringly, safe.

I got dressed quietly and went down to the deli where I selected some croissants and Danish pastries for breakfast and a couple of sandwiches for the car journey. Catherine was driving which was good. A sort of thank you for the shopping escapade I think.

I found myself wondering about Luke's life. I knew he'd been living and working in Sweden as an architect, but that was all really. And he didn't even have a Facebook page! So I'd been told…eh hem; moving on. So, what about girlfriends, wives… kids!? Surely Jenny would have said something though. The thing was, Luke rarely came up in conversation and, even when he did it tended to be in the context of his job and how well he was doing.

I'd only had two serious relationships since school. First there was Greg. We had lasted two and a half years, for the most part living in a small rented flat, goodness only knows how! We'd fought a lot and had certainly had our major differences. He was one of those men who insisted that pints shouldn't be drunk by women and that girlfriends should wear short skirts and high-heels and be perfectly turned out at all times, particularly when other lads are around. I was more of a jeans and tee-shirt girl, but Greg could be very persuasive. That was the thing about Greg, whilst he was pretty good looking – he certainly liked to think so – he was always, *always*, trying to change me and that was naff. I hadn't had much self-confidence back then, so I'd complied and hadn't felt very good about myself a lot of the time. However, despite everything, we'd stuck it out together for whatever reasons people stay in relationships that aren't good for them.

Then one day it had happened. I'd been sitting eating toast at the breakfast table and Greg had walked in to the kitchen and just stood there fixing his attention on me. He'd then cleared his throat and calmly said that it was time to move on. And by move on, he had meant go travelling to Thailand, alone!

'Move on? *Move on?* We were meant to be moving on together!' I'd shouted a bit but didn't put up too much of a fight. It wasn't really worth fighting for.

'I need time for me, Maggie, to get in touch with the hunter-gatherer inside me.' I knew I shouldn't have let Catherine lend him that self-discovery book.

Knowing Greg, the only thing he would be hunting would be a Thai bride.

Bloke number two was Rob: a lot safer and kinder than Greg. He just accepted me warts and all. He didn't moan when I left my dirty underwear on his bathroom floor, or forgot to wash the bath out. He never seemed to mind when I burned his best saucepan, or when I accidentally put weed killer on his flowers and 'Feed and Grow' on his weeds.

Rob was just, Rob. He was easy, comfortable and utterly dependable. I could have settled for Rob, I suppose, but despite all his pluses he really was rather dull. And eighteen months after we'd got together it had been my turn to say, 'I'm really sorry Rob, but it's time to move on!' Yes, I honestly did. What a cop-out but it was the only thing I could think of. I wasn't going travelling, but I did 'need time to find myself'. I possibly even said, 'It's not you, it's me'. Poor Rob.

During all that time though Luke had always been at the back of my mind and, despite the way things had ended, I needed to find out the truth. While the reunion was unlikely to bring him back into my life, it would at least bring me the closure I so desperately needed.

When I came to pack later that morning, I almost called the whole thing off though. I'd finally got round to fishing my black stilettos out of the back of the cupboard, squashed, slightly beaten looking and in need of a good polish, and I realised in horror the right heel was hanging off! Memories of a drunken night came flooding back.

Catherine and I had been on one of her work's parties, and let me tell you parties in nurses' quarters are just as wild as the rumours would lead you to believe. Catherine left so drunk I had to half carry her, which was embarrassing as she was wearing a Margaret Thatcher mask and kept hollering at the top of her voice to passers-by that she was the Iron Lady and did they want any ironing done.

Swaying all over the place, Catherine had managed to accidentally push me off the curb and my heel had ended up going down a grate. Unfortunately, the heel had stuck and after all manner of twisting and tugging, we heard a crack and my stiletto came free with the heel hanging off from the sole.

I had a vague memory forming of Catherine lending me her mask so no one would know it was me limping all the way home. I must have come in and thrown them in the back of the cupboard and… *hang on a minute…* I reached in amongst the jumbled up pile of shoes and, sure enough, there were Margaret Thatcher's beady eyes staring at me from the depths of the back of the cupboard. I pulled out the mask and groaned.

'Shit, shit, shit!' I swore loudly, surveying the flapping heel and cursing the Conservative Party.

'What's going on?' Catherine yelled back from the kitchen.

'It's my stiletto!' I wailed, feeling sick.

She came rushing out.

'My mask!' she cried, spotting the Iron Lady, 'I've been wondering where that went.'

'Never mind that, what about my stiletto?'

'Oh Mags, it's ruined!'

My face fell.

'Sorry, that was a bit dramatic. Let me see. She took my lone stiletto and surveyed the damage.

'Maybe it's not as bad as I thought. We'll go to Mr Fixit by the station on the way. He can fix anything and he'll do it while we wait.'

'But it'll never be as strong.'

'It's OK,' Catherine soothed, 'I've got some black insulating tape in the case; we can tape it up for a bit of extra support,'

I was incredulous.

'Why on earth have you brought insulating tape with you?'

She looked perplexed.

'Just in case something like this happens, silly!'

Of course, I should have known.

Having called, for the second time, to make sure Catherine's neighbour was tending properly to her beloved ginger cat Tom, we loaded our cases in the car and finally began our journey to Tillmouth. It was a gorgeous, warm, sunny day and we wound down the windows and turned on the radio.

First stop was Mr Fixit who, thankfully, managed to do a pretty good job of mending my heel, leaving me feeling much happier about things as a result.

Soon, we were on the motorway chatting excitedly and nervously about the evening to come.

As we left the city behind, making way for the greenness of the countryside, the hypnotic effect of the trees and fields whizzing past the windows set me off daydreaming about who we'd meet that evening. Would they be like older versions of the teenagers they used to be, or would they all have changed dramatically? Had I changed that much? My hair would certainly look different.

I glanced over to Catherine as she drove and wondered what thoughts would be going through her head. I knew she had got her hopes up about Joe Riggs. She'd never forgotten the 'wonderful kiss' they'd had and had never forgiven the bleached-blond third year who'd moved up from London, seemingly to work her way through as many boys at Tillmouth Academy as she could, including Joe. At least, being younger than us, she wouldn't be there tonight.

I thought back to *my* first kiss, around the same time as Catherine's actually. There would be no rematch going on there! It had been with Kenny Sykes also in our year and who I'd only practised with in readiness for when Luke declared undying love for me.

Kenny had suctioned himself on to me like a limpet and after a thirty second tongue fighting session during which I hadn't felt anything 'wonderful' or near to it, he had run off noisily flicking his fingers together in the direction of his best mate Elvis who had set us up and who was hiding in the bushes. Not his real name, but something to do with his dad owning a chip shop. Kenny had then turned back to me and called out 'nice tits, Magpie' (my nickname at school) before disappearing into the trees never to be kissed again, ever! I had heard a short while after, at school, that there was a new nickname flying about.

'Magpie' it seemed, had been replaced by 'Suction Pad'!

More and more memories came to mind but Luke managed to keep squeezing his way in again until his face became a permanent fixture in my head. The feeling of butterflies in my stomach was getting stronger and stronger the nearer we got. My chest felt tight inside and I was finding it increasingly difficult to breathe properly. After a while I felt like a prisoner in my own head, so I had to break the silence.

'Cat, I'm so nervous I feel quite ill,' I blurted out.

'About seeing Luke?'

'I know it happened so long ago but I keep playing the scene of seeing him over and over again in my head and it's driving me mad.'

'Couldn't you think of something different, like a tranquil desert island maybe?'

'I tried that one, only the big strapping islander building a mud hut for me, turned round and it was Luke, all covered in mud and wearing a loin cloth.'

'Nice.'

'Exactly! I don't know what the matter with me is. I know that the best thing is to just stop thinking about it and get on with enjoying myself, but it's like I have to put myself through this constant thought process, acting out every possible outcome.'

Back I went, straight into daydream number five, where Luke turned up really drunk and leered at me, spitting as he talked and telling everyone that I was a really easy lay. I'm not sure which was worse, that one or the one where he was the perfect gentleman, all smiles and white teeth, and then just as I thought he was really into me, his stunning wife turned up in a flurry of 'Very Valentino' and a mink stole. The only saving grace was when the crowds turned on her and started spitting, jeering and brandishing animal killer banners around the place. That one actually worked quite well in an odd sort of way.

'I wonder what Joe looks like these days? I must admit I haven't been able to stop thinking about him either.' Catherine said interrupting my thoughts, right after Sophie Potter had walked through my fantasy with a banner reading 'Foxes are for life, not just for Glacier Mints'.

'He's probably married with five kids and a receding hair line,' she continued.

'I bet he's got a dog called Rover and a cat called Fluffy,' I suggested 'and two kids at the local comp.'

'Yes, and he probably works in the local council offices and pushes papers around all day and goes on holiday for two weeks every year to the same campsite in Bognor Regis,' she said giggling.

There was a brief silence.

'I'm not sure he would work for council though,' she said thoughtfully. 'He was far too cool. In fact, I keep imagining him owning a string of Porsche dealerships and being married to his work and having a girl in every port.' Her expression changed and she looked a bit down.

'Surely if he owned Porsche dealerships, he'd have a girl in every showroom,' I pointed out.

'True. In that case, I'll make all the girls work in the garages out back and wear baggy overalls and smell of grease.'

'What are we like?' I said.

'Dumb!'

'I'm glad we're both dumb.'

'I feel as if we are going to a school disco,' Catherine said. 'Heavens, do you think any teachers are going to be there?'

'I doubt it. I can't see Tatty Spud, or Doughnut Dave, boogying the night away with us lot!'

'Why *did* they call him Doughnut Dave?' she asked.

'Something to do with lewd goings on in his father's bakery so I'm told.'

'What about Barmy Brenda with the toupee? Do you think she still wears it?' Catherine asked.

'Not if she's got any sense. Once she put that ridiculous bobble hat on that she used to wear, she looked like a bag lady.'

'Oh, but there is one teacher I wouldn't mind seeing again,' I went on.

We exchanged glances and groaned in unison, '*Gorgeous Graham.*'

Graham James had been our tennis coach and the only decent looking teacher by a long way. All the girls would eye up his brown legs in his short shorts and shout cat calls every time he went past.

'I always wondered why he left so suddenly,' I said, remembering his clandestine disappearance back in the fifth year.

'Didn't he move away? I seem to remember the head saying something at assembly.'

I shrugged. 'There was something strange, it was all very sudden.'

We finally began to recognise our surroundings. It was nice to be in the familiar countryside for a change. It was ages since either of us had been home to Tillmouth.

As we drove through the winding lanes it brought back childhood memory after memory. It was like going back in time, nothing had changed much.

After a while we rounded a very familiar corner into the old estate where we used to play. It was still a fairly modern group of houses with a parade of shops. Kids hung around and smoked on corners and sat on bar gates, which marked the beginnings of alleyways and wooded walks. We'd done exactly the same thing all those years ago although Catherine and I had only had the odd puff of a cigarette and had usually coughed it back up again. We had been so cool.

My parents lived slightly out of the village but Catherine's parents lived fairly close by, just on the outskirts of the estate in a little cottage. They were currently away for two weeks in the Lake District but we drove up the familiar narrow lane and stopped outside her old house. It was a small, detached cottage with a thatched roof and rosebushes adorning the front garden. Fields stretched out behind it as far as the eye could see and, at the front, there was a little garden gate in the middle of a low higgledy-piggledy stone wall. We got out the car, walked up the path and peered in the window, breathing in the familiar scent of the lavender bushes either side of the front door.

The grass was neatly mown and the pretty wooden bird table was stacked up with nuts and seeds as always. I felt a gnawing of homesickness in my stomach.

'Does it feel good being back?' I asked her as we slid back in to the warm seats of the car.

'It feels odd,' she admitted, pulling the car away slowly.

'Home sweet home,' I sighed looking out onto the streets, which seemed so small.

I was strangely calm as we headed back through the little estate, out through the parade and back on to the main street. The sun beat down on the car and songs for sunny days drifted out from the radio.

We drove over the little bridge at the end which crossed the picture-perfect twinkling brook, flanked by the greenest reeds and rushing fast over stones and rocks, after some recent days of rain.

The roads were swept clean as usual and the hedgerows were being trimmed back by a young lad with loud humming hedge trimmers that buzzed in my ears as we went past. The verges were edged with flowers. Everything was just the same as always.

We reached the hotel just after half past three, drove up the gravel drive and parked up in the car park at the front. The hotel was quite large and while the main front wasn't huge, there was a single-storey extension cleverly added to one side and what looked like another wing to the rear.

Getting out of the car we carefully retrieved our dresses on their hangers from the back seat then hauled our cases out of the boot (you'd never have thought we were only away for one night). We made our way across the gravelled drive to the big oak front door. Our footsteps crunched beneath us as we walked. Pretty hanging baskets were either side the large entrance and the whitewashed walls shone out in the sunlight. The front steps were old and worn down from all the visitors over the years. The flowerbeds at the front were full of brightly coloured flowers. It really was very pretty.

Inside, the reception area was quiet and, despite the warmth outside, felt cool with its stone floors and staircase. I could smell the wood that adorned the walls in deep wooden panels. Various leather chairs were dotted about adding to its stately appearance and in a small seating area, along from the reception desk, a couple of old gents sat and sipped their ale and read the paper next to a large fireplace. We signed in, feeling very grown up. I could see the main bar through some open double doors and my stomach did a somersault as I thought of the evening to come.

A young, dark haired, Latino-looking porter took our cases. Catherine and I raised eyebrows at each other and admired his bum while he took our bags up the stairs.

Jenny and Pauline were due to meet us around six in the lounge bar for a mini reunion of our own. This meant Catherine and I had a couple of hours to get ready. It was pushing it, but we'd do our best.

Ordering some tea and cakes from room service to line our stomachs, we settled ourselves in our comfy bright twin room and began in earnest the grand task of preparing ourselves.

For the next two hours we showered, scrubbed, shaved, buffed, oiled, and painted until we were glowing from head to toe.

Sitting round in fluffy white towelling robes, we started to apply our make-up, and with vodkas from the mini bar on the go, we both felt confident enough to go a bit more over the top than usual. Catherine added lots of purple glitter shadow and a lovely purple tinted lip gloss and I ringed my eyes with a rich dark kohl pencil and three coats of black mascara before adding a striking scarlet lipstick.

I helped Catherine restyle her hair, which didn't take too long at all and then I dried mine off with a hairdryer so we could begin the task of straightening it. My hand shook with anticipation as I plugged my new straighteners in. I felt like my life was about to change.

Half an hour later, after carefully going over each section of hair layer by layer, we sat back and surveyed our efforts.

'Wow!' Catherine whistled. 'It's like you're… a different person!'

'I don't know if that's a compliment or not.'

'Sorry, you know what I mean though. You just look amazing. I'd probably walk past you in the street!' Cat exclaimed as I tossed my hair for umpteenth time at my reflection.

'Maybe I can spy on Luke without him knowing who I am.'

'You'll be fine, Mags. Sometimes I don't think you realise how attractive you are. You'll knock him dead looking like that!'

'I think I might knock him dead anyway, after the way he treated me.'

She narrowed her eyes quizzically to see how serious I was.

'By the way, while I remember…' she began, 'did you ever confess to Jenny and Pauline about you and Luke… you know… back then?'

'No!' I howled. 'And you mustn't say anything to them, particularly Jen!'

'But why? She won't mind. It's all history now. Besides, she knew you fancied him.'

'How?'

'Because you used to shake every time he came near you, get your words all muddled up and your eyes went all dewy!'

'They didn't!'

Catherine started humming *Love Story*. I sighed.

'Anyway, I can't tell her, not now. It's been too long. It felt bad enough and weird enough when we were teenagers but if she finds out now I sneakily went out with her brother while she and Pauline were at summer camp, she'll feel really put out.

'I suppose… but don't you think she might feel worse if you don't tell her? She doesn't bite you know.'

I raised a quizzical eyebrow and Catherine's face gave in.

'OK fair enough… she does but it's more of a bark really and quite yappy if you think about it.'

'Forgive me for not taking my chances on being yapped at, barked at, bitten or worse thank you very much.'

Donning my sparkly black dress, I was more than a little worried that it seemed shorter than I remembered and my stilettos looked a little askew with one heel now covered in insulating tape. But once I had added my diamante earrings, necklace and bracelet, I had to admit the finished effect was pretty striking.

Catherine had replaced her usual round specs with contact lenses and, standing beside me, she looked fabulous in her new dress but, to be honest, I didn't think people would really notice her dress. Her boobs were like two giant milky white space hoppers and even I had a job to stop myself staring at them. At least she'd have somewhere to balance her drink; come to that, so would half the people there.

We stood with our hearts in our mouths, admiring ourselves in the long mirror.

'How do you feel?' I asked.

'Don't ask!' Catherine pulled a face at me from the reflection.

We gave each other a good luck hug, then clutching our evening bags and giving ourselves a final once-over in the mirror, we headed for the door.

The lounge bar was quiet. Six o'clock was that in-between stage when most people were up in their rooms getting ready for the evening. There were a few people milling around, some scanning bar menus and a small group of elderly folk in the far right hand corner.

It was a big old room with high ceilings, walled with wooden panelling. Red swirling carpet covered the floor. The large windows had crimson velvet curtains and matching velvet cushioned window seats. Low dark gleaming wood tables were dotted about with little stools and chairs set around them, covered in a rich, red velvet or leather.

Behind the long bar there were masses of different bottles on the wall against lighted mirrors. The bar itself shone out in deep mahogany and was laden with little bowls of olives and peanuts. There were ice buckets and shiny black jugs of water. The barman was busy polishing glasses and making sure everything was in order.

No sign of the others at this stage but we ordered up a bottle of Pinot Grigio and four glasses, pre-empting their arrival, and headed for a low table by the big middle window, which overlooked the drive and the array of flowerbeds at the front. I sat down nervously, my heart in my mouth. Luke Henderson could come through the door at any minute. I took a few sips from my wine and relaxed a little. It was still early. He wouldn't be around yet, surely. The reunion wasn't due to start until seven thirty and we could see through some double doors at the end of the bar that the main function room was alive with waiters and kitchen staff buzzing around laying tables and checking centre pieces.

Catherine and her space hoppers were clearly concerned.

'I'd forgotten we'd have to sit down for dinner!'

That got me alarmed. 'What if there's a seating plan which puts us on separate tables?'

'Don't worry, when Jenny emailed our acceptance she said that the four of us had to sit together or we wouldn't be coming.'

Suddenly, as if on cue, we looked up and saw Jenny doing a mad head-banging dance in the doorway, with Pauline standing behind her rolling her eyes to the ceiling.

If Jenny was here, did that mean Luke was with her?

She bounced over to us, followed closely by Pauline who smiled apologetically.

'Sorry, ladies, I forgot to bring her leash. It could be a long night.' Jenny's hair was a dark mass of newly head-banged sexiness.

Standing up to greet them both, we hugged warmly. I was so glad I'd come now. It was great to see them both.

I found myself peering through the doorway mid hug, just in case, but it seemed it was just the two of them.

Jenny plonked herself on the seat beside mine and immediately poured out another two glasses.

'Cool dress, Mags. Loving the hair!' she whistled with approval as I settled back into my seat.

'You look like a different person,' Pauline echoed Catherine, 'like a film star!'

I began thinking of all the years I'd wasted looking like a Rastafarian bush. God was most definitely a man.

'Jenny's been making me feel sick with all her head banging. I swear I am going to need to apply for a permit for that girl,' Pauline said.

'It's not my fault I have bags of energy. Besides I need it to jump up to people so they can see me!' she laughed loudly.

I reluctantly eyed her up and down. 'I don't think you need to jump up at all, Jen, people would notice you if you crawled along the floor in a sack.' She looked fantastic. Long dark messily layered hair, a full sexy mouth and large inky blue eyes glinting with mischief. Lookswise Jenny was a complete contrast to Luke. She wore a gorgeous emerald green mini dress and her legs were tanned and smooth. She was just like a model, only not a very tall one.

Unlike Jenny, Pauline's appearance was pretty plain. She'd dressed quite smartly in a trouser suit but it didn't appear particularly new and her hair, which she wore short, didn't have much style to it. Still, she'd stuck on a hint of mascara and lip gloss which was rare for her. I supposed she was normally in wellies and covered in mud with her only audience being the horses and Ralfie her Great Dane. I wondered idly if she and Terry still had sex.

'How's Terry?' I asked.

'Bloody hell, Mags, I'm here to enjoy myself! I certainly don't want to talk about Terry. In fact, I want to talk about anything but!' She laughed but looked like she meant it. Maybe they weren't having sex.

We caught up on each other's lives. Jenny's seemed to be the most exciting. She proceeded to tell us all about her job and her travelling and how, having been recently promoted, she was being called all over the world to cover stories on the rich and famous.

'I was in Marbella last month,' she said. 'Had to represent this shipping guy and get him some decent publicity deals. Carlos his name is. Shedloads of dosh. He's launching a new fleet of motor cruisers in a few weeks and wanted the top moguls to know he means business. He doesn't really need my help. The press are all over him anyway. Everyone on the Costa knows him. He's always throwing parties and charity events and donates obscene amounts of money to charities every year; pretty decent bloke actually.'

'Is he married?' Catherine piped up hopefully.

'Nope, not as far as I know but he's pretty ancient. Mind you, if you fancy trying your luck, Cat, he'll probably pop his clogs soon, and you'd end up getting the lot.'

'It's a thought,' Catherine replied, pensively.

More people arrived in the bar, younger people, some about our age and we all checked to see if we recognised anyone. We didn't.

Pauline was dying to meet up with her old friends from her school tennis class. She had been a heck of an acer back at school and the captain of the tennis club.

Which reminded me.

'Pauline, you'll know… whatever happened to Gorgeous Graham? He was your coach wasn't he? Remember he left really suddenly? I'm sure there was something going on there.'

I seemed to catch her off guard and she appeared a bit unsettled.

'Um not sure, moved away I think,' she replied.

'I fancied the pants off Gorgeous Graham!' Catherine said.

I think we *all* did,' Jenny added with a chuckle.

I thought back. 'I wonder why he left like that though.'

'Family reasons I think, not sure.' Pauline poured out a second glass.

'Oh.' I was disappointed. 'I was sure if anyone would know it would be you. Don't you know, Jen?'

'Don't ask me, I know nothing,' she grinned, though her face said she did.

'Why the interest anyway?' Pauline asked. 'He probably had very ordinary reasons for leaving.'

Jenny, taking a mouthful out of her wine nearly spat it out again. 'Yeah right,' she coughed.

'What's up, why are you laughing?' I asked.

'Me, laughing, no, I'm not laughing. Everything's fine. Isn't it Pauline?' Pauline shot her a look that I couldn't read and then turned to me.

'I'm just saying it was probably just something and nothing, you know how these things get blown up out of all proportion,' she continued.

'Oh for goodness sake, tell them will you?' Jenny said, leaning across and cuddling Pauline with her spare miniature arm.

Pauline looked uncomfortable and Catherine and I exchanged glances.

'What? What?' Catherine cried.

'Nothing, it's nothing, shut up, Jenny.'

'Go on tell 'em, Paul'. I would if I were in your shoes.'

Jenny pulled a 'pleeeease' face.

After a bit of an awkward silence Pauline tutted.

'All right, you tell them, but no snide comments,' she conceded, reluctantly.

Jenny cleared her throat and leant in close to the middle of the table. Catherine and I did the same.

'Gorgeous Graham didn't leave for family reasons.' She bent in even closer. And when Catherine's and my eyes were open about as wide as they could be, she leant back in her seat and said rather too loudly, 'Gorgeous and utterly naughty Graham was having it away with our Pauline!' With that she reached out her arm sideways and thwacked Pauline on the back.

'What?' Catherine shrieked, 'You're joking!'

'Nope. Our cool, sweet, vegetarian Pauline was seduced completely and utterly by Mr Lurv God James and turned into a meat eater overnight!'

'Jenny!' Pauline hit her on the arm, 'It wasn't like that!'

'Yeah it was, don't lie.'

'Oh my God, I don't believe it!' Catherine said, her jaw almost reaching the floor.

'So what happened?' I asked.

'They got found out, eh, Pauline,' Jenny said.

'And how!' Pauline admitted.

'But how come we never knew about it?' I was completely perplexed that one of my closest friends had got off with a teacher and no one had told *me*.

'I was sworn to secrecy. Jenny only knew because, in the end, I had to tell someone and even then she had to prise it out of me when she caught me in floods of tears one evening.'

'Come on then, tell us *everything*! We need details! What happened, where, for how long?' Catherine demanded.

Pauline took several gulps from her wine.

'OK, you know I had coaching with him?' she started.

Jenny sneered. 'Oh yeah; we know, we know… sorry, carry on.'

'Well, one day after school, in July it must have been, just before we broke up for summer holidays at the end of the fourth year, he was coaching me on my back stroke. It was only him and me in the indoor tennis hall and he came up and showed me how I needed to stand in order to play the best shot. He stood behind me and put his arms around me and held my wrists and placed my right arm across my body to show me what was what. It was at that point that his groin accidentally pressed up against my bum and there was no mistaking what stroke he was keen to play!'

'No,' Catherine and I said together.

'Yep. A large and very erect hard-on was pressing into my back.' She smiled at our expressions.

'Oh my God, what did you do?' I asked.

'I know what I would have done all right!' Jenny said.

'I flinched actually,' Pauline went on, 'and then couldn't move. I guess he must have realised I'd noticed, because he straightened up and slowly turned me towards him.'

'This is too much!' Catherine cried excitedly. 'Then what? Did he kiss you?'

Pauline nodded.

'I remember it like it was yesterday. He took the racket out of my hand, bent down and carefully put it on the floor. Then he stood up again and stared straight into my eyes. I remember thinking what a fantastic colour they were, amber and gold. He had really long eyelashes too.'

'You lucky mare!' Jenny said.

'Don't stop her flow! What happened next? Catherine urged.

'He kissed me really gently,' she said staring into space, looking almost puzzled.

'Wow!' Catherine and I said together.

'Did you kiss him back?' I asked.

'Well yes, I kind of felt I had to really,' she said.

'Had to…? HAD TO?' Catherine shrieked, 'I'd have bloomin' well had his trousers off given half the chance.

'Ah, the voice of experience,' Jenny said dryly. Catherine glared at her. They'd always had a bit of a jibey relationship.

'He was very handsome, I'll give you that,' Pauline acknowledged.

'I can't believe you!' Jenny said. 'We are talking Gorgeous Graham here; the only dishy guy in the whole school. Jeez woman, what gives with you?'

'Been married too long probably.' She smiled.

'OK, so you're alone in the tennis hall and he's kissing you, what then?' I asked.

'Well, we snogged for quite a while and then, without saying anything, he walked over and locked the main door. Then he came back and led me through to the girls' locker rooms where he just stood there looking at me. It was a bit unnerving at the time. I was really conscious of the fact that he was a couple of inches shorter than me. Anyway, he reached forward and started taking off my tennis kit! I remember he was like a little boy, all eager and desperate and he kept fumbling about with my buttons.'

'You must have fancied him, surely?' Catherine asked.

'Kind of.'

'God I sooo did! If he'd have come on to me, I wouldn't have been able to wait until the locker rooms!'

'There speaks a woman of the world,' Jenny said sarcastically.

Catherine's expression went from hurt to defensive.

'Just because I haven't had loads of men like *some* people,' she said pointedly, 'doesn't mean I wouldn't have had a bit of a kiss and a cuddle.'

Jenny laughed.

'Oooh, you're such a hussy!'

'Stop it you two. *Anyway…*' Pauline went on, 'we started off on the benches and then ended up on the floor!'

'Gosh, multiple positions, it sounds amazing!' Catherine shrieked.

'I suppose it wasn't bad for a first time, weird, but OK.'

'So, it was your first time then,' I said.

'Yes. That's what made it so weird I suppose. I mean I had no idea what to expect, or how I was supposed to feel. I had nothing to compare it with, so I didn't really know if it had been good or not.'

With a flash I thought back to my first time and knew exactly what she meant.

'What happened afterwards?' I asked

'Well, we straightened ourselves up and then it was all a bit awkward. He actually apologised for his behaviour, which I thought was odd. I mean, surely if he had been sorry, he would have stopped.' She shrugged. 'He said he couldn't help himself and that he had been attracted to me for, get this, almost two years! Can you imagine anyone fancying me at the beginning of the third year?'

'Yes, of course!' Jenny stuck up for her.

'Well I couldn't.' Pauline said 'I thought there must have been something wrong with him. I was tall, skinny and gawky!'

'Did you see him again?' Catherine asked.

'Yes, he was really keen; insisted on a repeat performance the following week, and the one after. Honestly, my tennis really suffered with all that going on. I was a bit miffed actually.'

The rest of us shot each other confused glances.

'When we broke up from school I didn't think we'd see each other again until term time and I assumed that was it. You know, us finished. I wasn't really that bothered to tell you the truth, only that obviously wasn't his plan.

Just before school was out, he cornered me in the playground. Said he wanted to meet me over the holidays. He was really insistent. I wasn't sure really but I said yes. I felt like I had to in a way, he was very persuasive.'

'What do you mean?' Jenny frowned.

'You know, him being a teacher and all that. I just felt like I should do what he told me to.'

'You never said that before! That's fucking terrible!' Jen said angrily. 'Did he force you?'

'No, no, nothing like that, it was me. It was just how I was at the time, that's all. He was a very nice guy. I liked him, as a person. I just didn't know...' she shrugged, looking pensive, '... I didn't know what I was doing. I suppose I was pretty much out of my depth.'

Catherine urged her on again. 'So what happened? How did you meet up?'

'He picked me up in his car a couple of times and we drove down to the old railway line. It was pretty cramped in the back of his car but we managed.'

'Was he good?' Jen asked.

'I suppose so.'

'How big was it?' Jen went on.

'Jen! For heaven's sake, I don't know, big probably, I can't really remember.'

'God, I'll never forget my first one! Huge great fucker it was!' she scoffed.

Catherine became more subdued.

'Did he use a condom?' she asked Pauline, quietly.

'Yes, he had to. I mean, can you imagine if I'd got pregnant?'

'Tell them about the last time you met,' Jenny insisted.

'OK. Well, it got very risky, being out and all that. Our break, if you can call it that, was when his wife went off to visit her friend in Milton Keynes for a long weekend and...'

'His WIFE!' Catherine and I shrieked.

Catherine was clearly shocked. 'He was *married*?'

'Er... yes. Not something I feel particularly proud about,' Pauline admitted. 'He said she didn't understand him and I just accepted it. Can you believe that? Oh the naivety of the young.'

'Forget that, tell 'em what happened,' Jenny urged.

'Like I said, she went off to see her friend because she wasn't well and needed her help. That was when Graham suggested going to his and staying with him while she was away.'

Jenny smirked. 'Get her! "*Graham*" eh?'

'Bloody hell!' Catherine swore, uncharacteristically.

'I told my parents I was staying at a friend's. They were pretty cool about things like that, they never checked up or anything. As far as they were concerned I was a model daughter. So, I stayed round at his place for a couple of nights and we got on really well. We ordered in pizza and talked and drank wine. That was the best bit really, the conversations. It was good to talk to a real adult, on a level, you know? But, it all went a bit pear-shaped.'

'Why?' I asked.

'His wife came back early, without warning, a day early to be precise and caught us in their bed! Talk about being caught in the act. It was pretty horrific. She was so angry standing there in the bedroom doorway and shouting and screaming, steam coming off her.'

'No! What did you do?' I asked.

'I just lay there. It was kinda disappointing because in the presence of his wife, Graham became pretty pathetic, begging her not to worry and saying he really loved her, which was a bit of a kick in the teeth for me at the time. She kept yelling about me *and* other women! In fact, I got the distinct impression she'd come back early thinking she might catch him up to something. I was just stuck there wondering what the hell to do, with the covers up to my face.'

'Wasn't his wife one of the school governors?' Jenny asked, thoughtfully.

'Yes, she was.' Pauline laughed. 'And I can remember wondering if her catching us would affect my exam results! She looked pretty menacing standing there screaming, I can tell you. She was a pretty big woman.'

'When she finally decided to deal with me she threw my clothes at me and ordered me out of her house; calling me a bitch and a whore and a filthy little slut, that sort of stuff. I got dressed really quickly and dodged past her in the doorway. It was awful. I couldn't meet her eyes. I felt really shitty, like I'd mucked up their lives. I know he'd made the running but I still felt like I should have known better.'

'You were only a kid for god's sake,' Jenny said.

'Did anyone find out?' Catherine asked, knocking back her drink, topping us all up and emptying the bottle.

'She told my Mum and Dad. I didn't think she would, I thought she'd be too embarrassed, but she wasn't. She was really angry.'

'Bloody hell! What did they say?' I asked.

'Dad went ballistic. I'd never seen him so mad. In fact, I'd never seen him angry at all until that point. He paced around, threatening to do Graham some damage and went on about what he'd do to him if he'd harmed me in any way.'

'What did your Mum do?' I asked.

'Nothing really. I think she found the whole thing quite exciting if I'm honest but she didn't say as much.'

'So what happened at school?' I asked.

'Well, between his wife and Dad, they got Graham sacked.'

'Oh so that's why he *really* left.' Catherine said.

'Durrrr,' Jenny scoffed, draining her own glass and belching.

'Don't be sarcastic, Jen,' Pauline reprimanded. 'His wife ordered him out the house and the last I heard he was building boats in Cornwall and doing a bit of private coaching on the side.'

'I bet he is, dirty old git,' Jenny said scornfully.

'Oh come on' Pauline defended, 'he was only about ten years older than us. In fact, the same age as we are now! Not so old really. I feel a bit sorry for him.'

'Well I don't,' Jenny retorted. 'I think he should have known better and kept his snake in the basket. You were a pupil for goodness sake.'

She paused.

'Although, I still wish it had been me!'

'Do you think he'll be here tonight?' Catherine asked. Then blushed heavily as she clearly realised how silly it sounded. The rest of us turned to her and all at once collapsed into howls of laughter.

'God, there's Elvis!' Pauline pointed out. We all squinted over towards the direction of the bar. A really tall handsome guy had just walked in.

'Never, that can't be him,' I said. 'He had blonder hair at school, didn't he?' And he was much skinnier. Bloody hell it is.'

I was astounded as to how much he had changed. Really dishy, tall, tanned and immaculately dressed in a DJ. And then there, right behind him was Kenny Sykes. Only, by comparison, he didn't look very good at all. His hair was very thin on top and he'd put on quite a bit of weight.

'Gosh Kenny looks a bit ropey,' Catherine said. I can't believe you snogged him, Mags.'

'You didn't!' Jenny said. 'You never told me!'

'I was much too embarrassed. Anyway, I don't think you've got any comeback on me, after what you guys have just told *us*!'

'Fair enough, mate. Was he any good?' she asked.

'Not really,' I said. I recalled the suction pad nickname and chose to move things along.

'Anyone fancy another bottle?'

'Only if you go to the bar.' Jenny kicked her sandals off and put her feet up on a spare stool.

Catherine became excited. 'Yes, go on, Maggie, go to the bar and talk to them at the same time,' she urged.

Happy to have the subject changed, I stood up, pushed back my chair and negotiated my way around tables until I reached the bar. I looked quickly around for Luke, my heart suddenly beating fast with anticipation, but he was nowhere to be seen. I relaxed again.

Kenny noticed me first.

'Magpie!' he called, smiling nervously. I went across to where they were standing. Hmmm, I'll give him Magpie. Suction Pad indeed! Still, it was a long time ago and I decided to be big about it.

'Hi, Kenny, how are you? Hi, Elvis, how's it going?'

'Not as well as with you it seems, Magpie.' He whistled, checking me up and down appreciatively. Then he glanced over to where the others were sitting. 'Tell me, how come the best looking girl in the room doesn't appear to have a partner on her arm, eh?'

'Who's to say I haven't left one at home?' My tone was playful.

'No way! You look far too sexy to have a man at home.'

We chatted for a while at the bar and, after that, it seemed only right that they join us. Kenny was being quite quiet though and every time I caught his eye he blushed.

Jenny wasn't having any of Elvis's patter, and clearly didn't take to him one bit. Every time he told a joke or a funny story, she just sneered and kept filling up her glass and knocking it back.

After a while the drink began to get the better of her and she started sniping at him.

'Still the smooth-talking wide boy then, Elvis?'

'Still the poisoned dwarf then, Miss Henderson? Things don't change,' he came back at her.

'Surprised your wife let you out,' she retorted, eyes flashing.

'Jealous are we?'

'Ha, of you? You must be joking; I know your sort.'

'Oh yes, just what is my sort then young lady?'

'Don't you young lady me!'

And so it went on. I had no idea what was afoot until Pauline explained to me later on that they had had a very passionate two-night stand after a boarding house party, just before they left, which Jenny had decided to keep quiet due to the fact he had dumped her and gone back to some girl in the comp who he'd apparently been seeing all along. If there was one thing Jenny couldn't abide, it was cheating and being cheated on. How anyone could ever have two-timed Jenny, the way she looked, was beyond me.

It seemed the best thing at this point was to break things up and go through to the main function room. After all, it was almost quarter to eight and people were bound to be in there already. So, we finished our drinks and headed through. On the way, us girls stopped off for a loo break leaving the lads to get the drinks in.

'That Elvis is such a fucking sleaze!' Jenny spat. 'Wouldn't trust him as far as I could throw him.'

'Oh come on, Jen, don't be like that. He was all right.'

'Well you're welcome to him. I meet his type all the time, in bars, all over the world. Little boy lost type, wife doesn't understand them, needs the love of a good woman. Just like old "Get your rocks off Graham". It's bollocks the lot of it. They just want to get their leg over,' she said nastily.

I left the subject and went to wash my hands. As I did so, I caught sight of myself in the mirror, taken aback by the sudden change of image. Tonight of all nights, I needed to look my best. I smoothed my hair into place, marvelling at how soft it had become. Then I carefully reapplied my lipstick and smiled inwardly at my reflection. I was ready. Apprehensive but ready.

We all headed out and along the wide, carpeted, corridor, Pauline and Jenny a few steps in front seemingly not worried at all. How I longed for some of their apparent nonchalance. Catherine and I hooked arms nervously as we walked. This was it. This was finally it. Once inside the function room, there was no turning back. Luke would be in there. He was bound to be by now. My stomach churned at the thought of it, despite all the wine and the earlier vodka. I was petrified. I felt acid in my throat and I couldn't feel my feet. The world outside my head seemed like a dream.

Catherine squeezed my arm with hers.

'I'll be here, don't worry,' she assured me. I gratefully squeezed her arm back. We reached the main door to the function room bar. I took a deep breath and we headed in to the mêlée.

The large room was grand, brightly lit and packed. The ceilings were high and decorations and balloons were hung or strewn everywhere. The noise was deafening. People everywhere, a blurred sea of faces talking, laughing and drinking. Pretty much everyone must have gone straight in to where the action was. We found Elvis and Kenny again and gratefully accepted some champagne. Shortly after, Elvis asked a girl I didn't know when her baby was due. Then there was an embarrassed silence after she said she wasn't pregnant. He headed off after that, Kenny in tow.

We hardly had time to breathe before being swooped on by faces from the past and, before long, we were all chatting away with people we hadn't seen for ten years as if it was yesterday we'd left school. So many people were instantly recognisable. The geeks were still geeks. Some of the good-looking girls had got fat, which Catherine and I thought was excellent. Some guys had gone from long hair to short and some were even going grey. People had put on or lost weight, so it took a little while to click who they were, but others were identical to how they'd been at school, only bigger.

I scanned the room, nervously, for signs of Luke but I couldn't see him.

Bernard 'Bernie' Hemmingway from our English class turned out to be gay. I think the giveaway was the big blue floppy hat and pink feather earring. He was a scream and I had to bite my tongue to stop myself laughing when he commented that Gina Turnbull's chin was so out of proportion that when God was handing out chins she must have thought he said gins and ordered a double! He then went on to comment that, with a nose like Ned McFarland's, he must have thought that God was handing out roses and ordered a big red one! And so the ribbing went on, and I was rather glad I was *in* his company.

Suddenly, I felt my legs go wobbly, and I had to steady myself. I felt the colour drain from my face. A cold trickle of fear ran down my body and I froze on the spot.

There, through a gap in the crowd, some distance away, was a face I couldn't help but recognise. A surge of anxiety flooded my stomach. I felt my mouth fall open and I went cold with shock.

'Cat,' I croaked, under my breath.

'What's up, hun?' She turned to me, saw my face and followed my gaze.

'Gosh! Is that... Luke?' She squinted her eyes.

Jenny overheard and peered over through the gap, raising her hand to wave.

'That's not Luke, that's Tony,' she said.

'Tony?' Catherine frowned, 'but he was in the year below us.'

'They moved him up remember. Little swot,' she mocked.

Catherine glanced in my direction.

'Where's Luke then?'

'He's not coming; couldn't make it back from Sweden, something to do with work, so he said. He's missing Dad's party too, the arse.'

The room seemed to spin round suddenly and I couldn't breathe properly. I felt like someone had knocked the wind out of me. I stood staring with a fixed grin on my face, trying to hide my feelings from Jenny. If I thought seeing Luke would be tough, realising it wasn't him – that he wasn't coming – was like being kicked in the stomach very hard and then being told to remain calm like nothing was wrong and not to let anyone know how much pain I was feeling.

I had to get away. I hung around for a few moments, so that no one would suspect anything then excused myself to go back to the loos. When I was out of sight of our little crowd, I practically ran until I reached them and locked myself in a cubicle where I remained until I was able to breathe properly again. This wasn't supposed to happen. This wasn't in the plan. This *wasn't supposed to happen.* What now? What the hell now?

Chapter Four

For ages that evening, I fought hard to hide my disappointment. I couldn't bring myself to ask Jenny about Luke and why his name had been on the acceptance list. I had so many questions. Had he asked about me? Did he send his love? Anything. Everything.

I had so wanted some closure; closure on the past, on my feelings. I'd come all this way in the hope of seeing Luke and sorting everything out and now I wouldn't get the chance. He wouldn't even be at his dad's birthday party.

At one point Catherine came up and put her arm gently around me.

'Are you OK?'

'No. Not really. I feel sick. What am I going to do, Cat? I never imagined he wouldn't show. His name was on the list. What happened?'

'I don't know hun but there's bound to be a very good reason for it. You'll find out soon enough,' she tried to comfort me.

'Will I? I probably won't see him for another ten years now!'

She squeezed my hand. 'And by that time, you'll be married to a fabulously handsome, rich man who adores you. You'll be spending your mornings in the gym and your lunchtimes with me in some gorgeous wine bar, where we discuss the latest fashions and beauty treatments and won't have a care in the world. So it won't matter then.'

'Do you think he really had to work?' I asked sadly.

'Of course! It was obviously unavoidable. He would have come if he could have. And he certainly wouldn't miss his dad's do if he could help it would he?' she assured me kindly.

'I suppose not.' I hated the way I was feeling; the weakness that was charging through my body. I felt so out of control, again; just like I had all those years ago.

My attention went back to Tony who was now standing at the bar.

'Apart from the hair colour, the resemblance is uncanny,' I said, just as Jenny snuck up beside me and punched me on the arm.

'Yeah, loads of people say that. They're both big oafs!' she said loudly in Tony's direction.

Right at that moment Tony looked over, straight at me, and smiled. It jolted me. It was such a lovely warm open smile and quite unexpectedly, I felt my stomach do a small somersault. Our eyes locked for a couple of seconds and then he looked away again and carried on with his conversation.

'So Tony moved up a year then, Jen?' Catherine asked, frowning as she tried to recall the past.

'Yup. Don't you remember? He was such a swot. Worked like mad to get good grades to match up to Luke. In the end they had to move him up. He's always been a smart arse. Still, it was great having someone to do your homework for you!'

'Actually,' Catherine said, thoughtfully, 'I do remember him joining my science class now you come to mention it.'

'So what's he been up to?' I asked, as casually as I could.

'Just split from his fiancée,' Jenny explained. 'I reckon it's because she's a shopaholic. They were living in London for a while but Tony reckons he hates big cities. I don't know why he doesn't just sell up but I suppose he has got a business there. Laura's gone back to live with her Mum quite near Tillmouth and Tony's still in their flat but he spends most of his spare time up at the farm with Dad. '

'Best go and say hello I guess.' She rolled her eyes and headed off to where Tony was talking in a small group from our year. I watched how he handled himself. He was self-assured, confident; full of wide smiles for the people around him. I saw how he touched a girl on her shoulder as she was talking. Immediately she seemed to become aware of herself and I observed as she blushed and focussed her gaze into her drink. Tony was certainly handsome. I wondered whether he and Luke really did look alike these days. I supposed there was a good chance I would never find out now. I sighed inwardly then gave myself a small shake to buck myself up. I knew I should at least try and move on and enjoy the night.

'Have you spotted Joe yet?' I asked Catherine, deciding that she at least stood a chance of meeting her man.

'No, not yet but we can always check the seating plan.'

'What seating plan?'

'C'mon I'll show you.' Catherine took my hand and pulled me through the crowds to the edge of the dining room where a big flip chart had been drawn up with all the tables on it.

While Catherine kept her eyes peeled for Joe, I scanned the plan for names we'd recognise and found Joe's almost immediately.

'Where are we sitting? Is it close by him?' she asked.

'I don't know,' I squinted at the plan. 'Oh, here we are. Look, we're all together thankfully. Joe's, a few tables away.'

Read the other names out on our table?' she insisted, still surveying the throng.

'Jackie Grayson,' I read out.

'Who?' she asked.

'Haven't the foggiest. Maybe it's her married name. And partner!'

'So people have brought partners,' she said.

'Well Jackie Grayson has.'

'Who else?'

'John Forbes. Ooh I remember him from Maths class,' I said. 'Big guy, dark hair.'

'Wasn't he the one who used to use the peashooter all the time?' Catherine asked.

'That's the one. He used to chase us round the playground when we were in the second year. Actually I think I had a bit of a crush on him. He was all muscles and shoulders,' I said thoughtfully.

'I don't remember that,' Catherine said.

'It was only a mild crush, Luke was the main one,' I said, feeling down again.

'Who else?' She quickly urged me on.

'Jack Higgs. His name rings a vague bell. George Littlewood, as in…' I allowed my voice to go deep and slow, '… *boring George*. Always the one to ask a question just as the bell went so we had to stay until the bloody teacher had answered it.'

'Who else?'

'Some girl called Kirsty Trotter, née Spears. Oh no! Not her! She threw a rope at me in gym class!' I said fretfully.

'Why?' Catherine asked.

'I never found out. But I was scared of her after that. All that red hair freaked me out. And she was part of a gang who frightened the life out of me. Every time I walked passed them they always gave me dirty looks. Typical she's on my bloody table!'

Catherine 'hmmmed' suspiciously; undoubtedly considering this *chance* seating arrangement to be the hand of fate working.

A bell was being rung behind us, and we turned round to see a bearded, rotund man looking like a town crier, clearing his throat ready for an announcement.

'Ladies and gentleman,' he sung out in a monotone.

'The Tillmouth Manor requests your presence in the dining area. Please make your way to your tables noting the seating plan which has been carefully prepared for your convenience.'

People cheered and started downing their drinks. Then the humming crowd began moving slowly in the direction of the tables to find their seats. Catherine and I found ours next to one of the external walls and our seats faced outwards into the room, giving us a great view of everyone. It seemed whoever had put together the seating plan had ensured that each table consisted only of those in one particular year.

After a few minutes of shuffling chairs and loud excited chattering, people began to settle down.

Our table was filling up. John Forbes remembered us. Well, he remembered Jenny, which didn't do my confidence much good so I turned my attention to Jack Higgs, according to his name card, who was sitting on my right. He was an attractive man and, while I kind of remembered his name, I didn't recognise him at all. He was wearing an expensive suit and wore his dark hair slicked back slightly. He had an infectious twinkle in his eye and I wanted to giggle each time I caught his gaze.

'Maggie Parsons,' he said slowly. 'I'd recognise you anywhere.'

'Would you? I don't recognise you at all. Sorry, that didn't quite come out right.'

'That's because I was a complete dork at school. We were in the same French class. I sat in the row behind you and used to admire your, um back.' He gave me a wink. 'Actually I used to admire your front as well.'

I blushed unwittingly.

'I always thought you were rather gorgeous back at school and I see nothing's changed there.' He blatantly gave me the once over.

'Well there's no accounting for taste,' I pulled a face.

'I'm sure you taste lovely,' he said.

'I can't say I've ever licked myself,' I blurted, and could have kicked myself.

'Now there's a picture I'm glad I've got,' he said thoughtfully. 'Of course, Maggie, I'd be more than happy to do the honours and tell you what you taste like. You just have to say the word.'

'Honestly, you're such a flirt. And we've only just sat down!' I shook my head pretending to be cross but the corners of my mouth curled as I did so.

'Takes one to know one. Besides I'm not flirting, I'm just stating facts.' He shrugged slightly.

'Well, you look nice too.'

'Nice? *Nice?* What kind of a word is nice?'

'I use it a lot.'

'Well stop! Find another word.'

'Sorry. Nice suit,' I said.

He laughed.

'What this old rag? Just something I picked up at Oxfam. I think they paid me to take it away.'

I peered more closely at his jacket then, pinching a bit of material between my thumb and forefinger, I nodded.

'Yes, on closer inspection I see what you mean. Quite tatty really. Honestly, Jack, you could have made a bit more of an effort. I mean, there's me assuming you'd made it big in the world but the suit, well, I don't know what to say.' I was beginning to enjoy myself.

'Na, not me, just a modest chain of bars and clubs across the South, nothing major,' he said humbly.

'Only a modest chain eh? Pity. Oh well, there's still time.'

The waiters interrupted our repartee, bringing wine over along with some bread rolls in readiness for the starters.

The room was alive with chatter and our table was no exception. Unfortunately, Boring George started boring me. I kept giggling as Jack began snoring under his breath, as I talked across the table to George. I had to kick him to stop.

Then the food started and we began tucking in.

The room was alive with the hum of conversation and our table chatted and laughed loudly. Even Boring George was telling jokes by the end of the main course, although I think everyone just laughed to humour him.

Kirsty Spears, or rather Trotter, kept throwing me strange looks. I wondered whether she had remembered what she'd done back in gym class. Although I briefly smiled back at her, I found myself unable to meet her eyes.

After the dessert plates had been cleared, people started to swap places and talk to different people. Pauline headed off to see some of her old tennis mates and I took her place next to Jenny who seemed to have sobered up somewhat after the food.

'How come you're not with a man, Jen?' I asked, feeling brave.

She shrugged dismissively.

'You know me, married to my job and all that.' She turned her face away from me a bit too suddenly, steering the conversation back to me again.

'How 'bout you then, Mags, anyone you fancy?'

'Well I was hoping that Lu…' I trailed off, realising too late what I'd done.

Jenny snorted a laugh.

'That Luke was going to be here,' she finished.

I stared down to my lap, feeling embarrassed.

'Look, babe, I know you always had a thing for him, I'm not stupid, but honestly he's not worth it. None of them are. Men are just after one thing and then when they get it, they're off in search of the next conquest or back to their wives,' she said bitterly.

'But Luke's your own brother!' I was taken aback. 'Anyway, it was a long time ago; things change.'

'Whatever,' she dismissed. 'Brother or not, he's a man.' She knocked back the rest of her wine and poured another glass.

'Who do you get on with the best out of Luke and Tony?' I asked, guiding the conversation back.

'Luke probably, although I don't get to see him much; him living in Sweden and all that.'

'What about Tony, don't you get on with him?'

'Yeah, he's OK, but I don't see him much either really. He freaks me out a bit sometimes. He gets kind of moody.'

'What happened with his fiancée?'

'Fuck knows. I never really liked her.'

'How come?' I found myself more than a bit interested.

'Too fussy and bossy. I hate bossy women.'

I bit my tongue.

'Anyway, he says she's always working – or shopping! Not much fun for him when she doesn't come home until all hours I guess,' she went on.

'But you're married to your job' I pointed out. 'You must know where she's coming from?'

She thought for a bit.

'Yeah but the difference is I'm not dragging anyone along with me. I'm just in it for me. As far as I'm concerned, my job is who I am and I'm not fool enough to get hitched to some guy who's going to resent me for it later,' she finished, just as Jack Higgs sat down beside her.

I was aware of someone moving into my line of vision on my opposite side and the next thing I knew Kirsty Spears had plonked herself down in the seat next to me.

I turned away from Jenny and faced her wondering what to expect. She clinked my glass clumsily and gave me a wry smile.

'I know this may sound silly,' she began awkwardly 'but I think I owe you an apology.'

'The rope thing?' I offered up.

'You remember!' She put her hand to her face to cover her embarrassment.

'It hurt!' I said taking a mouthful of wine.

'I can't believe I hit you with a rope! I didn't like you because you were prettier than me and had nicer hair.'

I nearly spat my wine out.

'Well that's a first!' I said.

'I always wanted curly hair, instead of this red mop!' She waved a lock of hair at me. I see you've discovered hair straighteners.' She grinned.

I tutted. 'Only fifteen years too late.'

'Anyway, I hope you won't hold it against me,' she said.

'As long as you promise not to do it again!' I smiled and clinked glasses back at her, mentally laying the ghost. At that moment I looked up and saw Catherine looking smug, and nodding wisely in my direction.

The waiters cleared away the remains of the debris from dinner and started moving some of the middle tables to the side of the room in preparation for the dancing. I felt like it had been a long night already and there was still so much of the evening ahead, so I decided to get some air before it carried on.

A few people had headed out to the terrace area. The night air was quite warm. It had turned dark and the moon was full and bright. Moths were flickering around the subtle outside lighting and the occasional owl called from the tall fir trees in the large grounds. I gazed up in wonderment at the stars shining down brightly from the midnight-blue sky, throwing a bright glow across the lawns. I could see a group of people running around and giggling by the fountain, shoes discarded and feet bare on the cool grass. Then they all raced off in the direction of the trees. I leaned over the ornate wall beside the wide sweeping steps down to the gardens and breathed in the fresh night air. My mind inadvertently went to Luke again. I sighed heavily and a voice sounded behind me, making me jump.

'Penny for them, Magpie?'

I turned quickly to see Elvis standing a few feet away from me.

'Hi you, need some air too?' I asked.

'Something like that.' He walked towards me.

And then he was beside me. Close. Very close. I became aware of how tall and handsome he was. He smelled good too.

He stood smiling down at me, his narrowed eyes burning through me, his confidence undermining mine.

'You know,' he drawled, 'people don't actually call me Elvis anymore.'

'O-o-h, I'm sorry.' I stammered feeling unnerved with him so close. 'Um, actually I don't know if I've ever been told your real name.'

'It's Sean,' he said, not taking his eyes off me.

I grew more awkward as he just stood there, his strong presence almost mocking me.

'That must be the first time I've ever heard you called Sean then.' I laughed nervously. 'It's much nicer than Elvis.'

'Do you think so?' He moved a step closer to me and leant down, breathing in the smell of my hair. I started getting butterflies in my stomach.

'You smell gorgeous,' he said gruffly.

It had been a long time since I'd been this close to a man. I had to admit that despite the inner turmoil I'd been through that evening Elvis was looking attractive standing over me, tall and handsome. I could feel the alcohol cushioning me from analysis. I had a feeling Elvis was about to kiss me and, right at that moment, I wanted him to. People had gone back inside and we were momentarily alone. He leant forward and I felt my eyes begin to close but instead of kissing me, he lifted a tendril of hair away from my face and tucked it behind my ear. My eyes shot wide open again and he smiled, the corners of his mouth twitching. Was he making fun of me? I'd obviously been wrong about the kiss and, feeling embarrassed, I began shuffling my feet unable to meet his eye. I suddenly wanted to get out of there. But Elvis seemed to have other ideas.

'Do you know, Magpie, back at school I reckoned you were one of the sexiest birds in the whole year. I used to fantasise about you.'

'Did you?' I was genuinely surprised. 'But you set me up with Kenny.'

'More fool me.'

I giggled, thankful for the respite.

'I'm kind of glad, though,' he said, looking thoughtful.

'What do you mean?' I found myself wanting him *not* to have been glad.

'Well, if you hadn't gone off with Kenny, I might never have found out what a good kisser you were and my fantasies would never have got off the ground.'

'A good kisser! But, I thought… I mean… what about the nickname?' I asked awkwardly.

He seemed confused. 'What nickname?'

'You know, the nickname I earned after the kiss – "Suction Pad"!' Goodness this was embarrassing.

He started laughing.

'What's so funny?' My face burned.

'That wasn't your nickname, Magpie, my little sweet darling, that was your mate Catherine's!'

My mouth fell open.

'Oh my God, Catherine's, what… after…?'

'Joe Riggs,' he finished.

'But she said it was a fantastic kiss!'

'Maybe she thought so, but Joe was quick to brand her a suction pad. I remember it well. He used to suck his cheeks in behind her back whenever she walked past.' He laughed. 'So you've been thinking all along that you were the bad kisser!'

'Pretty much!'

'That's the sort of thing people go to counselling for. So I'm told,' he added quickly.

'Oh God, poor Cat. You mustn't say anything, promise me,' I insisted.

'Well now, that all depends.'

'On what?'

'I promise not to say anything to Catherine, if you promise to show me what all the fuss was about.' He narrowed his eyes sexily at me.

I looked up at him, saying nothing.

He bent down and kissed me very gently on the lips. It was a nice kiss, very nice considering my previous drought period. And before I knew what was happening we were headlong into a fully blown snog. Until I became conscious of someone close by on the terrace, so I broke it off, suddenly uncomfortably aware that I was kissing a man I hardly knew. I glanced around but whoever it was had gone away again.

'Well, Kenny was right. And not a trace of a suction pad anywhere.' He grinned down at me.

'You promised!' I complained.

'I did, didn't I. I could have been lying though.'

I hit him hard on the arm in mock anger. The music started up inside.

'Best go in really,' I said.

'Yeah, Kenny's probably wondering where I am and having a breakdown. Maybe catch up with you later, Magpie?' he said

'Yes maybe,' I replied, taking the kiss for what it was. Just a bit of fun.

We started heading towards the French doors.

'You know, Sean,' I smiled, '… people don't actually call me Magpie anymore.'

And we went inside.

The lights in the function room were still bright and the dancing hadn't yet started. The high ceilings did little to deaden the noise of the room and conversation and laughter flowed, as did the drink. Lots of people, including Pauline and her tennis crowd, were standing up by the bar. I waved at her as I went past then ricocheted my way through the crowds, bouncing off various backs as I squeezed past, jogging arms and drinks as I pushed through. When I finally reached our table, I saw that quite a few people from other tables had joined ours. They were gathered round, either standing or having pulled their own chairs up. There seemed to be a bit of a commotion going on. I couldn't see what was happening initially then I realised what it was. Jenny was standing on her chair, now even drunker than before dinner, reciting Shakespeare.

'The Quality of mercy is not strained. It droppeth as the gentle rain from Heaven. Upon the place beneath… Never knew the bloody rest ha ha ha ha.'

Jack was leering at Jenny from the seat next to her, and laughing loudly when she did. He managed to pull her down from her chair and on to his knee where she began fighting to get back off again, her little hands pulling at his fingers laced around her stomach. She was no match for his strength, so she stopped struggling and gave in but started with her usual abuse.

'Ahhh fuck off ya lousy son of a bitch, you're just after my knickers!' She turned to face him and pushed his forehead, hard, away from her with her flattened hand. His head flopped backwards and almost disappeared down his back and then popped back up again, which Jenny howled at.

'You've got me wrong, I'm just after what's inside them,' he stated, laughing loudly, the rest of the table joining in.

'At last! A fucking honest son of a bitch! Well done! There's a first for everything. Cheers!' Jenny clinked his glass, and downed her drink in one.

'Ah, Jenny, Jenny, Jenny, you are but the loveliest sweetest maiden with the sweetest mouth, I could fair listen to your verse forever. Marry me?'

'Marriage is for idiots! Go and find someone else to marry!' But then she caught his eye and they both roared with laughter.

They weren't the only ones who were drunk, Catherine was completely trollied! All hell was breaking loose as she was demonstrating how to take her bra off through her sleeve without removing any other clothing. This was usually a pretty neat trick to entertain guys with but she didn't actually have a bra on, nor did she have any sleeves, so I wasn't quite sure what she was doing. I went round to her side of the table and tugged her momentarily free arm.

'You all right, Cat?'

'Absobloodylutely my bestest friend in the whole wide world. I have never been happier.' She hugged me very tightly before holding me at arm's length and telling me very seriously that she loved me *very* much. She stood up swaying rather badly and lurched forward to pick up her champagne glass, her left boob nearly falling out onto the table, much to the delight of the, by now, very drunk and disorderly George Littlewood, who licked his lips and flopped towards Catherine hungrily.

'Toast, everyone! Toast!' Cat announced, standing up.

'Couldn't eat a bloody thing,' came Jack's rather obvious reply but one which everybody seemed to think was hilarious.

It was at this time I remembered Catherine's weakness when it came to champagne; not that she couldn't do without it but that it made her completely and utterly drunk, almost uncontrollable. I had a feeling I might be needed, so I pulled up a chair.

'To friends,' she cried out.

'To friends!' we all chorused.

Swig, swig.

'To school friends.'

'To school friends!'

Swig, swig.

'To *absent* friends!' she went on.

'To absent friends!' People were shouting louder and louder and even the next two tables were joining in.

Catherine was highly excited.

'To men!' she cried, getting up on her chair and causing a few worried looks.

'To men!' the women shouted.

Gulp, gulp.

'To *absent* men!' Catherine cried, upending two glasses as she knocked the table hard with her shin.

'To absent men!' A few people began to exchange glances, clearly unsure where she was going with this.

Then Catherine's face grew more serious. She bent down and rubbed her leg frowning slightly, displaying even more breast, which caused a cheer in itself. Then straightening up slowly, she lowered her voice ominously.

'And in particular, to one *very* absent man!'

No one said anything but a few giggled.

'To Joe Riggs!' she cried, raising her glass high in the air. 'The most absent man here, although he's not here is he! So, to the very conspicuous (she actually said consickuous, but hey) man not actually here.' And she drained her drink in one.

'To Joe Riggs!' everyone joined in, though perhaps not entirely sure why.

I cringed slightly and before I knew what was happening Catherine was shouting for the music to be turned up so they could dance.

'Come on, people, let's dance the night away. I love you all!' she sang and started dancing on her chair which didn't appear at all safe. She was about to raise her glass again when she realised that her bias train had got caught on the back of the chair. She bent down and tried to pull it free but, as she did so, she completely lost her balance and came crashing down very unceremoniously on to the floor pulling Jenny on top of her. Jack followed, not entirely by accident I imagine, only just stopping himself from crushing them both. I think a chair broke at this point but there were so many people crowding around I couldn't really tell. I tried to move in to help but it was impossible. There was a lot of commotion, lots of laughing and hiccupping and the odd ouch which didn't sound too convincing. The whole escapade ended up with Jenny singing *Roll Me Over in the Clover* and Catherine struggling to get up but laughing so much she couldn't move. Jack seemed quite happy with two women writhing around beside him and lay back with his hands behind his head saying things like 'Bring it on girls!' and 'Have I died and gone to Heaven?' Catherine giggled and struggled for dear life clutching her crotch in case she wet herself. She finally managed to wriggle free and rolled onto her back, the tears of laughter streaming down her face. Suddenly though she stopped laughing and her face froze. Her mouth dropped open as she looked up from where she lay. There, towering over her with a rather puzzled expression on his face was a tall, somewhat confused man. Catherine went white. She had only landed at the feet of, yes you've guessed it, the not-so-absent Joe Riggs.

'Raaaaalph! Errrgh, raaaaaalph, blurrrrrch!'

In the ladies toilets, Jenny was being sick while Pauline stood behind her in the cubicle holding her hair out the way.

'Raaaaaaaaaaalph', came the repeated sound, from the cubicle.

'Ohhh Goddd, raaaaaaaaaaaaaaaalph, sniff cough.'

Yuck!

Pauline soothingly rubbed Jenny's back and assured her over and over that it would be all right.

Catherine on the other hand had almost sobered up.

'Bugger, bugger, bugger! Why then? Why *then*? Why did he have to turn up then? I feel so stupid. What must he think of me? Oh God he must have heard me toast him, he must have. Do you think he heard me toast him, Mags?'

'Probably not,' I lied. 'Anyway, it was a nice thing to do.'

She pulled an incredulous face at me. 'Oh yes, it was a lovely thing to do! Not like I had been desperate for him to turn up or anything like that. Not like I had been waiting and hoping all night that he was just running late and that he would turn up at any time. Oh no, none of that would have been apparent when I toasted some guy I hadn't seen for years! NOT!'

'I'm sure he wouldn't have read any of that into it. Besides, he offered to help you up,' I said.

'I knooooooow! Poor guy! Bet he wouldn't do that again,' she said, manically reapplying her make-up in the mirror.

'What do you mean?' I asked.

'Didn't you see? When I took his hand I was too heavy for him and I fell back down again and split my dress. Look! I have never been so embarrassed in my life. He only just managed to stop falling on top of me!'

I watched in amazement as Catherine pulled out a miniature sewing kit from her bag and proceeded to sit down on a little chair in the corner, hoist up her hem, turn the bottom of her dress inside out and begin in earnest to repair her split.

I tried to instil some calm in the situation. 'Look, I'm sure when you go back in there, he'll be totally cool about things. If you see him, just start up a conversation like nothing's happened. Act normal and make out you're having a whale of a time.'

Catherine paused, sewing needle suspended in mid air. After a long moment, she looked up to face me.

She spoke slowly. 'Are – you – mad?'

'What do you mean?'

'Go back in? Go back... GO BACK IN?' her voice rose hysterically. 'You honestly think I can go back in there after that?'

I calmly washed my hands and dried them, ignoring her hysteria.

'Well actually that's exactly what I think you should do.' I turned to her again. 'Hold your head high, link my arm and we'll walk in together, smiling and chatting like it's all been a breeze.'

'It may have been a breeze to you but you weren't the one who almost dislocated Joe's shoulder when he tried to help you up.'

'No, but...'

'You weren't the one who practically declared undying love for him to the whole room!'

'No, but...'

'AND, you weren't the one who displayed her thighs and goodness knows what else to all and sundry and is now being considered a laughing stock, as we speak!'

'You don't know that.'

'No, you're right, I don't. But I think it's a fair bet don't you?'

I paused, a little too long.

'See.'

I had to think on my feet.

'OK... well... maybe it was a bit embarrassing. I'll grant you that.'

'A bit?' she cried.

'OK, more than a bit. But look at it this like this. If you don't go back in, people will always remember you as the woman who did all that stuff and then was too chicken to face the music. This way, you'll be remembered as the really funny girl, who was a right scream, didn't give a damn about what other people thought and enjoyed herself the whole night.'

Catherine was clearly dubious but I detected a very slight flicker of interest in her eyes so I kept going.

'Plus,' I went on, 'they're too drunk to know what's going on anyway. Get back in there, with me, and we'll show them all what a great sport you are. It's the only way, Cat.'

She began to sew again and we sat in silence, apart from the sporadic coughs and retches from Jenny's cubicle.

'And you honestly think I'll get away with it?'

'If you're willing to laugh it off, then yes I do.'

I watched as she carefully cast off her sewing work, leant down and broke off the thread with her teeth. She calmly replaced the needle and cotton in the little plastic box, then turned her dress the right way and smoothed it down. You wouldn't have known anything had been wrong with it.

'And you really think it'll work?'

'If you want it to,' I said wisely. 'And remember, focus on what you want!' I grinned.

'That's what you're always telling me.'

'What I want is for the whole thing not to have happened.' She paused and sighed.

'I suppose you might be right though. I certainly don't want people to think I'm a chicken.'

'Exactly, so come on. Let's get back in there before you change your mind.'

I turned purposefully towards the door. Catherine tutted and stood up to follow me. We quickly checked on Jenny, still in her cubicle and looking mightily sorry for herself.

'My work here has just begun,' Pauline said solemnly and then shook her head as Jenny retched and groaned into the toilet bowl. Pauline assured us she would take care of her, so we headed out along the corridor towards the bar.

The party was in full swing and the disco had been started up at the far end. People were throwing themselves round the dance floor to music from our school days. They were all like giggling teenagers, as if transported back in time.

Catherine took a deep breath, linked my arm and off we marched in the direction of the bar. I saw a gap and headed for it, pulling Catherine behind me. I quickly ordered a couple of glasses of wine from a momentarily free barman and we settled into our position of power.

'Maybe he's left?' Catherine suggested hopefully.

'Why? He's only just got here. Besides, he'll probably want to make sure you're OK,' I said.

Bernie Hemmingway flounced up, minus his feather earring, doing a one-man version of the conga.

'Loved your display darls, fab legs by the way!' He blew Catherine a kiss.

And off he flounced again in the direction of the dance floor.

'See, Bernie thought you were fab.'

'It's not Bernie I'm concerned about,' she said, peering around the room and scanning for Joe. 'I'm so embarrassed. Oh God, where is he?'

I joined in the search, narrowing my eyes around the place for signs of Joe. We were so caught up in what we were doing it was somewhat of a surprise when a voice beside me said:

'Looking for me?'

And there was Joe, right next to us!

Catherine blushed and shot her hands up to her mouth.

'Joe!' she burst out.

'Catherine.' He smiled at her.

'Oh, Joe, I'm so sorry,' she said not being particularly cool. 'You must think I'm a complete idiot.'

'Not at all; I'm very flattered that you'd think so badly of me for not turning up. Fancy a drink?' He motioned his head over to the space beside him.

She hesitated.

'I won't bite you know. Not unless you want me to.' He winked at her

'Go on then,' I urged, 'best do as the man says. I'll head off and make sure Jenny's OK. OK?'

'OK.'

And Catherine joined Joe, looking suitably humbled.

Making my way through the crowd, I kept recognising people. It was difficult to go more than a few steps without someone calling out my name and demanding I stop and reminisce about old times. Before long I was totally caught up in the sheer, heady, energy of the evening and was actually really enjoying myself. I realised I hadn't given Luke a thought for ages, and that was a good thing. I spotted Elvis, or rather Sean, chatting up an attractive auburn-haired girl. It seemed like Jenny had been nearer to the truth than I had, considering the way his hands were wandering.

Then I spotted Kenny on his own looking a bit glum so I went over and sat down to keep him company for a bit. Poor bloke really didn't have much to say for himself and he would insist on staring into his drink as he spoke without once meeting my eye.

After a while, I made my excuses thinking I really ought to check on Jenny and Pauline. On arrival at the toilets, however, I discovered they'd disappeared; back to the room I assumed. So I headed back to find Catherine and hoped I wouldn't get in the way of romance. I found her still at the bar but this time she was being chatted up by Adrian Higginson from our year.

'Hi you two, what's going on?'

Adrian put his arm around Catherine's shoulder, unashamedly ogling her breasts.

'Ah, now your gorgeous friend Catherine was just explaining how the female hormones rise and fall through the course of your cycle; very interesting. A guy could learn a lot here.' He lowered his voice. 'Best keep it just between us though, Catherine, this stuff will keep me scoring time after time after time. What did you say that wonder hormone was, west... something or other?'

'Oestrogen! It's oestrogen, like east, not west. And it's probably only the equivalent for us as it is for you blokes all the time! It's not fair,' she said in mock crossness, 'you've got it great. We just get wonderfully horny and flirty for a week or so; life is great, we sparkle and our oestrogen levels are up and raring to go, and then bam! We crash back down again. Although I suppose things do climb up again just before, you know, our um...' Catherine blushed heavily, '... time of the month.'

'Uh oh, that's me done.' Adrian put his palms up protectively. 'Too much information, I'm off.' He laughed.

'Good to see you, Mags, you're looking swell!' He gave me a wink.

'Do people really say "swell" anymore?' I asked Catherine, when he was out of earshot.

'He apparently does, a lot, and he kept bloody winking at me. So did Joe, really annoying!'

'What happened to Joe anyway?' I asked.

'Put it this way. If he ever offers me a helping hand again, I won't be taking it. If I'd asked him what colour my eyes were, he'd have probably been more able to tell you the size, shape and colour of my nipples, despite the fact they're hidden. I don't think the guy understood that my face was actually *above* my neck!'

'Bit of a sleaze then.'

'Just a bit, but I managed to get rid of him when I told him I was a single mother and had two kids and an Alsatian.'

Bernie Hemmingway danced passed us yet again with a rose from one of the centre pieces in his teeth, he was pretending to play the castanets.

'Oh don't you just love life, darlings? Hurrah for Tillmouth and all who sail in her!' And he was off again, followed suspiciously closely by George Littlewood. Although George still managed a quick leer at Catherine's chest as he went past.

When Catherine started chatting to a group next to us, I felt an invisible pull; a feeling that someone was watching me. As I turned my head to the right, there, about twenty feet away, was the same face that had jolted me so much earlier on in the evening; a face which now had a different affect on me.

Tony smiled and this time I smiled right back at him. And in that moment, we connected. This is going to sound daft but I remember thinking as he walked towards me, that he was like Jesus walking through the Sea of Galilee, the crowds parting in his path and without question making way for him. I don't think we broke eye contact as he made his way over. It seemed to be happening in slow motion and finally he reached me and stood looking down at me.

'Maggie Parsons I believe.' He smiled a wry smile and bowed down dramatically in front of me.

'Tony Henderson if I'm not mistaken,' I replied, giving a mock curtsey then inadvertently blushing.

'I saw your name on the website,' he said, 'and I'm glad you didn't let me down.'

'What do you mean?'

'Oh, I don't know. Let's just say I thought it would be nice to catch up after all these years.' He gave me a smile that nearly took my breath away.

'I saw you earlier,' I said. 'Actually, I thought you were Luke at first.'

It might have been my imagination but I could have sworn I saw Tony's jaw tighten, just very briefly. But then, as quickly as it had happened, it disappeared.

'A common mistake or so I'm told. Luke's the old git though. It's us younger ones you need to watch out for. Footloose and fancy free and, unlike some, certainly wouldn't pass up an opportunity to meet up with the lovely Maggie Parsons again.' He raised one eyebrow flirtatiously.

'Are you enjoying yourself?' I asked.

He cocked his head to one side and looked at me.

'Is that the best you can come up with after ten years of not seeing me?'

'Sorry.' I grimaced. 'OK then, well I hear you've recently split up with your fiancée.'

'That's more like it, straight for the jugular.'

'Whoops, that was a bit forward of me wasn't it? I'm afraid that's the only bit of information I have about you since we last met.'

Tony didn't seem particularly offended.

'Let's just say, it was an unfortunate situation which needed resolving and, as far as I was concerned, dissolving it was the best way of resolving it.'

'I'm sorry to hear that,' I said, not feeling particularly sorry.

'Don't be, I'm not. Shit happens but then, sometimes, if you're lucky, there is something,' he paused, 'or someone, even better just around the corner.'

I blushed again and tried to change the subject.

'Well, forgive me for being boring again but what are you up to these days? What do you do for a living?'

'Stuck in the big bad city a fair bit of the time. I've got a little investment company which keeps the wolves from the door, but the rest of the time I stay with Dad.'

'How come?'

'Dunno really. I guess I prefer it in the country; less hectic, less polluted. Besides, Dad needs all the help he can get with that land of his. He's not as fit as he used to be and I wonder if he gets a bit lonely up there on his own so I do what I can to keep him company and share the load. You know how it is with family.'

A warm feeling spread over me. What a nice guy to look after his dad like that.

'Are you going to his party?' I asked, forgetting to put my 'Hi, I'm Maggie and I play hard to get' hat on.

'Well, I think Dad might object somewhat if I swerve it don't you?'

'Luke's not going though?' I unwittingly had a question in my voice.

He shrugged.

'More fool him. All work and no play makes Luke a dull boy. He'll just have to miss out on all the fun. I for one am rather looking forward to catching up properly with some old *acquaintances*.' The corner of his mouth lifted.

I felt yet another blush coming on, so I tried once again to steer the conversation but was growing increasingly aware of his eyes on me.

'Well, I hope the weather holds for it.'

'There you go again. We'll have to find some decent conversation in you at my Dad's bash, otherwise I won't be able to flirt very well with you,' he said, grinning, as I squirmed.

'I am sure I could think of some now if you'll just give me a minute,' I said.

'No can do I'm afraid. I'm on borrowed time. There's a group of us being picked up by a minibus right about now. I've got to go and wait in the lobby.'

'Will they fit a minibus in the lobby?' I asked.

He laughed.

'That's more like it. I'll expect much more of that quick wit next time we meet otherwise you'll have a lot of explaining to do. You've got a ten-year reputation to live up to.'

'I have?'

'You have, so don't let me down OK?'

'I'll do my best!'

Then he paused, as if deep in thought.

'The problem is,' he began slowly, 'I don't know whether I can let you loose at the party without a proper practice of slick conversation.'

I raised my eyebrows. 'Is that right?'

'Well, it just wouldn't be fair.-How would you compete?' he asked.

'Against who?'

He looked surprised. 'Well, me of course! I'd eat you for breakfast. Although, maybe not such a bad idea. No, it's no good,' he sighed, 'we'll have to meet beforehand and get in some decent hours of banter. It's the only solution.'

'You seem very sure of yourself. What exactly do you have in mind?'

'Hmmm, it's a tough one. I reckon I'll need a bit of time to think.' He began stroking his chin with his finger and thumb. 'I'll need to take your telephone number and we can discuss it.'

'I see. So, you're assuming that all this is fine with me then?'

'Of course. Like I said, you need the practice. It's the only way.' He shrugged, grinning like a naughty schoolboy.

Cheeky so and so, I thought, but Tony's smile was infectious and I was enjoying myself, so I went along with it.

'Well, I suppose if you're sure. I mean I'm not saying you're right or wrong, just that I might give you the benefit of the doubt, seeing as you seem to know so much about this "banter" stuff.'

'An expert, even though I do say so myself,' he said proudly.

'OK, I guess I could give you a shot; a sort of trial run.'

Suddenly aware of what I was doing, I couldn't believe I was about to give Tony Henderson my telephone number. I'd come here all set to see Luke and now I was flirting with his younger brother.

Tony took out his phone.

'You've got the same phone as mine!' I exclaimed with, probably, a bit more enthusiasm than was necessary.

'Ah, it's a sign,' Tony said nodding confidently.

I sent him a text attachment with my numbers on.

'So, that's that then. Now, feel free to practice before I ring you.'

I kicked him playfully on the foot.

'Watch it, you. A girl could go off a man you know.'

'Ah, now that would suggest she was on him in the first place.'

Without giving me a chance to protest, he was walking away.

'I'll see you soon,' he called over his shoulder. Then, before he'd gone far, he turned and walked back. Reaching me, he picked up my hand and kissed it, bowing again slightly.

Then he was gone.

It was quarter to midnight when Tony left and I found myself flagging. The party was still in full swing but I'd pretty much had enough, we'd been on the go for ages.

I spent a bit more time flitting from group to group but I really was past my best and sleep was beckoning. Time to find Catherine and see what she wanted to do.

I went over to where she and Adrian had been talking but she wasn't there. Scanning the bar I saw Joe who said he thought she was dancing so I headed off to the edge of the dance floor, smiling as I spotted Catherine singing away and dancing madly, along with what appeared to be half our year on the dance floor. They were laughing and whooping for the whole world to see. Onlookers were clapping wildly. They all seemed to be having a whale of a time. I smiled, and got a little happy/sad feeling in my stomach which, for some reason, brought tears to my eyes.

I turned and left them to it. I'd send Catherine a text from the room. She'd know to check her phone if she couldn't find me.

It had been a fun reunion. I'd had a great time. It had been nice to see old friends and realise that old enemies really weren't enemies at. All in all, it was well worth going and, despite Luke's no-show, I was getting an increasingly warm feeling when I thought about his brother.

I walked past the still-crowded bar for the last time that evening, glad to be escaping to the solace of my room.

'Oy, Magpie!' a female voice shouted.

As I looked over, I spotted my old netball pal Tracey Lovett towering above the crowd and waving frantically at me to go over.

'Maggie Parsons, get your arse over here,' she shouted, grinning from ear to ear.

I turned and walked over to her. I'd forgotten how tall she was. She'd been the best goal attack we'd ever had.

'Gimme five!' she cried as I reached her, putting her hand high in the air. I had to jump up to slap it.

There endeth the great night.

Up I jumped and 'gave her five', all good and well, but, as I landed, my heel collapsed, finally giving in to the evening. I felt my knees buckle and I fell, smack, in a very undignified and painful heap right in front of the whole bar crowd! Excellent!

I had landed, face down, cracking the side of my face on the floor – rather hard actually – drink still upright in my right hand (I had my priorities right at least) handbag still being clutched by my left hand and my body spread-eagled with my ankles at right angles to my legs! I'm not quite sure how one little heel could have caused so much damage but it had. My face was throbbing and I felt like I was having an out-of-body experience. If this had been a cartoon, I would have had tweeting birds and sparkling stars dancing in a ring around my head.

For a few moments, no one around me moved or appeared to want to help me. They'd probably decided I was just drunk and would crawl back up to my feet at any moment. But I couldn't move, what with both hands being full, and for all I knew I could have broken something. Pain was beginning to creep over my body and my face and head were becoming increasingly painful. The side of my forehead and cheekbone had obviously taken a nasty bang and my knee was throbbing too and had been scraped along the coarse carpet. Embarrassingly, I could feel tears welling up. On top of everything I was beginning to feel rather sick.

Suddenly, everyone crowded round me at once, the picture of concern and I was helped up by a couple of guys and a waiter.

'You all right?' came a voice.

'Is she all right?'

'What's happened?'

'Is she hurt?'

Someone brought a chair and I was guided down on to it with concerned faces all around me.

'Are you OK?' One of the guys who I thought I recognised as Jason Finch from my Biology class, asked me.

'Erm yes, I think so. Well no, actually, I feel a little strange.'

I sat for a few minutes to stop the room going round and someone got me a brandy. My left cheek felt really hot and painful even through the alcohol and my head was throbbing more and more by the minute. Luckily the sick feeling began to subside but I still felt like I was in another world.

'Seems like you've bashed yourself good and proper.' The middle-aged, somewhat portly, bar manager had been summoned and was offering his expert and tremendously helpful opinion. It turned out he was also the hotel's first-aider and had fetched a first aid box.

There was quite a crowd gathering around me by this time.

'She might have concussion you know,' someone offered up

'Yeah or she might have broken something.'

'Maybe she should lie down.'

'I think I'm fine, really.' I thought I'd better let them know I could hear them, before they started diagnosing surgery.

The room had stopped spinning, nothing felt broken and I think any temporary concussion was abating. Despite the pain, I reckoned I would live.

'I could just do with a bit of help up to my room,' I aimed at the bar manager whose name badge said Fred.

'Certainly, missy, you leave everything to me. I'll take over. Move along now, ladies and gentlemen, there's nothing to see here. Thank you,' he said, ushering people away and assuming military status.

I put my handbag arm around his neck and he helped me limp to the lift.

Safely inside my room Fred did some concussion tests (hotel policy) which involved him moving one finger from the corner of my left eye over to the corner of my right eye. I had to follow it while he watched my pupils and then I had to count how many fingers he was holding up. It was two. Content I was concussion-free he finished off by putting a dressing on my scraped knee. I felt like a little girl being tended to by her father.

Alone at last, I got myself ready for bed, limping round rather gingerly. I surveyed my face in the dimly lit bathroom mirror. Apart from a small cut, and a suggestion of some slight bruising, I was pretty much unscathed. My cheek and knee did throb though… and carpet burns. Carpet burns! They'd never let me live that down in the office.

I finally snuggled up inside my cool sheets and pulled the heavy covers up high to cover me. I texted Catherine to say I was in bed and that I'd see her in the morning. Finishing my brandy, and feeling suitably humbled by my brush with serious injury, I turned off the light, rolled over and went to sleep.

Chapter Five

I woke the next morning with a severely pounding head. I ached all over and felt rubbish. The sunlight was glinting through a crack in the curtains. I had no idea what time it was. For a few moments, I didn't recall the final part of the evening. I forgot about the floor-kissing moment and I assumed that the pounding head was simply a very bad hangover.

Then I became aware of an intense throbbing over one eye and remembered. I groaned, sliding down under the covers and pulling them over my head. It smelled too much like a brewery though so, pulling a face, I came back to the surface for air.

'Oh no,' I said out loud, embarrassment flooding through me.

'Oh nooo,' I wailed again as I remembered kissing Elvis, a practical stranger.

I did feel marginally better though when I recalled the flirting session with Tony. Would he call?

I wondered if I was in enough physical pain to make out that the terrible aching throughout my head and body was purely down to me bashing myself on the floor rather than being the result of a hangover. Hmmm.

It occurred to me that the room was rather too quiet and felt suspiciously empty.

Catherine? I turned my head. Her bed hadn't been slept in.

I went through the possibilities.

Seeing that Catherine was a virgin and had sworn she wouldn't sleep with anyone until her wedding night, the possibilities were few. I supposed this didn't stop her from being in a man's room though.

Joe? No, surely not.

Any of the forty or so men who had leered at her breasts all night? Possibly but unlikely.

Any of the forty or so women who had eyed her breasts warily all night? Stranger things had happened.

Perhaps she'd bumped into Pauline and Jenny and slept in their room so as not to wake me? Also unlikely. She'd be too keen to find out if I'd got up to anything.

Then where? Was she OK? Maybe she was in trouble. I pondered that possibility for a little while but it wasn't enough to start me leaping out of bed and banging on doors until I found her gagged and tied in the cellar or somewhere. I hurt too much to leap anywhere. I'd have to text her and hope that if she had been kidnapped, they would still allow her access to her mobile. If nothing else, for the possibility of letting me know she'd be OK as long as the ransom demand was met. Maybe they'd send a letter comprising solely of newspaper lettering so as not to identify themselves. Maybe they'd splice off Catherine's left ear or a finger and send it in a Jiffy bag as a warning. Maybe they'd…

My warped and, let's face it, somewhat unbelievable kidnapping chronicle was interrupted by the door opening slowly and quietly. In crept Catherine, looking a little dishevelled, still wearing last night's dress but un-gagged and with no sign of rope remains or missing body parts. I pulled myself up in bed.

'Hello,' she said sheepishly. 'Were you worried?'

'Not until about two minutes ago. I've only just woken up. Should I have been?'

'Not really, although… OH MY GOD!' she cried.

'What!!' I cried back, the fear of God instilled in me.

'What on earth's happened to your face?' She rushed over to the bed.

This was slightly worrying, as the curtains were still shut and the room wasn't exactly light.

'You need to upgrade your insulating tape.'

'Oh no! Your heel?'

'Yup. It gave way at the end of the night and I fell over in a heap,' I explained.

'Fell over? I thought you'd been mugged! Let me see.' She sat down on the edge of my bed, flicked on the sidelight and peered down at me.

'It looks awful! Your eye is purple.'

'It's probably just the reflection of your dress. What are you still doing in it anyway?'

'Never mind that, go and look in the mirror.' Without waiting for me to comply she pulled back my covers, displaying bare leg and a knee with bruises spreading around the edges of the dressing Fred had put on it.'

'You're black and blue, Mags!'

'And purple apparently.' I grudgingly manoeuvred my way out of bed and limped, painfully, over to the mirror. I clicked on the dressing table lamp.

'OH MY GOD, Cat, it's AWFUL! Worse than awful! It really is purple! What am I going to do? I don't remember it hurting that much, although… it was *quite* bad.' I decided I'd quite like a bit of sympathy.

'The wonders of alcohol,' she said wisely. 'It probably acted like an anaesthetic.'

I had a large purple ring round my left eye. From the bridge of my nose, all the way round to my cheekbone and up to my eyebrow. The corner of my eye was bloodshot and the lid was closing slightly. I just hoped I'd be able to conceal it with makeup.

As I fretfully inspected the damage, there was a knock on the door. Catherine answered it to Fred bearing a sachet of Alka Seltzer, two Nurofen and a first aid box.

He bustled in with his supplies, squinting in the darkened room.

'Just thought I'd check in on you; thought you might need… OH MY GOD, look at your face!'

Marvellous!

Despite his protestations and threats to call doctors and ambulances and such like, I managed to convince him I didn't need them.

There was a bit of a disagreement when we had to stop him from at least calling his wife Bessy, who did a mean compress for black eyes; she swore by them. She'd had lots of practice, due to their unruly teenage boys who'd spent more time in trouble than out of it, one of whom was currently spending a bit of time at Her Majesty's pleasure but was a good boy really. They blamed the system. If it hadn't been for the school not realising that having dyslexia didn't mean you were thick, he'd probably have been a doctor or a brain surgeon or something.

'They are never going to believe me at work that I fell over. They'll think I got in a fight,' I said to Catherine when Fred had finally left the room.

'So what happened exactly?' she asked.

I walked, or rather limped, her through the final steps of the previous evening. While she did make lots of caring and soothing noises, she also howled with laughter!

'You're meant to be my friend!' I reminded her.

'I am but you have to admit it is rather funny. You could always pretend you did have a fight. You know, build the drama.'

'I could say I was fending off a crowd of good looking men.'

'And were you?'

'Only Elvis. Although there wasn't much fending going on I'll be the first to admit.'

Catherine raised her eyebrows.

'Just a little kiss,' I said.

'How little?'

I sighed, thinking back to the terrace scene, wondering how many people had spotted us.

'Huge actually; a full-blown snog.' I cringed inwardly.

'Do you fancy him?'

'Not really, not much. It was nice to kiss someone though.'

I thought wistfully about Tony. Should I mention it at this stage? Maybe not a good idea. Catherine might well say I was on the rebound and I was too hungover to argue.

'Anyway, enough about me,' I said pointedly, 'where have you been all night?'

'Oh, Maggie, you'll never believe it! Promise you won't think I'm awful?'

'I promise. Let me guess, you decided to give Joe a second chance?'

'Yuck you must be joking.' She looked disgusted. 'He said he wanted to take me to bed so he could sleep with his head in between my breasts to stop the sounds of the party!'

I giggled.

'So what happened?'

'Well I was dancing away and Jimmy Morrison had us all doing some sort of line dance. They turned the music up and we got really lively, arms and legs flying about everywhere. It was a scream. But at one point, I flung my hand behind me and accidentally punched a passing waiter and sent him and his drinks tray flying!'

I laughed loudly, grimacing at the pain that suddenly shot through my head.

'Poor guy,' she went on, 'it was quite a blow!'

'What on earth did you do?' I was laughing helplessly by now, clutching my stomach.

'I started helping him clear up all the mess. I was so embarrassed. I'm surprised I didn't give him a black eye too! Anyway, while we were picking bits of broken glass up, I realised he was the porter who'd helped us up to our room yesterday afternoon and he was so cute. He kept telling me not to worry and that he'd clear it up, but we ended up mopping it up together and, by the time we'd finished, we were chatting away like we'd known each other for years.'

'OK… and what then?'

'This is going to sound awful.'

Surely Catherine wouldn't have slept with this guy, cute or not. It just wasn't in her game plan. She was after the full fairy-tale ending. The man of her dreams. Total soulmates and a huge white wedding with all the trimmings. This would be topped off by a springy four-poster bed with goose-feather duvet and rose petals sprinkled all over it to seal the deal.

'Well, I'd cut myself on a bit of broken glass, you see, and, when he realised I was bleeding, he insisted on getting me a plaster from the first aid box. So off we went to find the first aid key from some guy named Fred. Only he wasn't in his room.' Realisation spread over her face.

'Hang on… was that Fred with the Nurofen?'

'Yes!'

'Bizarre!'

'So what did you do?'

'Went to his room to find a plaster.'

'Cat! You hardly knew him!'

'I know, I know, but he was so sweet. His name's Nico and he's just lovely. He lit up a couple of candles and put a plaster on my hand and we sat by the window looking at the moon and stars and shared a bottle of lager he had in the fridge. Oh, Mags, I know I've only just met him but we had so much in common. We talked for hours. It was really lovely. He comes from Italy, Florence to be precise, and he's over here with his brother studying for a business degree at uni; it's some sort of flexible course which means he can also work at the hotel, to support himself.'

I had to ask.

'Did you…?'

'No! Of course not! You know I'm saving myself for my wedding night. He made up a bed on his sofa for him and let me sleep in his bed. It seemed like the natural thing to do. There was never really any question of me coming back to our room. He was worried I'd wake you up and insisted I stayed. He's so lovely and such a gentleman.'

'Did you kiss?'

She blushed.

'Yes! Several times! And guess what?'

'What?'

'He told me I was beautiful. And he says he hates skinny women and told me I had a lovely, comfy body and I made him feel safe.'

'Wow!'

'I *know*! Do you think it's too soon to be in love with him?' she asked.

'Probably,' I said.

She hugged herself.

'See, I did meet someone! My horoscope was right!' Then she shot me a glance and her face fell. 'Sorry, Mags, I didn't mean to rub it in about Luke.'

'Oh that's OK, don't worry. Besides…' I thought might as well come clean, 'Tony and I had a bit of a flirt.'

'Tony Henderson?'

'Yup.'

'Goodness, another Henderson!'

'I know.'

She hesitated.

'Could be a rebound you know.'

I shrugged.

'Does it bother you?'

'What?'

'That he's Luke's brother.'

'I don't know really. But Luke didn't show and Tony did and he paid me lots of attention and made me laugh so that's got to be worth something, surely.'

'Mind you', I swivelled back to look in the mirror again, 'I'm not sure he'd be so attentive if he saw me like this. How long do you think black eyes take to disappear?' I asked hopefully.

'Not long. Don't worry it's Touche Eclat to the rescue!' she grinned. 'Now, what time is it? I'm meeting Nico in the lobby at eleven o'clock, check-out time, to say goodbye.'

I peered over at my watch.

'Shit! We have precisely seven minutes to get dressed, cover my eye up, get packed and check out!'

I left Catherine in the lobby to wait for Nico while I limped out to the front of the hotel. The bright sunshine blinded my good eye for a moment.

'Good God,' a male voice boomed 'it's the Bride of Frankenstein and she's been in a fight!' So much for my attempt at a cover up.

The omnipresent Bernie Hemmingway appeared beside me looking decidedly less flamboyant than the previous evening; puffy-faced and piggy-eyed.

'I hope you sorted her out good and proper!' he said.

'Who?'

'The bitch who gave you that.'

'Oh her, yeah she's in hospital. They fear she might not last the weekend.'

'Did you try to nick her bloke?'

'I did, but she had two. It just wasn't fair,' I explained.

He nodded gravely, 'I understand.'

We both sniggered and he bent to kiss my good cheek.

'See you in another ten then!' And off he wobbled, still sporting his floppy hat and last night's clothes. I wondered if he'd actually been to bed.

I found Pauline and Jenny beside the rose bushes. Pauline still had the job of rubbing Jenny's back while Jenny threw up, yet again, over the flower bed this time. I was surprised there was anything left but, apparently, it was the cooked breakfast re-appearing which made me rather glad I'd swerved it. It didn't look too good from my angle.

'What on earth happened to your face?' Pauline asked between rubs.

'I had an argument with the floor and it was bigger than me.'

Jenny tilted her head up towards me.

'You look like a panda,' she croaked.

'Cheers, Jen, you look pretty good yourself.' I took in her puffy eyes, pink cheeks and dribbly mouth. But, despite everything, she was clearly still beautiful. It was totally unfair.

'This is my breakfast in bed. Flower bed!' she feebly attempted a joke. I didn't think the hotel gardener would look on the situation too favourably. Could sick constitute as fertiliser?

A voice from the hotel entrance crashed through my delicate head.

'OH MY GOD! Look at your eye! Your face!' Tracey Lovett cried. She looked as fit as anything, not a trace of a hangover and she was dressed in a baby pink tracksuit with whiter than white Nike tennis shoes. She bounced over to where I was standing.

'Are you OK, does it hurt?' she asked examining me with French manicured nails.

'Only when you poke it with your nail,' I replied, hearing my phone ting out a message alert from deep down in my bag.

'Sorry!' Tracey pulled her hand away quickly.

'I feel like this is my fault.'

'I guess it would have been better if you'd been shorter,' I admitted, ruefully.

Her face fell.

'But then you wouldn't have been the best goal attack in history,' I grinned.

She beamed down at me.

'At least let me take your case.'

She picked up my case, just as Nico and Catherine came outside glowing and shy.

'Who's lover boy?' Pauline asked from the vicinity of the flowerbed.

'Catherine picked up a hotel porter. Cute huh?'

'Don't tell me... she's in love!' Jenny straightened up and blew her nose on a tissue.

'Probably... and, by the looks of things, I reckon he might be too.'

Jenny started to protest but thought better of it and leant back over and started retching again mumbling threats about suing the hotel for food poisoning.

I let Tracey help me over to Catherine's car, where I waited patiently for Catherine and Nico to say their long, slow goodbye. Tracey apologised again, squeezed me sympathetically on the shoulder and bounced off to play squash with her friends. The idea of squash filled me with dread at the best of times but, with a hangover, a black eye, a dodgy knee and carpet burns, I would rather have been tortured by the fictitious gang that had supposedly kidnapped Catherine. They could even take my right ear too!

Catherine finally joined me. Her cheeks were flushed and her eyes sparkling. We packed away our luggage in the boot then she opened up the car and we both flumped down in our seats.

She let out a big sigh.

'Enjoy it?' I asked her.

'Oh, so much. You?'

'Well, it was eventful.' I checked my face in the sun visor mirror.

'So, will you see Mr Porter again?' I asked, as she drove off waving frantically out of the window at him.

'Yes! Well, at least I hope so. I hope he doesn't change his mind. He's promised to call in the week and we're going to meet up here again next weekend on his day off, and then, depending on my shifts, maybe the following weekend in London, if we still want to, which we will. Oh, Mags, I think this could be the real thing.' She sighed another heavy sigh.

We headed out through the country lanes and, with Catherine in her far-away love land I let my mind wander over the previous evening. Luke not showing had left me feeling bruised. I had thought that the reunion would be the night for him to make peace but he hadn't bothered. I wasn't sure if I was angrier at him or at myself; him for letting me down again or me for being so stupid to let a teenage romance take over my life like this. I wondered if we'd ever get the chance to put things right.

I thought about Tony. Maybe Catherine had been right. Maybe our horoscopes had predicted correctly for a change. Could it be that, after all these years, Tony was the Henderson brother I was meant to get together with? Anyway, Luke was probably fat and ugly by now and Tony was the handsome one. I thought about seeing him at his Dad's birthday party, maybe before, and a feeling of anticipation and excitement filled my stomach.

I suddenly remembered I had a message, so reaching down into my handbag, I located my phone and smiled as I remembered Tony having the same model.

I didn't recognise the number. Clicking on the message, my heart did a little leap as I read it.

Free Banter lessons available. Dinner included. Bring smart clothes & high heels 4 props & poss banter subjects. Dates TBA. Fridays & Sats special offers of free wine & cocktails. RSVP initial interest. Yours TH

I hugged myself, wondering how soon I should text back. I checked the time he sent it. Only fifteen minutes. Not long enough.

We sat in silence.

I started humming.

More silence.

Bugger, I had never been one to play hard to get.

I texted back:

Suggestion being considered. Pina coladas may swing decision. Agree, initial idea tempting, but still need 2 consider whether teacher suitable & qualified 2 run course. Maybe texter could advise textee?

I pressed 'Send'.
Five minutes later a message alert sounded.

Pina coladas confirmed. Only as special case. Teacher has over 15 yrs exp in banter & quals levels 1-4. Need level 5 2b achieved & request textee agree 2b guinea pig. Will even throw in free transport 2restaurant. (texter not used to begging, but bribery speciality!)

I texted back:

Ah, now guinea pigging is my speciality, especially if Thai food is present. Call me. M (GP)

I sent it and very quickly it tinged again. Catherine raised her eyebrows beside me. It read:

Dear GP (Doc!) This is 1 happy banterer X

'Tony by any chance?' Catherine enquired.
'Tony,' I confirmed, unable to stop smiling.
With the surge of excitement this new possibility with Tony gave me, I realised at that moment how lonely I'd been of late, going home to an empty flat every night. I'd not had anyone in my life for ages and while my independence was not to be knocked, my social life was good fun and Catherine was the best friend I could ever wish for... having a boyfriend, a relationship, was different; special; intimate. Weekends away, dinner for two, company in the evening watching films, surprise presents, engagement parties, wedding plans, more presents... *stop it, Maggie*; I inwardly told myself off.
Having said all that, I hadn't had much luck with relationships and the idea of one was quite probably better than the reality, but still... I lived in hope. Could Tony be different? Was this fate?
As I daydreamed about the possibilities, we turned a corner into Tillmouth and drove into the main street.

A final look at the little bridge and the babbling brook which glistened and twinkled in the sunshine. The village seemed sleepy on the way back. Sunday morning and all was peaceful. The church bells began to chime and it was really quite lovely. Catherine and I exchanged glances, her out of two eyes and me out of one and a half.

'Does kind of feel like home, doesn't it?' Catherine conceded.

'Mmmmm,' I agreed sleepily. 'It kinda does.'

Chapter Six

Monday morning, before I'd even limped to my desk, I was the talk of the office. It seems bad news travelled fast.

'Did you hear about Mike Tyson?' Craig quipped as I walked up. 'After going just two rounds with our Maggie, he's been forced into early retirement and is threatening suicide,' he finished, greedily scoffing down some toast.

'Ha bloody ha.' I sat down at my desk, putting my handbag down by my feet.

'Who's been spreading the gossip?'

'Mate, you were on the nine o'clock news last night. A satellite picked up on you and your shiner while it was scanning for alien life; thought we'd been invaded!'

'Surprised they didn't spot you then,' I said.

Maureen was silently staring at me.

'I've told you before about nicking others birds' blokes,' Craig said throwing a scrunched up ball of paper at me.

'Don't be so mean, Craig. I'm sure Maggie's got a perfectly good reason for having a black eye.' Maureen had found her voice.

'Haven't you, Maggie?' she enquired.

'My heel gave way on my stiletto. I fell over and hit the ground that's all. Nothing particularly earth shattering I'm afraid. So you can tell your friend Mike Ty thingy...'

'Tyson, dim bird.'

'*Tyson* then, that he's really got nothing to worry about and he's not to do anything silly on my account.'

I tried to act like I didn't care but I was pretty embarrassed. There had been a point in my life where I'd quite fancied the idea of a black eye, just to see what it was like but now I had one, I wished I hadn't. I felt like one of those women you sometimes see in the supermarket on a Saturday morning; one black eye and not much self-esteem. Four unruly kids hanging off her. Another baby in the trolley wailing for food and an expression on her face that says I need out but I don't know how to get there. That's how I felt. Although I didn't have a boyfriend or husband who had given me my black eye, people were sure as hell going to think I did. Either that or they'd think I'd got into some drunken pub brawl with another girl. Or maybe a fight in the taxi queue. The women would all think I was bad news and avoid me like the plague and whisper behind my back and the blokes would all be asking if we'd had lesbian sex while we were at it. My life was doomed.

'Are you all right?' Bill asked kindly.

'I'm fine thanks Bill, and *thank you* for asking,' I smiled sarcastically in Craig's direction.

Justin had been shooting daggers at me since I arrived; on time, I hasten to add. He was bound to say something soon enough.

'So how was the evening?' Maureen asked, 'Did your Luke chappy see you looking like that?'

'He didn't see me looking like anything, he didn't show up,' I explained.

'Probably heard about your left hook and decided to swerve it,' Craig said.

'Be afraid, be very afraid.' I glowered menacingly at him then turned to check my emails.

'I'll put the kettle on shall I? Cheer you up a bit?' Maureen pushed back her chair and headed off to the kitchen.

I was aware of people from the main office standing up and staring. Every so often someone would point in my direction. I slid further down in my seat and prayed for my eye to heal quickly.

From behind me, I heard Justin's door open. I held my breath. I let my fingers type something and nothing onto my PC and willed that he go off in another direction.

'Maggie,' he boomed. 'My office. Now.'

Here we go.

I stood up and followed him into his office, hanging my head, ready for my telling off.

Justin was standing with his back to me, attention fixed on the notice board behind his desk.

'Close the door and sit down please,' he said, still not facing me.

I shut the door quietly behind me and went and sat down on the small chair on the opposite side of the desk to Justin's monster chair.

Justin turned round slowly, leaning down and resting his hands on his desk; his eyes locked with mine.

'This has all gone that little bit too far now, Maggie, don't you think?' His voice was slow and deliberate, suspiciously calm. He should have been shouting at me; bawling me out for my black eye and lack of respect. Yelling at me for the way I was letting the company down.

Unnerved, I focussed on my lap, feeling ashamed.

'I'm really very sorry, Justin.'

'Are you? Are you really? What exactly are you sorry for, hmmm?'

Why wasn't he shouting?

I looked up.

'Well, I'm sorry for my eye. I'm sorry about coming to work with it.'

'Ha! That's a good one!' he said 'The one time you've actually got a decent reason *not* to come into the office and what do you do?'

'I…'

'Shut up, Maggie!' His voice rose. 'I'll tell you what you do,' (apparently the low voice thing had come to an end) 'you bloody well come in here looking like a battered fucking wife and give out goodness knows what message to the rest of the staff about what you get up to at weekends.'

'But I…'

'What the hell do you think this says about the company?'

Was this a rhetorical question?

'It really wasn't my fault, Justin, you see my heel…'

'I don't give a damn about your bloody heel! I don't give a damn about your lies and reasons. What I do, however, give a damn about is this company, this company's staff and this company's image. It's my responsibility to see that the staff here *respect* their jobs and the way this company is run, and it is not, I repeat *not,* run for people who want to waltz in after a weekend bender, having had a fight with their boyfriend, and expect things to be the same on the Monday morning.'

'But it wasn't…'

'I don't want to *hear* it, Maggie,' Justin bawled at me. Then, taking a breath in and exhaling steadily, he deliberately slowed and calmed his voice again. 'I don't want to hear it.'

Still leaning over the desk he looked directly at me and sighed, before sitting back down in his chair.

'This is it. You've had enough chances. No more.'

I felt the tears mounting.

'Quite frankly, this makes no difference now. It's the end of the line, Maggie.'

'What do you mean?'

'Just what I say: we won't be requiring your services anymore. I'm making some redundancies today. I thought it was going to be a tough morning but it seems you've made my decision easier than I thought it was going to be.'

He went to his computer screen and started moving and clicking his mouse around.

I sat there dumfounded. Surely this was a mistake. 'You mean... you're firing me?'

'No, I've just told you, I'm making you redundant, Maggie.'

What was going on? This was completely surreal. One minute I had a job, a boring but safe job, and the next minute I'd been made redundant. How?

'This doesn't feel like being made redundant. Where's the nice letter explaining everything? I feel like I'm being fired.'

'Perhaps you should have thought about that before you waltzed in here looking like that,' he said pointedly. 'Besides, if you were being fired, I'd want you to leave immediately. You've still got unfinished work to do here.'

'Well who else is going then?'

He hesitated.

'I suppose you'll find out anyway. From this office, Kevin is also going and, for the rest that's none of your damn business.'

'Kevin? *Kevin?* I raised my voice. 'But he's the office junior! You mean it's me and the office junior, like we are the lowest of the office or something?'

'Get your head into gear, Maggie. Think about it; we've just lost the Greenwich account and who's the account manager? You are. So use your brain for once and work out the logistics.'

'And Kevin? Why him?'

'Maggie, just worry about your own future, eh? Leave the rest to me. Now, we'll see you get what you're due,' he said perfunctorily.

'And what exactly will I be due after two years' hard labour?' I asked sarcastically.

'You'll need to discuss things like that with personnel. Now, if you'll excuse me, I have a lot of work to do.'

I was totally shocked. I really hadn't been expecting this. Why the hell hadn't I left sooner, of my own accord? How degrading! Bloody hell. Bloody Justin.

'Fine,' I said huffily, scraping back my chair and standing up. I didn't know what else to say. Nice working with you would have been a bare-faced lie. Thanks for everything and all your support also a huge lie. You bastard, after all I've done for you, would have been only partly true, after all I hadn't exactly worked my socks off, so fine it was.

I moved to the door but, just as I was turning the handle, Justin spoke again.

'Find Kevin and send him in, please.'

The cheek of it!

I silently seethed as I shut the door behind me. Mandy smirked and raised a condescending eyebrow at me as I came out.

The others looked up as I arrived back at my desk.

'Everything OK, Maggie?' Maureen asked.

'I'm fine,' I said, feeling shell-shocked. 'Won't be a sec.'

My pride was severely dented as I limped slowly down towards the photocopier where Kevin was doing his usual wodges of document copying, which head office still insisted on.

'Kevin, Justin wants to see you in his office.'

He looked up with the dopey expression he always had.

'Blimey, Maggie, what happened to your eye?'

'I'll tell you later. Better go in, he's not in the best of moods.'

Off he went, for some reason passing me a pile of papers to hold on his way and I stood there, like a lemon, while he headed off to see Justin.

I was quite fond of Kevin in a funny sort of way. He was a bit dippy but harmless and quite sweet. Erring on the quiet side, he only usually came alive when he'd had a couple of beers and would start getting all het up about some world crisis or another; saving the whale or the rain forest. He was obviously passionate about things that mattered to him. But, apart from that, he hardly said boo to a goose.

I felt sorry for him now; he didn't stand much of a chance in the big bad world. I hoped Justin wouldn't be too unkind to him.

Suddenly from down the corridor, I heard a crash and someone shouted. Quickly putting Kevin's papers down, I rushed to see what it was.

I saw Maureen first, standing up at her desk, a shocked expression on her face. She was staring in the direction of Justin's office.

'Do you think he's all right?' I heard her say to Craig.

'What's happened? Do you think who's all right?' I asked as I reached them.

Craig nodded his head towards Justin's office, 'It's Justin. Kevin's only gone and decked the bastard.'

I turned to see Justin on the floor of his office, making a grab for the edge of his desk to pull himself up.'

'Oh my God, that's because he's just laid him off,' I explained in horror.

Kevin stood looking down at Justin, a far cry from being, quiet, dippy and harmless. He was shaking and shouting at him.

'You bastard! After all I've done for you.' At least one of us could say that truthfully.

'What should we do?' Maureen asked fretfully.

'Do you think we should go and help him?' I asked, rather lamely.

Craig squared himself.

'I'll go and sort it out.'

And off he went, followed rather more slowly by Bill, just as two of the business managers from the main office came through the adjoining door with the same idea.

But they were too late, something had evidently been said to upset Kevin again, and, thwack, Justin was back down on the floor.

The men reached Justin's door just as Kevin was coming out.

'He's all yours, lousy son of a bitch.'

Justin was clambering up the desk again and shouting. His nose was bloody.

'Get him out! GET HIM OUT NOW! Crazy idiot, call security.'

Kevin turned back.

'No need, I'm out of here, arsehole!'

'You OK?' I aimed at Kevin as he walked out. I was actually quite impressed. Despite my anti-violence policy, I couldn't help finding the whole alpha-male aggression thing strangely attractive.

'Yeah, don't worry about me, plenty more companies around here. That bastard wouldn't know a good admin assistant if it hit him in the face.'

'And you did!' Maureen giggled.

This was the funniest thing I'd ever heard Maureen say.

'I'm off down the Brickman's,' Kevin said as Craig and Bill returned. And, with that, he grabbed his denim jacket and stomped out the door and down through the main office.

I thought I'd better get my news out the way.

'Listen guys, I'd better tell you now, Kevin's not the only one.'

Three shocked faces turned and stared at me.

'I've been made redundant,' I said, looking round at them all. Maureen's eyes filled with tears.

'But that's not fair, why? Oh, the eye I suppose?' she said.

'If it was because of the eye, surely you'd have been fired,' Bill rationalised.

'Not according to Justin but I think the eye made it easier to present the good news.'

Craig was unusually quiet.

Security had been called and two guards walked in but, by that time, Kevin was long gone. We didn't understand why Justin hadn't called the police, that is, until lunchtime.

Craig, Kevin, Maureen, Bill and I sat on a bench in the sunny beer garden of the Brickman's Arms, drinking cider.

'Didn't you think he'd call the cops?' Craig asked Kevin.

'Na, I told him if he dared to cut my notice money or call the police, I'd let his bitch-face wife know he'd been having it away with our Mandy. That shut him up.'

'Wow, nice one Kev!' Craig slapped him on the back for the fourth time in an hour. We sat united it our newfound admiration for Kevin. Who'd have thought it?

The boys began to swap fighting stories and Maureen turned to me.

'I don't want you to go, Maggie. Who am I going to share things with?' she asked dolefully.

'We can keep in touch and there's always the telephone and email,' I assured her.

'You'll have to teach me to use the email properly then. I keep sending all the naughty attachment things people send me on to Justin by accident. I'm sure he must think I'm trying to be his friend or something. But I'm not... especially not now!'

'What are you going to do, for work I mean?' she asked.

'I have no idea. It's come as a complete shock. Maybe I'll take some time out?'

I knew I couldn't really. After all, I was broke. I would have my notice money but that wouldn't exactly take me very far. I really hoped it wouldn't be too difficult to find something else. After all, people like me were always in demand, weren't they?

Mandy came looking for us not long after and announced that Justin had been called away and she'd been left in charge and we were all to come back to work because it was gone two o'clock.

'Cow,' Maureen said under her breath.

But we drank up and, leaving Kevin in the beer garden with cider-filled promises to keep in touch, trudged slowly after her.

I realised at that moment, that I might just be getting the kick up the backside I actually needed.

Chapter Seven

Two evenings later, after a pig of a day made bearable by the fact that Justin also now had a black eye (ha! – in fact – ha, ha, ha, ha, HA!), there was an unexpected buzz at my door. It was Catherine. I pressed the intercom button for her to come up.

She bustled in a few minutes later, red in the face and out of breath from the climb up the stairs, and flopped a big pile of brochures on the table.

'That landlord of yours is taking the mickey! Anyway, these' she said, puffing and panting, 'are the answer to the next bit of your life.' She took out a tissue and began her usual ritual of mopping her face and cleavage, then took off her steamed up glasses and started cleaning them.

I glanced at the pile suspiciously.

'Holiday brochures?'

'Exactly! Oh, Mags, it would be great, don't you think?' She stood beaming like a child.

'I think it's impossible, I'm skint!'

'No you're not, not really. Anyway, the way I figure it is this. You've lost your job.

You've got some notice to work but then you're a free agent. You can sign on with an agency before you go, get them to put your CV out there and then turn up for interviews when you get back, easy! And, in the meantime, live a little. It'll be good for you. You've been saying for ages you felt stuck in that job and now you're free and that's worth celebrating!'

'Cat, I can't! I need every penny I've got now. What if I don't get another job for ages? I can't tap my parents for money anymore.'

'But you've got a new credit card, I know you have. And that's what they're for, being a little bit risqué every once in a while.'

'But I need a job and, besides, I used my credit card for my reunion dress and I'm not sure I'm cut out for living life on the edge.'

'Oh, Maggie, Maggie, Maggie,' she said dramatically, collapsing down on my sofa.

'Think about it, this is your chance to do something different; something other than being stuck in an office. Something spur of the moment. It could be just the tonic you need and it'll give you a chance to think about what you want in life. You know, what's important to you.'

I sat down in the armchair, jiggling my knee.

'Even if I did go on holiday, I wouldn't want to go on my own,' I said, realising that if I was being sold to by a sales rep, I would have just given a 'buying signal'.

'No silly, I've got two weeks' leave coming up. I was going to spend half of it redecorating my kitchen but, now you're out of a job, I'd much rather go on holiday!'

'Thanks!'

'Sorry, but you know what I mean. Oh, please come, it'll be such a laugh.'

'Won't you want to see Nico though?'

'There's always the second week. Anyway, he can only get one week off, I've already checked!' She grinned.

'Jenny's well up for it,' she said, then blushed.

'So you're all in it behind my backs.'

'Not exactly, Pauline doesn't know yet. But she will!' She didn't even try to hide her glee. 'Jenny reckons Spain's a good bet; says she'll be able to sort us all out with a huge discount through work.'

'So how do you know that Pauline will come? Not that I'm going you understand,' I added.

'Jenny's going to work on her tonight; she says she's in a real rut.'

'Oh I see, so you're working on me and she's working on Pauline.'

'Listen, when else are you going to get a chance like this? Please, please, please...?'

'The last time you said please, please, please like that, I got roped into going to the school reunion and look what happened there!' I pointed to my only slightly faded black eye.

'Yes but... um... you had a great time! And you met Tony!'

'Mum would kill me.' I gave another buying signal.

'Don't tell her! Just send her a postcard and say what a wonderful time you're having. She'll be fine.'

'She doesn't even know I've lost my job yet.'

'Best not to let on then, at least not 'til you've booked the ticket.'

'I haven't said I'll come yet!' I insisted.

'Ah, you haven't said you'll come *yet*! That means, you will come but haven't said you'll come *yet.*' She lingered dramatically over the word yet and nodded to herself, knowingly.

'OK, OK! I'll think about it.'

'No!' She cried 'You have to decide now, it's the rule. The only way you are going to make some positive changes in your life is by changing the way you play things. Live a little, make a decision tonight. As a very wise man once said, I forget who it was now, "if you want things in your life to change, you have to change things in your life".'

I tutted. I was being ganged up on by Catherine and a nameless guru.

'You'll need to give me a bit of time to think.'

'I'll go and open the wine.'

'What wine?!'

'The wine I bought to go with browsing through these brochures silly! What wine indeed.' And off she went, muttering, to the kitchen.

I walked over to the lounge window and gazed out over the rooftops. It was a warm and sunny evening. The sky was hazy blue and the tops of the buildings were still soaked in sunshine. Opposite I could see a couple having dinner on a little table they'd put out on their balcony. They were sharing a bottle of wine and laughing easily together. I was suddenly gripped by the lack of outdoor life I'd been having recently. Being cooped up in the office, often until quite late, meant I hadn't exactly enjoyed lots of free time in the fresh air and sunshine.

Perhaps I didn't need to find a job immediately. Maybe this was the breathing space I needed. I'd said myself I was bored and that the job was beneath me, well what next? More of the same? Not a good idea.

'When are you talking about going?' I called to Catherine in the kitchen. *Buying signals, shmying signals.*

'As soon as you've worked notice and left that horrid *CrapiTel* job,' she called back.

The very mention of CapiTel coursed through me with so much negativity it seemed to make up my mind for me. I rolled my eyes to myself.

'Go on then,' I called out to the kitchen, 'let's do it. But it had better be good otherwise I'll want my money back. Or rather my credit card company will.'

Catherine came rushing back through with the wine bottle under her arm and two full glasses in hand.

'Yay! Quick,' she passed me one, 'let's have a toast to our holiday before you change your mind!'

I shook my head and chinked her glass.

'To wherever we end up and whatever we end up doing,' Catherine toasted.

Somehow I'd been convinced and before I knew it, we were all booked to go to Spain with the help of one of Jenny's very rich clients. I signed on with a central London temping agency. Over the phone I might add. I did, initially, attempt one interview with an agency but the bony-arsed, blue-suited recruitment consultant took one condescending look at my eye and raised her over-plucked eyebrow so high, that any higher and she may have lost it in her hair. I tried to explain what had happened but she said she was sure it was all very unfortunate but I needed to think of how it would look to a prospective employer. She was right of course. It had never crossed my mind when Justin had delivered his news. Still, the prospect of a holiday away with the girls was doing an increasingly good job of making the future seem rosier than it actually was.

Chapter Eight

Tony called me the following Friday. I found myself inadvertently checking my black eye in the mirror. I was very glad he couldn't see me.

'So, Doc, how goes it?' he asked.

I grinned down the receiver.

'I've been better,' I admitted.

'Ah, well that's where I come in. What are you doing next Friday?'

'Hmm, now let me think. I do have a couple of options.'

'Oh really?'

'Well, Brad Pitt popped round yesterday and asked if I was free for a little soirée.'

'Ah, you've been asked too, huh?' he joined in, seamlessly.

'Yes, but I don't know about you, I'm not keen. I never know whether he's on or off with Ang' or if those rumours about Jen were true. I really don't want to put my foot in it again.'

'No, I know what you mean, last time I went round I called Angelina "Jen", twice! And when Brad collapsed in a fit of giggles, you know what he's like, I thought she'd never invite me again.'

'Maybe they're low on numbers?' I suggested.

'Oy! Watch it, you.'

'Sorry,' I giggled.

'Still,' he said 'what say we swerve it?'

'Maybe you're right.'

'What about your other option though?' he reminded me.

'Ah yes, the council planning meeting. That one's more difficult.'

'Really, what's on the agenda?' he asked seriously.

'Well, first there's my gazebo, then the rooftop swimming pool. They're buggers to get passed you know.'

'So I've heard. I opted for a basement pool myself, bit dark sometimes but the fairy lights help.'

'Aren't you worried they'll fall off the wall and into the pool and you'll end up electrocuting yourself?' I asked.

'No, the fairies won't let that happen.'

'I see.' I giggled, thoroughly enjoying myself. 'So you think I should reschedule the planning meeting and put in new plans for a basement pool instead then.'

'Pretty much.'

'With fairy lights?'

'With fairy lights,' he confirmed.

'That only leaves the rooftop gazebo then.'

'Ah, but now you're moving the pool, you don't need one, at least not this summer.'

He had a point.

'So, you're saying I should decline my two options and go out with you instead then?'

'Well, if you don't come out with me, then we'll both have to go along to the Pitts' and they might not let me sit next to you. That just wouldn't do.'

'I suppose you're right. Last time they insisted I sat next to – God rest his genius soul – David Bowie. I mean, the guy's a serious legend, there's no denying that, but he kept bending my ear about how Ground Control wasn't what it used to be and did I want to make friends with his Major Tom.'

Tony laughed loudly.

'I think you may be playing the role of Banter Teacher if you carry on like that.'

'Maybe I don't need lessons then?'

'Oh, I think you do really. I'm just being kind.'

'Cheeky get!'

'Will you come then? I promise you can have as many pina coladas as you can drink and I'll be the perfect gentlemen.'

'Can I have an umbrella?'

'Do you forecast rain?'

'Ha ha… I meant a cocktail umbrella.'

'Well, of course, and a wedge of pineapple.'

'What about a sparkler and a singing waiter?' I asked.

'I can organise the sparkler but I'm not sure Billy's caff would run to singing waiters, not unless Doris the tea lady does an evening special in karaoke.'

'Then I'll settle for the sparklers and you can owe me one.'

'The next time maybe.'

'Maybe.'

'Good; sorted. I'll pick you up around… seven thirty?'

'Thanks, Tony,' I said, more seriously this time.

'Damn, there's my other line. Sorry, Mags, got to go, I'm expecting a call from my solicitor. Can you text me your address?'

I agreed and we said our goodbyes and hung up.

I was smiling from ear to ear as I texted him. I had a feeling our date was going to be really good fun but I sincerely hoped my black eye would have disappeared!

Chapter Nine

Around at my flat on Saturday morning, Catherine was up in arms.

'I've put on half a stone!'

'You don't look any different to me.'

'How on earth am I going to fit into a bikini? she wailed. 'We'll have to go shopping and buy a costume that hides my fat bits, if one exists. I hate the fact I've got no will power.'

I watched as she tucked into a Marks and Spencer's custard slice while I made a half-hearted attempt at the jam doughnut she'd brought round for me. I was supposed to be on a strict diet for my date with Tony.

'The thing is,' she began almost inaudibly, her mouth stuffed full, 'it's in my genes.'

'What is?'

'Well, my grandmother was really big. It was her metabolism.'

'Mmm hmm.'

'Apparently it was the same with her grandmother, so it must go in missed generations. I might as well accept it,' she said reluctantly.

'Don't your alternative therapy books talk about mind over matter?' I asked.

'Yes, but that's for people who don't have hereditary gene issues like mine.'

I considered my own grandmother. She was skinny and built like Kylie Minogue, so no generation gene skipping for me, more's the pity.

Looking down I sighed. The doughnut was all but gone.

Perhaps I'd book myself in for a mud wrap.

'So, are you excited about next Friday?' Catherine asked.

'Very.'

'Do you think your eye will have gone back to normal?'

'I don't know. I'm sure it's got worse!' I stood up and surveyed it for the umpteenth time in the mirror over the fireplace.

'He'll probably see the funny side,' she said.

'Either that or he'll wonder what kind of a mad woman he's asked out. If it doesn't disappear, I may have to postpone.'

'Sorry to mention it again, but are you sure Tony's not a rebound from Luke? I mean there's a definite resemblance.'

'It's an awfully long overdue rebound don't you think? It's been ten years.'

'Yes, but it was only a week ago you were all het up about Luke and now Tony steps in and sweeps you off your feet. I don't want to be a killjoy, I'm just saying.'

'Have you heard from Nico?' I asked, changing the subject.

'Every day, sometimes twice!' she bubbled excitedly. 'Honestly, I know he's foreign but he speaks better English than I do! I keep having to fetch the dictionary to understand all his big words. He says I'd love Florence, *Firenze*. Oh, I have to lose weight, Maggie! Being in a bikini with you lot is one thing but he'd probably take one look at me and run off in the opposite direction.'

'Don't be silly. He obviously really likes you. Who phones who?' I asked.

'Well apart from once, he always calls me.'

'There you go then!'

'Oh, he's so gorgeous!' she sighed, 'I just can't believe it's happened. It's like it's too good to be true.'

'When are you seeing him again?'

'Tomorrow, he's coming down on his day off. Then I'm seeing him the day after Mr Henderson's birthday party.'

'Oh, Maggie. I think I might be…'

'In love,' I finished. 'I know, I know.' We'd been here before.

Chapter Ten

The following Friday evening arrived and I was in a panic. I'd had the week from hell, trying to sort things out at work and leave them in a good enough state for Justin and that day had been particularly challenging due to Justin's tyrannical attitude. He'd kept me working way past five thirty, a complete sin for any Friday, and I was really late home. Honestly, I could have kicked him.

The good thing was, my black eye had virtually disappeared – with a bit of make-up it would look fine – but, even better, Justin's hadn't (ha, ha, HA!).

I only had an hour to get ready. I'd washed my hair the previous evening and was currently hurriedly going over it with the straighteners. It had rained a little on my walk home and I could hear the fizz of burning wet hair every now and then. I poured myself a glass of white wine to sip slowly through the process but, five minutes later, the glass was empty. Pouring myself a second, I promised myself I'd sip it doubly slowly this time.

Courtesy of my credit card, I'd bought myself an off the shoulder vivid blue top to go with my black, skin-hugging, satiny trousers and I finished off the look with some black, sling-back, mid-heeled strappy sandals. I figured the outfit was sexy and sophisticated and, not knowing what sort of evening Tony had planned, it would suit pretty much any venue.

I matched the blue of the top with some striking blue eyeshadow and added black kohl around the rims of my eyes before lengthening my lashes with some extra lengthening mascara. The straighteners were still a huge novelty and at seven twenty I stood back and happily surveyed my sleek appearance in the mirror. I felt all buzzed up with anticipation, pleased in the knowledge I looked good. I hoped Tony would appreciate my efforts. I observed my empty glass, which in fact had been empty for some time; so much for sipping. I cleaned my teeth instead and sat down to wait.

I was too jumpy though and got up and paced my lounge. Then I went to the window and stared out over the rooftops. Then I sat down again. Then I plumped the cushions. Then I polished the coffee table. Then I had to put on more perfume in case I smelled of Mr Sheen. With all the rushing about I was growing more hot and bothered by the minute and my tight trousers did nothing to cool me down.

I sat down again and tried to control my breathing.

Suddenly, the door buzzer went and I nearly had a heart attack.

I shot up out of the chair, my heart going like the clappers but, as I did so, I realised that my trousers had ridden my calves. I'd have to rearrange them before Tony saw me. Bending down to right them though, the sound of an awful rip rung through the air! I stood up quickly and felt behind me. Sure enough, a newly created hole had appeared right down the seam on my backside. Shit! There was no time to change. I'd have to brave it and hope it wouldn't be noticeable when I walked.

The door buzzed again and I went slowly and carefully over to answer it, praying the hole wouldn't rip any more.

Thankfully, it was only the landlord at the door telling me that my rent date was changing and could I amend my direct debit. I hurriedly agreed and got rid of him. Glancing at my watch, I decided I might just have time to do a speedy sewing job.

Quick as I could, I got out my travel sewing kit, the only one I had, and peeled down my trousers to my ankles. I was heating up again and wished fervently I had worn something a bit cooler. It was too late now though. I'd matched up everything with the outfit and I'd just have to make the best of things. My hands were shaking as I sat, sewing as neatly as I could, pleading loudly that Tony would be late. I managed to patch up the hole pretty well and sat surveying the results. I'd never been a good seamstress but, from where I was sitting, I'd done an OK job. I'd just got the trousers halfway up when the door sounded again. This time it was Tony and I buzzed him up. There then followed a succession of hops and jumps round the room as I pulled my trousers up over my now hot, swollen legs.

What with the lift being broken, I figured I had about one minute to calm and cool myself down. I poured another half glass of wine and, opening the window, I took a deep breath of the evening air which was only moderately cooler than my flat.

The door to the flat knocked and, taking a final breath, I exhaled slowly then nervously walked over and opened the door.

There stood Tony with a single red rose looking handsome and far from hot and bothered.

'Banterers Inc, at your service.'

He had on a pair of designer jeans with a deep blue linen jacket. His cream shirt was open at the collar, displaying a brown chest and thick dark chest hair. If truth be known, I'd always prefer a smoother chest, but it was a minor point. After all, there was always wax.

He whistled as he eyed me up and down.

'You look gorgeous, Maggie.'

'Thank you,' I nodded graciously.

Then he gave a puzzled frown.

'You been running? Your face is a little flushed.'

'Long story,' I smiled demurely, inviting him in while I got my bag.

At least he'd whistled at me, which was a good sign. So, feeling good about myself, I turned and wiggled my way over to the table.

'Erm, Maggie?' he called from the doorway.

'Yes, Tony?' I turned and gave him the benefit of another smile.

'Did you know you have a needle and thread hanging from, um, between your legs?

I looked down and, sure enough, swinging about merrily, was the needle and thread I'd forgotten to cast off.

Marvellous; bloody marvellous!

Chapter Eleven

When Tony had stopped laughing, he drove us to a new Thai restaurant which had opened up in Soho.

I admired the grey leather interior of his dark blue BMW and thought that, despite his love for the country, he seemed very at home in the city.

'My friend's little brother used to call BMWs black men's willies,' I said, totally without thinking. As Tony started the car and drove away, I stared out of the car window biting my lip, pulling a face to myself unable to believe what I'd just said.

'I see,' Tony replied.

Silence hung in the air and I prayed for the ground to swallow me up. Tony broke it.

'Well, mine's blue. Does that make it a blue man's willy?'

I shifted in my seat.

'It fits, I guess,' I said, still facing out the window with embarrassment.

'So that makes me a blue man.'

'Mmmm,' I agreed, mortified.

'Have you ever met a blue man before?' he asked, casually.

A respite perhaps?

'Yes, but I've never seen his willy!' I replied.

Oh God, I'd done it again. I inadvertently slunk lower into the seat.

Thankfully, Tony didn't give any of the obvious macho answers so I continued with the charade to try and save face.

'I've often thought that perhaps blue men don't have them at all. Maybe they are blue because they are so cold and they've fallen off,' I suggested, trying to avoid the word willy.

'You've often thought that?'

'Oh yes. Surprisingly frequently; I don't get out much.'

There was another brief silence.

'Either that or we are both talking a lot of rubbish,' I said.

Tony laughed warmly.

'That's as maybe, but the banter session is into the ninth minute, so rubbish can be spouted all night without recrimination.'

Phew!

Having parked the car, we walked the two blocks to the restaurant, which had a black sign with gold letters that read 'So Thai'.

Once in, we were led to a little table in the corner. The tables and chairs were wooden and the little Thai waitresses were in oriental dresses.

'Pina coladas for two?' he asked.

'Do they do them here, then?'

'Of course! I checked when I made the reservation. I had to ring around at least five other restaurants before I struck gold. But I made a promise, remember. Don't tell the other students though; they'll all want them.'

'Oh, so I'm not your only pupil then. How many do you have?'

'I'm afraid I'm not at liberty to discuss that. I could but then I'd have to kill you and I haven't brought my exploding ice cubes with me.'

I laughed, feeling relaxed and happy in Tony's company.

'Now then,' he began, 'time to really begin the lesson.'

He moved the menus and the small vase of flowers from the centre to one side, then took out a little notepad and pen from his inside jacket pocket and cleared his throat.

'So, Maggie, tell me, apart from recent conversations, have you had any previous experience with banter?'

I tried to look thoughtful.

'Well, I don't want to seem big headed or anything, but I do have a certificate.'

'You do?' He seemed surprised and made a note on his pad. 'Is it genuine?'

'Of course it is! I'll have you know I worked hard to get that certificate.'

'I see. So, tell me then, who gave it to you?'

'From memory, I think it was the "The UK division of the International Bantering Society".'

'Hmmm.' He took more notes.

'When did you receive it, may I ask?'

'Um, let me see.' I pretended to do some mental calculations.

'OK, so I left school, then – then there was college, and after that… no hang on, it might have been before college. Let me see.'

I glanced up and saw him smiling at me.

'Ah, I remember now. I was ten!'

'Ten! You got a bantering certificate at the age of ten?'

'Yes. Well I think I did… ohhh hang on, maybe it wasn't for bantering. I thought it was but I'm not so sure now. If not, it's for something that sounds similar. Umm…' I paused thoughtfully, 'oh wait a minute; it might have been for badminton. Yes.' I tutted. 'Sorry, Tony, it was for badminton. I was the junior school badminton champion.'

Tony laughed.

'I think you've been having me on.'

'About what?'

'You're a master of the fast talk. I've been had.'

'Oh well,' I sighed, 'guess you'll just have to buy me dinner now I'm here; shame to waste a good evening.'

'Who said anything about waste? The only wasting going on tonight is the expansion of ours. I intend to make sure you drink and eat until you can't speak. That way, I stand a chance of impressing you with my fast talking instead.'

And so the tone was set. Tony and I were officially comfortable spending time together. We laughed and drank and ate. I couldn't handle more than two pina coladas but Tony insisted on ordering some wine. The food was delicious and I was really enjoying myself.

'So, Maggie, how goes it in the world of telesales?' he asked me.

'Telemarketing!' I corrected him.

How did he know I worked, or rather *had* worked in telemarketing? Had I told him?

Had Jenny?'

'I got sacked,' I admitted. 'They said it was redundancy but I know I was sacked.'

Tony smirked.

'A bit more exciting than a straightforward *fine thanks,* I'll give you that. Go on, tell me; no on second thoughts let me guess. Did you try to steal a telephone? No, that's not it, not your style. Let me think. I know! You didn't sell enough tellies.'

'Shut up you. We don't sell tellies and I told you, it's telemarketing, not telesales. That's the sort of slanderous thing you can get sacked for these days.'

'Well I give up then.' He tilted his head to one side, 'What did you do?'

Oh, what the hell.

'I got a black eye and I don't think the management liked the image change.'

He studied my eyes, squinting from one to the other.

'They don't look very black to me.'

'Thankfully it's pretty much cleared up, but I don't know what I'd do without the aid of make-up.'

'So, what happened to your opponent?'

'Flat out.'

'Seriously?'

'It was the floor!'

I explained what had happened at the reunion and Tony laughed long and hard.

'I knew you wouldn't let me down. I was counting on you to keep me entertained.'

'I wasn't going to tell anyone, it just slipped out.'

'What your eye?'

I kicked him under the table.

'I should have said I walked into a door.'

'Maybe, but it's been done to death don't you think? The floor is much more original.'

'Would you have believed me if I'd told you it was a door?' I asked, looking across at him and thinking how handsome he was when he smiled.

'Of course.'

'Liar!' I grinned.

'So what's next on the job front then?' he asked. 'More of the same?'

'No chance. And no joy anywhere else either so far. Apparently there's a lack of vacancies for women with black eyes.'

'That's racial discrimination against eyes you know,' he said.

'I know but I didn't have a leg to stand on.'

'Had you forgotten to take them with you?'

'Now you're just being silly.'

'Or did you just get legless the night before?'

I giggled and shook my head.

'You could have worn a patch over it,' he suggested.

'What my leg?'

'Ha, ha. Touché!' He laughed.

I grinned. 'Well, I suppose I could have done, if I'd been going for a Gabrielle look-a-like job, or perhaps the lead in the *Pirates of Penzance*.'

'I would have hired you.' He raised one eyebrow and my stomach did a somersault.

'What for exactly?'

'Oh, I don't know,' he shrugged, 'just to sit there and be pretty probably.'

'That's very sexist you know.'

'I prefer to think of it as honest.' He narrowed his eyes slightly and stared straight at me.

'I might have got a bit bored though, just sitting there.' I was feeling very aware of myself under his intense gaze.

'Well, I am sure I'd have found you something to do, something that satisfied both of us,' he flirtatiously raised both his eyebrows up and down.

I blushed at that and Tony was astute enough to move the conversation on.

We talked through dinner, and it all went really well. Better than that. Tony, it seemed, knew how to charm me and I was right in the mood to let him. He also came across as very kind. He talked well of everyone and always had something good to say about people. A refreshing change from some. We talked about his dad and the farm, he asked after my family, particularly my mum whom he remembered with fondness and saw fit to tell me he could see the resemblance between us. I chose to let him off that one. The most wonderful thing though, was that he was so confident. I loved that; a man who knew his own mind. It made me feel safe and secure. And he took care of everything in the restaurant, making sure I had exactly what I wanted and wouldn't hear of me contributing to the bill.

After dinner, we walked through the streets of Soho. The shop windows were lit up and the theatre billboards beckoned us in to see magical shows for all the family, while certain other 'establishments' beckoned us in to see shows certainly *not* for all the family. As we turned off the main road, the remains of the day's market stalls and crates stood silhouetted on the side street we walked down, ready for the next morning's early start. Tony took my hand. I was a bit disappointed to find that his hands weren't quite the right shape for mine. They were smaller than I'd thought they would be. Not to worry, I adjusted mine and they fitted better then. It felt nice to hold hands with someone after my long drought without a boyfriend.

Back at the car, Tony opened my door for me. A girl could get used to this, I thought. The doors whoomphed shut and when he'd climbed in beside me the locks clunked into place. The sounds of the streets outside were all but drowned out. I felt warm, sleepy and contented sitting in the passenger seat. I pulled the smooth-running seatbelt around me and clicked it easily into its counterpart, comparing it, fleetingly, to the rigid and unreliable one in my old car. Sitting there in easy silence before we moved off, I felt relaxed with Tony, maybe in part because I'd sort of grown up with him. It was strange to be sitting with someone who had been in short trousers when I'd first known him. I looked across as he started up the car. He seemed so confident as he took the wheel, indicated then pulled out, changing gears and smoothly negotiating the late evening's flow of traffic. He must have felt me staring because he turned towards me and smiled and my stomach did a familiar leap. That smile would be the death of me.

As we drove back to my flat, I began to anticipate how we'd end the evening. Definitely too soon to invite him up. Besides, it would only remind him of the needle and thread incident. No, best to say goodbye at the main entrance. But would we kiss? I hated this bit. Kissing was lovely, the best bit really, but the wondering if and when it would happen was awful.

All these rules nowadays about how far to move forward, who should make the first move, at what point did you close your eyes, and I'd recently seen a film saying that when you were about to kiss, the guy had to go ninety per cent of the way towards the girl and wait until she came the other ten per cent! I hoped it wouldn't end up being too technical.

I needn't have worried though.

Tony parked outside my place and was the perfect gentleman. We both got out the car and he walked me to the bottom of the steps up to the main front door. There, he simply took my hand and kissed it. He promised faithfully that he'd be calling me for another banter session then he waited to make sure I got in safely. He walked slowly backwards towards his car, grinning at me as I waved half way up the steps. There was an embarrassing moment when I tripped up the last step and felt like a real eejit. Finally, with a final wave to a still-grinning Tony, I closed the main door behind me and we were out of sight of each other. He hadn't kissed me. Well, that was OK, I supposed. Shame though, I could have done with a good old snog! My phone rang as I got through the door of my flat; probably Catherine eager to get the gossip.

'Hello?' I answered not recognising the number.

'You have the most gorgeous bottom I've ever seen,' Tony's voice came down the receiver.

I felt myself redden.

'Have I?'

'I only wish I'd been the needle and thread,' he said.

'Cheeky.'

'Exactly!'

I laughed.

'Thanks for a lovely time, Tony.'

'You've already thanked me. It's my turn to thank you.'

'OK, go on then.'

'Thanks for a lovely time, Maggie. Listen, I'm off to my dad's place for a while now, so I won't see you before the party. I think I might miss you, you know?'

I smiled, thinking I might miss him too.

'Oh, by the way,' I said, 'that certificate. It wasn't badminton after all.'

'Oh no?'

'No, silly me, it was backgammon.'

'Ah, well that's OK then. Backgammon is my other speciality. I hereby challenge you to a match.'

'You're on.'

The certificate was actually for backstroke but I wouldn't be admitting that just yet.

Chapter Twelve

There had to be a work leaving party for me of course, I couldn't have escaped that easily; in fact, it was the done thing at CapiTel. Anything, and I mean *anything,* which could be semi-construed as warranting a celebration would be celebrated. There had been Bill's divorce, with cakes in the office, celebratory drinks in the pub and an impromptu game of tenpin bowling, where we all imagined his wife Cheryl as being the pins. Bill won the match. Then there had been Maureen's cat's birthday; Maureen bought some cream at lunchtime to take home that evening for a special birthday treat but, thanks to Craig nipping down the 'offie' and to Justin for being out of the office, by three o'clock we were all plastered on Irish coffees, remembering to toast good old Fluffy along the way. When Craig had had his wisdom teeth out, we'd celebrated by having a pretend pub quiz round at his flat, where we played for intelligence points so that Craig could regain some of his lost wisdom. Unfortunately, he lost rather badly but we made up for it by playing another round for tequila shots and somehow he took the lead.

So, my leaving was, in true team fashion, something to be celebrated or rather commiserated.

On my last day, as I walked down through the main office, I saw Maureen up ahead, scuttling off in the opposite direction when she saw me coming. Her cheeks were bright red and her face was flushed.

I soon saw why. The whole area around my desk had been elaborately decorated and she'd even brought balloons in and tied them up all around my desk. Oddly, they had 'Happy 21st birthday' written on them.

'Sorry,' she said, 'but they'd sold out of "Sorry You're Leaving" balloons and it was a choice between these and "Congratulations on your New Baby"!'

Craig had brought in a load of wine and beer. Amazingly, Justin had agreed we could finish at four o'clock to have a drink and some fruit cake that Bill's mother Dolly had baked. She was the office cleaner. I insisted Bill call her up to come and join us for a slice and a glass of wine and, grudgingly, he called and arranged it. After the last experience of Dolly coming out with us, he was reticent to repeat it. Dolly had little to no control when it came to alcohol.

It was a strange last day. Everything seemed surreal, like it was happening to someone else. I felt odd as I sat down at my computer for the last time. In my head I'd already left and didn't feel I should be there anymore. I considered what it would be like after I'd gone. Would my remaining work be distributed to other people? Would they miss me? Would people just forget me after a week or so?

Maureen jolted me from my thoughts.

'Do you remember when you started, Maggie?' she reminisced. 'You were so scared. Now look at you, all grown up and capable.'

'Capable? Me?'

'Well, maybe not capable' she admitted, 'perhaps more confident.'

'Thanks.'

'No, sorry, not that you're not capable, because of course you are, but you've become more assertive. Yes, that's it, assertive,' she finished happily.

It didn't sound like me at all.

Craig stepped in. 'Streetwise, I think she means. Probably because I keep teaching you stuff.'

'Of course, that's bound to be it.' I pinged a rubber band at his arm.

'You've definitely changed though, Maggie,' Bill joined in. 'Maureen's right. You've grown a lot more confident, especially lately.'

Had I? What could they see that I couldn't?

As I worked, their words washed over me. I thought back to when I'd joined CapiTel.

I'd certainly been less sure of myself then, partly due to being on the phones and partly because I hadn't really wanted the job in the first place. But then when I'd moved across to marketing, it had been because I'd seen an opportunity to do something I thought I'd be good at. For a while at least, I'd enjoyed it and had been challenged by the role. Something twigged inside me. The reason I'd been so bored of late was that I'd achieved what I'd set out to learn. I'd got on top of my job, and there was nowhere else to expand to. Just because we'd lost a client and, OK, I'd mucked up a bit with the black eye, didn't mean I hadn't done a good job, because I had. I'd been promoted and I'd also been given more responsibility as time had gone on. I'd actually done this job well, despite any impressions that Justin may have given me to the contrary. I began to feel differently about what was happening. Differently about what my leaving meant to me and my life. This was absolutely the right thing to do.

Suddenly my future looked different, brighter. I actually *had* a future. I saw myself through the eyes of my colleagues – my friends. They were right; I *had* changed and now I needed more of a challenge, whatever that might be. Catherine had also been right. The holiday would be a chance to think things through and plan my next career move. A feeling of well-being washed over me and I beamed at the others.

'Hope you've got me a decent leaving present!' I said, 'Unlike my birthday, *Craig!*

'Every girl should have a blow-up doll, it's the rule,' he answered, defensively.

'A female one?'

'Yeah, well, I'd have felt like a bleedin' poof in the shop asking the geezer for a bloke doll. Besides, this way, it gives me something to think about when I'm...'

'Yes, OK, OK,' I showed him my palm, 'I think I get the picture. Anyway, I don't actually use it you know.'

'Shut up! You'll ruin a good fantasy.'

The day sped past. It was like every moment was a last moment. Everything I did was the last time I'd do it. Emailing people became their final email. Saying hi or bye to other people became the last time I'd ever see them. It was strange but at the same time exciting. Everything I did gave me time to think about all the skills I had and all the tasks I undertook and never even thought about. I realised what I enjoyed and what I really didn't. And I began to think of some of the things I'd be looking for in my next job. The more aware I became the brighter and clearer my future seemed.

At three fifty-eight on the dot we downed tools, me for the last time. This time the following day I'd be at the farm, happily getting ready for Mr Henderson's party and this would all seem like it had happened to someone else, but right now, here in the little office I had known to be my second home for the last two years, I felt sad; sad to be leaving my friends. We'd been like a little family together, although I hadn't really appreciated it until now. The Monday morning hangovers and the stories that accompanied them, the faddy diets, the stories of one-night stands and all-night parties. The time Craig's mum had walked out on his dad and he'd been in tears and we'd all looked after him and kept Justin off his back. The time Maureen had to have her gallstones out and had cried like a baby before and after but had kept her stones in a Robinsons jam jar and proudly showed us all afterwards. The time when Bill's wife had actually left him for the milkman; we still couldn't believe that had happened in real life. It was OK anyway because he had subsequently got together with Tina (Teens), one of the secretaries at head office and everything had turned out for the best. And they had all been so sweet to me when I had broken up with Rob and it had really meant a lot to me when they had dosed me up with sweet tea and jam doughnuts and Maureen had knitted me a scarf. I wasn't quite sure of the significance of the scarf but she meant well. I was going to miss them all and I hoped we would stay in touch.

A few people I knew from the main office came through to wish me luck and to have a plastic cup of wine.

We drank all the wine and the beer and ate some of the cake which, I have to say, was soooo heavy! At one point I saw Craig and Maureen clutching their stomachs in pain. But we couldn't say anything. Dolly had been so sweet to think of me, although I suspected we may have been palmed off with last year's (or maybe the year before's) Christmas cake. I thought I detected a faint mark on the icing where a sprig of holly once lay. Dolly had insisted I take the rest home with me but I wasn't looking forward to carrying it.

At one point during the party, I think Dolly, who had become very merry, may have fallen asleep in the loo. Maureen had gone to fetch her but Dolly had insisted that the call of nature had been longer than expected, so we'd left it at that.

They gave me a presentation. By rights it should have been Justin's job but, apart from a few short, cold, words of good luck earlier in the day, which were more grudging than giving, that's all we saw or heard from him all afternoon.

Maureen had chosen the present.

'It's just in case you get lonely,' she said beaming at me.

Craig kept winking at me as I opened it and hinting at it being something to take to bed with me at night for those long nights in on my own, so I had suspicions he might have swapped whatever Maureen had chosen for a sex toy. It was a teddy bear though. A large, cute, teddy bear with huge doleful eyes and we all attempted to think of a name. Bill suggested we find an anagram from the word CapiTel but, when Craig suggested things like Pat Lice and Clae Pit, I settled on Mobear as Maureen had chosen it and Mo was short for Maureen. Mobear looked like a girl bear anyway. Maureen was very pleased indeed and I knew Mobear would always bring me fond memories of them all. Craig, true to form, had also bought me a mini plastic penis on legs. And when you wound it up and let it go, it jumped around the desktop.

'Something to remind you of me,' he said proudly.

'It's not very big,' Maureen pointed out.

'Exactly, something to remind her of Craig!' Bill chortled, then hiccuped.

Everyone in our office – and some from the main one – had signed my card, which was huge! I was more touched by that than anything.

'Good luck and stay in touch' seemed to be the general theme but some had taken the trouble to write something more personal.

Maureen had written:

'I don't know what I'll do without you, missing you already, please don't go!' Which made me cry.

Bill had sellotaped a Werthers Original into the card and drawn a sad face and put two kisses, which was nice.

Craig had written:

'Roses are red, Craig is blue, cos Maggie you're going and I haven't shagged you!'

When we all left to go to the pub, Dolly wanted to come but Bill insisted on taking her home. I think he'd been a little worried she'd embarrass him after the last time.

She'd come out with us on his birthday in January. We'd all gone to the pub and she had ended up singing *My Old Man's a Dustman* (but she'd actually said dustbin) and dancing with the barman round the pub. The rest of us had all thought it hilarious but poor Bill was red as a beetroot, especially when she'd asked the barman to come home and tuck her in!

So a crowd of us from both offices went to the Brickman's Arms for a final drink to see me on my way and Bill hugged me goodbye and we both got rather teary.

'I'll miss you, young Maggie,' he sniffed. 'Don't be a stranger now.'

'I won't and thanks for the Werther's Original, it meant a lot.' I smiled.

'Remember to find something that's worthy of you. Don't you go accepting the first thing that comes up. Promise me?'

'I promise,' I said, meaning it. And we said goodbye. He bundled his mother into a black cab and the last thing I heard as it drove away was Dolly singing 'All I want for Christmas is my two front teeth'.

Four more glasses of wine later and another piece of Dolly's brick cake to prevent the hangover, and to reduce the weight of my parcel, the barman rang the bell for time at the bar, so we grudgingly drank up.

Apart from one instance when Craig nearly got into a fight with a rather fat lady in a wheelchair, who had apparently stolen his pint, the evening had gone smoothly. Most people had left and gone off to their regular Friday nights out so, when we finally made it outside, there was only a handful of us still there. Maureen started crying and kept hugging me and telling me she loved me.

Craig also hugged me but, mid hug, he tried to put his leg over me while jeering at a couple of the IT lads.

I was too drunk to fight him off.

There was talk of clubbing but I couldn't walk particularly straight and I had the cake with me, so a cab was called and it was finally time for me to go.

'Promise you'll stay in touch and email and everything,' Maureen sniffled, handing me 'Mobear'.

'I promise. I'll miss you, Mo'. I hugged her. 'And you, Craig, you bugger.' I let go of Maureen and hugged him again.

I may have imagined it, but I think Craig might have had a tear in his eye.

My cab arrived and I clambered in with a helping hand from Craig on my bottom. I slammed the door.

Sitting down, I leaned forward and smiled at them all through the partially opened window.

'See ya soon,' I yelled.

'Not if I see ya first!' Craig yelled back, pulling a face then squashing it up against the window.

Maureen waved her hanky at me and the little group cheered as the cab pulled away.

Then, that was it. Over; finished; finito.

As the cab turned the corner, I leaned back against the red leather seat and sighed. Even through my haze, I knew that I was doing was the right thing. Exit one old, safe but boring life; enter one unmapped, unplanned, new and exciting one. I had no idea what I would be doing after Spain. For the first time in my life, I didn't have any plans. I didn't have a safety net, just a bit of cash and some big hopes.

I knew I was taking a risk, but something deep down told me it would all be OK and I'd land on my feet. Sometimes in life, I decided, you needed to take the odd risk; escape the safety zone, push yourself a bit harder than you're used to and take a chance. After all, this was my life and if I didn't take the odd chance in it, who else was going to?

Chapter Thirteen

The following morning, as I woke, my eyes fell on 'Mobear' sitting happily on my chair. I smiled sleepily and stretched. Judging by the lack of headache, I reckoned Dolly's cake must have soaked up all the alcohol. I let my mind drift over the previous evening. Now that it was all over, I felt freer. I was in an in-between place – in-between jobs, in-between lives; a sort of limbo where nothing and no one could get me; nothing could be demanded of me. I was absolutely without commitment. I was certain I'd easily find a job after the holiday and, for now, I was going to enjoy this feeling of being between past and future.

I got up and for some reason felt an urge to clean the flat. I was happily going round with the duster and singing along to the radio when the phone rang. I saw it was Mum and my mood sank. I hoped she wouldn't ask about work.

'Maggie?' she said as I picked up.

'Yes, Mum,' I said warily.

'You know those CB things we talked about?'

'Yes'

'I've got one!' she cried excitedly.

Good grief.

'It's the latest model and it does all sorts of things like…'

'Mum, what on earth have you got a CB radio for?'

'Well, you know I told you about Mrs Banbury's son Trevor. Nice lad, very tall…'

'Yes, Mum, I remember.' A hangover was threatening.

'Well, he went away to work in France and left it behind and you'll never guess.'

'What?'

'Mrs Banbury started using it! She's been talking to all sorts! Now let me see, there's Old Farmer Giles, no, no that's not it, Old Father Miles. See? Clever isn't it, him being a long-distance lorry driver, you see like a play on…'

'I get it, Mum.'

'Yes, of course you do. Anyway, then there's a woman called Flo' who's also using her son's radio and another woman who calls herself Aunty Bessie. I think it's a code name; maybe she makes cakes?'

'Or Yorkshire puddings.'

'Well, quite. And then…' she hushed her voice to a whisper and as usual, annoyingly, I found myself leaning in closer to the receiver, 'there's this one chap called Joe Ninety who's divorced with two kids and he's on the lookout for a new wife, and Mrs Banbury says she's sure he's got the hot rods for her.'

'The whats?'

'Hot rods! You know, the hots! Only they call it hot rods in their CB language.'

'Do they? Are you sure?'

'Well, Mrs Banbury and her gang do.'

'Anyway, she says he sounds a bit old and I wondered whether Joe Ninety meant he was actually ninety. I told Mrs Banbury and she thinks she'd better stop being so friendly with him.'

'I thought she was married!'

'She is, she is, happily so. But it never hurts to have a little flirt every now and then.'

'Mum!'

'No, no, not me of course, your father is all a woman could wish for, but I'm just saying.'

She didn't sound too convincing and I pictured Mum using the radio and flirting outrageously with Joe Fifty, Sixty, Seventy and possibly even Joe Forty and having all sorts of illicit conversations about secret codes and FBI agents.

'Anyway, Mr Parkinson from across the street found out what Mrs Banbury was up to, and it seems he's also been doing it for years! That's when I got involved.'

'How?'

'Well, Mr P – nice man, grows his own cauliflowers – he pointed out that I was the only one not joining in all the fun, so we went off to some big out-of-town warehouse place that sells everything you could imagine and he showed me what's what and now I've got one!'

Barbara Parsons: (Babs Sixty?) Clandestine pensioners CB club member and truckers friend; who knew?

'Can you actually work it?'

I had visions of Mum tapping in to a private police conversation and getting herself arrested.

'I'm still a bit of a novice but I'm getting the hang of it and Mr Parkinson's been very kind. Nice man, grows his own...'

'Cauliflowers, yes, Mum, you told me.'

'I was going to say marrows... *and* tomatoes *actually*. Honestly, sometimes Maggie you can be very cutting.'

'Sorry, Mum. I hope you have lots of fun with your new toy. What does Dad think of it?' I couldn't imagine Dad getting involved. The only technology he was interested in was the telly.

'Your father's refusing to discuss it, thinks I'm completely barking. Anyway, he's still angry at me.'

'What for?'

'I cleaned his beloved chair when he was on one of his golf weekends and he's not forgiven me yet. I was right about the colour. It doesn't go with the room now. I've told him he'll have to redecorate.'

'It's only one chair, Mum.'

'That's beside the point. The more I go on at him about it, the more likely he'll cave in and we'll have a lovely new front room before you know it. Remember, I know how your father's mind works. Anyway, I was just ringing to make sure you were still coming to the party.'

'Of course; I said I would.'

'That's good. I must say, it'll be wonderful to have all the children there, just like old times. I spoke to Rex Henderson earlier. He said he's going to be making some announcements. Got some news from his lot I believe.'

My stomach tightened.

'What kind of news?'

'Oh I don't know; something to do with one of the kids; one of the boys possibly? I can't remember, he was a bit cloak and dagger.'

My stomach wound up another notch.

'Um... only Jenny and Tony are going,' I told her, nervously. 'Do you think it's about Tony?'

'Perhaps; we'll have to wait until later. Anyway, I'm very glad we'll be seeing you.

Nice to show a united Parsons front.'

'Yes, I'll be there, Mum.'

'And wear something pretty for goodness sake, none of those Doc Malcolm boot things you always used to wear with that horse jacket.'

'It was a donkey jacket and I was fifteen at the time, Mum! And you mean Doc Martens not Doc Malcolms.'

'Whatever they were, these things have a habit of coming back into fashion and I know what you're like darling.'

Huh?

'What do you mean…?'

The echo of door chimes sounded in the background.

'Sorry, darling, that's the door, must dash. Toodle ooh. Don't drive too fast now. Kiss kiss.'

And she hung up, leaving me mouthing down the other end of the phone.

As I replaced the phone in its cradle, I wondered if she really had any idea what I was like these days.

Catherine and I had thought it only fitting to do a last-minute clothes shopping trip for our holiday so the plan for the morning was to go into town. We decided that the dresses we had worn for the reunion would be perfect for the party that evening seeing as, apart from the girls and Tony, no one would have seen them before. If truth be known, I'd have quite liked to have had another option to show off to Tony but I'd only just met him and was in danger of reading too much into things. Maybe I'd keep my eye out though, just in case.

By midday, we were in amongst the hoards of shoppers, fighting for pavement space, being bumped about among Saturday crowds. The shops were packed. Catherine was on a high though and nothing would dent her mood. After having had a blissful day with Nico the previous weekend, she was over the moon at the thought of seeing him again on Sunday. Her high spirits buoyed us both up and, with the promise of sun-kissed beaches ahead, we had a ball. Between us, we managed to spend almost five hundred pounds on new summer outfits, sun creams and make-up, even some *Miss Dior* for Catherine which was described as 'a fragrance for an elegant and spirited young woman in love' and which she spritzed all over both of us. I had definitely acquired credit card fever. It was almost as if by using it for my reunion dress, then again for the flights and insurance, then again for my new blue top and then *again* for Jenny's Dad's birthday silver tankard, it had an energy of its own and was pulling me along behind it, just calling on me to punch in my pin number at the appropriate moment. I was torn between the addiction of shopping, knowing it wasn't real money so I wouldn't notice a hole in my pocket, and buyer's remorse. I worked myself up into such a frenzy trying and buying, even not trying and buying... and then once I'd paid and experienced a short period of excitement, kaboom, I'd crash down into the doldrums feeling dreadfully guilty.

Still, it didn't stop me. I was on to the next shop for more of the same until I had four shopping bags. I always knew when I'd had a good shopping trip. I'd come back with those large expensive-looking, laminated carrier bags with cord handles that certain shops only give you if you've spent loads and bought lots.

Of course we had to buy swimming costumes. I owned three bikinis but the white one was more yellow than white, one had polka dots on it and I hated it (Mum had bought it for me) and the third had been a Marks and Spencer purchase when I had put on a fair bit of weight one year and it really needed to be condemned. No, it was definitely time for an overhaul in that department.

The bikini trying-on session was an interesting experience. You know some shops seem to want to go the extra mile and really *sell* you clothes and thus the changing rooms are nicely lit with flattering mirrors and comfy chairs and a little bell you press when you need assistance? And then there are the others where you have to queue for ages, their entrances are guarded by truculent teenagers who have the music up really loud and who nod, dance and gesture to each other in some sort of code which alienates everyone over twenty-five. And the worst thing is that their curtains don't close properly and they have fluorescent lights that shine *directly* down onto your legs and show up *every inch* of cellulite, making your fat look like it's put on weight and your face appear ten years older than it did before you went in there? Well that's where we first tried on bikinis. We laughed throughout of course, we had to, but I'm not sure if it was laughter really. We just pretended it was funny to hide the sheer horror of how we looked. We tried on three bikinis each then left hurriedly to find a shop which fitted into the first category.

'Lighting like that should be banned,' I remarked.

'I know I'm fat,' Catherine acknowledged, 'but by bikini number three I was contemplating suicide!'

In the next shop, most definitely in category one, we both found what we wanted.

Catherine had opted for a plain black one piece with loads of Lycra. It suited her larger build and made her boobs look astonishingly massive.

Nothing new there then. I, on the other hand, had a moment of exhilarating recklessness and opted for a bright, rainbow-coloured, string bikini.

'Crikey! You look stunning!' Catherine whistled, as I came out the changing room to show her. The lighting was low enough for me to venture out of the safety of the cubicle and I must admit I liked what I saw in the mirror.

I was exceptionally pleased when one of the other shoppers also told me how good it looked on me.

So, adding a bright blue one in the same style to my basket, we made our purchases and the bikinis were added to our other goodies. These included a really rather striking dress, for me, for going out in the evening. It was made up of silver meshing, with a split up one side and thin diamante straps, no back and very little front. I was a bit concerned about how my boobs had been squished up together giving me a rather tarty cleavage, and they didn't look that secure either, but Catherine insisted that, after the amount of alcohol we were bound to drink, I wouldn't care. So I bought it.

We headed back home to pack the new additions before setting off. We were due to get to the farm by about four, get ready, and then have early drinks before the masses arrived. Catherine was driving, again. I knew it was my turn really but even the idea that I might have a hangover and might cause an accident was enough for her to insist.

Surprisingly, the roads were pretty clear. We drove along with the windows wound down, the wind whooshing through our hair and the radio turned up loud, so we could sing along.

We made good time and arrived at the entrance to the Henderson's track, leading up to the farm a little early.

'Stop a minute, Cat.' I tugged at her arm as she was about to turn off the road. Catherine pulled up beside the verge. The late afternoon sun was gradually falling in the distance and the farm sat silhouetted on the rise against the hazy blue sky; birds swooped and wispy webs of cloud were gathering across the horizon. A tractor from a neighbouring farm chugged along in a field across the other side of the valley and I was filled with a longing for days gone by. The farm looked as it always had: warm, friendly and inviting, just as a home should be. It had been special to us all; a place of many warm memories which had tied Jenny, Pauline, Catherine and me together forever – families and friends, adventure and laughter, memories of childhood that stay with you for the rest of your life. Catherine and I sat for a few long moments in silence, soaking in the feelings then Catherine spoke:

'I don't think I've ever been happier than when we all lived around here.'

'Me neither,' I agreed.

'Do you ever think about us getting married to blokes and settling down in a place like this?' she asked.

'Frequently!' I admitted.

'Me too; funny isn't it,' she said, 'I don't think a week goes past without me dreaming of a life like that with a happy ending.' I knew she'd be filling the dream with Nico now.

'Come on…' I sat up straight, rubbing my hands together, 'we'll be late for kick-off if we're not careful. Let's get in there and get things started.'

We turned into the track, bracken clicking at the sides of the car, dried mud splattering from the wheels, and headed up to the farm where our holiday was about to begin.

Chapter Fourteen

Rex Henderson greeted us at the big oak front door and I could smell the familiar smell of my childhood as a big whoosh of farmhouse air came towards me. His rather trussed-up, summer-suited appearance was a far cry from the green woolly cardigan and gardening shoes he normally wore. His white hair and beard had been newly groomed so he didn't look quite as much like Father Christmas as he normally did. I always expected him to say 'Ho Ho Ho' when I saw him.

'Girls, girls,' he boomed, with a voice far belying his five foot seven height. 'Come in, come in. Splendid, splendid! What a pleasure indeed. My, *my*, you're all grown up and beautiful.' He enveloped us, in turn, in a big strong bear hug and a loud kiss.

'All set for our hols, are we?'

'Shhhsh, Mr H!' I whispered stepping past him and into the hallway, 'Mum and Dad don't know I'm going. Bit of a secret. I asked Jenny to let you know.'

He slapped his hand dramatically over his mouth then lowered his voice.

'Profuse apologies! A momentary lapse of the old grey matter. Worry not though; I've not said a dicky bird. Leave it to me.' He tapped the edge of his nose with his forefinger, 'Soul of discretion, mum's the word.'

The grandfather clock struck four with loud echoing chimes and, despite the early hour, it was obvious that alcohol had been consumed as we heard bottles clinking from the direction of the kitchen. I wondered whether Tony had arrived. I hadn't seen his car in the driveway but it could have been tucked away in the big garage.

'Happy Birthday, Mr H,' Catherine said, handing a carrier bag full of wine from us both. 'This isn't your present but I'm sure it will come in handy!'

'Splendid! Thank you, thank you.'

From behind Mr H, my Mum bustled through sing songing her 'hellos'. She was clearly pleased to see me and bundled me into a dramatic hug. I could smell White

Linen and powdered foundation. Her lips were painted perfectly in 1950s' coral. She wore a floaty Laura Ashley dress with a full skirt, which swirled around as she did.

'Darling. What a divine little top,' she gushed, in a somewhat staged voice. Then whispered, 'Glad you took my advice about the Doc Malcolms.'

I grimaced inwardly.

'Hi, Mum. You look very nice.'

'Do I? Do I really?' she peeled off me and checked her hair in the hall mirror, turned and reached out dramatically for Catherine's hand, pulling her towards her and holding her at arm's length so she could view her properly.

'Hi, Mrs Parsons.'

'Oh no, no, no… do call me Barbara, we're practically family and you're a grown girl now. Now let me look at you; lovely as ever. It's been too long.' She emphasised the 'too' and spoke as if she were in one of the old movies. There followed another elaborate hug.

Catherine raised her eyes at me from over Mum's shoulder and I raised mine back. We had been subjected many, many times to Mum's theatrical movie-star tendencies. She loved to live and act like she was playing the part of some big-screen starlet and her life was like the stage that she *so* should have acted on. It got more pronounced when she drank and, no doubt, later, when things really hotted up, she'd be heard uttering things to Dad like 'Frankly my dear, I don't give a damn'.

She broke away from her embrace and hustled us both in the direction of the country-styled kitchen, announcing 'the girls have arrived' and 'how beautiful they've become' and 'aren't they just peaches?'

Peaches?!

We stood awkwardly in the doorway, as we had done in many a dinner party doorway when we were younger. Us turning up after a teenage night roaming the streets with bottles of scrumpy, arriving to see all sets of parental drunken, sparkling eyes upon us glowing and proud. 'Here are the girls', they'd be saying. Thinking things like 'The fruits of my loins', 'A reflection of me', 'A chip off the old block'. Luckily there wasn't a piano in the house anymore, or I'd be asked to sit down and do a quick rendition of *Für Elise* to much applause and shouts of 'More, more' and 'That's my girl' and 'Do you know, I think she must get it from my side of the family, my mother was musical you know…'

Catherine's parents Marvin and Joyce were in the kitchen, so was my Dad,

Douglas, and, by the way his arm was slung casually round Catherine's mum's shoulder, it was pretty clear they'd had a few. Joyce didn't usually drink much but her pink cheeks suggested that today was an exception.

Dad's dishevelled hair was sticking up on one side and his warm but mischievous eyes shone out and I smiled at him. He winked back. He was a softy, all heart and forgiveness which was good seeing as he was married to Mum but he had a definite naughty side which usually got him into trouble with her. At the end of the day though, Dad was Mum's rock; her comfort zone. Whenever Mum was flapping around in a strop or worrying herself into an early grave, Dad was always there with a soothing voice and a cuddle until she'd calmed down. Strangely, they made a good couple although it wasn't always obvious from the outside. I think that without each other, they really would have struggled.

'We've been having a rather long lunch!' Mum giggled, winking at Mr H, who was pouring another round into crystal glasses on the large wooden kitchen table which was strewn with bottles, glasses and the remains of what looked like a ploughman's lunch.

We suffered another round of too-tight hugs and several more moments of being held out at arm's length so whoever it was could, 'Let me look at you' and marvel at 'How you've grown!' And everyone could agree again that, yes indeed, we had grown.

We eventually managed to escape, saying we needed to unpack our nice dresses for the evening. The mention of nice dresses had them all agreeing. Time was getting on after all, and we'd need to get a move on so as to be ready on time.

'Middle room girls, just like old times, eh?' Mr H thwacked me on the back as we left the room.

'The others are already up there, best get a move on if you want to get ready by seven,' he chortled teasingly.

'Goodness, it's only just after four,' Catherine said as we headed out to the car to get our stuff. 'They'll be annihilated by the time the party starts. Makes us seem like amateurs! Anyway, if anyone says I've grown again, I'll swing for them. Don't they know I'm on a diet?'

'Quick let's get these cases in before my Mum and Dad start asking why we've brought so much stuff for a weekend.'

'I don't think they'd notice if we'd brought the New Zealand rugby team, the state they're in,' Catherine replied.

'I think my Dad would. He'd have had them all out in the back garden scrummaging and weaving in and out of the trees with a watermelon before I'd even made the introductions!'

We took our cases and made our way back to the house, as fast as we could across the gravel drive. Then we started to haul them up the wide wooden staircase. Halfway up, pulling our cases behind us, I felt the back of my neck bristle and all the little hairs down my arms sprung into life. I felt his presence before I even saw him. It was almost like it had been at the reunion but this time there was a difference, a marked difference – a stronger pull. I knew he was there before I saw him. I knew without looking that this time it wasn't Tony, this time it was Luke.

As I climbed further up the stairs, I could sense Luke behind me on the landing. I don't know how I knew for sure it was him, I just did. I could almost smell his presence. I'd always loved the smell of Luke. He was like no other. It may sound a little strange but it was just the way it was. I could feel my stomach react and all the nerves in my body stand to attention. My heart began to beat faster and I felt dizzy with the shock.

I let my head turn very slightly and, sure enough, out of the corner of my eye, I saw the shock of blond hair and tanned skin. What the heck was he doing there? He was supposed to be in Sweden. My chest had tightened and I could feel my breathing quicken as we reached the top. Any minute now we'd have to acknowledge each other.

But before I could start worrying about how to react, Jenny burst out of her room in the roof, bounding, excitedly, down the top stairs and meeting us on the landing, hugging Catherine and me where we stood fixed to the spot.

'Am I glad you're here! The oldies are doing our heads in down there. I've never seen your mum pissed, Cat, she's well funny! Come on, you're in that room, as always!' She yanked my case from me and, pulling up the long handle, wheeled it away leading us towards the spare room we used to stay in when we were kids.

'Pauline's in the shower and I'm left having to deal with Luke and my cousin Leon. *Plus,* Honey's still got her four Andrex puppies, Dad won't get them re-homed, so the bedrooms are like world war three! Poor old Parliament refuses to purr and keeps hiding in the barn! Come on up as soon as you're settled and let's get this party started.' She let go of my case again and I grabbed onto it, as if for some sort of protection.

I couldn't bring myself to look behind us. I knew he was there and I was sure he knew I knew he was there. My mouth had gone dry and I could feel my palms grow sweaty on the suitcase handle. But as I turned to go into our room, there he was in my peripheral vision and I couldn't help myself. I turned and stared straight at him.

He stood tall, tanned and blond as ever – stunning. Age had done nothing but be very, very kind to him. If it were possible, he was more handsome than I remembered him. My stomach lurched and my breath caught in my throat. I couldn't speak and felt the colour draining from my face.

Catherine, behind me, stepped in and saved the moment.

'Luke, hi!' she gushed. 'It's been ages! How *are* you? How's Sweden?' She left her case and moved confidently over towards him, her arms outstretched for a hug.

'Hello, Catherine, you look fantastic.' They hugged warmly. And why wouldn't they? We'd all been close, once. 'It's so good to see you,' his voice drawled, deeper and sexier than ever. He kissed her on her both cheeks catching my eye as he did so.

As he broke away from her, our eyes met properly and I could see he was as unsettled as I was. His expression was quizzical, questioning, as if waiting for my reaction.

'Hello, Maggie,' he said slowly, allowing his lips to form the mere suggestion of a smile, which quickly disappeared as my own face remained void of expression. His eyes seemed to be urging me to respond. To show him something, anything, but I felt frozen from the inside out.

I stood there, still clutching at the handle of my case, my knuckles growing white and stiff from holding on so tightly. I was unable to move but it didn't stop the intense panic which engulfed me as Luke moved forward slightly. Walking apprehensively towards me, he bent to kiss me and we awkwardly bumped cheeks. My whole body tightened with resistance. I had to get away from him.

'How are you?' His watchful eyes bore down into me and, try as I might, I couldn't look away from him.

From deep within me I heard myself reply, something nondescript. Something like, 'Fine thanks, Luke.' I think he may have answered me, but I couldn't seem to hear or see properly. I was in some sort of tunnel. The world around me had ceased to be real and I felt as if I were in a dream.

Again, from somewhere deep, deep inside me, I spoke. Not words of conscious choice, but my subconscious needed to know.

'I thought you were going to be in Sweden.' The quiet words came out, as if from somebody else's mouth.

But before he could answer, Jenny bounded back down again, unintentionally interrupting the awkwardness.

'You still here? Forgot to say, the bathroom's in there now, ladies,' she pointed to the corner of the landing. 'Dad's had a bit of an overhaul, Tony's idea. Just put all your stuff in the wardrobes and make yourself at home. And hurry up!' She started to head downstairs. 'I thought you'd at least be unpacked by now!'

'And…' she ran back up a few steps again, her little head visible through the banisters, '… don't let my brother annoy you while I'm not around!' She grinned.

'I think that was aimed at me.' Luke turned and smiled at Catherine, seemingly glad to break the uneasiness. 'I'll see you later then.' And with that, he turned and walked to one of the bedrooms across from ours. Then turning back slightly, he said; 'It's good to see you… both.' He smiled uncertainly at me before entering his room and closing the door behind him.

'First round's on you!' Catherine called after him. Then turned to me and pulled a face.

'I didn't know what to say to him.'

I didn't reply. Instead, I hurried into our room and, hardly waiting for Catherine to make it in, I closed the door behind us and leant against it. Then I found myself shooting away from it as if, somehow, I could feel Luke's energy emanating through the wood. Even behind the closed door, he felt too close.

I could feel my heart pounding in my chest; my breathing had quickened even more and my legs were unsteady. I left my case in the middle of the room and sat down heavily on a pink eiderdowned single bed, putting my head in my hands.

Catherine sat down beside me and put her arm around me.

'I wonder what he's doing here?' she said.

'I don't know but… he's here. I… can't believe it. He's actually here.' My voice faltered.

'How do you feel?' she asked.

'I don't know. I just don't know. I feel… I feel… I don't know.'

I stood up and went to the window. Opening it I breathed in the fresh air, inhaling deeply. I waited for a sense of reality to come back. I was back in my childhood, back at the farm. It was the same farm, they were the same people but so many years had passed in-between. They were different worlds, different lives. I shook my head, trying to will myself back into the present, instead of into the string of memories that were pouring from my subconscious into my conscious. *Hey, Maggie, remember us? We're all these memories you stopped recalling because they hurt too much. Remember? Well, here we are. We're back. And we're ready to be aired good and proper. You have to deal with us, you know. You have to. Otherwise we won't go away; we'll just keep taunting you until you do.*

So much for putting the lock on the door marked 'Memories of Luke. Do not open until dead!'

Visions flooded my mind. I saw the two of us sitting in Clementine's cafe in the high street sharing a coffee milkshake. None of our friends liked coffee flavour, just us. Then, the first time we went to the cinema. I told my mum I was round at a school friend's house. We didn't really want people to know about us; it seemed weird, even to us. After all, we'd known each other for so long, how would they react? We hardly saw any of the film, sitting in the back row kissing and kissing, unable to let each other go. And then, then…I willed my mind not to go there. Not to go to the time we'd been by the river. I willed it to come back to the present but, too late, I was back there, holding Luke, wanting him so badly, wanting to be near him, always. Loving him. Not caring I was still too young to be with a boy like that, to be that close. I really had been so young. And then I felt it, the pain. The same pain I'd felt all those years ago, when he'd turned his back on me, when he'd moved away from me. Why? Why had he done that? Ten years on and I still needed the answer to that question; so much depended on it.

I could hear Catherine's voice somewhere in the distance. I inadvertently put my hand to my chest, as if to support my breaking heart. I felt Catherine beside me.

'Maggie. Did you hear me?'

'What?' I turned and stared blearily at her. 'Sorry, did you say something?'

'I just asked if you were OK. You're obviously not.'

I took a deep breath, somehow managing to push the old thoughts away, for now.

'Sorry, I was miles away.'

'Miles away… or years away?' Catherine asked quietly.

'Do you think he feels anything?' I asked her.

'By the look on his face when he kissed you hello I should say he feels a lot like you do.'

'Only not enough to have got in touch sooner,' I said sadly, walking over and sitting back down on the bed.

'We don't know what happened, Mags. But a lot's happened in the last ten years. At least you get to ask him the truth tonight.'

'I can't ask him anything. I can't even speak to him. You saw how I was. What am I going to do?'

'I don't know,' she replied honestly.

'What about Tony?' she asked.

The sudden thought of being in the same room with the two of them was almost too overpowering to handle. I had to break out of this fog.

'This can't happen, Cat. I can't go through the evening feeling like this. Everyone will know something's wrong. I couldn't bear everyone looking at me pityingly. Jenny and Pauline don't even know what happened between us; they don't even know we dated. No, I need to keep this between you and me. I need to snap out of this somehow. I'll have a shower, a cold shower.' I smiled slightly. 'That'll help.'

'Will you be OK?'

'I'll have to be,' I said sadly, finding the strength in me to stand up and hoist my case on to the bed.

I jumped at a knock at the door. It was Pauline; a thankful interruption. She was obviously fresh out of the shower, ruffling her short hair with a towel.

'Am I glad you two are here. It's been insane; all these parents and not a drop of self-respect between them!' She laughed, coming over and kissing us both. If she sensed any tension, she didn't comment on it.

'I'm not sure who's worse, Mr H or your mum, Mags. I just hope my folks keep it together when they get here!'

'What do you mean?' I asked.

'Typical them, they've just been to some nudist thing in the Caribbean and, if we're not careful, we'll have a naturist party going on. I don't think that lot downstairs will need much encouraging, they've been on the sauce since one o'clock!'

Pauline's dad had died about eight years previously and, after a couple of years, her mum had met, and soon after married, Wally, a wonderful old rogue who everyone adored, especially her mum. The two had formed a match made in heaven and, much to everyone's amazement and amusement, had settled into a life of travelling and nudist beaches.

'I'm not sure I've ever seen anyone over fifty naked,' Catherine said thoughtfully. Jenny hurricaned in then with a bottle of chilled white wine and four glasses. I could see the condensation forming on the cold bottle and realised that, if anything was going to get me out of this headspace, a glass of wine was.

'I'm fed up with waiting. I need a drink. It's nearly five o'clock for goodness sake and we're on holiday!' Jenny started careering round the room, singing a rocked-up version of *We're All Going on a Summer Holiday* using the bottle as her microphone.

Soon it was just like old times and we were chattering away like teenagers. Our laughter was infectious and I felt my mood lift gradually. It was hard to stay so low when Jenny and Pauline started re-enacting the time when we'd stolen a football from Mr Sampson's farm but there was pig's muck all over it and Jenny had got covered in the stench. So much so, that it wasn't long before we'd been caught and the whole story had come out. We laughed so much as Pauline did an impression of Mr Sampson, puffing her cheeks up and waggling her finger at us. Before long, I'd managed to build a kind of wall in my mind, protecting me from the fact that Luke was across the landing from us.

Just before six, we felt we really ought to get a move on. The house had suddenly turned into a free-for-all charge for the bathrooms. There may have been three of them but it was hellish trying to get ready with so many people in the house, especially drunk people. There was a rather embarrassing moment when I walked in on Catherine's dad in the loo, but all he'd done was to carry on peeing, turning his head slightly to smile sheepishly at me, so I smiled back, apologising, and left as quickly as I could.

Catherine and I got ready for the party. As I blow-dried my hair, she turned to me.

'How are you feeling now?'

'At least I've seen him and got that bit out of the way. I'll just have to play the evening by ear,' I rationalised, sitting down at the dresser and turning on my straighteners.

Catherine looked slightly worried.

'You did get awfully hurt you know,' she reminded me. 'I mean, I love Luke, he's like a brother, but I couldn't bear to see you get hurt like that again. Be careful won't you,' she said, turning her back to me and crouching down beside me, so I could zip her up.

As I straightened my hair, pleased with the reflection forming in front of me, I thought about how I'd changed and I wondered how Luke had changed. I began to apply my make-up and found that with each line of kohl and each stroke of mascara (and each mouthful of wine), my confidence was building. In fact, the more I let my mind think about the past and everything that had happened, I found myself feeling something other than pain. I began to feel anger. I wasn't 'throwing things around the room' angry, just quietly, simmeringly, angry. I was angry with Luke. I recalled things like they were yesterday. All the love, the hurt and the pain that I'd felt; God, the pain. I remembered the denial stage too. Insistent that I was being silly, that of course Luke would be in touch. But then, as time had gone on, I had experienced the next progressive stage of grief. The angry stage that ultimately arrives when you realise you've been had. It was standard psychology stuff, according to Catherine. And here I was again, reliving those feelings. I mean, it was ten years, ten whole years, and there had been nothing. No call, no letter, no apology, nothing. What on earth was I doing? This was ridiculous. I wasn't going to let Luke ruin my evening. I was a grown woman. I had made a life for myself in London and the past couldn't just step in and take over, washing away the years. No, it had to stand in line and I'd deal with it when I was good and ready. So what if the door to the Luke memories was open? Great! I'd deal with each and every one of them. It was good that Luke was here. Finally, I'd get the answers I needed. And when I got them, I could carry on with my new and exciting life with even more freedom than before; freedom from the past. I could then shut Luke's door in my mind, and get a big eraser and rub it out completely!

I picked up my wine and drained it in one. Surveying the result of the last hour's preparation, I winked confidently at my reflection, raising an internal eyebrow at the amount of kohl around my eyes. I looked as if I was ready for battle, adorned with sexy war paint.

I stood and admired myself in the large dressing table mirror, twisting and turning this way and that, exceptionally pleased with the results. I was aware of my alter ego rearing its confident yet slightly dangerous head, encouraged by each glass of wine to come out and play. I felt a wicked streak bubble up inside me. I was ready for whatever Luke Henderson had to throw at me.

With both of us now ready, it was like the reunion all over again. All dressed up in our stunning dresses; hair and make-up perfect.

'You seem better?' Catherine observed with a slight question in her voice.

'I feel better,' I said confidently.

'Well, here we go.' She linked my arm. 'I'll be there with you, don't worry.'

'I'm not,' my alter ego answered.

I switched off the light over the dressing table and we headed out in the direction of the hubbub below.

Chapter Fifteen

The big open lounge was already heaving with people and we made our way through the throes of familiar faces. Friends and families. Hugs and kisses. More '*haven't you growns*' interspersed with '*it's been ages!! The last time I saw you, you were this high!*' There was a bit of a dodgy moment when old uncle Clement, a distant uncle of Jenny's, decided that Catherine was his dearly departed wife returned from the grave, but cousin Leon intervened with a large glass of sweet sherry and a ham sandwich and led him out to the garden to admire the chrysanthemums, which seemed to calm him down.

We added our gifts to the growing pile of presents on the large dining table which was set through a big archway leading from the lounge. Past that, the double French doors were open to the garden and the bright, warm, summer evening drifted in, carrying smells of wild flowers and countryside. The room was decorated with balloons, streamers and tiny white fairy lights for when it got dark. Conversation and drink was already flowing freely. Most people had dressed up to the nines in summer suits, or shirts and trousers for the gents and colourful dresses with special occasion jewellery for the ladies. I glanced nervously around for Luke but he was nowhere to be seen. Inhaling deeply, I took stock of the situation. There was nothing to be nervous about. I was in control.

I saw Mum and Dad and Catherine's parents in the thick of things. Mum's garden-party hat had, for some reason, been donned for the occasion but it was looking a little askew and, if I wasn't mistaken, a touch of fifties coral had escaped onto her face. Dad, with multi-coloured lipstick kiss marks all over his cheek, was telling one of his only three jokes, luckily the cleanest one, and Pauline's stepdad, Wally, was laughing loudly as if it was the first time he'd heard it. Mr H was deep in conversation with Pauline's Mum, Phyllis, who was tanned and glowing and sporting a rather strange sari type thing with huge bright pink and red flowers all over it; no doubt bought in the Caribbean for those occasions when clothes were mandatory.

She caught me watching and beckoned me over, gathering me to her in a whoosh of colour and a strong whiff of Opium, which, I assumed, was the perfume variety. You never could tell with Phyllis and Wally.

'Darling, Maggie, you look so well, your hair! Whatever happened to all those curls?'

'The wonders of modern technology,' I admitted.

'Can't beat the natural you though, Maggie.' Wally had joined us and cuddled me to him with his bronzed Caribbean-shirted arm and huge gold ring. 'Still as lovely as ever I see.' He bent and kissed me on the cheek. 'So, how are things with you and the big city?'

'Interesting,' I said.

'Interesting good or interesting bad?'

'A bit unbalanced in favour of the latter I'm afraid.'

'Is it boy trouble?' Phyllis asked and I remembered where Pauline had got her directness from.

I shrugged slightly.

'And life trouble,' I admitted, feeling my newfound confidence slipping away.

'It's such a shame;' Wally began, 'young people seem to be having so many problems these days; everything moves so fast, so many choices, so much stress with work and life and all these issues with the opposite sex. Makes me all the more glad I met Pauline's mother.' He gazed lovingly into his wife's eyes and put his arm round her shoulder. 'I knew she was the one for me as soon as I saw her, that very first time. Never any doubts. It was just so easy.' He smiled. 'I hope you find someone special. Someone who it's easy with,' he said. 'That's how it's meant to be you know.'

'You make it sound so straightforward. Life doesn't tend to happen to me like that.'

'Ah, now there's your problem,' he said confidently.

'What do you mean?'

He cleared his throat.

'Well now, you don't want to let life happen *to* you, make it happen *for* you. In fact, make *you* happen to life!' he said, looking pleased as punch with his philosophy.

'I'm not sure my life is quite that straightforward, it always seems full of new problems round every corner.' I thought about Luke, checking round the room yet again.

'Maybe they aren't problems,' he suggested,' maybe they are just forks in the road. Signposts to show you it's time to make new decisions and change your life. And remember, Maggie, you always have a choice you know. Every single situation gives you options. You *always* have a choice.' He nodded wisely in conclusion.

Phyllis intervened.

'Don't worry dear, he subscribed to *Women's Health and Healing* last month by accident, instead of *Yachting Monthly.* The boxes were too small on the application form and he ticked the wrong one. Next, he'll be telling you your hormones need rebalancing and your chakras could do with a spring clean. He means well though and he's probably right, you know.'

Donald and Betty Finch stepped in then, causing a diversion with questions about the Caribbean, and I stood to the side and let Wally's advice sink in.

Fuelled by his words and my third glass of wine, I knew what I had to do. I had to find Luke and I had to have it out with him. I wasn't going to wait for him to maybe come and talk to me; I was going to approach him, in control, and ask him the questions I wanted answering. It was my right to know. This was me dealing with the past so I could get on with the present and the future.

I stared down at the empty glass I was now nursing. I knew I used alcohol to soften life and make things like this easier and I also knew it couldn't always be this way. Decisions made on white wine had a tendency to be the wrong ones – ones I might regret the next day. But I needed these answers and had done for more than ten long years so white wine or no white wine, nothing was going to stop me. I had to do exactly what Wally had been talking about. I had to make life happen *for* me not *to* me. *That* was my choice. I was going to find Luke Henderson and say my piece and if he wanted to interrupt – then tough!

Chapter Sixteen

I scoured the place twice over looking for Luke, and almost gave up thinking he was going to do another of his no-shows but finally he appeared through the doorway from the hall. His hair was still wet from the shower and his sky blue shirt clung to his smooth, bronzed, chest (damn that smooth bronzed chest). I realised, however, I'd have to be patient as people had started to sing Happy Birthday to Mr Henderson. I stood in the corner biding my time. I could wait.

'Happy birthday to you, happy birthday to you, happy birthday dear Reeeeeeexxx/Daaaadd/Mr H, haaapy biiirthdaay toooo yooooouuu. Hip hip hooray, hip hip hooray, hip hip hooray. Bumps! Bumps!'

Mr Henderson looked more than a little disturbed at the suggestion.

Suddenly, from my position by the French doors, I spotted Tony, staring at me from the entrance to the hallway. He was wearing his sunglasses pushed back on his head and looked like he'd only just arrived. Our eyes met and he gave me a big smile. I smiled back, unwilling at that stage to think properly about what seeing Tony again might mean to me.

'To Rex', 'Mr H', 'To Dad', people chorused, and we raised our glasses to the birthday boy.

I stole another glance at Luke.

'Speeech!' we cried. 'Speeech!'

Mr H started shaking his head; then, as if he'd been intending to make a speech all along, he waved his hand away at us theatrically.

'Oh if I must, if I must!' He clambered carefully up on to a little footstool next to the archway. We all cheered him and he had to use his flattened hands to quieten the room.

'Thank you so much. You are most kind.' He smiled around at everyone.

'Friends, family, neighbours,' he began, 'I am delighted you could all join me tonight for this little celebration.'

'Hear, hear.'

'I have known many of you for so long. You are just as much a part of me as I am.'

'Awwww' we chorused, the whole room one big smile.

'There are times in a man's life when he realises just who his friends really are and tonight, as I look around this room, there is not one person who I don't consider to be a dear and valued friend to me. And judging by the numbers, that makes me a very, very lucky man indeed.'

I spotted my mum wiping her eye and Dad put his arm around her and gave her a little squeeze.

'I'd like to make a few very special toasts though,' Mr H continued.

Like a flash, my mother's words from that morning came rushing back to me.

'Rex said he's going to be making some announcements...some news from his lot ...*one of the boys possibly.*'

I felt my body tighten again. Something inside me didn't want the news to be about Luke. Was that why he was here?

'Firstly to Leon, my lovely nephew and son of my late sister Flora.'

I relaxed slightly, although Mr H had said 'firstly'. Who was next?

'Leon is responsible for the wonderful decorations in the house and the garden, which I am sure you will agree look rather splendid!'

People clapped and cheered Leon, who blushed heavily. Not the most confident member of the family.

'And also for bringing me the wonderful news today that through his studies with The Open University he has been awarded a 2:1. Well done, Leon. I'm very proud indeed. To Leon!' He raised his glass.

'To Leon!'

We clapped and cheered even louder and Leon blushed more fiercely.

Was that the main news? Leon's 2:1?

When the noise had died down, Mr H moved on.

'And now to Jenny,' he turned to her, 'my adorable if not somewhat unruly daughter, to whom I lost my heart when she was just a baby. She took hold of my finger in her tiny hand, gazed up at me and said, "Dadda", and I was smitten.' He smiled warmly, his eyes glistening.

Jenny smiled back at him, blinking back her own tears.

'Jenny has proved to me that this is no longer a man's world, not that I ever suspected it *was* you understand.'

Laughter rippled around the room.

'She has proved that, against all odds in this very machismo world of ours, a very beautiful and extraordinarily talented woman can run rings around any man, despite the gruesome conditions that we, as a species, seem to want to place in the way.'

'Hear, hear!' Some of the women's voices rang out.

'So, Jenny, my darling,' her father continued, 'I raise my glass to your courage, your strength and your determination.'

'To Jenny!'

'To Jenny!' we followed.

Without warning, tears pricked my eyes too and Pauline linked my arm beside me.

'And now Tony, my dear son.' I turned to Tony, watching his reaction.

'I know things have been a bit tough on you lately and I can't say anything to make things better. But I can say this: You have made me a very proud father indeed with the support you have shown over these past years, putting your own feelings on hold for the benefit of others. You have helped me enormously with the farm, especially recently, and I couldn't have coped with all this land without your help. I know you have so much responsibility in London with your company but you still choose to come and help me and I will always be so thankful for that, son. It takes a very special kind of person to put his family first.' And with that Mr H stopped and took a hanky out of his pocket, removed his spectacles and dabbed both his eyes before replacing them again. The room went quiet. I don't think there was a dry eye in the place.

Mr H composed himself again.

'To Tony.' He raised his glass.

'To Tony!' we cheered loudly, clinking glasses with those closest to us. Tony smiled but looked down at his feet.

'And finally to Luke, my oldest son. The first born and the first loved.'

I tensed. Here we go. I allowed myself to glance briefly in Luke's direction then steeled my gaze back to Mr H again.

'When my lovely wife Amelia was alive, God bless her, she used to say he had the charm of an angel, even as a child. His blue eyes captured our hearts and we could deny him nothing. He has grown into a strong and intelligent gentleman of whom I am very, very proud. From an early age, he knew he wanted to be an architect and to see more than just these green and pleasant lands. And travel he did, setting himself up in Sweden and making a tremendous success of his career. I always wondered whether he had chosen a career over a family and I have to admit I've been a tad hopeful that one of these days, being the oldest, he might make an honest woman of some lovely lady and bring me some grandchildren while I'm still young enough to play tag with them.'

Laughter peeled round the room again. Everyone but me was relaxed and happy. I didn't like the way this was going. I didn't want to think about Luke with another woman.

Not yet at least.

'So you can imagine my delight when Luke turned up last night, quite out of the blue, and brought me some very pleasing news.'

Horror shot through me. I caught my breath.

'Yes, my oldest son, Luke Henderson is to be married! There's hope for my being a grandfather yet!' He nodded his approval at Luke.

'What?' Jenny swung round in Luke's direction, looking perplexed.

'It's just a pity she couldn't be with us tonight so that we could have welcomed her into the family properly. Perhaps a fitting idea would be to throw another party for them both!'

Everyone cheered.

'To Luke. To Luke and, um, Sian I believe is his fiancée's name, isn't that right, son?'

'Yes, that's right, Sian.' Luke said, clearly a little embarrassed but smiling warmly. I looked away as he glanced over at me, unable to meet his eyes and see in them the love that he felt for his new fiancée.

I found myself caught up in the crowd's cheering and unthinkingly raised my glass to the air, feeling my legs begin to shake.

The room swam around me, blurred and distant. I managed somehow to create a smile. One which would fool the room but inside I felt dead. All those years of feelings, squashed. Luke was getting married. I felt very unbalanced, so I quickly put my glass down and headed for the downstairs loo. There I locked myself in, standing with my back to the cool wooden door, trying to breathe normally. I could hear the party going on outside, a blur of muffled, animated voices, laughing and joking, unaware of the pain I felt. My previous determination was gone. My confidence shattered.

I sat down on the wooden toilet seat lid, my head in my hands for the second time since I'd arrived. I couldn't go back out there, not yet. So I just sat and sat, my head reeling. Every so often someone would come down the hallway and try the locked door, rattling the brass handle. I'd hear them tut, or mutter their apologies or annoyance and then head up the main staircase above me, their footsteps thudding overhead as they went off to one of the bathrooms, leaving me in peace. The mixture of the bright light overhead and the blur from the alcohol made things seem once again surreal. The sound of Mr H's voice still rang in my ears. *My oldest son Luke Henderson is to be married.*

Gradually, my beating heart calmed and my senses quietened. I stood up slowly and turned to the mirror, where I appeared like a young girl with her mother's make-up on. I washed my hands under the cold tap then pressed my palms to my temples to clear my head. I reached up and took a fresh hand towel from the shelf, putting it to my face and breathing in the familiar scent from my childhood. I felt pain through my chest and my head. Ten years on and now this, still the same old feelings. Why? *Why?* I clenched my fists, banging the sides of the basin. Why couldn't I just forget him? He had been a complete bastard to me. Was that why? The fact that he had been so unkind? Was I one of these women who were attracted to the pain that unrequited love brought? Love was shit sometimes. But I wasn't in love. How could I be? This was just a boy from school, someone from the past and these were just old feelings that needed to go away. I would deal with this. My previous assertiveness began to swim through me. I thought of the night by the river and allowed the anger to surface again. I was not going to let this guy get to me a second time. I'd suffered enough.

I steeled myself to return to the party. Checking my make-up and flushing the toilet I took a deep breath and went back out.

In the hallway, Catherine was suddenly beside me.

'I've been searching everywhere for you, I thought you'd left! You must feel awful, I'm so sorry,' she said.

I leant against the wooden wall panelling in the hallway, still feeling unsteady.

'I'm OK, I'm just not quite drunk enough.' I grabbed a glass of white wine from Leon as he walked past. He seemed slightly taken aback but took one look at my face, while I downed half of it, and walked off without a word.

'Are you going to say anything?' Catherine asked.

'No. No I'm not. It would be pointless.'

'Don't you want to ask him why he didn't get in touch?'

'Yes, but…' I thought about what good it would do and closed my eyes, gathering strength. 'No. It wouldn't do any good now. It's time to put the past behind me. I'll just wish him all the best and leave it at that. It was over years ago. I've been living in the past and kidding myself. This is just what I needed to realise that Luke Henderson was a complete shit to me and I've had a lucky escape.'

A male voice sounded behind me.

'Hey, Luke, how's it going? Congrats by the way.'

I turned to see a smiling Luke heartily shaking hands with one of the neighbour's sons and realised, too late, that he must have heard every word I'd just said.

He stood there staring at me.

Catherine made her excuses and left us to it.

Neither Luke nor I said a word and you could have cut the tension with a knife. Several people came through the hallway and we both just smiled at them as if nothing was wrong. Then it was just the two of us. I fixed my gaze straight ahead, unable to look him in the face. He was the one to break the uncomfortable silence.

'I didn't want you to find out like this Maggie. I'm really sorry.'

The cheek of it, like he thought I gave a damn.

'Nothing to be sorry about, Luke,' I said aloofly, knocking the remains of my drink back and wondering briefly how many I'd had.

'I hope you'll be very happy,' I snapped, still embarrassed at being caught off guard.

Luke spoke slowly, his tone hinted at regret.

'Thank you for that.' He paused, 'I hope so too.'

A moment of silence filled the air before he continued.

'There are some things I need to say to you though...'

I cut him dead.

'Luke, just leave it. It's history. Life's moved on. I've moved on.' I was almost convincing myself. 'Now if you'll excuse me, my glass is empty.' I tried to move past him.

He put his hand out to stop me.

'Mags, I'm sorry.'

'I've told you...' I allowed myself to look into his face feeling drawn into his deep blue eyes. I forced myself to turn away.

'About before I mean. After we, well you know.' He was clearly embarrassed. I sniffed a retort.

'That was ages ago, Luke, it was kids' stuff. I got over it,' I said.

'Did you?' he asked quietly, scanning my face. 'Did you really? Cos I didn't.'
I blushed, taken aback by his tone.

'I need to talk to you properly about what happened,' he said.

I found my knees weakening at his voice. He was so close I could breathe in the smell of his body. The way his shirt clung to him showing off his strong body and broad shoulders. His smooth chest was tanned and agonisingly sexy, just begging to be touched. I knew that all I had to do was reach out to him and touch him and all the love I'd felt those years ago would come flooding back. I could beg him for the answers. I needed to know. I so desperately wanted to have his reassurance. And he wanted to tell me. Maybe he still wanted me. Maybe this marriage was a huge mistake, a sham, and it was really me he wanted. I could feel the connection we'd always had. This was Luke, my Luke. The thoughts and feelings were still all there, pounding at my head, begging me to take notice. But…I couldn't. I wouldn't. And as quickly as the thoughts and feelings arrived, I managed to stop them in their tracks. Reality kicked in, hard and cold. There was no point in falling for this guy a second time. He was getting married. This was a road to nowhere. I had to be strong. I'd promised myself.

I turned and faced him full on. Holding his gaze and staring determinedly from eye to eye.

'You don't need to explain anything, Luke. Nothing whatsoever,' I said firmly.

'Please, Maggie, I need you to understand,' he pleaded. 'Things back then they…'

My anger snapped. 'Understand? Understand what exactly? Why you took the one thing that was precious to me then completely ruined my life? Is that what you want me to understand, Luke?' I spat, close to tears.

I stood shaking, shocked and embarrassed at my own outburst. Luke's face had fallen. I immediately regretted my words. I tried to compose myself.

'Look, just forget it, Luke, it's gone. You're getting married and I'm very pleased for you, truly, so please, let's just leave the past where it belongs.'

Luke seemed taken aback, hurt, confused even.

'Maggie, please, it wasn't …' he began, but a male voice interrupted him.

'You OK, Maggie?' Out of nowhere Tony had appeared.

He and Luke exchanged looks and then Tony's attention turned to me, his face a picture of concern.

Luke seemed to give up then. He stared down at the floor for a few moments then back up at me again. His expression showed pain. There was no mistaking I'd hurt him with my words. Well tough, it was about time he knew how it felt.

He spoke quietly, sadly.

'I just want you to know I am sorry, for everything.' And with that, he turned and walked back towards the party, leaving me wrecked and empty.

'You look like you need a drink,' Tony said.

He guided me towards the kitchen and I let myself be led, unable to comprehend the world outside my head. But before I knew what was happening, Jenny collared me and having no strength or will to stop her, she dragged me to the dancing area.

My body was limp. My heart was heavy and my emotions were tumbling over each other.

The more the evening wore on, the drunker I became. The more I drank, the more I became numb. I smiled outwardly and no one would ever have known what I was feeling. But though the lights may have been on, Maggie was out. Catherine tried talking to me about things but I shook my head and mouthed 'not now'.

I remember the clock striking. I tried to count the dongs, so I knew whether I could feasibly go to bed without being missed, but I lost track after six or seven.

As I stood at the side of the lounge, vaguely aware of the revelry going on all around me, suddenly, I was aware of a presence beside me.

Turning, I was taken aback, once again, at the resemblance. Similar features, especially around the nose and mouth, the eyes were different but still with that alluring twinkle, the hair was also quite similar although his was darker and coarser, and then that strong solid appearance which had always made me feel so safe. Tony smiled down at me and, despite everything and even through all the wine, my stomach flipped slightly and I smiled back.

'How's the under twelve's backgammon champion then?'

'OK.' I smiled weakly at him.

'I've been watching you,' he said with a hint of mischief in his voice.

'Have you? Was I interesting?'

'Very. Do you know you've got eyes like Elizabeth Taylor?'

'You've been talking to my grandmother,' I said. 'She always says that.'

'Only yours are a bit,' he paused 'blacker!'

I elbowed him in the ribs.

'Shhhh, don't mention the black eye! My Mum would never forgive me.'

He grinned, not appearing at all sorry. 'Your secret's safe with me, for now anyway.'

I felt my spirits lift slightly but then I noticed Luke approaching and I was suffocating again. He walked towards us, stopped, and looked at us both from one to the other. Then his attention settled on Tony. I glanced apprehensively up at the two of them. They seemed less alike now they were together. There was something in the way they looked at each other but it was unreadable. I felt strange, like I was witnessing something I shouldn't have, so I stared down into my wine glass until Luke turned and walked off out of the room.

Tony appeared unperturbed. Had I imagined the tension?

'I didn't think he was coming this evening,' I said, braving the subject.

He shrugged. 'Must have been a change of plan.' He looked down at me. 'How are you feeling now?'

'What do you mean?'

'After, you know, earlier.'

I studied his expression, trying to read his mind.

'You knew then?'

'Brothers talk you know.'

'How much do you know?' Suddenly I realised that Tony may be able to shed some light on things. Things I was so desperate to know.

'Enough I guess.'

'Do you know everything?' I searched his face.

'I know he hurt you.'

My gaze fell to the floor.

'I heard you talking earlier,' he said gently. 'Guess things are well and truly over now that he's getting married?' There was a slight question in his voice.

'Tony, they were over years ago.'

He looked through narrowed eyes at me.

'Were they?'

'Absolutely,' I said firmly.

'Maggie, tell me to mind my own business but you don't seem very sure.'

'Well I am.'

'You deserve someone better.'

I was shocked at the way he was referring to his own brother.

'I tried to convince him to do the right thing you know,' he said.

'What do you mean?' I stared up at him, sure now that he knew the truth.

'Back then when he didn't come home to see you.'

'I assumed he'd just gone off me,' I said.

'If it had been me, I'd have wanted to stand by you, whatever happened.'

I looked up at him completely confused now. *Stand by me?*

'Tony, I must be missing something. What on earth are you talking about?'

'Oh... Oh no...' He was clearly uncomfortable. 'He didn't tell you, did he?'

'Tell me what?'

'Look, Maggie, I'm sorry.' He touched my shoulder. 'Can we just forget I said anything?' I moved his hand away, almost roughly.

'No! No, we can't. Please, Tony, you've got to tell me. What didn't he tell me?

He paused, took a mouthful of his beer then sighed, exhaling slowly.

'He thought you might be pregnant. In fact, he was convinced of it.'

I felt the colour drain from my face.

'What?'

'That's why he wouldn't come back from uni. Honestly, Maggie, I thought that's what you were talking about out in the hall.'

'No, he never said a word,' I said quietly.

My mind was reeling, none of this made sense.

'But... I don't get it. How come he thought I was pregnant? He never even got in touch!'

Tony seemed twitchy and started looking nervously around the room.

'Tony, please, if you're covering up for him, don't. I just need to know what really happened. I need some closure on all this.'

This apparently gave Tony the permission he needed.

'Look, the thing is, Maggie... God this is embarrassing.'

I stood there, watching his uncertain expression, willing him to tell me.

'The condom broke, you know, when you... got it together. Luke panicked. He came running back home afterwards and told me everything. He was scared. He was convinced you'd get pregnant.'

I tried to take it all in – *pregnant? But why on earth hadn't he tried to find out for* sure?

Tony carried on.

'He went off to university and said he was going to lie low. I think he was the only guy that didn't come back for the holidays. I tried to get him to face up to you but he wouldn't do it; refused point blank. I guess he was still scared, after all he was only a kid really.'

I stood back against the wall of the lounge, putting my hand to my forehead, trying to piece together the past.

'But… but…' I felt my lip begin to quiver and I had to bite it to regain control, '…we were so close.'

The thought of Luke running away and not feeling able to come to me with something like this, left me feeling cold inside. We had been like two peas in a pod. And now, after all this time, I find out he couldn't even face me.

'But you were still around, Tony, why didn't you tell him I wasn't?'

He turned to me, his eyes apologetic.

'Maggie, I couldn't. I didn't know. For all I knew you could have been pregnant.'

'Surely you must have noticed the lack of a bump!'

'Yes, but you could have had a…' he faltered, '…a termination for all I knew.'

I must have looked incredulous.

'Oh come on, Mags, I wasn't to know. See it from my point of view. You girls were always round at our place up in Jenny's room; as far as I was concerned, you might have been covering up all sorts. I couldn't tell Luke you weren't pregnant because I thought you might have been.'

I didn't believe what I was hearing.

'And you're saying Luke wouldn't come back, even though, as far as you were both concerned, I could easily have been pregnant with his baby?'

'Like I told you, I did try to get him to come home.'

'So then what?'

'Eventually, I realised it couldn't be true. I mean, when people referred to you, you know, in conversation, there was clearly nothing going on. No one mentioned a baby or a… termination and no one had a go at Luke for anything and so I figured the coast was clear for him to come home. Anyway, you moved away after a while and rumour had it you were practically married so that was that.'

'I think I need to sit down.' I felt my legs start to go from beneath me and Tony just managed to catch me as I began to slide down the wall.

He led me to a nearby chair and got me some water. Then he pulled a second chair up and we sat in silence until I felt better.

It was then I began to feel angry again; really angry this time. The damn cheek of Luke Henderson. It was all beginning to make sense. No wonder he hadn't bothered to come back. Luke was a coward, a chicken. I felt sick. The spineless git; I couldn't believe I'd been so upset, when all along the guy I supposedly loved, wasn't even man enough to support me when I was carrying his child. Well, obviously I wasn't but that was beside the point.

'You OK?' Tony put his hand on my arm.

'You're damn right I'm OK…now.'

I turned to him feeling the adrenalin coursing angrily through me, giving me a second wind.

'Thanks, Tony.'

He seemed puzzled. 'What for?'

'For being so honest; I know it can't have been easy talking about Luke like that. He is your brother after all.'

'Don't I know it,' he said. 'Listen, can we just keep this between you and me though? He'd kill me if he found out I'd told you. He made me promise to keep my mouth shut. And I would have done only… well… I just got things wrong earlier.'

'Don't worry I won't say anything about it. In fact, I probably won't say anything to Luke ever again,' I said bitterly.

'So, you're well and truly over him then?' He looked at me with a slight smile, clearly trying to lighten the mood.

'You'd better believe it.'

'Good. In that case, perhaps you won't mind his little brother stepping in and keeping you company for a while? Remember we've got a backgammon match to play.'

'Backstroke,' I said partly to myself.

'Sorry?'

'Nothing.' A vague smile twitched at my lips.

'Come on then!' He stood up, took my hand, pulling me up too, and led me off to where people were dancing.

As I looked up at him smiling down at me, I couldn't help but smile back, suddenly unable to stop his infectious mood breaking mine.

It was only when Catherine and Leon left the space beside Tony and me on the dance floor, that I caught sight of Luke through the gap. He was sitting in his father's armchair and staring directly at us, totally still, his expression hard and cold. I shivered.

The party continued into the night. The lights were dimmed, the fairy lights twinkled and all manner of music was played at high volume. I think everyone must have danced with everyone, apart from Luke. He'd disappeared. I hadn't seen him go. I just knew he was gone. I couldn't feel his presence any more. I was able to breathe again.

Tony was attentive and kept getting me drinks and food from the buffet and pulling me up to dance but, after a while and despite my earlier insistence, he seemed to sense I needed some space to piece things together. I sat in a blur most of the time, smiling and laughing at the appropriate moments and watching the party in full swing, but in a little world of my own. The world outside my head could have been a fictional drama playing out on a television screen or in a dream. Any minute now I could have woken up, I felt so detached. Every time I allowed my thoughts to go back to Tony's words, it was as if a safety mechanism kicked in and steered me back to oblivion again. The thoughts would wait and I hoped that, in my fragile state the next day, I would be able to handle them.

People sang, danced and drank and the atmosphere became extremely lively. Jenny passed round tequila shots at about one in the morning; thankfully I declined. She was full of it, dancing one minute, singing the next. Her face was radiant. Her eyes were wild. She reminded me of Cathy in *Wuthering Heights*. There was a moment when she looked a bit scary. She stopped flinging herself about the floor and glared into space but then her face softened again; her expression became mischievous and she skipped off in the direction of the hall.

At one point, I remember the phone ringing. It was Pauline's cousin Timmy, to wish Mr H a happy birthday and then to chat to Pauline. Timmy was an absolute scream; we were all very fond of him. He'd lived quite close by while we were all growing up but he'd moved away in search of bright lights.

I remember the music slowing down and I think, as the lights were dimmed even lower, Tony was about to ask me to dance but my dad came over and grabbed me so he could dance with his 'lovely, lovely daughter'.

Pauline was the most sober and kept clearing up, much to Mr H's protestations. I recall Mum having to sit down, while Dad, face like a beetroot, did his rendition of the Gay Gordons with Wally and Phyllis.

Great Uncle Clement started singing *The Green, Green Grass of Home* until Jenny began booing him and Pauline had to drag her off into the garden where I think she was sick.

It's all very patchy after that; alcohol had finally got the better of me, but sometime after three o'clock I think, I clambered up the stairs, leaving the party behind, stepped out of my dress and fell gratefully onto my bed and into a welcome abyss of nothingness.

Chapter Seventeen

I woke at ten wrapped in a pink eiderdown, very aware I was still drunk. The room was blurry and my head felt like cotton wool soaked in methylated spirits. I got up carefully, my inner voice reminding me of the previous evening's events, but once again I pushed the thoughts to one side. I couldn't deal with things yet.

I turned to the second pink eiderdowned single bed under the window. It was empty and hadn't been slept in. Once again, no Catherine.

I stood up slowly; so far so good. I walked over to the mirror above the little basin and was not best impressed when I inspected the evidence. My eyes still showed last night's make-up and were very red indeed. The bags underneath them would have been enough for hand luggage for the flight.

Making my way out across the landing, the carpet felt cool under my feet. The house was in near silence apart from the grandfather clock in the hall. I crept along to the bathroom and quietly shut the door behind me. The hand towel was strewn across the floor and the door to the airing cupboard stood open. The cardboard toilet roll sat empty on the holder and a new roll sat on the back of the cistern with its end hanging down over the toilet seat. Also on the cistern were two wine glasses, one half full, and a beer can perched on the edge of the basin with a cigarette butt stubbed out on the top of it; the aftermath of a party.

I caught sight of myself in the mirror, grimaced and began wiping the eyeliner from beneath my eyes. What a mess. I groaned out loud. And bizarrely, someone groaned back! Shocked that I was apparently not alone, I turned round quickly; no one. The bathroom seemed to be empty. The window was open above the bath. Perhaps someone was out on the roof. The groan came again!

'Hello?' I questioned, feeling extremely self-conscious.

'Ohhhhhhh.'

The groan sounded familiar.

'What happened?' The very ill sounding voice belonged to Jenny and I soon saw why I hadn't seen her the first time. Tucked up into a tiny ball, clutching her stomach, she was curled up at one end of the large deep bath behind the shower curtain, which was pulled halfway across.

'Jenny, it's you! I thought I was hearing voices. Are you all right?' I leant over the bath and helped her up to a sitting position.

'I'm not sure.' She looked bemused. Her face was white and she had traces of lipstick smeared up one cheek. Her eyes were bloodshot and her makeup was smudged. But, despite all this, she *still* looked beautiful. I sighed, sitting down on the lid of the toilet seat.

'How long have you been here?' I asked.

'I don't know. I remember I was sick, maybe twice, and then I must have crashed out here. And… what's this?'

She moved her hand underneath her and pulled out a half-eaten ham and pickle bread roll. Her face turned decidedly green.

I saw there were several towels underneath her from the open airing cupboard.

'What time is it?' she asked quietly, lying back down again and clutching her stomach.

'About ten fifteen.'

'Oh God, the tequila. It must have been that. I was the shot queen for the night. Wish someone had shot me before I reached the bottom of the bottle.'

'Do you want a cup of tea?' I asked helpfully.

'Oh nooooooooo!' she shot up to vertical and threw her hands to her face. 'What?'

'Oh God, no, no, no! Maggie, did I… did I call… anyone?'

'Like who?'

'Just anyone? Please tell me you didn't see me on the phone.'

'I don't know; I don't remember much myself. Why? Do you think you might have been?'

'I can't bloody think straight. Oh what have I done?'

'Who shouldn't you have called?'

'Someone I really, really shouldn't have, that's all. Fuck, fuck, fuck.'

I pulled a sympathetic face hoping it would encourage Jenny to spill the beans. She didn't and I wasn't sure I was brave enough to ask any more questions. Even after all these years I still didn't feel able to approach her about certain things, especially if she didn't give the impression she wanted to share anything.

Having said that, she had a hangover, so I ventured forward a little.

'Was it a man, Jen?'

'It might have been.'

'Oh well,' I said 'just blame the tequila, I shouldn't worry, you probably didn't get through.'

Another look of shock crossed her face again.

'Fuck!' she said again, pulling herself quickly out of the bath and pushing me off the toilet, loudly slamming the wooden lid up.

'I think I'm gonna be...'

'Raaaaaaaaaaaalph.'

And she was. Very Ralph indeed!

Despite my offers of help, she waved me out of the way so I closed the door and left her to it.

Back in the room, my mobile began to ring. I fished it out of my evening bag. For some reason it was covered in candle wax!

It was Catherine.

'Hello' she said sheepishly. 'Were you worried?'

'You're making a habit of this. Should I have been?'

'No.' I could hear her smiling down the phone. No prizes for guessing where she'd got to.

'How are you?' she asked.

'Pretty dreadful.'

'What happened with you and Luke?'

His name sent jolts of violent electricity through me.

'I'll tell you later.'

'Where are you?' I asked.

'I'm over at the hotel with Nico,' she admitted, guiltily.

'Did you...?'

'No! Absolutely not. I'm still intact but I have to admit I was very tempted. I called him about one in the morning and he came and picked me up! Sorry I didn't say goodbye but you looked like you and Tony were quite cosy together.'

'Did we?' I asked, slightly alarmed.

'Yes, you were lighting lots of candles in the garden. You put them in a circle then had a slow dance in the middle of them. It was very romantic.'

'Was it?' A fuzzy memory was forming and I wondered if my phone had somehow got in the way. I also wondered if Luke had seen us together. Not that that mattered of course.

'Is Nico with you now?'

No, he's just gone to get us some breakfast. It's his day off. I hope he hurries up. I need something to cover up my alcohol breath! I haven't got any mints, I don't have a toothbrush with me and I've been talking to him through his sheet all morning.'

I chuckled.

'He's so lovely, Maggie.'

'I know, you've told me. A hundred times!'

'Yes, but I keep finding out so much more about him. And guess what? His mum has

two cats and one of them is just like Tom apparently and he's got a wheat intolerance too!'

'Has Tom got a wheat intolerance?'

'Yes! I've told you before.'

'Have you? Sorry my head's a bit foggy. How on earth did you find that out?'

'He kept eating the bread I put out for the birds and then blowing up like a balloon. Honestly, he looked like a boiled sweet; a little head and little bottom and a huge stomach. I got so worried I thought he might just up and drift off like a balloon he was so big. Alfie, my neighbour down the hall said the vet would have to stick a pin in him to let the air escape but I think he was just trying to wind me up.'

'Or "wind" you up!' I attempted a joke. Catherine didn't laugh.

'Anyway, Nico says I'll have to meet his mum because she's bound to be able to help Tom. They've got a homeopathic vet in Florence,' she said excitedly.

'Why don't you just stop him eating bread?'

'Ah, but he'd find some. Cats are clever you know, especially Tom.'

Apparently not clever enough to avoid wheat though, I thought, but chose not to comment.

I considered how the conversation might have got onto the food intolerances of a cat and then wondered if Catherine really had met her Mr Right.

'Are you guys still planning a barbeque?' she asked.

'I didn't know we were.'

'It's such a nice day. I thought maybe I could bring Nico along. What do you think? Do you think Mr H would mind?' she asked tentatively.

I said I'd check and call her back if there was a problem. We chatted for a few more minutes about the wonders of Nico and my rather worrying candlelit dancing, before hanging up. I wondered what else I couldn't remember. Emptying the contents of my handbag out and finding a half-eaten profiterole, I decided I was probably best not knowing.

Catherine was right. It was a gorgeous day outside and, despite my hangover, I managed to get showered and dressed. Opening the window, I leaned out and gulped in some fresh air. Surprisingly, my head was beginning to clear.

Pauline wandered into my room looking tired, but rather too unhungover for my liking.

'Thank goodness, someone's actually up!' She came and sat down on Catherine's bed. 'Jenny's lying on the bed groaning and feeling dreadful. You look pretty rough yourself,' she said.

'Gee thanks! You don't, though. Didn't you get drunk?'

'No, I didn't drink much. I wasn't really in the mood.'

'Hang on… you were trying to tidy up! God, how times change,' I said, remembering parties gone by.

Pauline laughed.

'I put that down to being married. Someone's gotta do it.'

'Wait a minute, where *was* Terry? Sorry Pauline, I didn't even think to ask.'

'Working, where do you think? Some "out of town" conference.'

'At the weekend?'

She pulled a face.

'Sorry, none of my business.'

'No, that's OK you're right. But he's the boss and I guess that's what bosses do.'

'Didn't he ask you to go with him?'

'Yes, but only because he knew I'd say no. Besides, I wouldn't have gone if he'd paid me! Think of it, I'd have missed your mum doing the cancan and you singing *Happy Birthday* like Marilyn Monroe! Not one to swerve in a hurry.'

'No!' I cried. 'Tell me I didn't! Did anybody see me?'

'Er… everyone. Don't worry, it was very funny. You should have been on stage. You did all the actions and everything.'

Another vague memory was beginning to take shape.

'Did I… did I use Mr H's tablecloth as a wrap?'

'Yup.'

'And did I, oh no, did I use a rolling pin as a microphone?'

Yup,' she confirmed.

'Oh jeez, did I sit on Mr H's lap at the end and give him a big kiss?'

'Oh, yes. But I think he was quite happy about that.'

'I'll never drink again,' I vowed.

'I think Tony was rather enamoured with your performance. He didn't take his eyes off you.'

I felt my face redden.

'Don't worry, Mags, your secret's safe with me.' She smiled an enigmatic smile.

'Now listen, I have a proposition for you and the others. How would you feel if my cousin Timmy came out to Spain with us? Well, not actually with us but on the first flight he can get. He called last night and he's a bit down. His bloke chucked him and I think he was rather fond of him.'

It must have been serious. Timmy had always been a 'one-night stand if you're lucky' merchant; a total commitment-phobe and a complete party animal to boot. Any man that stayed in Timmy's bed more than a night was a relationship.

'You're joking aren't you?' I smiled, happily. 'Of course he can come!' We all loved Timmy. He was very camp, very naughty and very funny.

'I'm glad you're cool with it. I'm a bit worried about him to tell you the truth.'

'How come?'

'Call it women's intuition but I don't think he's very happy. Not just about the break up but about life.'

'Best we cheer him up then.'

'Thanks, Mags. I'd better check with the others. Where's Cat?'

'Loved up with Nico at the hotel; she'll be back later. By the way, are we having a barbeque?'

'Yup, two o'clock start. I hope they've got some veggie sausages.'

And she headed off to get Jenny up.

Shortly before kick-off I stood at the French doors dressed in a deep red halter neck dress that I'd bought for the holiday, which I'd decided had already started so it was OK to wear it. Pleased with the way it flattered my body and accentuated my cleavage, I thought at least I could try and look decent, even if I didn't feel it.

Unfortunately, in my attempt to be cool, sophisticated and demure, as I headed outside through the French doors, I caught my foot on the step and went flying out into the garden where I ended up on all fours, only just avoiding being face down in the irises. Marvellous! I remained there for a moment, wondering who might have seen, then clambered up again, my eyes flitting around for the crowds of spectators rolling about in fits of giggles at the daft cow in the red dress playing dog. Thankfully, the only person who seemed to notice was Great Uncle Clement, in a nearby deckchair, who, instead of laughing at me, began spouting off about the war.

'Lying low and hiding from the Jerry, eh? Good girl! Splendid idea! In the flowerbeds, eh? Good plan. Wish I'd thought of that; bloody Jerry.' And he continued mumbling away to himself until suddenly he appeared to pull out a pretend rifle and, much to my dismay, began shooting up at imaginary planes.

Dusting myself down, I breathed in the sweet smell of the country garden. Up above the sun was beating down from high in the clear blue sky. There was a good breeze and little puffy white clouds drifted about, colliding with each other like teenage bumper cars. Not a Jerry plane in sight thankfully. I'd downed half a pint of orange juice with two paracetamol and managed to force down a cheese sandwich on Pauline's insistence so, luckily, I felt my hangover improving.

All those who had stayed were finally up and about. The majority of guests had left the previous night but immediate family and close friends were still here, milling about the house or wandering around the grounds and waking up slowly.

Unfortunately, Luke was one of the people milling around. I knew that because as I'd walked passed the dining room I heard his voice and whoever was talking to him laughingly referred to him as 'half of the happy couple'. Unwilling and unable to deal with Luke issues, I left without being seen.

Jenny had apparently braved the outside world and she and Pauline had taken Honey and the puppies out across the meadows.

I made my way down the lawn saying my hellos and tried, but failed, to avoid Great Uncle Clement, who gave me a right start as he jabbed me with his invisible rifle as I went past.

Thankfully, I saw Mr H down the far end of the garden putting some coals on the barbeque and I headed towards him. Beside him was a large table, laden with cool boxes crammed full of ice, beer, cider and wine, and a tray of glasses. My parents were close by in the shade of the big old oak tree.

Even from a distance, I could sense some serious hangovers. They were both looking rather sheepish and were certainly quieter than the previous night. Mum sat in an upright chair beneath the sheltering branches. She was wearing another one of her Laura Ashley dresses, of which there seemed to be a never-ending supply, along with, for some odd reason, one of Mr H's gardening hats. She had also donned her darkest, largest, sunglasses. I wandered over. Mum was making green-gilled conversation with Mr H as he lit and stoked the barbeque.

'I have to be careful you see', Mum was explaining. 'The sun can make me feel awfully wobbly. It seems to affect me more than most.'

Mum *definitely* had a hangover.

Dad gave me a wink as I sat on a fold-down chair beside Mum, grateful for the shade of the tree. Gazing up into the ancient branches, I remembered how us girls had climbed the old oak tree as kids. It had been one of our little hideaways when we'd played together as a four. We'd clamber way up high into the thick branches. Hours could go by in our little camp. We'd sit and talk about school and boys. We'd swap secrets and swear we'd always be friends. We'd often pretend we were in a woodland den and carve spears from pieces of wood with Jenny's penknives, just in case her brothers decided to invade us and declare war. I lived in hope. We'd even used the penknives to perform a childlike ritual to become blood sisters. We'd hardly even scratched the skin, but we'd been so serious about it. It had meant so much to us back then. I smiled at the memory.

Mum, yawning, brought me back from my daydream.

'Where's your nice hat from last night, Mum?' I asked.

'It's vanished. I can't imagine where. Who'd want to steal a hat?' she replied, fanning herself with what appeared to be a leaflet on colonic irrigation.

Dad was doing his best to appear normal but looked decidedly peaky, though I did spot a half empty lager bottle beside him on the grass.

'You OK, Dad?' I asked, going over and kissing him on the head, changing chairs to sit beside him. He was wearing another of Mr H's hats. One of those Australian wide brimmed jobs with corks all round.

'Ah you know me, love.' He gave me a sideways cuddle, 'I'll be good as gold with a bit of food inside me, won't I my sweetness,' he aimed at Mum, his corks jiggling as he turned.

'You'll be OK if you don't throw any of that Benny Hill stuff down your neck again. I think it's best if you stick to water today, Douglas.' She dabbed her face with a hanky and took a large sip of her lemonade.

Dad reached down surreptitiously and tucked the lager bottle under his chair.

'Benny Hill stuff?' Dad and I chorused. 'What's that?' I asked.

'Oh you know, Benny what's it thingy drink. I always forget the name. It reminds me of monks. Your father was a disgrace last night, an absolute disgrace. It was abnormal all that jumping around and behaving like a teenager!'

'I seem to remember you doing a rather lively rendition of the cancan oh innocent one; hardly what I'd call "normal" behaviour. And, I don't think you mean Benny Hill if monks are involved,' he pointed out.

'No, I can't imagine Benny Hill as a monk,' I agreed.

'More of a monkey!' Dad grinned.

Mum tutted impatiently.

'I think Mum's probably talking about Benedictine, Dad. Weren't you on that last night?'

'... and Rex Henderson if I'm not mistaken,' Mum said pointedly. 'They were both as bad as each other!'

Dad rolled his eyes in my direction and I rolled mine back.

Mr H joined us in his chef's hat and blue and white checked apron. His face was red from the barbeque and his moustache wet with beer froth. He had a bottle of stout in one hand and was clutching his barbeque tongs in the other, just like they were a conductor's baton. There was a twinkle in his eye and he looked just like a naughty schoolboy.

'Ah,' he said wisely, with a flourish of his tongs, 'but you must allow us gents a little scope for fun once in a while, Barbara. How else will we be able to keep up the pace? A little tipple, particularly one so fine as my dear friend Benedictine, keeps us young and alive, just like you are my dear.' He placed his beer on the table, bent down and picking up my mother's hand he kissed it chivalrously.

Mum blushed but then went rather white.

'I'm afraid this sun is a trifle strong for me,' she said 'I think I may have to lie down for a few minutes. Would you mind, Rex?'

'Not at all,' Rex boomed, clearly the only one not suffering. 'Make yourself at home. Now, Barbara, can I tempt you to a cold glass of something naughty to take with you? A little snifter of chilled white perhaps? Hmmm?'

I was sure I saw my mother retch and her hand went protectively to her stomach but she shook her head and smiled sweetly as she stood up. 'Thank you, Rex, most kind, but I think I'd rather just have a little lie down in the shade indoors and then…' Before she had time to finish her sentence, one of Honey's Andrex puppies came bounding out towards Mr H and nearly knocked Mum over. Pauline and Jenny had evidently returned.

The puppy had hold of Mum's hat from the party, battling with it and dragging it alongside as it ran. It stopped and shook the hat from side to side, growling playfully. Then it let go of the hat and retreated a little way back, its front paws stretched out in front and its little bottom still high in the air, tail waggling ten to the dozen. It obviously wanted to play. But whenever Mr H tried to grab the hat, the puppy lunged at it again and swept it off round the garden. The hat was decidedly bigger than the puppy, and everyone except Mum thought it was hilarious.

'Douglas, do something!' she shrieked. 'That's a Vivienne Westwood hat! And it's *this* season's!'

There followed an amusing kerfuffle as Dad ran around the garden, followed by Mum barking orders at Dad and the dog. The dog careered around the flowerbeds, growling away happily into Vivienne's latest hat, unaware of the damage and uproar it was causing.

Dad finally managed to catch hold of the puppy's tail and delay it long enough for him to get hold of the rim.

'Careful, Douglas, don't let him rip it!' she yelled.'

'I'm doing my best!' Dad was clearly exasperated as he began to prise the puppy's jaw open and extract the hat.

'There you go! Good as new.' Dad presented Mum with the chewed up hat.

'Good as new? Good as new? I'll be the laughing stock of the neighbourhood if I go out wearing this!' Mum shrieked, inspecting the tattered rim.

'You're very welcome to borrow mine again if you like,' Mr H offered.

Mum hmmphed loudly and marched off to the house with her chewed hat. Dad shrugged his shoulders and followed behind her.

Thirty seconds later, Dad doubled back again, grabbed a fresh bottle of lager from the table and ran back the way he came.

Mr H's laughter rumbled heartily beside me.

'Ah the joys of married life. Now then, young Maggie, you'll not be refusing the demon drink will you?'

'Absolutely not! White wine please Mr H, second thoughts better make it a spritzer.'

The drinks prohibition would start after the holiday. Thinking of the holiday suddenly made hangovers and drinking OK; par for the course really.

Mr H handed me the tongs and headed back up the garden to get some soda.

I stoked the coals cautiously, standing back to stop the sparks flying onto my new dress. I was in a world of my own when a familiar voice sounded behind me.

'You look stunning as ever. How's the head?'

I turned to see Tony casually dressed in cream shorts and a petrol blue tee shirt. His hair was still wet from the shower, making it appear darker than usual. There was a glint in his eyes and a knowing smirk played on his lips.

I tried to act cool. 'Who's to say I've got a hangover?'

'Well if I've got one you've definitely got one! He sat down on one of the chairs and patted the one beside him for me to join him.

'Why? What did I do? Please tell me I wasn't awful.' I put down the tongs and sat down quickly.

'Awful? Not at all.' He looked amused. 'I've just never met a girl who can match me drink for drink. I'm afraid it's a biological fact that guys can drink more alcohol than girls before getting a hangover, something to do with the amount of muscle we carry, I believe.'

'You'd get on well with Catherine,' I said. 'I thought you meant I'd done something terrible. I can only remember certain things and I get kind of paranoid when I've got a hangover.'

'Ah, so you have got one!'

'Don't, it's embarrassing enough that I did an impression of Marilyn Monroe.'

'Oh yeah, I'd forgotten that. That tablecloth really suited you. And as for the rolling pin, well, what can I say?'

'I made a fool of myself didn't I?'

He laughed. 'Not at all. Not many people saw really, and I won't tell if you don't.'

He paused, 'although…'

'Although what?'

'You'll have to promise to sit with me all afternoon and not leave my side.'

'What if I need the loo?'

'Hmmm, OK I'll allow that.'

'That's good of you. I'll think about it.'

'You will huh? Well I'll think about not telling anyone about you doing a strip tease with the tablecloth.'

'I didn't!'

'Only a pretend one.'

'Noooo.' I groaned. 'Right, I'll stay here but just don't remind anyone and you'll have to keep topping up my glass if I'm not allowed to move.'

'Done.'

'I think your mum's feeling a bit worse for wear. She looked pretty white just now. I hope she's OK and they don't have to head off early. I'm really fond of your folks. I don't see enough of them as it is.'

I glowed with pleasure at the kind reference to Mum and Dad. He really seemed to like them. I wondered if he'd feel the same if we were marrie… *Stop right there!* I inwardly showed myself the hand.

Of course he'd like feel the same.

Mr H came back with my drink, which I accepted gratefully before he turned back to the house again to see to his guests.

I took several welcome gulps, feeling my hangover easing away with each mouthful. People seemed to have gathered in the coolness of the kitchen and Tony and I were temporarily alone.

I became aware that he was watching me.

'You don't look like you've got a hangover. You look pretty good actually. And your eyes seem very clear indeed, not a trace of… black.' He laughed as I whacked him on the arm.

'You promised you wouldn't mention it!'

'I won't let your secret out, don't worry, but I'm afraid you'll have to do one more thing to guarantee my silence.'

'Typical. What is it this time?'

'You'll have to let me kiss you.' He stared intently at me then shot me such a gorgeous smile, that I realised how much I fancied him.

Sure, I wanted to kiss him, but the big question was, had I remembered to clean my teeth? Had I? Had I? Aggghhh. Now, I had been in the bathroom but then there had been the groaning incident with Jenny and then the chat and then she had pushed me out the way to be sick in the toilet. When had I had time to do my teeth? Oh no, I hadn't done them! Oh no, oh no, oh no, oh… yes! A memory flashed, I *had* done them, in the sink in my bedroom. Phew!

'Well?' Tony had his head cocked to one side.

I smiled shyly, taking another mouthful of my spritzer for Dutch courage.

Tony reached his hand up to my cheek and began to caress it, watching my face as he did so. Then very slowly, he leant towards me and kissed me gently on the lips.

Right at the same time as Luke decided to make an appearance!

'*Jesus!*' Luke's voice was unmistakeable. I opened my eyes to see him coming down the pathway beside the house. He had on faded denim shorts and a white tee shirt and, despite my situation, I felt my stomach lurch. I broke away quickly from Tony, only to watch Luke stride angrily towards the kitchen and into the house, shaking his head and muttering to himself as he went.

I could have sworn Tony was pleased that Luke had seen us.

'I never doubted it.'

'What?' I asked quietly, feeling shell-shocked.

Tony leant back in his chair, raised his arms high into the air behind him and stretched his long body beside me.

'You're one heck of a kisser.'

I smiled vaguely.

He nodded towards my glass.

'Come on, you, drink that last bit and I'll get you a refill. I did promise after all. And I reckon you deserve it after that.'

I did as I was told and he took my glass and refilled it from the drinks table.

'Thank you,' I murmured, as he handed it to me. Despite everything I'd learned about Luke and the past, I wasn't sure I'd been ready to have him see me with Tony, whether he was engaged or not.

'Now if you'll excuse me a sec, this gent needs to visit the little boys' room.' And making me promise to keep his place, Tony wandered off.

Left alone, I allowed my mind to journey back over the previous evening.

Mr H's speech, me running off, Luke trying to talk to me. What would have happened if I'd let him? Would he have gone on to explain the past? Would he have made sure I understood? How different would I have been feeling about things now?

Before I had time to dwell on it further, two more puppies bounded out of the house. They were closely followed by a hot and bothered Jenny in the tiniest pair of denim cut-offs and a pair of green wellies, which made her legs look like dolls' legs. I inadvertently hid my calves and ankles under the chair.

Pauline followed, holding her sides as she laughed loudly.

'Never again!' Jenny yelled disappearing behind the shed for the second time.

Pauline joined me.

'How you feeling? Nice dress by the way.'

'Thanks. I'm feeling better now, hair of the dog mainly. I'm with Jenny… never again!'

'You always say that,' she pointed out.

'I know but, after the holiday I intend to stop drinking so much. I'm fed up with always having hangovers. Goodness only knows what my liver looks like.'

I took a sip of my drink.

'Catherine told me once that the liver's the organ where people keep all their unresolved anger,' I said dubiously. 'She said she'd always been put off eating liver because of it.'

Pauline was thoughtful.

'What does she think would happen to her if she ate it?'

'I don't know. Perhaps one minute she'd be fine and calm and the next she'd be conjuring up angry memories and beating up the waiter!'

'And they'd be cow memories,' Pauline pointed out.

I giggled. 'Like the farmer having his hands all over her udder!'

Pauline laughed. 'Then she'd be remembering the time that the cows in the next field snubbed her, and wouldn't moo at her for weeks.'

'All because she got off with one of their heifers,' I added.

Pauline sniggered.

'And then,' I continued, 'just as she thought all was well, she'd be whisked off to the abbatoi…' I trailed off, realising how awful that must be to be going to your death.

'Thank God I'm a vegetarian,' Pauline said.

'I do eat free range meat,' I said, thinking it probably wasn't enough of a defence.

Pauline gave me a slight, resigned, smile.

One of the puppies finally came to rest at Pauline's feet, panting hard as Jenny ran up and flumped down on the grass beside it.

'Little bastards! They'll be the death of me.' Jenny sat panting, trying to get her breath back. The puppy and Jenny had reached a stalemate.

Pauline scooped up the puppy and held it in the air for me to see.

'How can you possibly call this cutie a bastard? Just look at his little face!'

And with that, the puppy did a little jiggle in Pauline's hands and promptly pee'd through the air onto her tee shirt!

'Little bugger!' she cried, leaping up and hurriedly setting the puppy down on the grass.

Jenny creased up.

'Told you! They may look cute but don't be fooled. There's enough projectile urine in those little bodies to put out the barbeque.'

Up the garden, the side gate opened and I spotted Catherine begin to make her way down the path. Behind her, handsome and shy, was Nico.

Catherine's face was all lit up. She came down the lawn to where we were sitting, leading Nico behind her like a shy animal. The poor guy seemed totally overwhelmed.

'Hi, everyone, I'd like you to meet Nico,' she introduced, as they reached us. 'Nico, this is Jenny, Maggie and Pauline.'

'Forgive me for not shaking your hand,' Pauline said, 'I've got dog pee all over it! Back in a mo.' She ran off up to the house.

'Watcha!' Jenny grabbed Nico's hand and shook it hard.

Nico nodded, smiling tentatively.

'Do you like dogs, Nico?' Jenny asked.

'I luff dogs,' he said, enthusiastically. 'My parents, they have three.'

'Good, well in that case you can take this little arse!' And she picked up and handed Nico the thankfully empty-bladdered puppy. 'Just keep it away from the flowers! Must dash, there's a special bottle of cider in the fridge with my name on it!' She grinned and ran off up the garden.

'Would you like to sit down, Nico?' I asked.

He sat down beside me, and Catherine pulled up another chair just as Tony returned.

'Sorry I took so long, Wally's in there with the holiday snaps. My hangover's taken a significant turn for the worse having seen him and Phyllis naked. Not a fig leaf in sight either!'

Tony eyed Nico slightly suspiciously.

'This is Nico,' Catherine explained. 'We've been seeing each other. He's from Italy.' She beamed proudly and Nico smiled lovingly at her. He sat, still holding the puppy, stroking its head and tickling it behind the ears, much to the puppy's delight.

Tony nodded in a typically alpha male way and pulled up a fourth chair.

I leaned over to the puppy and gave its chin a scritch. Nico smiled gratefully at me.

'Italy huh?' Tony sounded a little brusque.

'Yes, I come from *Firenze,* Florence,' Nico replied.

'Do they have Labradors in Italy?'

It was an innocuous enough question, but the way Tony had asked it, it sounded rude. I looked over at him and frowned slightly.

'Actually, Nico has got three *Black* Labradors. His mum and dad have always kept

them, sort of like a family tradition,' Catherine explained.

'In my country, it is sad that many people do not treat the animals well. It is not my way, nor the way of my family. We luff dogs and cats and I have grown up with them all my life.' He scratched the puppy on its tummy as it writhed around in ecstasy.

For some reason, there followed a rather uncomfortable and unexplained silence. It was as if there was something unspoken between Nico and Tony. Maybe it was a male thing. Catherine broke the tension.

'Who's for a drinkie then? Nico?' Catherine stood up.

'I come and help you.' He passed the puppy to me and it wriggled on my lap but then settled down again as I made a fuss of it. Tony and I were left alone again under the tree.

'He seems nice,' I said, fishing for Tony's reaction.

'Mmmm, I guess.'

'Didn't you like him?'

'Didn't really get a chance to get to know him,' Tony shrugged. 'Anyway, I've got you on your own now, that's the important thing. Shame we were interrupted before.'

'Looks like it's going to happen again.' I nodded in the direction of Mr H who was returning with some plates of meat.

'When am I going to get you to myself? With you wearing a dress like that, a man could be forgiven for all sorts.'

'Such as?' I asked playfully, deciding I may have misjudged Tony's mood with Nico.

'Don't tempt me. I'll just have to take you out again when you get back from this holiday I've been hearing about.'

Mr H reached us.

'I hope you've been stoking my coals,' he said.

'Sort of,' I admitted.

People were heading out into the garden now. More tables were brought out and chairs and tablecloths were added.

Before long, everyone had gathered under the tree and tables had been set ready for the feast. Bowls of salads were carried down, French sticks and cheese, burger buns and condiments. More drinks were added to the cool boxes and two big containers of strawberries were placed on the table with some extra thick double cream.

Mr H cooked happily, brandishing his tongs. Dad, who had snuck away from my sleeping mother, helped. I think he was rather relieved to be able to enjoy a drink without being nagged at.

It was actually Mr H's birthday that day and, before long, there was another party starting.

Every now and then I would catch Tony staring at me and we'd smile secretively.

Thankfully, Luke didn't put in much of an appearance saying he had urgent work to do. He grabbed a few bits from the barbeque at one point and glanced over at me, looking less than friendly, but apart from that I hardly saw him.

Nico settled in and it soon seemed like he'd been in the family for years. When he was in full flow with Wally, Catherine took the chance to ask my opinion.

'Well?' she asked excitedly, 'What do you think? Do you like him?'

'He seems really lovely, Cat. Be good to get to know him properly though?'

'You will, you will; I promise. Oh, Mags,' she hugged herself, 'I can't believe my luck!'

'He's lucky too you know!' I pointed out.

'I know but… I think I might be falling for him.'

'Even though you've only seen him twice.'

'Oh don't you start too, that's what Jen's just said to me. Besides, we talk for hours every day.'

'We just want you to be careful. We know what you're like.'

'What do you mean?' she asked indignantly.

'Well, and please take this the right way, you do have a habit of falling in love quickly and not always for the right men.'

'Like who?'

'OK, for one, there was that builder bloke, Jim?'

She tutted. 'I wasn't to know he was a bigamist.'

'He would have been a trigamist, if you hadn't found out about the other two. And then there was that bloke, what was his name, Johnston... Johnny?'

'Johnno. And he was nice!' Catherine defended him. 'He bought me flowers.'

'Er, correction! He stole you flowers!'

'Not really *stole*.'

'Yes really *stole*. Did you think a bunch of chrysanthemums with "Rest in Peace Aunty Mabel" written on the label, were really meant for you?'

'He meant well.'

'So did the nieces and nephews of dear old Aunty Mabel but I bet they didn't mean for their chrysanths to end up on your coffee table!'

Catherine giggled. 'I did feel a bit guilty.'

'Look, all I'm saying is that I, for one, just want to make sure you don't get hurt.'

'I know and I won't. I'll be *really* careful, I promise. But he's so gorgeous! I'm sure he's right for me. I've just got this feeling. Anyway,' she went on, 'what about you? How did things go last night?'

'It was certainly an interesting night,' I said thoughtfully.

I lowered my voice and quietly explained all about Luke trying to talk to me and then what Tony had said.

She was shocked.

'But that's awful!' she cried, then lowered her voice. 'What are you going to do?'

'Nothing,' I replied.

'Nothing?'

'Cat, I've spent ten years of my life wondering what happened and now I know.'

'Surely you'd want to say *something*.'

'Nope. Besides, I think I'm rather interested in his brother.'

'Of course! How's that going?'

'He kissed me,' I said.

'Really!' she shrieked.

'Cat, keep it down!' I eyed Tony who, thankfully, was talking to Mr H.

'Was it a nice kiss?'

'I think it would have been but Luke turned up in the middle of it.'

'No!'

'I know. It kind of ruined the whole thing.'

'Where is Luke anyway?' She looked around the tables.

'Urgent work to do, apparently.'

'Maybe that's for the best', she said. 'Just think how confusing it would be, having them both sitting round the same table!'

And then some. I thought.

After a feast of a barbeque, just when I thought I'd never eat another thing, Jenny appeared carrying a cake ablaze with candles.

We started singing *Happy Birthday* as she placed the cake on the table in front of Mr H and hugged him. On the final 'yooooou' he blew all the candles out with one breath and a great cheer went up.

'Wish! Wish!' we all cried.

'I wish we could do this every year!' he laughed.

We stayed and ate, drank and laughed, late on into the evening.

I didn't get much of a chance to talk to Tony but as dusk was setting and Catherine and Nico went off for a walk around the meadows, he took the opportunity to slip into the chair beside me.

'I've got to go in a minute, early start back in London tomorrow. But I was hoping we might be able to meet up again, when you get back from Spain. What do you think?'

'This would be for the backgammon match, right?'

'Only if you promise not to do too much practising on holiday.'

'I hardly think we'll have time for backgammon,' I laughed.

Tony put his head woefully in his hands.

'Oh no! She's going to be out every night without a thought for poor old me, cooped up in polluted, boring old London. What am I going to do?' He looked up with a hangdog expression on his face. 'Perhaps you could spare just a little time to drop me a text or even send me a postcard.'

'I tell you what, I'll drop you a textcard.'

'Will you give me weather reports?' he asked, pretending to be eager.

'If you're good. And bar reports probably!'

'And beach gossip?' he asked hopefully.

'Definitely beach gossip.'

'What about...' he hesitated 'nightlife gossip.'

I could see he was fishing.

'That's if I can fit it in between all our mad partying,' I replied, jokingly, trying to keep things light.

He seemed genuinely forlorn then and I found I couldn't keep it up.

'Then again,' I sighed, 'it all depends on whether you consider being in bed by midnight with a cup of cocoa, nightlife worth gossiping about.'

He smiled.

As long as you describe exactly what you're wearing, then I'll be happy.'

'You, Tony Henderson, are a dreadful flirt.'

'Takes one to know one.'

'Wish you could fit me in your suitcase,' he said, looking like he meant it. And at that moment, I rather wished I could too.

Chapter Eighteen

The next morning, I was rudely awoken at seven o'clock by my phone bleeping.

The room was already bright and, feeling remarkably awake, I stretched where I lay wondering who had texted me – perhaps Mum? She and Dad had left late last night, with Mum feeling suitably puritanical after her rest. She'd issued strict instructions for me not to drink too much so I wouldn't have put it past her to check up on me at the crack of dawn.

Turning, I remembered Catherine had gone back to the hotel with Nico and I was alone.

I eased myself up onto my elbow and reached down into my handbag on the floor, retrieving my mobile. I discovered two texts including one from the previous night.

The recent one wasn't from Mum, it was from Jenny.

GET UP you old bag! We're going on holiday! Jen XX

I couldn't believe it. In just a few hours we'd be in Spain, no doubt heading for the beach.

I tapped open the second text. It was a number I didn't recognise. Timmy!

FAB news! Got flite4 Tues! Will have a ball (or several!!) Hate Brazilians! (men – not waxes) Will mayb love again 1 day, prob Thurs! In need of girlie chats and COCKTAILS. Hugs Timmy XXX

I smiled and thought back to the last time I'd seen him remembering he'd got me completely annihilated and convinced me to have my hair streaked vivid blue (!)…while he got a Mohawk coloured like a parrot! Not one of our finest moments I have to say. Justin had done his nut and I'd been a laughing stock in the office.

I sent him a text back:

Can't wait to see you again!! We'll find you a scrummy Spaniard instead (or several!!) Well up for 'cock'tails but no 'parrot'heads! XXXXX

Down in the kitchen Jenny was crashing about looking alarmingly angry and far away from the mood of her earlier text.

I sat down at the large wooden kitchen table and watched her for a few moments, banging things around and huffing and puffing.

'What's up?' I ventured, wondering where Luke might be.

'Huh? Oh nothing, just men,' she snapped. 'Everyone around here thinks I'm their skivvy and I'm not, right? I'm fucking not!' She picked up a load of mugs from the table and put them noisily in the dishwasher.

'They're always bloody walking all over us bloody women. I can't stand it.' She started running the hot water to wash the frying pan.

'Who are?'

Jenny didn't seem to hear me.

'Next time I'm coming back as a man; they've got it easy!'

'Do you believe in reincarnation then?' I asked, having rather assumed she probably didn't.

'Definitely! Basically, women are going to rule the world one day and we are just going to keep going round and round, coming back life after life and being reborn until we've sussed out how to overturn those bastards and nick it back off them again.'

'But then why are you going to come back as a man?'

'Just to see what goes on in their thick skulls so I can kick them into touch the next time round.'

'I see. So…' I sing-songed, trying to sound cheerful, 'All packed then?'

She stopped what she was doing for a moment and turned to me.

'Sorry, Mags, I know I'm a bear with a sore head. I didn't sleep too well and work's pretty full on at the moment. It's all just catching up on me a bit. Yep, I'm packed, passport and tickets at the ready, and raring to go. You wait. The apartment we've got is awesome. I checked it out on the website.'

'We'd better sort you out with some money then,' I said, wondering how much it was all going to set me back. I knew Jen was getting a good deal, but still; if the apartment was *that* good…

'You don't need to give me anything for the apartment. *I'm* not paying for it, so I don't see why you guys should, not unless you want to!'

'You got it for nothing?' I asked incredulously.

'That's what happens when you know guys in the business. A client reckoned he owed me a favour and I'm not complaining. I guess some men have got their uses,' she admitted, as she started to dirty up the frying pan again with our cooked breakfast.

'So, where's Cat?' she asked. 'With "Lover Boy"?'

At that moment, with great timing, Catherine's face appeared at the open top of the stable door.

'I'm back!' she sang, opening the bottom part of the door and walking in before collapsing on a chair beside me.

She sighed dramatically.

Then when no one said anything, she sighed again even more dramatically.

'Don't tell me...' Jenny said 'you've just got laid and now you're going to talk us through all the gory details.'

'Jenny!' Catherine exclaimed. 'No, of course not, but...' she sighed yet again, 'I think

I'm...'

'...in love!' Jenny and I finished together and Jenny began to laugh.

'What's so funny?' Catherine demanded.

'You're always in love!' Jenny said.

'I am not!'

'Are too.'

'Am not.'

'Are too.'

'I AM NOT!'

'Stop!' I put my palm up before world war three broke out.

Catherine usually came off worst in these infrequent bickering sessions. Unlike Jenny, she didn't possess the ability to stun a person with her words, bringing them down to the floor as if she had a gun to their head. I was rather glad we had always got on so well.

Catherine turned away from Jenny and sat huffily at the table.

Jenny banged cupboard doors about and started cooking very noisily. I wondered who would break the silence. Unusually, it was Jenny.

'I'm just saying; that's all. You're too soft, you're always falling for guys and I hope this one's worth it.'

This was Jenny's rather veiled way of saying she cared about Catherine and didn't want to see her get hurt.

'He is,' Catherine said sulkily.

'Good,' Jenny confirmed.

'Yes it is good actually.'

'It wants to be.'

'Great! Then everything's settled.' I concluded. 'God I'm starving.'

There followed an awkward silence but as the smell of cooking filled the air the tension seemed to dissipate and Catherine broke it.

'Is Luke still here?' She glanced briefly at me.

I knew she was asking for my benefit.

'Nope, he left first thing to get back to his bird; must have been gagging for it.'

I felt a little sick.

'Can't believe I'm gonna have a bloody vegetable for a sister-in-law.'

Catherine looked puzzled.

'A Swede!' Jenny chuckled, giving me a kind wink.

I had a feeling she was trying to slag off Sian for my benefit.

So, he'd gone. Well, so what, good riddance to him and good luck to him and his Swedish Shmedish fiancée. I didn't care. OK, so I hoped that Sian looked like the back end of a bus but I was entitled to the odd personality defect, considering.

Pauline came in looking decidedly tired.

'Ha! Now you've got a hangover!' I pointed accusingly at her.

'Nope,' she smiled. 'Still not; I'm just knackered. I think that rock hard army camp bed has seen better days.' She rubbed her lower back.

'Not the same one as you had when we were kids?' I asked Jenny, dismayed.

'The very same; Dad won't part with it. Luke and I were playing Peanuts and Eggcups on it the other night. Remember that?' My stomach gave a huge lurch.

The game Peanuts and Eggcups had been invented when we were young teenagers; discovered quite by accident, when Pauline had been eating peanuts and dropped one, from some height, on the camp bed. We realised then how far a peanut would travel once it had bounced on the taught surface of the regulation army bed. There began Peanuts & Eggcups.

Equipment needed: 1 regulation army camp bed, fully assembled; 1 bag of peanuts, preferably not dry-roasted, for the sake of mess; several containers of differing sizes, e.g. Tupperware boxes, bowls… and most importantly an eggcup.

Rules: Sit one side of the camp bed, bounce said peanuts one by one on the camp bed aiming them at one of the containers lined up on the other side.

The idea was to land a peanut in a container; the bigger the container, the smaller the number of points; the smaller the container, the greater the amount of points awarded and the more kudos. And the eggcup held the most points. Actually, in all the times we'd ever played (loads) only two of us had ever got a peanut in the eggcup – me… and Luke. It was of those special things we'd shared. He even used to joke that one day we'd teach our kids to play it. I wondered whether he'd managed to get a peanut in the eggcup with Jenny. And if he had, would he have thought of me? But of course, *I didn't care!!* I reminded myself forcefully.

The four of us sat at the kitchen table and had a stodgy breakfast which left me feeling a bit woolly. I was beginning to feel like alcohol was running through my veins instead of blood. After two cups of strong coffee, though, I felt a little more alive and we piled off excitedly to finish packing our stuff up ready to set off for the airport.

In our room, Catherine chatted excitedly about Nico.

'He's going to phone and text all the time while I'm away. He says he's going to miss me so much and he didn't stop kissing me. Do you think he could be the one Maggie?'

'Do you?' I asked carefully, feeling a little worried about losing my best friend to a bloke.

'Maybe, oh I do hope so.' She danced about the room with her floppy sun hat on.

I thought about Tony. Would *he* ring? Would he text? Watching Catherine so happy in her newfound romance, I suddenly ached for a bit of the same.

Mr H was running us to the airport. We had to travel in the old Land Rover van he used for carting stuff about. I clambered in the back with Pauline and Catherine while Jenny sat up front with her dad. We perched on the dusty old seats and shared our space with a pile of dustsheets, a pickaxe and one of Honey's puppies who'd jumped in the back with us and clearly had no intention of going back into the house.

We headed out on to the country roads and towards the airport. As we passed Tillmouth Manor, Catherine waved frantically out of the back window.

'I know he's working but, you never know, he might have been looking out of the window.'

The further away we got from Tillmouth, the easier it was to think about the holiday rather than the past and the pain that went with it. I didn't want to mope around feeling bad about things. I wanted to empty my head of anything unhelpful so I could think clearly about my future.

After an hour of being thrown about and watching the puppy skating from one side of the van to the other, much to our amusement, we reached the airport and, apart from one almost catastrophic moment when Jenny thought her passport had been left in her bedside cabinet only to discover it down the side of her seat, we were ready.

Chapter Nineteen

Several long hours later, we found ourselves at our destination. Finally, we'd arrived but not without incident. Jenny had nearly got into a fight with a poor unsuspecting man wearing sandals with white socks.

I'd felt a bit sorry for the guy really. I don't think he'd done anything wrong apart from be a man and, from my point of view, been seen in public wearing sandals and white socks. One minute the poor guy was happily carrying coffees and soft drinks back to his wife and kids in the queue and the next, Jenny was giving him a right earful for apparently treading on her toe. It was only when his wife intervened and threatened to call the police that Jenny let him off with a warning and a threat to make him repaint her toenail where the nail varnish had been chipped. His wife pulled him off in the other direction at that point. Angry or not, Jenny was too much of a threat to have her husband do *that*.

Our seats on the plane were right on the wing and, being in the window seat, I found myself spending most of the flight thinking that the wings were far too wobbly and debating whether to ask a member of staff if they normally juddered about like that.

Catherine's cheese and ham toastie turned out to be just cheese and she wasn't happy – she'd been looking forward to 'said toastie' since we'd arrived at the airport. The steward informed us that 'these things sometimes happen'; one of the perils of the budget airline I imagine. Catherine was only slightly placated when the nice lady with the severe bun and blusher which could well have been visible from the moon, managed to sneak her a free mini can of salt and vinegar Pringles. Fair play to her.

Noticing that the stewardesses on the plane had incredibly firm-looking bottoms, I began to feel really paranoid about my string bikinis and prayed to goodness that the daylight was as flattering to me as the category one changing room had been.

Then there was the baby in front of Jenny and Pauline. It had cried so loudly that I was sure Jenny was going to jump out of her seat, lean over and smother it with the in- flight blanket. Either that or I was going to! Strangely enough though, when I opened my eyes from my post gin and tonic doze which had been sorely interrupted by the baby's screams, Jenny was sitting forward on the edge of her seat, making funny faces at it through the gap between the seats, while it gurgled at her.

When we landed it took an absolute age for our cases to come out and when Catherine's finally turned up, having clearly been opened, it was journeying round the luggage conveyor belt with one of her bras hanging out of it!

Then when we headed off to find the swanky new red Jeep that Jenny had organised through a small local company, we found that the last person to bring it back had left it without any fuel in the tank and no one had picked up on it. Luckily, with Pauline's pidgin Spanish and the pidgin English of the rep from the car hire company, they got the Jeep filled up for us and finally we were zooming along beside the sea amongst the wonderful white villa'd landscape of the Costa del Sol. The sun beat down on us and the wind whooshed in our hair while the music blared out of the car stereo. At last, we'd arrived. We really were on holiday.

Now we stood, hot and exhausted, on the roof terrace of the most amazing apartment block I had ever seen. Four luxurious storeys high, painted in dazzling white with pink bougainvillea creeping over the walls, it nestled against a gently rising landscape, overlooking a stunning private sandy beach. Below us, the vivid, sparkling, blue sea calmly drifted in and out lapping against the immaculate shore. And every now and then, little white waves took turns in crashing and frothing up onto the sand before bubbling and fizzing back into nothing and disappearing out to sea. Above us, seagulls called to each other as they floated and swooped against the matching expanse of blue, cloudless, sky. Waves of wobbling heat rose through the atmosphere distorting the handful of white motorboats powering through the water in the distance. Majestic white villas, almost blinding from the sun's rays, were sprinkled around the surrounding hillside, each with little pathways winding down to moorings at the sea's twinkling edge. Everywhere we looked there seemed to be shocks of pink, red, orange and purple as flowers adorned every wall of every villa and pathway. We scanned our surroundings and stared down, awestruck at the beautiful little cove below, unable to believe our luck. It was breathtaking.

'How did you do it, Jen? How did you get this place for nothing?' Catherine's incredulous face was pink and shiny from the heat.

'Remember that shipping mogul I told you about at the reunion?'

'The one I'm going to marry? Only temporarily you understand,' Catherine added.

'That's the one. Apparently he was so impressed by the work I'd done and the amount of free publicity I managed to secure for him that when I told him I wanted to book up a decent holiday for us all he insisted we stay here! Amazing, huh?' she said happily, leaning forward over the balcony so far that I felt sick.

'And guess what?' she continued from her ninety-degree angle.

'What?' Pauline asked, pulling her up and telling her off for being so reckless.

'We've got a party to go to on Saturday night. He's organised some charity thing on one of his yachts in Puerto Banus.'

'One of his yachts? He's got more than one?' I exclaimed.

'At least three and those are just the one's I know about.'

'Puerto Banus… isn't that where all the rich and famous go?' Pauline asked.

'Pretty much.'

'Will they let us in?' Pauline asked dubiously.

'Don't be daft, of course. Anyway, we can pretend we're rich and famous too, if you're that fussed.'

'Ooh!' Catherine said. 'I could pretend I'm some famous film actress in Hollywood.'

'They'd probably suss you, Cat,' Jenny said.

'Why?' She looked indignant.

'There'll be a whole load of people there who actually *are* famous actors and actresses in Hollywood; best to choose Bollywood or something.'

'I'm not Indian though!'

'You'll have to work on your tan then.'

'Will we be able to dress up?' I asked hopefully.

'You'll *have* to dress up!'

'I hope they have veggie food,' Pauline said.

Jenny smirked.

'They'll have shedloads of everything, I bet you.'

'Wonder who'll be going,' I said dreamily, envisioning film stars being snapped by cutting-edge paparazzi; lots of flashing camera bulbs going off with me, accidentally on purpose, in the background of each shot.

Jenny was scornful. 'It'll be full of rich people lording it about and thinking they're better than us, but at least we'll be able to drink loads of fizz and have a laugh. And you know what, my client's a decent sort,' she added.

I was already working out what I'd wear and wondering what I'd text to Tony about the party.

I spotted Catherine checking her mobile for about the tenth time since we'd landed.

'He'll call soon,' I whispered, trying to reassure her.

'He's probably still working,' she said.

'He's probably doing lots of overtime so that he can take you out somewhere special when you get back,' I suggested.

'Yes, probably.' She managed a brave smile. 'I wish he'd hurry up though. As far as I'm concerned, no news is bad news!'

'He's probably shagging some other bird, now you're out of the way,' Jenny butted in.

'Jenny!' Pauline said, 'That was uncalled for.'

'Sorry, I'm just saying. They're all pigs. Be careful.'

Jenny glanced across and, seeing Catherine's crestfallen face, bounced over and put her arm around her, giving her a friendly punch on the arm.

'Look, don't mind me, I'm just a cynic. I'm sure he's the epitome of loveliness, as are you. Now, come on, let's go down for a swim before we unpack.'

The sun was high in the sky still, beating down relentlessly, as we stood on the edge of the golden sandy beach in shorts and flip flops, carrying bags full of towels, water and books to read. I was almost too frightened to put a foot on the sand in case someone asked us to leave.

'This way you lot!' Jenny ordered, racing off in the direction of some empty loungers. She began hauling two more from another umbrella, so we could all sit together.

Sun-worshippers from the various luxury apartment blocks surrounding the bay lay stretched out in little groups, while scantily clad waiters and waitresses delivered their cool bottled beers, iced wine and elaborate cocktails from the beach bar.

This was no ordinary beach. It was private and it smacked of money. It came with all the trimmings that a large wodge of dosh could buy. Immaculately pruned palm trees and sand that could almost have been hoovered, it was so smooth and clean and completely free from any litter.

Behind us to our right where the edge of the beach met the hillside, there was a huge swimming pool with a stunning fountain at one end that rose high in the air then cascaded into the brilliant blue water. There was even a bridge across the pool leading to a bar in the middle of it with stools in the water and a large canopy so people could swim up and have a drink in the shade.

I laid my towel out on a lounger and, sitting down, eased out of my shorts to reveal my new rainbow-coloured, string bikini. Embarrassed, I quickly covered myself with sun cream and lay down before anyone could really notice me and pass judgement.

'Check you out!' Jenny called over. 'You'll have the helicopters circling round wearing that!'

Jenny could afford to be complimentary. She looked utterly perfect in her itsy bitsy teeny weeny black and very sexy bikini, more like a perfect model doll than ever and, by contrast, Pauline in her Nike power swimmer Lycra-filled one-piece, looked like she was about to enter the school swimming contest. They both fancied a swim and, when Catherine and I declined to join them, headed off insisting that when they got back we were to have a large jug of sangria and four glasses at the ready.

A welcome sea breeze cooled the air. I stretched where I lay, aware of the sound of the waves breaking against the shore. I was reminded then of how much I needed this holiday. How much I had needed to get away from the hustle and bustle of the big city. I could feel my head clearing gradually as I breathed in the sea air.

Out of one eye, I spotted Catherine on the far lounger checking her mobile yet again.

'You know what they say. "A watched pot never boils",' I called over to her.

She came over and sat on the lounger next to me.

'But I can't understand it. He said he'd phone and text all the time and I just thought... well I thought he'd have phoned by now.'

'Don't worry! Like I said before, he's probably busy working. He'll be in touch when he finishes his shift.'

'Yes, I suppose so.'

I reached over to my beach bag and pulled out my own phone, turning it on. I didn't really expect any messages but I was in fear about Mum finding out I had no job and was spending what little redundancy money I had on a holiday. It would be just my luck for me to unwittingly answer a call from them and have to explain what the hell seagulls were doing in Clapham.

It took a while for the network to register but then suddenly a ting sounded. Catherine jumped.

I had a text. From Tony!

I savoured the moment of anticipation before tapping open the message. It read:

Are you back yet? I'm sure you must have been away for at least a week! T X
P.s tell that damn waiter to stop staring at you!

I grinned.

'Tony?' Catherine asked.

I nodded.

There was a part of me that wanted to text straight away and start up a fun texting session but there was another part that didn't want to think about life back in England and, despite my feelings for him, that included Tony.

Soaking up the sun and the atmosphere and listening to the seagulls and the sounds of the sea, I was really beginning to properly relax and feel detached from my everyday life; my old life. I needed this feeling and wanted to avoid texting or talking to anyone back home, for now anyway. I switched the phone off again. I'd text him later.

After our lazy afternoon swimming and soaking up the sun, Jenny and Pauline had driven down to a local supermercado and had come back laden with bags of shopping. Bags, I hasten to add, that mainly clinked. Jenny had then proceeded to make us all Cosmopolitans, which were currently slipping down like Ribena.

'I've got a Jacuzzi in my room!' she yelled from the other end of the hallway, while Catherine, Pauline and I stood comparing tans in the room that Catherine and I were sharing. Pauline and Catherine were both already bright pink.

'I look like a lobster,' Catherine complained. 'That sun's stronger than you think. It'll take me ages to tone this red down to go out tonight,' she said, checking her mobile for the umpteenth time. 'What time is it, Mags?'

'Still early.'

'At least you haven't come out in a million freckles,' Pauline said. 'My face is like join the dots!'

'I'm more like join the spots!' Catherine grimaced at the amount of little spots the sun and her sun cream had already brought out on her forehead and chin. 'No one's ever going to look twice at me now.'

'What about Nico?' Jenny poked her head through our door. 'I thought you weren't interested in anyone else.'

'I'm not, I'm just saying, I'm a complete mess.'

'Hasn't phoned, huh?'

'Not yet but we've only just arrived!' Catherine's tone was more confident than she looked. 'He's probably still working anyway.'

'I'm sure he is.' Jenny rolled her eyes and disappeared off in the direction of the kitchen.

'Excuse me,' Pauline said, heading for the bedroom door, 'I'm off to put a sock in Jenny's mouth before she does any more damage. Just ignore her, Cat; I think she might well have some man trouble of her own.'

With that, Pauline left us to it.

'What man trouble?' Catherine asked.

'Goodness knows. Anyway, what are you wearing?' I thought it might be best to change the subject.

'I don't know. I don't care! Why hasn't he phoned, Mags?' she asked dolefully, plonking herself down on her bed. 'He said he'd phone when I got here. That was hours and hours ago. Maybe he's just lost interest.'

'What since this morning? Don't be ridiculous.'

'I wouldn't be surprised,' she said sadly, pulling a brush through her hair. 'This always happens to me.'

I sat down beside her. 'What does?'

'Guys dumping me before we even get off the ground. I think I've done it again.'

'Done what?'

'Let a guy run rings around me. You're right. I do pick the wrong guys. I always end up falling for them and then I get hurt.'

I gave her a cuddle.

'I just thought we had a connection.'

'I'm sure everything's fine. Seriously, Cat, it's only the first evening.'

'Yes, but he's supposed to have called by now. Something's happened. I can feel it. He's gone off me and reckons that, now I'm gone, he doesn't have to pretend anymore. He's probably decided that, because I won't sleep with him I'm not worth all the bother.

'You've told him then.'

'Yes. I've told him that I'm waiting for the right man.'

'What did he say?'

'He said he totally respected that and hoped he would be the right man. I really believed him.'

'Well then, it's not that is it. Besides, it's not even eight o'clock! There's probably a perfectly good reason,' I insisted.

'Yes, or maybe he just got bored and thought better of it. Without me actually there with him, he's obviously decided to just forget it.' She stood up.

'You could always phone *him*?' I suggested.

A look of horror crossed her face.

'No! I can't do that! It wouldn't be right. I'm not going to make my usual mistake of chasing after a man. I'm going to, at least, keep some dignity.'

She took a couple of gulps of her drink and headed for the en-suite to put her face on.

I thought it best to leave her to it for a while so I got ready in the bedroom.

I chose a red skirt and a white string tee shirt and put on some little white sandals. I finished the outfit off with red bangles and a red necklace. Surveying my appearance in the mirror, I felt a bit like a strawberry Cornetto. I was just considering whether I should change into something different when Catherine let out a squeal from the bathroom.

'My face is on fire!' she yelled.

I ran in, closely followed by Pauline who'd been passing our room.

'What on earth's happened?'

Catherine was frantically splashing her face with water.

'It's this toner of yours!' She reached out blindly in front of her, her face all wet and eyes screwed up. 'Oh, by the way can I borrow your toner?'

'But I haven't brought any toner with me,' I said puzzled.

'This!' She held up a clear bottle half full with orange liquid. It's practically taken the skin off and nearly blinded me as well!'

'Cat, that's not toner, it's nail varnish remover!' I picked up the bottle and saw the label was badly faded.

Pauline had to work hard to stifle a laugh.

'What?' Catherine grabbed it from me, squintingly trying to read the side.

Pauline and I lost control then and the two of us collapsed into fits of giggles.

'Don't laugh! I'm all patchy. I look like I've got measles!'

So Pauline and I sat her down and attempted to calm her face down, while trying desperately not to laugh in the process.

Chapter Twenty

Later that evening, after eating out in a fish restaurant in the local port, we stopped off at a bar where Jenny and Pauline got very drunk. Jenny nearly got into another fight, this time with a six-foot-two woman from Slough, who Jenny insisted was a man in drag. Pauline got uncontrollable giggles then had to run to the loo to be sick. She returned soon after but despite being rather green around the gills, she was still giggling, so we didn't worry too much. Catherine had her boob pinched, twice, and I was chatted up by a drunk guy from Dundee who kept calling me Ken. All in all, I thought it was probably time to leave so, with a collective burst of second wind, we decided to go to a nightclub we'd seen from the cab on the way in. We found a taxi rank and another cab took us across to the edge of the town where we spotted the club's neon sign shining out against the night sky: Angelo's.

The front entrance was on a street full of shops and cafes shut down for the night and the back seemed to lead out towards the sea.

A wall of loud music hit us as we headed down the dimly lit stairs in search of the bar.

Downstairs, the pumping club was painted with deep purple walls. Tiny lights lit up the ceiling like stars and motorised beams of pink and purple lights flashed across the darkness. The floor was edged with neon lighting, which pulsated with the music. Over on the far side the club opened up to the elements and we could see smokers lounging around on sofas and beanbags and great plumes of smoke mixed with dried ice and moonlight.

A long bar stretched the whole of one side of the club. Large mirrors ran behind it and four or five tanned and hunky barmen were rushing around trying to keep up with the constant orders. We spotted a space and a couple of bar stools up at one end and eased in through the crowd, to settle ourselves in.

Jenny hopped up onto one of the high stools and Catherine eyed the other hopefully but slightly dubiously, given its distance from the floor. Jenny had other ideas though.

'You'd better sit down before you fall down, Paul,' she said. 'I don't want you throwing up on me!'

Pauline sat, gratefully. 'I think I got rid of most of it at the last place.'

One of the barmen stood shaking a cocktail shaker before effortlessly decanting some green frothing liquid into several little shot glasses.

'Oooh! We must have a cocktail!' Catherine clapped her hands together like a little girl in a sweet shop.

'I'm not sure I could face one quite yet,' Pauline said, looking almost as green as the shots.

I spotted Catherine surreptitiously checking her mobile. Jenny saw it too.

'Face it, Cat, he's not going to ring. They never do!'

'Stop it Jen,' Pauline warned.

Jenny's dark eyes flashed dangerously as she checked out the menu, her head wobbling slightly as she tried to read it.

We scanned the long list of possibilities.

'I hope they sell vegetarian ones, Paul' Jenny chuckled.

'Don't be silly, Jen, they'll all be vegetarian!' Catherine insisted, frowning slightly.

'Won't they?' she added quietly to me.

I assured her they would.

'What about a *Saucy Senorita*? Or a *Spanish Orgasm*?' Catherine suggested.

'Or perhaps a *Long Lingering Kiss*?' I said, thinking of Tony.

'Whoa I fancy this,' Jenny said, '*Sex in the Sea.*'

'A woman after my own heart,' a voice beside her cut in. A tall, dark and seriously good-looking guy shot her a wink.

'Shove off, wanker, we're not into blokes tonight,' Jenny retorted.

'Aren't we?' said Catherine dolefully. 'Maybe I should forget about Nico and find myself a lovely Spanish man.'

Jenny started squinting and peering over Catherine's shoulder.

'Hey! Isn't that... Nico?' she asked rather too innocently.

'Where?' Catherine's head shot round quickly.

'Oh no, my mistake,' Jenny went on, 'It just looked a bit like him.' She sighed, going back to the menu.

Catherine turned on her, 'What did you do that for?'

'Just thought it was him, that's all,' she said calmly, still scanning the menu.

Catherine went into a sulk until the cocktails arrived.

In the end we all opted for the house special *Angelo's Artillery*. Four fizzing, sparkling cocktails arrived ten minutes later, each equipped with a banana and two plump cherries, strategically arranged, sticking out of the top.

Pauline tried a few sips of the one Jenny had insisted on ordering her but then had to disappear off to the loos. When she hadn't come back after ten minutes, Catherine went after her.

I climbed up onto the bar stool and joined Jenny. For a while we sat and watched the dancers, passing comment every now and then. But I was just biding my time because there was something I wanted to ask her. When I'd plucked up the courage, I took a large mouthful from my cocktail and took my chance.

Why are you so anti men at the moment, Jen?'

I was met with silence

'Man trouble?' I ventured.

She shrugged non-commitally.

'You know, you *can* talk to me, to us, about it, if there's stuff on your mind.' I wondered if she'd open up or just get mad.

She was about to say something but Catherine came rushing up, her cheeks red and flushed.

'Guess what?' she cried excitedly, a rather sickly looking Pauline in tow.

'What?'

She beckoned us to huddle inwards.

'There's a load of people outside smoking dope!'

'Pauline smelt it and then I saw them bold as brass smoking this long white thing.

'Maybe it was a tampon,' Jenny suggested sarcastically.

Catherine ignored her.

'They're all leaning back with their feet up on the tables, as if they own the place,' she said excitedly.

'Maybe they do,' Pauline said.

'I'm going to the bog,' Jenny announced.

'I think I might have to go again too,' Pauline clutched her stomach and followed Jenny.

'Anyway, why would they be smoking tampons?' Catherine asked indignantly, when they'd gone.

'I think Jenny was joking.'

'Well I don't think it's very funny. Honestly, I don't know what's up with her at the moment. She's so snipey. And she's being horrid to me; worse than usual.'

200

'I reckon Pauline's right. I think she may have man trouble.'

'Really?' Catherine's eyes were wide. 'What's she said?'

'Nothing yet but I'm pretty sure she called a guy at her dad's birthday party. I don't know for sure but I suspect she was going to spill the beans just now when you were in the loo, only she didn't get the chance.'

'Why? What happened?'

'You two arrived back with tales of long white tampons.'

'Oh.' Disappointment spread across her face.

'She'll tell us in her own time. You know Jen.'

'She'd better! I'm dying to know now,' Catherine replied.

'Anyway,' she said eagerly, 'do you think a lot of people are on drugs?' She squinted her eyes and began scanning the place.

'How come you are so interested?'

'I'm not, really,' she lied.

'Yes, you are! It's written all over you.'

She tutted. 'I don't know; I just fancied trying some. I never do anything naughty and look where it's got me.'

'I hardly think that's why Nico hasn't rung.'

'Well, why else? It's the same with all men. They just want to get you into bed and once I tell them I'm not willing to give them "you know what" until I'm married, they dump me.'

'But you told Nico how things were. And you said he wanted to be "the one"'.

'I know but either he's changed his mind or he wasn't being honest. Whatever it is, something's gone wrong.'

'That doesn't mean you need to go and do something out of character though,' I pointed out.

'Maybe not but, whatever's happened between us, I'm fed up with always being Miss Goody Two Shoes. It would be nice to do something bad for a change, you know, like getting drugged.'

'I think the expression is "stoned" Cat.'

'Stoned then. Anyway I've got a feeling about this; we'll be smoking away and getting stoned by the end of the night. I'm sure of it.'

'I think they call it "toking"',' I said, feeling very streetwise.

'Look!' Catherine pointed to the outside terrace. 'Over there. Through that big archway, by the pillar! Those are two of the guys I saw before with the drugs. Come on let's go.' And before I could stop her, she'd grabbed her cocktail and my hand and was off, making her way through the crowds, pulling me behind her trying not to spill my drink.

We weaved in and out of bodies flinging themselves all over the place, gyrating to the music and punching the air.

I managed to get kicked once, elbowed twice and then get propositioned one and a half times. The half was when a semi naked guy with mad eyes lurched forward, and licked my cheek. Nice.

We reached the edge of the dance floor, walked the final steps to the large archway leading to the outdoor area and felt the warm night air tinged with tobacco drifting in. There were little lights dotted around outside and groups of people sat talking and laughing, drinking and smoking, the ends of their cigarettes glowing against the relative darkness as they dragged on them. Others danced to the music which was being fed outside by speakers but wasn't as loud as inside. You could just about hear the sound of the waves on the shore and the smell of salt reached my nostrils. Catherine pulled me towards a tall, wide Grecian-style pillar in the centre of the terrace. It had a shelf running all the way around it. On her lead we set our drinks down on the shelf only a few feet away from her targets on the other side.

Catherine stood a little too casually, leaning against the pillar. She rested her short chubby arm on the shelf, which was a bit too high for her, and, all in all, she looked rather awkward.

One of the men was incredibly tall with ebony black glossy skin. He was probably the tallest man I had ever seen and he was clothed from head to toe in black leather, apart from a velvet squishy top hat in a black and white zebra print, which made him appear even taller. His black leather waistcoat showed off his sculpted muscley arms. He wore thick gold chains around his neck and wrist and his long dark fingers were covered in striking gold rings.

As I surreptitiously watched him talk, I saw a flash of yet more gold and assumed he either had a gold tooth or was chewing some sort of expensive gum.

The guy with him was, by contrast, short and skinny, puny even, and very white. Seedy would have been a good word to describe him had I needed to; seedy and speedy as he was moving very jerkily. He looked like a Billy or a Jimmy or something else ending in an 'ee' sound. He had a pair of faded jeans on and a cut-off sleeve tee shirt with a big Union Jack on it. Just the sort of tee shirt one would want to wear in Spain. Not.

If Catherine's meaningful glances in their direction were anything to go by, it wouldn't be long before we would find out what both their names were.

Zebra-man started swinging and swaying along to the music which pumped out from the club and which had thankfully slowed down from the high-energy techno stuff, which I couldn't handle at the best of times.

Catherine nudged me.

'Here's my chance,' she said.

'To do what?'

'Just watch,' she said in an uncharacteristic 'I'm the woman' kind of way.

She moved round the pillar and leant on the shelf again. I shook my head to myself.

From the top of his seven-foot frame, a very white-eyed zebra-man peered down at Catherine.

'Great music don't you think?' she shouted up to him.

I held my breath, in case he took a swipe at her. I had visions of him hoisting her up and bouncing her up and down like a basketball into the main club, then swiftly aiming her at one of the light fittings and scoring poor Catherine right up and into the safety net which hung between the lighting and the floor in case anything fell down.

However, strangely enough, a flicker of something that could well have been intrigue crossed his face as he answered her, his booming Carribean-sounding voice cutting through the sounds of the club.

'Yeah, maan,' he drawled. 'Music is de key of life; the sound of the soul; the breath of the gods.'

Catherine shot me a confused glance but she nonetheless turned back and continued her mission nodding earnestly.

'Oh absolutely; you're so right, the breath of the gods. It's very groovy isn't it,' she enthused, in a very 'I'm *not* the woman' kind of way.

Zebra-man looked down at her quizzically but kept swaying and swinging away, with the occasional bob to add a bit of variety.

Catherine tried to copy him.

Now, Catherine is good at a lot of things. She's a great nurse, a fabulous hostess, a whiz with a needle, creative in the kitchen and a fantastic friend but she can't for the life of her dance. Oh she thinks she can but, quite honestly, when she moves she resembles a duck dancing like its great aunt, all elbows and shoulders up too near her head and a movement which involves sticking her bum right out. All in all, it's hilarious. Try as she might, she's never been able to get the hang of it. The only thing she *can* do well, for what it's worth, is Scottish country dancing but apart from those rare occasions that one might be planning a wee jaunt to the Highlands for a grouse-shooting ball, not much use really. Hence, as Catherine started strutting her stuff to the music, I had to turn away to stop giggling.

Unfortunately, as I looked away, I accidentally caught little 'Jimmy's' eye but it appeared he had been staring at me anyway. He grinned and flipped his head upwards by way of a 'hello' in my direction.

I smiled reticently and quickly turned away.

Catherine was still on the attack.

'So, um do you come here often?' she began.

Oh lord.

'Yeah, maan. It's always ma first starp of dee evening,' he drawled.

'I see, I see and where's the next um… stop?' she asked politely.

'Dee night will take me where it waants to, you know what I'm sayin'?'

Catherine clearly didn't but she stood there persistently bobbing away and trying desperately to keep in rhythm with him.

'So, um, what's your name?' she asked.

Zebra-man peered down at her again, clearly trying to work out what her objective was. I noticed Jimmy/Billy/Thingy was now darting back and forth on the other side of the pillar. Not a bob or a sway in sight. He seemed to be sussing Catherine out too.

Zebra-man, however, must have decided Catherine was harmless, especially having witnessed her dance.

'Dey call me Jye,' he said, closing his eyes to the music as he moved.

'Jyyyye,' Catherine repeated slowly, as if trying it on for size. 'Ooh!' she looked thoroughly excited, '…as in Tarzan's friend?'

Zebra-man slowly shrugged his huge shoulders and whoomphed them down again with such a force, I thought that somewhere in the world a tidal wave might be forming.

'I don' know y'ur friend Taarzaan, but if he's garta friend called Jye, den I'd like to meet him.' And defying his size, he suddenly spun round nimbly on the spot, in a three-hundred-and-sixty-degree turn, clicked his fingers twice and then continued bobbing.

Catherine had apparently decided not to copy this particular move. Jimmy/Billy/Thingy on the other hand wasn't a bobber. He was more of a poker. He poked his head up and down and in and out a bit like Flat Eric the Levi's puppet. He looked like he was trying to kill mosquitoes with his head. It was like two of his pokes were equal to one of Jye's bobs.

Quite suddenly Jimmy/Billy/Thingy circled round the pillar and stood beside me.

''Right?' he flipped his head up again.

I eyed him suspiciously.

'Fine thank you,' I replied, keeping my head exactly where it was.

He continued staring.

Oh crap.

'You?' I asked warily.

He replied in an incredibly fast-paced Cockney accent.

'Yeah, really great thanks; really great. You enjoyin' it? It's good isn't it? Great night, good club, yeah? D'ya like it?'

I wasn't sure which question to answer first.

'I'm Mexxy,' he said, before I could reply. He put out his hand to shake mine.

Mexxy. It figured.

I shook his hand politely but it was rather clammy and unpleasant to touch.

'What's your name then, gorgeous?' he asked.

Oh dear.

'Maggie,' I said, reluctantly.

He shifted beside me.

'So, er, what ya doin' dan 'ere then?'

'Just out for the evening with some friends.'

'Right,' he said, jigging about on the spot beside me.

Then he bent his head a little too close to my face.

'I reckon your mate's got somefink on her mind, yeah?'

'What do you mean?' I moved away slightly.

'I clocked her earlier givin' us a right eyeful and now here yous bofe are over ere where we are! Somefink you want to tell me?'

'Errrr, no, like what?' I frowned, wishing Catherine hadn't decided to stalk them.

'You're not undercover pigs, are ya?' Mexxy asked, quite matter-of-factly.

'What?'

'Pigs, coppers, fuzz,' he explained.

'Oh, police, I see. No we're not.'

If we were, we'd hardly be announcing the fact.

I paused.

'Do we look like the police then?' I asked, rather curious to know.

He shrugged.

'Na, not really but best to ask outright, don't you fink?'

'Mmm, I suppose so.'

'In that case then, you must wanna score yeah?' he nodded expectantly.

'Must we?'

'I can get whatever you want. You name it I can get it. I can always tell the ones who want stuff, dead giveaway, all sort of eager like. Your mate's definitely after somemink, ain't she? Yeah? Am I right? I am arn' I? I'm usually right about these things.'

'What would you do if I said I was a policewoman?'

Mexxy stopped dead. A look of fear crossed his face.

'You're messin' wiv me, right?'

'Just wondered what you'd do.'

'Oh, right hyperfetically like.'

'Yes, hypothetically, like.'

There was a pause.

'Shit meself!' he answered, laughing loudly. I couldn't help but laugh back.

'Just as well you're not though.'

'Why's that?'

'They always expect a discount.'

I began to laugh again but he was evidently serious.

Glancing over at Catherine, I noticed that it was either a joint in her hand or she had in fact taken to smoking tampons. Super Plus by the looks of things! She gazed over at me with a big sleepy smile on her face.

'Looks like my friend's sorted herself out,' I said to Mexxy.

'Fair enough; but if you want anything else, anything at all, I'm your man right? You'll find me doing the rounds of most of the clubs. Just ask for Mexxy. That's Mexxy with a 'y' by the way. Not one of them poncey 'i's, can't be doin' with all that shit.'

'I'll make sure I remember if I'm ever writing to you,' I said.

'Well, in that case, remember, it's two 'x's as well.'

Then he was off, dodging in and out of the dancers and leaving me alone.

I surreptitiously moved round the pillar and stood beside Catherine. I caught Jye's eye and smiled and apparently taking this as some sort of sign, he passed me the Super Plus.

Now, the last time I'd smoked a joint had been with Timmy at some underground bar in Manchester. The whole place had been stoned or drunk or both, so I tried it. I'd heard all these stories of people just getting tired or it not having an effect at all. Well, it'd most certainly affected me! Maybe it had been the alcohol but I got completely smashed on the stuff. First of all, I'd had a great time talking and giggling and finding everyone soooo interesting. I had several very deep conversations where I discovered all manner of things about life and the universe and I was rather proud of my newfound ability to inhale smoke. I did have rather a lot though and suddenly along came the head spins and, after a while of wondering if I was OK, I became very aware of myself and then after spending about fifteen minutes with my head on Timmy's shoulder, I finally went and threw the whole lot up in the toilet.

I supposed if I didn't have as much this time, I could give it another go. After all, Catherine was clearly enjoying herself, bum stuck out, swaying away to the music, with a huge grin on her face stretching from ear to ear.

I took it from Jye and had a couple of puffs, coughing most of it back out again but, as no one seemed to be paying any attention to me, I tried again.

This time, I managed to keep it down and I waited a bit to see if anything happened.

I wasn't sure, so I tried again and inhaled a bit more.

Did I say that I didn't like techno? Well, I was wrong! Right then, I loved it. Along with every track they played. In fact, from where I stood, Catherine was actually a *good* dancer!

I smiled lazily around and smoked some more before passing it back to Jye for the second time. He passed it straight to Catherine, who nearly took his hand off snatching it from him.

'Sorry,' she apologised, laughing nervously, 'co-ordination's gone a bit.'

I caught Catherine's eye as she finished her turn and handed it back to Jye. Suddenly, I wanted to be nearer to her. I felt a bit weird standing next to this big giant stranger who, although very nice, wasn't as safe as my best friend. I think she must have felt the same because, before we could plan it, we both circled round to our original side of the large pillar and practically bumped into each other.

'Oops!' she giggled.

'Sorry,' I said.

'Me too, sorry.'

'Can you feel anything?' I asked.

'Yes, I have hands!' She giggled again.

'No, I mean from the stuff?'

'I know what you meant, ha ha ha ha.'

'Ha ha ha ha,' I laughed back.

'Good isn't it? I feel all squidgy,' she said thoughtfully.

'Yes. Yes! I do too!' I said, my eyes widening and feeling very excited at the realisation.

'Squi-dgy,' I said slowly, trying the word on for size.

'I think those people must be stoned too,' Catherine said confidently, nodding over to a crowd lying around on sofas. 'And them, through in the club, look at the way they're dancing.'

'Yeah, probably. Maybe everyone is stoned?' I suggested.

'Yeah, probably. I am. Are you?' she asked.

'Yeah, very actually. You?'

'Yeah, very,' she agreed solemnly.

'Me too. How stoned are you though?' I asked seriously.

'Oh very; you?' she asked.

'Very.'

Then, out of the blue, I found I wanted to laugh so I started giggling.

Then Catherine started too, which made me laugh even harder and my eyes started watering.

'Tee hee hee hee,' she giggled, 'what are we laughing at?'

'Haa haa haa haa,' I almost cackled, 'I do-o-n't kno-o-w!' I gasped breathlessly.

Then Catherine let out a snort through her nose and I nearly wet *myself* for a change.

In the end we were laughing so much we both had to turn in opposite directions from each other and, even then, I knew she would be shaking uncontrollably just like I was. Thank god it was pretty dark!

Then I had a sober realisation and had to turn back.

'Cat, we can't stay here. What will he think?' I nodded in Jye's direction, nearly cracking my head against the pillar.

There was Jye, all alone. We'd deserted him! We both pulled a face.

'Shall we go back round to him?' Catherine nodded sideways in his direction and she nearly cracked her head on the pillar too. This time we lost it completely.

'Ha ha ha ha HA HA HA HA.'

'HAHAHAHAHAHAAAAAAAAAAAAAAAAAAHAAAAAAAAAAAAA
HAAAAAAAAA.' We 'ha'd' uncontrollably, clutching our stomachs, tears
rolling down our cheeks.

Then we both got paranoid about laughing too loudly, so we laughed in
silence, with our mouths open and it almost got too much as Catherine had
to put her hand between her legs to stop her wetting *her*self, which got me
even more hysterical. Then we had to turn back away from each other again.
We stood back to back, shoulders shaking, tears running down our faces,
unable to look at each other.

Finally, after some deep breaths, we managed to calm down. I had no idea
how long we'd been back there for. Time seemed to be standing still.

'Best go back round don't you think?' Catherine said, trying to be sensible
and refusing to give in, when her face almost cracked.

'Yeah, best,' I agreed, sucking in my cheeks for good measure.

'You first,' she said.

'No, after you,' I insisted

'I can't, after you.'

'No, you.'

'No, you, I'm too stoned. I feel really weird going back there,' she said.

'But so do I! What if people look at us?' I asked.

'Exactly. They'll all be staring at us. I feel a bit strange.'

'Me too,' I agreed.

Before we could decide who went first, Jye poked his head round, eyebrows
raised.

'You ladies ar right?' he enquired.

'Er, yes, sorry, Jye; just needed a bit of a girlie chat. We're just coming back
now,' Catherine informed him.

'No prarblem.' He nodded slowly and moved away again.

'Let's go back then,' I said confidently.

'OK.'

'You go first though.'

'OK,' she giggled and I followed and stood beside her, holding onto her
arm.

'Um, Jye?' Catherine said.

'Yeah maan?'

'Do you think um we could buy some of this stuff of yours?'

I tugged her arm.

'Cat! What are you doing?'

'Well? Why not?'

Catherine had turned into a disco diva drug queen.

'How much you wantin'?' he asked.

Catherine turned to me. I shrugged.

'A quaarter maybe?' Jye drawled.

'How much is a quarter; I mean how big is it? We probably don't need very much.'

'Catherine, are you sure?' I whispered.

'Unless you think we do?' she asked me.

'Do what?'

'Need more.'

'No, I don't mean that. I mean are you sure we should buy some?'

Catherine's voice dropped to a whisper. 'Yes; why not? The others are bound to want some and Jenny needs to chill out.'

Good grief, she'd even taken on the language.

'How much is the smallest we can buy? We don't really smoke this usually,' she explained.

Jye reached into the front pocket of his black leather jeans and passed something to Catherine.

'Take this, lovely lady. It's not so big, but it'll see you ar right.'

'Gosh thanks. How much is this bit then?' Catherine examined it closely.

'No prarblem, take it; s'too smaall to sell.' He gave her an unexpected wink.

'Oh no, no we couldn't,' she protested, 'Could we, Maggie?' she looked at me.

I thought we could actually. It was free after all. But I thought I'd better put up a bit of a fight too.

'No, no, really we couldn't, it's very kind of you but we must give you something for it, really.'

'You can just buy me a drink sister. Large rum and Coke would be super cool,' he drawled.

I wasn't sure that, even with my part suntan, I could be classed as his sister but the sentiment was nice.

'Well, if you're sure?' Catherine said.

Jye nodded in rhythm with the music.

'OK then, come on Maggie we'll both go. Back in a mo, Jye, and thanks ever so much!'

We linked arms and headed back inside before bumping our way across the dance floor again and over to the bar.

Having delivered the drink to Jye, we went off in search of the others and found them in the loos.

'Where have you two been?' Pauline asked looking worried. 'We were about to send out a search party!'

'Sorry, we got a bit waylaid.'

Jenny squinted at Catherine's eyes.

'Uh huh. More like 'way hayed!' She perched herself up on the basins.

'Come on, spill! What've you been up to?'

We told them about our little escapade.

'You could have been kidnapped,' Pauline said.

'Where's mine?' Jenny demanded.

So Catherine gave them a peek of her little lump. She seemed to take great pleasure in being queen bee for once.

'You got papers and fags?' Jenny asked.

Catherine's face fell. Her reign had been short lived.

'So, you've managed to score a lump of hash and no papers or baccy to roll a bloody joint with.'

'We were going to get some!' Catherine said indignantly, clearly worried about losing her kudos.

'Maybe Jye could give us some?' I suggested.

Catherine brightened up.

'Yes, let's go back! Come on, you two, I'll introduce you,' she proclaimed proudly.

So we all bumped our way back across the dance floor and back outside where Jye had been joined again by Mexxy.

I think Mexxy fell in love with Jenny at first sight and there was a bit of an odd moment where he asked if he could sniff her hair but when she answered kindly, 'Of course! As long as you don't mind wearing your testicles as earrings for the rest of your life,' Mexxy left her alone.

After another Super Plus, another half an hour of bobbing, swaying, poking (that was mainly Mexxy) and nodding, we left Jye and Mexxy equipped with a packet of papers, two cigarettes and four very monged out heads.

We decided to leave after that.

'I feel sick again,' Pauline said after we'd climbed the stairs and made it outside.

So we headed down to the beach kicking off our sandals, feeling the cool sand beneath our feet. But after swaying about, bent over, with her hands on her knees for several minutes Pauline informed us it was a false alarm and she managed to wobble along, her face vaguely green, behind Jenny, Catherine and me as we wandered along the shore, giggling.

We couldn't help wowing every time we saw something worth wowing at, like the moon, or the stars or a wave. As we meandered, haphazardly, the night breeze was cool against my skin and, in my little summer strawberry Cornetto clothes, I felt unrestricted and uninhibited.

We must have walked for a good hour along the beach and up along the coastal path but the time just passed us by and before we knew it we'd arrived back at our apartment block happy but exhausted; the sound of the sea was still ringing in our ears and the salt from the sea spray made our faces slightly sticky and tight.

There was a panic when Jenny couldn't find the key and then another one when we thought we'd found it but it wouldn't open the door. Then Pauline, having fallen asleep on the step, woke up and returned the real key, which Jen had given to her for safekeeping. Poor Pauline, she didn't look very well at all and, once we got inside, she headed off for bed.

Jenny, Catherine and I settled into the big squishy white sofas and, after Cat had made us huge mugs of sweet tea each, Jenny began to roll another joint or 'spliff' as she called it. I didn't feel particularly streetwise when I was with Jenny.

Catherine and I watched in awe at the construction being made before our very eyes. It was all going so well, for a while anyway.

Panic set in when Catherine realised she had lost her little lump.

After turning out the contents of her handbag and purse twice and then crawling about on our hands and knees scouring the floor, we discovered it sitting bold as brass, on the magazine that Jenny was using to roll the joint on. All three of us swore blind it hadn't been there the first time we'd looked.

Catherine was worried that the apartment might have a ghost who'd taken it, then put it back, just to spook us.

'What would a fucking ghost want with a lump of hash?' Jenny retorted. 'He's already out of his skull!' she sniggered.

'Maybe he wants to get into the spirit of things!' I suggested.

'But if he got too wrecked, how could we tell if he was having a whitey!' Jenny added, then creased up at her own joke.

Neither Catherine nor I dared to admit we didn't know what a whitey was.

'Bugger,' Jenny said, when things seemed near to completion.

'What?' I asked.

'I've rolled the skins the wrong way round and now I can't find the gluey bit, see?'

She showed it to me.

'Oh yeah, right,' I pretended, not seeing much at all.

'Damn, I'll have to put another skin over the top of it. Sorry ladies it might be a bit harsh on the old throats.'

I shrugged at Catherine, who belched loudly then giggled.

'See?' she said happily, 'I've always told you I get what I focus on.' She put one hand over her left eye. 'I knew we'd get some of this hash stuff tonight, I just knew it.'

When Jenny had finished we headed out to the chairs on the balcony and Jenny lit it up. I was a little nervous, feeling it was perhaps a bit close to home doing it at the apartment... it didn't, however, stop me.

We talked and giggled so much I thought we might wake Pauline.

At one point, Catherine leant close into our little triangle and said in hushed tones:

'Between you me and the goat paste, I think Jye was rather cute.'

There was a pause.

'GOAT PASTE?' Jenny roared, GO-O-O-AT P-A-A-ASTE? What go-o-oa-a-t pa-a- s-ste?' she howled with laughter.

Catherine and I fell about and laughed so much that the two of us had to clutch our crotches once again.

'Ha ha ha I me-e-eant ga-a-a-aate po-o-o-sst.' Catherine could hardly speak.

'Ha ha ha ha ha ha HA HA HA GA-A-A-A-ATE PO-O—O-O-O-ST.' We laughed 'til we cried.

And so it went on until about five in the morning, when we all decided we really ought to head for our beds.

Once in our room, Catherine and I must have bumped into each other at least ten times trying to get ready for bed. At one point Catherine roared from the bathroom and I found her bent over the basin holding the nail varnish remover, helpless with laughter. Of course that started me off again. It took ages to get to bed and even then we couldn't stop giggling so we stayed chatting for a bit longer.

I think we redesigned the bedroom four times, having it all manner of bright colours.

'Oooh yes and the fireplace would look really good in ochre, or maybe sea-blue,' Catherine suggested excitedly.

'Yes, blue, that's the best so far, blue marble even,' I said.

'Can you get blue marble?'

'Well, maybe, I don't know. But, if not, wow it would be so good to invent it don't you think?' I suggested.

'Yes! What a great idea, blue marble. We could start up a factory or something for different colour marbles,' she said.

'Marbles or marble?' I asked.

'Well, maybe both, although I don't know who would want to buy marbles, apart from kids, unless we did designs with marbles.'

There was a pause.

'YES!!' we both cried, as if we'd discovered a sure fire way of winning the lottery.

'MARBLES!! Just like we had when we were kids and we could make glass things out of marbles, you know like lampshades and maybe coffee tables.'

'Ooh, yes. Imagine a coffee table with marbles embedded into it; that would be fantastic!' I said excitedly.

'Ohhhh and what about…?'

And so it went on and we finally crashed out at about six o'clock in the morning, into a very, very dream-filled sleep.

Chapter Twenty-one

The next morning, we all felt rough.

'Ohhh I feel awful,' Catherine giggled.

'Why are you laughing then?' Jenny asked.

'I don't know; I think that stuff is still in my system.'

'I just feel horrid,' Pauline said, looking like she did. 'Whose idea was it anyway?'

'Catherine's,' Jenny and I chorused.

Catherine started to object but then conceded and went off to fetch her mobile, just in case Nico had texted in the last five minutes.

'Actually, I think it's the drink that's got you, girl,' Jenny aimed pointedly at Pauline.

'Never seen you sink so much.'

'It seemed like a good idea at the time.' Pauline nursed her mug of tea.

The only thing for it was to go for a swim and wash the cobwebs away. So, packing up our things we headed down to the bay.

The lounger man, who introduced himself as Enriqué, was on us before we'd even got to the loungers, offering to carry Catherine's bag. She kept giggling and, in the end she let him, even though we were only going a few feet.

Before two minutes had gone past, Enriqué, clearly taken with Catherine's breasts, was dropping strong hints that he worked every day except Thursday, which was his day off. 'Yes, THURSDAY, ees my DAY OFF'. This, he elaborated several times until she eventually replied that she hoped he enjoyed his DAY OFF and that we would be spending THURSDAY, his DAY OFF, on a day trip to MARBELLA.

I think, with his big biceps and shiny brown skin, he thought was in with a chance but it was possibly his slightly crossed eye that had Catherine giggling uncontrollably every time he came within ten feet of us. He soon left her alone.

We stayed on the beach all day, only moving to swim and eat. None of us had much energy at all and when the evening came, it was all we could do to watch a DVD on the huge television.

Still, we were on holiday and I, for one, was happy to relax. I still hadn't texted Tony, so I decided to send him one that evening. I went into the bedroom and, sitting down on my bed, I turned on my mobile.

I waited for the network to register and, a few moments later, it bleeped with an incoming text.

From Tony.

So, Shirley Valentine, will you ever be coming back...or texting me again??

My body tensed. Pressure!

I couldn't think what to say back. He seemed so far away from where I was, in my head. Every time I typed in something, I deleted it again. In the end I settled on:

Sorry! Phone's been off. Been full on here. Eating & Drinking 2 much. The place is fab, weather's hot, but waiter's not! p.s he was looking at Catherine!

I sent it but still wasn't happy. I found myself trying to picture his face but, for some reason, I couldn't get it right.

Then, despite feeling distant, I began to wonder whether the text had been too formal? Had I been friendly enough? Should I have sent him a kiss?

I was busy trying to analyse if I'd mucked the whole thing up when Pauline stuck her head in the doorway.

'I think I'll go back to bed now, Mags. I'm knackered and I've still got a hangover.'

'OK, hun, sleep well. Hope you feel better. Tomorrow's another day.'

She smiled but was clearly far from happy.

I wandered into the lounge to join the others, just as Jenny's phone rang out. Maybe it was Tony checking up on me?

I berated myself for being so silly.

'Timmy!' Jenny exclaimed then put her hand over the mouthpiece.

'Fuck,' she whispered, 'it's Tuesday night! We forgot Timmy!'

'What's up, mate? Where are you?'

There was a pause.

'In the where?' she cried getting up and pushing the door to. She lowered her voice again. 'What on earth's happened? What are you doing there?'

Chapter Twenty-two

Jenny and I arrived at Marbella police station at around eleven o'clock that evening and took possession of a rather disgruntled Timmy. His bleached blond hair was tousled and his eyes were glazed and tired.

He cuddled us both, looking a little sheepish but more indignant than anything.

'Does Pauline know?' he asked, worriedly.

Jenny shook her head, 'Not yet.'

'Oh pleeease, Jen, I'll love you forever. Don't tell her, she'll only worry. I'm supposed to behave responsibly or I'm not allowed to come on holiday.'

'You've started out well then!'

'It wasn't my bloody fault!'

'Oh no, I suppose it was that little old lady that came in on the same flight. Framed you for the whole thing did she?'

'That's just plain silly,' he giggled. 'Anyway, if you must know, it was all a complete mistake; an utter mishmash. If it hadn't been for my shirt…'

'What shirt? Jenny and I asked in unison, as we made our way down the steps of the police station and into the warm night air. We started walking down the quiet street towards the car.

Timmy tripped along beside us, wheeling his pink suitcase with a leopard skin strap behind him.

'Well, me and my shirt have got this sort of "relationship," he said. 'It's my lucky shirt you see.'

Jenny scoffed. 'You mean your pulling shirt?'

'They're all pulling shirts, darls!' he winked at me and hooked my arm.

'No, it's a sort of good luck shirt. It keeps me safe and lucky and I wear it if I've got something important or special going on, like a hot date or if I'm on holiday, or I've got a job interview where I really want the job, you know the sort of thing.'

'So, what's your shirt got to do with all this?' Jenny asked.

'Well, as a lucky shirt, I take good care of it. You know special care. I always wash it by hand and hang it up and all that.'

'Yes and…?' she said impatiently.

'I'm getting to that. Keep your hair on, Oh Feisty One. Anyway, so when I packed, I decided I would pack some of my super-soft, baby-soft washing powder. I wouldn't trust what these Spaniards were selling, could be anything. I'd never understand what it said on the bloody packet. Heaven knows what I'd have done if I'd washed it with bleach or something.'

I had a feeling I knew what was coming.

'Well the bastards only searched me and discovered this nice little container of fine white powder in my hand luggage, all neatly wrapped up so it didn't leak. Get my drift?'

'Or your *Dreft*,' I giggled.

'Anyhow, the poor bastards assumed it was Charlie and whipped the handcuffs out.'

Timmy laughed loudly.

'I mean, if it hadn't been for the nasty mean looks on their faces, I might have thought my luck was in!'

'What are you like, you daft tart!' Jenny shook her head.

'And, they cuffed me in front of everyone! I mean, the whole airport is standing there having a right old butchers at me as I get hauled off. I tried to tell them but they kept babbling away in Spanish and I didn't have a clue what they were talking about. In the end, I just gave in.'

'So what happened then?' Jenny asked.

'They hauled me over here, threw me in a cell and didn't even give me a cup of tea! I ask you. Mind you, Spanish tea isn't exactly Earl Grey, so probably just as well.'

'How long were you in there for?' I asked.

'A whole bloody hour! I s'pose it took them that long before they could get someone who could speak English to come and tell me it had all been a big mistake. Poor sod was really embarrassed. I don't even think he was a copper. It looked like he was some random they'd got out of bed.'

Jenny laughed. 'Maybe he was their *spin doctor*?'

'Was he *awash* with guilt?' I chuckled.

'Well the case was a complete *wash out,*' Timmy replied.

'If they had nicked you, they'd have *hung you out to dry*,' I added.

'*Taking the shirt off my back*, no doubt.' Timmy said.

And we laughed our way back to the car.

'You're such an idiot,' Jenny said as we got in, 'only you would be caught and arrested by the Spanish police for being in the possession of washing bloody powder.'

'I'll have you know, I'm turning over a new leaf,' Timmy said sincerely. 'I intend to *clean up* my act.'

Jenny started the engine.

'Just as soon as I've finished this little lot!' he added.

We swivelled round in our seats to see Timmy take off his baseball cap, undo the lining and, from underneath a piece of spongy padding, pull out a little bag of white powder and a see-through packet of rather suspicious looking pills.

'Timmy, you didn't!' Jenny frowned.

'Rather ironic when you think about it,' he giggled.

'You idiot, you could've been caught!' she said.

And then realising how silly that sounded, we all collapsed into more laughter and sniggered our way back to the apartment.

Chapter Twenty-three

The next morning Pauline gave us all the third degree. She didn't for one moment buy our story that Timmy had arrived unexpectedly in the middle of the night. In the end we had to *come clean* about the washing powder experience.

Pauline was indignant. 'Anyone would think I was Attila the Hun the way you treat me. I know what Timmy's like. I'm just glad it was only washing powder.'

OK so we hadn't told the whole truth.

It was another gorgeous day and Pauline didn't stay mad for long, so we decided to go for a swim and a picnic on the main public beach. First, though, we went into the town for coffee and pastries.

We wandered down a pedestrianised street, full of cafes, bars and boutiques, then found a pretty cafe on the corner and sat down at one of the round tables. The big umbrellas above us were red and white and complemented the checked table covers. We settled in and began to watch people as they sauntered past, carrying bags of shopping and chatting idly to each other.

A middle-aged waiter came over and took our order from Catherine's breasts.

The café con leches were the biggest creamiest coffees I'd seen in a long while. I stretched where I sat and sighed happily. This was what holidays were all about.

We sat lazing about in near silence, soaking up the sun.

'I could get used to this,' Pauline said.

'God, me too,' Timmy agreed.

I spotted a shop across the street with racks of postcards outside. A wave of guilt washed over me. This was ridiculous. I should have told Mum and Dad the truth about my job and the holiday before I left. Now it looked worse, like I'd been lying to them. Whichever way I considered things, I was doomed. Mum was going to make my life a misery.

I sat with my guilt until my coffee was two-thirds empty and then nipped over to the shop and bought a card which I started writing the moment I got back to the table.

Dear Mum and Dad
I'm in Spain! Forgot to mention it Saturday – you know how things go.
Also, more great news, I've left my job! No prospects there so decided to
temp until something more suitable comes up. Sure you'll be pleased, I am.
In a lovely area – the postcard says it all. So much culture! Ring you when
back, café con leche calling. Wish you were here!
Loads of love Maggie xxxx

Question was would they buy it? I decided I'd better buy a tourist guide and swat up on some Spanish history before I saw them.

A new waiter delivered our pastries to Catherine's breasts and topped up our coffees, just as Jenny's mobile rang.

'Dad! Hi!' she smiled openly. 'How's it going?'

'Hi, Mr H,' we chorused.

'Yeah, uh huh, I know the one,' she said. 'Tony knows where it is, he filed it.'

My ears immediately pricked up Catherine shot me a glance.

He hadn't texted me back yet and I couldn't help wondering whether he was there and knew his Dad was on the phone to Jenny. If so, would he want to talk to me? Suddenly the thought of him not texting or not wanting to talk to me made me want to talk to him. *Ah, the contradictory mind of a woman.*

'Oh, OK, well I think it's in the Grounds file under G,' Jenny continued. 'And tell Tony, if it's not there then he's an arse for moving it. He's always knocking about in that filing cabinet. It's not his bloody farm Dad. ... I know, but make sure he tells you where everything is in future.... OK, I know, I'm just saying. ... Yes, it's great! You should see our apartment! ... Thanks, we will.... Say again? ...What? .... Luke is? ... When?'

My heart caught in my mouth.

'All right, Dad, don't worry. You get the other phone. I'll call you soon, yeah?... Love you too, bye.'

'Bloody Tony,' she said when she'd ended the call. 'He's always moving stuff so Dad can't find it. I need to have some serious words with that man. Thinks he knows it all; just cos he's got his own business.'

At this point I didn't care what Jenny thought about Tony. I had to know what her Dad had said about Luke.

Infuriatingly, Jenny didn't seem to be going to say anything and calmly clicked her fingers to call the waiter.

'Oh, by the way,' she said.

I held my breath.

'Looks like Luke's bringing his bird back to live in Tillmouth.'

I felt my heart crash in my chest.

'Why?' Pauline asked. 'I would have thought they'd stay in Sweden because of his job.'

'Dunno, Dad didn't say. The other phone rang before he could tell me.'

I felt sick. It was one thing him getting married to some blond Swedish goddess with a tiny waist, slender calves and platinum blond hair but quite another when he was bringing her home to live in Tillmouth!

'Hold on…' Jenny frowned, 'he's not bloody having my room.'

'You're hardly there!' Pauline exclaimed.

'I don't care. It's my room.'

'Besides, why would he?' Pauline asked. 'He's got his own room.'

'Yeah, but it's not as big as mine and they'll want more space to get all cosy and loved-up in; blurrch.' Jenny pulled a face.

'Just think Mags that could've been you. You had a bloody lucky escape if you ask me. Imagine having to resort to living in one bedroom in the farm!'

Once again, I knew she meant well. But right then, nothing she or anyone could have said would have helped. I felt as if I was in suspended animation. Luke was coming home.

Jenny continued to chat about her Dad and the farm. But I could hardly hear her. I was trying hard to make sense of my feelings. I'd only just got used to the fact he was getting married and now this.

Despite the heat, I felt myself go cold as I considered Tony. The thought of getting together with him had been a real possibility when Luke hadn't been around but now he was coming back things seemed very different.

I inadvertently put my hand to my forehead.

'You OK, girl?' Timmy asked.

'Yes, just a bit hot. Anyone fancy a swim?' I needed to get away and immerse myself in the cool sea. To wash away the lingering effects of the phone conversation.

'But you haven't touched your pastry,' Pauline pointed out.

'I know. For some reason I've lost my appetite.'

Chapter Twenty-four

That night, Catherine and I talked.

I'd been quiet all day, keeping my thoughts to myself, and she'd known not to say anything in front of the others.

'It won't be that bad, surely. I mean, you'll never see them. How often do we go back to Tillmouth?' she asked.

'Well, counting recently and including when we go back, it'll be three times in the space of a few weeks!'

'Yes, I know, but usually.'

'Not very often.'

'So there you go. By the time you see Luke Henderson again, you'll be snuggled up in some lovely relationship. Maybe even… with Tony.' She didn't sound too enamoured.

I looked up from my doldrums. 'You don't seem too keen on me seeing Tony.'

'I am… it's just…'

'Just what?'

She paused.

'Well, if I'm honest, I'm a little concerned because he's Luke's brother; like he's a sort of close second.'

'Well, he's not,' I retorted, immediately regretting my snappiness.

'OK… I'm sorry. I just don't want to see you hurt, again.'

I thought back to our first date. Tony had been a great laugh and so lovely to me. We'd had fun and I'd felt relaxed. He was kind and generous and attentive and attractive. Maybe I was just being silly about things being weird with Luke coming back. I liked Tony, I liked him a lot and considering how badly Luke had treated me, perhaps Jenny had been right. I'd had a lucky escape. Catherine was right about one thing. I wouldn't be seeing Luke and Miss Sweden, with her long tanned smooth legs and eyelashes the length of blades of grass, for ages. Tony would be there, waiting for me when I got back. Maybe he'd be the way to put all this into perspective. Tony wasn't a close second, not at all, he was just… different.

We turned out the lights.

Catherine turned over and went to sleep but I lay there staring at the ceiling. Things had been so clear before this morning. It struck me that I hadn't turned my phone on all evening. I was bound to have got a text from Tony by now.

I reached over to the bedside cabinet and picking up my phone, I turned it on putting it on silent to hide the bleeps so as not to disturb Catherine.

I waited patiently for the network to register. I waited until it finally sprung into action.

My breathing quickened as I steeled myself for a text coming through and then I waited …and I waited.

After five minutes, I stopped waiting and turned the phone off.

Tony hadn't texted. It had been practically two whole days and he hadn't texted.

That, I decided, was not a good sign.

Chapter Twenty-five

The following day my head had cleared and I felt much more positive about things. I was worrying over nothing. Tony would text me, I was sure of it. I didn't think he was the kind of guy to hold a grudge.

After yet another lazy beach day, during which my tan improved enormously, I was looking forward to a night out. However, when we arrived at the club Timmy had chosen, we found ourselves in the gayest nightclub I could have ever imagined.

'Timmy!' Catherine cried as she realised what we'd just entered.

'Oh, come on. It'll be fun! Anyway, you get straight guys here.'

'Er, where?' Jenny retorted scornfully, eyeing several handlebar moustachioed gentlemen in leather boots and matching underpants.

The five of us sat outside under the stars, in the warm night air, drinking yet more cocktails and people watching, or rather gay men watching.

'If it wasn't for Nico, I think I might assume I'd died and gone to Heaven,' Catherine admitted, as yet another scantily dressed, nubile body shimmied past covered in baby oil.

Timmy pretended to bite his bum as he walked past and he shot Timmy a playful glance back.

'Nico still not phoned?' Jenny said to Catherine, almost kindly.

'No.'

'Do you think he will?' Pauline asked.

'No,' she mumbled, sadly.

'Well, in that case, he wasn't worth it. You deserve much more than a guy who can't even be arsed to ring you,' Jenny said, surprising us all.

'Do you think I will ever find anyone nice?' Catherine said to me, while the others were contemplating whether the person in the leopard-skin leotard was actually male or female.

'If you don't find someone nice, there's no hope for any of us, Cat.' I nudged her with my shoulder.

'By the way, thanks, Mags.' She smiled, weakly.

'For what?'

'For not mentioning it too often; I know how it must look.'

'Cat, none of us can really tell what a guy's like, not straightaway. They can spin all sorts of yarns. You weren't to know. Besides, you still don't know what's happened. You really could try ringing him you know.'

She paused for a moment.

'Cat…?'

She gazed down at her lap.

'I have rung him.'

'And…?'

'The number's been disconnected, so it looks like he's pulled out all the stops to stop me from contacting him.'

'You can always ring the hotel, or even just turn up when you get back,' I suggested.

She shook her head.

'I wouldn't do that and I'm pretty sure he knows that I wouldn't. No, I just have to face it; we were over before we began.'

'You really liked him though.'

'I know I did. I still do! And I thought he liked me but I can't start chasing him. I've done it before, more than once, and it's degrading and demoralising.'

I put my arm around her shoulder.

'Listen, don't give up yet. Just see what happens when you get back. There could be a perfectly good reason for things.'

'Maybe, but to be honest, I don't want to put myself through all that hoping again. I've been there already in the past. It's so draining; it's just not worth it.' She looked very sad. No usual happy, brave, Catherine face covering up her feelings; just sad.

Seeing my concern though, she did her best to perk herself up again.

'Oh, don't you worry about me.' She sat up straight and slapped her palms on her lap. 'I'm as resilient as they come, you know that.' She turned back to the others. 'Oy you lot, your drinks are still half full! We're on holiday for goodness sake. Come on, Pauline, help me at the bar will you?'

Without another word about Nico, Catherine leapt up and, linking arms with Pauline, marched her off in the direction of the terrace bar for another round of cocktails.

'Fancy popping one of these naughties, ladies?' Timmy offered when they'd gone, giving us a quick glimpse of the packet of pills he'd produced from his baseball cap when he'd arrived.

'What are they?' I asked.

''Es probably!' Jenny scoffed, 'I'm not taking any of that stuff, Timmy. You know it fucks me up.'

'You mean it makes you love everyone for a change and you don't know how to handle it, sweetheart!'

I couldn't help feeling curious. 'What do they do?'

Timmy closed his eyes and hugged himself.

'Ahhhh, these particular ones are great! They'll make you all lovely and floaty and warm and fluffy. You'll love life and everyone in it. Not a word of a lie.'

Jenny rolled her eyes and shook her head.

'Yeah and they'll make you dance like a tosser and cuddle every Tom, Dick and Harry in the place. Waste of time if you ask me!'

'Just because you cuddled that beautiful big hunk of a bouncer last time, doesn't mean it was a bad thing,' Timmy said.

'Maybe not for you but it wasn't you he picked up and shook upside down searching for evidence in front of the whole flaming queue to the club,' she replied.

'More's the pity; I wouldn't have minded being picked up and shaken about by Jethro.'

'Jethro!' I exclaimed.

Timmy giggled. 'It's a nickname. His name's Jet but cos he throws people out, we call him Jethro.'

'Jet's not his real name, surely. He sounds like a gladiator!'

'And looks like one,' Jenny said.

'And shags like one actually,' Timmy added.

Jenny tutted loudly, 'Timmy, you're a whore.'

'Why thank you, ma'am.' He bowed graciously from his seat.

'Actually,' he went on, 'I think his real name's Gladstone but who'd hire a bouncer named Gladstone? Anyhow, enough about my love life, do you want one of these little beauties or not?'

Before we could answer, we were interrupted by Pauline and Catherine coming back from the bar.

'Say nothing,' Timmy hissed from under his breath.

'What are you lot whispering about?' Catherine set the drinks down on the table.

'Nothing,' Timmy replied, quickly.

Jenny intervened.

'Timmy's got some pills.'

He shot her a look.

'Shut *up*, Jen!'

'Well, it's true, might as well be honest about it. It's no big deal. By the way, I said no,' she said pointedly to Pauline.

'And you thought I'd disapprove?' Pauline asked, sitting down opposite Timmy who wasn't meeting her eyes.

'I didn't want you worrying,' he lied badly.

Catherine was clearly excited. 'Goodness, it's all very cloak and dagger. What kind of pills are they, Timmy?'

'Oh not you as well!' Jenny responded. 'One night on the hash and she's a junky.' She gulped the remains of her first cocktail and pulled the fresh one towards her.

'I'm just interested,' Catherine said, sulkily.

'What do they do exactly?' Pauline asked.

We all turned to her.

'*You* don't do drugs, Pauline, and certainly not ones that Timmy gets!' Jenny said.

Timmy took umbrage.

'Oy, you! I'll have you know these are the best on the market, guaranteed to make you high as a kite without a care in the world.'

Catherine's eyes grew wide. 'Ooh, that sounds rather nice!'

'That sounds more than nice,' Pauline added thoughtfully.

Actually I had to agree.

Chapter Twenty-six

I woke the next morning from a very strange and fitful sleep to find the sun high up in the sky. What a night.

Despite Jenny's previous refusal, we all ended up taking one of Timmy's pills, even Pauline. In fact, strangely enough, she had been the first one to agree to it. Pauline, it seemed, had a new take on life; one which, apparently, included taking illegal substances, copious amounts of alcohol and not phoning her husband.

I, on the other hand, had taken a little more persuading but after the second cocktail, I have to admit, drugs had suddenly taken on a much more innocent persona and after a full explanation on the ins and outs of ecstasy, I was pretty much convinced that the whole illegal thing was somewhat out of line. Waking up that morning though, I had decidedly mixed feelings.

We'd swallowed the little tablets, in Timmy's case in a very blasé fashion which involved pinging a pill up in the air and catching it like a peanut ('lucky he didn't miss' I had said at the time) ('and if he had missed, I'd have been down on my hands and knees and taken it myself' Catherine had said), and, in Catherine's, Pauline's and my case, very surreptitiously waiting until we were sure no one was watching us.

Then we nervously counted time. Actually, Jenny and Timmy looked completely relaxed like it was the kind of thing they did every day.

It was explained we'd have to wait for a while before feeling anything. That bit was really quite stressful. We waited and counted and shuffled our feet. Catherine, Pauline and I began to wonder whether anything was going to happen. Time moved on and we grew increasingly fretful but suddenly Jenny started 'coming up', as she'd called it. Catherine then panicked so much that hers wasn't going to work, that she started jumping up and down on the spot to make hers come up too. It was Timmy's idea and, had I not been so nervous about my own escalation, I might have laughed loudly as Catherine and her large breasts filled my vision and turned more than a few heads, despite the majority of onlookers being gay.

She had ended up getting really cross when everyone else was feeling the effects apart from her. But after angrily going to the bar when no one seemed to care, she wasn't gone two minutes when she bustled back in such a hurry, without the drinks and, much to our amusement and probably that of everyone else on the terrace, announced, 'I'm coming, I'm coming!'

I have to admit that, while this morning in the cold light of day things appeared and felt very different, at the time I'd felt lovely! I hadn't imagined it would be anything like that. I now understood what people meant when using the expression 'as high as a kite'. Floaty, deliriously happy, out of this world and giddy with this magical feeling I can only describe as ecstasy! There's definitely a downside, but it has to be said that whoever had named them, hadn't been wrong.

Finally, we were all up in the same place. Evidently, there was a general need to loll about all over each other. There also seemed to be another imperative of proclaiming undying love for each other. We were, after all, completely beautiful and very lovely people.

Jenny, true to apparent form, wanted to cuddle the world and did. She really had looked the most beautiful I had ever seen her and the fact that she smiled so much made her unusually approachable. I am sure I could have got lots of information about her love life from her that night, if only I hadn't been so mushed up and unable to think coherently about anything! Timing is a cruel player.

In fact, it wasn't just Jenny who looked fabulous, everyone was beautiful. Oddly, for a spell, even Timmy developed a rather manly appeal. I wondered idly if it was possible to turn a gay man straight but then he had opened his mouth and promptly proclaimed, very camply, more undying love for a fourteen-year old (or so he appeared) bar 'boy' with a G-string, a bow tie, a top hat and very little else on, so the moment of my misplaced worship was short.

The 'I've turned over a new leaf, it's a bit muddy, and I'm loving it, Pauline', was sparkling in the seat across from me.

'I'm in love! With Es!' she proclaimed. 'Why has no one ever introduced me to them before? I think I'm going to be on them forever!'

I think we all thought that – at the time anyway.

Going to the toilet had been a completely new experience. Catherine and I went together to look after each other and smiled our way across the dance floor, ricocheting merrily off slightly annoyed dancers and then bumping happily into the next set, completely convinced that our actions were nothing less than totally forgivable and that we were wonderful. In fact, why on earth weren't people hugging us?

In the toilet cubicle though, despite being desperate to go, I had dried up. Catherine was the same.

'I can't pee!' she cried from the cubicle next to me. Luckily, understandably, the ladies loos were practically empty.

'Me neither!' I called over.

'What will we do?'

'Wait?' I suggested, happily sitting in my spaced-out, fluorescent lit, little world.

'How long for?

'I don't know, until it comes out I guess.'

A few moments passed in silence.

Someone came in and used the loo. Then they came out, washed their hands, unzipped a handbag, applied some make-up (I know because I was listening to every step with the greatest of interest) and then left again. I found myself wondering if whoever it was might be on drugs too. Was the whole world taking things and I just hadn't realised it before now?

'I still can't pee!' Catherine cried when the coast was clear.

'Me neither. Oh hang on, try pushing your stomach.'

Catherine then farted as she did so and started giggling lazily.

'Oooooh, here it is!' she exclaimed.

Never could peeing have been so enjoyable.

Then there came the hand washing. Now I would have thought that washing your hands would be the same whenever you did it; pretty boring, pretty necessary but, overall, pretty ordinary. Oh no. Just like techno music, it had taken on a whole new persona.

'Mmmmmm', Catherine said sleepily, as she ran her hands underneath the stream of warm water.

'Mmmmmm', I agreed, smiling happily at my best friend in the whole wide world.

'It's soooo soft,' she said

'I knoooow,' I agreed.

'I don't think we've ever looked so gorgeous!' she said, drying her hands and gazing lovingly at her own refection. 'You look amazing, Maggie!' She stared at me in the reflection of the mirror. 'Your pupils are so big!'

'Yours are MASSIVE!'

'Like eyes like boobs,' she said and tried to laugh.

I tried too, but laughing didn't seem to be on the cards. All we could manage was to make silly sleepy half laughs and then sigh again.

'Mmmmmm,' we chorused.

Then there were an odd couple of minutes where we proceeded to stroke our own arms! Because of course, like everything else, they were sooooo soft.

Then we became aware that we were both chewing our cheeks and licking our lips and swallowing a lot.

'My saliva tastes like metal,' Catherine said, lolling against a wall.

'Mmmmm, mine too,' I agreed lazily, lolling against another wall with my eyes closed.

Soon after, we were joined, quite unexpectedly, by a six-foot-something transvestite who shimmied up to our mirror. After oohing and ahhing at his/her gold sparkly seven-inch platforms, discussing star signs and then sitting on the wash basins and talking for what seemed like hours, we felt like we'd known each other all our lives! It was obviously a fated meeting.

We finally bid our goodbyes and went back out to find the others, discovering that Jenny, true to form, was hugging a bouncer.

I'm not sure how she managed it but the next thing I knew Catherine was on top of one of the dancers' podiums! However, after some odd shuffling, totally out of time with the music, she then promptly fell off into a crowd of onlookers much to their annoyance.

'Whoopsidaisy,' she sing-songed, clambering up. 'Just like at the reunion!' she called out to me, smiling lovingly at the crowd who didn't smile back.

'Did I look good up there?' she asked as we made our way off again.

'Yes, great.' I half lied. She'd looked better than she normally did.

Then there had been the Jye incident. Now there's a story and a half.

While Jenny and Pauline were off for their turn of stomach pushing in the loos, Timmy, Catherine and I were dancing away (rather expertly I have to say – even Catherine's duck dancing had taken on a rather sensual appeal), when suddenly Catherine pulled my arm.

'Look!' she cried. 'There's Jye!'

I swivelled round to where she was pointing and peered through the crowd. 'Where?'

'There, over there outside through the doors, I'm sure it's him.'

I followed her gaze over to the little cocktail bar on the terrace.

'That can't be him, he's hardly wearing anything!'

'I know!' Catherine said excitedly. 'Come on, let's go and talk to him.'

We left Timmy gyrating around with a five-foot-high Spanish guy with miniature rippling muscles and a bulge between his legs so big I suspected he might have shoved a chorizo sausage down there, and headed off in the direction of the Jye look-a-like.

Catherine had been right. It *was* him. This time he wore a leopard-skin hat in place of the zebra one, and on his lower half all he had on was a leopard-skin loincloth!

Catherine went up and touched him on the back but immediately snatched her hand away because it was covered in grease. Jye turned and saw us. Recognition flickered and he cleared his throat somewhat self-consciously.

'Er, hi there.' His deep voice rang out and a few people turned round.

'It *is* Jye, isn't it?' Catherine asked a little bewildered.

He cleared his throat again. 'Yeah, sure, it's me'.

'You look, um, nice,' she said, staring at his loincloth.

Jye nodded in thanks.

Just then a couple of teeny-tiny-tight-bottomed guys, who could well have been trying to smuggle drugs up their backsides, wiggled up beside him. One pulled him down from his giraffe-like height and kissed him full on the lips, telling him he'd see him back at his place later. Then they both wiggled off, bottoms all ripe for striking matches on, and settled themselves on cocktail stools round the other side of the bar.

Jye didn't seem to know where to look.

'Jye?' I questioned.

'Yeah maan?' He drawled, unable to meet our eyes.

'So you're…' Catherine started. Jye let out a big sigh.

'Oh, heck,' he camped in a voice several octaves higher than before. I've been nobbled! Me cover's blown!'

It was very surreal. Catherine and I exchanged incredulous glances. Catherine's mouth had fallen wide open and, as she didn't seem to be doing anything about it, I physically pushed her chin back up to close it again.

I couldn't stop staring at Jye's body. He was like something off the cover of Chippendales monthly and 'what a waste' was a phrase that sprung to mind. Although I'm sure the entire gay community of the world would contradict me on that.

'But what about last night, your voice… your clothes… your… your… everything!?' I asked, confused.

Jye seemed a little defeated.

'You promise not to tell?'

We promised. Catherine even crossed her heart and hoped to die. Then she took it back and went into a lengthy explanation of why she didn't *really* want to die and it was just metaphorically speaking. She actually said metaforkily speaking.

Jye explained his double identity.

'You see on Friday through to Tuesday, I'm Jye the Jamaican drug dealer,' he giggled, 'but on Wednesdays and Thursdays, I'm queer as travel sickness!'

'Wow!' We both wowed.

'So, do we still call you Jye or is that your Jamaican drug dealer name?' I asked.

'Jye's totes fine, my little sweet peas, that's my name, but up here everyone calls me Jyelo!'

I giggled and then said I had to sit down. I was still very high and felt a bit wobbly. We all sat down in the comfy chairs next to the bar.

Even in our sleepy, surreal, states, Catherine and I were fuzzily confused. Here was a seven-foot Rastafarian drug dealer, dressed in a loincloth and talking like someone out of *Carry on Camping*!

'Swear you won't tell on me though,' he fretted again. 'It's just that I've got my reputation to consider.'

We swore.

He then reached into a pouch under his loin cloth and Catherine and I weren't sure that we should be looking. We gawped anyway. I wondered if he might be going to perform some lewd sex act. He didn't. Instead, he pulled out a joint and proceeded to light it with a lighter he produced from amongst his dreadlocks.

'Isn't that dangerous?' Catherine said.

'Not for me, I smoke it all the time. I love the stuff!' he camped. 'Makes me feel all warm and cuddly.'

'Not that. I meant keeping a lighter in your dreadlocks,' she explained. 'They might all go up in flames and then what would you do?'

Jye giggled, took off his hat and promptly lifted up his 'hair', revealing an almost shaved head underneath.

'Go out a buy another lot!' He grinned a big white toothy grin.

He pulled it back down into position, replaced his hat as Catherine and I stared on in amazement, and with his previous Jamaican drawl said, 'Hi, sisters. My name's Jye!'

'Wow,' Catherine said.

'Wow,' I agreed, pinching myself to make sure that this whole experience was actually happening.

'But what if someone recognised you; like we did,' I pointed out.

'Oooh no, you got me muddled up, darls. I'm Jye-*lo*, you're thinking of my twin brother; lovely bloke, name's *Jamaican* Jye!'

He grinned and I spotted his gold tooth and wondered if that too was a fake.

'Besides', he went on, 'It's never happened yet, apart from yous, and I reckoned you were cool. And if anyone I knew from my other life came up here, they'd be far too embarrassed to let slip they'd seen me, cos they'd have to explain what they were doing here in the first place! None of the gays up here would blow my cover.' He paused. 'Not unless I asked them nicely!'

I stretched in my bed and thought back over the night as a whole. All in all, I guess the experience had been a good one but I had been aware, as the E had worn off, that actually people didn't seem so attractive anymore and, come to that, neither did I. I also noted that the two guys I had been pouring my heart out to didn't in fact look like they were the sort of guys I would normally have chosen to pour a drink out for, let alone my private life. 'Coming down', as Jenny called it, had a lot to answer for.

I had a feeling that Pauline might have taken more pills with Timmy because, despite numerous attempts to get her to come home with Jenny, Catherine and me, it seemed they were both there for the night.

Catherine was still fast asleep and snoring. Bless her. She had done her best to have a good old flirt, but when I'd noticed her sprawled over the laps of three rather unimpressed gay guys, I had to pull her away and sit her down while she told me, in detail, how Nico was the one for her and about every little thing they had ever done or said to each other.

I slipped out of bed, swinging my feet down onto the cool marble floor. I stood up, waited for the room to rebalance itself and headed for the kitchen for some welcome orange juice. No one else seemed to be up yet and I wondered whether Timmy and Pauline had stayed out all night. Timmy's door was ajar so I crept over to take a peak, but there he was tucked up in bed, cuddling Mr Peeps, his childhood soft toy dog who travelled everywhere with him.

Noticing the clock, I saw it was eleven thirty. I'd had enough sleep and thought perhaps I could top up my tan on the roof terrace while I waited for the others. The wrought iron spiral staircase leading up to the roof felt cool under my bare feet, and the metal pattern dug into my soles. At the top, I was surprised to find the door to the terrace open.

I stepped out onto the roof and into the blinding sunlight, covering my eyes while I got used to the glare. It was too hot to stand in the sun, and the concrete under my feet burned by comparison to the staircase, so I moved over to the shade by the generator hut and gazed out to sea, marvelling at the three hundred and sixty-degree view of the beach and landscape. I stepped forward a little and leaned over the railings, gazing down at the beach below. The water looked very inviting and I considered whether a swim would wash the previous night away. It was worth a try.

I breathed in the very warm summer air and sighed to myself, fleetingly reliving the evening again and wondering if I'd done anything to worry about. Then, suddenly, out of the corner of my eye, I noticed something move. Startled, I turned to see what it was. There, crouched down in the corner, sitting on a pile of cushions with her head in her hands, looking completely desolate, was Pauline.

Pauline glanced up and I saw her eyes were red like she'd been crying. Pauline never cried. She looked terrible, her skin grey even through her suntan.

'Hi, Maggie,' she sniffed.

I padded over to where she sat.

'You look terrible.'

She winced.

'Sorry, but you do.'

'I feel terrible.' She wiped her nose with a wrinkled tissue. I sat down beside her. 'How long have you been up?'

'All night.'

'Couldn't you sleep?'

'No. Not a wink. That bloody stuff kept me awake.'

'You weren't calling it "that bloody stuff" last night', I joked, trying to cheer her up a bit.

'Last night and this morning are very different. I wish I'd never touched anything now.'

I gave her shoulder a friendly rub. 'We were all a bit drunk though; don't be too hard on yourself.'

She shook her head. 'I've been so stupid, Mags.'

'I think we were all pretty stupid. I blame Timmy completely,' I said ruefully. 'Did you take more when we left?'

Pauline shook her head, as if in disbelief, and put her face in her hands.

'I was such an idiot. I shouldn't have done it.'

I gave her a cuddle.

'How many?'

'Three,' she said into her lap.

'Wow! And there was me thinking you were practically tee-total.'

She straightened up.

'How long have you been up here?' I asked.

'Since about five I think.'

'Maybe you should give sleep another try,' I suggested.

'I can't. I've tried and tried and… god I feel so shitty! My mind won't stop reeling, over and over…I just can't go on like…,' she paused mid track and glanced at me with a worried expression then seemed to gather herself. 'Look forget it, you're right. I do need sleep.'

'Can I get you anything?' I offered.

She blew her nose and groaned as if she was in pain. She sat and stared out to the horizon and was silent for so long, I was about to repeat my question. But then she spoke.

'I feel so ill.' Tears began running down her cheek.

Poor Pauline; but I knew what she meant. I was feeling worse as time went on and I had just remembered copying Timmy and trying (and almost succeeding) to bite a man's bum in the club. I hoped that had been the worst I'd done.

'Don't worry, hun, you'll soon feel better when you've slept, honestly. I don't feel too hot either but we'll be fine. We'll just have to make sure we don't do it again. I must admit, I feel a bit guilty. I mean, what were we thinking!?'

'No, Maggie, I don't mean that. I mean I really think I might be ill, properly ill.' And with that, she broke down completely.

My eyes widened in shock. Like I said, Pauline never cried. She was usually so serious. So quiet and contained.

'How do you mean, Paul?'

'I don't know what's happening to me,' she continued. 'I've not been well. I mean, really not well, for months and it's getting worse.'

'What kind of not well?'

She fished out a new tissue from a packet beside her, dried her eyes again and tried to compose herself.

'I've lost all my energy and I'm so run down I keep picking up viruses. I sleep so much and half the time I can't even get up to eat. I get exhausted from walking down the street and sometimes I have to pull myself upstairs by the banisters, my legs get so weak.'

I have to admit she had lost weight. And there had been me feeling jealous.

'Have you seen a doctor?'

She laughed but there was no humour.

'A doctor? Yes, I've seen a doctor. I've seen three doctors.'

'And…?'

'Apparently, I'm suffering from stress, according to the first doctor. The second said I had what they call in the profession "multi-viral syndrome" whatever that is. And the third said it was a simple case of chronic fatigue. A simple case… can you believe that? Like I can just be swept aside with a phrase and that's that.'

'But, do you think it's serious?'

'Maggie, I don't know. I have no idea. The doctors seem to think I'm fine and I just need to rest and sleep more. Huh! If that was possible! But I'm scared. For the first time in my life, I have no control. It's like my body is working against me and all I can think of is… is… that I must be dying!'

The tears started to fall again.

'Pauline, don't say that. You're not dying. If there had been anything that serious going on, the doctors would have told you.'

'But what if they don't know or they're missing something?' she cried.

'Have they done any tests?'

'Yes,' she sniffed.

'And…?'

'All the blood tests are fine; completely normal.'

'Well then, you're not dying. The tests would have shown up anything bad. So for a start, you have to stop thinking that.'

She blew her nose again and cleared her throat.

'Am I being melodramatic?' She glanced at me, her eyes piggy and bloodshot.

'Maybe, but you're obviously worried. Look, we can all talk about this when the others are up. There are bound to be solutions.'

Pauline's face seemed to drain of what little colour she had left. She turned to me full on.

No, Maggie! Absolutely not; I don't want anyone else to know. At least not until we get back.

'But why? They're your friends. That's what friends are for.'

She was insistent.

'Please, just promise me you won't say anything. I'll tell them when we get back but not now. I really need to deal with this my way. If I thought people were feeling sorry for me all the time, it would be a hundred times worse.'

She paused, as if thinking about what would happen.

'No, definitely not. I don't need their sympathy. Not on holiday. I want everyone to carry on and enjoy themselves. At least that way, I stand a chance of enjoying myself too.'

'Jenny'll kill you for not telling her, you know,' I pointed out.

She sniffed a laugh.

'Don't I know it.'

I had a thought.

'So, is that why you've been acting so out of character? You know; all this drinking and taking drugs.'

She smiled ruefully.

'Seemed like the easiest way. I didn't want anyone to notice how low I've been feeling. Besides, you were right about last night. It did seem like a good idea. But now this! Now I haven't bloody well slept, I haven't eaten and I have even less energy than before. I feel so awful and so guilty. I mean, here I am having being told not to overdo it and I'm caning it every night. Shit, Maggie, what if this has made me worse – all this E stuff? What if I've buggered myself up completely and for what, all for a stupid high? Just so I could forget for a bit?'

She stood up and walked over to the railings.

'Fuck, fuck, fuck! I am so stupid. I should have known better.'

She ran her fingers through her cropped hair and shook her head.

'I should have known better,' she said more quietly, to herself.

I clambered up off my low cushion and walked over to join her.

'So, what's Terry said?'

She shook her head.

'I haven't told him, not really. I've simply said that I'm overtired and not feeling so good but you know what he's like. He just tells me to buck up and eat some more greens. Terry is the world's worst nurse. He seems to think people can just snap out of it. I must admit, until I felt like this, I thought pretty much the same way, but now…' she trailed off.

'Look, things will seem brighter once you've had a decent amount of sleep.'

'Maybe.'

'Why don't you at least give it another go? There's some camomile tea in the cupboard, or I could heat up some milk and honey. What do you think?'

She shrugged.

'S'pose it can't hurt to try.'

Somehow it felt odd playing nurse to Pauline. She wasn't the sort of person who needed looking after.

We made our way down the metal staircase. I felt awful for her handling this alone. Terry was an arse, fancy not being able to rely on your husband. I'd thought that was what being married was all about! Being able to count on each other at all times.

My thoughts suddenly went to Tony – strong, dependable Tony. At that moment I wanted him to text me. I *needed* him to text me. I needed to know that things were OK between us. It had been too long since our last contact and I had a feeling it was all down to me. The question was, should I text him?

Chapter Twenty-seven

Saturday night – our last night – and still no text. I had toyed constantly with sending Tony one but I kept stopping myself. I really wanted *him* to text *me*. Luckily it was the night of the party on the yacht, so a lot of time was being taken up by deciding what to wear and how to wear our hair, etc. And, despite my reservations on the home front, I was very excited about the possibility of rubbing shoulders with the rich and famous.

Pauline had me on a solemn promise not to say anything about our conversation or to seem remotely concerned about her, so I carried on as normal and, to look at her, you would never have guessed the turmoil she was going through.

We'd all had showers and hair washes and divided up to get ready. Jenny did her usual trip round with the jug of cocktails. Tonight's *cocktail del dia* was margarita. And lots of it! By the end of my second drink, I'd decided to wear my new silver mesh dress. It didn't seem nearly as risqué as when I'd tried it on that morning and dismissed it as too revealing.

Catherine was in a strange mood. It had switched from being sad and forlorn about Nico, to thoroughly pissed off and as yet she hadn't shared with me the reason why.

She was stomping around the bedroom, complaining about everything.

'You OK, hun?' I asked, tentatively.

'Fine.'

Hmmm.

I was in the middle of debating whether to probe her further, when she saved me the trouble.

'Do you know, Mags, that's it. I've had it!'

'Had what?'

'I've had enough of being Goody Two Shoes.'

'What does that mean?'

'If Nico doesn't want me, then I'm going to go out and find myself a man who does.'

This was worrying. 'Meaning what?'

'Answer me one thing.' She stood looking down to where I sat on the dressing table stool, her hands on her hips and her face red with frustration.

'OK,' I said, slowly.

'What's the point of holding out 'til I'm married? Where has it got me?'

Her virginity had never come into question before. I felt it warranted defending.

'Cat, don't say that! It's lovely; romantic. I wish I could say the same thing.'

She didn't seem to be listening.

'Maybe I've been missing out all these years. I mean whoever heard of a twenty-seven-year-old virgin?'

'Well, for starters there was the Virgin Mary,' I grinned.

'Apart from her.'

'OK, well… what about Mother Teresa? Ooh and Charlotte the barmaid from The Brickman's Arms! She's still a virgin, I overheard her telling someone.'

'I thought she had two kids.'

'Ah, does she? Well perhaps she just thought it was a good front. A lot of women wish they were still virgins you know.'

'Do they now?' She didn't seem that convinced.

She angrily pulled out her new low-cut red dress from the wardrobe, the one she'd bought on our shopping spree before the holiday, and laid it on the bed.

'This should do it. I hoped that I'd be able to wear it for Nico when we got home but it doesn't look like that's going to happen now does it!'

I surveyed the dress and then Catherine as she took off her towel turban, sat down firmly on the bed beside me and started roughly towel drying her hair.

'Right,' I began, wondering how to handle this. 'Um, so what you're saying is, you've decided not to wait until you're married after all?'

'Exactly.'

'OK. Um, so when exactly are you planning to act on it.'

'Tonight,' she said matter-of-factly.

Ri-i-ight.

'Cat, this isn't the way, surely. I mean, you're better than this.'

'I'm sick of being better; I want to be badder… I mean bad.'

'But are you really certain? I'm not so sure it's your best idea yet.'

She turned to me, looking slightly less manic. Then she sighed.

'Maggie, I know you're trying to help, really I do, but it's no good, my mind's made up. Besides,' she rationalised, 'I might get lucky and meet the *real* man of my dreams.'

'Maybe,' I said dubiously.

'Anyway, I don't care if I do or not. I just want to find a man who'll pay me some attention and show me what it's like to be a real woman.'

'You are a real woman!' I protested.

'Am I? Am I really? I don't think so and I certainly don't feel like one. I feel like a freak,' she exclaimed, then stood up and disappeared into the en-suite closing the door and locking it behind her.

Twenty minutes later, Catherine emerged from the bathroom, fully made up, just as I was pouring myself into my new dress.

I eyed her warily but she calmly helped me slot myself into place then collapsed on the bed laughing as my left boob fell out. At least she was in a better mood.

Despite the margaritas, I began to have doubts again.

'I don't remember the front being this little.' I anxiously studied my reflection in the mirror. 'It won't stay in place properly.'

'I've got some clear Duck tape with me?' she offered helpfully. I used it on a split on my suitcase handle. It might help?

Was she serious?!

One look at her face told me that she was.

'I can't put Duck tape on my boobs! What if I get hot and the glue melts?'

'Well, it's up to you but I hope one doesn't pop out on the yacht. It's not like you'll be able to run out of the party and hide, not unless you'd consider swimming ashore.'

I was momentarily taken aback.

'What do you mean, "swimming ashore"? Will we be out at sea then? I assumed we'd be moored up safely to the marina.'

Catherine thought about it.

'Perhaps, but it's a party and they're bound to want to play music quite loudly. I should think there's a good chance they'll sail out a bit so no one in the port can hear it,' she rationalised.

My fear of deep water was suddenly introduced and I began to feel a bit faint.

'I wonder if there will be a cute pilot,' Catherine went on as I fretted.

'Er, don't you mean captain?'

'No, I mean pilot, as in a guest. Millionaires' parties are bound to have pilots invited, don't you think? I've always fancied marrying a pilot,' she continued wistfully. 'All those duty frees.'

I began straightening my hair. Seeing as we'd been on holiday, I'd left it natural all week but tonight was special.

'Cat, are you sure about this manhunt thing? I mean, going out and getting off with some guy you happen to meet doesn't sound like a good idea at all. What if he's a nutter or something!'

'Don't worry. I'll pick a nice one.'

She saw my look of concern and sighed.

'I'm just fed up with being the token virgin. Guys never want to know me once they find out that being a virgin doesn't mean I'm a challenge waiting to be conquered and they're the one to do it.'

'Nico wasn't like that.'

She stiffened at the mention of his name.

'I think I just need to forget about Nico, don't you?'

'Please don't do anything you'll regret though, hun. You're so lovely, you just need to believe in yourself a bit more. You don't need to do anything you don't want to.'

I watched her squeeze herself into her own dress and flatten down her skirt in the mirror, turning from side to side and back to front. She pulled a face I couldn't read. Then she turned and sat down on the bed again looking up at me smiling very slightly.

'You don't get it though, do you?' she said.

'Get what?'

'I wouldn't expect you to know,' she said, not unkindly. 'And why should you? I mean, look at you. You're gorgeous. Slim, tanned, really attractive. Mags, I may be lovely but I'm fat, and guys don't like a fat girl unless she puts out. That's a fact.'

'That's just not true!' I exclaimed.

'In my experience, it's completely true.'

I tried to argue with her and convince her it wasn't but she was adamant and headed off to the en suite again.

As I applied my make-up, I found myself mulling over what she'd said. Could it really be true? Were we living in a world where beauty and glamour mattered that much? I mean, hadn't I been on every diet known to mankind?

Didn't I rush to the nearest newsagents every time the latest issue of a glossy magazine came out just so I could keep up with fashion and fads and diets? Had I not fretted myself silly every time my clothes got tighter or I got a spot on my chin? Well, the answer was yes. But surely that was beside the point. It was still no reason for Catherine to…

A shriek from the bathroom broke my thoughts.

'Oh no!' Catherine wailed.

I rushed in to find her sitting on the toilet hand over her mouth.

'Oh, Maggie, I've got a rash!'

'What sort of a rash?'

'It's in a very embarrassing place,' she blushed.

'Go on…'

'Don't laugh but earlier I kind of went a bit mad and shaved everything off down there…'

'Everything?'

She pulled a face. 'Everything!'

'Eek.'

'Now it's all horrid and red and no one will want to go anywhere near me.'

'They won't know!'

'They will if they get down there! What on earth am I going to do? It was those disposable razors, I'm sure of it!'

'You used a disposable razor… down there?'

'I didn't have anything else!' she cried, defensively.

There followed a succession of to'ing and fro'ing from the bedroom to the en-suite, while Cat put a variety of lotions on her 'area' and eventually things apparently calmed down. She was so oiled up though if anyone did venture down below they'd probably end up sliding off.

However, finally we were both ready.

Jenny bounced in, wearing a short black mini dress and little stilettos. She'd piled her hair up and diamante earrings hung from her ears. I wondered why I'd bothered and made a mental note to stand next to someone else all evening.

'Blimey, Mags, your tits look nearly as big as Cat's in that dress! You'll need to be careful, they'll be using you as a lifebuoy if someone falls overboard.'

Which reminded me.

'Do you think the boat will go out to sea tonight?' I asked.

'Na, wouldn't think so. "Health and safety" and all that. Why?'

246

'I'm not sure I'm cut out for being in the middle of an ocean at night. There might be sharks.'

'Don't worry,' she said. 'The only sharks you'll have to worry about are the ones *on* the boat.'

'Do you think there'll be a pilot there?' Catherine enquired.

'Probably; there are always pilots at these sorts of things.' Catherine threw me an 'I told you so' look.

'Can I take it that you're setting your sights higher than him back home, then?'

Jenny asked.

'There was nothing wrong with Nico. I don't need to set my sights higher.'

'Ah, so you still like him then. And there was me thinking you might have moved on.'

'I have!'

She didn't sound very convincing.

I found myself checking my own mobile and not for the first time that day.

'Expecting a message?' Jenny asked.

'Er, no, not really, I just thought Mum and Dad might have tried to get through, that's all.'

Pauline came in with the margarita jug.

'I think I'll need a gallon of this stuff!' She cringed at herself in the wardrobe mirror.

She had on an oriental patterned dress with a high collar. I couldn't remember the last time I'd seen her in a dress and no wonder! She was clearly very trussed up and uncomfortable.

'Do I look as awful as I feel?'

I worriedly scanned her face to see what she meant but it seemed she was just talking about the dress.

'I'm like a Chinese carpet!'

Jenny laughed.

'It's not that bad. Don't think I've seen you in a dress since we were kids.'

'No wonder, if they make me look like this!' Pauline swivelled and observed her back view. 'Nope, no difference, it's definitely a Chinese rug. It was all right in the shop mirror.'

Catherine and I glanced at each other and chorused 'Category One Changing Room!'

Pauline frowned in confusion.

'At least it doesn't look like you'll fall out of it at any moment,' Jenny remarked, giving me the once over.

'Don't you start. Catherine's all for taping me up with Duck tape.'

'I wish I had tits,' Jenny said, looking down at her own chest and giving her small breasts a squeeze. 'I went out with this guy once who kept telling me to turn round when I was talking to him. Said I was so flat-chested he assumed he was looking at my back!' she sniggered.

Catherine said, 'If I turned my back on blokes when they talked to me, they'd have nowhere to focus their eyes. They'd soon lose interest. I shouldn't think it would matter which way you were turning, Jen, men will propose marriage to you within minutes right up until the end of time.'

Jenny sneered.

'Where's Timmy,' I asked her, 'is he still getting ready?'

'He left a while back, to see a few "local sights"', she finger quoted.

'Huh?'

'He's gone off to meet some guy he met at that club we went to; said he'll see us at the party.'

'And you trust him to turn up?' I asked.

'Oh he'll be there all right. I told him Ricky Martin was on the guest list.'

A taxi ride later, we arrived at Puerto Banus and wandered into the throes of the port.

I hadn't been ready for quite how rich looking it would be; heaving with breathtaking yachts and speedboats. People were even having parties on some of the decks. I wondered if our boat was nearby.

The shops were out of this world; stylish leather, art galleries, high-end jewellery, chic boutiques. All the things I couldn't afford. Then the bars and restaurants began and glamorous people stood inside and out, dressed up to the nines, talking and laughing animatedly.

The night was so warm and lights sparkled up and down the boulevard making it seem quite magical. Crowds formed as street theatre was performed, market stalls were pored over and lounge bars, full to the brim, spilled out onto the walkways. People stopped and stared as motorboat after yacht after mansion with engine became the centre of attention. Jazz bands played on the decks and swishy cocktail dresses mingled with dinner jackets, laughter and the hubbub of conversation. Champagne glasses clinked and the distant sound of a piano drifted through the air. It was alive with energy and excitement. I felt my eyes grow wide with anticipation and my stomach fill with butterflies.

As we made our way through the port, the crowds got thicker, the air became hotter and the whole experience suddenly became a bit daunting. The heat from the suntanned bodies was becoming too oppressive and I think we were all glad to finally come to the end of the boulevard and reach the barrier marking the entrance to seemingly the most exclusive area of the port. We opened the little gate beside it, went through, and were met with row upon row of huge white powerful boats and nothing much else. Thankfully the air seemed to cool then. The bright lights had been reduced to dimly glowing street lamps and tiny floor-level spotlights to mark where the jetty stopped and went over the edge to the water. The sounds of the crowds were gradually left behind us, growing fainter and fainter as we walked. They were replaced by crickets chirruping enchantingly in the dark evening air. Jenny held her piece of paper with the details on and scanned each boat for its name. The huge vessels nestled up against each other, creaking against their moorings. Most of them had no lights on but about two hundred yards up ahead, the largest boat I'd ever seen was buzzing with activity. There were several tiers of decks and, on the main one, all the lights shone out across the sky. Music and crescendoing laughter filtered through the warm night and reached our ears.

I fretfully began to wonder what I'd talk about to the other guests. People who, I imagined, lived in a different world.

We walked, unusually silent, every now and then shooting sideways glances at each other and smiling nervously. When we'd nearly reached the boat, all at once, we looked down at ourselves as if to suss out whether we measured up to the evening ahead. I think each of us felt a bit out of place, even Jenny.

She was the one who finally broke the silence.

'So, that Enrique bloke from the beach then, Cat.'

'What about him?'

'What's the betting he wanted to get into your knickers?'

I smiled, happy to hear familiarity.

'Is your client really as wealthy as that boat makes him look?' I asked Jenny worriedly.

'And then some!'

'I hope Timmy finds it all right?' Pauline said. 'You know what he's like after a few drinks.'

'Told you; he'll be here. Ricky Martin beckons remember? Besides, he loves turning up late. He has an innate need to make an entrance.'

We reached the ramp that led upwards to the decks. A thick rope cordon was hooked across the entrance and a couple of huge bouncers stood waiting to hear who we were.

'Names?' the first bouncer demanded. He distinctly resembled Odd Job out of *Goldfinger*.

We gave our names and Odd Job checked his clipboard, taking an age to scan the list and find us. It took so long that I wondered if maybe Jenny had got it wrong and we weren't invited after all. Eventually though, he unhooked the rope and nodded us through.

We traipsed up towards the sound of the party and my butterflies grew more fluttery by the second.

'I think I might pee myself,' Catherine whispered from behind me.

'Me too!' I whispered back.

We reached the second deck and glanced round at our surroundings. Even before we'd got inside they were nothing less than palatial. The great white *Genevieve* was gleaming, glossy and stunningly finished off with huge golden rails; probably even real gold.

We stood nervously just outside a set of glass double doors which led through to where the party was. The entrance was manned, this time by two men who could easily have been born into the army. Their thighs were so wide you could have fitted two of mine into one of theirs, which was actually surprisingly comforting. I noticed nervously that they had long holsters containing intimidating black guns, on which they each rested one hand. I glanced at them both in turn, hoping not to catch their eyes, but I needn't have worried. They were not unlike the sentry guards at Buckingham Palace, seemingly aiming to avoid all eye contact.

They opened both doors for us and we had little choice but to go through, finding ourselves in a narrowed area with a little room on the right to hang any coats. We gingerly walked a few steps towards the throng then, as if to get our bearings, all stopped just short of the main area, and stared. It was huge. Nothing like a boat really, more like a movie star's apartment – plush, expensive and very glamorous. It was alive with people talking vivaciously and looking decidedly rich and famous.

'Do you think they'll let us in?' Catherine asked nervously.

'We're already *in* Cat,' Jenny answered impatiently.

'I don't feel very in.'

I didn't either.

'My dress is beginning to itch,' Pauline complained. 'I wish I'd worn something more comfortable.'

Suddenly Jenny spotted her client in the crowd. On sight of Jenny, he gave her a wave and began to make his way towards us.

A small, fat, cigar-smoking man of about sixty-five at a guess, arrived a few moments later. He was dressed in a white tuxedo, white shirt and a red bow tie. His hair was also white, a startling contrast to the deep brown, lined, skin of his face and hands.

'Jennifer, Jennifer.' He took both her hands warmly and kissed each cheek in turn.

'Come, come, why you stand out here?' he asked, in a thick Spanish accent. 'You must join my little party.' His eyes turned to the rest of us. 'And of course, you have brought your friends weeth you, I am so pleased.' He smiled a very even white-toothed smile at us all. 'It is a pleasure to haff your company tonight. Any friends of this leetle treasure are friends of mine.' He tipped his head.

Jenny smiled confidently at him.

'You look well, Carlos.'

'I haff good surgeon; effryone in Puerto Banus look well!' he acknowledged in good humour.

Catherine piped up.

'What a pretty... um... little ship, you have. Thank you for inviting us,' she said, blushing.

'Mi casa es su casa,' he replied, graciously.

And with that, he extended his arm in the direction of the crowds and urged us to go through into the mêlée.

I could hear Jenny mumbling incredulously under her breath as we went in.

'A twenty million quid, three hundred sodding foot motor cruiser, and she goes and calls it a pretty fucking little ship!'

We stood at the huge glossy ebony and gold bar, drinking Dom Perignon champagne out of crystal flutes.

The main party area was lit up everywhere with little sparkling white lights, and a huge twinkling chandelier hung from the centre of the room. There was a definite black and white theme going on. The ceiling was shiny and black with tiny lights embedded in it like stars. The walls were a brilliant white mix of buffed wood panels and padded leather and two-thirds of the way down they became gleaming ebony wood which then moulded into the backrests to the white leather seating that edged all around the air-conditioned room. Black and white fur cushions were placed strategically around the seats and glamorous people lounged around confidently as if they came to parties like this one every day.

White-jacketed waiters and bar staff buzzed around attentively, filling up glasses and pointing people to the cloakrooms. I could see a lavish buffet through some adjoining doors. It looked like no expense had been spared.

Having speedily finished my first glass of champagne, I was beginning to relax. The more we all talked the more we drank and as soon as our glasses were empty they were filled again. Despite Pauline's previous decision to calm down with the booze she too was knocking them back.

Women and men chattered animatedly around us and the smells of expensive scents filled the air. Heads were thrown back dramatically as jokes were imparted and laughter rang out. The women seemed to merge together in a sea of swirling, elegant, dresses and sparkling earrings and the men might have stepped off the set of a Hollywood movie. All square-jawed and white-teethed, wearing black or white tuxedos. Some appeared like they probably owned multi-million-pound companies and others like they directed movies or were movie or TV stars. We tried to spot famous people and soon the comments were flying as we shouted over the noise of the party.

'Isn't that…?'

'I think it might be.'

'No, I think he's moved to Australia.'

'Maybe he moved back.'

'Didn't his wife leave him for the butler?'

'No, silly, that was on the soap he was on.'

'Oh, right.'

'Oooh, that's thingy from thingy on ITV, isn't it?'

'I thought it was him from *The One Show*.'

'Who Chris Evans?'

'No, he left ages ago, the other bloke.'

'I haven't got a clue, but he's definitely on something.'

'Talking of Chris Evans, isn't that him over by the buffet?'

We all squinted through the doors.

'Yeah, maybe.'

'Shit…it's Prince Harry.'

'No…seriously?'

There was a pause.

'That's a woman!' Pauline exclaimed. 'I'm pretty sure it's Anne Robinson.'

'Oh my goodness, it's Cilla Black!' Catherine said.

'Unless she's visiting from beyond the grave, I doubt that very much,' Jenny mocked.

'Oh of course,' Catherine looked mournful. 'I forgot. Poor Cilla. I loved her. Shame, she might have been able to get me on *Blind Date* if it came back on?'

'Maybe she could've got you a date who was blind!' Jenny cackled and Catherine glared at her.

'I'm not sure, but I think that's the bloke who used to be on *Eastenders* over by the ice-sculpture,' Pauline indicated. 'Timmy's always harping on about him.'

'Where?' I asked.

'Over there, talking to the guy who looks like he's a film director.'

'Which one? There are tons of blokes who look like they direct movies,' Jenny said.

'I see him!' Catherine cried. 'Yes! It's him from the pub, the Queen Vic. I must get his autograph. How do I look, she turned to us, smoothing down her dress and plumping up her boobs.

'Careful, Cat, you'll have his eyes out with those!' Jenny said.

'Then he really would be a blind date!' Catherine laughed. 'I wonder if he's with anyone.'

'I thought you wanted a pilot?' Jenny pointed out.

'Pilot, actor, film director. I'm not too fussy,' she said, knocking back her third glass of champagne.

'I'm going to talk to him.'

'But you don't even know him!' Pauline cried.

'Ah ha, but I will in a minute! Byeeee,' she sang.

And she was off.

To give us our dues, we did mingle. Buoyed up by champagne, the rich–poor divide became smaller as our confidence grew. One of the many film directors with square jaw and tuxedo started telling me about a current movie he was making. I was fairly interested until I noticed the way he was eyeing my breasts. For one awful moment I thought one might be peeking out the side of my dress but luckily it wasn't. Then he went for the kill and looking me up and down blatantly asked if I fancied a part in it. I decided the only part I would be getting was the one between his legs, so I declined, politely, explaining I was camera shy. Unfortunately, Pauline chose that very moment to take a photo of me with her phone, for which I unashamedly posed. I promptly found myself minus one film director.

I spotted Catherine chatting away to a couple of tall men. By this stage, she was decidedly wobbly on her feet. What with it being champagne in her hand, one never could tell quite where it would lead her. The guy from *Eastenders* had left her to talk to a woman I swear used to be on *Casualty*, or was it *Holby* or possibly *Corrie*. Maybe even all three. Catherine had been left with a Mr Square Jaw, who could have been related to my Mr Square Jaw, and another quite tall guy with dark hair and a white suit that made him resemble a navy captain. Or even a pilot! He was quite good looking in an obvious kind of way but was getting a bit too cosy with Catherine for my liking. As I observed, he kept touching her lower back before casually sliding his hand down to her bum. Unfortunately, apart from one time where she coquettishly shooed his hand away and giggled, she seemed to let his hand remain there without any complaints.

The evening was quite a success but we had all drunk so much in anticipation, it was turning out to be one of those nights where everything that happens, happens in one long line of blur.

I was always chatting to someone or other, usually a man. I remember checking my mobile a few times but, in the end, I gave up. Tony had obviously decided to give me the cold shoulder. I knew there was nothing I could do right then. Besides, in my haze of alcohol, I almost didn't care; only almost though. I was in the middle of talking to Mr 'I own three companies, a fleet of cruise liners in the South Pacific and two wives who don't understand me' – he was a Mormon – when Jenny wobbled up, very unsteadily and stood beside me. She swayed but said nothing.

She was nursing an empty glass and as a poor unsuspecting waiter came past with a tray of champagne, she grabbed his arm so hard he nearly upended them all over the floor.

'Give us a drink, mate,' she insisted loudly. The waiter courteously obliged and smiled a little hesitantly before heading off past other guests who were beginning to shoot wary glances at Jenny.

'Wassa matter with them, haven't they ever seen a bird pissed before?' she slurred. I excused myself from my Mormon 'friend' and turned to Jenny.

'Dunno what all the fuss is about,' she said.

'What fuss?'

'This lot! All these so called rich and famous, lording it all over the place.'

'Shhh, Jenny, keep your voice down. We'll get thrown out.'

'Wouldn't care if we did!'

'Come on let's sit down for a bit.' I indicated a spare seat behind us.

But Jenny was having none of it.

'I don't wanna sit down I wanna leave,' she announced, loudly.

'Why? I asked. 'What's the matter?'

'Nothing's the fucking matter. I've had enough, that's all.'

She sat down heavily then and I joined her. I continued warily.

'Listen, Jen, you can tell me to mind my own business but something's bothering you. I know it is.'

'I told you, I'm fine.'

'Look, I've known you practically all my life and I think by now I can tell if there's something up. I might be able to help you know.'

She swayed where she sat then struggled to her feet again as if she was going to walk off. I looked up at her, unsteady on her pretty little heels. I thought she might be going to fall over or be sick but then, all of a sudden, she slumped back down, her face crumpled and she burst into tears.

I was shocked. I'd only ever seen Jenny cry once when we were kids and she'd told me about her mum dying.

'Jenny, hun, what is it?' I glanced round, noticing people staring at us, so I stood up and pulled her up with me then ushered her out of the side exit and into the night air.

Checking left and right, I thought we'd be best to head away from the crowds so, following the golden safety rail, I led Jenny down the side of the boat and up towards the front. The pointy end (sorry, I'm not very nautical). We passed a couple of the staff who were having sneaky cigarettes. As soon as they saw us though they scuttled off, throwing Jenny, who was now sobbing loudly, quizzical looks.

At the front of the boat, the deck opened up to a wide seating area. The majority of seats were protected for the night by royal blue covers but a couple of chairs resembling nautical director's chairs were left uncovered to one side, facing out to sea, so I brushed them off, sat Jenny down on one, pulled the other closer to her and sat down beside her.

Her pretty eyes were full of mascara filled tears.

'Are you going to tell me what's wrong?' I ventured.

She sniffed back her tears and wiped her eyes on her wrist. A black line of make-up smeared across her cheekbone.

'Maybe.'

I sat quietly, waiting for her to speak.

Then she looked across at me, like a little girl.

'Promise you won't judge me.'

'Of course I won't.'

She picked up her evening bag from her lap and rummaging around she found a tissue.

'Courtesy of Catherine,' she smiled weakly through her tears. 'She said a woman should always carry a tissue in her bag, just in case.'

And with that she burst out into tears again.

I reached across and let my hand rest on her shoulder.

'It's John.' Tears rolled down her face.

'John?'

'Remember, the guy I phoned from Dad's place, the one you asked me about that time in the bathroom?'

'I remember. Who is he?' I asked gently.

'He... he... he's my boss,' she sobbed even harder.

I waited until she'd blown her nose and composed herself again. I could hear laughter from the main deck and I hoped no one would turn up and interrupt us.

'OK... so this John... your boss, is something happening at work?'

'It was.'

'What do you mean? Did you do something wrong?'

'You could say that,' she sniffed.

Once again, I waited for her to explain.

'But he's here. Right here at this party. I had no idea he'd be here or I'd never have come.'

'What? Why's he here?' I asked.

'I don't know. I don't fucking know. I didn't think I'd have to see him again. He was supposed to be leaving and sodding off to one of the other offices but he's here. Why is he here, Mags, why? Why couldn't he have just left me alone? I don't understand.' She began shaking.

'But, Jen, what's he done? Why did you want him to leave you alone?'

She blew her nose again.

'I couldn't tell you before. John and I…we were seeing each other. It was all kept a secret. I suppose you'd call it an affair, but we were in love. I know we were. I'm sure we were. I was anyway…' she trailed off.

'So what happened? Did you finish?'

'He did.' The tears came again. 'He finished with me. It was the only thing he could do.'

'Why?' I asked, incredulously.

'Oh, Maggie, I've been so stupid. I can't believe I've been so stupid; me of all people!'

She was shivering now, despite the heat of the evening. I moved closer and gave her arm a comforting rub.

'It was …his wife,' she said falteringly. 'She found out.' Jenny looked down at her hands, playing with the strap of her evening bag.

'He's married?' I was shocked.

'Exactly! A married man. Jenny Henderson, hater of all married men playing away, goes and lands herself in a fully blown relationship with one. And not just any one, her boss!' she said scornfully, tears falling steadily down her cheeks.

'How did it start?' I asked carefully.

She gazed wistfully out to sea then her face lit up through her tears, like she was remembering the past.

'We never planned it, we just fell in love. We were so… connected. For the first time in my life, I felt like someone… got me, you know?'

Somehow my mind found its way to Luke.

'I know,' I agreed quietly.

'I'd never have done it, I'd have found a way to stop it but his wife was such a bitch,' she continued. 'I know that for a fact. I met her, several times. She'd turn up at the office, always laying down the law and looking down her nose at all of us. She'd talk down to John in front of the whole office. It was… it was horrid. He'd worked so damned hard to build up the London office, there's no way we'd be anywhere near as successful without John. And he's so amazing and so clever and I love him so-o-o-o much.'

As she cried, I thought about her life and how I'd imagined she had everything just so. Jenny had always been tough, together, strong, and appeared to be completely in control; and now this? It seemed she was human after all. As much as I hated to see her so upset, for the first time since I could remember, Jenny seemed more accessible. Her guard was down and she was perhaps more real at this moment than I think I'd ever seen her. I shook my head to myself. How wrong can you be?

She was crying more softly now. In the background the distant sounds of the party were barely reaching us. The occasional seagull called overhead from the darkness and little waves lapped comfortingly up against the side of the boat.

'So, did he go back to his wife?' I asked, gently.

She nodded, her eyes full of sadness.

'He told me he had to go back to her. He said he didn't want to. He said he didn't and I believed him.'

'Did she know he'd been seeing you?'

She shook her head.

'She found out he was having an affair but she didn't know who with. They had a massive row and she begged him to stay and swore she'd change. Thing is, she's got a kid, a boy, and even though John's not the father, he's been there for them both since they've been together so I think he went back for the kid as much as anything. I know how guilty he felt and he loves kids. That's the thing about John, he hates the idea of letting people down and hurting them. He's a great believer in marriage and a stickler for loyalty; he would have planned to be in it for life. But his wife was such a bitch to him; he found that out the hard way. So when I came along I don't think he could help himself.'

'God, Jenny, I'm so sorry; what a difficult situation.'

'I know and it got worse after we broke up.'

'Why, what happened?'

'I'd moved into a different office on a different floor. We thought it was best. I'd been promoted by head office anyway, so no one suspected. Plus, I was travelling a lot and so was he, so we just got on with life without each other. Somehow, after a few crap weeks, it started getting a bit easier because I never saw him. Only after a while he chased me up the street and caught me on my lunch break. He pulled me into a shop doorway and said he couldn't handle life without me. He said he'd been so wrong and wanted us to try again.'

'Well, that's good isn't it?' I asked.

'I didn't know what had hit me, though. I wanted him back so badly but I didn't say yes. I couldn't, not straight away. I told him I had to think things through. I'd spent all that time without seeing him, so I said I needed time. But it backfired.'

'Why?'

'His wife announced she was pregnant.' Jenny shook her head, pursing her lips bitterly and went still for a few moments. She stared out at the black ocean.

'Oh, Jen, you must have felt terrible.'

'You don't know the half of it. It was like going through all the pain again and this time there would be no going back, I know how John feels about kids. The worse thing was I knew then that they'd actually slept together. I mean, of course it was bound to happen, that's what people do when they're married, but it still came as such a shock to have it confirmed. Up until then, I'd convinced myself that there wouldn't be any sex.'

She put her face in her hands and shook her head.

'Maggie, I can't bear having him so near and not being able to touch him.' She sat up her eyes wide with anguish. 'What am I going to do?' Tears were sliding down her perfect face.

'Sssh now, it'll be OK. You don't have to see him if you don't want to.' I wondered if we could slip away without people noticing.

'But that's just it, I do want to. I want to see him so much. I miss him. We shared everything. I don't think I can take this. I love him.'

'But what about you?'

'What about me?' she asked, perplexed, blinking back her tears.

'Didn't he care enough to support you? You needed looking after.'

'I didn't give him a chance. I made out it was the right decision to go back to her. If I'm honest, I know if I'd begged him to stay with me, he would have done but I didn't. I couldn't. That poor little baby; I know what it's like to grow up with only one parent and I couldn't be responsible for that. I couldn't have lived with myself, so I told him to go back to her and I refused to see him.'

'My god, you must have been so strong.'

'I wasn't strong at all. After he left, I broke down. I had to take time out. I couldn't handle being around people. I went back home to Dad's and hid in my old room for days. Dad was really worried about me, but I couldn't talk to him. I so wished Mum was still here. She would have known what to do. I miss her. I miss having a mum.'

Her expression was desolate and I felt dreadful for her. She never talked about her mum. She must have felt so alone.

'There's… something else,' she faltered.

'Go on,' I encouraged.

'I was pregnant.' Her eyes flicked quickly to mine, as if to catch my reaction.

'What?'

'Two months to be precise.'

'Oh my god, Jen, are you pregnant now?' I inadvertently glanced down at her tiny stomach.

'No. I lost it. I had a miscarriage. I'd just come back from Dad's when I realised I was pregnant. I didn't know what to do. I didn't know whether to tell John or not, after all he had his own family to think about. The only person I confided in was Tony and that was only because he turned up when I was in a right state and wouldn't leave until I'd told him what was wrong. I just put my head down and buried myself in work. God knows how I did it. I mean, I know I'm tough but this was different. It was shit.

'And then it happened. I remember the pain; the bleeding. At first I thought… you know just normal stuff but something right down inside me told me it was more than that. And then, one minute I had a life growing inside me and the next… it was gone.' Her face was ashen, like she was living the whole experience for the first time.

'I wouldn't have felt so bad if…'

She stopped.

I paused.

'If what, hun?'

'I mean these things happen, don't they, losing babies. It happens to lots of women.

If something's not meant, then surely it's just not meant, yeah?'

'Yes, of course. You mustn't blame yourself.'

'But I do. I so do.'

'Jen, why? You said yourself, these things happen.'

'I know.'

She went quiet.

'Jen?'

She swivelled round in her seat and looked into my face.

'Promise you won't think badly of me, Mags.'

'Of course; I promise.'

She continued, with an odd expression on her face.

'About a week after I found out I was pregnant, I… Oh Mags… I was so stupid.'

Tears streamed down her face again.

'Jen, whatever it is, just tell me.'

'I booked in to have a termination. I can't believe I did it. All this talk of how important babies are and I was going to get rid of mine. I was going to kill my own baby. How could I have even thought of that? That's why it didn't want to be born. That's why I miscarried. It knew. My baby knew I didn't want it. Two days before I was due to go in, it just died anyway. It's all my fault, Mags,' she sobbed.

I pulled my chair around to face her and took her hands. She looked up at me, and seemed to search my face for my reaction.

'Jenny, listen to me. You've been through a lot, an awful lot. It's so sad and such bad luck but you have to believe me, having a miscarriage wasn't your fault. It really wasn't. So many babies don't go the full term. You said before how you hated the idea of a child being brought up with one parent. You also sent John back to his wife for the sake of their baby. You were just trying to do the right thing. I know you. You wouldn't have done this if you hadn't thought, at the time, that it was the right thing.'

'But then I lost my baby anyway.'

'Exactly. I think that happened to save you the decision and who's to say you would have even gone through with the termination anyway? Do you know, I think the baby just helped you and decided that it wasn't the right time. Sometimes these things happen for a reason.'

Her face showed a glimmer of hope. 'Do you really think so?' She appeared no more than a child herself. Her make-up had practically gone and her long glittering earrings looked like they belonged on someone older.

'Yes.' I nodded. 'I really do. Jen, one day you'll make a perfect mum, when it's the right time. I know you will.'

She was silent for a few moments.

'I will get another chance, won't I?'

'Of course you will, at the right time and with the right man.'

'But John was the right man. He *is* the right man. Despite everything that's happened, I know he is. I still love him, Mags. If it wasn't for his horrid wife, we'd still be together. Now he probably thinks I don't give a damn. I sent him back to her. I know I wanted the best for the baby but I didn't realise how much it would hurt me. I can't stop thinking about him. I hate the thought of them together – a family, a little unit – and I'm alone again.'

'We're here,' I said. 'We'll always be here. Does John know about the baby, the miscarriage?' I asked.

'No, no he doesn't and he mustn't. It would crucify him. Please, Mags, promise me you won't tell him. Promise me?' her eyes pleaded with mine.

'Of course I won't. Besides, I don't even know who he is.'

She seemed relieved. 'No… of course you don't.'

We sat, unspeaking, for a few more moments. Then Jenny sighed and composed herself.

'We can't stay here. The others will be worried. We'd better find them.' She stood up. 'I just need to get cleaned up and put my face back on. I couldn't bear him to think I was upset.'

'Has he seen you?' I asked.

'I don't know. I don't think so. One of the benefits of being short I guess.' She gave me a bleak smile. 'I just saw him, froze on the spot and then ran off in search of alcohol.'

We walked back down the side of the boat again and were just about to go in through the side entrance and slip to the toilet when Jenny stopped suddenly, and I walked into the back of her. A man was standing near the doorway smoking a cigarette. He was a gorgeous man with jet-black hair and dark eyes. I could see signs of a five o'clock shadow and he looked tired but, if anything, it made him appear more attractive. He was leaning against the side railing of the boat, staring out to sea. He started when he saw Jenny and the two of them stood facing each other, eyes locked, like rabbits caught in the headlights. This I presumed was John.

'Jenny?' I asked quietly, 'Do you want me to leave you to it?'

'No, Mags, I don't need…'

'Jenny, please,' John interrupted, 'we've got to talk.' His voice broke slightly and there was so much anguish in his eyes, I felt almost embarrassed to witness it.

'I'll leave you two alone. If you need me, Jen, text me and I'll come out and find you. We can leave when you want to. Will you be OK?' I asked, looking from her to John.

Jenny nodded and I moved to pass her.

As I did so, she grasped at my hand and squeezed it very lightly.

'Thanks, Mags.'

I gently returned the squeeze and walked back into the party.

I made my way back through the crowd and scanned the place for Catherine but couldn't see her anywhere. Spotting Pauline sitting on her own on a window seat, I went over and joined her.

'You OK?' I asked.

'Not really. I don't think champagne's the answer. I'm already getting a hangover and I haven't even managed to get properly drunk yet!' Her laugh was filled with irony.

'I think maybe you and Jenny could do with each other's support.'

At her look of confusion, I explained about John. Not all the details, Jenny could do that herself, but enough.

'But what's he doing here?' she asked

'Your guess is as good as mine.'

Before we could cast aspersions, we heard a loud crash which sounded like it had come from the direction of the main entrance. Several women's voices cried out and we heard a high-pitched male voice shouting abuse.

'Ah shove off and feed your crocodile handbag. Haven't you ever seen a drunken poof before? Now then… where's Ricky? Where's my lovely Ricky?'

Timmy.

Pauline and I leapt up from our seat and rushed forward to where a crowd was forming near the entrance. Through the onlookers we spotted Timmy sprawled out on the floor surrounded by smashed champagne flutes. A poor dishevelled waiter was beside him and trying to clamber up from the slippery floor. It wasn't working. As the waiter tried to stand, Timmy grabbed onto the back of his jacket and pulled him down again saying he was lonely all on his own on the floor. Then Timmy collapsed into fits of giggles. From outside, Odd Job had been summoned and was heading towards the scene. Then as I became aware of some commotion behind Pauline and me, I turned to see Jenny's client Carlos on his way over from the buffet area, accompanied by another couple of henchmen looking far from happy.

'Pauline, quick,' I whispered. 'We have to do something. Carlos is coming!'

As he made his way angrily towards Timmy, Pauline put her hand on his arm as he went past.

'Carlos, um sir, remember me? I'm Jenny's friend Pauline. I thought I'd better explain about the gentlemen on the floor.'

Carlos gave her an indifferent sideways glance and showed no sign of stopping so Pauline and I were forced to follow him as he made his way through the circle of people surrounding Timmy.

'Well?' He demanded as we reached Timmy, who grinned up at the three of us like a naughty teenager.

The stares from people around us were full of disdain.

'I'm so dreadfully sorry,' said Pauline, 'but he's with us.' She lowered her voice. 'He's just arrived and has evidently had one too many. But the thing is he had some dreadfully upsetting news earlier today. It's his grandfather you see, and while we all thought he'd handled it incredibly well, I think the whole thing's caught up with him.'

Carlos' eyes narrowed suspiciously. He appeared momentarily unsure then his face softened a bit.

'Hees grandfather you say?'

'Yes, such a shame.' Pauline looked down sadly.

It was obvious her words had hit home and Carlos clearly took them to mean the worst. His attention went from Pauline to Timmy and then unnervingly to me. (Don't look at me mate. I didn't even know he had a grandfather!) But with a sharp nod to Odd Job, Carlos called him off, indicating that Timmy should be helped up.

'Oh, loving the pistol darling!' Timmy made a grab for henchman A's weapon but henchman B firmly removed his hand and swung it round his shoulder.

'Ooooh lovely! You… him… me… tight black uniforms; two, no make that three large weapons and a hoofing great yacht… I make that Pimms o'clock, or should I say Pimms a COCK!' Timmy 'hurrahed' for good measure.

The two henchmen half-carried him off to the main doors and Pauline and I exchanged worried glances.

Carlos immediately took control of the situation inside and turned to his gawping guests, gesturing with open, apologetic hands, a broad smile on his face.

'Ah, the demon dreenk; our friend and our enemy!' He smiled. 'Pleease, pleease forgeeve my young friend there, my champagne does not always mix weeth thees heat, no?'

Some people laughed, and a relieved feeling seemed to ripple around the crowd.

Carlos continued, 'Please honour me by continuing to enjoy yourselves and mind your feet, we have had a few breakages over here; notheeng to worry about.'

What a lovely man, I decided.

Pauline and I followed Timmy and the henchmen outside and down to the quay, where he was led to a bench and forced to sit down, much to his obvious annoyance. Carlos was behind us all the way.

I turned to him.

'Thank you, Carlos. We'll make sure he gets home and sleeps it off.'

'Please do, I theenk it would be better for everyone,' he said, brusquely, looking somewhat less friendly now. *OK, maybe not quite so lovely.*

'Well thank you for being so understanding and… um… it really has been an amazing party,' I added, just in case he saw fit to add me to the guest list for his next one. It's not every day one gets to rub shoulders with Chris Evans or was it Anne Robinson?

Carlos nodded briefly and headed back up to the party again, Odd Job and the Hench Twins in tow.

Pauline was trying to keep hold of Timmy who was struggling to get up again.

'What grandfather!?' I asked her.

'It was the only thing I could think of. I thought that Carlos might relate to a grandfather story. Anyway, I didn't say what the news was. I just said it was very upsetting. He could have stubbed his toe or lost his favourite watch!'

Timmy had escaped and was prancing off down the quay, dancing and singing loudly. I glanced up to the boat but luckily Carlos and his crew had disappeared back into the party.

'I am well and truly off my trolley. And I love it!' Timmy cried out drunkenly, reaching up to the stars, his hands outstretched, twirling himself round.

Pauline called after him, 'My God, Timmy, how much have you had?'

'Not enough my darling cousin; not nearly enough.'

Then he turned back to face us and a mischievous expression crossed his face. Without warning, he charged towards us and, as he reached us, pulled his arms strongly around both of us in an attempt to swing us round. Pauline almost toppled over and spun away to the side.

'Let's dance!' Timmy cried, whizzing me round and round by my arm. We twirled off in circles and the lights from the boat became long streamers of gold against the dark sky. He had hold of me so tight that I kept losing my footing. Round and round we went and I was getting so giddy that at first I didn't notice that one of my boobs had lost its battle against the force of all the movement and popped out the side of my dress.'

'Timmy, stop!' I cried. 'My boob's fallen out!'

Odd Job, who had returned to his bouncer duties at the bottom of the ramp, nearly fell into the water. I was vaguely aware of him scuttling back up to the party. I sincerely hoped he wasn't going to fetch Carlos for a second time!

Suddenly though, the whole thing seemed really funny. Timmy was still holding on to me and I was out of completely out of breath, giggling badly. At last, Timmy stopped from his current attempt at the tango and saw what I was talking about. He screamed with laughter so loudly that everyone on the main deck above us swivelled round to take a good look. Timmy and I were becoming helpless and I couldn't even move to sort my boob out! Then Pauline started and we laughed and laughed until we were gasping for air. It took me ages to put it away again and Timmy was all for taking the other one out to make it match!

Finally, red cheeked and breathless, we sat down on a nearby wall panting heavily.

'I haven't laughed that much for years!' Pauline gasped.

'I've got a stitch,' I half groaned, half laughed, clutching my side.

'Look,' Pauline pointed back up to the deck, 'there's Jenny. Is that John with her?'

I followed her gaze. Jenny was leaning over the side of the boat grinning and waving down at us; John was beside her. I watched as they began to make their way down off the boat.

'Yep, that's John,' I said.

'Well bugger me sideways with a bargepole!' Timmy exclaimed 'He's gorge'!'

He covered one eye with his hand then took it away again.

'And how convenient; he seems to have brought his twin brother along too!'

Timmy attempted to stand to get a better look but was so unsteady, he ended up falling back down again, almost tipping backwards over the low wall.

'Timmy, calm yourself will you,' Pauline insisted. 'Go and lie down on that bench, we need to sober you up or we'll never get a taxi to take us back to the apartment.'

'It's too far away, I'll get lonely!' he protested.

'I'll come and read you a bedtime story in a minute, now just go!' Pauline ordered.

Amazingly, Timmy obeyed and headed off but stopped short of the bench and lay down on the wall a little way up from us. He began singing up to the night sky.

'*Are the stars out tonight? I don't know if it's cloudy or bright. For I only have eyes for you, dear…*'

Pauline and I stood up as Jenny and John stepped off the ramp. As they walked towards us, I saw they were hand in hand.

Jenny was still without her eye make-up, and her lips were suspiciously void of lipstick too. John looked decidedly happier than the last time I'd seen him and as they reached us he put his arm protectively round Jenny's shoulders.

'I'll explain later,' she whispered to us.

As we made our introductions we became aware of an odd growling sound which was growing louder and turning we realised that Timmy had fallen fast asleep where he lay and was snoring. With a gasp, Pauline shot off towards him and only just managed to catch him before he rolled off the wall and smack bang into the side of a large rubbish bin.

All of a sudden, we heard a terrified cry from the very top deck.

We all looked up and saw what appeared to be a man and a woman struggling. The man had hold of the woman's shoulders and seemed to be trying to push her down. It was hard to hear everything but one sentence was clear and hung on the wind.

'I'm sorry; please stop!' the woman's voice cried out.

'Oh my God,' I cried, 'that's Catherine!' I ran towards the boat in horror. Clambering over the unmanned rope I began to race upwards. Once on the first deck, I checked both ways, searching for a route to the top. From behind, John overtook me. 'This way!' he cried.

Dashing past the noise from the party he ran towards some steps in the far corner, taking them two at a time. I raced after him.

At the top, there was another, smaller, flight of steps.

As we headed up even further, we heard a man's voice, nasty, threatening.

'Fucking prick tease, I know what you want.'

Hardly out of breath, John reached the top first and as I struggled up breathlessly behind him I could see Catherine being pushed about by the guy I'd seen her with earlier, the one who'd had his hand on her backside. I watched in horror as he reached out and caught her ankle with his foot, tripping her down onto the deck.

I screamed out.

'Cat!'

The guy turned, alarmed, his chiselled face registering fear as John reached him and forcefully pulled him off poor Catherine, hurling him across the deck with such brute force that he landed with a loud smack against the railings opposite.

Catherine lay shaking in a heap. I rushed over to her. Her dress was pushed up showing her thighs. I could see the material was torn. Her red lipstick was smeared across her face. She looked terrified. I crouched down beside her and covered her up, helping her to a sitting position.

'My God, what happened? What did he do to you?' I urged as Jenny and Pauline reached us, puffing and panting.

Catherine sat quivering, holding her knees close to her and rocking backwards and forwards. It was a few moments before she spoke and when she did her voice was weak and scared.

'I couldn't do it, Maggie, I just couldn't. I thought I could but I couldn't.'

'Couldn't do what?' Pauline asked gently, kneeling down beside Catherine and putting her arm around her shoulders.

'I'll tell you later,' I said quietly.

'But he just wouldn't take no for an answer,' Catherine went on obliviously. 'He wouldn't get off me! He kept trying to force me...' She covered her face with her hands and began to cry into her lap. 'What have I done, what have I done? This is all my fault.'

'Nothing is your fault!' Jenny, still standing, glared down angrily, immediately taking in the situation. 'A no is a no and that's that. Catherine, did that arsehole try to rape you?' She pointed accusingly over at the dishevelled guy, who at this point was being pinned down tightly by John.

'Don't you go fucking blaming me,' he shouted defiantly. 'She's the one who started it, all tarty and giving me the come on. What's a man supposed to do, have a cold shower just cos some bitch changes her mind? Fucking little whore!' With that, John hauled him up and lamped him one straight to the chin, sending him flying across the deck and into a pile of tarpaulin.

'But he's right, it is my fault, I am a tart. I thought I wanted to lose my virginity but when it came down to it I was too afraid. I'm sorry, I'm so, so sorry,' she wailed in the direction of the tarpaulin.

Jenny was fuming. 'He's not right at all. You said no and that's the end of it, Cat. Whatever you thought you wanted, you said no, so that bastard deserves everything he gets,' she said angrily as John returned, bent down and put his jacket around Catherine's shoulders.

By the time we looked back over to where the man had been lying, he'd done a runner.

Gradually Catherine began to calm down and we managed to get her shakily to her feet just as Carlos turned up with Odd Job, clearly less than pleased for the second time that evening.

'Jenny! Pleease tell me what ees happening now!' He put his hand to his head in disbelief. 'One of my best customers ees complaining that a man up here hass heet him.' He looked accusingly at John.

'He bloody well deserved it,' Jenny yelled angrily. Then, taking account of who she was yelling at, added 'Sorry, Carlos, but he tried to rape my friend!' John took matters in hand then, and led Carlos off to explain. The rest of us carefully helped Catherine to the flight of stairs and slowly began our descent.

From the boat, we could see that Timmy was still fast asleep on the wall but, as he snored away happily unaware of the goings on, we began to make out a figure in the shadows. Getting closer we saw it was a very tall dark man wearing a dinner jacket and staring down at Timmy. Almost off the boat, to my dismay, I realised it was Jye!

Jye stood striking and impressive in a black dinner jacket and maroon shiny shirt, with his usual dreadlocks replaced by a virtually shaved head. All signs of his macho drug dealer image had completely gone. He looked so different, almost unrecognisable. He stood gazing down at Timmy as he slept with a very soppy expression on his face.

'Jye, what on earth are you doing out here?' I asked reaching the wall and sitting down with Catherine who still had John's jacket on.

'Where there's a party, there's a Jye. Or should I say Jye*lo*!' he camped. He'd completely dropped his drawl.

'Jye! Be careful! People might hear your voice.'

His face became one big wide grin, his white teeth appearing like neon lights in the darkness.

'Frankly, my dear, I don't give a damn!' He sat on the wall next to Timmy's head, looking down adoringly. 'I saw this beautiful specimen of a boy shake up that bunch of upper-class toffs up there and I fell completely in lust on the spot,' he sighed. 'I think he's just taught me it's time for me to be me for a change. If he can do it… so can I!'

We were all quiet on the way home.

Thankfully Catherine dozed on Pauline's shoulder in the back of the people carrier. I sincerely hoped she would be OK. She'd been so badly shaken.

Timmy also slept on and off, every now and then stirring and asking where Ricky Martin was. Poor Timmy, as he'd woken on the wall he'd come face to face with the rather substantial Jye and had been decidedly sheepish ever since. Jye had apparently asked for his number and Timmy had been too frightened to refuse.

John sat up at the front with the driver, giving Jenny the chance to fill me in on what had happened between them. Apparently John's wife Jane had been lying all along about the so-called pregnancy. It had just been a ploy to make John stay with her but of course it had soon become apparent that there was no baby. So no baby meant the marriage was over, leaving John free to be with Jenny. The irony was he had no idea Jenny would be at the party and was simply there doing the PR coverage. He'd thankfully been able to talk Carlos into letting the whole thing with Catherine drop, by promising him some free PR consultancy for his new golfing complex.

Tucked up in bed that night as Catherine slept soundly, I stared at the ceiling and went over the evening's events.

I thought about how sad Jenny had been earlier, so desolate. She'd even spoken about her mum. That had really jolted me at the time; the thought of not having a mum, of not having *my* mum.

It was strange, no one in the Henderson family talked about Amelia Henderson really. Apart from Mr H referring, briefly, to her on the night of his birthday party this was the only reference to her I could remember anyone making… since…

I allowed my mind to drift back to that afternoon all those years ago.

Luke and I had been sitting up amongst the solid branches of the big old oak tree in their garden. It was a warm, balmy, summer's day and we'd been wiling away the hours together, talking about whatever teenagers talk about. And for some reason known only to him, Luke had chosen that particular afternoon to tell me the full story of how his mum had died.

He'd only been eight, which would have made Jenny six and Tony five. Luke and his mum had been going out in the car for ice cream because Tony had thrown a massive tantrum and wouldn't stop screaming until his mum had finally given in and agreed to go and get some.

They hadn't seen the lorry until it was too late. It had appeared, suddenly, seemingly from nowhere and crashed into the driver's side of their car. Luke had made a *smack* sound when he'd told me, hitting his fist into the palm of his other hand. I remember because it had made me jump at the time.

His mum hadn't died immediately. Luke, from his position in the back seat diagonally behind her, remembered staring over as she sat with her head slumped, face down, on the steering wheel. He'd wondered, stupidly he said at the time, if she was just asleep. People had surrounded the car and he remembered the muffled voices and cries of the faces outside his window, like he was in a goldfish bowl and was hearing them through water.

Luke had had tears in his eyes as he explained that she had died in the ambulance on the way to the hospital. I listened to him and felt his anguish as if I'd gone through it all too.

At the hospital, his father, in an attempt to soothe the situation for his young son, had said she'd gone to Heaven and wasn't in any pain anymore. Luke said he'd often wondered about, worried about, what pain she might have felt in the first place.

Lying there in our apartment reflecting on it made me think about my own mother. OK, she could be a bit exasperating; we didn't always see eye to eye. In fact, she was downright nutty sometimes, if I'm honest, but I loved her. She was *my* mum and I *really* loved her. No one could ever take her place. I thought about how awful it must have been for Luke actually being in the car with his mum and then how dreadful it would have been for the three of them and their dad to have to learn to cope on their own. It must have affected them all so terribly. How did anyone get over something like that?

I sighed sadly, suspended between the pain of the past and the pain that thinking about Luke, *anything to do with Luke*, still somehow managed to bring to the present.

Catherine stirred fitfully beside me, breaking my thoughts. I looked across to see if she was OK but she quickly settled again. I wondered how she would feel the next morning. Something told me she wouldn't be trying to lose her virginity again until the right man came along. I considered Tony then and in a mad moment almost texted him. Despite all the champagne though, I decided against it.

Chapter Twenty-eight

It was time to go home.

We rose the next morning and began our packing. Catherine had perked up a little but was still very quiet.

'How you feeling?' I ventured.

'Ashamed. Embarrassed, you know…' She gave me a weak smile. 'I'm OK though, no bones broken.'

I squeezed her shoulder affectionately.

We heard the front door open then slam shut and Jenny bounced in from her night away at John's hotel. She was full of the joys of spring and sprung up onto Catherine's bed then off the other side and on to the floor again before circling round the room, looking incredibly pleased with herself.

Thankfully, she wasn't the only one who seemed happier. Pauline wandered in, her eyes smiling.

'Do you know,' she said, 'I think I laughed so much last night when your boob fell out, I've got away without having a hangover!'

'Whose boob fell out?' Catherine swivelled round from her packing.

'Mine,' I admitted ruefully.

'I seem to have missed out on quite a lot last night,' Catherine said sadly.

'Yeah well, at least you managed to swerve what that arsehole on the boat was offering,' Jenny pointed out.

'Only just.'

Jenny then proceeded to do something so out of character I had to rub my eyes to make sure I wasn't seeing things. She bounced over to Catherine and gave her a huge hug followed by a big smacking kiss on the cheek and said 'One day, Cat, you'll know how lovely you really are and then you can stop knocking around with arseholes who don't.'

And, with that, she skipped back round the beds and out of the room shouting:

'Coffee anyone?'

Catherine and I exchanged puzzled looks.

'She's in love,' Pauline explained. 'I've only seen it once before, back when we were in the first year. Michael Larson his name was, from the third year.'

'What the tall guy with the big ears?' I asked

'No, that was his brother James.'

'Oh.'

'Michael was the shorter one with really blue eyes,' Pauline described.

'God yes! Him that looked like a young Robbie Williams,' I said.

'No, that was his cousin Simon.'

'Oooh I remember Simon!' Catherine said looking much more cheerful again. 'I rather fancied him actually,' she admitted.

'I seem to remember most people did,' Pauline said. 'Michael was the one who looked like the lead singer of Green Day; the dark one with the spikey hair and makeup.'

'Oh *him,*' she realised. 'I know who you mean. He was really cool; far too cool for me. Now you come to mention it, I do vaguely remember Jenny quite liking him,' Catherine said.

'Er, she was *in love* with him,' Pauline corrected her. 'She didn't really let on how hard she'd fallen. You know what Jen's like about people knowing her business. But I can tell you now, I recognise the signs. She's well and truly hooked on John. When she was into Michael, she kept wanting to dance the waltz with me around the school playground.'

'In year one?' I exclaimed.

'Her dad taught her.'

'Right.'

'And you'd always catch her humming while she did her homework. Jenny never hums.'

At that moment Jenny came back along the corridor. She was humming. Pauline shot us a 'told you so' look.

'What?' Jenny snapped indignantly, placing the tray on the dressing table.

I laughed. 'We've just never heard you hum before.'

Jenny's face recovered its more familiar scowl. 'Give it a rest will you. I hum all the time.' And she half stomped, half skipped, back up the corridor.

Timmy poked his head in then, looking very dishevelled. He wandered over and sat down beside Catherine's case.

'I had a really bad dream.'

'What was it about, honey bun?' Catherine asked, kindly.

'I dreamt I was being attacked by a dark, menacing, seven-foot bloke with a gold tooth and a skinhead. And he wouldn't let me wake up until I'd given him my phone number.'

'Did you give it to him?' Pauline smiled.

'I can't remember. I think I might have done.'

'So do I,' Pauline said.

'How do you know? You weren't in my dream!'

'Maybe not but we were all there when you gave the guy your phone number.'

Timmy was clearly horrified. 'You mean he was real!'

'All seven feet of him.'

Timmy slumped down with his head in his hands. Then his head shot up again.

'Did someone flash their tits?'

'Maggie did.' Jenny was back.

'Not on purpose!' I pointed out indignantly.

'I remember lots of stars,' Timmy said thoughtfully.

'That was probably when you fell on the floor. Perhaps you banged your head,' Pauline said.

'What floor? When? Oh hang on… Oh God, the party!' he cried in horror.

'The party,' we confirmed in unison.

'I remember being outside though.'

'We got chucked out.'

'Because of me?' he asked meekly.

'Kind of.'

'Shit, sorry.'

'My back hurts this morning,' he went on.

'You fell asleep on a wall.'

'Oh… now I remember, that's when I saw all the stars. There were loads of them and then…' he faltered. 'Oh God, the guy in my dream! He wasn't in my dream was he?'

'No!' we cried, laughing at Timmy's expression.

'And I think I did give him my number didn't I.'

'Yes!' we chorused.

'It's not funny! He could have eaten me for breakfast!'

'Thought that's what you liked,' Jenny said.

'There'd be nothing for him to eat, I'd be too scared.'

Catherine looked puzzled.

'He's just being pornographic, Cat,' Jenny explained.

'I knew that,' she lied.

Pauline explained to Timmy what had happened. 'Apparently when you did your diving impression on the boat, he decided you were God's gift to men. He reckoned that the way you put your two fingers up to the snobby guests was, how did he put it, "quite beautiful".'

'I didn't put my two fingers up to anyone, did I?' Timmy asked, shocked.

'Just metaphorically, Timmy,' I clarified. 'Anyway, I think it's rather lovely. I mean because of you, Jye, that's his name, is "coming out" to the whole world; and it's all because you were the natural you that he wants to be the natural him. Sweet don't you think?'

Timmy appeared far from sure.

'Jye,' he said slowly. 'Even his name sounds dangerous.'

'But Jye was the name of Tarzan's little friend in that old TV series and he was really sweet.' Catherine pointed out.

'Must have been a very, very distant cousin then,' Timmy's face was downcast. 'I guess that means I missed out on seeing Ricky Martin?'

'Never mind,' Jenny soothed, 'he didn't look so hot.'

Hauling my case onto the floor, I wheeled it out into the hall. Then, checking to make sure I was alone, I surreptitiously turned on my mobile. After a few minutes it bleeped out an answer phone message alert.

My heart leapt; Tony perhaps? I'd woken up with a far from clear head and any confidence I might have had that all was well between us and I was just being silly, was quickly diminishing. In fact, I was fast concluding that not only must he have gone off me, I'd obviously done something very wrong and I needed to do something to make it very right. Maybe this would be my chance?

However, the message wasn't from Tony. It was an answer phone message from my mother.

I listened to several minutes about the perils of not having a job and then a couple more on the dangers of mosquitoes and Spanish men and then she was cut off halfway through the part where she was sounding off about me never telling her what was happening in my life.

I sighed as I turned my phone off again. Back to reality.

Chapter Twenty-nine

The flight home was reasonably uneventful. I sat next to Timmy who, after downing three Jack Daniels and Coke, slept most of the way.

Jenny sat excitedly, as if new life had been breathed into her. I'd never seen her so alive. John would be flying back in a couple of days and coming over to meet her dad. Needless to say she was like a cat on a hot tin roof with anticipation.

Left alone with my thoughts my mind found its way unhelpfully to my job…or lack thereof. Damn. All my good intentions to sort out my life while on holiday had been completely scuppered. That horrid feeling that comes over you when you've blocked something out that's got to be let back in again was washing over me as the landscape changed beneath us and the miles before landing grew fewer and fewer. I was jobless and broke. And worse still, my parents were bound to be on my case. They would be aware I had no real means of support and they would no doubt be fretting; Dad, because he couldn't bear anything bad to happen to me, and Mum, because she couldn't bear the thought of me having to shop in the Co-op.

And then there was the temping issue. Temping had seemed such a viable option when I'd had the holiday stretching ahead of me as a bargaining tool. I was currently managing to get myself into a right tizzy about working with strangers week after week. What on earth had happened to my plans of spending endless days contemplating life and my future? Every time my thoughts had touched upon something sensible like what sort of career options should I be considering, or what was it about my previous job I liked or wanted to avoid, or what geographical area did I prefer, my mind had switched to automatic avoidance, offering up helpful suggestions such as 'nah, not the right time to be thinking about that, you're on holiday!' or 'plenty of time to think about that tomorrow, you're on holiday!' Well, I wasn't on holiday anymore. I was heading, rather too quickly, back home. The feeling of angst got stronger as I also considered the fact I would probably have to temp in areas of work that, although I had experience, I really would rather move away from. All in all, the prospects, which had seemed fine – even exciting – before Spain, now loomed ahead in a far more threatening manner.

I sighed loudly and the woman in the window seat beside Timmy glanced over at me then went back to staring out at the sky again.

I actually felt quite afraid. After all, who was I kidding? I couldn't just up and leave everything and start afresh. Could I?

I tried my best to be rational. I mean, it was only temping and temping did mean temporary. Yes, it would give me a chance to think about what I really wanted to do. I gave an internal sigh feeling deflated. Where had I heard that before?

My thoughts went to Tony again. Another feeling of nervous butterflies coursed through me. I felt unsettled at the thought of seeing him. All the confidence and 'couldn't care less' attitude I'd found in copious amounts of alcohol, had disappeared. The fact was that, over the next however long, I was bound to bump into Tony. And that felt very disconcerting.

I wasn't really sure what had happened. I mean, one minute I was really into him and the next here I was thinking about seeing him again and almost dreading it. I tried to put my finger on why. I wasn't sure whether it was because I'd gone off him – I didn't think so – or whether it was because I'd felt pressure when he'd texted me on holiday or whether it was actually because I was frightened I'd put him off and was worried I'd have to start apologising as soon as I saw him.

Letting my thoughts drift over the future, I realised suddenly that I didn't actually *want* to go off Tony. I wanted at least one thing to be able to look forward to when I got home – a nice man. A man who made me laugh. A man who took care of me and a man… who had more money than me! But there *was* a problem with Tony. He was Luke's brother and the thought of them both being around made me acutely uneasy, despite trying to convince myself otherwise.

For the last couple of days, I'd half forgotten that Luke was due back with his bride to be. And then a shock of a thought hit me. Unless they'd done a quick in and out registry job in the last week… they'd be coming back and getting married over here. And I'd be invited! I'd have to stand in the church with a big fake grin on my face as Luke and his 'supermodel with an off the scale IQ' wife, moved gracefully back down the aisle having said at the altar, 'Of course we do, we were made for each other'.

I shook my mind away from the disturbing daydream, annoyed at myself for allowing such negative thoughts to unfold so easily. It was, of course, rubbish. I had to forget this and move on. I *had* moved on for goodness sake. It was just that a person who I'd once loved was back in my universe again and it was going to take a little time to shake the memories and feelings off completely.

Timmy stirred in the seat next to me and then – how embarrassing – started muttering and moaning, *really* loudly. The people in the seats in front of us turned round to see what was happening. I smiled apologetically and they turned away again and began whispering to each other. Then the woman in the window seat next to him nearly jumped out of her seat as he gave a final resigned groan, uttered some loud expletive and flung his arm in the air and straight across the front of her body! Poor woman, she was pinned down for a good few seconds before cautiously lifting and moving his arm away from her.

'Don't worry, he's gay,' I said comfortingly.

I have to say, she didn't seem particularly comforted.

As the plane started its descent, my stomach did several familiar lurches, partly due to the air pockets but mainly because we were about to land back into normality. My suntan suddenly appeared a bit faded against the greyish, overcast light of the British sky.

I woke Timmy, who looked like he had been crying in his sleep. He came to with such a jolt and let out a little whimper, like he'd been in the middle of a bad dream. He seemed so like a young boy I felt sorry for him. I was glad he wouldn't have to go back to his empty flat quite yet. We all had one night left together at the farm then Timmy would be heading down with Pauline to stay with her and Terry for a few days.

I turned across to where Pauline sat in the opposite aisle, staring out the window at the fast approaching land beneath us. I had been firm with her. She wasn't going anywhere before talking to Jenny and the others about her health problems.

We were almost on the ground. I began to anticipate the touchdown, pulling my stomach in so it didn't make me jump.

The end of the holiday.

The sky was overcast and the air muggy as we stood waiting with our cases in the long taxi queue.

'Hang on a minute,' Jenny squinted past Catherine's shoulder, '...isn't that Nico?'

'Yes, yes. OK, OK. Nice try, Jenny, but I didn't fall for that one in Spain and I'm not going to fall for it now,' Catherine replied.

'No, I mean it. Look.' Jenny pointed behind Catherine who turned, just as a dark haired guy with a large holdall could be seen paying a taxi driver up ahead. He then broke into a slight run, as he headed towards us.

Despite her suntan, Catherine went white.

'Oh my God, it *is* him. What's he doing here? Quick, hide me.' She ducked down behind the three of us.

'He's bound to see the rest of us, though,' Pauline pointed out. 'He knows we've been on holiday together and we can't all hide!'

'By the looks of that bag, I reckon he's leaving the country, Cat,' Jenny said. 'Must have heard how pissed off with him you are and decided to do a runner.'

'Oh no, oh no, he's going to see me, what will I do?' Catherine panicked.

'Ah so what,' Jenny sneered. 'He never bloody contacted you. Just ignore him.'

So we did. We all faced the other way as he came towards us. Well actually, that's a lie. We started that way and then all ended up turning back and staring at him. We needn't have worried though as he turned and headed inside the airport without spotting us.

'Ohhh that was close,' Catherine breathed, her face flushed. 'My heart's going like the clappers. I wonder where he's going.'

Timmy was now wide-awake again and gave a whistle. 'My, my, what a *cutie*! You guys are going to have to learn to share.'

'Hands off, you!' Catherine said a little too abruptly.

'I thought you didn't want to know!' Jenny pointed out.

'I don't, not really,' she said sadly.

'Just a minute,' Pauline frowned. 'If he's leaving the country, how come he was going into the arrivals and not the departures?'

We exchanged confused glances.

'Maybe he's meeting someone?' Catherine suggested.

'Or maybe he's *hoping* to meet someone?' Pauline said pointedly to Catherine.

'What do you mean?'

'He's here to see you, you daft bint!' Jenny scoffed.

'She's right, Cat. He must be!' I agreed.

Catherine thought about it for a moment or two then her eyes opened wide with realisation.

'Do you really think he is?'

Jenny answered, 'Think about it. Why else would he turn up here, just as we arrive, and go into arrivals? Bit of coincidence don't you think?'

'But he was carrying a bag. Maybe he's just gone into the wrong entrance.'

'Or maybe he's planning to go to the gym later, I don't know.' Jenny shrugged impatiently.

Catherine started to panic.

'Oh my God, you could be right.' She started flapping about and searching in her handbag. 'Quick, someone give me a mirror. Where's my lipstick?'

All hell broke loose then, as we scrabbled to get Catherine into a proper 'greeting' state.

'How do I look?' she asked fretfully. I held up the little mirror for her, while she dabbed a piece of tissue on her lips.

'Stunning,' I soothed.

'Like you're shitting yourself,' Jenny added helpfully.

'He'd better hurry up and see you; we're nearly at the front of the queue,' Pauline remarked.

Suddenly, there was an out of breath voice from behind us.

'Cathereen!'

We all swivelled round. There stood Nico, handsome and desperate. Like I imagine Heathcliff might have looked after a night on the moors.

Catherine tried hard to compose herself.

'Hello, Nico,' she sniffed aloofly. 'What are you doing here?'

'Please, Cathereen, I know how theesa look but...' he paused suddenly aware that we were all staring at him. 'Please excuse,' he aimed at us then he gently pulled her to one side. But we could still hear everything, primarily because we were listening intently.

Nico shook his head and held his open hands to the heavens.

'My phone wassa stolen weeth alla my numbers, just when you leave. Samone at hotel they theenk. I had to haff the phone company put stop on my number and everything! I could not phone; I had no number for you. Nothing! I was so worried. I try to contact you through the airport but I only haff thees main number, with lot of recorded voices, and no real people. Eet tooka so long to find anyone to 'elp me. Eventually, I get through to the airport and then it take soo long to get through to right desk and when I do, you take off already! I try to theenk of a way to reach you but it ees impossible. I no know the name of your 'ospital so I cannot call your work. I even drive up to the farm where the party was and I leave a note for Jenny's brarther Tony to contact me but I hear nothing, so I theenk maybe he is away also. I am so sorry, Cathereen. I did not know what to do or where you are staying, but I knew what flight you were returning on so I come here. But then I nearly did not arrive on time! There was so much traffic and we get stuck for so long but I am here now and you are looking so lovely,' he finished breathlessly, reaching out and touching her cheek.

Catherine flushed.

'Can you forgeeve me?' he asked, anxiously.

'Yes!' Catherine cried, happily. 'Yes, of course I forgive you!'

They threw their arms around each other.

Jenny raised her eyebrows.

'I'd have kept him hanging on for ages.'

At the front of the queue Pauline, Jenny, Timmy and I took a taxi, leaving Catherine and Nico (carrying what did in fact turn out to be his gym bag) behind to get a second one. They were going to his hotel but Catherine would see us later.

No doubt she would have been hugging herself that her plans the previous evening had been stymied, albeit dangerously so.

As the rest of us settled into our journey back to the farm, my mobile rang. Grappling around in my handbag, I fished it out.

'Hello?'

A strangely familiar and somewhat distant voice came down the line.

'Timmy?' the voice enquired.

'No, sorry, this is Ma... Jye? Is that you?'

I swivelled round from the front of the cab to see Timmy slide, guiltily, down the back seat.

'I'm not here!' he mouthed.

'Yes, Jye, it's Maggie... No, this is *my* phone. I think there's been a bit of a mix up...

Yes, probably. He must have got our numbers muddled up. Don't worry; I've got your number now... Oh yes, you can be sure I'll be passing it on to him... I see... really? ... Well, yes, of course... Yes, I will, I will certainly be telling him to call you... Bye, Jye, nice to hear from you. See you... soon then.'

I ended the call and glared at Timmy.

'Please don't be mad at me?' he pleaded, still cowering in the back. 'I must have panicked and given him your number instead. Sorry, Mags!' He cringed guiltily.

'Well, that's all well and good but I don't know what you're going to do when he comes over here next week. He sounded pretty insistent about seeing you.'

The smile faded and Timmy's eyes went wide with horror.

'What? No!'

I clicked my mouth.

''Fraid so.'

'Oh, shit, no! You'll have to hide me. He mustn't find me. Oh God.' And Timmy went on ranting and raving away as we drove along.

I turned and surreptitiously winked at Jenny and Pauline.

Maybe I'd wait just a little bit longer before telling Timmy the part about Jye's visit hadn't been strictly true.

Chapter Thirty

As our taxi drew up to the farm my mobile rang again. This time it was Mum. I quickly put it on to answer phone. Now was not the right time to deal with a tirade of abuse.

Looking up ahead, I saw Mr Henderson's van and I smiled inwardly as a vision of a puppy sliding from side to side in the back came into my mind. Behind the van, I could see another car peeping out. I squinted but couldn't make it out properly. As we drew nearer though my heart began to beat faster. There was no mistaking it now.

The taxi pulled up on to the gravel in front of the house.

Mr H must have seen us as the front door opened and he stood there all smiles. He came out and opened the back door of the taxi wearing his long shorts and gardening shirt, his face ruddy from the oppressive heat and his eyes twinkling. Somehow he made coming home slightly more bearable. As we clambered out he hugged us one by one, genuinely pleased to see us all.

'Welcome. Welcome!' he boomed. 'Come on in. The lawns are mown, the flowers are tucked up in their beds for the night and we're all about to have a cup of tea in your honour.' He ushered us towards the open door and into the hallway, taking each of our cases and putting them to one side at the bottom of the stairs.

All? I wondered. *Who's all?*

Once in, the others followed Mr H into the kitchen where he immediately made a fuss of Timmy who he hadn't seen for ages. For some reason, I found myself heading for the lounge. Another one of those invisible pulls? And there he was. Sitting slightly hunched on one of the old sofas, elbows on his knees, head in his hands, staring at the floor. He looked startled as I came in and our eyes met. He appeared… worried?

'Hello, Tony,' I said quietly.

I started to give him a shy, neutral, smile, one that I hope wouldn't suggest one thing or another but, as I did so, it froze on my face. From the door leading to the kitchen, entered a slim, pretty, fair-haired woman carrying a tray full of tea and cake.

She glanced up as she came in and her face also seemed to stop mid expression. Placing the tray down on the coffee table, she straightened herself up, brushed her hands off and smoothed down her skirt with her delicate little hands.

'Hello,' she smiled rather too sweetly, holding out her hand to shake mine.

'I'm Laura. You must be... let me see, Maggie? Am I right?' I may have imagined it but I could have sworn I detected a note of disdain in her voice.

My mind was working overtime. *Laura? But wasn't Laura... Tony's Ex!?*

Bewildered, I shook her hand, which was like shaking a limp lettuce leaf. Yick.

Glancing across to Tony, this time he wouldn't meet my eye.

From behind me, Pauline and Timmy came in and Mr H entered from the kitchen. Full of bonhomie, he introduced Laura to Pauline and Timmy who took turns in shaking the lettuce leaf.

Laura smiled a fake smile at them.

'I've made the tea, just what we all need. Shall I be mum?' she simpered.

I think I hated her on the spot.

Delicately – no make that annoyingly delicately – Laura began to pour tea into the china cups before sitting on the edge of the sofa like a little Kylie Minogue doll. I felt like a baby elephant by comparison.

We were still standing like lemons when Jenny skipped in. She stopped in her tracks staring at Laura then frowned.

'What are you doing here?' Her stare became a glare.

Her father interjected.

'Jenny! That's no way to talk to our guest now is it?'

Jenny shrugged, collapsing into the other armchair. Sliding round so she was sitting sideways she swung her legs over one arm like a little kid.

'Sorry,' she shrugged. 'Just thought these two were history.'

It didn't appear anyone was going to offer any explanation about the reappearance of Laura. Tony seemed jittery and an awkward silence settled over the room. Mr H broke it.

'Cake anyone?'

'For goodness sake you lot, sit down will you,' Jenny exclaimed. 'I'll break my neck having to talk up to you all!'

Pauline and Timmy sat on the two-seater, Mr H on his favourite armchair and before I realised what was happening the only space left was the one on the sofa, next to Tony and Laura.

I glanced nervously at the empty seat, then at Tony who was beside it and then back at the seat.

'Come along, Maggie, sit yourself down now. You're making the place look untidy!' Mr H chortled. He'd always said that when we were kids.

I sat down tentatively, aware of Tony's knees next to mine and trying desperately to stop them actually touching. Trouble was the sofa was a really old squashy one that dipped in the middle. It was, therefore, almost impossible not to fall into the centre of it and onto Tony. I held on tightly to the arm so as to keep myself as upright as possible but it kept creaking whenever I moved and drawing attention to me. I sat perched as still as I could, hoping no one would ask me why I was doing an impression of someone riding the waltzers.

Jenny began regaling entertaining and suitably virginal stories of the holiday, which kept everyone amused. Timmy disappeared halfway through to go to the toilet. Then, when he came back about ten minutes later, he was considerably more animated than when he'd left.

When he refused a piece of cake, I feared my suspicions had been correct.

At least while everyone was talking, no one was apparently the slightest bit aware of the tension over on our sofa.

'… and then Maggie's tit fell out!…Sorry, Dad,' she added to her frowning father.

'… But it did; Pauline told me.' Jenny fell about laughing. 'I wish I'd been there!'

I felt myself instantly redden.

Tony's foot started tapping beside me.

Laura complained. 'Stop it, Tony, you're jiggling me.'

'… and Timmy pulled a thirty-foot Rasta bloke.'

'I did not!'

'Did too!'

'Did not!'

'Did too. OK, he pulled you then.'

'Jennifer, please! Leave the boy alone.'

'Thanks, Mr H,' Timmy pulled a face at Jenny, who pulled one back. 'Anyway, you can make fun all you like, I'm off for a jaunt round the garden.'

Pauline and I exchanged puzzled looks as Timmy headed out the French doors.

'... You should have seen the size of the cruiser! It was like a flipping mansion! I've never seen so much champagne and, Dad, you'd have died for the lobster. Honestly, it was like walking onto a Hollywood film set.'

'Sounds *fabulous!*' Laura simpered.

'It was,' Jenny deadpanned.

'So, with all these rich and famous people milling about, who did you meet then?'

Tony sounded a bit offish.

'Prince Harry was there,' Jenny replied flippantly.

Pauline tutted. 'It was Anne Robinson!'

'OK bloody Anne Robinson then. Anyway, there were loads of soap stars and movie folk who kept lording around like they owned the place. Bit in your face for me but it was worth an eyeful. Most of it anyway,' she added tactfully, no doubt thinking about Catherine.

Pauline headed off to the kitchen having offered to make a fresh pot of tea, and then it was Laura's turn to go to the toilet. As the others seemed to be having an involved discussion about some building work that Mr H had had done while we were all in Spain, Tony took his chance to talk to me.

'Maggie,' he whispered.

'Yes, Tony?' I replied quite loudly and innocently.

'Look,' he hissed, 'this is not what it...'

Jenny interrupted him. 'What are you two whispering about?'

'I was just saying what a great tan Maggie has. It really suits her,' Tony deflected, skilfully.

Jenny pulled a face. 'Yeah she was getting loads of looks from all the men while we were out there.'

'I wasn't!'

'You were too! What about that Scottish bloke?'

'He doesn't count; he was really drunk.'

'Well there were loads of others.'

I could feel the tension growing beside me.

Before Jenny had the chance to say any more, Laura came back. I must admit, I couldn't help being hopeful that there was a perfectly innocent reason for Laura being around but I certainly wasn't going to give in that easily.

Just then, my phone bleeped a text from my bag. I pulled a contrite face.

'Excuse me,' I apologised, reaching down into my handbag and taking out my mobile.

286

Clicking quickly through the screens, aware of Tony beside me, I saw a number I didn't recognise.

As I read the text, I still didn't know who it was from but when the name came into view at the end of it, I was taken completely off guard. What the hell…? It was from my ex, Greg!

I excused myself feeling the need to take a minute to digest the text in private.

Hi Babe! Back in London, working in the City as a trainee solicitor. Running my own firm soon tho! Fancy a meet? Lots to tell. Greg XX

What on earth was Greg doing getting back in touch with me? The last time I'd seen him, he'd been planning his trip to find his perfect Asian woman. A perfect woman to replace a far from perfect woman – me! Fancy a meet indeed; bloody cheek.

He was acting like the last two years had never happened. Mind you, I supposed if he'd been away all that time, coming back might seem exactly like that. Well things had moved on, for me in any case.

I composed myself and went back into the lounge again.

'You OK, Mags, you look like you've seen a ghost,' Pauline said.

'Maybe not seen one but… do ghosts send texts?'

She frowned quizzically.

'Don't worry,' I said. 'Just someone I haven't heard from for a while.' I sat down again on the sofa again but, in the process, I accidentally brushed Tony's knee with mine. He started jiggling it up and down.

Laura shot him a contemptuous look then turned to me from her opposing corner.

'Old flame perhaps, Maggie?' she enquired, all sickly sugar. But for some reason, there did seem to be masked venom in her voice.

Would it be wrong to reach across and pull her hair?

'Um, yes that's right, Laura. It was an old flame actually. How perceptive of you.' I could feel Tony's agitation once again and I decided to play things up a bit.

'Seems he's doing really well; he's got an amazing new job in the City as a solicitor. Wondered if I'd like to go out for dinner.'

'Not that wanker that buggered off to Thailand?' Jenny said scornfully. '… Sorry, Dad,' she added.

Mr H raised his eyebrows. 'You're as bad as your Aunt Josephine!'

'Nowhere near as ugly though!' Jenny smirked at her dad who shook his head and sighed, exasperatedly.

'How long since you've seen him?' Pauline enquired.

I thought back to our break up.

'It's at least two years.' I had a vision of me in my long teddy bear nighty, buttering toast while Greg did the dirty deed of breaking up with me.

'So, you gonna go out with him again or what?' Jenny asked.

I decided it was worth milking the situation, for Tony and Laura's benefit, regardless of the fact that I'd rather have gone out with my old maths teacher than Greg.

'Maybe; I'm not sure. He was always pretty *reliable*,' I shot a brief sideways glance at Tony.

'But he fucked off to Thailand!' Jenny cried. 'Sorry, Dad.'

She had a point.

'He was OK up until that point though,' I lamely attempted Greg's defence; in actual fact he'd been about as reliable as expecting Basil Fawlty to keep his mouth shut at a tea party for the WI.

'Surely that's not the best reason in the world to go out with someone, Maggie,' Mr H offered up.

'Perhaps you're right Mr H but it helps, don't you think? You know, having someone to *rely* on. Someone honest, someone you trust.'

Mr H nodded in concurrence.

'Besides,' I went on, beginning to enjoy my little charade, 'He was very attractive.'

Once again, Tony's leg began jiggling beside me and it was gathering momentum.

'For goodness sake, Tony, stop it! You're rocking the sofa!' Laura snapped sharply.

Tony stopped immediately. *Well* under the thumb!

I noticed Pauline staring out the window to the back garden.

'What on earth is Timmy doing?'

We all swivelled round to see.

'I believe he's pruning my ornamental pear!' Mr Henderson said. 'What a good lad.'

The wonders of class A drugs.

We all swivelled back again.

'So he's a solicitor then, Maggie? This Greg chappy,' Laura said, 'I understand that's a very well paid profession.'

'Oh, um, yes, I believe it is. Yes, he went off travelling around Thailand after his exams and now he's been accepted by a City firm. Fantastic prospects so he says. But no more than he deserves,' I continued proudly, thinking Greg sounded a lot more glamorous than he actually was.

'How wonderful,' Laura said. 'Perhaps you should give him another chance then. You never know, you could be married off within a few months and living happily ever after just like Tony and I will be doing, won't we Tony.' She turned slightly and tucked a bit of hair behind Tony's ear.

Tony looked annoyed and un-tucked it again.

Happily ever after, eh? So they really were well and truly back together. Well I'd show him.

'Do you know, Laura, I think you're right. I'm going to phone him right now and arrange something; might as well see him while I've got this tan to show off.' I stood up, smiled sweetly at her and left the room with my mobile.

Unfortunately, despite having pulled the door to, there was no mistaking the fact that while I was in the middle of a fake conversation with Greg making our date, my phone actually rang and I was momentarily lost for words. So I quickly put it on to answer phone and tried to pretend to the fake Greg that it had been a call waiting notification. I ended the bogus conversation quickly in case it rang again. I thought this would be a good time to head upstairs with my luggage, to escape any onslaught.

Not long after that, I heard Tony and Laura leaving.

'Say goodbye to Maggie for us won't you?' Laura gushed to Mr H, 'And do wish her lots of luck with her scrummy man.'

I snarled from the safety of my bedroom.

Catherine came back late that night full of the sparkle of someone in love. What with her and Jenny beaming big smiles about the place, we hardly needed to put the lights on. Things changed however, soon after Mr H went to bed.

We were lounging around in Jenny's room and Pauline spilled the beans about her health situation.

There was a temporary loss of words.

Catherine broke the silence. 'But why didn't you say anything sooner? We could have supported you!'

'Sorry,' Pauline said ruefully. 'I just didn't want my problems ruining the holiday.'

'But we could have helped!' she cried.

'How?'

'I don't know. We could have…'

'Please don't tell me you would have given me a tincture of Catherine's Special Brew.'

'I might have,' Catherine replied indignantly.

'Thanks, Cat, but I kind of preferred keeping quiet; nothing personal. Anyway, you know now.'

Timmy sat on the floor, tears running down his cheeks. 'But what if you're really ill!' he sniffed.

From my position lying across the foot of the bed, I gave his shoulder a gentle nudge with my foot.

Pauline shook her head. 'Yes, thanks Timmy, I hadn't thought of that!'

'So what now?' Jenny asked flatly. She was the only one who hadn't reacted.

'I'll wait to see what the test results show.'

'What test results?' we all chorused.

'Oh sorry, of course I haven't told you.'

'No, you bloody haven't,' Jenny snapped.

'I'm having some tests done privately.'

'Such as?' Jenny said angrily.

'I don't know. A whole series of stuff, stuff that the GP doesn't deal with. The grey areas, so I'm told.'

'What does that mean?' Timmy fretted.

'You know, the grey areas; the bits that don't fit into the black and white.'

'Grey sounds really morbid; like doom and gloom. You wouldn't even catch me buying a pair of grey socks!'

'Shut up, Timmy!' Jenny snapped again.

Pauline tried to lighten things, 'You never buy your own socks anyway. You've always got some man buying them for you!'

'Not the point. I'm just saying grey is bad.'

'Grey isn't bad sweetie,' she continued in a motherly tone, 'not in this case. These are tests for things that might not show up on run of the mill blood tests. They're looking a bit closer from different angles hoping they might reveal something else. The consultant explained that there are a lot of things that GPs and the NHS aren't aware of, that's all.' She gave a light shrug.

'Isn't your GP recommending anything?' I asked.

'Not really. Although this private guy suggested I go for a full medical, just in case.'

'Just in case what?' Jenny pushed, crossly.

'Jen, I really don't know. I guess with the symptoms I've had… I've got, they simply want to rule everything out. They're probably just covering their backs.'

Pauline seemed remarkably relaxed about things. It was weird that she should be trying to convince us and not the other way round.

'That's all very well for you to say, but we're worried sick here,' Jenny blurted, clearly quite angry at Pauline's calmness. 'What exactly are they checking for? Are we talking bad stuff? I mean, are you saying you could have cancer, leukaemia, multiple sclerosis?'

Pauline remained unruffled.

'Let's hope it's nothing like that; I'm sure the initial blood tests would have ruled out most things. Like I say, I don't know exactly but I assume they'll check me out for all sorts, just to be sure. Listen, Jen, guys, just stick with me, yeah? I'm not finding any of this too easy and well, put it this way, I need you on my side right now. OK?' She looked round at us all for a response.

Jenny spoke first.

'OK but make bloody sure you don't keep anything from us. We're all in this together right?'

Silence hung in the air. I could sense tension, and it mainly was coming from Jenny. She sat at the other end of her bed leaning up against the pillows and playing with the corner of her bedspread, just like she used to do when we were kids.

I got up to try and break the mood.

'Who fancies a nightcap?'

Before anyone could answer, Jenny suddenly banged her pillow, hard. We all turned to stare at her.

'And anyway, how come you didn't tell me first? Why did you tell Maggie and not me?' She promptly burst into tears.

Pauline stood up from the dressing table stool and went over to her. Sitting down beside her she put her arm comfortingly around her shoulder.

Pauline tucked a stray lock of hair behind Jenny's ear and smoothed her hair down on the top of her head, just like a mother might have done.

'I'm sorry, Jen, but Maggie stumbled upon me when I was at the end of my tether. The last thing I wanted was to burden you. I had no idea how I was going to tell anyone, or even *if* I was going to tell anyone. You know me, bin it or bottle it and deal with it on your own. Maggie was just there at the wrong place at the wrong time.'

Jenny looked up at me through her tears.

'Sorry, Mags,' she sniffed loudly, wiping her eyes on her sleeve. 'I just fucking hate people not telling me stuff. And I especially fucking hate being the last to know!' she aimed at Pauline.

'OK. OK! Message received and understood!' Pauline conceded. 'Now stop beating the hell out of that pillow and yes, Maggie, I'd love a nightcap!'

Chapter Thirty-one

The following morning, Pauline and Timmy were leaving to go back to Pauline and Terry's place. In our bedroom Catherine was on her phone to Nico and looked like she was there for the duration.

I left her to it and wandered into Pauline's room where Timmy was rushing around trying to pack for her.

'Timmy, that's not even mine!' Pauline retrieved a half chewed teddy bear from her case and threw it over to Honey, who was lying panting in the corner of the bedroom.

'You don't have to pack for me, Timmy. In fact, I really wish you wouldn't.'

'You need taking care of. I'm not letting you overdo it.'

Pauline rolled her eyes at me.

I shrugged, unsure who to side with.

'Besides,' Timmy went on, 'If I'm going to be staying with you for a while, I'll need to earn my keep, so I want to help.'

'For a while? But I thought you were only staying…'

'No, no, I won't hear another word about it,' Timmy interrupted. 'You need help and I'm staying.'

'But you don't…'

'I know, I know. I don't know the area and there are no pubs and clubs but I'll be fine and, really, there's no need to thank me. We're family and that's what families do. They look after each other when they're in trouble.'

Now it was Pauline's turn to shrug, rather uncertainly.

I had a sneaking suspicion that Timmy might need Pauline a little more than she needed him.

'Well, I suppose I could phone Ter…'

'Good, well that's settled then, Terry's a crap carer anyway.'

Timmy hauled Pauline's suitcase off the bed and onto the floor, where it landed with a great thud. Righting it then wheeling it out through the bedroom door and on to the landing, he turned back. There was a tear in his eye.

'I know you think I'm being a drama queen over this but...' he hesitated, gave a small sniff and turned away, '...well that's just the way it's going to be, OK?' And off he went, bumping Pauline's case down the stairs.

'I think you've got yourself a live-in nurse,' I said.

'Seems that way, although I'm not entirely sure who's going to be the one doing most of the nursing.'

Downstairs, Jenny and her dad sat drinking tea and flicking through the papers at the kitchen table. I sat down to join them and wondered, not for the first time, when the subject of Luke would come up. No one had mentioned his name since we'd been back and I didn't want to be the one to do so. It was possible of course that Jenny had already spoken to her dad about him and had just forgotten to mention anything to the rest of us. In fact, why would she mention anything? Why should she think anyone but the Henderson family would be especially interested in when Luke was bringing his beautiful, blond, straight swingy-haired, slim, Nordic, ice-blue eyed, goddess of a fiancée back to taunt us all.

Spookily, as if Jenny had read my mind, she brought the subject up.

'Oh, Mags, I forgot to tell you. Remember I said that Luke was coming home?'

I caught my breath.

'Yes, I remem...'

But, as I started to answer, the doorbell sounded echoing around the house in resonant chimes. There was no chance then to finish the conversation as Honey, four puppies and Parliament the cat, came tearing through the kitchen heading for the hallway, skating, sliding and scrabbling their way across the wooden floor. And all apart from Parliament began barking and yapping madly at the partially visible figures silhouetted through the glass section of the front door.

Jenny scraped back her chair on the kitchen tiles.

'I'll go. It's probably some of those Jehovah's witnesses come to tell us that Christmas is bad for us.'

'They'll not be wrong,' I said ruefully. 'Last Christmas was extremely bad for me. I spent a fortune and my last credit card died.'

Mr H lowered the corner of his newspaper and peered over his reading glasses, frowning in confusion.

'I had to cut it in half,' I explained.

'Ah,' he said. 'The perils of modern day living.'

I heard the door being opened and voices carried through to the kitchen. I strained to hear what sounded like a man and a woman. I was right, moments later Tony and Laura entered the kitchen.

'Eejit forgot his keys,' Jenny announced sitting back down at the table.

Laura appeared ready for a workout. Her hair was up in a ponytail with a very annoying baby-pink scrunchie thing holding it in place. She had white flared drawstring shorts on, with baby-pink piping around the bottom of them, and her tiny little whiter than white pumps were matched up with little white and baby-pink socks. The only thing stopping her resemblance to an ice cream was the stripy blue and white tee shirt which clung to her (thank you, God) very small chest.

'Christ, anyone for tennis,' Jenny mocked, under her breath.

Tony, clearly unsettled, kept flicking his eyes over mine and then away again. My heart began pumping fast.

It transpired that he'd left his sunglasses the previous afternoon and we were all roped in to hunt for them. Jenny, Tony, Laura and I went from room to room, upturning cushions and lifting up chairs and sofas; discovering coins and biscuit crumbs and our fair share of dog hair. Mr H joined in and unearthed his old reading glasses from down behind a cushion.

'Marvellous! I'd wondered where these little fellas went!' he announced happily.

'But the new ones are really trendy, Dad,' Jenny said. 'They make you look like Sean Connery.'

'The namej Bond, Jamej Bond,' he chortled.

'Don't call *us,* Dad.'

Tearing about all over the place, sniffing frantically, the puppies had obviously decided we were playing a game and insisted on helping us, which led on to us having to play hunt the puppy. No sooner had we discovered one in the downstairs loo, another disappeared and it turned out to be a much longer 'game' than we'd anticipated. And still no sign of the sunglasses.

'For goodness sake, Tony,' Laura eventually called from the hall. 'They're in your jacket pocket.'

'*To-ny!*' Jenny and her dad groaned. I would have done the same but I was still at the Ignoring Stage.

We traipsed back into the kitchen and Laura joined us, shaking her head in disbelief.

'Honestly. Men! Sometimes I think we have to do everything for them. And fancy not looking in there first!'

Huffily Tony mumbled, 'I'm surprised *you* didn't look, if you knew how unreliable men were.' He pulled up a chair and sat down at the kitchen table.

We all sat and joined him but I made sure to take a seat as far away as possible, avoiding eye contact.

Tony's comment apparently flew over Laura's head, as she pranced over and flicked the switch of the kettle.

'Nothing like a nice cup of camomile tea, to soothe a crisis.'

Mr H swivelled round clearly a little alarmed.

'Ah, now, um, I'm afraid we don't actually have such a delicacy.'

'Not a problem,' she sing-songed, in a baby-pink voice, 'I never go anywhere without them.'

Tony sat quietly, idly examining his fingernails while Laura enthused about infusing.

'I've peppermint if anyone would prefer? *So* good for soothing the tummy.'

Mr H was clearly finding all this tea business a little 'New Age'.

'But of course camomile is top of the tree for calming the nerves,' Laura continued, taking a deep breath of fresh air through the open top of the stable door.

'Just what I need,' Tony grumbled.

As the kettle boiled, Laura came and stood behind Tony, putting her hands territorially on his shoulders.

'So, where are you staying?' I asked her, thinking I should at least try to be amicable.

'Oh, my mother lives quite close by in Buckley. That's where we met, all those years ago.'

'Really? What happened?' *So shoot me for being curious.*

I was aware of Tony's foot tapping somewhere under the table.

Laura puffed up like a peacock.

'Well, you see, coincidentally, I went to university with Luke, such a duck that boy!' I felt my stomach tighten. 'And Luke and I got talking and he suggested, because I lived so close, that I should get in touch with Tony when I came back in the holidays. And I did, and... well...' Laura sighed dramatically, '... the rest, as they say, is history.' She gave Tony a hug around his neck, closing her eyes in ecstasy.

Tony shifted uncomfortably in his seat.

'He's such a love, apart from when he's losing things. She scrunched up her nose causing it to crinkle at the bridge and proceeded to playfully pinch his cheek and wiggle it between her thumb and forefinger. 'Such a *silly Billy*,' she said in voice which should have only been used for babies and very small children. Tony's face was a picture of pent-up annoyance and I saw a muscle clench in his strong jaw.

Jenny, beside me, pretended to scratch her foot and made throwing-up gestures under the table at me.

Giving him another squeeze round the neck Laura proceeded to come round the front of him and sit on his lap. Honestly, what on earth did he see in her? I could imagine her being one of those cheesy models that jump out of cakes with a loud 'Ta-da!' on bachelor nights and I would have placed money on her having been a cheerleader.

Under the table I noted her alarmingly slender ankles. I reckoned that both her ankles put together might well equal one of mine. And although no one could see, I saw fit to hide mine under my chair.

'Careful, Laura!' Tony said. 'You don't want to crush my sunglasses now that you've found them.' He tipped her forward and pulled the sunglasses out from his lap. She had little option but to move back to stand behind him again, putting her hands back onto his shoulder. A brief look of annoyance was replaced by a simpering smile.

Tony's phone rang then and, as he answered it, I noticed it was a different model from the one he'd had before. He stood up and moved away slightly to get some privacy. Suddenly I was aware of Laura's dagger-like eyes boring into me as I watched him, so I quickly shifted my attention. She then proceeded to tell us all about how she and Tony had got together and fallen in love and how silly they'd been to ever split up and how lucky it had been that Tony had seen sense and come back to her.

Finishing his call and rejoining us at the table, Tony gave her a look that I couldn't read but, whatever it meant, he seemed far from happy.

My phone bleeped out a message.

'Bet that's Greg,' Jenny said. 'When you going out then?'

'Um, nothing's finalised,' I faltered blushing hard and resisting the temptation to check my phone.

'I thought you arranged things last night?' Tony's tone was blatantly sarcastic and for a moment our eyes met.

He stood up quickly making his chair scrape loudly on the kitchen floor, causing Laura to have to step back.

'I'm going to watch the tennis. Coming, Dad?' He sounded annoyed. Mr H was clearly relieved.

'Marvellous idea.'

'I'm off to phone John,' Jenny announced.

The idea of being left alone with Laura filled me with dread, so I excused myself too and said I had to shower. Climbing the stairs, I checked my phone. Jenny had been right. The text was from Greg.

'Mags! Call me! You know you want to ;-) Greg xxx'

Grrrrr.

Then, I noticed a second message. It was from Mum. However, on closer inspection, I realised it was from Dad using her phone. Strictly speaking it was his phone but he'd only got it on Mum's insistence. And she'd only got it so she could show off to her next door neighbour and so-called friend Mrs Partridge, whose husband wouldn't allow her to have a mobile phone of her own. When I'd asked Mum why, she had explained that Mrs Partridge 'although I wasn't to breathe a word…' had an awful habit of calling those premium rate numbers you find in the backs of women's magazines. The ones that play you recorded messages from men with names like Conan the Barbarian and Jed the Jedi claiming to be able to 'take you up to the dizzying heights of sexual fantasy'. Having met Mrs Partridge, I found this hard to believe. She had a mono bust and wore an omni-present rain mac. Although maybe that was some sort of clue?

Anyway, the reason Mum had wanted to lord the phone in front of Mrs Partridge was because she had, allegedly, made unwelcome advances to Dad at last year's annual golf club dinner. Right after his election to the committee had been announced.

I read the text.

Maggie, your mother is making me type this to you. Please call her, or I'm not allowed to play golf! Love Dad xxx p.s whatever she says as long as you are happy, I'm happy x.

Bless him.

I headed for our bedroom but Catherine was still on the phone to Nico. So I went and sat in Pauline's room and composed myself to make the dreaded call.

Their phone rang for ages before finally Mum picked it up.

'What took you so long?' I asked.

'Your father was his usual lazy self and didn't get up in time. So I had to get it instead!'

'But it's your phone Mum!'

'Yes, but he pays the bill.'

Exactly!

'Anyway, never mind about that, what's all this nonsense about *temping*?'

She'd made it sound like a dirty word. Anything other than permanent, secure and with plenty of prospects had Mum declaring that I was selling my soul to the devil. The only other acceptable option was to find myself a rich man.

'Mum, there's nothing wrong with temping. In fact, it has a lot of benefits.'

'Hmmph. That remains to be seen. So, what exactly happened to your last job?'

'Um… things weren't working out.'

'Weren't working out how?'

Let's see, first there was me being late all the time, I kept coming in with hangovers – and if I'm honest my work suffered – once I came in with blue hair, I was generally bored, the boss hated me, oh and I think the final straw was I turned up for work with a black eye. In the end they just sacked me.

'No real *prospects*,' I said using a parental buzzword.

In the pause that followed I could hear Mum's brain ticking over. She sighed, a resigned sigh.

'Well, why didn't you look around while you still had a proper job?'

'Um… I… felt it was only right to let someone else have a chance. It wasn't really fair to stay when I wasn't happy. Besides,' I said, getting into the story, 'the more positions I try, the more chance I have of finding a job with *real prospects*. It often happens that temping positions end up in a more permanent position. Something a lot better paid with loads more *prospects*.'

Another pause. I knew she'd be weighing up what I'd said to see whether it fitted into her ideal model of the world.

'I don't know why you can't just find yourself a nice rich man and be done with it. You wouldn't have to work at all then!'

I rolled my eyes at the bedroom wall.

'Maybe I'll meet a man at one of the firms I join.'

She inhaled in quick excitement.

'Ooh, might you get a job in one of those swanky City firms? You know the ones with those tasteful glass fronts and impressive gold signs outside and receptionists who sit behind long high desks and look important?'

'Probably. And who knows, they might even have glass lifts that go up the outside of the building,' I said.

'Oh, I love them. Mr Fairweather from across the close works in a place like that. Such a lovely man; he drives one of those sporty Porch cars. Mind you, it's a bit hip for him I think. If you ask me, they suit a younger man. Maybe your next man will drive a Porch.'

'I think you'll find they are called Porsches, Mum, not porches.'

'Whatever,' Mum dismissed, sounding like she'd been watching *The Jeremy Kyle Show* again. Daytime TV had taken on a whole new meaning since Dad had finally given in to them getting cable. Mainly because he realised what Mum hadn't. That there were a large number of channels dedicated purely to sport.

Anyway, my fate was sealed. I was to work in the City, travel to my office via a glass lift and take my lunch breaks in exclusive wine bars until I met the man of my mother's dreams, and lived happily ever after, spawning grandchildren called Grace, Olivia and Thomas, for Mum to parade around in front of Mr Fairweather's Porsche, Mrs Partridge's phone-free front room window and any other unsuspecting neighbours whose noses she might want to put out of joint.

Ending the phone call with promises to pop over on my way back to London, I headed off to have a wash and clean my teeth.

As I walked passed Luke's old room, my stomach did one of its unhelpful lurches. I was suddenly catapulted back in time to when Luke and I had somehow managed to be in the house alone.

We'd been lying on Luke's bed together and Luke had been leaning over me and playing with my hair. Despite my protestations that it had a life of its own and was more like a mad wig than real hair, he was having nothing of it. In fact, Luke had a habit of making my hair seem... sexy. He'd said that it made him want to put his face in it and breathe in the smell of me. You might think that sounds weird but, to me, it sounded so romantic. The idea that somebody might want to sniff me was very erotic, even at my ripe young age. I remembered how he'd threaded his finger through one of the many naturally forming ringlets then pulled his finger back out and laughed as the hair sprung away from him and straight back into place again.

'One day you'll love your hair,' he'd assured me.

'One day, I'll find a way to straighten my hair,' I'd assured him.

'One day our kids will all have mad, sexy, hair like yours,' he'd insisted.

I think we'd probably kissed a lot after that.

The thought of kissing Luke jolted me back to the present. I had to stop this damned daydreaming about the past. After all, Luke's kids were going to have white blond, straight, swingy hair that fell immaculately back into place whenever they shook their heads. They were going to feature in Nordic magazine adverts for minimalist furniture. Luke and Sian, as the doting parents, would be lounging happily on their bed, holding each other fondly and gazing at their two point four (or whatever the stats are in Sweden) children as they laughed and played at the foot of the bed, lapping up their roles as child models and looking forward to successful careers in merchant banking or as managing directors of top fashion houses. Kids with mad hair? Pah!

Grabbing my toothbrush and toothpaste from the bedroom and making pretend snogging actions in front of Catherine who was still glowing into her mobile, I went to the bathroom and closed the door behind me.

Catching site of my face in the mirror I realised how brown I was. Actually, I was quite pleased with the reflection. Not a sign of mad hair in sight, just smooth, straightened, long dark locks. I did my teeth and was just marvelling at how white they looked against my skin, when a knock at the door made me jump.

'Just a mo…' I began but the door, which I'd apparently forgotten to lock, opened slowly. Whoever it was, was coming in anyway!

In came Tony's head, followed by Tony's body.

I stood there unsure what to do.

He shut the door quietly behind him.

'I need to talk to you.'

'I'll be down in a minute, Tony. You can talk to me all you like.'

He shook his head.

'Not in front of the others, I mean I need to talk to *you*, *properly*, about…'

'The fact that your wedding plans are back on again?' I challenged, snappily, facing the mirror again and pretending to check my make-up.

'No. Well yes, but it's not what you think.'

My reflection frowned at him.

'Listen, like I tried to tell you yesterday, it's not how it looks. Laura and I aren't really back together.'

'You're right. It does look like you are back together. In fact, from every single angle, I'd say it looks exactly like that.' I began washing my hands.

'Maggie, for goodness sake, why are you doing that?' he said.

'My hands are dirty. I thought you were the clever one in the family,' I said sarcastically.

Again, I pretended to check my make-up in the mirror, wondering how much longer I could do so, without having to turn and face him again.

'Don't mock me. You know what I mean. Please don't be like this, Maggie, I'm trying to explain.'

I turned to him very aware he was only a few feet away.

'Go on then, Tony. Why don't you enlighten me? Tell me exactly how things *aren't* how they seem, hmmm?'

'Just don't listen to what Laura says. There's a lot you don't know.'

'Such as…?'

He took a step towards me and I felt my nerves jump to attention.

'Oh come on, Maggie, you must know how I feel about you! Why on earth would I suddenly go back to Laura?'

'I don't know. Isn't that what you're supposed to be explaining?' I sighed loudly. 'I just don't get you Tony. One minute we're starting to date and you're insisting I text you and keep in touch while I'm on holiday, and then next…'

'Yes. And on that note, exactly why *didn't* you text me?'

'I did!' I said, indignantly.

'Hardly.'

'Well, you didn't either!'

'Ahhh, so you do care.' A teasing smile formed on his lips. He stepped even closer and I could smell his musky aftershave.

He put his hand up and brushed my cheek with the tip of his finger. I stood rooted to the spot.

'An eyelash,' he explained, lowering his hand to rest briefly on my shoulder before letting it drop.

'Maggie, I know how this seems but just listen.' He took hold of my hand as I stood at the basin.

'While you were away, Laura had a bit of a breakdown.'

I must have looked shocked.

'Don't worry she'll be OK but, right now, she's got it into her head that we're back on.' He sighed. 'The thing is, I went round to her place to pick up some of my stuff that I'd left there and …well, it was obvious she was in a bad way and needed looking after. And like a mug, I did the looking after. I suppose I felt I owed her. After all, according to her, I was the reason she was so unhappy.'

'And I s'pose you felt so bad, you went back to her!'

'No! I've told you, it's all in her imagination.' He appeared genuinely fraught and ran his fingers through his hair.

'If I'm honest, and it's pretty tough to say this, I think she's losing it.'

I thought of Laura, downstairs with the others, ice-creaming her way through her camomile tea. Could she really be losing her marbles? Could she have been so upset that she'd formulated a life in her head that didn't exist? It didn't seem possible.

'Hang on, Tony. You're a smart guy. You wouldn't keep up this so-called pretence if there wasn't some truth in it. It would do more harm than good, particularly long term.'

'I know what it sounds like…but it is exactly that: pretence. And you're right.' He shook his head. 'I've been a class idiot.'

I shifted uneasily.

'You see, I feel pretty guilty about the way things ended between us. I wasn't exactly Mr Nice Guy, on more than one occasion, and I guess I saw this as an opportunity to make things right. I said things she needed to hear, to make her happy and to make me feel better about myself.'

'What… like "Will you marry me Laura?"?'

'No, not like that, I've told you. That's her stuff.'

'Well, what then?'

'I just tried to comfort her you know; saying it would all be OK. I wanted to help her see that things would be fine again. She took that to mean that *we'd* be fine again and clung to me like this messed up kid. Back came the guilt with a vengeance and, somehow, I ended up going along with it. Her mum told me she'd been in a right state since we split. I certainly didn't want to make her any worse.'

'So you decided to let her think you two were back on and going to spend the rest of your lives together. Don't you think that's going to be worse for her in the long run?'

Tony tutted, 'It all got a bit out of hand.'

'I should think it did!'

'Worst of all, now her mum thinks we're back together!' He grinned then.

'It's not funny, Tony.'

'I know! Her mum's terrifying! I don't know what to do! Stick it out for the duration with a complete loony or finish it and get my bollocks lopped off!'

I knew I shouldn't have but I couldn't help the corners of my mouth twitching.

'So you see I'm stuck.'

He was so close now; I could feel his breath on my face.

'I've got Laura downstairs, telling whoever'll listen that we're set for church bells and bridesmaids and all I want to do is be up here with you.'

My heart was pounding faster by the second.

'And…' he went on, 'to add insult to injury, you're wearing that sexy little sundress and taunting me with those lovely long brown legs.'

With that, he moved his hand slowly across to my thigh and began caressing me, gently, through my dress. He held my gaze and, for a few moments, I forgot to breathe. I felt my dress being lifted slightly and his fingers circled expertly down the material and onto my skin, creeping gently round to find the softness of my inner thigh. I inhaled quickly and my breathing became short and quick. There was no mistaking my reaction to Tony's touch. I felt aroused. Despite everything he was telling me, I couldn't help it. There was something in the way he smiled at me; a knowing smile; a confident smile. Like he knew he had won me over; like he wanted to tease me, gently, until he had me just where he wanted me.

'It's you I want, Maggie,' his voice was husky.

He leant forward, put his hand behind the back of my head and guided my mouth towards his. Without losing eye contact, he kissed me lightly on the lips. I felt my mouth open to him and, as I did so, his other hand grasped my backside with sudden urgency and he pulled me roughly towards his groin, forcing me to arch my back.

But, despite the unmistakeable ardour, despite the feelings of lust that were now coursing uncontrollably through my body, from somewhere within me, a little voice reminded me that he had a fiancée downstairs, albeit a crazy one. It was no good, I couldn't do this. It didn't feel right.

I broke away but I wasn't going far. Tony's hands remained tightly gripped.

'Tony, stop! We can't.'

'Can't we?' His eyes remained fixed on mine. His mouth twitched, mischievously, as he held me to him, his left hand still full of my right buttock, which I was trying desperately to keep clenched. *Why, oh why hadn't I done more swimming?*

'Laura's downstairs and, whatever you say, you've got to tell her. Not because of me but because of her. She needs to know if you're not serious.' This time, I managed to pull away.

I allowed my breathing to calm down to normal and went to rinse my hands; anything to deviate from what was happening.

'There's no point in washing your hands again, Maggie. I know you feel it too.'

I didn't reply.

Tony caught hold of me again and pulled me back to him, kissing me and forcing my mouth open teasing his tongue around mine.

But suddenly, without warning, from behind us, someone opened the door. I froze.

Breaking away from the kiss, I looked over Tony's shoulder but whoever it was had gone.

'Shit!' Tony said, swivelling round.

'Who was that?' I gasped.

He went to the door, locking it. He seemed as unnerved as I felt.

'Fuck knows.'

'Why didn't you lock the door?' I accused, shaken and shocked.

'I must have had other things on my mind.'

'Do you think it was Laura?'

He thought for a moment and then visibly calmed down.

'No, it wasn't Laura.' His confidence returned. 'If it had been Laura, she'd have come right in and yelled the place down.'

I breathed a heavy sigh of relief.

'Don't worry, Maggie. She won't be having a go at you.'

'Why should I worry about that?'

He sat down on the edge of the bath and paused for a moment before answering.

'The thing is, she kind of knows about you and me.'

'How!?'

'I told her.'

'You *what?*'

'Hear me out. She found my phone. Or more to the point, she went looking for my phone. I suppose she wanted to find out what I'd been up to since we'd split up. Anyway, when she found it, she read one of your texts.'

'And?'

'And she wanted to meet you.'

'Meet me?'

''Fraid so.'

'What on earth have you told her?'

'I said we went out. I didn't want to lie.'

'Oh you didn't want to lie? Is that right? Well you sure as hell seem to have got yourself into several big whoppers at the moment.'

He pulled a sheepish face. 'It'll be fine, don't worry.'

I thought back to the phone I'd seen him use earlier.

'Where did your old phone go?'

'Under Laura's foot, several times! She wasn't best pleased I can tell you.

'So that's why she's been shooting daggers at me.'

'I imagine so.'

'Well… is she going to say anything?'

'Na, doubt it. It's not her style. She just wanted to see what the competition was, that's all.'

'Oh what a relief,' I said sarcastically, wondering how wary I should be of a mad woman who stamped on mobile phones.

'Listen, Maggie, don't worry about it. I've just got to hang in there for a while and make sure she's OK. To be honest, I am worried about her. She threatened all sorts when I went round.'

'Meaning?'

'You know, the worst.'

'*Suicide?*' I asked incredulously.

'Pretty much.'

Now it was my turn to run my fingers through my hair. What was I doing here? Tony was checking his reflection in the mirror. He wiped his mouth of any traces of my lipstick and straightened himself up. 'I'll have to go downstairs now Mags. She'll be wondering where I am. But I need to see you, to talk to you properly without people walking in on us. Will you meet me?' his eyes pleaded.

My expression must have shown I wasn't sure.

'Maggie, please. You deserve more than a sneaky meeting in a bathroom for goodness sake.'

Well, that much was true.

'Please?'

'OK,' I heard myself say.

'Thank you. It'll be OK, you'll see. Can you text me tomorrow? My number's the same.' I frowned, taken aback. After all, surely *he* should have been contacting *me*!

He pulled an apologetic face. 'Thing is, your number, along with everyone else's, is splatted to pieces on my old phone. Stupidly I didn't have a backup and I'm not very good at guessing people's mobile phone numbers.'

I tutted. 'Yes, all right then.'

I watched him walk to the door and unlock it before turning back to me.

'I think we'd better keep this between you and me, just until I can sort things out.'

'Someone saw us though!'

'I'll deal with that. But shtumm for now, eh?'

I nodded and, as I did so, Laura's voice sounded up the stairs.

'Tony, hurry up, what on earth are you doing in there?' she called out.

Before I knew what was happening, I heard her footsteps mount the stairs.

'Shit!' he whispered, locking the door again. 'She's coming up here. You'll have to hide.'

'*Whaaat?*'

'Quick, it's the only way. Get in the airing cupboard!'

'You must be...'

But, before I could finish protesting, Tony had opened the door and was pushing me inside.

In I went, reeling from the imposition. Luckily it was large enough for me to stand up in. Beside me in the darkness, I could feel the heat from the boiler and smell the clean, warm, towels and sheets.

Silently, with my ear to the closed door, I listened. Laura knocked on the bathroom door then tried the handle.

'Tony, open the door, you've been up here for ages! What's taking you so long?' she shrilled.

Honestly, talk about not respecting someone's privacy. What was her problem?

'Coming, Laura.' Sounding cool as a cucumber, he flushed the loo and put the seat down. 'Won't be a minute.'

'Hurry up, I need the loo!'

Excellent! She was coming in. Now I was going to be subjected to her going to the toilet while I was a prisoner in the airing cupboard!

Tony unlocked the door and in she came.

Despite everything, I had to bite my lip as I felt the urge to laugh. I mean there I was hiding like a mischievous schoolgirl!

'At last!' Laura's voice shrilled.

I heard the toilet seat being lifted up again and making contact with the cistern. I heard the seat move as she sat on it and I held my breath as I waited for the sound of peeing to come. Catherine was going to fall about when I told her.

'Can we hurry up and get out of here, Tony? I just want to get home. I can't stand being here for a minute longer. You know how difficult all this is for me. I'm dying to say something.'

'Just leave it, Laura. We'll talk about it in the car, OK?'

So, she was obviously itching to have a go at me. It wasn't my bloody fault that she'd found my text in his bloody phone. OK, we'd been out but so what? They weren't together at the time and she had no right to think badly of me. A thought crossed my mind. No wonder she'd been so keen to get me to see Greg again.

I listened as she flushed the loo, washed her hands and they both left. The bathroom became silent again. For a while, I waited in the warmth and silence of the airing cupboard to make sure the coast was clear. I was about to open the cupboard door when I heard the bathroom door open again, and someone else came in. I slunk back holding my breath. Who was it? I listened hard.

It was a man. The footsteps were heavy; definitely a man. Timmy? Mr H? I heard the sound of the seat going up. Trousers were unzipped and I had to stand there while he went for a pee. Thankfully, only a pee!

Whoever it was finished, flushed and then washed his hands. I remained as still as I could. The room outside became silent and I strained to hear what was going on. Nothing. Just silence. Had he left? Several moments went passed and I stood there unable to move or breathe properly.

Then I heard a floorboard creak outside the airing cupboard and I let out a little gasp as, suddenly, the door was opened and light flooded in.

There in front of me, tall, tanned, blond and as handsome as ever, was Luke.

Luke stood there staring at me. I stared back, unable to think of a reasonable excuse for being in his father's airing cupboard. He narrowed his eyes slightly then shook his head. His expression seemed somehow... disappointed? Whatever it was, it wasn't good. Without a word, he turned and walked away leaving the cupboard door wide open.

For several long moments I stayed there, stunned and rooted to the spot. Then, dumbly, I stepped back out into the bathroom shutting the door behind me. Going over to the bathroom door, I locked it and stood with my back against it, numb with shock. Gradually though my brain started to function and, like a Polaroid photo, realisation began to develop. The more it developed, the faster reality came into focus. Then with a sudden whoosh, it hit me. Luke was home from Sweden. Luke was here, in this house ...and very probably with Sian! Luke had found me in the airing cupboard and Luke, therefore, must have known I'd been in here with Tony. *He* must have been the one to come in while Tony had been kissing me. OK... while Tony and I had been kissing.

I began to wash my hands – again. It was becoming a habit. Maybe I was in the early stages of that awful condition that caused people to have to wash their hands a hundred times before they felt safe. I wasn't entirely sure that anything would make me feel particularly safe right then. I dried them on the hand towel beside the basin, hoping that in fact three times would offer some sort of haven. I realised that it was the same slightly damp towel that Luke had just dried his hands on. It was disconcerting. Like in some way, Luke and I had touched hands. I folded my arms protectively across my body.

The question, or at least one of the questions, was: what was going to happen when I went downstairs? I considered possibilities:

1. Luke could have told the whole family, including the Nordic Nymphet, about Tony and me and they'd be waiting there, lips pursed, brows furrowed, ready to launch into a tirade of abuse as soon as I walked in the room.
2. Luke might have kept his mouth shut but there would be an awful tension in the room, which people would start to question.
3. Laura would immediately know something was up and leap up and start brandishing vases around and smashing them, before hurling herself towards me with a piece of broken glass to slit my throat with!
4. Due to unforeseen circumstances, Luke had gone back to Sweden,

taking his... Swedish, Oscar-winning, Mount Everest conquering, Peanuts & Eggcups World Champion, fiancée with him. That would be the favourable option.

The dreadful realisation that Sian could be downstairs hit me properly. Everything else seemed to pale into insignificance by comparison. I looked in the mirror again. How would I compare? It was as if my reflection was saying: 'It's no good, you know you're only covering up what's natural. Your hair's a great big curly bush. One Ice-Queen glance from the blond bombshell from the land of Swedes and you'll be sussed out and branded a fraud.'

Damn those Swedes.

I listened intently at the bathroom door, my ear pressed up against the frosted glass. I held my breath in the hope I'd be able to catch any conversation that might be going on.

There was the distant sound of a shower and I could hear the grandfather clock ticking loudly, echoing through the hall but that was it; nothing else except for the sound of my heart banging frantically up against my ribcage. I allowed myself to exhale.

It was no good. I couldn't stay in there. I had to go downstairs.

I composed myself and went to unlock the door, just as I heard footsteps coming down the landing.

Shit, could it be Luke again? Whoever it was tried the door handle and rattled it both ways.

'Sorry!' A voice apologised from the other side of the glass.

Catherine!

I quickly unlocked the door.

'Cat,' I hissed, 'get in here quick!'

I leant out and practically pulled her arm out of its socket, dragging a dismayed Catherine inside the bathroom and shutting the door quickly behind her.

'What on earth...?'

'Have you been downstairs?' I demanded urgently.

'Not yet, I was on my way via the loo. Why? What's going...?'

'Shhh, just listen.'

I told her what had happened.

'Was it a fully blown snog?' she asked eagerly, clasping her hands together.

'Pretty much.'

'Tongues and everything.'

'Yes.'

'How exciting.' Her face was a picture of glee.

'And you're sure it was Luke that saw you?'

'How else would he have known it was me in the bloody airing cupboard?'

'You're probably right, unless...'

'Unless what?'

'Well, unless he meant to leave the bathroom and got the wrong door.'

I frowned.

'Yes, because that's very likely isn't it. He was born and grew up in this house and suddenly, just because he's been away for a while, he inexplicably forgets the layout of his dad's house and tries to make his exit via the airing bloody cupboard!'

'All right, I'm only trying to help.'

'I know but you're not.'

Seeing her crestfallen face, I rubbed her arm in apology.

'Maybe he wanted a clean towel,' she suggested.

'Well, if he did, he sure as hell didn't reach in and get one. In fact, he looked exactly like a man who knew that, as soon as he opened the door, he'd find me behind it.'

'A bit like knowing what you're getting on Christmas morning when you open your presents.'

'In that case, he didn't seem particularly pleased at what he found.'

'I was never one of those people.'

'Which people?'

'The ones who like to sneak a peek at their Christmas presents before they're actually given to them. They go searching for them in all the possible hiding places and when they find them, tear a little corner of the paper, or carefully unpeel the...'

'Cat!'

'What?'

'What's this got to do with Luke?'

She appeared momentarily puzzled.

'I don't know... it seemed relevant when I started it.'

'What am I going to do? What if he's told everyone downstairs that I've been snogging Tony?'

'Why would he do that? Laura's here.'

'Exactly!'

'No, he wouldn't do that, Luke's not a stirrer, never has been. He's a peacemaker. That's one of the things you used to love abou…' She hesitated. 'Sorry, I didn't mean to bring that up again.'

'S'OK.' I shrugged staring down at my feet.

'But you know what I mean. Luke is more likely to say nothing to keep Laura from finding out. Besides, he wouldn't want to embarrass everyone. If anyone was likely to cause a scene about something like this, it would be Tony.'

I looked at her incomprehensibly.

'Tony? Why Tony?'

'Oh you know Tony. He's OK really but he's always been a bit of a drama queen.'

'D'you think?'

She must have realised she wasn't being very tactful.

'Well, not in a really bad way but you must remember what he was like when he was younger.'

'Must I?'

'Sure. He was always acting up and trying to get his dad's attention.'

'Was he?'

'Yes. In fact, he was either playing up or sulking.'

I wasn't sure I liked the sound of this.

'I don't remember that.'

Catherine saw my expression and changed tack.

'I'm sure he's different now though,' she added. 'He's bound to have grown up a lot. Look, all I'm saying is, Luke's not the kind of man to make a scene or cause trouble, that's all.'

'S'pose.'

I glanced in the mirror again and went to wash my hands, but stopped myself just in time.

'Do you think she'll be better looking than me?' I asked quietly.

'Who?'

'The gorgeous Sian, that's who.'

Catherine was clearly bewildered. 'Who said anything about her being gorgeous?'

'All Swedes are gorgeous. I think it's the hair. Stick some long, straight, white blond hair on a woman and she's turning heads before she's even walked into a room.'

'What about Ulrika Johnsson? She's not *gorgeous*. Oh actually, she has got a certain something,' she said thoughtfully.

'Exactly.'

'I think it's her hai... oh.'

'EXACTLY!'

'I can't think of another Swedish...oh yes! There's that Malin someone who was on The Proposal with Sandra Bull...' Catherine's trailed off.

'Good looking?'

'...a bit.' She had the good grace to look apologetic.

Catherine pulled a resigned face. 'Yeah...I see what you mean now. All right, what about Carolina Kluft?'

'Who?' I frowned.

'She's a Swedish athlete. I wouldn't call her gorgeous.'

'She's bound to have some foreign blood and is only part Swedish on her great grandfather's side. Anyway, how do you know any Swedish athletes?'

'I read the papers,' she said indignantly.

'No, you don't.'

Catherine paused.

'OK, I don't. But she was on a game show the other day and she's got the same birthday as my sister so I remembered her name. Anyway, what about Brigitte Nielsen? She's *certainly* not gorgeous.'

'No, but she's terrifying! And some men find that a turn on.'

Catherine shook her head.

'Those Abba women... oh, no, bad example.'

'Exactly! Swedish women all have *something,* whatever that something might be; even if it's only by reputation.'

'Maggie, have you ever met any Swedish women?'

I shuffled my feet, looking down at the floor.

'Not exactly.'

'Not exactly?'

'OK... no, I haven't. But I've seen those ads for Ikea kitchens and stuff and they've all got beautiful Swedish people in them.'

'Yes, but they're all models, Maggie. Models are paid to be beautiful.'

'And thin.'

'And thin,' she agreed reluctantly. 'But who's to say Sian's a model?'

'Can you imagine Luke going out with an old dog?' I pointed out.

She thought for a moment.

'No, but neither can I imagine him going out with some woman just because she's beautiful on the outside. Luke needs a woman who's individual, independent, beautiful inside *and* out, and who makes him laugh. He needs someone like you.'

I blushed.

'Have you ever heard of a funny Swede?' she asked.

'No, but I've met a few amusing cauliflowers in my time! Boom boom!'

'See! There you go. You're funny!'

She had a point.

None of the people in the Ikea catalogues were guffawing their heads off. You never caught Abba cracking jokes on stage and I was pretty certain Bjorn Borg hadn't served up a smile since nineteen seventy-seven.

I relaxed a little.

'So what shall I do?'

'Go down and face the music.'

I sincerely hoped the music wasn't Abba.

Clattering noisily down the wooden staircase with Catherine by my side, we were met at the bottom by Pauline and Timmy.

'We're off,' Pauline explained, when I eyed her suitcase.

'We were just coming up to say goodbye.' Timmy bent down to peel off a piece of sticky label from Pauline's case, which had got caught on the wheel.

'I'm surprised your ears weren't burning,' he said to our feet.

I reeled in horror. Was he talking to me? Had Luke said something?

'What do you mean?' Catherine asked as he stood up.

'All that time on your mobile to lurver boy, you're bound to be radioactive by now!'

Thank God!

'Have you said your goodbyes?' Catherine asked.

'Yes, and did you know, Luke's back!' Timmy swooned. 'To die for, that man!'

Jenny came out then.

'Haven't you gone yet!?'

'Thanks!' Pauline replied.

'Tony and Laura are going as well. I was just coming up to get you two,' she aimed at Catherine and me. 'You've been causing a right stir.'

'Who me?' I squeaked.

'Yup; we were trying to remember what your middle name was. Couldn't for the life of us think of it.'

'It's Geraldine,' I admitted, reluctantly. Whatever bad stuff I'd ever done to my parents in my life, they'd more than paid me back before I'd even come into the world. In fact, I reckoned I still owed them.

'Ha ha ha ha,' Jenny laughed. 'I know, we remembered in the end. I said it was like a boy's name but the girl's equivalent. Actually, it was Luke who told us.'

My stomach lurched.

'Oh by the way, I still didn't get round to telling you. Luke's back! And you'll never guess…'

Just at that point, Mr H came into the hall interrupting her flow.

Aghhhh! Was she ever going to get to finish her sentence?

'Are you still here?'

Pauline rolled her eyes.

'Still here Mr H.'

He was followed by Tony and Laura. No sign of Luke. He was no doubt keeping Sian company in the lounge. Maybe he'd been translating for her. After all, she might not be able to speak English. I felt a quiet satisfaction at this thought and had a momentary vision of me using really difficult words in all my conversations, so she wouldn't be able to understand a word. Unfortunately, then, I began to feel guilty. Damn, I'd make a useless bitch.

Suddenly I locked eyes with Tony. His face softened, but I had to turn away.

'It's been wonderful seeing you again Mr Henderson, sorry, *Rex*.' Laura simpered.

'Such a *lovely* home.'

'Pop in anytime. Open house, you know that.' He firmly embraced his son and kissed Laura on both cheeks.

'Oh yes, and you must come over to us, especially when…' Tony shot her a look that stopped her short.

'Cheers, Dad, great to see you again. I'll be up to stay soon,' Tony smiled warmly and I felt my stomach flip.

'Thank you for the mint tea, my dear,' Mr H. said to Laura. 'I'll certainly give it a try but, speaking candidly if I may, I'm not so sure it'll be quite me.'

'Three to four minutes in a cup of boiling water. You'll see; perfect for the tum.' She cupped and gently patted her 'tum' protectively. Tony, seemingly impatient now, hurried her out the door.

Silly cow.

I hugged Pauline tightly and promised to go down and visit her soon.

Finally, the cars had been waved off and the front door was closed. The inevitable time had come.

'Cup of tea anyone?' Mr H offered.

'As long as it's not that peppermint shite!' Jenny said scornfully.

'Jennifer!'

'Sorry, Dad.'

'I have to say, I rather agree though,' he chortled.

We trooped into the kitchen; still no sign of the happy couple. Jenny, Catherine and I sat down at the kitchen table, while Mr H put the kettle on and started taking mugs out of an overhead cupboard.

'Where's Luke disappeared to, Dad?' Jenny asked him.

'Garden I think.'

'What do you reckon's going on with Sian then?' she went on.

Catherine and I shared puzzled expressions.

'Shit!' She whacked her palm on her forehead. 'You still don't know do you!'

At that moment, Luke's head appeared over the stable door. Blond and tanned, his white tee shirt smeared with earth and bits of grass.

Noooooo! Would I ever find out what was going on?

'Hi, Luke!' Cat said, 'Couldn't keep away then?'

He smiled. 'Something like that.'

His gaze shifted to mine.

'Hello, Maggie,' he said pointedly. 'Been a while, huh?'

I blushed.

'Ages,' I mumbled down to the table.

Luke turned his attention to his father. 'There are so many apples on the ground,

Dad. We could make cider.'

'Or apple tea,' Jenny said. 'I'm sure Laura would approve.'

Luke looked perplexed.

'Long story,' she explained.

Where was Sian? I glanced through to the lounge, trying to catch sight of her, but the door wasn't open enough to see in properly.

'Cider it is then. I'll go and get the apples in.'

'Yeah, go on, Luke,' Jenny said, clearly delighted. I'll get John onto it; he'll be putty in my hands.'

'Jennifer!' Rex said.

'Sorry, Dad.'

Luke disappeared outside again.

'What were you saying about Sian?' Catherine whispered.

Jenny urged us into a huddle over the table. Catherine and I moved forward, our eyes wide.

'He's only gone and dumped her!'

Chapter Thirty-two

So, it was one thing Luke being home and sporting a fiancée but quite another him being home and single! Talk about short engagements.

That night in bed, I tried to make sense of my feelings. Unable to sleep properly, I semi-dozed, waking up in starts, filled with visions of my teenage years interspersed with fearful interludes of Luke and Sian laughing at me and making fun of my hair.

I'd spent the whole of that afternoon trying to avoid Luke. Avoid seeing him, bumping into him, talking to him or catching his eye if he was in the room.

Luckily, he'd gone out for the evening and the feeling of suffocation I'd had while he'd been in the house abated. There had been one very uncomfortable time earlier on when we'd found ourselves alone in the kitchen together. He was peeling apples and I was sitting at the table flicking through the local paper. Never one for silence, I eventually had to break it or explode.

'So, I hear commiserations are in order then?' I said without looking up and trying to appear like I was concentrating on a particularly uninteresting article entitled 'Who is watching the Neighbourhood Watch?' It was all about the misdeeds of a local committee head who'd been caught burgling his neighbours while they'd been out at a committee meeting and he'd supposedly been laid up with an in-growing toenail.

Luke stopped what he was doing and slowly turned round. I couldn't help myself, I looked up and our eyes finally met. A muscle twitched in his strong tanned jaw. His blue eyes were fixed and cold.

'I think that all depends on which one of us you're talking about, don't you?' he said evenly.

Then without another word he turned back, sploshed down a peeled apple into the bucket of water beside him and walked determinedly out of the kitchen and into the garden. I was left staring for ages at the sub heading which read, *Neighbourhood Watch Committee Head, Nailed!* The words swam out at me, moving in and out of focus. Luke had just walked out on me.

Bloody cheek.

Bloody hell!

There was no getting away from it. I desperately wanted to know what he was thinking, why he'd dumped Sian and whether he was going to spill the beans to Laura. But I couldn't talk to him. I *wouldn't* talk to him.

After a few minutes though, he walked back in, carrying another basket of apples. The air was filled with tension.

Again, more silence.

I turned over the page and found a double-page article on the prime differences between types of potatoes; riveting.

'Well?' he asked suddenly, just as I was almost getting interested in a comparison between a King Edward and a Maris Piper.

'Well what?' I flicked over another page, still avoiding eye contact.

'Who were you talking about?' he asked. 'Who exactly deserves commiserations? Me?'

I wasn't sure exactly where he was going with this but I certainly wasn't going to rise to any bait.

'You of course; I heard things were off between you and Sian.' I shrugged, still concentrating on the paper in front of me.

'And you thought you'd say how sorry you were.'

'Well… yes, that was the idea.'

'And what about Laura? Are we going to be offering commiserations to her soon?'

My head sprung up to vertical. There. He'd gone and said it. The truth was finally coming out.

I tried to lie.

'I don't know what you mean, Luke.' I quickly looked down again and turned another page, determinedly scouring the contents.

'Save it, Maggie, I saw you both. No point in lying is there.'

His deep voice was filled with sarcasm, but something else too. Hurt? Regret?

'What's it got to do with you anyway?' I asked, truculently, closing the paper, folding it in half and pushing it to one side. I folded my arms in front of me. *Go on then, Luke,* I thought, *bring it on.*

'First of all, Laura is a friend of mine and I don't like to see friends being shat on.'

I felt my eyes widen. Luke never used to say words like shat. He must have been angry.

'I'm not…'

'And secondly,' he interrupted, 'of all the people you could have gone for, Maggie, of all the people in the whole fucking world, you could surely have chosen someone other than my brother!'

Splash – an unsuspecting apple was hurled into the bucket, causing water to spray back out. This time, when Luke exited the kitchen, he stormed off via the hall mounting the stairs fast and hard. I didn't think he'd be back.

Luke never used to swear! He must have been *very* angry.

I listened to the silence around me, straining for sounds of Luke moving around. I heard a stereo go on somewhere above my head, the bass pumping through the ceiling; loud, angry music.

Shit. I felt bad then. There was me, totally concerned with my own stuff and Luke was probably going through hell. For all I thought and felt about the situation, there was no denying that Luke would be suffering from the Sian situation and I didn't wish that on anyone.

He stayed up there until he clattered noisily back down the stairs a couple of hours later while I was in the lounge watching TV with Catherine and Jenny. I stole furtive glances through the open door as he stormed out the house, a holdall in hand, slamming the front door behind him without a word of goodbye. Moments later, we heard a car door slam, an engine start and car tyres crunch and noisily spray gravel as the car tore off down the drive.

Jenny and Cat exchanged knowing looks.

'Woman trouble,' Catherine stated.

I nodded silently in agreement.

'Bloody women,' Jenny scoffed.

Bloody Luke, I thought.

By the time I got to bed Luke still wasn't back. In the morning, I'd be leaving. Would that give him the opportunity to talk things through with his family? Would he say anything to Tony? How long before I found out?

And with thoughts of bugging the whole house before I left the next day, I'd fallen into my fitful sleep where one of my dreams saw Luke as the head of a Neighbourhood Watch meeting and, in front of the whole committee, accusing me of stealing Tony from Laura. Laura had turned into a small and lumpy Maris Piper potato-woman wielding a tennis racket, so at least things had a slight positive spin.

Chapter Thirty-three

Catherine and I lugged our cases down to the hall. This was it. It really was back to reality, plus I still had to visit Mum and Dad on the way home. I'd had very little decent sleep and I knew Mum would complain I wasn't looking after myself. On the plus side, she'd probably send me away with a load of the free beauty samples, from Decleor and Guinot, which she was always given when she went for her regular beauty treatments. It was almost worth going without sleep just for that.

'Where's Luke? I need his expertise,' Mr H said, coming into the kitchen carrying some kind of an engine part.

My ears pricked up.

'He's upstairs on the phone,' Jenny said.

He was back then.

'It's probably Sian cos it sounds like they're having a row. I heard Luke raise his voice and he never raises his voice.'

Or swears. I thought.

'Ah well, probably best not to disturb him then,' Mr H said reluctantly. 'Trouble with the fairer sex and all that.'

'Bloody women!' Jenny sniggered.

'Jennifer!'

'Sorry, Dad,' she sing-songed happily. John was joining her today. She had every reason to be happy.

'You ready then?' Catherine asked me. 'Best get on the road before too long, otherwise your mum'll have us staying for dinner and we won't get back to London before midnight.'

We took our cases out to the car.

'Better go to the loo before we go,' I said, heading back inside again.

This was only partly true. Yes, a sensible idea but the idea of hearing Luke on the phone rowing with Sian had a strange, sickly appeal, which was far too strong for me to ignore.

On my way up to the bathroom, I couldn't hear anything at first then I heard Luke's slightly muffled voice coming from his bedroom. I crept past, straining to hear but it was no good he was talking too quietly. I moved towards the bathroom but, as I did so, Luke's voice rose up loud and clear. What he said stuck out like a sore thumb.

'*What*? Tell me you're joking. You're *pregnant*? For God's sake, Sian!'

I froze in the bathroom doorway.

Pregnant? Did he say *pregnant*?

Without thinking, I crept back over to his door and listened intently.

'Sorry, sorry, sorry…' I heard him apologise, his sorrys fading as he seemed to move further away.

There was silence for a few moments then he started speaking again, his voice was too quiet to hear properly but then suddenly he seemed to get closer again, his voice louder and far from happy.

'For heaven's sake, what are you going to do? Now of all times!'

There was a short pause…

'I know, I know… oh hell… I realise I'm being insensitive but how am I supposed to react, it's a shock!'

As I moved slightly, a floorboard creaked beneath my foot and, startled, I shot quickly away to the bathroom again.

My mind was reeling. I felt sick.

I closed the bathroom door behind me, locked it and sat down on the edge of the bath.

Fuck. Sian was pregnant. What would she do? What would *he* do? I felt like I'd been punched. It wasn't unlike the feeling I'd had at Mr H's party when he'd announced Luke's engagement. And here was Luke back home again, unengaged… but with Sian pregnant. Sitting quietly alone, I allowed the feelings to wash over me. Then it hit me why I was feeling like this. It was totally ironic. All those years ago I'd been the one who was supposedly pregnant and he'd gone running off to university and avoided me completely. Now, here he was with another girl pregnant, once again having run out on her. He'd been *shouting* at Sian, like she'd done something wrong. And by the sound of things he was pinning all the difficult decisions on *her*. I thought of Sian far away in Sweden and I felt kind of sorry for her. I wished I'd had the chance to warn her about what he was like; that he was unreliable and probably wouldn't stick by her.

At that moment, it was like having the kick up the backside I needed. I realised, even after everything that had happened the old feelings I'd had for Luke had almost crept back again, almost. This was just what I had needed, a reminder that Luke Henderson was bad news and, more to the point, old news.

Luke's life was nothing to do with me anymore. It was up to him to sort things out with Sian on his own. This time, he'd at least have to face up to his responsibilities. There would be no running away now, he wasn't a kid anymore. He may have treated me like shit all those years ago but this was different. Divine retribution I wondered? What comes around goes around? If he had any decency left inside him, he'd be on a plane back to Sweden straight away. But, hey, this was their business, not mine.

After a few moments, I could hear crashing and clattering sounds coming from Luke's room. Despite my reluctance to have any involvement I once again found myself with my ear pinned up against the door. Then, through the frosted glass, I saw his door open and I quickly pulled back out of sight. He slammed his door shut and ran down the stairs and out the front. I hurried over to the bathroom window and watched as he sped off in his car again, tyres screeching and gravel shooting upwards off the drive.

Chapter Thirty-four

'Do you think he's gone back to Sweden then?' Catherine asked, as we headed off for a quick pit stop at Mum and Dad's.

'He didn't say goodbye though,' I pointed out, battling with myself not to care.

'People do funny things when they're stressed,' she said.

'Yes, like buggering off to university never to be seen again.'

Catherine went quiet.

'What?' I challenged.

'Nothing; I didn't say anything.'

'That silence was loaded; I could hear your mind going over.'

'No, really. It was nothing,' she insisted.

More silence.

I looked sulkily out the window at the passing fields.

'Well, OK, maybe not *nothing* nothing,' she admitted.

'What then?'

'Well… I'm just not sure it's doing you much good dragging up the past all the time.'

I frowned and kept my gaze on the distant horizon.

'I mean, it really was a long time ago… And,' she continued, when I made no attempt to speak, 'Luke and you. Well, maybe it just wasn't meant to be.'

'What do you mean?' I swivelled round to look at her, slightly surprised at her words.

'Just what I say; maybe it's just one of those things that happened between two people, two teenagers. And it's just… over, in the past, gone. Sometimes we have wonderful love affairs when we're young but they don't usually last, so we move on. It doesn't mean they meant any less, far from it.'

She glanced across at me staring blankly at her.

'Listen, all I'm saying is that what happened before, you know… the bad stuff, it's the past. It's over, dead and buried. Maybe you should just put it down to the inexperience of youth. Remember the good times…?'

'But…'

'And before you say anything, there were good times, lots of them.'

I shut up again.

'So, remember the good times and get on with the rest of your life,' she concluded.

Neither of us spoke as she overtook a tractor but it seemed her conclusion had a caveat.

'I read somewhere that if someone has hurt you and you don't feel able to get over it, you know what you need to do?'

'What?' I said huffily.

'Forgive them.'

I tried to interrupt. 'But…'

'Because then what happens is, you release all the bad feelings and emotions and memories that you have and you release the person. And most importantly, you release yourself and you get to feel a whole lot better about everything.'

I went to object but found I couldn't. Instead, I let her words sink in.

'Just like that?'

'Just like that,' she confirmed.

I paused but only briefly.

'I don't want to forgive Luke.'

Despite my earlier resolve I wasn't even sure I wanted to release Luke.

'OK, well maybe not quite yet but think about it yeah? Soon maybe?'

I hmmphed. 'Dunno.'

'After you've had a good old moan about him of course.'

Her eyes flicked sideways at me.

'I mean a real humdinger of a moan.'

A slight smile crept across my lips.

'He deserves it,' I said.

'Absolutely.' She grinned. 'I'll even help you and have a good old moan too… maybe on my next day off?'

I felt myself perking up a bit.

'We'll need chocolate then,' I pointed out.

'Well, of course, and maybe a DVD for after.'

'Possibly even two… and wine,' I added.

'Lots of it. A good old moan is thirsty work.'

'The thirstiest,' I agreed.

I couldn't help but smile out the window.

325

Catherine dropped me off at my flat that night, laden down with my suitcase and a goody bag from Avon of all places, courtesy of Mum.

There would have been a time when she wouldn't have allowed Avon in the house!

Apparently Mum had taken to buying from door-to-door salespeople. Avon, Kleeneze, Innovations. You name it; she had a catalogue for it.

'They're just as good as the quality brands you know,' she'd said.

'Your mother fancies herself as a rep,' Dad had said from behind the sports pages.

'I do not!'

'You do.'

'Well, maybe I do but I'd be very good at it.'

'You mean you'd get to find out what all the neighbours' houses looked like inside, instead of from your normal viewpoint of through their front windows,' Dad chuckled.

'Douglas, that's an awful thing to accuse your wife of. I am not a snooper.'

'I thought you'd been in to all the neighbours' houses,' I said.

Mum waved her arm in some invisible direction outside the house.

'Yes, but there's the big estate, and…'

She blushed, aware she'd been caught out.

Catherine and I managed to get away with a short visit. Just long enough to assuage Mum's concerns about temping yet again and to convince her that before too long her daughter would be earning hundreds of thousands of pounds from a top job in the City and married to a highly successful barrister who'd be able to sort out all sorts of things like contracts for Mum's new job with Avon.

It felt strange to be back in my flat. Everything was the same but it seemed to have a sort of haze around the place. The air appeared to be hanging, like it hadn't moved much since I'd left and needed to be broken up and circulated again. The flat had a non-lived-in feel and it made me look at it like it was the first time I'd seen it. It needed a clean, a proper spring clean, that was for sure and somehow I felt in the mood to do it. I opened the windows and breathed in the cool, crisp air of London; the smell of the city. It was dark by then and the air that reached my nostrils was tinged with chilled traffic fumes and the aromas of back alleys and takeaway joints. A lone dog barked in the distance and a couple of silent pigeons, flying home to their nests, flapped and swooped across my eye line. Gazing down I blinked against the harsh street lamps which glowed like fluorescent orange dandelion clocks waiting to be blown away and wished upon. They appeared to burn so much brighter and harsher than those in Spain had. I began to get that awful Sunday feeling of knowing you had to be at work the next day. Only, I didn't have to be at work, I just had to go out and find work. The feeling was the same though.

Of course, it wasn't just getting a job that was on my mind. The next day, I was due to text Tony. Should I even be considering it after what he'd told me? I thought back to the kiss in the bathroom and there was no mistaking the lurch to my groin but could I get past the Laura situation? Then Luke's sniping words sailed into my head about Tony and me, and why, out of all the people in the world I could have chosen, it had to be him. I recalled his telephone conversation to Sian, and his angry voice shouting at her when he found out she was pregnant. Frustration bubbled up inside me again and right then, texting Tony seemed like an excellent idea.

I wasn't going to let Luke Henderson affect me or my life ever again. My future was starting now, without him in it – and Tony, well, I'd start with a text and go from there. I'd give him a chance and I'd make up my own mind about him. In fact, maybe I'd just leave things in the hands of this so-called fate that Catherine kept talking about.

Chapter Thirty-five

I woke feeling strong and resolute.

'Today is the first day of the rest of my life,' I announced to my bedroom ceiling, quoting some undoubtedly wise person. I was going to find a job and maybe start a relationship and forget the past and Luke smelly, bum-faced, Henderson. I was on a mission and I would succeed at all costs. In fact, I was so committed to my cause, I was going to find out who'd coined the wise phrase I'd cited, and perhaps drop it intelligently into a conversation – maybe someone would offer me a job on account of my impressive knowledge. I grabbed my phone from beside my bed and Googled the answer:

Charles Dederich, a reformed alcoholic and a member of Alcoholics Anonymous.
Oh.

Not quite Eleanor Roosevelt, but still. My mission would continue. My future was paved with love, gold and abundance.

By midday, my mission had failed.

'Haven't we met before?' said the recruitment woman sitting opposite me.

Without realising, one of the temping agencies I'd pre-booked before our holiday to Spain had been the temping arm to the permanent agency where I'd met Miss Condescending-Bony- Arsed-Blue-Suit, when I was sporting my black eye. I could actually see her in the adjoining office, busying herself at the photocopier.

'You look kind of familiar, I'm sure I recognise you,' Miss Slightly-Less-Condescending-Not-So-Bony-Arsed-Blue-Suit was saying.

'No, I don't think so,' I replied, 'although people say I have got that kind of face. Something about my eyes,' I challenged, feeling a bit 'couldn't care less' about the whole situation. Mission shmission.

Eleanor, as her desk sign read, sat superiorly on the edge of her chair clicking the end of her pen in and out; in and out, in and out, as she read through my CV.

'Hmmmmm,' she deliberated, skimming over the lines.

'Uh huh,' she uh huh'd, turning to the second page.

'Hmmmmm,' she said again.

Annoying!

'Ri-i-i-ight.'

Perhaps news had got out about my being sacked, sorry, made redundant. Perhaps, knowing my luck, Justin had been in touch and warned all the agencies not to take me on.

However, she put down my CV and started clicking her mouse and scanning her monitor, behind which I was surreptitiously doing the V sign.

'How's your typing?' she asked.

'Rusty,' I admitted.

'Filing?'

'I'm not doing a filing job!' I said indignantly.

'Ohhh... kaaay,' she said slowly, glancing up at me. Then made a note on her pad without letting me see and moved on.

'Hmmmm,' she continued.

Shut up!

'Here's a possible. I notice you've done some research work with this *CapiTel* company (the way she said 'CapiTel' made it sound like a dirty word – she wasn't wrong) Would that interest you?'

My ears pricked up. Research sounded quite appealing. I thought back. I'd done two types of research. Firstly, a campaign I'd worked on, on the telephone, for CapiTel. Only a short campaign but research none the less. It had been quite fun, much better than selling and the client had been a blue chip company so I decided I could pad out the importance for Eleanor.

Secondly, I'd done hoards of internet research. OK, so maybe surfing for Christmas presents and the latest fashion items wasn't exactly Eleanor's idea of research but I knew I had a knack for wheedling things out and finding things I wanted at the best price so, with a few blags, I made out that internet research had also been part of my previous role.

There was a position covering maternity leave. A research company in Islington was after an assistant to fact find and help put together statistics for reports. Nothing like the stuff I'd done for CapiTel but I could relate to what they needed. It would involve a lot of legwork on the web and collating information and I was sure I could do it standing on my head, so Eleanor called and arranged an interview for me.

Mission reinstated. Back on course. Success in sight. Celebratory white wine calling.

I took the train from Victoria Station back to Clapham Junction and as I walked back home the hazy sun was doing its best to filter down through the layer of cloud. It was close and quite muggy and I didn't have the energy or inclination to do any further job searching that day. I started making my way via Lavender Hill. Checking my watch, I realised it was quarter to one; perhaps a good time to text Tony? I wondered whether he'd be at work, maybe just about to take lunch?

Where would Laura be? Mind you, Tony had simply said to text him 'tomorrow' and hadn't specified a time, so surely they weren't going to be together.

Cutting down one of the side roads, I sat down on a handy bench. Pulling out my phone I contemplated what to text. Despite having been out on a date with him already, it didn't seem right to just go straight in for the light-hearted approach, what with everything that had happened since.

I wanted to get in touch, I knew that much. Memories of the previous date were good and those of the bathroom incident were not all unpleasant. But the Laura thing was unsettling. However, once again Luke's irritating, interfering, words about Tony and me floated into my mind. That did it.

Nervously, I punched in a simple, straightforward message.

Hi Tony. Text as promised. You've got my number now, so over to you. Maggie.

Not exactly ultra-friendly but at least I was giving him the chance he'd asked for. It was up to him now.

I didn't have to wait long. After a couple of minutes, my phone sounded a message.

Despite myself, I was excited that it might be him.

It was.

Oh Maggie…No kiss! You're killing me! I'll have 2 put that right when I c u. I'll call u soon, pleeease meet me XXX

I couldn't help but smile. Maybe I was being too paranoid about the Laura thing; I mean all this talk of kisses didn't sound like someone who was hell bent on making his engagement work! Besides, if Laura really did need help, then she could get it and surely any woman, mad or not, wouldn't want to be going out with a man who didn't really love her. I certainly wouldn't.

I carried on with my journey feeling lighter and brighter. As I got closer to my flat I spotted the off licence a little way ahead of me. I was still in holiday mode really and the thought of an ice-cool glass of wine was too good to ignore. Besides, my mission was back on track and I had an interview! Plus, Tony was clearly into me. Definitely all points worth celebrating.

The door jingled as I went through and Charlie looked blearily up from his paper and gave me a lopsided grin.

My eyes widened in shock. His lip was all swollen and bruised.

'Charlie! What happened to your mouth… and… where's your tooth?'

'It got knocked out. I got in a fight.'

Go figure.

'I'm sorry to hear that. Did it hurt?'

'Yeah! She really lamped me one.'

She?

'Um, I see. Did she? Who?'

'My girlfriend's mum.'

Good grief, I was on *The Jeremy Kyle Show!*

'I wouldn't go out with her.'

'Really?' I said nervously.

'Silly tart.'

Probably a good time to wrap the subject up.

'Well, I hope you get it fixed soon,' I said, scanning the fridge for some wine, hoping to make a swift exit.

'The bitch'll have to pay for me to get it fixed,' he said angrily.

'Sure,' I squeaked, opening the fridge and speedily choosing a light Californian white. I took it warily up to the counter and Charlie rang it into the till.

'Seven forty-nine, please.' He held out his hand for my card.

'My God, Charlie, your hand! What happened?'

Charlie's hand was cut and bruised. He turned it over front and back.

'I lamped her back of course! Then put my hand through her window.'

'Oh….um…wow…' I hurriedly punched in my pin then glued my eyes to the small screen waiting nervously until I was instructed to remove my card.

'Well, I hope you sort everything out soon.'

He shrugged.

'Ah, no worries there. All sorted.'

'Really?'

OK, I was curious. So shoot me.

'Yeah, yeah, I set her up with me mate. He's much more 'er sort. Anyway, her daughter's well fit. Why should I want to mess around with her mum? Mind you, the offer of cash was pretty tempting. You know?'

I didn't.

'We're all going out as a four on Sunday. Be right smart, the old bird being so loaded and all that.' He winked.

Strange but true.

I left the off licence and wondered if I'd somehow stepped into a parallel universe without realising it. I also considered whether there might be another off licence nearby to go to next time. Having said that, I couldn't help being a little intrigued as to how the double date would go.

The bakery loomed to my left and I popped in for a chocolate éclair. The diet was most definitely starting tomorrow.

Chapter Thirty-six

I went off to my interview with the details and directions of the company and the name of the man I was to ask for.

Arriving at Highbury and Islington tube station I headed down Upper Street. The company was based in a big old house, quite a way down a tree-lined side road which looked to be mainly residential. While the road was a pretty one, this particular building looked a little scruffier than most of its neighbours and the main front door was painted a rather depressing black. A small sign on the front wall showed that the offices I needed were round the back and, as I made my way down the overgrown side path, I felt a sinking feeling in the pit of my stomach. The good thing about CapiTel, as well as being local, was that, despite the building being old, inside it had been modern and bright. It had big windows and was high enough up that you could see right across Clapham. The only view from the back of this house was the back of another one. There was a garden though, so that would be nice for eating my lunch in… I supposed.

I rang the door buzzer and waited. From the names on the plaque on the door, it appeared there were four companies there.

''Lo?' A disembodied female voice rang out from the dirty white entry-phone box.

'Hi, I'm here about the research job. Maggie Parsons.

'Right; just push the door. We're on the fourth floor, up the stairs in front of you; sorry the lift's bust.' An accented voice of some sort buzzed me in.

Busted lifts seemed to follow me around.

By the time I'd got to the top of the stairs, I was completely out of breath and red in the face. I waited a moment to recover and then went tentatively into the office in front of me. The sign on the door said 'Welles & Mayer'. It sounded more like a solicitors than a research company.

Pushing the door open, it also appeared more like a solicitors. Old furniture surrounded me. Old computer screens, desks and a beige carpet that had seen better days and was full of spills and marks. I saw a woman through a glass door in the next office, audio typing (*audio* typing. Did people still do that?). She was about sixty-five by my reckoning and didn't look up when I came in.

Glancing left and right I spotted a sign saying 'Reception' and headed for that. I was met by the girl I assumed was the one who'd answered the door to me. She greeted me from behind her desk.

''Lo.'

Definitely her.

'Hi, we spoke on the door.' I smiled.

'Yeah right. Take a seat, Mr Welles won't be laarng.' She sounded like she was from somewhere in the West Country which led me to thinking about Cornish pasties. My stomach rumbled unhelpfully. Damn this diet.

I thanked her and went and sat on a low brown sofa, which had also seen better days. Sinking down into it, I tried not to touch it. Again, I made a mental contrast to CapiTel's offices. I had a feeling that 'type of building' and 'location' would be featuring reasonably highly in my long-term career criteria. If my mum could have seen me then, she'd have been straight on the train and whisked me back out again.

The girl behind the desk surveyed me for a bit, then turned away and started doing something on her computer. She couldn't have been more than twenty-three. She had bleached white blond hair, really short and spiky, and a stud through her nose and thick black mascara with bright pink lipstick. When she went round to the photocopier, I observed her clothes. The top part might pass for being officey; short black skirt and open necked white shirt but, on the bottom, she wore purple and black striped tights and huge clompy black goth shoes.

She sat back down and we remained in silence apart from the tapping on her keyboard and the odd click of her mouse.

After a few moments she turned to me, chewing her gum noisily. She stared hard, making me feel uncomfortable.

'You smoke?' she aimed.

'Um, no, sorry, I don't.'

'Figures.'

'Sorry?'

'I said it figures. I've run out and no one in this office smokes. They're all too old and stuffy. I just thought you might, cos your nart.' She gave me a friendly smirk which I returned, feeling pleased to have made a possible friend. One who didn't appear like she'd audio type. She probably didn't even know what audio typing was.

'Margot,' she offered.

She didn't look like a Margot in the slightest.

'Maggie,' I said.

'Yair I know,' she said chewing away merrily.

'Sorry, course you do.'

'I don't look like a Margot do I?'

'Um…?'

'It was my mum's idea you see. She was really into that ballet stuff and called me aafter some bird called Margot Fontaine, some famous ballet daancer.'

'Did she make you go to ballet classes?' I asked.

'Yair, but I was really shite at them, so she gave up.'

I decided I rather liked Margot, nose stud and all. The phone sounded on her desk.

''Lo?' she answered.

'Right, Mr Welles, I'll send her in.'

'Boss is ready to see you now.'

'Thanks.' I stood up. 'What's he like?' I asked tentatively.

'Old and stuffy,' she gave a laugh.

I pulled a face and headed for the door she pointed out to me.

She was right. Mr Welles was old and stuffy and my grandmother would have described him as being 'a tad on the portly side'. Actually, it was more than a tad. He also had a most unfortunate comb-over and a really, really bad treble chin. No sign of a neck anywhere. But he had kind, smiley eyes and I warmed to him almost immediately.

His desk, like all the furniture, was brown and the top was covered with green embossed leather. He had a fountain pen resting in a penholder beside a blotter pad, and the phone on his desk could easily been shipped in from Eastern Europe, it was so dated. I was soon to find out that when he laughed, which he did a lot, his turkey chin wobbled about rather unattractively. But he was very charming and friendly, 'old school' I think you'd call him.

The interview went really well and, almost an hour later, I felt pretty chuffed with myself. He'd offered me the job on the spot. And I'd accepted it. This meant that, starting from the following Monday, for the next three months at least, I had a bit of security back. And it paid better than my previous job so, while it wasn't high tech, and while the furniture left a lot to be desired and the carpets were in need of a good scrub, I had a feeling it would be a pretty good temporary measure.

When I went out the main door again, Margot was there leaning against the red brick wall, dragging hard on a cigarette.

'Scrounged one off the gaardener,' she said.

I smiled.

'D'ya get it then?'

'Yes.' I smiled.

'Cool! Nice one; I reckoned you would.' She looked really chuffed. You have no idea

how good that made me feel.

I didn't hear from Tony that day or the next. And by day three I was convinced that either Laura had found his phone again and Tony was therefore looking at a second smashed-up mobile on the floor wondering how on earth he could get in contact with me, or that he had decided the whole idea was a really bad one and had made up his mind to forget 'we' had ever happened. However, as I sat down with my Weight Watchers meal for one that evening he finally sent me a text.

Sorry4silence…been seriously hectic! Let me make it up 2 u. How does being totally spoiled Sat week sound? Yr place 8pm? Then off 4 some serious eating & not so serious banter?XX ps Can u text yr address again??

Of course, my address had been previously annihilated. Thoughts of the mad Laura came to mind. I imagined her stamping on Tony's phone, and therefore the text with my address, in her pink and white tennis gear. Up and down, up and down, chamomile tea spilling from her mug as she did so, doing nothing to calm her nerves. What was I letting myself in for? I have to admit to being a little put out that Tony hadn't actually remembered my address. If it had been important to him, might he not have had it etched in his mind?

I texted back, still not quite ready to be all romance and roses.

Sounds good, thanks. Maybe some serious talking too? Address attached. Maggie X

He wasn't going to get away without some explaining, but, regardless, I'd added a kiss.

Chapter Thirty-seven

Monday morning – time to start work. It took me two cups of strong coffee and a cool shower to finally wake me up properly. I *had* to be on time this morning. This meant getting up at the unearthly hour of six forty-five a.m.

Wandering around the flat in my dressing gown, I felt cross with myself at my lack of 'house-proud-ness'; I had to do a decent clean. There were far too many drinks rings on the coffee table and the dust was so thick I could write my name in it. Tonight, maybe, when I got back?

I arrived early to the office. I'd been bumped into twice, hard, on the tube, then a very large woman with an eye patch had nearly poked *my* eye out with her umbrella (although it wasn't even raining so goodness only knows why she had it) and finally the guy at the kiosk short-changed me on a packet of Rolos, which I shouldn't have bought in the first place because I was on a diet. Feeling flustered, I was quite glad to be early to catch my breath a bit before starting.

Margot was out in the garden again having a Silk Cut. The box was in her spare hand.

''Lo,' she greeted me.

'Hi, want a packet of Rolos?' I offered. 'I'm on a diet.'

'Not while I'm smoking ta but I'll take 'em for later.'

I handed her the Rolos, feeling slightly better about myself as I did so. Maybe she'd offer me one later though.

'Had to scrounge these off my mum.' She waved the Silk Cut packet at me. 'She's not well pleased, I'm always doing it.'

'Are you broke then?' I asked.

'Na, just stingy!' She grinned and I spotted a little silver star sparkling in her front tooth.

'Do you like it?' she asked, when she saw me staring. 'I had it done on Saturday at the tattoo place.'

'Um, yes, it's very um… trendy.' Beside Margot, I felt very *un*trendy in my plain light grey suit with my hair sensibly up in a ponytail.

'Don't you have to go to a dentist for stuff like that?' I asked.

'Na, the tattoo place does lots of things like this you know, beauty stuff.'

I nodded.

'You can even get that Botox out the back.' She pulled thoughtfully on her cigarette. 'It's all needles I s'pose. Anyway, this is my last one.' She threw the cigarette end down on the path and stubbed it out'

'Are you giving up then?'

'Hell no!' She looked quite horrified. 'I meant the pack's finished. I s'pose I'll have to buy my own now.'

'Morning, ladies.' Mr Welles ambled round the corner, smiley and wobbly.

'Morning, Mr Welles,' Margot and I said together.

'All ready for your first day then, Maggie?'

'Absolutely.' I smiled.

'Come along then, let's get you settled.'

'Good luck,' Margot called after me as I followed him in. 'I'll show you the sandwich place at lunchtime if yous want.'

My office was small. Pretty dated (no surprise there then) and kinda dingy. There was one little window but it was too high up to see out of it.

Having had a talk through my responsibilities with Mr Welles, I settled myself in and, using the password that Tommy the IT youth had given me, I signed on to my computer. Tommy, a noisy gum chewer, had leant over my desk giving me a close-up view of his late teenage acne as he set me up. It felt very odd working in such a little office all on my own. Apart from Margot and Tommy, I hadn't spotted anyone young and no one had really paid me much attention as I'd walked through. It didn't appear like there could be more than fifteen employees at a guess, and they were all tucked away in their own separate offices. I felt rather alone. I took out my lucky snow scene globe from my handbag. Catherine's nieces had given it to me two Christmases ago when I'd complained it never snowed at Christmas in London. I'd picked it up last minute that morning for good luck and was rather glad I had. It was my way of making the office my own. Mr Snowman was happily snuggled up in his red hat and scarf with his carrot nose and little buttons and there was an igloo behind him. I gazed at the scene for a few moments then gave the globe a quick shake and placed it on my desk, watching as the snow settled.

I felt around in the bottom of my bag for my low cal protein bar and put that on the desk too. I was starving already and it wasn't even ten o'clock. The diet wasn't going particularly well but I was determined to stick to it and lose a few pounds by Saturday.

I got stuck into my work. I had to gather together information for two reports on investment opportunities in China, with particular emphasis on manufacturing and the current opportunities and implications of the legal and illegal internet cafes in China and in particular Beijing. I used the web, called up the BBC News website, a couple of private investment sites, all of which were really helpful, and I even called the desk officer for Beijing at UK Trade and Investment. The woman I spoke to was actually Chinese.

'Wha' you wan' know?' she asked abruptly.

I explained my quest.

'Beijing big place; Lo' of pee'po. Lo' of cafes.'

But she gave me some tips on additional sites to browse and info on the their on and off-line libraries, and advised I book a meeting with Colin Jennings – a whiz with corporate statistics – so I arranged a time the next day to meet him and be shown around. I was actually finding the project pretty motivating and I would get to go out of the office, which I loved.

By lunchtime I was really hungry. The morning had flown past and I'd hardly had time to think about anything but work. My protein bar sat unopened on my desk; I'd been too ensconced in my research to even think about it. I was just checking my emails on my phone when Margot's head poked round the door.

'Come on!' she said, 'I'm staarvin', let's go eat.'

We headed up past green trees and pretty Georgian houses and turned into Upper Street. The sun was shining and it was a perfect summer's afternoon.

'So, you married or what?' Margot asked sucking loudly on what I could only guess was a Rolo. 'It never said on your CV.'

'Married? No. Why are you?' The thought quite alarmed me that she might be.

'Me? Nope. Not on your life. I'm too young. I don't think I'll ever get married.'

'How come?' I was already feeling comfortable in Margot's company.

'My brother got married a couple of years ago, and he said they only ever have sex once a month. What d'you think of that then?'

She didn't let me answer.

'If I could only have sex once a month, I think I'd die,' she continued. 'I love sex, me. It's well good. Don't you think?' she aimed.

I thought about my current drought and didn't want to admit to it.

'Yes. Great!' I enthused. 'Really great!'

We walked in silence for a few moments.

'You're not getting any are you?'

Damn. A psychic receptionist.

'Um, what makes you say that?'

'Dunno, you can just tell, I s'pose.'

'Really?' I was intrigued.

'Yair, you don't look very smiley.'

'Oh.'

'Bet you're a Virgo too aren't you,' she said.

Wow!

'How can you tell?'

'You can always tell Virgos. They're always so nice and polite and everything has to be "just so". Probably why you're not getting enough sex – too choosy.'

I was astounded.

'And you sussed out my star sign just by knowing me for all of a few hours?'

'Pretty much.'

We continued in silence for a bit.

'That and the fact that I saw your date of birth on your CV!' Margot laughed. I laughed too.

'I'm a Scorpio, you know? It's well known that Scorpios love sex. You see, the way I reckon is, sex is there for the 'avin', right? I mean if God, or whoever's up there telling us all what to do, meant for people not to 'ave it, he wouldn't have given us all bits, would he?' she said.

'I guess not,' I agreed.

'I mean, I know some folks say it's all about 'avin' kids and stuff but there's so many kids in the world already aren't there? And people need to stop 'avin them really, don't they, so we can sort out all this poverty stuff, right? But you don't see God or Mrs God reachin' down and cutting all our bits off, now, do you?'

I was beginning to realise that Margot was a master of the rhetorical question.

'So you see, we may need to stop getting pregnant but we've still got our bits, so we might as well use them. Don't you think?'

She paused.

'I said, don't you think?'

340

Apparently, this was the end of the rhetorical questions.

'Maybe, but aren't *you* choosy?' I was still smarting over the 'too choosy' comment being a little too near the truth for my liking.

'Kind of.' She put another Rolo in her mouth and put the packet back in her bag sucking noisily for a moment or two.

'Nah, not really!' She laughed. 'I s'pose they've got to be fit though. A good body is always a plus. Oh, and I likes nice eyes, thems that look right deep into you like you caan't hide anywhere.'

I thought about Tony.

'And I likes a nice bum; nice and firm and tight.'

This was a heck of a conversation to be having with someone I'd only just met!

'But apart from that, anyone'll do: tall, short, dark, blond, Liverpudlian, Brazilian, not fussy really.'

I wondered how she had gone from Liverpool to Brazil but could only assume she'd been out with at least one of each.

'Here we are,' she said, indicating Sue's Sandwich Bar.

'I'm going for a jacket spud with sausage and beans. Heaven help Paulo this evening!' she laughed. And off she went to join the queue.

Chapter Thirty-eight

That evening, my flat remained un-spring-cleaned. I did have an excuse though; Pip had turned up in a bit of a state. What can I say; he *needed* me. Andrew had found out Pip had got off with another bloke and was threatening to throw him out.

'It wasn't my fault, *he* came on to *me!*' Pip sniffed, in tears. 'I didn't stand a chance.'

'Couldn't you just have said no?' I asked.

'But I did! I really did.'

'And...?'

'Then I said yes,' he admitted.

'Do you think Andrew will really kick you out?'

He thought for a moment.

'I don't think so, not really. Besides,' Pip stopped crying and straightened up, 'he cheated on me once, big time.'

'Did he?' I couldn't imagine Andrew being the type.

'He did. It was awful. Some guy from work, one of his trendy City types; all master's degrees and designer suits. How was I supposed to compete with that?'

'I bet he was really boring,' I said.

'Yeah me too!'

'So what happened?'

'I found a note from this guy. Leo, his name was. Poncey name don't you think?'

'Um, a bit maybe.' I rather liked it actually.

'It was obvious what was going on. You can tell if someone you're with is doing the dirty, they act all strange, so I had it out with him and he 'fessed up everything.'

'And you forgave him?'

'I had to really; didn't have anywhere else to go at the time. Besides,' Pip became reticent, 'Andrew's all right really, just a bit uptight sometimes.'

I refrained from telling him that one drunken night I'd nicknamed him the 'Uptight Squirrel'. Probably not the time.

'I think that's why he's so mad about me and this German guy I met at the club last week. Because he's done it to me, he thinks I'll have an affair like he did.'

'Sounds like a lot of pressure for a relationship.'

Pip sat thoughtfully for a bit, staring into his lap.

'It is really,' he said sadly.

'I'll open some wine shall I?' I suggested.

'Thanks.'

'Look,' he called out, as I headed for the kitchen. 'I can write my name in the dust on your coffee table with my finger.'

I sighed.

Tomorrow. *Really*, tomorrow.

Chapter Thirty-nine

Saturday arrived and despite the best will in the world (ish), I still hadn't cleaned my flat. I tried to blame it on having such a heavy workload but I knew it was really because I kept watching umpteen back episodes of the soaps I'd recorded since before our holiday. Catherine was round flicking through a diet magazine at my kitchen table while I made coffee.

'So…' she began, 'this stomach stapling stuff…'

I spun round in horror. 'What stomach stapling stuff!? Cat, please don't tell me you're thinking of doing anything like that!'

'Me? No. No, of course not! I'm just saying that it can't be very good for you. I mean, what would happen if people accidentally over-ate? The staples might burst.'

She put her hands protectively over her stomach.

She flicked over another page. 'Do you think it works though?'

I frowned.

'Cat, don't even think about it. You're fine, just as you are.'

'No, I'm not,' she said. 'You're just being kind. I'm very podgy and that's me being kind.'

'If you're really unhappy about it, maybe you could try a bit of exercise.'

She pulled a face. 'I know I should but I just can't seem to get myself motivated. Besides, I get so exhausted after a shift at the hospital. By the time I get home, I can't be bothered to do anything except flump down in a chair and put my feet up with Tom and watch telly. And talk to Nico on the phone, of course,' she added, picking up her phone to see if he'd been in touch.

I put the coffees on the table and sat down with her.

'They'd probably rust anyway,' she went on.

'What would?'

'The staples; the ones in these people's stomachs. I mean, can you imagine a staple being wet all the time, it would rust surely.'

344

'I should imagine they use special material that doesn't rust.'

'Hmmm, you're probably right,' she said thoughtfully.

'Anyway, why all the sudden interest? Why the magazine?'

She shrugged.

'Cat?'

'It's probably nothing.'

'What's probably nothing?'

She sighed. 'Nico showed me some photos of his sisters.'

'And…?'

'And… they're really thin, all three of them.'

'So…?'

'So, he's really slim and fit and they're practically waiflike and then there's lardy old me. What if I meet them one day and they think I'm horrid?'

'Cat, for goodness sake, you're far from horrid. You're lovely. *Everyone* loves you. You haven't got a bad word to say about anyone. No one could ever think anything other than nice things about you.'

'That's what Nico said.'

'There you go then.'

'Yes, but what if one day he wakes up and realises that all this time he's been missing out and he could have someone really thin. What then?'

'Do you really think that would happen?'

She thought for a moment.

'I don't know,' she answered sadly. 'I really don't know,'

'Well I do. I think you're worrying over nothing. Nico really likes you. For goodness sake, the guy was up in arms about almost missing you at the airport and he's been phoning you every day, more than once a day, for weeks and he keeps telling you he likes you just as you are! You have to start believing him.'

Catherine nursed her coffee.

'I s'pose.'

'Good.'

'Maybe a mud wrap though?'

'Cat!'

'OK, OK, but I do want to lose weight, for me. Not just for him.'

'Well that's different. Do it for you, by all means, but don't do it for anyone else and certainly don't go making up stuff about people's sisters, that's just plain silly.'

She gave a reticent smile. 'OK.'

She turned over a couple of pages in the magazine, scanning the contents.

'Got any biscuits?' she looked up, pulling a face.

I stood up and went over to my hideaway place under the sink and pulled out a packet of Hobnobs. It's the place I hide things I don't want to eat when I'm on a diet. Bizarre I realise, seeing as I know where they are, but it's a case of 'out of sight out of mind', in theory anyway. I put them on the table and we both had one.

Munching away, I had a brainwave.

'I know how you could lose some weight.'

'How?'

'Help me clean this place! Tony's picking me up later and I need to make it all sparkling and lovely for him.'

'Sorry, no can do. I'm on shift at three and I need to go back and eat and get changed.'

'Oh well, worth a try.' It was no good, I'd have to get started.

At six o'clock that evening I was rushing like a mad woman, trying to clean up. Only two hours until Tony arrived and I still had to get ready. I needed to wash my hair and I really wanted to straighten it. Tony had only seen me with straight hair since I'd hooked up with him after all these years and I wasn't sure I was ready to show him the real me quite yet.

Sod's law, the Hoover decided to blow a fuse on me so I had to run down to Andrew and Pip's flat to get a replacement.

Andrew came to the door in a dressing gown. It was the first time I'd seen him since the Tequila night and I swear he blushed when he saw me. There still hadn't been any sign of my lost knickers and I had visions of him harbouring them in the back of one of his anally tidy drawers, sneaking them out every now and then and doing with them whatever people who steal knickers do with knickers they've stolen.

However, then I saw Pip in the background wandering around in just his underpants so I assumed I'd caught them making up in an afternoon of steamy lovemaking. I wondered briefly how squirrels made love. After profuse thanks and apologies for the interruption, I left, fuse in hand, to mend the Hoover. But evidently, it wasn't the fuse after all, so I had to go back down to ask to borrow their Hoover. This time, Andrew came to the door very red in the face with his dressing gown on inside out. He was clearly not happy.

I finally finished cleaning the place, utterly shattered. I hadn't even begun to get ready. I realised, with alarm, it was ten past seven. Somehow I'd lost track of time. I'd never have time to straighten my hair! I tried to console myself that it wouldn't matter and, besides, I'd done it so much since I'd bought the straighteners, my hair really did need a rest. But I felt panicky. What if Tony didn't like my hair curly?

I showered and changed and put my make-up on, then worked some expensive serum through my hair. I was just being silly. I looked fine, good even. I just looked like me. Maybe not quite the movie star Pauline had called me but good nonetheless.

Bang on time the main doorbell rang and I buzzed Tony in. Smoothing down my white trousers and tweaking my appearance in the mirror, I gave him time to climb the stairs then went to open the door.

I was greeted by a lovely bunch of red roses covering up Tony's face.

'These roses wanted to be the first to tell you how lovely you look,' he said, then took them away from his smiling face.

It was only a small change but a change never the less.

To the untrained eye it would have been and gone before being noticed but I noticed it. Tony's face had fallen, very slightly, as he'd taken in my new appearance.

'Thank you, Tony, I'll put them in water. Come in,' I smiled, taking the roses from him.

'Cheers.' He came in and closed the door.

'New hairstyle?'

'No, this is just how it goes naturally.'

'Nice,' he managed. 'Great!' he added.

Not so great, I thought.

We ate at a little Italian place he knew tucked out the way of the crowds. Unless you'd known about it, you'd never have found it. Luckily, despite some earlier surreptitious glances at my curls, Tony seemed to have got used to my hair and I began to relax. Conversation was a little stilted for a while though and, while it was nice to see him, I wondered if things had lost their edge. I knew it was partly down to me and I decided that if we were going to get past any unspoken discomfort, I had to broach the subject that was constantly on my mind.

'How's Laura?' I ventured, when the waiter had cleared the starters away.

Tony's jaw clenched.

'As well as to be expected,' he said, signalling a different waiter.

'Really?'

'It's just like I told you at Dad's, nothing's changed.' He looked at me and smiled, reaching over the table and taking my hand. 'It will though, given time. Trust me, yeah?'

'Could we have another bottle of the red, please?' he asked the waiter who'd come over.

'Tony, we've not even finished this one yet!'

'Better hurry up then. I plan to get you very drunk then make you tell me all your childhood secrets.'

'I don't have any really.'

'Don't you? What about your hair? That was a secret until tonight.' He laughed. 'Don't get me wrong, I like it… it's kinda funky!'

It was an odd comment and, while I smiled, I wasn't sure I liked it.

'Please tell me a bit more about Laura, Tony. I think I've got a right to ask, don't you?'

I felt his foot start to jiggle under the table.

'Can't we just forget about Laura tonight? I seem to spend all my time thinking about her and what to do for the best.'

I couldn't meet his eye.

'Listen, Maggie, I am sorry. I know this is hard and I will tell you things, important stuff but, just for a little while, can't it just be you and me? Mmm?'

I paused thoughtfully then gave a reticent nod.

'OK, but I don't like seeing you behind her back.'

'You're not! I'm only with her because I feel sorry for her. Just give me some time and I'll sort it all out. It'll be fine. I'll *make* it fine.' He cocked his head to one side, his eyes beseeching until I couldn't help but smile.

'That's better. Now then, this backgammon award of yours. When are we going to have a match?'

'You'd have to be very good to thrash me.'

He narrowed his eyes. 'And you'd have to be very, *very* good for me to thrash you.'

'It was actually backstroke,' I admitted, not feeling ready for sexual banter.

'What was?'

'My certificate; I won it for backstroke.'

'Ah ha! Now there's a challenge. You are looking at the Tillmouth Academy boys backstroke champion.'

'Since when?' I exclaimed.

'Since, ooh, about ten seconds ago probably!'

I laughed then. The ice was broken.

Tony reached across and took my hand again tilting his head to one side.

'It'll be OK you know, Maggie. Really it will.'

I smiled over at him.

'Yeah… of course it will.'

Chapter Forty

Later that week Pauline rang me in the evening. She'd received her test results. Strangely, they were all negative.

'And they did a full set of blood tests?' I asked her.

'Yep, they did everything they could think of. They're now talking about me meeting up with one of their in-house counsellors.'

'They think you need therapy?'

'Perhaps; who knows?'

'You poor thing, you must be feeling pretty naff.'

'I'll survive.'

'Is Timmy still with you?'

'Oh, yes.'

'Is he helping?' I asked.

'That depends on your definition of help. If you mean is it helpful having him and Terry arguing all the time, then he's being very helpful indeed, thank you.'

'Oh dear, still don't get on, huh?'

'Nope; never did, never will.'

'Is Timmy helping round the house at all?'

'Yeeesss…'

'But…?'

'I think he makes more mess than he actually clears up.'

'Sounds like Timmy.' I chuckled. 'I should imagine it's nice to have the company though, while Terry's at work?'

'True, very true; and I have to say, he is great with the animals. He gets up and feeds the horses and walks the dogs every morning, which is a real help. For all his minor faults, he's a good lad. And I am glad he's here,' she admitted.

'You up for a visit soon then?' I asked.

'Maggie, you're welcome here anytime. You know that surely. Don't even bother asking.'

'I know but, what with you feeling so lousy, I just thought…'

'Well, un-think immediately. Just make sure you call first, in case Timmy's whisked me off on some special surprise outing.'

'Like where…?'

'I'm usually the last to know, it could be anywhere! He's got it into his head that I

need more fun in my life, so he keeps taking me on trips to the strangest of places. We've been to feed the ducks at the school pond; we've even played bingo. *Bingo*! Can you imagine, me playing Bingo?'

'Did you win?'

'Yes! That's the irony of it all. Maybe I should have taken it up years ago. Don't tell him but I actually rather enjoyed it. And fifty quid is not to be sniffed at.'

'Why don't you go back again?' I asked.

'Fun as it was, I was so knackered afterwards I slept for three hours and missed *Question Time*.'

This didn't sound entirely unfortunate to me.

'Then yesterday,' she continued, 'we ended up going on a coach trip round rural Berkshire!'

'Whatever for?'

'Apparently we have some of the most beautiful countryside in England. That's as maybe but I've seen it all before. I got so tired that I fell asleep and when I woke up Timmy was sitting and playing gin rummy with what appeared to be half the Women's Institute. We were the youngest people on the coach. Timmy was fussed over by the blue rinse brigade from start to finish and, if I didn't know better, I'd say it was him that needed the trip, not me.'

'Really?'

'He was positively lapping up all the attention. I think he rather liked being cosseted by all the old dears.'

'Maybe he needs looking after then?' I suggested, remembering I'd thought the same on holiday.

'You know Timmy,' she went on, 'bit of a chequered past. I wouldn't be surprised if it was catching up on him. He's seemed as tired as me lately.'

'Do you think he's been burning the candle at both ends?' I asked, carefully. I wasn't sure how much of Timmy's past Pauline actually knew about.

'You mean has he been going heavy on the drugs again? Maggie you don't have to protect me, or him. I know what Timmy's like. I wasn't born yesterday.'

'Sorry, I wasn't sure…'

'I'm not a hundred per cent but, yes, I think he has. I may not be a world expert in these matters but, if I was a betting woman…'

'What are you going to do?'

'What can I do? I've tried talking to him about things but as soon as I start probing he clams up. The good thing is that while he's here I can keep an eye on him. But he's not happy, I know he's not. Sometimes, when he doesn't know I'm doing it, I watch him and he looks very sad, just like a little kid. If I'm honest, I am worried.'

'Poor Timmy.'

'Indeed. If I ask him if he's OK, he tells me off and says I'm not to worry about anyone else except me. He won't let me do anything but rest. If it wasn't for the fact that half the time all I want to do is sleep, I'd be probing further but right now he's right. I need to get better as soon as I can. I can't have him nurse-maiding me forever.'

'Do you want me to have a word when I come down?' I offered.

'Would you, Mags? I'd be very grateful actually. I think he needs taking in hand, only I'm not in a position to do that right now.'

'Pauline, try not to worry about Timmy, he's made of strong stuff you know.'

'Mmm, I know. But he's been taking strong stuff too. And that's what I'm most worried about.'

Chapter Forty-one

'Your horoscope's pretty dire,' Margot informed me one lunchtime.

'That figures.' Tony hadn't been in touch since our date and I'd wondered if it was because I hadn't asked him in for coffee afterwards.

'What does it say?'

Margot took her chewing gum out her mouth, rolled it into a ball between her finger and thumb then pinged it towards the bin. It missed and stuck on the wall behind. It was not alone.

She cleared her throat.

'It says you've been hiding your true feelings and your love life needs a shake up.'

'Great. What does yours say?'

She took a few moments to read Scorpio to herself.

'It says I'm going to meet a rich man, have plenty of sex and go shopping a lot.'

'Nothing new there then.'

'Huh! Chance would be a fine thing,' she scoffed. 'I never seem to bag a rich bloke. I don't think I've got the knack. Darius keeps asking me for a lend.'

'Darius?' What happened to Paulo?'

She shrugged. 'He's kickin' around still.'

'And Darius…?'

'I met him at salsa.'

'I didn't know you went to salsa!'

'I don't normally but my mate goes and she said they had some really haart guys there. That was it. I signed up on the spot.'

'And you met Darius.'

'Yair, but he wasn't one of them whoosy daancers, he was the barman. Go figure. What do you think of that then?'

'Ironic. So, is it serious then?'

'Dunno. I like him though. He's a bit like a guy I went out with in year six. I wondered whether it might be him at first, you know, when I saw him with the cocktail shaker. Reminded me of when Jason, that's the boy from school, used to play the maracas in the school band. Well, not so much a band, more of a dodgy noise really. I played the triangle. We used to nip off for a snog between sessions.'

'How old were you?'

"Bout eleven; old enough!' She grinned. 'Anyway, it wasn't him cos when I asked his name, he said it were Darius. So I figured, unless Jason had taken to changing his name, it probably wasn't him. You know?'

I knew.

'Only trouble is, there's Paulo to think about. I'm not sure he'll be too happy.'

'Still seeing him then?'

'Not really seeing, more like sleeping with. You know?'

Not really, I thought and went quiet.

'You still not getting any then, Mags?'

I shrugged. 'I just haven't met the right person yet.' I chose not to mention Tony.

Margot snorted.

'How on earth are you gonna find out if a bloke's the right person, if you don't sleep with him? I mean, imagine you get really into a guy, you know, likin' 'im and all that, but you don't sleep with him. What 'appens if, when you do, he's only got a little wiener? That's not gonna be much good now is it? You'll 'ave wasted a good "like".'

Margot's phone tinged out a text which she read and snorted with laughter then swiped a reply and shoved the phone in her bag.

I wondered if Tony had a little 'wiener', and thought probably not.

'But what about personality, sense of humour and all that?' I asked.

'That's all good and well but they's gotta have a big wiener, that's all I'm sayin'. See now Darius, he's got a *massive* wiener; too big, if you ask me. I once got this email right? There was this photo of this massive great tribal lookin' bloke with a maaaasive great wiener. Longest I've ever seen.'

A memory flashed across my mind.

'Was he in the jungle by any chance?'

She thought for a moment.

'D'you know, I think he waas.'

'I think I saw the same photo.'

'I mean, imagine me sitting on that? He'd have me in the air for goodness sake. I wouldn't be able to reach my feet to the ground!'

I decided Jenny and Margot would probably get on quite well.

'So anyway, you've gotta get out there, Maggie my love. You've gotta try before you buy. Know what I mean?'

'Maybe…'

'There's no maybe, girl. Get shaggin', that's my motto. When I die, you know what I want on my gravestone?'

'What?'

'"Margot – Laid to rest"; and I will've been!' She laughed loudly and headed off to the coffee machine where I could still hear her chuckling to herself.

Why had I been born a Virgo? I wondered.

Chapter Forty-two

Tony did get in touch of course. Deep down I'd known he would but with him things were never straightforward; never easy.

'I'm really sorry, Maggie, it's a work thing,' he explained one afternoon. He'd cancelled our date, for the second time, for work reasons.

'How long will you be away?'

'Couple of weeks, maybe ten days if I can tie up all the loose ends.'

So far we'd only been out twice since the holiday: once to the Italian place and the second to Ronnie Scott's. I thought back to that evening. I'd never been to Ronnie Scott's and, while I didn't have a clue about the ins and outs of Jazz, I really loved it. I loved the way the musicians all supported each other. I loved the way they all took their turns while the other musicians so obviously appreciated them and smiled encouragingly tapping their feet or clapping along. It seemed like one big happy family. No one I knew was into Jazz but Tony said he'd take me.

I knew by the end of the first number it had been a mistake. Tony was bored. It was written all over him. He was nice enough to try and hide it but I kept catching him, out the corner of my eye, looking at his watch. I asked him if he wanted to leave and, full of smiles, he assured me he didn't but I knew he was pretending. It really took the edge off things.

We went on for a meal afterwards and while I took a little while to defrost after Ronnie Scott's, we had fun. I think Tony realised he'd been a bit of a killjoy and spent most of the evening either flattering me or making me laugh. He'd even mentioned us going away for a weekend together, somewhere quiet, just the two of us. By the end of the evening any discomfort between us had dissolved.

'Can you forgive me?' he pleaded down the phone, bringing me back to the present.

'I really would get out of it if I could but my partner's off to the Maldives with his family and there's no one else I can trust to go. You don't mind, do you?'

I kind of did but I said it was fine; I knew I was being a bit unfair.

'How about I take you to that new club when I get back? We can make a night of it.'

'Won't Laura mind?' I said deliberately then regretted it feeling like a child. He tutted.

'I won't tell her, of course. You're not going to start on about that again are you?

Maggie, come on, I won't be able to see you for a couple of weeks. Don't let's end on a bad note, eh?'

He'd tried two or three times recently to put my mind at rest about Laura, once even without my mentioning it first. I felt guilty then. Perhaps I should be more supportive.

'Sorry,' I said.

'I'll call you,' he said.

'OK.'

'And text.'

'OK.'

'"OK"? Is that all I'm going to get?'

'Sorry.' *I really was being unfair.* 'I hope it goes OK. Don't work too hard,' I managed, thinking I'd be bored now for two weeks, what with Catherine on nights.

'I'll bring you something nice back from Paris.'

Ah ha!

'Really?'

'Only if you promise to miss me.'

'I might,' I conceded. 'But only if you promise not to chat up all the French women. I've heard they can be very predatory.'

'No kidding? I'll have to remember that!'

'Oy!'

'Gotcha.'

And got me he had. I didn't want him to go away; Paris of all places. I was jealous, in more ways than one.

'What will you buy me then?'

'You'll have to wait and see.'

'I don't like Nougat.'

'I was thinking more like a French letter.'

'Ha ha.'

This had been one of the very few references to sex that had been made between us. We'd kissed goodnight after our dates together but nothing more. I felt a bit odd at the innuendo.

'I'd rather have chocolates,' I said.

'Maybe I'll go for both,' he said slowly. 'I'll miss you, Maggie. Mind you behave yourself while I'm gone.'

Chapter Forty-three

That weekend, I decided to visit Pauline. I rang first to make sure she was in and Timmy answered the phone.

'I'm very glad you're coming down. I think she could do with the extra company. I don't think I'm doing much good.'

'I'm sure you are, hun.'

'You say that but wait 'til you see her. She's not herself.'

When I arrived, Timmy met me at the door.

'How is she?'

'Oh, Mags, I don't know what to do!'

'Why, what's happened?'

Timmy came outside, pulling the front door to behind him.

'She's not eating.'

'What, nothing?'

'Hardly; I'm sure she's gone downhill. She seemed better last week but something's happened to her.'

'What's she said?' I asked.

'Nothing, absolutely nothing; she won't tell me how she feels. She keeps going all quiet on me. Every time I ask her how she is, she drifts off into a dream. I can't understand it,' he wailed. 'She's just not fighting anymore. It's not like her.'

'Have you spoken to any doctors?'

'Some bloke turned up the other day. One of these hospital types, all medical spiel and brown suit.'

'What did he come round for?'

'God knows. Paul' never even mentioned he was coming. I don't know if she forgot, or what?'

'And...?'

'And bloody nothing. She didn't even want me in the room but I kept walking past and peeking through the crack in the door. He took her pulse,

359

listened to her chest, took her blood pressure and got her to fill in some forms.'

'Forms? Why?'

'I don't know. I only caught useless snippets of conversation.'

'Do you think she's hiding something?' I was feeling decidedly uneasy.

'That's what I've been thinking! Maybe the docs have said something to her and she's not letting on!'

He was clearly very upset so I took hold of his hand.

'Timmy hun, don't worry. Pauline would tell us if there'd been any developments. I'm sure of it.'

I was, in fact, far from sure of it. Pauline had kept her poor health a secret for months, what was to stop her keeping more from us all now?

'And bloody Terry makes matters worse,' Timmy added.

'What's he been doing now?'

'That's just it. Nothing! Nada. He's such a prick, that man.'

'Timmy, come on. That's not fair. He is Pauline's husband.'

'Yeah? You think so? Well, if Pauline was my wife, not that I'd have a wife but you know what I mean, I'm buggered if I'd be out all hours of the day and night working. That's if he *is* working.'

'Do you think…?'

'Fuck knows; arsehole. If it was up to me, he'd be out permanently. But it's Paul' I'm worried about. She needs support and he should be giving it to her.'

'Come on, let's go in. She'll be wondering what we're doing out here,' I ushered him back into the hallway. Go and stick the kettle on. I'll talk to her.'

We wandered down the hall and Timmy headed off to the kitchen. I made my way to the downstairs bedroom, which Pauline had recently moved into. She'd said it was because it was nearer to everything she needed. Of course it meant she and Terry were sleeping apart.

She was lying on the bed, staring out the window, when I walked in. She turned and smiled. I could see she was tired but she sat herself up, adjusting the pillows and cushions behind her to make her more upright.

'I hope Timmy hasn't been bending your ear out there.'

'He's just worried about you.'

'He's fussing over nothing. Some more rest and I'll be fine.'

'He says a doctor came round the other day.'

Her eyes were red and I wondered if she'd been crying.

She looked blankly out the window.

'Pauline…?'

'It was nothing, just routine.' Turning back to me she patted the bed.

'Come on, sit down you. I need cheering up. What's happening in the wild and hectic life of Maggie Parsons?'

I went over and sat down on the bed.

I considered my news and thought it best not to say anything about Tony just yet, not until the Laura thing had been cleared up.

'I've started a temping job.'

'Great. How's it going?'

'Actually, I like it. It's really interesting.'

'Better than the last place, then?'

'In some ways; I do miss the people though. There's one girl called Margot who's really nice; a bit daft but very friendly. Trouble is, apart from some teenage I.T. guy who's always picking his nose and playing computer games, she's the only young one there. It makes me realise what good fun my old crowd at CapiTel were.'

'So what next then?'

'How do you mean?' I asked.

'Well, if it's not what you want…?'

I thought for a bit.

'I like it. I really do. I just think that in future, I'll aim to put a bit more thought into what I really want out of a job.'

'Such as…?'

'Such as more people, a better location, nicer offices. You know, that sort of thing.'

Pauline smiled.

'Sounds to me like you're growing up, Miss Parsons.'

'Shut up! I am doing no such thing!' I complained, giving her foot a firm nudge beside me.

'OK, that's the work bit done; now, how about something a bit juicier – love life?'

'Complicated,' I admitted.

'In other words, mind my own business.'

'I didn't say that.'

'You didn't have to.'

'How's Terry?' I ventured.

'Complicated!' She laughed.

'In other words, change the subject.'

'Change the record more like. I've had Timmy bending my ear about him since he arrived.' She shook her head and sighed.

Timmy came in then with the teas.

'Ralfie's shat in the middle of the lawn; looks like you've been invaded by a herd of small horses!' He placed the tea tray down on the side table.

Ralfie was Pauline's Great Dane.

'Oh, just stick it on the compost heap. It's good for the roses,' Pauline said.

'I'll do no such thing! I'm not going near that steaming pile of germs.' Timmy folded his arms indignantly.

'You can use one of the pairs of rubber gloves you bought me,' Pauline added.

His face brightened.

'The ones with the leopard fur round the cuffs?'

'With my absolute pleasure.'

Chapter Forty-four

'Ow's your new bloke then?' Margot asked, one day at work.

'I never said I had a new bloke!'

'You didn't 'ave to. It's written all over your face.'

Was it?

'Big time,' she added.

'What exactly does my face say?' I wondered, not for the first time, if Margot really was psychic.

'It says you like this guy but things aren't exactly rosy.'

I shook my head.

'I don't know how you can work all that out just from looking at me.'

'I'm an expert, me. I studied human behavioural psychology at college.'

'Did you?' I was taken aback. I didn't think Margot was the type to have gone to college.

'Yair, it were really smaart. We had this bloke come in from the local shrink place and give us a talk on body language, facial expressions; that sort of thing. You know?'

I didn't.

'Besides, you've been gawpin' at your phone every time I've seen you. Waiting for a call?'

'No, just a text,' I admitted.

I thought I might as well tell her about Tony. She didn't know him, after all.

'I've been seeing this guy called Tony. And he's... well... it's complicated.'

'Married?'

'No!'

'Complicated how then?'

I considered the situation.

'Well, first off, he's the brother of a guy I was once in love with.'

'And you still like the first guy?'

'No, no… no,' I faltered. 'It's not like that… anyway, that's not the point.'

'Sounds like it might be.'

'No really, you don't understand.'

'Hmmm.' She narrowed her eyes.

'What do you mean hmmm?'

'Nothing. Carry on.'

'Well, he's kind of engaged.'

'Who the bloke you're not in love with?'

'Not him, Tony the guy I'm seeing.'

'Kind of engaged? Surely he's either engaged or not engaged?'

'You'd think so wouldn't you?' I said, wearily. 'Thing is, his fiancée's got a bit of a problem in letting him go, so he's seeing me too.'

'Uh huh.'

'It's not as bad as it seems. He's only with her until he can make sure she's well enough to handle him not being with her anymore.'

As I said it, I knew how it must have sounded.

'Ohhkayy. And you believe him, right?'

'Well, yes… of course.'

Margot's face spoke volumes.

'I know what you're thinking, but I really like him. And I… trust him. He's just trying to do the right thing.'

Margot shrugged. 'And the sex?'

I blushed.

She shook her head.

'You've not shagged yet then?'

'No.' I felt like I should apologise.

'How come?'

How come indeed?

'There hasn't been much of a chance really.'

Was that the real reason?

Whatever Margot thought on the subject, she kept it to herself.

'What's his star sign?' she asked.

'I, er, don't… know.'

She shook her head.

'It'll never work.'

'Why?' I said indignantly.

'If you really like a guy, you find out his star sign on the first date. It's what we do, us girls. It's our way of finding out whether the bloke is compatible. You know? Marriage material and all that…'

'I didn't think you believed in marriage,' I pointed out.

'I don't but I still aask. You never know, I might change my mind one day. Best to find out quickly, don't you think?'

I began thinking back over the serious relationships I'd had: Greg, Rob, Luke… and then some of the not so serious ones. She was right. Margot was right! I could tell you the star signs of each and every one of them. How come I'd never asked Tony? And come to that, it was my birthday coming up and, unless I told him, Tony would have no idea either. Now, *that* was worrying!

Chapter Forty-five

Tony was due back at the weekend.

He'd called three times since he'd been away and despite my truculent behaviour before he'd left we'd been getting on really well. We'd had long lazy conversations and lots of laughs. Plus, we'd had a rather sexy text fest, which had lasted a good few days and had left me more than a little excited about his return. And what with Paris serving as a distraction from his current situation, I'd almost managed to forget the fact that he was coming home to lead a double life again.

But then when he'd phoned the previous day we managed to have a mini row. The conversation had started out fine but I made the mistake of bringing up the subject of Laura. As we'd been getting on so well, I thought it would be safe to at least ask him his plans.

'Look, Tony, I don't want to get heavy about this…'

I could feel him tense up the other end.

'It's just that I want to be clear.'

'About what?' he said, a little tersely.

'Well, when you come back, will you be…' I hesitated, 'will you be talking to Laura? It's been a while now. Surely you could say something to her?'

'For crying out loud, Maggie!' he exploded. 'I'm in Paris, working my butt off. Don't you think I don't know what a shitty situation this is? Don't you think I'm going to do it as soon as I can?'

I felt sick.

'I don't know, Tony. But you keep avoiding the subject.'

'That's because I don't fucking like the subject.'

'Well neither do I!'

'There you go then. I'm dealing with it, OK?'

No, it wasn't OK.

'How?' I challenged.

'What do you mean, how?'

'What I say. How *exactly* are you dealing with it Tony? I know you keep telling me you're dealing with it and you've got things under control but I haven't got a clue what you're actually saying to Laura. Or even whether you're saying anything!'

'Oh for goodness sake, what do you take me for? Some sort of a sick liar?'

'I'm not saying that.'

'Aren't you?

'No...'

'Well, what then?'

'I don't know, Tony. You tell me.'

Silence.

Had I gone too far? Then he sighed.

'Listen, Maggie, it's like this; Laura's not well, you know that, and I'm the shit who is making the situation worse. And I don't feel entirely happy about what I've done. I know you've been taking a lot for granted...'

That was putting it mildly.

'... but just bear with me, OK? I *will* talk to her.'

'Good. Because if you don't, then... well... I just might.'

'Oh yeah?' he challenged, a sarcastic snigger creeping into his voice.

'Yeah,' I confirmed, sounding braver than I felt.

'Don't do anything stupid, Maggie, for God's sake.'

That did it.

'Stupid? STUPID?' My voice sailed up. 'It's not me who's leading a double life. It's not me who's making his ex-fiancée think everything's fine, is it?'

'You know what I meant.'

The conversation was really bringing me down.

'You know, I was telling Margot about us, if there is an "us", the other day and...'

'Who the fuck's Margot?' he demanded.

'Just this girl at work. Never mind about that...'

'What do you mean never mind about that!? I hope you're not going off and telling every Tom, Dick and Harry about this.'

'Not every Tom, Dick or Harry, Tony. Just Margot. She doesn't even know you!

Anyway, as I was telling her about you and about the situation, you know, it sounded *crap*.'

'Meaning...?'

'Meaning that, as much as I tried to convince her you were a good guy and that I really liked you and trusted you, I…' I paused, trying to think of how to say what I wanted to say, '… well, let's put it this way, I suddenly wasn't very sure who I was trying to convince, OK?'

There was silence at the other end. Then he spoke slowly and deliberately.

'Well, if that's how you feel, Maggie?'

'It is Tony,' I confirmed.

'Right, that's that then.'

'It is,' I confirmed again.

'I've got to go, Maggie. I have work to do.'

'Fine.'

'Seems like there's nothing left for us to say to each other then, doesn't it?'

'Seems that way.'

'In that case I'll say goodbye, Maggie.'

'Goodbye, Tony,' I said curtly and hung up.

'Bastard!' I said out loud, staring at the silent phone.

'BASTARD!'

The *cheek* of him. Honestly, anyone would think *I'd* done something wrong!

I went crashing and banging around my flat but five minutes later my phone sounded out the harmonious ting of a message alert and I raced over to the table, scrabbling frantically to pick it up.

Good, an apology. And quite right too.

Not an apology though.

It was Greg.

Chapter Forty-six

I guess it had been a question of timing. Any other time and no way would I have gone out with Greg. NO WAY! Particularly with hindsight. But, what with not having got round to saying no and what with him being so persistent and what with Tony being such a PIG (and still not having apologised), I somehow found myself agreeing to go to dinner with Greg. I knew I was just doing it to spite Tony, which was probably stupid, but I went anyway.

I arrived first at the Chinese restaurant. No change there then. Greg had always been purposely late so he could make an entrance. I sat in the waiting area by the small bar aimlessly 'liking' Facebook posts, as the waiters bustled about polishing wine glasses and clearing and laying tables. Not for the first time I was regretting turning up although, if I ever got the chance, I'd at least be throwing the occasion in Tony's face. I pushed guilty thoughts of Tony to the back of my mind reminding myself that he hadn't rung. He hadn't apologised and I was therefore perfectly within my rights to have an innocent meal with a friend… *or a dodgy ex.*

Greg finally turned up fifteen minutes late, shaking the rain off his umbrella from a freak shower. He appeared quite grown up, with his smart jeans, white shirt and linen jacket. He hadn't changed much really; still good looking in a boyish kind of way. A little more grown up, maybe, but the proof of the pudding and all that…

The maître d' was suddenly on hand, perhaps deciding that Greg would be a good customer.

Greg gave me one of his fake smarmy smiles as I stood up and I felt my insides deflate. I was a good three inches taller than him in my heels.

'Hello, Greg.' I smiled down at him, remembering how disappointed I had always been that he wasn't taller.

We kissed on the cheek and, as we did so, I breathed in his smell and was reminded of the fact that it had never actually turned me on.

'Maggie Parsons; looking good, girl.' He whistled, eyeing me up and down.

'It's been a while hasn't it? How was Thailand?'

'Oh, you know,' he shrugged coolly.

The word 'prat' inadvertently popped into my head.

'Come on, let's get you sat down first. We can talk then.'

I recalled how controlling Greg had been when we'd been together. I was already feeling like his younger counterpart.

We were led to our table in a corner. It was covered with a white linen cloth and silver cutlery had been laid out, with a little flower arrangement and an unlit candle in the middle of it.

The waiter ushered me to my seat, shaking out my napkin and placing it across my lap. Greg sat down opposite and smiled across at me as the waiter took out a lighter and lit the candle. Then taking some menus from the next table, he passed one to me and the other to Greg.

'The wine list, sir.' The waiter then passed Greg a third menu and left us to it.

'Maggie, Maggie, Maggie,' Greg said, looking over at me and shaking his head slowly. 'It's been too long, toooo long.'

'How are you Greg?'

'Oh you know,' he shrugged again.

Grrrrr!

I wasn't going to pander to him. If he wanted me to probe him, desperately wanting to hear all about his wonderful travels and amazing career, he'd have a long bloody wait.

I simply smiled innocently.

'Um, well actually,' he continued, 'I'm doing rather well at the moment. I'm a legal executive in the City firm I joined. I might have mentioned it in my text?'

Might have mentioned it indeed; he knew exactly what he had and hadn't mentioned.

'It's an impressive organisation, Maggie. I've done well to be accepted.'

I smiled again. 'I'm sure.'

'We get all sorts of interesting cases. Bet you'd like to hear about them. Remember when I used to come home every night and tell you all about my day and what I'd got up to. You used to love it.'

Oh I remembered all right and I'd be glazing over more like. At the time Greg was an estate agent and there had been nothing more boring than listening to him going on and on about interest rates and house prices. I remembered also how disturbing it was that he could happily convince couple after couple to borrow more than they could afford, to get what he had convinced them was the house of their dreams. The thing with Greg was he was a born achiever. Governed by success, he'd always strived for the best; probably why we'd finished in fact. I thought about how manipulative he once was and wondered if he'd changed. Somehow I doubted it. My regrets over the evening were already being compounded.

We studied the menu.

'Guess you'll be watching your weight then, Maggie?'

I shot him an annoyed look.

'Sorry, no harm intended. I just meant, you know, you always did. You were always very careful about your lovely figure.'

To be precise, *he* was the careful one. If I so much as glanced at a bar of chocolate, he'd be there to remind me of my *precious* figure. Greg liked me to be 'just so'.

'Actually, I wasn't going to watch my weight at all. I don't need to these days. In fact, I'm not sure I ever did,' I said evenly.

Greg eyed me warily.

That may well have been true but, when we'd been together, I'd had a real thing about my weight, born from Greg's continuous criticism no doubt. I'd been really paranoid about putting on the pounds. On more than one occasion Greg had made the fatal mistake of telling me I'd put on weight. Once he'd even called me chubby! I'd taken it so much to heart that I'd practically starved myself for a month.

'Well you're looking fit, Maggie; *really* fit. Go right ahead and tuck in to whatever you like. This evening's on me.'

I inadvertently went to say, 'I should think so', but Greg interrupted me.

'No, not another word,' He put his hand up. 'I won't hear of you paying a penny toward this evening. In fact, I've just been given a pay rise. Even though I've not long joined the firm,' Greg continued proudly. 'So, you can help me celebrate.'

I wanted to punch him.

'Lovely,' I said vaguely, as I contemplated the menu. I wanted to go for the deep-fried everything but annoyingly Greg's weight comments were still floating about, so I began to consider a more slender selection before an angry light bulb moment occurred. God he was infuriating! To hell with this; I was going to order whatever the hell I wanted!

Unaware of my bitter inner conflict Greg proceeded to tell me about his travels.

'… and you should have seen the beaches, Maggie, stunning. You'd have loved them.'

'If I'd been with you, I probably would have,' I responded – not meaning anything particular by it.

A wry smile crossed his lips.

'Oh, come on, Maggie, you're not going to hold that against me are you?' He reached across and took my hand. 'I had to go, you know that? It was in my blood. I needed to travel and get it out my system.'

Smug git!

'Oh trust me, Greg. It's fine; *really* fine.' I smiled at the waiter, as he came over to take our drinks order.

Greg ordered some expensive white wine, without consulting me. Oh well, more fool him. If anything was sure to loosen my tongue and remove my self-control, that would be the drink of choice… but, hey, what could I say, his choice not mine.

The wine arrived quickly, which was a godsend. I downed my first glass with rapid speed and ignored Greg's quizzical frown as I poured a second one.

'Still like a drink then, Maggie?' he commented. I wondered how much damage I could do with a chopstick; perhaps an accidental stab in the eye or up the nose? Yes, the nose. Then I could whip it back out again, having punctured his brain, and no one would be any the wiser. I could place the chopstick in his hand and feign complete ignorance when all the waiters rushed over to find out why he was slumped over face down in his won ton soup.

The waiter returned with his pad and pen and, as I placed my order for a starter, I glanced surreptitiously over at Greg to watch for his reaction when I went for the prawn toast. True to form, he raised his eyebrows.

The chopstick saga returned for part two. His ear seemed particularly inviting.

And so it went on. Despite having told me how good I looked, everything I chose throughout the boring conversation-stilted meal got a comment.

'Chow Mein eh? Yes, I remember how you used to eat that by the bucket load from the takeaway, back in the good old days.'

'Spring rolls, eh? A moment on the lips, a lifetime on the hips.'

'Apple fritters? Wow, Maggie, are you sure you've got room?' he remarked, when we – or rather I – ordered dessert.

Bastard! I was seriously close to hating him. Tony would never have treated me like this. That did it. Suddenly I wanted to be with Tony. Mad ex-fiancée or not, he was gorgeous and he *did* want to be with me and he was intelligent and funny. Bloody Greg, I thought, finishing another glass of wine and helping myself to the last of the bottle.

The alcohol was really beginning to affect me.

I couldn't be bothered to check out Greg's no doubt critical expression but I was aware of his fingers starting to drum on the table. I avoided his gaze, even when I grabbed the arm of a passing waiter and ordered a second bottle, nearly knocking the tray out of his hand in my vigour. White wine, particularly decent white wine, had a lot to answer for at the best of times. While I loved it, when drunk in quantity, it was well known for its ability to knock my head off and make me say all sorts of outrageous stuff. Causing me to get: a) feisty b) angry c) emotional d) way hey! e) all of the above.

Tonight was evidently an 'e) all of the above' night and I found myself getting more and more sarcastic through my apple fritter course. Having finished my last mouthful, I leant back in my chair, riding it slightly, and rubbed my tummy. And quite forgetting, or maybe not caring, where I was, I belched. Loudly! I thought for a minute about excusing myself and then decided I might as well be hung for a sheep as a lamb so I did it again!

I giggled provokingly, sensing fear from the other side of the table.

Greg was quite obviously embarrassed and hastily scanned the faces of the other diners.

I stopped riding my chair, pushed it away from the table as I stood up and went to the loo without a word. When I came back, Greg's leg was nervously jiggling under the table.

I sat down heavily, aware of how wobbly I'd become. Regardless, I wanted more and poured out another very full glass from the newly arrived bottle ignoring Greg completely and glancing drunkenly round the restaurant, smiling at whoever would dare to look at me.

'Don't you think you've had enough now, Maggie?' Greg hissed.

I allowed myself to face him putting on what I intended to be a scary, predatory expression. Then I leant forward and narrowed my eyes.

'D'you know, Greg, you're right. I *have* had enough. I've had enough of you. All fucking night (oops, here we go, and it gets worse) you've been jibing on about my weight, my appearance, the past, what you like, what you don't like... all the *bloody* time, going on and on and on...' I could actually hear my own voice sounding more than a little drunk.

'But I...'

'Shut up! I feel like you are slowly picking me apart and stripping off the bits you don't approve of. Well, if that's the case, why the bloody hell did you want to go out with me in the first place?' I slurred, gulping down some more wine.

'Well, I...'

'In fact, I need to take some of the flack, cos it was *me* who agreed to go out with *you*, so really this is *all my* fault. I don't give a shit (I said shit really loudly and all the waiters looked over at once, as did some of the diners, who'd gone rather silent anyway) about how much you earn or what your stupid job title is or how fat you think I am (luckily the guy at the next table shook his head disbelievingly at the idea and I thanked him loudly, then his wife got cross). I also don't give a damn whether you think I've had enough wine, or whether an apple fritter is really a good idea cos, actually, Greg, it is. It's all a good idea. The whole menu would be a good idea, if you weren't so bloody stingy...'

He started to protest but I was having none of it.

'... all the fat, stodgy, sloppy, yummy lot of it. I'm out for a meal and I'm eating exactly what I want and how I want it. The only let down is that you are most *certainly* not the man I want to eat it with. So there!' And I leant back in my chair, drained my glass, then bent down and groped around on the floor for my bag, which had temporarily disappeared. I had a feeling that the guy at the next table was tempted to clap but his wife didn't appear particularly enthusiastic, so he winked surreptitiously at me and carried on eating.

Poor Greg was shocked. I say poor Greg because, had I played back the scene in the sober cold light of day, I may well have seen myself over-reacting somewhat. But, it had been building over the course of our past relationship and that night all it had taken was a few jibes and I'd let him have it.

My bag was finally found in the cloakroom – left there accidentally when I'd gone to the loo. This unfortunately put a stop to the quick and dramatic exit I had planned to do after my little speech. So Greg and I had to walk out together.

'Thank you, Gregory,' (he hated being called Gregory) I said, as I flagged down a cab and got in, feeling very light headed and completely fearless.

Before shutting the door, I turned back to him. 'It's been a ball! Ring me sometime, why don't you – NOT!'

I slammed the door. And off we drove, leaving the stunned Greg nursing a bruised ego and a dented wallet. Despite what he'd said about treating me, Greg had always been stingy and he would have hated 'wasting' money on the evening. The wine we were drinking had cost over thirty pounds a bottle. I suppose, therefore, it was lucky that I'd sneaked out the rest of the second bottle under my coat with me.

'You didn't!' Catherine said, agog, when I told her the following evening on her night off.

We sat drinking cups of sweet tea, curled up on her big squashy sofa.

'I did; twice! Loudly too!'

She rolled up with laughter.

'Not going back to him then?' she said.

'God, Cat, it was like going back in time, only worse. Never ever in a million years could I go back there again, urgh, never!' I felt ill at the thought, although it could have been my hangover.

'Well good for you. I always thought you could do better.'

'Did you? You never told me that,' I said indignantly.

'I know but, if I had, you'd have felt bad and anyway he went off "to find himself", so I didn't need to.'

'He may well have found himself but I just found him irritating!'

'Any word from Tony?'

'No.' My insides sank.

'Think you're going to?'

'I think I might have blown it.'

It had been four days now and I'd heard nothing. I'd been staring at the phone all morning, willing it to ring. I hoped that if I stared at it long enough Tony would somehow pick up my vibes and contact me with an apology. Mind you he had apologised, hadn't he, or at least he'd tried. Only I'd dismissed it. It may have been the anxious feelings my hangover had brought with it but I'd begun to seriously doubt myself again. While I'd been truthful with Tony, as with any impromptu outburst of feelings, I was left with the awful notion that I may have gone too far.

'It's not on though, Maggie,' Catherine said, interrupting my anxiety. 'He can't go around expecting you to accept the situation. I think you did exactly the right thing. Oh, Tom, stop it. You're digging your claws into me, you naughty boy.' She pushed Tom off her lap and he huffily strutted over to the opposite armchair, totally ignoring me.

'How come I feel so horrid about it all then?'

'Maybe because it *is* horrid.'

'I think I might have ruined things.' I gazed gloomily into my lap.

'*You*? How?'

'By not trusting him.'

She sighed. 'Maggie, listen, Tony has treated you pretty badly in my opinion.'

I looked up. 'You think?'

'Yes, I do. I'm sure you get on well and I know he makes you laugh and you find him attractive but this Laura business… he's not exactly making things easy for you, is he?'

'I know, but if I'd really trusted him I'd have left him to do what he said he was going to do and just forgotten about it.'

'And you think that would have been possible do you?'

'What?'

'For you to have just forgotten about it, just acted as if nothing was going on with Laura?'

I considered it.

'Well… no… perhaps not completely. But if I had, we wouldn't have had the row in the first place. I could at least have given him a chance to do things his way.'

'And if you hadn't had the row, you'd still be sitting here worrying about the situation. At least this way you've made your feelings clear. You've been true to yourself, Maggie, and that's the only way.'

I wasn't convinced. I'd been feeling very lonely for the last four days, especially since the charade with Greg, and had begun to realise just how much I'd been relying on Tony, what with Catherine working so much and me in a new job; one that didn't exactly offer much of a social life because Margot was always out with one her cosmopolitan bunch of men. My thoughts flickered to my old friends at CapiTel. Maybe I could give Maureen a ring?

'When's he back?' Catherine asked.

'Saturday. Shit – tomorrow!'

'Well, I'm not going to tell you what to do but I really don't like you being taken advantage of.'

'I'm not.'

'You can be too soft sometimes, Maggie. Whatever you do, don't contact him. Leave it for him to get in touch with you, OK?'

'OK.' I didn't mention the fact that I'd been seriously toying with the idea of texting him ever since I'd woken up.

Chapter Forty-seven

Saturday came and went; nothing – not a peep from Tony Henderson. He'd have been back since the Saturday lunchtime and by Sunday evening I knew I'd blown it. Self- respect had never been my strong point and it was currently not occurring to me that I might have done exactly the right thing.

That evening I went to see Pip who had invited me down for a drink as he had the flat to himself.

'You look dreadful, Mags, you OK?'

'Thanks! No, not really. I think I've mucked up my already dire love life.'

Pip grinned. 'Join the club!'

'Trouble in paradise?' I asked.

'I'm not sure we ever reached the paradise stage.'

'What's the latest?'

'We nearly broke up again last night.'

'How come?'

'It's never quite got back to where it should be, since Poncey Leo reared his ugly helmet.'

'Yuck! Pip!'

'Well, I bet he has got an ugly helmet. Red and swollen and really veiny.'

'What will you do?'

He shrugged.

'What I always do probably, sit tight until something major makes me move on or stay put.'

I knew that feeling of old.

'I'll get us something to drink, shall I? Andrew's out bowling tonight with work. He invited me along but I'd probably have wanted to smash one of the balls over Poncey Leo's head.'

'Aren't you worried about them being together, since, well you know, what happened between them.'

He started searching through Andrew's drinks cupboard.

'Not really. Do you think that's a sign I should move on?'

'Probably,' I replied honestly. 'But I'm sure you'll do the best thing when the time's right.'

Pip's muffled voice echoed from the depths of the cabinet. 'Apart from a million litres of mineral water and cartons of cranberry juice, there's only Drambuie or advocaat. Oh, hang on, what's this?' He reached his arm further in to the back. 'Ouzo! Must be the one we brought back from Mykonos last year.'

One and a half ouzos on the rocks later my phone tinged with the sound of a text.

From Tony!

I felt my heart quicken as I swiped the phone's face and opened the message.

Hello Gorgeous. Sorry4 being an arse. I've got some news. At my dad's for a couple of days, but meet me Wed eve? TX

Through my ouzo haze, I decided this could be very good news and for the first time in four days I began to properly relax.

Chapter Forty-eight

Margot had been off on the Monday so I had to wait until Tuesday to tell her about

Tony's text.

'You gonna meet him then?' she asked.

'Yes. He's picking me up at my place.'

'He's probably a Gemini,' she said thoughtfully.

'Why?'

'Double lives and all that. Never trust a Gemini, that's my motto.'

'I thought your motto was, if it moves shag it,' I pointed out.

She smirked. 'That's my other motto.'

'Surely saying all Geminis shouldn't be trusted is a bit of a generalisation don't you think?'

'Maybe, but as far as I'm concerned as star signs go Gemini's the one to watch.'

Despite my misgivings, I sincerely hoped Tony wasn't a Gemini.

That evening I came in through the main front door and spotted a pile of post on the side for all the different flats that no one had bothered to sort out. Sifting through and depositing mail into the various pigeon holes, I found that all I had was a bill, a reminder from my dentist that my check-up was due, two free papers and a magazine on seated corner baths for the elderly and infirm. Brilliant!

I made my way up to my flat, wondering for the millionth time when the lift was going to be mended. I let myself in, put my mail on the kitchen table and poured myself a glass of red wine. It had been a long day.

Several leaflets fell out of one of the papers as I opened it. MFI were having one of their omnipresent sales and I could get fifty per cent off selected kitchens and bathrooms. Homebase were having their own sale and I could get twenty per cent off selected home ware. The AA were promoting personal loans and if I applied and was successful I'd be eligible for a twenty-five pounds M&S voucher (tempting actually) and then finally Peabody and

Peabody (the bath people) were also having a sale and I could get twenty-five per cent off selected seated corner baths, with a free – guaranteed non-slip – rubber mat thrown in.

I sighed loudly. It all seemed to be about money these days. Half the adverts on television were about either sorting out all your money problems with a big fat, high-interest, loan, claiming back 'wrongly paid' PPI or suing your employer for just about anything that didn't fit into stringent health and safety guidelines.

I very nearly chucked out the envelope. I didn't see it at first. It had got caught up between the two free newspapers and, had it not slipped out from between them on my way to the recycling box, I may have never read it.

It was a typed white envelope, with a Tillmouth postmark. Tony? Was this his news?

Butterflies began to flutter in my stomach as I carefully opened the envelope, making sure not to tear anything inside.

His way of apologising? Was he sending me tickets to Ronnie Scott's with promises of enjoying it more this time? Perhaps this was the present from Paris. Maybe it was two tickets to somewhere romantic, Paris even, and he was planning to spoil me rotten for a weekend.

I unfolded the letter.

My eyes widened in shock. It wasn't from Tony at all.

I sat at my table, staring at the note in front of me. A mixture of sick, excited, terror filled me and I smoothed the letter flat in front of me.

Maggie

… it read

So, I was right not to trust him around you. Women's intuition, always a good barometer. I hope you'll be very happy.

Good luck. I think you'll need it.

I won't be seeing you again.

Laura.

Laura!

Tony had told her. *He'd really done it.*

But what did she mean? 'I won't be seeing you again?' I sincerely hoped she wasn't planning to do anything drastic!

I thought back to the phone conversation I'd had with Tony just days earlier. Perhaps Catherine had been right. Maybe by telling him how I really felt, he'd finally decided to take some action. Suddenly I felt proud of myself for speaking my mind and standing my ground. It was like I'd somehow turned one of life's corners. On top of that, I felt free. Free of the situation and free of all the bad feelings I'd had recently. Tony had really finished with Laura and, in twenty-four hours, he'd tell me himself, face to face. I guessed it wouldn't have been easy for him though. Well, I would let him know that I understood and was on his side but, also, that it hadn't been easy for me either. Whatever had happened, I was glad. Finally, we could move on, together.

'See! I told you so,' Catherine said, when I rang her. 'Honesty really is the best policy.'

'OK, Mrs Know-It-all...you were right.'

'I know.' I could hear her smiling down the phone.

'So, how are things with you and Nico then?'

She sighed dramatically. 'Lovely, just lovely. I really think he could be the one, Mags. And before you say anything, I know I've said that before but this time I mean it. He's so perfect, I feel like I've met my soul mate.'

'What's his star sign?' I asked suddenly.

'Cancer,' she answered, without hesitation. 'Nurturing, generous and home-loving.

Why?'

'Oh...no reason,' I replied, despondently. 'Just wondering.'

Chapter Forty-nine

Tony came round at seven thirty the following evening. I opened the door and he leaned lazily in the doorframe. I'd forgotten how lovely and tall he was. Bloody short arse Greg Smeg.

I smiled. It was good to see him.

'Now then, are you going to pour me a drink and tell me all about what you've been up to for the past two weeks or are you going to pour me a drink and throw it in my face for being such an arse?' he asked.

I took the bottle of red wine he was holding out and headed towards the kitchen.

'You'll just have to find out, won't you?' I replied teasingly over my shoulder.

'Shut the door on your way…' I paused… 'in.'

Smiling to myself in the kitchen, I took down two glasses from the cupboard.

'Make yourself at home, Tony,' I called out to the lounge.

'Very formal, I must say,' he called back.

Carrying a small tray with the clinking glasses and bottle, I placed them on the coffee table. Tony sat on the sofa.

'Open that, will you?' I said airily then wandered off to check my makeup, feeling rather proud of myself for playing it so cool.

'My pleasure, *Maam*. Like the hair by the way,' he called after me.

I'd straightened it, knowing he preferred it that way. I hoped he didn't mind it natural either but there was no harm in a bit of give and take I'd decided. I'd made up my mind that we were going to have a lovely evening. I'd even put on my sexiest, black, low-cut, top; one that I knew gave me a lot of cleavage. I'd paired it with some fitted, deep purple, cotton trousers, which hugged my bum, then I'd donned a pair of black strappy wedges to give me height but stability; and finally I'd added a hipster-style chain belt, for effect. My make-up was quite light, but a dash of daring purple at the corners of my mascaraed eyes, along with a pout of lip gloss gave the exact effect I was after.

'So, aren't you going to ask about my news, then?' Tony quizzed as I walked back in. 'By the way, have I told you how utterly stunning you look this evening?'

'You haven't. But thank you.' I remained demure and sat on the armchair.

'Oh, Maggie, so far away! He rolled over onto his side, clutching his heart. 'I've been pining over you every moment of every day in that bloody hellhole they call Paris and you reward me by sitting as far away as possible? Perleeease! You'll be the death of me.'

'That's the first time I've heard Paris called a hellhole.'

'You wouldn't believe it,' he said. 'All those fancy restaurants, glamorous shops and glitzy bars. You'd have hated it. And they actually expect you to eat all that haute cuisine muck. It's just plain wrong!'

I smiled.

He'd already uncorked the wine and proceeded to pour out two glasses.

'Well?' he asked.

'Well, what?'

'Aren't you going to ask me what my news is?'

'No.'

'Why not?'

I shrugged.

Tony passed me my glass.

'Thanks.'

He studied me quizzically.

'You'll tell me when you're ready, Tony, I'm sure.' I sipped my wine. I wasn't going to mention the letter just yet.

'You're a hard woman, Maggie Parsons, a hard woman.'

'Is that right?' I stood up slowly moving over to join him on the sofa.

He put his glass down and took mine from my hand, placing it beside his on the coffee table.

As his eyes met mine I saw his pupils dilate.

'Or maybe it's just me that's hard.'

He leant forward and kissed me gently then slowly pulled back again.

'I've missed you, you know. Have you missed me?'

'Might have.'

He shook his head and sighed.

'You're not letting up yet, are you?'

'I don't know what you mean, Tony Henderson.'

'Of course, if you don't want to hear my news, well that's perfectly fine I guess. I can wait.'

I shuffled around in my seat.

'Up to you. Is it worth it?'

'Oh, it's worth it all right,' he assured me.

I breathed out a sigh. 'Ohhhh, go on then, I can see you're dying to tell me.'

His expression became serious then and he picked up my hands from my lap.

'First of all, Maggie, all joking apart, I care about you OK? And I never wanted to hurt you in any of this. I know how patient you've been and I'm sorry if I overreacted in Paris. It's just that the whole thing was really getting to me. I've been a real jerk and I realised that when I was out there. So I went back to my dad's and I called Laura.'

He searched my face but I remained silent. I squeezed his hand slightly and he continued.

'I went over there and sat her down and told her the truth. About us, I mean.'

'What did she say?'

'Nothing much; that was the weird thing, she was pretty calm about it.'

He picked up his glass and took a mouthful before carefully placing it back on the table.

'She's always been pretty good at hiding her feelings but, to tell you the truth, I really think she was OK about things. She mouthed off a bit about knowing that there was something between you and me and that she'd been right all along. You know woman scorned and all that... sorry,' he added, seeing my look of disapproval. 'But that was it.'

'And she was really OK? I mean you were so worried about her; how she'd handle it.'

'I know. I'm beginning to wonder whether I imagined it all. She was so calm. I spoke to her mum today.'

'What for?'

'You know, just to make sure she hadn't fallen apart when I'd left.'

'You conceited bugger!' I whacked him with a cushion.

'Ouch! No, seriously, I didn't know and I needed to,' he said.

'Fair enough. And what did she say?'

He laughed sardonically.

'She was back to being good old Laura's mum. Any excuse to give me the cold shoulder these days, not like it used to be.'

I was curious at this sudden reference to the past.

'What was it that attracted you to Laura? I mean you must have loved her once.'

At last, I felt it was OK to discuss her.

Tony gazed out into a scene that only he could see.

'Yes, I did, once. It used to be great.'

I steeled myself to hear the words I needed to hear but didn't totally want to.

'She had an amazing smile. I think that's what first drew me in. And I guess... she made me feel... cared for. I liked that. I needed it... back then.' He smiled at a distant, private memory. 'We used to go up and stay at her mum's place. It was pretty great. When you grow up without a mum, you don't realise all the things you miss out on until you spend a lot of time with someone else's. I know things have changed now but her mum and I used to be close.'

'Do you miss her? Your mum I mean?' I ventured.

I watched Tony's face intently for his reaction and a muscle tightened in his jaw line.

Had I overstepped the mark?

But he simply shrugged, coming out of his daydream.

'I guess,' he answered flatly.

He didn't seem to want to dwell on it.

'Anyway, Laura's mum pretty much confirmed what Laura had said. That basically, I am a no-good loser and Laura is better off without me.'

'She's probably right.'

'Hey you!' it was his turn to hit me with the cushion. 'I'll have you for that.'

'So, it's all off, officially. You're a free man then?'

He swivelled round and faced me full on, reaching across to touch my cheek.

'Maybe not *free* free.'

I blushed.

'Just a little bit tied down perhaps?' He leant across and kissed me again. This time, it wasn't so gentle.

'God you're sexy, Maggie,' he said gruffly, nuzzling into my neck in between kisses.

'Couldn't we just stay in this evening? Eating out can be very overrated you know.'

I pulled away from him pushing him back to his side of the sofa.

'Oh no you don't, Tony Henderson; you promised me a night out... and a present come to think of it! Don't think you're getting away with things that easily.'

'Damn!' he said, in mock crossness. 'Seems like I'll just have to wait then, doesn't it.'

'All good things come to he who waits.' I leant over, this time, and kissed him.

'Now come on, call a taxi while I redo the lip gloss you've managed to kiss off, and if I find you haven't brought me a present back, you might be waiting an awful long time!'

I went to the bathroom and touched up my face, feeling good as I spritzed perfume over neck and cleavage. Coming back out I gave Tony the benefit of a wide and confident smile.

'Ready?'

'Ready,' he confirmed.

'Oh, by the way, I knew you'd finished it with Laura,' I said, slipping on my jacket.

The evenings were cooler now the summer was all but over.

He looked puzzled.

'Am I that predictable?'

'No, but Laura kind of spelled it out in a letter for me.' I picked up Laura's letter from the hall table and handed it to him.

Saying nothing, he unfolded it and read it to himself.

'What do you think of that then?' I asked.

His brow furrowed pensively.

'You don't seem very shocked,' I said.

'I suppose I'm not really. It's the kind of thing Laura would do. She likes to tie up loose ends. Remain in control. It'll be her way of giving the seal of approval.'

'You think she approves then?'

'Probably not but she'll want you to think she's being cool about it. And she knows you'll tell me.'

He handed me back the letter.

'I wonder how she got my address?' I said.

Tony was thoughtful.

'Off your text in my phone knowing her or maybe my email address book, I don't know,' he smirked. 'She'd have smuggled it from somewhere though. What did you think when you read it? Were you shocked?'

'Totally! Although I was glad she'd written it,' I admitted.

He narrowed his eyes at me searching my face.

'Good. Well, if you're sure.'

'I'm sure.'

The beer garden was busy despite it being midweek. The trees around us were beginning to turn, indicating the end of the summer. It would be autumn soon, my favourite season. I loved the changing colours, the new smells in the air and a different wardrobe after months of summer clothes. It had always made me think about the future and new starts.

We'd managed to find a table by the little water feature and were already on our second round. On an empty stomach, I was beginning to feel very loose-tongued.

'So did you really miss me then?' I asked.

'Every day from morning 'til night.'

'Good. Where's this present then?'

'I'd forgotten that. Hang on.'

He slipped his hand inside his jacket and pulled out a little box.

'Hope you like them.'

I opened it up and inside was a little pair of earrings. Not my usual taste but... yes... they were nice.

'They're lovely, Tony,' I said.

'You hate them.'

'No! Of course I don't. They're really sweet.'

'I didn't know your taste but I thought these would look good on you.'

'Thank you. I'll wear them next time I see you.' I put the earrings away in my bag and we sat in silence for a few moments, sipping our drinks.

A family were on the next table to us; a mum and dad with a young boy of about five and a small baby – possibly also a boy. I watched it gurgling away, shrieking happily while the dad kept blowing raspberries on its tummy. I suddenly realised that I hadn't even mentioned Sian being pregnant to Tony.

Initially I'd decided not to say anything; after all, it really wasn't up to me. Besides, Luke had been a touchy subject and I'd tended to avoid talking about him completely. But now I felt a bit bad. If Tony and I were together, we'd tell each other stuff like this. And right then we were getting on really well so maybe it was a good time. Besides, I really didn't want Tony to think I was keeping secrets from him.

'So, what do you think Luke's going to do about the baby?'

Tony's face froze. *'Whaaat?'*

'Sian and him.'

He went almost white. 'What do you mean?'

'She's pregnant, oh god, didn't you know?'

'Sian's pregnant?' he asked shakily.

'Well…yes, so I understand. I'm so sorry, Tony, I thought you must have known. Didn't he say anything at all?'

'Er no, not a thing; how… how do you know?' he faltered.

'I overheard him on the phone to her. Looks like for once in his life he'll have to face up to his responsibilities.'

Tony went very quiet.

'I had no idea,' he said eventually.

'Maybe he's embarrassed to say anything to anyone. It could be a secret.'

'Maybe,' he agreed.

We sat in more silence. Had I been wrong to mention it? Tony had gone a bit strange.

I needn't have worried, though. Soon after, he seemed to gather himself together.

'Poor Luke.'

'Yeah?' I said. 'How come?'

'Well if you think about it, one minute the engagement's off and the next she's pregnant; must be a bit of a shock.'

'Probably, but it's not my problem.' I took a mouthful of my drink.

'Who else knows?' he asked.

I shrugged. 'Dunno. Catherine, I suppose. I told her at the time but I haven't mentioned it to anyone else. It's not really down to me is it.'

'No, I guess it's not. Actually, Maggie, maybe it's best not to mention it to Jenny or Dad then. Leave that for Luke to do, yeah? I know how you feel about what he did to you but it's not really up to us to start spreading it before he's ready.'

'OK, it's no biggie to me,' I said, meaning it. 'Besides, Jenny'll probably tell me next time I speak to her. Anything to do with love and babies is right up her street at the moment. Have you met John?'

Tony was clearly distracted.

'I said have you met John yet?'

'What? John… er… yeah. Yeah.' He straightened up again. 'Decent bloke, I liked him.'

As it was late, we ordered some pub grub where we sat. It was getting quite dark by the time the food arrived and I wondered what we'd do when we got home. Tony was still a bit preoccupied.

In the cab back to the flat, I put my hand on his leg.

'So, coming back to mine then?' I said warmly.

He yawned. 'Do you know Maggie, I'm actually dead beat. I think this thing with Laura has taken more out of me than I thought. I didn't get much sleep last night. Do you mind if I take a rain check?'

I have to admit I was taken aback.

'Oh… OK then.'

I took my hand away and he glanced across at me.

'Please don't be upset. I really want to be with you, but I want our first time to be special and I'm completely bushed. The last thing I want to do is to fall asleep on you. And the way I'm feeling right now, that's exactly what might happen, despite how amazing you look in that top.'

I relaxed a little.

'A rain check it is then.'

'Good. I'll need to cash it in soon though. I won't be able to wait long!'

I smiled sleepily and drunkenly at him.

Letting myself into my flat, my landline phone was ringing.

'Hello?'

'You really are the sexiest girl alive you know, Maggie.'

I smiled into the receiver.

'I know,' I said playfully. 'You'd better remember that the next time you turn me down.'

'Oh you can be sure there won't be a next time. In fact, I'm already thinking about how to make our next date extra special.'

'Oh yes? You're making the assumption that I'll accept the offer of another date then.'

'You want me to jump on you without wining and dining you first?'

When he put it like that…

He ended the call with the promise of phoning me very soon to set something up. I replaced the receiver, feeling happily merry. Finding the remote control, I went to turn on the TV but the phone rang again.

'That was quick!' I said, assuming it was Tony.

'What was?'

'Sorry, Cat, I thought you were Tony.'

'I've got some news,' she said excitedly.

'Not you as well, it's been my night for news. Go on then, what is it?'

'You'll never guess,' she gushed.

'You're probably right. I'm too drunk.'

She took a deep breath.

'Maggie…'

'What? Tell me!'

'I'm getting married!'

Chapter Fifty

'But you've only just met him!' I repeated when I went round the next day.

'Oh don't keep saying that. I haven't just met him, it's been ages! Besides, when you know, you know.'

We sat at the little dining table in front of her lounge window, drinking some mulled wine she was testing out the recipe for. It seemed to mark the start of the cooler weather and I sipped it gratefully, feeling the warm liquid cuddling my tummy. I eyed her glittering diamond engagement ring and felt bad. I knew I was spoiling her news.

'I'm sorry, hun, but are you sure? I mean *really* sure? It hasn't been that long and *marriage*... it's a big commitment.'

'I know but I'm sooo sure; absolutely, definitely. We're like two halves of the same book. We fit together. We... complete each other.' Catherine blushed. 'We like the same things, finish each other's sentences, laugh at the same jokes and we share so many of the same values. We even have birth marks in the same place!'

'Maybe you're brother and sister, separated at birth.'

'Yes, or maybe we're soul mates and were meant to meet and get married.'

It crossed my mind that I might be jealous.

'Listen, Mags, I know you're just looking out for me but you don't need to. Honestly. I don't think I've ever been so sure about anything in my life. I want to marry Nico and have his babies and live happily ever after.'

'That means you'll have to sleep with him,' I pointed out.

'I know! How fab is that?' she exclaimed, hugging herself. 'Oooh, I haven't told you how he proposed have I?'

'Go on.'

'Well, we went down to Brighton for the day and later on Nico said he'd always wanted to go on one of our British piers. I hadn't been on one for years so I thought why not! Oh Mags it was magical; we had so much fun and went in the amusements and laughed and laughed like kids...and then when we went outside again I went to the loo and when I came back Nico had bought all these doughnuts, you know those lovely little hot ringed ones they fry up in front of you? Anyway, we sat down on a bench and looked out to sea as the sun was setting and it was just perfect, and he passed me a doughnut on a little square serviette and I wasn't really paying attention because the sky looked so pretty, all pinks and oranges and bright yellows but then I realised Nico was watching me. So I asked him what he was staring at, you know how you do when you think the other person's thinking something nice about you but you want them to say it anyway. He had a big smile on his face and kept glancing down at the doughnut so I looked down and, in the middle of the doughnut, in the hole, was the ring! This ring!' she admired it for the millionth time.

'What did he say?'

'He got down on one knee, there and then, right in front of everyone. Not that it was very busy but still. He gazed up at me and said my name, really slowly, and he had tears in his eyes and everything and he said that if I would say yes to staying with him forever, then he would do everything he could to make me happy forever.'

Catherine's eyes filled with tears. (So did mine.)

'He really loves me, Maggie, I know he does.'

I leant over and squeezed her hand.

'Even Tom likes him and you know what a cross old bugger he can be,' she added.

That cemented it for me.

'Well in that case… congratulations.' I went round and hugged her. 'If you're sure and really are happy, then I'm happy too.'

'I am and I'm sooo excited! I'm going out to meet his family in October and we're having a winter wedding with fireworks and everything. I can't wait! She said, clinking my glass.

'OK. Well this is serious then. When exactly?'

'You might think it's a bit over the top.'

'I doubt it.' I considered my thoughts around my own fantasy wedding.

'November the fifth.' She pulled a face, waiting for my reaction.

I thought it was a fantastic idea.

'You don't think it's too much?'

'I think it's perfect,' I said honestly.

'Sooooo…' she began, 'that only gives us a couple of months. I think you and I have got some planning to do, don't you?' She stuck out her hand. 'Pen…'

I handed her the one which was sat right in front of her on the table.

'Paper…'

I went over and picked up a pad from the coffee table and passed it to her.

'Now then, the guest list,' she began. 'What do you think an acceptable number should be?'

'Do you think you should maybe include Nico in the planning bit?' I asked.

'Oh I will, only not quite yet. You and I have planned enough fake weddings over the years, I think it's only fair for us to be let loose on a real one for a change, don't you?'

I did.

And we were off. List upon list, just like when we were mucking around at school pretending we were marrying whoever we idolised at the time. Only now Catherine wouldn't be marrying Gorgeous Graham or Joe Riggs and I wouldn't be marrying Brad Pitt or… Luke. His face flashed in my mind.

'You OK?' Catherine asked.

'Yes, I'm fine. Just thinking of things I shouldn't be.'

'Luke?'

'How did you guess?'

'I know that look of old.'

'Come on, forget about all that, we've got a wedding to plan.'

And so we remained there at Catherine's little dining table, our only concerns being how many white doves would be allowed in the church and what kind of confetti was biodegradable. It was a tough job but somebody had to do it.

'By the way, you will be my chief bridesmaid, won't you?' Catherine said.

As if there had ever been any doubt.

'That's a bit quick isn't it?' Tony said when he rang and I shared Catherine's news. I wasn't sure I liked him saying that. It was OK for me to say it but not him.

'When you know, you know,' I said, a little curtly.

'Oh really. Is that right?'

'Yes. Anyway, they're happy and I'm happy for them.'

'OK, keep your hair on, I didn't mean anything by it. Maybe I'm just a bit more careful, that's all.'

'Mmmm, maybe.'

'So, when am I going to see you then? Or will you be too busy planning a wedding?'

'Probably, but I might just be able to squeeze you in.'

'I feel very privileged.'

'You are.'

'OK, Miss Playing Hard To Get, how about next week then? I'm seriously tight after that, I'm away for ten days at a conference in New York, which will be unbelievably full on, and then there'll be a load of meetings off the back of it.'

'Away *again*!' I couldn't help sounding upset.

'Sorry, babe, but I really need to go. We get shedloads of business from this conference every year.'

'When exactly do you leave?'

'Monday week.'

I realised, thinking about the dates, that he'd be away for my birthday. I still hadn't told him when it was. Should I mention it?

'You OK?' he asked when I fell silent.

'Yes. It's just you're away a lot. I didn't realise.'

'Aw, you're gonna miss me, aren't you.'

'No.'

'I think you are,' he sing-songed.

'If you don't shut up, I definitely won't.'

'Consider this me shutting up then.'

'Will I get another present?' I asked.

'Have you worn the last one yet?'

I hadn't.

'Of course!'

'Then I might. If you're good.'

'I think you *should* buy me one actually.' It was no good, my birthday was too special to me to keep a secret.

'Oh yes? Why's that then?'

'Well, it's my birthday on the second Saturday you're away.'

'You're kidding!'

''Fraid not.'

'Oh, Maggie, I didn't know. I'm so sorry.'

'S'OK,' I said, a little sulkily.

'Well, I promise we'll do something special when I get back. And why don't we get together next week and have an early birthday for you. If you don't fancy going out I could come round and cook you something.'

I had a thought.

'Why don't you cook me something at your place? I've haven't seen it yet.'

There was a pause.

'Er, well, I could but…'

'What's up? Are you ashamed of it?'

'No… but it's a bit…'

'Untidy?'

'No. It's not that.'

'What then?'

'It's just that… a lot of Laura's things are still there.'

'Oh.'

Oh indeed.

'She did used to live there you know.'

'I know.'

'We just haven't got round to sorting out when she's going to pick them up, that's all. So, if it's OK with you, I'd rather go out or come to you. Do you mind?'

'S'pose not.' I kind of did actually. Although I have to admit there was something peculiarly sexy in the jealousy I suddenly felt. I became quite possessive thinking about Tony and Laura together. But Tony was mine now, not hers.

'We could even go to that new club you mentioned?' Tony interrupted my rather unhealthy daydreaming.

'Maybe… but not midweek.'

'Friday then? I'm pretty snowed under until then.'

'Really?'

'Yes, really, work's never been so busy. How about we meet up for lunch before Friday though? I'm dying to see you. I can't get the vision of you in that sexy top out of my head.'

All was forgiven.

We agreed to meet the following Wednesday near my office. I toyed with the idea of inviting Margot but she'd probably try and suss Tony out. That reminded me.

'So, when's *your* birthday then?'

'Not until the twenty-first of June. You've got plenty of time.'

'June? That means you're a… Gemini!' I said in horror.

'On the cusp, so I'm told,' he said happily.

Was that OK? I wondered.

Chapter Fifty-one

Catherine was busy tidying and wiping her kitchen worktops while I sat at her pine table, idly flicking through her bridal magazines. Suddenly she cleared her throat.

'Um, Mags, could you do me a favour?' She took the kettle over to the sink and filled it with water, her back to me.

I looked up, hearing something in her tone I wasn't sure was very good. 'What?'

'It's nothing really. Nothing bad anyway.' She came back and replaced the kettle on its base and flicked the switch, avoiding eye contact.

'Then how come you look like it's bad.'

I watched her face as she looked up at the ceiling as if searching for words then she turned to face me.

'You know I said I'm going out to meet Nico's family in October?'

'Mmm *hmmm*.'

'Well, I was just hoping…that you might be able to take care of Tom for me?'

'But…'

'Otherwise, I'll have to hire some stranger through the vets and I don't think I could bear that,' she was babbling very quickly so I couldn't interrupt. 'My neighbour, who usually looks after him, will be on holiday and no one from work is near enough and I'd be really, really, really grateful and I'd love you forever and you can borrow anything of mine that you like, not that we're the same size, but maybe scarves and things and… and… anything you want really, anything,'

'But Tom hates me!'

'No, he doesn't. He just hasn't got to know you properly, that's all. Oh please, Mags, I'd hate anyone else looking after him for that long. Please, please, please?' She cocked her head on one side and stuck out her bottom lip.

'I've known him for four years. He's had plenty of time to get to know me. He hates me!'

'He doesn't, you're being paranoid. Besides, this would be the perfect time for you to spend some quality time together without me. He's probably just jealous of our relationship.'

She was serious.

I sighed as the kettle, billowing out white steam, clicked itself off.

'Do I have a choice?'

'Not really.' Catherine poured boiling water into two cups with teabags in.

I tutted. 'All right then, but only if you bring me back something nice.'

'Done.'

In front of Catherine Tom gave the impression that butter wouldn't melt in his ginger headed mouth but, as soon as she was out of the room, I just had to walk past him and he'd swipe me with his massive ginger paw.

'I owe you one,' she said, smiling as she stirred milk into our cups.

'I know.' I looked down as Tom entered the kitchen and ignored me totally, schmoozing over to Catherine and meandering in between her legs.

'Oh and remember his wheat intolerance,' she added, bending down to stroke him.

'Who's Mummy's little gorgeous boy? ... Actually don't worry, I'll make a list of the things he needs and buy as much up front as I can. It's just it needs to be as fresh as possible otherwise he gets dreadfully constipated. Or, well, the other, you know.'

'He's got his routine too. He goes out down the fire escape in the morning for his fresh air, but don't worry there's a cat flap, and then he likes to come back in and snuggle most of the day and then go back out again at night for a wander. But be careful, some of the neighbours' cats keep sniffing around him and I don't want him picking up any bad habits.'

'Such as what?'

'Such as...' Catherine paused, screwed up her face and shuddered, seemingly shaking an image from her mind. 'Oh never mind.' She placed the teas on the table and sat down to join me.

'Will you come shopping with me to find a wedding dress?'

'Of course, when?'

'Not quite yet, there's still a bit of time and I'm going on a diet, so there's no point in choosing anything right now. Anyway listen,' she said, 'talking of dresses, I wanted to talk to you about the bridesmaids' dresses.'

Visions of red silk and bouquets of white flowers flooded my mind; or maybe silvery satin with delicate strappy sandals and mother of pearl accessories.

'What do you think about this in baby pink?' She picked up another magazine from the chair beside her and pushed it across the table to me.

'Page sixty-one. I've put a yellow sticky in it.'

I found the page and opened it up.

It wasn't red silk or silvery satin. There were no delicate strappy sandals or mother of pearl accessories in sight. Catherine was showing me the most *awful* meringue-style bridesmaid dress I had *ever* seen.

I was stunned. My best friend was going to make me dress up like a toilet roll dolly, be the laughing stock of the guests and scare Tony off for good. What on earth was I going to do?

I glanced up and took in her eager face.

'Do you like it?' she asked.

'Well I… it's… um…'

She looked expectantly at me, her eyes wide.

'You do like it, don't you?' she pleaded. 'Oh please say you do. I want everything to be just perfect.'

Oh god, she looked so worried.

I sighed inwardly. I wasn't sure whether to laugh or cry. But I gave in graciously; if this was what she really wanted.

'Of course, Cat; whatever you like. It's lovely.' I smiled warmly at her.

She watched my expression, like she was searching for signs that I might not be telling the truth. I kept smiling.

Then she breathed a sigh of relief.

'Thank goodness. I was so afraid you might not. I know it's a bit different but it's the kind of bridesmaid dress I've dreamed of since I was a kid.'

We sipped our teas in silence. I flicked over some more pages and pretended to study an advert for a florist service.

Then Catherine collapsed into fits of giggles beside me, clutching her sides.

'Maggie, please! You don't honestly think I'd make you wear that revolting thing do you? For goodness sake, I thought you'd guess I was joking the minute I showed it to you!'

Phew!

'Thank God! I thought you were really serious. Mind you, I suppose it is rather fetching.' I looked at the photo again. 'I'm sure our mums would approve.'

She pulled the magazine away from me and replaced it with another one, turning to a page marked with another yellow sticky. 'This is the one I really like.'

It was lovely; shimmering deep red satin, very simple with spaghetti straps. It was long and fitted, almost down to the ground. Along the plunging heart-shaped bust line, tiny little red hearts were embroidered. I thought it was gorgeous.

'Cat, it's beautiful, absolutely one hundred per cent yes!' I reached over and hugged her.

'Of course,' she said, 'if you'd prefer the pink one, I'd quite understand.'

Chapter Fifty-two

The following week, at work, Tony called.

'Still on for lunch?'

'Are you buying?'

'If you're good.'

'And if I'm bad?' I asked.

'Then I'll buy you dinner as well.'

Margot stuck her head in as I ended the call.

'That lover boy?' she asked.

'Yes,' I smiled happily. 'We're going for lunch.'

'You done it yet?' she asked.

'No, Margot, we haven't "done it" yet.'

'What is it with you Virgos?'

She came in and sat on the chair opposite. Picking up my snowman scene, she gave it a shake.

'I wonder what they use inside. Water maybe?'

'Gloopy stuff I reckon,' I said.

She replaced it on the desk and we sat and watched the snow settle.

'So, have you found out what star sign he is yet?'

I shifted uncomfortably in my seat.

'He's on the cusp,' I said.

'Of...?'

I tutted and raised my eyes.

'Gemini, if you must know.'

'Told you! I knew it! Which end, Taurus or Cancer?'

'Which is which?'

'Durrr, Taurus is before, Cancer's aafter.'

'Cancer then.'

She looked thoughtful.

'What? What's wrong with that?' I demanded.

'Nothing; I was just thinking I once had a boyfriend who was on the cusp of Gemini and Cancer.'

'And…?'

She shrugged.

'I suppose it depends on what time he was born. He might be more Gemini or more Cancer. You'll have to find out.'

'What difference does it make?'

'Oh loads. Go find out his time of birth and we'll work it out this aafternoon. What year was he born?'

I worked it out in my head and told her.

'He's a Monkey,' she confirmed.

'A Monkey! I thought he was a Gemini.'

'No daaft head, a Chinese Monkey. What are you then?'

'I don't know!' I was beginning to panic.

I gave her my birth date and she worked it out.

'You're a Horse.'

'What does that mean?'

'You don't wanna be hangin' round with Monkeys.'

Bloody hell.

Lunch was almost a disaster. Margot had left me in a right state. What if it was true? What if Tony and I were doomed?

After our lasagne and salad there was a period of post-food silence which I was finding increasingly uncomfortable. But suddenly Tony shot me one of his famous smiles and my stomach lurched.

Not a hint of disaster.

We made arrangements to meet on the Friday.

'By the way, what time of day were you born?' I asked as we said goodbye.

'Dunno exactly, you'd have to ask Dad. But it was sometime in the early hours of the morning I think. Why?'

'Oh nothing, just women's stuff. Margot's really into star signs.'

I saw him tense.

'Margot, huh?'

'Yes.'

'You're still discussing me with her?' He raised one eyebrow, reminding me of Luke.

'Tony, it's what girls do. Don't worry.'

'I just don't like other people knowing my business that's all.' He wouldn't meet my eyes. At a bit of a loss, I tried to assure him he had nothing to worry about but I felt tense when he kissed me goodbye.

Back at the office, Margot questioned me as soon as I got in the door.

'Well?'

'Well what?' I replied, grumpily.

'Did you ask him what time he was born?'

'Not that it makes much difference but it was sometime in the early hours of the morning.'

'Figures.'

'What now!' I snapped.

'Definitely *all* Gemini.'

Bloody, bloody, hell.

Tony called me the next day to confirm Friday's date.

'Wear something special. I've decided I'm going to take you somewhere really posh and spoil you.'

I was relieved that all signs of the previous day's tension had gone.

The only thing suitably special in my wardrobe was the dress I'd worn to the reunion and he'd seen that. There was no choice in the matter I'd have to buy something new. Margot offered to come with me and we headed off into the centre of town after work.

It was odd going shopping with someone other than Catherine. Margot was good company but she kept eyeing up blokes and we had to keep stopping while she ogled through cafe windows or smouldered at cab drivers.

Wandering along Oxford Street, she spotted a stunning scarlet pencil dress in a shop window.

'That's you all over, Mags. Try it on. Bet you anything you buy it.'

I saw the sign at the mannequin's feet and nearly had a heart attack. 'Have you seen the price!?'

'Just try it. Trust me on this. Some dresses are worth splurging on especially if you're using it to pull a guy.'

'What?'

'Come on just try it.' She dragged me in to the shop.

'Who said I'm trying to pull Tony,' I asked, as I admired myself in the changing room mirror; twisting this way and that. I have to admit it did look very good on.

'I can tell these things.'

'You should have been a psychic.'

'I knows. My mum is. She's always trying to get me to "develop my gift".'

'Really?'

'Yeah she wants me to farlow in her footsteps.'

'Do you want to?'

'Maybe, but right now, I need to get some sensible stuff on my CV so I can start expanding my life in more creative and fulfilling areas when the time's right.'

I frowned at her quizzically. Margot never ceased to amaze me.

'Told you you'd buy it,' she said as we left the shop, equipped with the dress and some very high designer stilettos, all courtesy of my credit card.

'That's because you're psychic.'

Margot nodded seriously.

'I'll tell you another thing I knows for sure.'

'What's that?'

'I knows it's your round.'

And off we went to the pub.

Chapter Fifty-three

On Friday night I came home in plenty of time to get ready. I was very excited and ever so nervous. This would be the night. Tony and I would almost certainly be sleeping together and I was like a cat on a hot tin roof.

I showered and relaxed in my bathrobe while I blow-dried then straightened my hair. The dress warranted sophistication so I piled my hair up onto my head, letting the odd tendril fall sexily down around my face. Nice, I decided, very nice; sexy; mature. Just the look I was after. I carefully darkened my eyes with kohl and three coats of mascara then rounded it all off with scarlet lipstick to match the dress. Some months before I had treated myself to some gypsy-like undies in red and black lace but had never got round to wearing them. This was most definitely the night. I took them out of my bottom drawer and put them on, admiring my reflection in the long mirror. It had been ages since I'd slept with a guy and I felt my stomach churning. I added the striking, fitted, dress and stilettos and took stock of the woman staring back at me. I was pleased with what I saw and I hoped Tony would appreciate it. If only my nerves weren't so frayed.

I poured myself a vodka and tonic. Vodka as I didn't want Tony to smell alcohol on my breath; but I was so nervous I needed something. Unfortunately, it tasted like acid in my throat as the fear mounted up in my chest. I began to pace the room, taking off my stilettos in case my feet and ankles swelled up.

Finally, seven thirty arrived and I sat at my little dining table with my heart in my mouth. I'd managed to get the vodka down but I didn't feel any calmer. Any minute now the door would go. I sat down and took a few deep breaths to prepare myself for the sound of the buzzer. I was sure I would jump right out of my skin when I heard it. However, seven thirty came and went and no sign. I started pacing the room again. Seven thirty-five, seven forty and, after fifteen minutes, I was convinced he wasn't coming. I kept checking my phone for texts, then I checked my emails but nothing; not a word from him. Why wasn't he contacting me! I was so anxious I had to pour myself another vodka to steady my nerves, then I had to clean my teeth just in case Tony did smell it on my breath.

At five to eight, anger and frustration were bubbling up inside me. I was all over the place. Had he said eight o'clock? The thought flashed through my mind. Maybe I'd got the time wrong? With a surge of hope, I checked my phone again and found his original text but, no, it definitely said seven thirty. He'd obviously stood me up. Bloody Tony had stood me up! Maybe Laura had decided she wasn't going to let him go so easily. Maybe she'd come down and he was currently trapped back at his flat, yet another broken phone in front of him, unable to call me. Maybe she'd cut up all his clothes, so he only had underwear and half shirts to wear. Mind you I could have coped with that; might have quite liked it actually.

I was just in the middle of mentally cutting up Laura's clothes by way of revenge when the door buzzed and, as expected, I jumped – my heart ending up in my mouth. Not wishing to tempt fate, I crossed my fingers and answered it. It was Tony.

'Sorry!!' came the out-of-breath voice.

I buzzed him up.

Slipping my stilettos back on I waited for him to climb the stairs then opened the door. I was met with a breathless man, half covered by a very, very large bouquet of gorgeous, expensive-looking, flowers.

'Can you ever forgive me?' He peeked out from behind them, looking furtive.

'Jees!' he took in my appearance. 'Wow! Oh god, wow, wow, wow!'

'Hmmmm,' I said thoughtfully. 'The flowers might help but you've still got some way to go.'

I leant on the wall beside the door, not ready to let him in yet.

'You've gotta let me in looking like that! If I told you my train had been held up by robbers and then there were no taxis the other end, because the police had blocked the road off, would you believe me?'

'I'd ask what you were doing catching a train.'

'Ah, that's the other thing, I had to go up to Dad's today, last minute thing, and my car broke down. I had to get the train back and stupidly I left my phone in my car.'

'And the robbers?'

'They had their own phones.'

'Ha ha. Right, you can buy me dinner, ply me with wine and then I'll decide whether I forgive you.' I stood aside and sideways-nodded towards the direction of the lounge.

Tony came in and passed me the flowers.

'For you, oh gorgeous creature.'

'Thank you, they're lovely.' I took the flowers and headed off to find a vase.

'The guy who arranged them took forever! I was ready to punch him,' he called out.

'I'm glad you didn't punch him. I'm not sure I'd have liked having to come and put up your bail money to get you released from prison.'

As I walked into the lounge, Tony was taking out a bottle of brandy from a carrier bag. He placed it on the coffee table.

'For later maybe…?'

I felt my stomach come alive with anticipation again and I was aware of a mounting excitement I hadn't felt for so long rushing through every inch of my body.

Without asking whether he wanted one, I poured us both a vodka and tonic on the rocks. I even added a slice of lemon – organic lemon. (Catherine's insistence – it was a wax thing.)

Handing it to him on the sofa, I felt very pleased at the way he was staring at me.

I put on some music to soften the mood and, as it wasn't all that bright, flicked on the sidelight.

'Maggie, you look sensational,' he whistled and I sat down beside him. 'Maybe we should just stay in.' He put his drink down and moved a little closer.

'What and waste a good dress?' I said jokingly (but I seriously meant it!!).

'Oh, I can assure you it wouldn't be wasted.' His smile was lazy and he let his fingers idly caress my bare arm.

But eventually he conceded. At first I felt a bit awkward. Whilst Tony had been here before, this felt different. It was like there was an unspoken certainty that tonight would be the night; the brandy bottle said it all, and it took a little while for me to relax fully. After a while though we were talking and laughing and, with the aid of a couple of drinks, I settled in to what was soon feeling like the perfect evening. Tony was attentive and considerate and I thought how particularly nice he was being. Really funny and kind and suddenly the past weeks and all the issues with Laura seemed non-existent. There was only here and now; Tony and me; us; a perfect couple; our futures ahead of us; Mr and Mrs Henderson. *Shut up, Maggie*, I berated inwardly.

We finally left the flat, hand in hand, and climbed into the minicab waiting outside. Tony directed the driver to a wonderful new French restaurant in Mayfair, which he had been to with clients the previous week.

The evening went from great to perfect. The restaurant was fantastic; a huge sprawling room with high ceilings and glittering, shimmering chandeliers that cast a subtle, romantic, glow over the room. White-clothed tables were spread around. The walls were covered in a deep red, flocked, wallpaper and huge gilt-edged mirrors hung around the place catching the light and making the room appear even larger than it was. The floor was chequered black and white then met with rich red velvet carpet at the edges and over the steps up to a raised mezzanine area, surrounded by ornate banisters, where more tables subtly overlooked other diners down below. Everyone had dressed up for the evening. Some women were in full-length eveningwear. Waiters glided around attentively, serving and taking orders, their little notepads never in their pockets for long.

The maître d' greeted us warmly and, clearly remembering Tony, proceeded to give special instructions to our waiter, in French. We were then led up to the mezzanine and over to an alcove with soft, plush, red leather seats and a little round table for two. The waiter lit our candle and moved the exquisitely designed red rose table decoration to the side, so we could see each other. He handed Tony a thick leather-bound wine list and I watched as Tony confidently studied it briefly, before choosing a bottle of some Chateau blur de blur de something or other. I thought about my dreadful experience with Greg; this was so far removed from it. How could I have been so stupid?

'Do you approve?' Tony asked, taking my hand.

'Stunning,' I breathed. 'Really gorgeous.'

'I was thinking the same thing.' A smile played on his lips.

The red wine arrived and I sat nervously as Tony tasted it nodding his approval. The waiter poured out two glasses and left us with some menus. The wine was delicious; velvety smooth and almost warm.

'Shall I order for both of us? I had some amazing food here last week. I'd love you to try some of it.' He appeared so eager to please me, I happily agreed.

As I watched him study the menu in the candlelight, I thought he had never looked so handsome.

The order placed, we chatted idly about everything and nothing. Tony made me laugh and I felt feminine and enchanting. It was as if that night signified the start of our future together. We were relaxed and happy and everything was perfect.

The food started arriving in little courses.

I tried my first oyster, nearly threw up, but then had another one to show how much of a woman I really was. Whoever said oysters made you horny was just plain wrong!

There was a bit of a 'moment' when some snails arrived (I hate snails) and I had to politely refuse them. So Tony ordered me a goat's-cheese tartlet, which melted in my mouth. I thought I'd never tasted anything so delicious. I was mistaken. The rest of the meal was just as gorgeous.

Dishes of the tastiest meat, fish and vegetables were served up in miniature portions leaving plenty of room for more. I suspected that the truffle pate which stuffed the tiny pieces of fillet steak would attach itself to my thighs upon contact.

Later we were sitting grinning at each other over the most delicious strawberry pavlova in the history of cuisine when, in amongst this perfect evening – an evening I thought was one of the greatest in my life – it happened. I dropped the bombshell.

I mentioned Laura.

'D'you know, when you didn't turn up, I thought Laura had arrived at your place and cut up all your clothes and was holding you hostage!' I laughed but caught sight of his face and stopped abruptly.

Suddenly, Tony went from Mr Smooth, Mild-Mannered, Super Cool, Macho Stud, to Mr Leg Jiggling, Finger Rapping, Shoulder Twitching, Eye Darting, Manic Man. I could have been with his evil twin brother.

'Look, Maggie, I really don't want to talk about Laura tonight. OK?'

'Oh… OK. Sorry, I was just saying…'

'Well don't,' he snapped.

We sat in silence. A large ball of dread crept up from my stomach and into my throat.

'She's not like that anyway,' he said after a while. 'That's not her style.'

I'd offended him.

'No, I'm sure it's not. I'm sorry,' I apologised again.

Tony's leg was still jiggling under the table.

'I'm really sorry, Tony, I didn't mean to overstep the mark.'

I began playing with my dessert. 'Am I not allowed to mention her at all though?'

'I told you I didn't want to talk about it, OK?' He glanced briefly at me then started shovelling pavlova speedily into his mouth.

'Okaay,' I said slowly, 'what shall we talk about instead?'

He shrugged in a very unbecoming, little-boy fashion. I found myself getting annoyed.

'Well, you'd better say something or I might get it wrong again. And clearly, we don't want that do we?' I said sarcastically.

He shot me a look but remained silent which really got my goat. Fuelled by wine, I began to get my dangerous head on.

'Have you asked Luke about the baby and Sian?' I asked, calmly licking cream from my spoon.

He glared angrily at me.

'No, why?'

'Just wondered.' I avoided eye contact.

'About what exactly?'

'You *are* his brother. I would have thought you'd have asked him about it, that's all.'

'You seem very interested in Luke all of a sudden, Maggie. Is there something I should know?'

I'd hit another nerve. Well, good.

Actually, this was silly. It wasn't good at all, it was crap. The evening was fast going downhill and I wasn't sure why.

'No, no there's nothing you should know. Tony, what's wrong? Why are you so upset?'

The whole atmosphere had changed. My fine wine tasted sour and my strawberries tasted like straw. Glancing around, I was sure everyone could hear us arguing and were listening in. Feeling embarrassed I lowered my voice.

'Why can't I mention Laura, or Luke come to that? They do exist you know. We can't keep pretending that they don't. Anyway, it's me that should be upset about Laura.'

He snapped.

'Oh yeah? How do you figure that out then, huh?'

'Well, Laura came back on the scene when you and I started seeing each other and…'

'Oh, for God's sake, grow up, Maggie. Not this again,' he spat.

'Not what again…?'

'It always comes back to this doesn't it? Is it going to be like this every time we get together?'

'Like what?' I asked.

'You harping on about the past, about Laura. About how bad you've been feeling, about how awful it all is for *you*.'

'I'm just saying…'

'Well, don't.'

My face was hot with embarrassment and I seemed to lose my nerve to fight. I wanted to turn the clock back. I tried to back down.

'Listen, it's fine. I'm sorry. If you don't want to talk about it, then we won't OK?' I took a sip of my wine, thinking how bitter it tasted now.

'It's a bit bloody late for that.' He removed his napkin from his lap and threw it down onto the dish. 'Let's get out of here, I've lost my appetite.'

I sat in stunned silence as he caught the attention of our waiter and signalled for the bill.

Bang! Perfect evening over. I felt awful. Was this really my fault? Why was he so irate?

Without a word, Tony stood up and headed off in the direction of the toilet, leaving me to gather my thoughts. I watched his angry back as he disappeared from sight. I'd obviously misjudged how hard this was on him. Clearly I'd really spoiled things but there was no escaping the fact that I was smarting from his words and felt horrible. Part of me wanted to apologise but part of me wanted to punch his lights out.

I scanned the restaurant, watching to see if anyone was looking at me but thankfully no one seemed in the slightest bit interested. It wasn't long before I spotted Tony coming back from the loo and turned my head away to avoid his gaze as he headed back up to the table. He sat down and moved his plate to the side.

'Maggie?'

He reached out and took my hand across the table. I flinched at his touch but didn't pull away.

I looked up. His face had softened and he'd clearly calmed down.

'Maggie, I am *so* sorry.'

'Really,' I said flatly.

'God, I don't know what I was thinking! You didn't deserve any of that shit I gave you. And it wasn't really aimed at you, more… at me probably. I totally overreacted. It's just this Laura business; it's taken it out of me. Work's hectic – manic! I've got a mountain of stuff to do before I leave for New York on Monday and things are just getting on top of me, that's all. It's been a pretty trying time lately.'

'OK,' I said quietly, thinking it was probably best to try and smooth things over and put the horridness behind us. 'I understand. I'm sorry too.'

'Please don't be. It was all me, OK? Can we forget it ever happened and move on? We were having a great time before, weren't we?' He cocked his head, his lovely eyes pleading with me.

I smiled very slightly and nodded.

He gently stroked my hand. 'Thank you.'

The waiter came up with the bill but Tony sent it back and ordered two large brandies and some coffee. Then he turned back to me.

'What I'd really like, Maggie, is for us to finish up here, then just go home to your place and talk about us. Would that be all right?'

I nodded, thankful it was all over.

We had our coffee and brandy but, despite the truce, I couldn't help feeling that the evening had taken a nosedive. I wouldn't be broaching the subject of Laura again, not for a while.

Back at my place I made more coffee, unwrapping and using the new coffee cups my mum had brought over when I'd moved in over a year ago.

'You can't have enough nice crockery,' she'd said, 'you never know who might pop in unannounced.' Apart from Catherine, Pip was probably my one and only unannounced guest since I'd moved in. I giggled inwardly as I imagined him trying to drink nicely out of these petite coffee cups. Tony, on the other hand, may have had large hands (oh please let the old adage be true) but I thought he'd appreciate them.

I took the coffee into the lounge and Tony had poured brandy into the only crystal glasses I possessed (another gift from Mum). He had put on my Adele CD, loosened his tie and taken off his jacket.

He patted the sofa and I sat down beside him. We toasted on his instigation.

'To us and to the future,' he said, clinking my glass.

'To us.'

I took a largish gulp, grimacing at the harshness against my throat, then placed it back on the coffee table and snuggled in to Tony.

'You do look gorgeous in that dress, Maggie,' he said.

I smiled, kicking my stilettos off and tucking my feet up femininely underneath me. I was beginning to feel much better about things again.

'A man could get used to this you know,' he said, 'being waited on by a charming, beautiful, woman who makes great coffee and has the most exquisite legs.'

I looked up at him with what I hoped was a sexy, seductive, expression.

'Well, you paid for the meal, now it's my turn. Just relax and make yourself at home, OK?'

'Fine by me. In fact, in that case, do you mind if I smoke?' he asked.

I didn't know you smoked.'

'I don't really, only these.' He took out a packet from the inside pocket of his removed jacket.

Oh no! The dreaded cigars!

Now if there is one thing in this world which I HATE, even more than snails and liquorice, it's the smell of cigars. I absolutely abhor them with a vengeance. The smell quite literally makes me sick. Every time anyone so much as talks about smoking a cigar, I immediately start to feel queasy!

However, the evening might still have been on rocky ground so, for the sake of keeping Tony onside, I braved it. Besides, it had been a while since my last encounter, maybe things had changed and I wasn't quite so sensitive anymore?

'Sure, like I said, make yourself at home. I'll just open the window a bit if you don't mind. It's a bit stuffy in here at the best of times.' I stood up to go to the window.

'Maggie, are you sure? I don't have to smoke, it's just something I do after a meal sometimes. No big thing.'

He'd given me my chance but I didn't take it.

'No, no, it's fine,' I assured him, 'you carry on.'

So he did and, true to form, after a few bellowing puffs, I began to feel sick. He kept lighting the big fat ugly cigar and then putting it down to burn. Then it would go out and it would have to be relit again, causing even more great puffs of thick cigar smoke to bellow out into the air and down my throat. After a while I couldn't bear it, so I excused myself to make more coffee but he pulled me down and told me not to bother.

'Stay here, Maggie, we don't need it. Don't go. Please?'

So I stayed. And got greener and greener until I simply *had* to go to the loo and get away. I threw open the little window in the bathroom and tried to inhale the night air but because the lounge window was also open I could still smell the smoke. There was no escape. This time I really was sick, throwing up all my lovely food from the restaurant into the toilet. I felt dreadful. My nose was running, my head was throbbing and I still felt nauseous. I looked in the mirror and saw my eyes were piggy and bloodshot and my make-up had run.

I splashed my face with water and quickly sorted my face out as best I could. Then I cleaned my teeth, which helped a bit, and went back in. Luckily, the cigar was finally out.

I sat down beside Tony again, grateful for the relatively fresh air.

'You OK?'

'Fine.' I smiled. 'Just fine.'

I sipped some more brandy, so Tony wouldn't know I had cleaned my teeth and, after a few moments, began to feel more or less normal again.

'Maggie...?' Tony said slowly, his voice questioning.

I turned and met his eyes.

'I think I need to kiss you now, OK?' He gazed intently at me.

I felt my face grow warm, and nodded.

Tony reached forward and put his hand up to my face, caressing my cheek. Now, under normal circumstances this would have been lovely but, seeing as his fingers stank of cigar smoke, it was actually quite horrendous! I could smell his fingertips oozing out the foul smell.

He leant forward to kiss me and I had to will myself not to gag at the smell also coming from his mouth; blurrch.

And then we kissed. I really tried to enjoy it but his mouth tasted awful. I concentrated intently on swirling my tongue round with his but I couldn't wait for it to end. Poor Tony must have sensed my reticence because he pulled away and frowned slightly.

'You OK?' he asked

'Yes, sorry, it's just...' I had to say something, 'well the cigar smoke is a little strong. Sorry.' I repeated.

'Oh, Maggie, I'm the one who should be sorry. Why didn't you say something? I know some women love the smell, Laura always...'

Ah ha, now it was his turn to put his foot in it.

'Shit!' He grimaced.

Keen for there not to be a repeat of the restaurant, I stood up, taking his hand.

'Don't worry, Tony... Shall we...?' I smiled down at him and gave a sideways nod towards the bedroom.

He stood up, a little apprehensively, and I led him through.

'I'll just, er, wash my hands and stuff.' He grinned ruefully at me. 'Don't want you going off me completely.'

When he'd disappeared into the bathroom, I began to feel nervous again.

Would Tony have brought a condom? Maybe more than one? What if he hadn't? I did have one but it had been in my bedside drawer for ages and I wasn't even sure where it had come from. I wondered if condoms had a use by date.

I sat down on the bed and tried to arrange myself seductively, swinging my legs up. I pumped up the pillows, then leant on them, shaking my head a little and posing in what I hoped was a sexy pose. I felt really daft though, like some would-be porn star, so I swung my legs back down onto the floor and leant back on my hands. This was ridiculous.

I could hear the tap running and then what sounded like my tooth mug being knocked over. He must have been using the toothpaste to get rid of the cigar smell. For some reason that made me feel uneasy. He was trying to make things good to impress me. It felt oddly uncomfortable.

I glanced down at my ankles. They'd swollen up during the course of the evening and I started to get a little paranoid. Would he like my body? I was bigger and broader than Laura although, to be fair, most women would have been. Maybe he liked really small women though. Maybe because he had a small penis! Oh no! *Shut up Maggie*, I scolded myself silently. Relaaax… Deep breaths… It was all going to be fine. It was only sex. I'd done it all before; been there, worn the tee shirt and all that.

The door to the bathroom opened and I tensed up again, wondering whether the tee shirt had been redesigned since I'd last worn it. Tony came out and smiled at me.

'Scrubbed and cigar-free, Ma'am.' He winked then came over and sat beside me.

Then we kissed, rather awkwardly at first, bumping mouths but it didn't take long to get into it.

I pulled away slightly. 'Have you got…?'

'Protection?'

'Yes.'

He nodded and patted his trouser pocket then leant forward and kissed me again.

I put my hand inside his shirt. He tensed a little but then relaxed. He was very hairy. Not like Lu… I tried to stop the thought but it was too late.

416

Damn that man, didn't he know I was busy and didn't need to be reminded of him.

Tony moved his hands to my shoulders and gently slid the straps of my dress down, then reaching round he slowly undid my zip. Moving away from me slightly, he slipped my dress down over my arms uncovering my new bra.

I sat feeling self-conscious.

'Gorgeous,' he breathed. 'Just gorgeous.'

He stood and pulling me up peeled the dress over my hips until it slid the rest of the way down to the floor, revealing my thong, stockings and suspender belt.

'I'm liable to have a heart attack before this happens you know.'

I felt shy standing there in front of him almost naked while he was still fully clothed. Glancing down I saw him straining in his trousers, so I reached down and began to undo his belt. He tensed again leaning forward to kiss me, more forcefully than before.

With his belt loose, I undid his trousers and reached in and pulled him free. He felt hot in my hand.

Tony groaned and moved closer to me.

'Oh, Maggie,' he moaned, his voice thick with longing.

I began to move my hand slowly and gently up and down him. I tried to relax but, for some reason, I was finding it difficult. I felt tense. I glanced down between kisses to get a good look at what I was holding. There was a slight kink in the end, but that was ok. After all, I wouldn't be able to see that where it was going, now would I? So, what was the problem? Why had I just gone rigid? Surely that was his job, not mine. And by the looks of things, despite my efforts, things had taken a backward step. Perhaps Tony had picked up on my tension? Now we weren't talking uncooked sausages here but let me say that, if it had been one of those long party balloons you get, I'd be searching for the pump.

I don't know if he sensed my thoughts but he gently took my hand away then and guided me back down onto the bed.

'Lie down,' he instructed.

I lay on my back. Quite suddenly, I found myself feeling a little like I had done the first time with Luke. Unwanted memories of Luke and me on the picnic rug filled my mind but, as much as I didn't want them there, unnervingly I became more aroused.

I watched Tony deftly remove his shirt, socks and trousers, discarding them on the floor then he joined me on the bed and began to kiss me again. His kisses became more and more urgent and I could feel his now hard erection digging into my thigh. His hand moved down between my legs and I gasped as he slipped his fingers underneath my thong. Gently his fingers began exploring. I pulled my mouth away from his and gasped, laying my head back on the pillow.

In and out he gently probed his fingers, then circled them around me, teasing me to him. I felt myself rising to his touch, gradually, sensuously; infuriatingly slowly, I began to climb to the peak. In and out he moved again, round and round he circled. Touching me, caressing me, probing me, teasing me until I was arching my back and practically begging him to take me to the brink.

Closing my eyes in ecstasy I breathed deeper and deeper getting closer and closer. I found myself gasping I was so close. So near, sooo near but still not quite there – just a little further… But Tony seemed to have me exactly where he wanted me. He was enjoying this, whispering tantalisingly in my ear, soothing, seducing, calming, enticing, keeping me waiting, on the edge, wanting more. He kept going really slowly until I couldn't stand it anymore. I was so close, so near, oh please, I thought, please, please. And then I could feel myself finally reaching the peak. My back arched further.

'Yes, that's it, that's nice, oh yes, oh God, oh God, oh yes, oh please…'

'That's it, just let it go.' Tony's voice came from somewhere distant in the room.

'Oh yes, that's it, please don't stop, oh yes, oh yes…' I began thrashing my arms as I came so near then infuriatingly dipped down again. It was exquisite agony. I could hardly bear it.

Tony coaxed me back up again until I was nearing the summit again.

'Yes, yes, yes, that's it, yes, oh God, yes, yes, yes, ohhh, ohhh, ohhh. Oh Luke, oh God, oh yes, yes, yes …'

And just as I was about to have what proffered to be a rather lovely climax, Tony stopped… so I didn't!

I opened my eyes, shell-shocked. *What on earth?* I stared up at him. He was clearly angry.

'What… what are you doing? Why, why did you stop?' I stammered, confused and flushed.

He whipped his hand away from me and sat up on the edge of the bed. Then he turned back to me, scowling.

'You fucking well called me Luke, that's why I stopped!' he exploded angrily.

'What? I didn't!'

Shit, had I?

'You called me fucking Luke!' he said again, adjusting himself and rescuing his trousers from the floor. He started to slide them on again.

Jeees! Had I really called him Luke? Had I? Oh no, I had. I could hear myself saying it. Crying it out even! In the heat of passion, in the heat of such a crucial moment, I'd called him by his brother's name! Fuck! Poor Tony.

He wouldn't look at me.

'I can't fucking believe you called me fucking Luke! My own fucking brother!' He'd put his shirt on now and was buttoning up the front.

'Tony, I'm so sorry,' I pleaded, 'please don't go. It was a mistake, just a silly mistake. Come back to bed. I am so very sorry.'

He was threading his belt through the loops of his trousers.

'It's too late for sorry, Maggie. It's ruined everything.'

I sat up, watching him while he reached under the bed for his sock.

'No, no it hasn't,' I begged. 'We can try again. It was just a slip of the tongue. It's because...' I searched for a reason. 'It's probably just because I feel awkward talking about him. You don't like me mentioning his name and, because of that, it slipped out by accident. Bit like, you know, when someone tells you bad news and you laugh. It's not because you want to, it just happens accidentally.' I was gathering speed now, desperate to make things right.

'Oh, so it's my fucking fault now is it?'

'I didn't mean that! I just meant I probably just let it slip because I've been worried about saying his name all evening.'

'Maybe that's because you've been seeing him behind my back!' he raged.

'*What?* No, of course I haven't. Why on earth would I?'

'You tell me, Maggie. You seem to be very interested in whether he's going to have this baby. Maybe that's because he's already told you what's going on but, for some reason, you're checking up on him.'

'Tony, this is *ridiculous*. I'm hardly likely to be seeing you and Luke at the same time, am I? Besides, as far as I'm concerned, Luke is history. And if he and Sian are having a baby together, that's another huge reason to stay away. Don't you think?'

He sat down on the bed again, running his fingers through his hair.

'That's as maybe but calling out his name when you...' he tutted '... at that particular point is hardly likely to instil confidence into me, is it?'

I reached over and placed my hand on his shoulder.

'I'm so sorry. I don't know what else to say.'

He shook his head, staring at the wall opposite.

'I'm sure you are sorry, considering.'

Considering I've just been robbed of a rather lovely orgasm.

I didn't say that though.

'I am sorry.'

He sighed then, turning back to look at me.

'I just wanted this to be perfect.'

'So did I,' I said slowly.

We managed to call a truce and he ended up staying the night but nothing else happened. I lay awake for hours while Tony slept beside me, breathing heavily. It had all gone so horribly wrong. I could have kicked myself. Fancy calling out Luke's name; then, of all times! What on earth had I been thinking about? But there lay the problem.

Somewhere, on some level, I'd been thinking about Luke; comparing Tony to Luke. I knew I shouldn't have been but it seemed to be happening of its own accord. This was all wrong. Something had to change if Tony and I were to stand any chance at all of making a go of things.

The next day, I woke up to the sounds of someone in my bathroom. It took me a few moments to realise it was Tony and to piece together the events of the previous evening. A feeling a dread crept over me.

Moments later Tony came out of the bathroom. His hair glistened wet from the shower, a towel was wrapped around his waist and another slung around his neck. He smiled – a look of acceptance in his eyes.

'You OK?' I asked.

'Yeah, you?'

'Yeah.'

'Good.'

We didn't say much that morning. He had to leave to get ready for his trip so after

a quick glass of orange juice while I put my clothes on, Tony was ready to leave.

'See you when I get back then?'

'OK, have a good trip.'

'I'll try.' He smiled, kissing me bumpily on the cheek. His face was cool against my skin and he smelled of shower gel. He quickly slid his jacket on and, opening the front door, let himself out without turning back.

As the door closed behind him I turned just in time to see one of the petals from my flowers fall unceremoniously down onto the floor.

Well, if that wasn't a sign, I didn't know what was.

Chapter Fifty-four

'Well?' Margot came in to my office on the Monday. 'How was it?'

'Don't ask.'

'That bad?'

'Worse.'

'Ohhh. What happened?'

'I thought you were psychic,' I let out a heavy sigh.

'Have you ever called out someone else's name when you were… you know…?'

'Fuck, Mags! You never!?'

'I did.'

'Don't tell me. His brother.'

I shot her a look.

'I am psychic remember.'

'I couldn't help it. It just came out. What on earth am I going to do? I wish I could turn the clock back and start the evening again.'

'Good old hindsight, eh?'

I rolled my eyes.

'Er, Maggie?' Margot said slowly.

'Yes?'

'Ever heard of Freud?'

'Don't even go there,' I warned.

Chapter Fifty-five

I didn't hear from Tony for a couple of days and, when he did text, it was cooler than I was used to; brief and to the point. He would be away for ten days and would be in touch when he could. No mention of meeting up again. I had a sinking feeling in my gut that it might be over and guessed I was to blame. However, early on the morning of my birthday, I answered the door to a deliveryman, who was carrying a large pink teddy bear and a bottle of pink champagne. There was a card.

'The champagne is pink, teddy is too, I wish I was with you, I'm feeling so blue!'

I extricated teddy from the man and took him inside along with the champagne. All was OK again; just a rough patch. After all, circumstances surrounding the start of our relationship hadn't exactly been rosy so we were bound to uncover some blips along the way. Best to get them over with sooner rather than later.

I wished I felt completely convinced.

Despite the teddy, who was staring dolefully at me from his new position in the bedroom next to Mobear, it didn't feel very much like my birthday. Unfortunately, Catherine was working all day and most of the evening due to a mix up with the rosters, so I'd made arrangements to go and visit Pauline and Timmy. Pauline probably wouldn't feel much like celebrating though. Timmy had been on the phone to me earlier in the week saying how worried he was about her and how insular she was becoming. I hoped I'd be able to cheer her up.

I checked Facebook and saw sixty-eight friends had wished me a happy birthday, a large number of whom I didn't even recognise. Great. After going through the standard 'liking' routine and replying to those who'd taken the trouble to write something other than 'Happy birthday Maggie' or similar, I went through and searched for Tony's name. He didn't actually do Facebook so didn't have a presence but I randomly checked just in case he'd decided to set one up. Suddenly a strip of 'people you may know' sprung up and one of the first photos jolted me. Luke Henderson's smiling face sat looking up from my phone screen. I willed myself not to click on it; it could ruin my birthday if I did.

Bugger. As if with a will of its own, my finger clicked on his name and his page sprung open. My chest hurt as I saw some random entries from people and a photo of a funny cat...but thankfully an inner voice screamed 'Nooooo!' so I quickly hit the back key before I could do any further damage.

My attention turned to the morning's post. Maureen had sent me a card. Craig and Bill had signed it too and Maureen had written the message.

HAPPY BIRTHDAY MAGGIE!
We miss you loads! It's not the same without you!!
How's the new job? Let's meet up for a huge drink. Sooooon!
Xxxxxx

I smiled. A large drink with the old crowd was a great idea. I'd get in touch on Monday.

I got ready then decided to call Tony and thank him but when I got through his phone was on voicemail. He was probably at the conference. I left him an upbeat message saying how lovely my present was and that I hoped he wasn't working too hard.

Perhaps he'd call back later? It would be a good opportunity to smooth things over.

My Dad rang soon after.

'Your mother wants to talk to you but I thought I'd get in first otherwise I'll never get a word in edgeways. She is, as you kids say, "on one". And I'm getting an increasing urge to tell her to "do one".' Dad laughed, good-humouredly. 'Anyway, happy birthday, my darling girl.'

'Thanks, Dad, and thanks for the gift card.'

'Sorry I know it's probably a bit boring, but this way at least you can buy something you like and not something you'll have to return. Your mum was all for buying from M&S but I managed to stop her. She seemed to think you'd look good in their, er... Prune range? Something like that.'

I laughed loudly. 'I think you mean Per Una. But thanks, Dad. You did good. So what's up with Mum then?'

'Avon; bloody Avon, that's what's up with her. It was only last Monday she signed up as a trainee and she's already gone and won "Door-To-Door Sales Person of the Week". I don't think I'll ever hear the last of it. You'd think she'd picked up an Oscar!'

'She really went for the job then. I wasn't sure if she was serious.'

'Oh, let me tell you, she's serious all right. Insists this is the career of a lifetime and I need to watch out. Because now that I've retired, she's going to be the main breadwinner and I won't like it when she's wearing the trousers. Huh! What does she mean *when* she's wearing the trousers? She's been designing, producing and modelling a whole bloody range of trousers ever since we got married!'

'Oh dear, is she being really awful?'

'Worse than awful; and she insists on singing all the time. I'm currently being subjected to verse and chorus of *I Believe I Can Fly* morning, noon and night.'

'At least she's got an interest.'

'Another one! She's got that CB flippin' radio fad going on as well.'

'Still? I thought that might have fizzled out by now.'

'Nope! Plus, she's met this new friend from work who insists on filling her mind with all sorts…including ideas about keeping our marriage alive. Marlena Dietrich Van Heldergelder someone or other. She's Dutch and apparently thinks she knows everything there is to know about putting the spice back into things. I think she's from Amsterdam. We've to go on *European City Breaks*; to so-called *boutique* hotels, with… *themed* rooms!'

'That sounds quite fun.'

'And pricey.'

'Maybe you could try one,' I suggested.

'Oh, don't you worry, your mother's already got one booked. I'm the last person to have any say in it. Hang on, love, she's calling something out. WHAT?' he shouted.

'What's she saying, Dad?'

'Something about a change being as good as a rest, I don't know. She's shrieking about something. I'll give her a change, you wait. I'll hide the ruddy credit card so she can't keep spending on it.'

Poor Dad.

'Anyway, love, she's here now, wants to have a word. Don't say I haven't warned you.'

I heard him pass the phone over, amidst loud rustling and some annoyed-sounding muttering. Mum came on the phone.

'I suppose he's been bending your ear about me, has he?' she demanded.

'No. He was just saying you've booked a short break.'

'And you'd have thought I'd signed him up for kung fu lessons in China, all the carrying-on he's been doing. Harping on and on about money. Honestly, it's his retirement fund and there's no point in sitting around waiting for it to gather dust now, is there?'

'I suppose.'

'Anyway, Marlena at the office says she convinced her hubby to take her to Italy last year for a long weekend. Stingy bugger didn't want to go. Huh! I know that feeling. Still, she won him over in the end and guess what?' she said excitedly.

'What?'

'They're expecting their second baby in March,' she gushed.

'Expensive trip then,' I said, dryly.

'Anyway', she continued, 'it's not as if I'm not earning.'

'So I hear. "Sales person of the week", eh?'

'"*Door-to-door* salesperson of the week", Maggie, there is a difference you know.'

'Is there? Sorry.'

'Oh yes, "Door-to-Door" have to do *so* much more than those silly telephone people who call up at all hours. Honestly, the cheek of them. Did you know that your father answered the phone to some young upstart the other day and he had the nerve to ask your dad how he was! Like he was his best friend, I ask you.'

I thought of CapiTel and of my short spate on the phone and said nothing.

'And… I even beat Marlena,' Mum continued proudly.

'Is it a competition then?' I enquired.

'No…!' she said a little too quickly, then paused. 'No, of course not, not really, but I did do rather well and Marlena's been in the top slot since February. I don't think she was very pleased.'

Mum was sounding ever so slightly smug.

'Oh well, it doesn't matter now. Besides, I shared my Belgian choccies with her. Marlena's never been one to turn down a cappuccino mousse, you know.

If it wasn't for her weekly Weight Watchers meetings, I swear she'd be the size of a house. Which reminds me... you know Mrs Hartford from across at Holly Close?'

'Not personally, but go on...'

'Well, listen to this,' Mum's voice took on an air of scandal. 'Her cousin's wife went to Weight Watchers and ended up selling ampheti-watsits to everyone there.'

'Ampheti-watsits?'

'You know, that whizzy stuff.'

Dad shouted out from the background. 'You mean "speed", love.'

Good grief, my parents were druggies.

'Yes, that's it, speed, Ampheta... watsits.'

'...'mines Mum. Amphetamines,' I explained.

'Yes, like I said...'

I rubbed my bewildered brow.

'Anyway, they all lost weight though so I suppose it worked.'

'How do you know all this anyway?' I asked.

'Apparently, Mrs Hartford's cousin's wife got caught. It was all over the local papers. I can't believe I haven't mentioned it before. Your father was in stitches at the time. Couldn't stop him laughing for love nor money.'

'Why was he laughing?'

'Well half the women at the meeting kept disappearing to the toilets to take the ampheti-watsits.'

'...'mines.'

'Yes, I know... and the woman who ran the meetings was so worried she had a group of women suffering from mass bulimia that she called for backup from her brother, who brought along his friend who just happened to be one of those Special Constable types and, would you believe it, he arrested the lot of them, even the woman who ran it; poor cow. Your father got all unnecessary over the headline.'

'What was it?'

'Oh I can't remember. Something about Coca Cola I think.'

Dad shouted out again. 'Diet "coke" in the can!' I could hear him laughing away.

Mum tutted huffily. 'I didn't understand it at all, but your father seemed to think something was most amusing.'

I smiled.

'Anyway, never mind that. Happy *birthday*, my darling!' she gushed. 'Did you get lots of scrummy presents?'

'Not yet, but thank you for the gift card.'

'That way you get to choose something you like…although I did see this super top in M&S, but…well, I suppose we do have different tastes,' she sounded a little sad.

'Thanks, Mum. Gift cards are always a winner.'

'Any nice men to buy you flowers?' she enquired, demurely.

I hesitated a little too long. 'No.'

'Maaaggie?'

'What?'

'Don't give me that "no". I'm your mother. Tell me *immediately!*'

'Mum, there's not really anything to tell.'

'Not really? That means there is.'

'No, it means there's nothing to tell. I'll let you know if anything changes,' I insisted. I managed to convince her nothing was going on but, when we'd hung up, I wondered why I hadn't told her the truth. In fact, I wondered why I felt it was all still a secret between Tony and me. Surely when you are with someone, you want to go round singing it from the rooftops. Perhaps with all the previous secrecy, I'd got used to keeping it quiet.

As I was getting ready to leave, Jenny called.

'How's the birthday girl then?'

'OK. How's the love life?'

'Amazing!' She sighed heavily down the phone then continued on with her reason for phoning. 'Look, we've all been secretly plotting and John and I are going to be at Pauline's too. I'll bring your prezzie there. You'll love it. John helped me decide what to get you. We've got to leave quite early though, we're off to Edinburgh for a couple of nights and then, next weekend, we're off on holiday for three weeks! John sprung it on me. I had no idea! The whole thing's been arranged behind my back. Even Dad's been in on it.'

'God, you lucky thing. Where are you going?'

'That's the really awesome thing. I've been wanting to go travelling through South America for yonks and John's gone and sorted out this amazing trek through all these stonking places. Mountains, jungles, cities, beaches; honestly, it'll be like the trip of a lifetime. I can't believe that work agreed to it. One of the benefits of going out with the boss, I guess.'

'God that's seriously amazing! Hang on… what's in Edinburgh?'

'His *mum*. Get *that*! He wants me to meet her! I'm *fucking* nervous.'

It was like talking to a different Jenny.

'Unlike you to be nervous.'

She laughed. 'Love's got a lot to answer for. I'm in a right two and eight about things.'

Two and eight?

'Is his mum Scottish then?'

'Very, so John says. She's originally from Glasgow. I've got visions of her in a kilt insisting I finish up my haggis and neeps, washed down with a wee dram. God, I seriously hope she drinks. I don't think I'll be able to face meeting her without a drink of some kind.'

'Jen, I'm sure she'll love you and I don't think you'll find the Scots eat haggis and drink whisky all the time, or wear kilts come to that.'

'D'ya recs?'

'Besides, Edinburgh is lovely and the people are really friendly. You'll have a great time.'

'Reckon I will.' She was clearly over the moon. 'Gotta go, John's calling. He's just loaded the car and we need to get on the road. Drive carefully, Magsie, and we'll make a big fat fuss of you at Pauline's.'

The drive down did me the power of good. As I left the busyness of London and the trees and fields starting rolling past, I was reminded once again of how much I loved the space and the freshness. I found myself daydreaming about moving back someday; maybe with Tony? He'd said he preferred the countryside; would he be prepared to move out of the city? I thought of Jenny and John and how happy they were together. I wanted that for myself and hoped Tony and I might lead somewhere similar. I really did like him, despite everything that had happened. I couldn't help myself. I felt a kind of connection to him at some level. That was why it was so difficult when he changed and got angry. In that way he reminded me of Jenny. She'd always had a problem keeping a lid on her temper. Catherine had cited her bibles to me one evening.

'Anger is generally an emotion used to cover up a different emotion, sadness or fear. So really, angry people are just frightened or sad or both. They don't know how to express those emotions, so they use anger instead. See?'

I hadn't really at the time but I thought back to when Pauline had told Jenny about her being ill. Jenny had stomped angrily around the place with a black cloud over her head before breaking down in tears about not being the first to know. Perhaps there was more to the theory than I'd realised? After all, when Tony had exploded angrily in the restaurant, he'd come back and apologised and explained how tough things had been; perhaps the anger really had just been covering up all the grief and stress and was the only way he knew how to deal with things? I would try to get more of a handle on this; start seeing Tony as a challenge. I could be the one to help him through his fears and worries and take care of him when he felt sad. I'd be Nurse Maggie, Saver of Tony. The one he turned to in a crisis; the one who really knew him, right to the core. Yes, that's what I'd do. I might need to borrow a book from Catherine though.

I straightened up in the driving seat and opened the window a little. Taking in a deep breath I inhaled the wonderful autumnal smell in the air. New season, new beginnings, new attitudes.

As I turned into Pauline and Terry's bumpy lane, I saw their jeep being reversed out of the drive up ahead. As it came towards me I recognised Terry in the driver's seat, with his curly dark hair and beard. He was accelerating pretty fast for a country lane. Although I waved to him, he either ignored me or didn't realise it was me, because he sped past and screeched off in the opposite direction.

Charming I thought, as I parked up.

Getting out of the car I took in several long breaths. It was good to be away from the city again. The air was so different, so clean. I was blissfully aware of the near silence apart from the occasional cheeping of birds and the rustling of leaves as the wind whispered through the trees.

I approached the impressive old house, so full of character, and I admired the wonderful creeper that was turning a glorious red and covering virtually the whole of the front wall. In the silent, covered, oak porch, I pulled on a long, rigid, iron bell-pull beside the large front door and heard the chimes ring out inside.

Through the bevelled glass panes at the top of the door someone's distorted shape was coming down the wide hallway to let me in. The door opened and all five-foot-nothing of Jenny leapt forward and threw her arms around me, squeezing me tight.

'Happy Birthday. Come on in, you old trollop.' She pulled me by the arm into the spacious hall. The grandfather clock tick-tocked methodically beside me.

'Hmmm.' She held me at arm's length and cocked her head to one side; 'Yep, you definitely look older.'

'Shut up, you,' I protested.

'Nothing to be ashamed of, we're all heading there. Old age, wrinkles, saggy tits; not that mine will ever sag, they're too small to sag. They'll probably stay like this 'til the day I pop my clogs. Timmy says they're like fried eggs.'

'What does John say?' I asked, slipping off my shoes, which were a little muddy from the driveway, and leaving them by the coat rack.

'Says fried eggs are his favourite.' She grinned.

I wondered how Tony would describe my chest.

'Great timing by the way,' Jenny said. 'You've just missed Attila the Hun.'

'Who, Terry?'

'Who else? Miserable git.' She shook her head.

'Yes, what's up with him, he didn't even wave to me just now?'

'Dunno, probably got a question wrong on *University Challenge*. Timmy calls him "Tefal head". Personally, I prefer "shit head"!'

I laughed. 'He's not all that bad really.'

'Yes, he is,' she complained, loudly. Then, casting her eyes down the hallway in the direction of Pauline's room, she lowered her voice. 'He's been stomping around the place like a big kid. He keeps on at Pauline to do some work stuff, sort out some forms or something. Honestly, I don't know what can be that urgent and anyway, she's so tired she shouldn't be doing anything! He's been getting really narked with her. I'm seriously thinking of cornering him and giving him a piece of my mind. If he comes back before we go, he'd better watch out,' she said angrily.

'Do you think that's wise though? After all, he is Pauline's husband. Perhaps we shouldn't interfere?'

'I think we should. Thank God Timmy's here otherwise Terry would still have her running around after him all the time.'

I slid my coat off, hung it up on the rack and followed Jenny down to Pauline's bedroom, past the many photos of the family's animals; horses and Golden and Black Retrievers in the main. I spotted one particular shot of Pauline with her favourite pony Star. She could only have been about seventeen. Her cheeks were flushed and her eyes were alive with excitement. She seemed full of vitality. She'd just won a local gymkhana and was sporting a yellow rosette with 1st on it. It was a shock, therefore, to see the contrast of the Pauline in the photo and the Pauline who was lying stretched out on her bed as Jenny led me into the room. Despite her welcoming smile, she looked even more drawn than the last time I'd seen her. Her eyes were tired and lined and her skin was sallow. She looked dreadful. Still, she gave a cheer when I walked in.

Timmy sprung out from behind the door, wearing a silly hat with flashing lights on and blowing noisily on an unfolding paper party whistle. Jenny went and sat on the arm of the bedroom armchair where John was stretched out. He began singing *Happy Birthday* at which point Pauline, Timmy and Jenny joined in.

'Happy birthday to you, happy birthday to you, happy birthday, dear Maaaaagie, happy birthday to you. Hooray!'

I stood embarrassed in the doorway, waiting for them to finish. Then Timmy ushered me to sit down on the end of the bed.

'We've all got you something, so you have to come in and open your presents and pretend to like them,' he insisted. 'Especially mine.'

'I'll try,' I agreed solemnly.

I turned to Pauline. 'How are you?'

'Never mind about me, I want to hear all about what you got for your birthday and whether your new man got you something nice.'

'What new man??' Jenny and Timmy cried.

'I haven't got one!' I frowned.

'Damn,' Pauline said. 'Thought I might catch you out.'

I tried to keep a blush from creeping up over face.

'Well, Mum and Dad got me a gift card,' I said.

'A gift card!' Jenny exclaimed. 'Why is it that old folks always buy young people stuff like that? Do you run out of ideas when you get to that age or something?'

'Possibly,' I agreed.

'Maybe the bit of the brain that thinks up new stuff dries up and withers away,' Jenny suggested.

Pauline looked appalled. 'Jenny, that's a hideous notion! My folks are much older than Maggie's and they have wonderful ideas about things.'

'They also take all their clothes off and parade around with other oldies with all their bits dangling about. I don't think we can count them, Paul'.'

'If you'd seen some of the presents my mum and dad have bought me over the years, you'd want a gift card too,' I explained.

'Mine too,' John said. 'My mum bought me the most awful yellow jumper once, from BHS. It's still in the back of the wardrobe gathering dust.'

'Dad's always been bloody brilliant at birthdays,' Jenny said proudly. 'Last year he got me tickets for Les Mis.'

'I didn't know you liked all that musical opera stuff,' Timmy said.

'Well, I do,' Jenny replied, a little indignantly.

I saw John give her hand a squeeze.

'At least you've got parents to buy you presents,' Timmy said sadly. He'd never known his dad, and his mum, an alcoholic, hadn't been much use to him at all. She'd moved to Tenerife with one of her many boyfriends when Timmy had been only sixteen, leaving him to pretty much fend for himself. With no parents of his own, he'd frequently holidayed at Pauline's house as a teenager and had been a big part of our lives growing up.

I reached up to where he stood and rubbed his arm.

'You can share my dad, Timmy,' Jenny said. 'He thinks of you as one of his own anyway.'

Timmy cheered up at that.

'Now then' he said, 'you've got to promise not to open any presents until I get back with the tea.' Timmy reached down under the end of the bed and drew out a tray with several presents on it. He placed it on the bed.

'No peeking. Promise?'

'Promise,' I agreed, crossing my heart.

When Timmy had gone, I surveyed the pile.

'Who got me the one wrapped in naked men?'

'Timmy,' Jenny and Pauline chorused.

'You should see the card!' Jenny said.

'Enough to make a man jealous,' John added.

'Hardly!' Jenny exclaimed.

I think John blushed.

Moments later, Timmy backed his way in through the door with a large full tea tray including some side plates and a long knife then he disappeared again.

'No peeking still,' he called out from the hallway.

'You've got to humour him, I guess,' Pauline sighed.

Back he came. The door opened slowly and a sumptuous looking, highly decorated, chocolate cake appeared, covered in lit candles, followed by a singing Timmy.

'Happy birthday to you, happy birthday to you…' he sang for the second time.

The others joined in again and Timmy placed the cake on the side table so I could blow out the candles.

'The cake's from Choccywoccydoodah. We all chipped in,' Timmy explained happily.

'It's amazing! Thanks guys!' I exclaimed, examining the swirls and curls of dark, milk and white chocolate which adorned the thick chocolate coating over what promised to be the most delicious cake.

'Wish! Wish! You have to make a wish,' Timmy cried, when I managed to blow them all out in one hit.

Thoughts of Tony came swooping in but I wasn't entirely sure what to wish for, so I settled on a money angle.

'I wish I was rich, and in the meantime find a permanent job I really like,' I said.

'You mustn't say it out loud,' Timmy said, 'it might not come true!'

'Button it, Timmy, course it will,' Jenny reprimanded.

'This one's from John,' Jenny said proudly, passing me a little odd-shaped gift. 'It's really from both of us but he chose it all on his own, so it's more from him than me.' She slid down from the arm of the chair and squeezed herself onto John's lap like a little kid, kissing him noisily in his ear. He pretended to complain.

I smiled at John and carefully opened the wrapping.

'Just rip it open! The suspense is killing me!' Timmy cried.

Inside was a very chubby little silver Buddha with a smiley face.

Jenny pointed out, 'You're not supposed to buy one for yourself; someone has to buy it for you so its magic works.'

'You rub his tummy and make a wish and it'll come true,' John explained. 'I used to have one when I was little and, I kid you not, it really works.'

What a gorgeous man! I went over and kissed them both.

'Thank you, John… Jenny, I love it!'

'That's from me.' Pauline said pointing to a large box on the floor, wrapped in green and blue tartan paper. 'I know you said you wanted one ages ago; I hope you still do!'

I opened it up. It was an icebox.

I'd always wanted an icebox. Every summer I loved to go and sit on Clapham Common and although I always complained I didn't have anything to keep a picnic chilled I'd still never done anything about it.

'Bit cold for it now, I know, but there's something else inside,' she said.

I reached inside.

'A thermos flask!' I exclaimed. 'Perfect!'

'That way you can take your flask of coffee out to the common and huddle up in a fleece. So you've got summer and winter covered.'

'I love them!' I kissed her.

'I'd stick some brandy in there too,' Jenny said. 'I'm buggered if you'd get me sitting outside in winter with only coffee to keep me company.'

'I'd keep you company.' John smiled and the two of them shared a 'moment'.

'Now mine, open mine,' Timmy insisted.

'Timmy, you're not working, you shouldn't have got me anything!' I said, although I was rather glad he had.

I opened the paper, finding myself compelled to stare at one particular model's huge penis.

Timmy spotted me staring.

'I went out with him once,' he said proudly. 'Stefan. Went like a train!'

'Oy!' Jenny scolded. 'We have company remember.'

'Sorry, John.'

John grinned. 'I think I can handle it. Why did you finish?'

'If truth be known, I'm more of a Beetle convertible man at heart, trains make me feel sick.'

Inside, was a large photo frame and turning it over, I gasped in delight.

'Timmy! It's fantastic.'

It was a signed photo from my all-time hero, Sting. I'd grown up with his music playing in our house throughout his music career. Dad had been a huge fan. He'd be very jealous!

'How on earth…'

'It's not what you know, it's who you know.' He winked at Jenny. 'So, with a bit of help, I pulled a few strings and hey presto. One signed photo.'

I stood up and flung my arms around him.

'Now mine!' Jenny insisted. 'You're gonna love it. Dad helped me sort it.' Jenny's present was a large box but when I opened it there was another one inside it. I unwrapped that and yet another box was in the middle. Inside that was a parcel which, when I opened the paper, revealed masses of bubble wrap. I eventually got to the middle of it. And there was a single envelope inside.

'The suspense is even getting to me now; and I know what it is!' Pauline said.

I opened the envelope and inside there were two tickets.

'OH MY GOD!' I shrieked.

'Tickets to see Sting!'

'That's Dad for you,' Jenny said. 'Told you he was good at sorting these things out; he knows all the right people.'

'He was one of my string pullers,' Timmy admitted.

'But I'm surprised this wasn't sold out months ago!'

'It probably was; but you know Dad, he rubs shoulders with so many famous luvvies and musos through the theatres he goes to, he probably just called up an old mate and sorted it out in one phone call.'

I rushed over to Jenny and hugged her tightly, with profuse thanks.

'I might even keep you company, if Cat's not up for it.'

'She may have met a sexy man by then,' Pauline suggested.

As I sat down again, I felt myself colouring up and hoped no one would notice.

'Come on, let's get this cake cut. I'm starving,' Timmy said, clearing the paper off the bed. 'I'll be mum.' He went over and began to pour the tea.

'How's Luke doing?' Pauline asked Jenny. I did my best to keep my face neutral.

She shrugged.

'Dunno really. We went up last weekend but he was out a lot, just walking and stuff; seems to have gone into his shell a bit.'

'Can't be easy, all this stuff with Sian,' Pauline reasoned. 'It must surely be getting him down.'

'I think you're right,' Jenny said. 'I mentioned we were coming down today and asked if he wanted to come along but he went really funny on me. I don't think he's into socialising much right now.'

I looked for signs to tell if they knew that Sian was pregnant but certainly no one mentioned it. One thing seemed apparent though, Luke obviously hadn't gone back to Sweden.

'Well, tell him if he wants any company, I'll be there like a shot!' Timmy offered.

'What I wouldn't do to get my hands on those pecs!'

'Yuck, Timmy, you're practically related!' Jenny said. '*And* he's my brother!'

'Ah, but *practically* isn't the same as *actually*. Besides, I've hardly seen him for ten years, so it would be like wiping the slate clean and starting again.'

'There is the small matter of him being straight though,' Pauline pointed out.

'Soon change that. I'm an expert don't you know.'

I was feeling decidedly uncomfortable and unable to join in the conversation.

'You OK, Maggie?' John asked kindly. 'You've gone a bit quiet.'

'Have I? Sorry, I think I'm just hungry,' I said brightly.

'Yes, Timmy, hurry up with that cake!' Jenny exclaimed. 'The birthday girl needs feeding.'

As we drank our steaming mugs of tea and munched away on the heavenly chocolate cake, Jenny started worrying about meeting John's mum.

'Will she like me?' she asked fretfully. 'I'm not exactly every mother's dream.'

'She'll love you, because I do,' John said calmly.

'Awww, sweet,' Timmy said, putting his fingers down his throat.

'You're just jealous,' Jenny said.

'I know,' Timmy admitted sadly.

Jenny turned to John. 'Will she wear a kilt?'

'Um, I don't actually think she owns a kilt.'

'That's good then. I don't really do kilts and I'd have to be really polite and say I loved it.'

'Is that right?' John said, an amused expression creeping over his face. 'You know, being half Scottish, I've got a kilt.'

'You!' Jenny exclaimed.

'Yeah, me. Problem?' he challenged, teasingly.

'I love kilts,' Timmy said. 'All bare legs and bums and dangly bits, covered only by a piece of easy-access cloth, bliss.'

'But surely you wear boxers or something?' Jenny said.

'Not if you're a true Scot you don't,' John informed her.

'Wow,' Jenny said. 'And, er, are you... do you...'

'Wear anything under my kilt?'

'Yeah, do you?'

'I couldn't possibly tell you that. You'll have to wait until our wedding day then you'll get to find out.'

The rest of us exchanged glances.

'You mean you'd wear one to your own wedding!' Jenny squealed.

'Of course! I'd be piped up the aisle with a full pipe band and you'd have to pray that there wasn't one of those floor-laid air vents chucking up a blast of air when we all walked over it, otherwise the guests might get a bit of a shock.' He winked at me over Jenny's shoulder.

Jenny looked perplexed then realisation dawned on her.

'But… er… what do you mean… "our wedding day"?' she stumbled, her eyes wide. John shrugged.

'You'd better hope and pray that mum likes you, that's all I'm saying.'

Before Jenny could reply, Ralfie the Great Dane interrupted, bounding into the room with great gusto. He had a Wellington boot in his mouth and was looking very pleased with himself. He promptly dropped it on the carpet and barked, wagging his huge tail and nearly knocking the cups off the tray.

'I think he needs a walk, Timmy,' Pauline said.

'I think he needs a manservant!' Timmy replied. 'He needs a permanent walk. It's a full-time job running about after that mutt. And he's always running off chasing rabbits, he never comes when I call, and he poos like a bloody horse! Come on, Ralfie; let's get you out then before you drop more than that Wellie.'

'We'd better be off too, Jen,' John said, 'Don't want to keep Mum waiting. You wouldn't want to see her when she's angry.'

Fear crossed Jenny's face. Once again, John winked.

Timmy and I saw them off at the door. John drove Jenny off in a huge Range Rover that made Jenny look like a doll sitting up in a high chair. She grinned through the window, rotating her hand like the Queen and then squashed her nose up to the glass and pulled a face at us.

Timmy went off with Ralfie so I thought I'd go back in and take the opportunity to have a one to one with Pauline.

She appeared exhausted again and I wondered if having visitors was taking it out of her.

'How have you been feeling? You look awfully tired.'

'I am. I've got another viral thing and it's really draining me,' she admitted.

'Would it be better if I left, gave you some peace to get some sleep?'

'No! For goodness sakes it's doing me good seeing people. Sane people!' she added. 'Besides, it's your birthday and Timmy's done sandwiches for lunch and there's fizz too, so you have to stay. I think he's even got some paper hats but don't tell him I told you.'

We sat and chatted for a while and heard Timmy coming in the backdoor, complaining loudly about Ralfie's misdemeanours. Then suddenly, the front doorbell sounded, making me jump.

'Hang on, I'll get it,' Timmy called from the utility room. 'Once I've got these dog poo covered shoes off!'

'You expecting anyone?' I asked Pauline.

'It's probably just Terry. He went off in a mood earlier, so just ignore him if he kicks off again.'

'Hasn't he got any keys?'

'Yes. But I wouldn't put it past him to ring the bell just so I had to get up and let him in. He thinks exercise will make me better.'

I shook my head. 'I'm sorry to say this, Paul', but I don't think he's looking after you very well at all.'

She turned away. 'Let's not talk about it eh? Not today.'

'OK, but you know I'm here if you need to sound off.'

'I know.'

'Why don't I put the kettle on again and top up the pot,' I offered. 'One more cup and then I could be convinced to sample some of that fizz!'

I met Timmy in the hallway, padding along in his socks on his way to answer the door, just as the doorbell rang again.

'You'll have to ignore the smell from my shoes back there. Blame Ralfie, I swear he's been on the sprouts.'

'If that's Terry at the door, tell him he's an arse, from me,' I said as Timmy headed off.

'Join the queue,' he called back.

In the kitchen, I put the kettle on and waited for it to boil. I could hear muffled voices in the hallway. It didn't sound like Terry and whoever it was, was here to stay, because I heard Timmy shut the front door and take the person in to see Pauline. I thought I'd better check to see if whoever it was wanted tea, so I headed back along the corridor to Pauline's room.

As I opened the door, I caught my breath. There, sitting in the low armchair, long legs stretched out and looking painfully handsome, was Luke.

Luke was clearly as taken aback as I was and for a moment the two of us gawped at each other. Then I composed myself.

'Hello, Luke,' I said firmly. 'I'm just making us all a cup of tea. Would you like one?'

'Or there's squash or coffee or bottled water if you'd prefer, Luke,' Pauline offered.

'Actually, why don't we open the bubbles instead?'

'No really, tea's fine. Thanks, Maggie', he added, then turned away and spoke to Pauline. 'I'm driving and I can't stay long. Jenny said she was down today and I thought I'd drop in and see how you were.'

As I left the room, I was shaking. Back in the kitchen I had to sit down. Despite my conscious decision of putting thoughts of Luke in the past, my body seemingly hadn't caught up with the process and was still doing a rag doll impression.

Had he known I'd be here too? He certainly hadn't looked pleased to see me.

I made the fresh pot of tea and carried it through, embarrassed at how my hand shook as I placed it on the tray.

'More cake anyone?' I aimed to the air as I poured the tea.

'It's Maggie's birthday, Luke,' Timmy said, cutting a slice off and handing it to Luke.

There was a moment's silence then Luke spoke.

'Happy birthday, Maggie.'

'Thank you.' I smiled politely.

I knew it was silly but I couldn't help feeling a bit peeved that he'd obviously not remembered.

I heaped two sugars into Timmy's cup and passed it to him, then poured milk into Pauline's and Luke's. 'No sugar, isn't it Luke?' I said without thinking. I could have kicked myself. It was too intimate, too personal.

I glanced up at him. He smiled very slightly and nodded.

I blushed and passed him the mug, annoyed that my hand continued to shake. For a while, the conversation turned to Pauline's health. Luke showed genuine concern and it crossed my mind that, while I'd told Tony that Pauline wasn't well, he hadn't once asked how she was. Still, he was busy and he'd had so much on his mind lately.

I noticed how kind Luke was being. At one point, he went over and sat on the bed beside Pauline and engulfed her in a big hug. He squeezed her tight before letting her go.

'It'll be OK, you know. I promise you. We'll find out what the problem is and we'll sort it. You're not on your own.'

Tears filled Pauline's eyes and I had to turn away as mine sprung a leak too.

While I didn't like to admit it, whatever I thought about Luke, whatever had happened in the past, it was obvious he was a genuinely kind person. I wished the thought didn't make me feel quite so sad.

As the conversation flowed around me and Luke and I avoided eye contact, I couldn't help but wonder about Sian and the baby. What had been going on since she'd told him? Luke may well have been kind but the Sian thing really got to me. Surely he should be with her right now. Had he told anyone at all? Could Tony, Cat and I be the only ones who knew?

I played around with the crumbs of cake on my plate and listened as he told Pauline and Timmy about some work he'd be doing reasonably locally for the Swedish company he worked for. So it looked like he was here to stay.

Suddenly, as I went to put my plate back on the tray, Luke replaced his at the same time and our hands brushed each other's. A wild shock of electricity passed between us and shot through my body. Luke must have felt it too because he jerked away and almost spilt his tea.

'Careful, you two, you'll be setting the place alight if you're not careful,' Timmy laughed.

Luke and I both mumbled apologies into our laps.

Fuck! Why did that have to go and happen?

Pauline needed the loo, so Timmy helped her up and led her to the door and along to the bathroom, leaving Luke and me on our own. The silence was painful. It went on so long I could hardly breathe.

'Did you get anything nice?' Luke asked. 'For your birthday I mean.'

OK, so we were at least being pleasant here.

'Yes. Yes I did. Timmy got me this. I reached over to the pile of presents and handed him the photo frame.'

'Wow! This is fantastic.' He was clearly extremely impressed. 'I wonder how he pulled that one off.'

'I think your Dad had something to do with it.'

'Ah, sounds about right.' He smiled warmly. 'Good old Dad.'

Now he was even being friendly. What was going on?

'And Jenny and John got me two tickets to see him in the new year.'

'Lucky you…'

There was a horrid silence again and Luke's mood seemed to alter.

When he spoke, his voice was strained. His expression had changed and he stared fixatedly out the window.

'No points for guessing who you'll take then.' He carried on staring.

It was obvious he was talking about Tony.

I shrugged.

'It's a long way off.'

More silence.

'And anyway,' I said, 'I'm not sure it's really any of your business.'

He turned back to face me holding eye contact, his gaze intense.

441

'Not any of my business?'

I shifted in my seat.

'Well... no.'

'Is that a fact?'

I could see quiet anger simmering beneath the surface.

'So, how is my wonderful, loyal brother then?'

Honestly, he had a nerve; clearly the friendliness had come to an end.

'He's fine thank you, Luke. And tell me, how is Sian?' I asked spitefully. 'I'm surprised you're not over in Sweden with her.'

'That's out of order, Maggie. And it really *is* none of your business.'

'Touché.'

We both sat silently smouldering. You could have cut the atmosphere with a knife.

'So, are you going to sort things out with her?' I finally felt compelled to ask. It was making me angry now, just thinking about how she might be feeling.

'Just forget about Sian will you?' he said crossly. 'I don't want to drag that up again.'

'Forget about her? *Forget about her?* Is that what you're doing? How can you sit there and say that? She's your responsibility and you've let her down.'

Just like you did me.

'What?' he snapped. 'You don't even know what's going on. You haven't even met her. Anyway, why the sudden interest?'

I smiled sarcastically.

'Let's put it this way; I have a feeling I might know what she's going through.'

He looked a little puzzled, then a slight flicker of realisation crossed his face and his expression softened.

'Meaning?' he said slowly.

I fell silent, aware of him running his fingers through his hair and sighing heavily.

His gaze dropped. 'Look,' he began, '...about what happened...'

'Just forget it, Luke. All I'm saying is Sian's your fiancée. The least you could do is be with her through all this; she obviously needs you right now.'

Luke's head shot up to vertical and his anger rose again.

'Ha! That's rich coming from you! How the hell do you think Laura feels, eh? You're the one who needs telling; I've got nothing on you!'

I was seething now.

'And how the hell do you work that one out?'

I watched as he banged his clenched fist on the arm of the chair, like he wanted to punch something. Instead though he took a deep breath and exhaled slowly.

'Maggie,' he said, calmer now, 'if you can't see what you're doing, then you're more of a fool than I had you down for.'

This was really pushing things too far.

'*What?*' I fumed. 'How can you *say* that? After all you did…' But sounds of the others returning stopped me mid-sentence and Luke and I went back to a moody silence.

Oooh, I was so frustrated, so… *furious* with Luke, I wanted to scream! I had to get out of the room and away from him. I stood up and went to the door to help Pauline back in then said I was going to get a glass of water.

'You'll be peeing all day at this rate, Mags,' Timmy said as Pauline hobbled over to her bed and collapsed back on to it.

'Better still get the fizz and the sandwiches,' she suggested; 'everything's set up in the kitchen, you just need to get the bottle out the fridge door. Let's get celebrating,' 'OK.' I half smiled and shot out the door ignoring Luke's eyes boring into me. Once in the kitchen, I flung open the glass panelled doors to the garden and breathed in the fresh air. The trees had turned a gorgeous array of reds and oranges and the sun shone brightly, casting shadows over the lawn. Autumn – my favourite time of the year and it was my birthday. I should have been happy and yet I felt unable to enjoy it at all now. Such a beautiful day marred by *him*. I let out an exasperated sigh and Ralfie opened one eye then the other, peering up from his position on the kitchen floor. His tail thwumped a couple of times on the cool flagstones and I knelt down to pet him. He rolled over on his back while I stroked his tummy. He stretched and yawned where he lay then looked up at me, his upside-down head and lolling tongue a comical picture, in complete contrast to my mood. I was really annoyed with myself. Yet again, I'd nearly fallen into the trap of seeing the good in Luke. Fancy him dishing out all that stuff about Tony and me when he was doing something far worse!

Along the corridor I heard the front door shut and making my way back to the room with the tray of sandwiches and fizz, I found Luke had gone.

'Did you see Luke?' Pauline asked.

'No, why? Has he left?' I asked, innocently.

'He said he'd say goodbye to you in the kitchen,' Timmy said.

'I must have been in the loo. I didn't see him. Never mind. Who's for this lovely fizz then?' I was relieved he'd gone. Perhaps now I could feel normal again.

'Count me in,' Pauline said. 'Just a splash though, doctor's orders and all that.' She pulled a face.

'Oh by the way, Luke left you this.' Pauline handed me a red envelope.

'Seems like he knew it was your birthday after all.' She smiled knowingly.

'Thanks.' I accepted the card with a shaky hand. 'I'll open it later. Right now, I need a drink!'

I slipped the card into my bag and poured the pink sparkling wine.

And so we remained for another couple of hours until Pauline was really flagging and I made my excuses and left, promising I'd be back down very soon.

At the door, Timmy gave me a big bear hug but as I pulled away I noticed again how tired and drawn he looked.

'Timmy.'

'Yes?'

'Well done.'

'What for?'

'For taking care of her so well. You're a diamond, you know that?'

I left him standing in the drive, a tear in his eye.

On the drive back, the sun was dipping; there was a cool breeze now. It had been just the sort of day I would have liked to have been in a country pub that smelt of real ale and had a crackling open fire; it would serve delicious, fresh, country food and have cosy nooks and crannies to snuggle in. Perhaps the sort of pub that Tony and I would go to? On a sunny day like today we would sit out on a picnic bench in the pretty garden all snuggled up in warm clothes. He would wrap his thick jumpered arms around me, while we lazed happily soaking up the last of the sunshine, still slightly warm from the summer. Maybe we'd even go on a long country walk. Not too long though.

'How was your day, birthday girl?' Catherine asked on the phone that evening.

'Interesting. Luke turned up.'

'No! How come?'

'Dunno; said he'd dropped in to see Pauline.' I suddenly remembered the card. 'And he gave me a birthday card.'

'Gracious! So he knew you'd be there then?'

I thought about it.

'I suppose he must have done.'

When I replaced the receiver, I took the red envelope out of my bag. 'Maggie', was written on the front in Luke's still familiar handwriting. More grown up than years ago but nevertheless pretty much the same.

I opened it carefully.

It was a lovely card, beautiful even; a weeping willow bowing down over a river. It reminded me of the river at Tillmouth. Had Luke meant it to? It didn't necessarily convey any type of message but it was… touching somehow. I opened it up and read the words.

Despite everything, I still care
I'm sorry Mags
Happy Birthday
Luke x

I sat staring at the open card.

Ohhhh nooo.

Chapter Fifty-six

'A belated happy birthday for Saturday,' Margot said from behind the reception desk, as I arrived on the Monday morning. 'Sorry it's late.' She handed me a little gift and a card. She'd been off sick the previous Friday.

'Oh thank you! Are you feeling better?'

'What? Oh right, Friday.' She lowered her voice. 'I wasn't really ill.'

'Don't tell me, you met a new bloke and were up all night on Thursday.'

'No, not a new bloke, it were Darius.'

'Darius, you're still seeing him?' I was surprised. It had been, well, in Margot terms, ages!

She shrugged. 'Quite like him I s'pose.'

'Quite like him, or really like him?' I asked. 'You're not in *lurrrrve* are you, Margot?'

'Just shut up and open that, before I take it baack,' she complained.

I opened the wrapping to reveal a little box. I lifted the lid off and inside was the gorgeous pair of earrings I'd seen when we'd been out shopping for my new dress.

'You remembered!' I cried, going round the desk and giving her a hug.

She shrugged again.

'Don't go gettin' all sarppy on me, they's only earrings.'

I tilted my head to one side and surveyed Margot who was blushing slightly, even under her pink streak of blusher.

'If I didn't know better, I'd say you were covering up a great big heart underneath all that tough exterior.'

'The only thing I'm covering up is a Stranglers tee shirt under this blouse. Now get off to your office and stop swearing at me.'

I grinned and began chanting as I headed off down the corridor; 'Margot's in love, Margot's in love.'

I got on with my work but I was distracted. It was only a few days until Tony got back. Due to his intense workload, he'd only really been texting while he'd been away at the New York conference and we hadn't actually talked properly. I'd just had one brief message from him, on my answer phone, saying he was looking forward to seeing me and hoped that teddy was protecting me from all the men who were bound to be pursuing me relentlessly.

I opened my bag beside me on the desk and took out the same red envelope Pauline had given me yesterday. Inside, Luke's card felt like it was alive; full of energy; full of danger. Why had he gone and written that? Why had he gone and confused things even more? It was easier hating him. It was much easier to forget he even existed than to try and make sense of cryptic birthday cards that arrived out of the blue. It hadn't felt right to put it up on the mantelpiece. And it had seemed somehow wrong that anyone else apart from Luke and I knew what he'd written. That's why I'd put it in my handbag. I needed to keep hold of it. Keep it close to me until I knew what to do about it. At least, that was my excuse. I'd actually tried to throw it away but that had seemed petty somehow. I mean, it was just a birthday card; pretty innocuous really. I'd thrown it, no... placed it, in the waste paper basket in the lounge. It had sat there for all of ten minutes but I couldn't concentrate on anything else, so I'd had to take it out again. I mean what exactly had he meant? 'I still care.' What was that all about? And more to the point, why did I care so much what it meant? I was busy staring down at it, when Margot walked in.

'Guess what?'

'What?' I replied, half-heartedly.

'Old Wellesy's asked me to set up a meeting with you.'

'With me? Why?'

'Dunno. He was pretty keen for it to be sooner rather than later though. Sometime this afternoon suit you?'

'Any idea what it's about?' I fretted. *Was he unhappy with my work?* I thought I'd done really well and he'd praised me no end on my reports.

'Nope, probably wants to tell you when Chloe's coming back. She was on earlier; gave me a right earful about that bloody bairn of hers.'

Chloe was coming back!? That was quick. I mentally tried to work out the months she'd been gone. Surely she wasn't due back for a while, yet.

'Jake, she's called him,' Margot continued. 'As if there aren't enough Jakes in the world.'

'I like the name Jake,' I said.

'It's a bit *over* though, don't you think? Anyway, whatever, better get back to the boss man with a time; after lunch suit you? Say two thirty?'

I nodded.

Margot glanced down at my card.

'Don't tell me; let me guess.'

I rolled my eyes to the ceiling.

'You couldn't possibly know who it's from.'

'Hmmm.' Margot rubbed her chin. 'I think I'll need to sit down for this one.'

She sat in the chair opposite and, leaning her elbows on my desk, put her fingers up to her temples.

'Nope, I'm not getting any Gemini vibes, so it's not from that Tony bloke. Besides, if it were, you wouldn't have brought it to work with you. Nope, I reckon there's more to that card than meets the eye.'

I sighed.

'Margot, I haven't really got time for this.'

'Don't gimme thaat. Now shush, let me carncentrate.'

She went silent and, just as I was wondering if she'd gone into a deep trance and might need shaking out of it, she sat up straight and banged the desk.

'I'm pretty dumb aren' I? Of course; it's from his brother, innit?' It was her turn to roll her eyes. 'Should 'ave seen that one comin'.'

'Why? Um, not that I'm saying it is from him.'

'You don't 'ave to, it's written all over your face. Anyway, it's the Law of Attraction, see?'

I didn't.

I tried to sound bored. 'Go on, enlighten me then.'

'Well, see, when you shouted out his name, what was it…?'

'Luke,' I said regretfully.

'That's it, Luke. See when you called out his name, you sent a message out into the universe.'

'Saying what!?

'Saying that really, underneath, that's who you wanted to be with. See? I mean Jung and Freud and all them, they weren't theck, you know?'

I didn't.

'It was a Freudian slip. And by putting that message, albeit unconscious, out there, you've created an Aka cord, see?'

'What on earth's an Aka cord?'

'It's an attachment. It's a thin string; invisible, mind, to the untrained eye anyway.' A knowing look appeared on her face. 'A sort of psychic cord that attaches itself to people when you've got a connection. And this Luke bloke's got hold of the other end and he's responded back to you with this card. And you know what that means don't you?'

Er, no!

'He wants you just as much as you want him, see? Like I said, Law of Attraction. Long story short, you're attracting what, or in this case who, you're spending time thinking about... like it or not. And he's doin' the same... so it's a done deal; you mark my words.'

I frowned.

'Oh don't look so down in the mouth. Sounds like it's destined now so you might as well just accept it.'

And with that, she stood up and walked out, leaving me alone. Then poked her head back round the door. 'Don't forget the meeting. Oh and remember to tell me what Wellesy says, after. I 'ates not knowing stuff round 'ere, all right?'

'All right,' I replied.

Then I had a thought.

'I thought you were psychic though!' I called after her only to hear her chuckling to herself down the corridor.

I opened up the red envelope and sliding out the card I studied it again; the picture on the front, the words, the handwriting. Then I inadvertently lifted the envelope up to my nose and breathed in the smell of it. I was flung straight back into the past, to the time when it was just Luke and me. One little card and my world was threatening to turn topsy turvy. Didn't he know I was trying to get him out of my head? Didn't he know he had been mentally banished to the past? And didn't he know that I was supposed to be hating him and not... well, not other stuff; other feelings. And anyway, who was this Jung bloke? And what business did he and Freud have interfering with my love life?

I got ready for my meeting with Mr Welles and, as I was doing my best to de-frizz my currently curly hair without much joy thanks to the day's drizzle, the phone rang at my desk. Margot's voice came down the line.

'Some bird named Catherine for you.'

'Thanks, put her through,' I said.

Catherine was in a panic.

'I think Tom might be gay!' she exclaimed.

???!

'Er... gay? Why? And more to the point, how do you know?'

'I have my reasons,' she said, sounding like a school matron.

'What reasons?'

'I'd rather not say.'

'So, let me get this straight, sorry no pun intended. You're saying Tom is a gay cat with a wheat intolerance.' My voice cracked slightly.

'Don't laugh. And yes, exactly! Isn't it awful; poor thing.'

'Oh, Cat. You are funny.'

'I wonder if the other cats know?' she went on.

'What, that he's got a wheat intolerance?'

'Maggie, be serious. They're hardly likely to have worked that one out. No, I wonder if they know that he's gay.'

A vision of Tom came to mind. Standing on his back legs, dressed in a smoking jacket and cravat, and smoking a cigarette in a cigarette holder, puffing mice-shaped smoke rings.

'OK, come on, how exactly do you know that he *is* gay, or that he might be?'

'I've been watching him.'

'And...?'

'I don't really want to say.'

'It's only me. I won't say anything.'

As if!

'Cat, what's he done?'

'I'm sure it's not his fault,' she began.

'What isn't!?'

'Well, he's been sniffing some other cats that have just moved into the flats.'

'Yes. So...?'

'... in their...' she dropped her voice, '...nether regions.'

I sighed.

'Cat, that's what they do? That's them just being friendly.'

'Friendly maybe; but he's been sniffing the behinds of other male cats and that can't be right can it?'

'I think you'll find that it's perfectly normal.' I shook my head to myself. 'I thought you were the cat expert. You've enough books on the subject.'

'Yes, well, I skipped that chapter. I didn't think I needed to read about it.'

I could feel her shuddering on the other end of the phone.

'Anyway, you probably think I'm silly but it's just the *way* he's doing it. There's something not right, I'm sure of it.'

'Maybe he's bisexual,' I offered up, trying to keep a straight face.

There was a moment's silence.

'Yesss, maybe; oh I hope so or rather I hope he's straight.'

'Why? I thought you were very liberal about these things.'

'Oh I am, I am,' she said quickly, 'but I don't want the other cats picking on him, that's all.'

Oh dear....

'Have you checked his chart?' I asked, smiling to myself.

'Of course!'

'Cat, I was joking!'

'This is a very serious business, Maggie. You may not think so but I do.'

'OK, I'm sorry; really. What did his chart say then?' It was best just to run with it.

'Well, apparently he will be prone to adventure during his life and likes to experiment,' she explained. 'Which kind of says a lot, don't you think?'

'Is the chart for humans or are you reading one especially for cats?'

'For cats of course! What would be the point of reading a chart for a human? He's a cat!'

Exactly!

It was probably time to move on.

'Look hun, we'll talk things through later on but I really have to go. I have a meeting with one of the partners and I need to get my skates on.'

'OK, but maybe you could ask your friend Margot. From what you've said about her, she sounds like she might know about these things.'

I agreed to have a word but could already see the look on Margot's face.

I replaced the receiver.

Suddenly the thought of cat-sitting while Catherine and Nico went off to see his parents filled me with dread. A gay or possibly bisexual cat with a wheat intolerance, who didn't like his water too cold, absolutely had to have fresh food on a daily basis and, who knows, may have a penchant for Gauloises, didn't sound like my idea of fun.

'Come,' Bob Welles's voice rang through the door.

I let myself in.

'Ah, young Maggie. Just the person.' He smiled warmly and motioned to the chair.

'Sit, sit.'

I sat.

'Did you have a pleasant weekend?' he asked amiably.

'Yes, thanks. It was my birthday on Saturday.'

'Well how very nice…and I'm most apologetic; I wasn't aware. I'm sure we could have spoiled you a little on Friday.'

I shifted in my seat. 'Thanks but there was no need, really.'

'Out gallivanting no doubt? Burning that proverbial candle?' He smiled knowingly.

'Not quite, but it was OK.'

He nodded.

'Um…did you have a nice weekend?' I asked awkwardly.

'My wife and I partook in a spot of end of summer gardening. Makes one feel like one's achieved something, don't you think?'

I thought about my neglected window box with some dried-up basil and coriander and a lone daffodil (a plastic one come to that) and said nothing.

'We did, however, manage to sample some of our homemade nettle wine, the first batch this year. And rather good it was too!' He chuckled, making his chins wobble.

'Now then, Maggie, I wanted to have a little talk with you. I'm afraid…'

Here we go.

'…. I've been slightly lax.'

'How do you mean?' I asked.

'I think I've left you a little too much on your own.'

So, he *was* unhappy with my work. He didn't think it was up to standard and that would be his excuse for letting me go. Even though I knew it was because Chloe was back on the scene sooner than planned.

He cleared his throat.

'How have you been enjoying yourself whilst you've been here?' he asked.

I frowned slightly; an odd question.

'I've…well, I've enjoyed it. It's been fascinating …and rewarding…' I tried to think of other words to sound impressive, '…and I hope I've risen to the challenge.'

'Good. That's very good. I'm pleased.'

He was pleased?

'You see, there's been a bit of a development.'

'Oh?'

'Yes, indeed. Young Chloe. I believe you know she's had a baby.'

I nodded.

'Well, it seems that motherhood is rather agreeing with her.'

I suddenly realised what was coming. I had seriously misjudged the situation.

'Chloe has decided she'd rather carry on being a full-time mum, it's rather more um, let me see, "where she's at" I believe the expression is with you young people today. Understandably so, I have to say. I'm rather in favour of it myself. Too many young women these days doing both, careers *and* motherhood. Not too healthy, if you ask me.'

'No, um, absolutely,' I replied.

'So you see this leaves me in a bit of a pickle. Her position, or should I say your position, is now very much a full-time vacancy.'

'Right' I replied, wondering how I felt about what was coming.

'And I thought, or should I say we the partners thought, that you might consider joining us on a rather more full-time basis?'

I adjusted my position. 'I, er…er…'

I realise it's all a little sudden, my dear. Perhaps you'd like some time to have a think, hmmm?'

'Yes.' My body breathed a sigh of relief. 'Yes, please, a bit of time would be really appreciated. But, thank you. Thank you very much for asking me.'

'No, I believe it is I who should be thanking you. You've taken to the job like a duck to water and I'm very hopeful that you'll take the position.'

He smiled his warm fatherly smile.

'Terrible lack of skilled young people these days. I'm always telling my wife that if only we could find more skilled young people, the future of this company would be far more secure.'

Pressure!

'Well, you go off and have a little think and perhaps you'd let me know by, oooh, shall we say the end of the week, hmmm?'

I nodded. 'Of course, the end of the week would be fine. And thank you again, Mr Welles.'

I stood up to go.

'I think you'll find young Margot has taken to you rather fondly. We'd all be very pleased to have you on board.'

'Yes, of course. And um, thanks again,' I faltered, letting myself out of his office. I headed back along the corridor. Margot was pretending to clean one of the plastic plants in the reception area.

'Soooo?' she enquired, clearly impatient.

'So what?'

'What happened?'

'I thought you knew everything.'

'OK then, I reckons he's offered you a jarb.'

'Bloody hell, how on earth did you work that one out?'

A big cheeky grin spread across her face.

'Chloe's been back on, asked for her P45. Worked it out from there.'

'Oh Sneaky One.'

'So... you gonna take it or what?'

'Dunno. Need to think about it.'

'Bloody 'ell. You're not gonna take it are you?'

I shrugged.

'He's given me 'til the end of the week. I just need a bit of time.'

Her face fell.

'Don't worry you'll be the first to know,' I said.

She looked away.

'What?' I asked. 'What's wrong?'

'If you leave, I'll 'ave no one to talk to. I've got kind of used to 'avin' you around. Even if you are a big soft mush.'

'Cheers!'

'But you'll think about it yeah?'

'Yeah,' I confirmed. 'And don't worry, whatever happens, we can still be friends.'

'See! You've made your mind up already.'

I thought for a moment. *Had I?*

I headed back to my office. I didn't feel so good. I don't mean physically, but emotionally. I felt like I was back to where I'd been at CapiTel. Sure, I liked the job, sometimes I really liked it, but did I love it? No, definitely not. But once again there was nothing to go on to, and this time I had no cash to support myself if I looked around for something else. More temping? Not that I'd really temped, not like some. Not a week here and a week there, always with different companies, different people. I shuddered. I'd dreaded it the first time I'd decided to temp and if I left here, I'd dread it again. Suddenly I felt really unsettled. What now?

I picked up my snowman paperweight from my desk and gave it a little shake. It was the wrong time of year for snow but somehow the little winter storm scene matched my mood. In fact, it matched my life. Everything seemed upside down and up in the air. Like I was waiting for it to settle. Staring at the little snowman, enclosed in the see-through bubble of glass, I began to feel trapped. The job; the future; Luke; Tony; none of it was settled; even Catherine and Nico. Their being together meant she had less time for me. Understandable, of course, but still unsettling. For once, I wanted some security. Not boring security, like I thought I'd had at CapiTel, but real security, in life. I wanted to be happy with my lot. I wanted a good job, one that I really loved with people I really loved and… I wanted to be in a relationship that I really loved. With a lovely man who I loved and who really loved me back. I thought of Tony and inadvertently shook my head. I hadn't meant to; it had just happened. Surely if a relationship was meant to be, it wouldn't be so hard. But then again, like the job, for the moment at least, I didn't have anything else.

I sighed loudly just as my phone rang on my desk, making me jump. It was Margot.

'I've decided.'

'What?'

'If you leave, then I'm leaving too.'

Chapter Fifty-seven

'She's asked me to leave,' Timmy's fretful voice came down the phone that evening.

'Really?' I was quite surprised. 'Why?'

'Not forever, just for a few days. She says she needs some space.'

I relaxed a little then tried to be tactful. 'I guess we have been crowding her a bit.'

'I thought I was helping.'

'You were, Timmy. You are.'

'Well then, why does she need space? I don't like it. What's she up to, Mags?'

'Listen, try not to worry. We all need time alone sometimes.'

I heard my mobile ting a message from my bag.

'When are you leaving?' I asked.

'Next week. I've agreed to a few days, no more though. I don't want to leave at all and Terry's off on business again so she'll be on her own.'

'Surely she can't be left alone. Who's going to look after her?'

'That's what *I* said! Apparently one of the stable girls is coming in to sort Ralfie out and she's got Mrs Mop to do a few extra chores in the kitchen.'

It was my turn to worry. 'I'm not sure this is a good idea.'

'Join the club but you know Pauline, when she digs her heels in there's no way she'll change her mind.' Timmy sighed, sounding tired.

'You OK, hun?'

'Me? Yes of course, sweets,' he replied.

'You sound a little down yourself.'

'Don't you go fretting about me, I'm fine. Just a bit worried about Paul' that's all.'

'Are you going back to your flat then?'

There was a pause before he answered.

'For now. I... um... might be looking around for somewhere else soon though. It's far too big for just me. I'm rattling around like a pea in a box.'

That was strange. Timmy had always loved his flat.

'Timmy? You would tell me if something was wrong wouldn't you?'

'Of course! You daft bint. I told you, I'm fine. Now I'd better dash, I've arranged a trip to an organic farm this afternoon. They've got ducks and hens and all sorts. Thought it might put some colour in the old girl's cheeks.'

Oh dear, poor Pauline.

I replaced the receiver and almost immediately it rang again.

'Ah, you're there! I thought you might be avoiding me.' It was Tony.

'Tony! No, of course not, why?'

'I've been trying for half an hour and, when you didn't answer my text, I thought you'd gone incognito.'

'What text? Oh, yeah, I did hear my phone.'

For two people who'd hardly spoken in the last ten days, this was not the kind of conversation I'd been expecting. Whatever happened to 'Hello'?

'Never mind, I've got you now. I just called to say I'm back on Thursday and I was really hoping we could get together. I've missed you.'

I went quiet.

'Have you missed me?'

There was a pause.

'Maggie? You still there?'

'Yes, I'm here.'

'Well, have you missed me? Or have you found some other poor sod who's fallen for you hook line and sinker and you've broken his heart.'

I laughed nervously.

'No, silly. Of course I've missed you. What time are you back?'

'Early evening. I was thinking I could come straight round from the airport. Maybe we could order in?'

'Er, yes, fine. That would be nice,' I managed.

'Fine? Nice? Is that all you can say after ten days apart. What about: Tony darling! Of course, come round and let me ravish you. Or maybe: How are you? How was your trip? What have you brought me back? I can't wait to see you. Or even...'

'Tony, I'm sorry. I've had a bit of a day and I've got stuff on my mind, that's all. It'll be lovely to see you and, yes, what have you brought me back?' I joked.

'That's more like it… and you'll have to wait and see. So, what did you do on your birthday then? Sorry I missed your call but I'm glad you liked teddy.'

I thought back to the day at Pauline's and immediately felt guilty.

'I, er, went down to see Pauline. She's still not well you know but we cheered her up and they all bought me lovely presents. I got two tickets for…'

'Who's all?' I could hear the slight edge to Tony's voice.

'Oh you know, the usual. Except Cat, she wasn't there. She had to work, which was such a shame because I don't think I've spent a birthday apart from her since, well since forever really.' I was talking fast, trying to skirt over the truth.

'So, who else was there?'

Honestly, it was like the third degree.

'Well, Pauline, obviously.' I laughed nervously. 'And Timmy, of course, you know he's been staying there; I did tell you didn't I? Anyway,' I continued, when Tony didn't answer, 'Jenny and John also came down as a surprise. It was so good to see them. They're leaving for South America on Saturday. They won't be back until just before Cat's wedding, so they'll look all tanned and healthy. I'm so jealous. Aaand, John took Jenny up to see his mum in Edinburgh. She was so nervous and…'

'So no one else then?' Tony probed.

That was the moment of truth. The moment I could have come clean. I could have been honest and said that Luke had dropped in. Pretty innocuous really and I should have been able to share that sort of thing with Tony. But something stopped me. And I didn't.

'No, just us lot. Even Terry bailed out on us. Honestly that man's a pig. I don't know how Pauline puts up with him.' I was gabbling now, desperately trying to divert Tony off track.

Luckily he seemed to have bought my story.

'Well, you can tell me all about it on Thursday evening. I'll probably be pretty tired so perhaps an early night?' There was no mistaking what he meant.

I agreed tentatively and we ended the call.

I caught sight of teddy, who was sitting with Mobear, leaning sideways and squashing her under his big bulk. Poor Mobear. I was beginning to know how she felt.

Chapter Fifty-eight

Thursday night came around and I was a bag of nerves. Apart from a short text, I hadn't spoken to Tony since the phone call and I'd felt the same pressure ever since. Plus, I still hadn't decided what to do about my job. I had to give Mr Welles an answer the next day and, all in all, I was in a panic.

'You'll know what to do when the time comes,' Catherine said down the line, as I was whizzing around cleaning my flat, the cordless phone under my chin.

'That's easy for you to say, you're in a job you love, doing things you love to do with lovely people. You've got it made. You've even got a lovely bloke too!' I wailed. *And a gay cat*, I thought, trying to make myself feel better.

'You will find a job you really want. Just give it time,' she soothed.

'Yes, but what if I've already found it and I just don't know it yet! What if my perfect job is exactly where I am and, if I just give it a couple more months, I'll realise that. What if the things I don't like change! I might love it then. They might even decide to move offices and we might up sticks and go off to New York or Paris or Milan even.'

I gave the coffee table a final swish with the duster then sat down to survey my efforts. It would have to do.

'Have they talked about doing that, Maggie?'

I sighed. 'No.'

'Is it likely they will?'

I thought about Bob Welles, with his treble chin and fatherly smile, mildly complaining about the future of the company and not having enough skilled young people, and decided it wasn't.

'Not really.'

'And do you think all the things you don't like about the job are going to magically disappear?'

'No.'

'So perhaps you think you're not good enough to go out and find a job you really love?'

I hesitated.

'Maggie?'

'I don't think I think that.'

'Well that's a start. So, do you think you deserve a lovely job, one that you simply adore, working alongside people who you think are lovely and great fun?' she finished.

Damn those self-help books.

Did I? Or did I assume it was only other people, better people, who got all the good jobs. Who got to do what they truly enjoyed and were paid well for it too?

'I don't know, Cat,' I admitted.

'Well,' she said, 'I can tell you this for nothing. You *do* deserve that. You just haven't realised it yet. Tell you what, here's something to try.'

'You're not going to make me do anything weird, are you?'

'No, it's not weird. It's very sensible.'

'Go on then.'

'Write a list of all the things you want in a job. Go as mad and crazy as you like. Sky's the limit. Think of your dream job; whatever you like. And write about it. Then, when you've written out your perfect job description, try it on for size.'

It all sounded a bit 'American'.

'What do you mean, "try it on for size"?'

'Live it. Imagine you've got that job and think about what it would be like to do it. Imagine the offices, where they are, the kind of work, the people, all of it. Imagine how happy you are and realise why. Like I said, live it, try it on for size.'

'And is that what you did before you became a nurse?' I enquired.

'No,' she laughed. 'I always knew I wanted to be a nurse, so I didn't need to, but I'll tell you what…'

'What?'

'I did it with Nico.'

'Huh?'

'I tried him on for size before I met him. I imagined my perfect man. Ooh, I made him so lovely! I knew what I wanted, the sort of looks and personality, and how I wanted things to be and everything. I even saw us getting married.'

'And you're saying it's happened because of that? You meeting Nico?'

'Who knows? But it seems to have worked. All of it's come true. Goodness knows I spent long enough dreaming about it and not just dreaming, planning too!'

'And you reckon I can do the same with my job. I'm not so sure.'

'Just give it a go. I'm not saying you'll get your dream job straight away but who knows? Your next job might be a stepping stone in the right direction. Think of it, Mags!' she exclaimed. 'You could be really happy if you'd just realise that you deserve it as much as anyone else does. It's got to be worth a go.'

'Maybe…'

'No maybes! Just do it. And Mags…?'

'Yes?'

'It works with everything, you know. Not just your job. All of your life. Don't just settle for what… or who, you don't really want.'

'Meaning…?'

My door buzzer interrupted.

'That's all I'm saying,' she finished. 'Anyway, I hear your door. Have fun tonight.'

'I'll try,' I said.

'Don't try! There's no such thing! You either do…'

'… or you don't,' I finished. 'I know, I know.'

The buzzer sounded again.

Here we go…

Tony stood there with more flowers. The last lot still stood drooping and dying slowly on the hall table. They were beginning to smell.

'Because you're worth it!' He stepped in and kissed me on the mouth.

'They're lovely, Tony, thank you. Welcome back. How was your flight?' I asked.

'You're not going all polite on me, are you?'

'Sorry, force of habit I guess. Good manners have been drummed into me all my life.'

'Are we a habit already then?'

I felt myself tense.

'No! I didn't mean that. Look, never mind.' I took the flowers. 'Let's start again.

Come in and give me a hug. I've opened a bottle of red.'

I put the flowers down and we hugged, a little awkwardly.

'I've missed you,' he said.

'Me too,' I sang chirpily, breaking away and whisking the flowers off to the kitchen.

'Sit down and make yourself at home,' I called. 'There's a pile of menus on the table.'

I returned with a couple of glasses, my heart beating uncomfortably fast.

'I've brought you something.' Tony handed me a plain white bag.

Inside was a large box of Lindt chocolates.

'New York chocolates?'

He looked guiltily at me. 'I'm afraid I had to buy them at the airport. I hardly had time to think over there, I hope you don't mind.'

I forced a happy smile.

'Of course not, I love chocolates. These are great, my faves.' I could hear myself sounding fake, unnatural.

'Are you OK?' he asked, with a puzzled expression.

'Yes, I'm fine. Why?'

'Oh I don't know, call it male intuition. I just thought I detected a note of something.'

'Like what?'

'I don't know, just something. Come on then, sit down and you can tell me all about what you've been up to.'

'I haven't been up to anything,' I accidentally snapped.

'OK, OK, calm down. I just meant in general. What have you been doing?'

I had to apologise again.

'Sorry, it's been one of those weeks. Why don't you tell me all about New York?' I poured us both a glass of wine and leant back on the sofa beside him, taking a couple of large gulps and trying to quell my feelings of discomfort.

'Well,' Tony began, 'a lot of boring business men and women going to a lot of boring conferences and talking about a lot of boring financial stuff; usual thing.'

I thought about what Catherine had said earlier.

'Why do you go then if it's that boring?'

'It's work. Money, more to the point,' he admitted.

'But do you enjoy it?'

He looked at me quizzically.

'I mean, do you actually like your job, Tony?'

'It pays me well.'

'Yes, but do you *really* enjoy it. Is it what you really want to do?'

He shrugged. 'Like I said, it pays well. I'm not sure I've ever thought about what I really want to do. Not in the work sense anyway,' he added turning to me. 'I know what I'd really like to do right now though.' He leant over and pulled me by the arm to kiss him.

It hurt and I wriggled away.

'Careful! You nearly made me spill my wine.'

He backed off looking put out.

'Why the sudden interest anyway?'

'I just wondered. Catherine said that… oh never mind. It's not important.' For some reason, I found I didn't want to share it with him.

'No, don't do that. Catherine said what? That I should be doing something better?

What does she know anyway, she's just…'

'No, it wasn't about you. We were talking about work and I've been offered a permanent position so…'

'That's great! When do you get your new contract?' he asked clinking my glass.

'It's not as simple as that. That's what I'm trying to explain. Catherine's made me realise that there might be other possibilities, better ones.'

'And you take everything that Catherine says as read do you?' he sneered.

'Tony! That's not fair. She made a lot of sense,' I said, defensively. 'Besides, what were you going to say about her, she's just… what?'

He shrugged.

'Dunno, can't remember.'

He took several mouthfuls of his wine in quick succession and there was an awkward silence.

'It's not all about getting what you want in life you know, Maggie. It's pretty tough out there and who's to say you'll find something else that good?'

'Thanks!'

'I didn't mean that. But maybe you should start looking at what you've got and stick with it for a bit. Good jobs don't grow on trees,' he finished.

I was beginning to feel very stifled. Whether I was with Catherine on this one or not, I certainly didn't need someone telling me that I had to settle for something I didn't necessarily want. A bit of encouragement would have been nice.

'Look, forget it,' I said. 'Let's change the subject.'

'OK.' His tone was flat.

More silence.

Tony had already finished his wine and leant forward and poured some more.

'So, where's teddy then?'

'In my bedroom.'

'Lucky teddy,' he said ruefully.

This was all wrong. Tony, the man I was supposedly seeing, was here after a separation of nearly two weeks and rather than feeling pleased to see him, I was wondering if we had any common ground at all.

We sat sipping our wine and I twiddled the stem of mine. The only sound was the clock on the cooker ticking away in the background. The silence was palpable, until Tony broke it again.

'I really have missed you, you know, Mags.' He turned to look at me and reached out to touch my cheek.

I smiled.

'Me too.' Although the words sounded a little empty. 'Perhaps we could start again?'

Again.

'Sorry,' he said.

'Me too.'

'What for?' he asked.

'Same as you probably.'

We both grinned. This time, when he leant across to kiss me, I didn't pull away.

After a takeaway curry and half a bottle of wine each, Tony began to yawn.

'Said I'd be tired.' He smiled lazily at me. 'Cuddle?' He lifted his arm for me to slide under it. I snuggled up to him, aware of a faint smell of cigar on his jumper. 'Mmmmm, that's nice,' he murmured into my hair.

We stayed like that for a few minutes and I finally felt relaxed. This was what it was all about. Companionship, comfort, being at ease with each other. I now relished the silence at the end of a stressful few days. I snuggled closer, feeling safe and girlie and had just relaxed to the point of closing my eyes, when suddenly Tony let out a great snore!

He stirred, half waking.

'Mmmmm, lovely,' he murmured, cuddling me closer to him, obviously unaware he'd fallen asleep.

Within seconds, he was off again, his arm growing heavy on my shoulder and I realised I needed the loo. I managed to extricate myself from under him and went off to the bathroom, leaving Tony snoring unawares on my sofa. On the way, my phone's message alert sounded from the table, I turned quickly to Tony but he was dead to the world, clearly exhausted from his travels. I considered why I felt relieved he'd fallen asleep.

I walked over to my phone. A number I didn't recognise showed up in my messages.

My eyes widened in horror as I opened it. It was from Luke.

Maggie. You're making a mistake. Please don't get involved with
Tony. We need to talk. Luke.

Chapter Fifty-nine

I woke the next morning from the most fitful night's sleep I could remember. Visions of Luke and Tony merging into one had wracked my dreams. At one point Tony had taken on the guise of a gangster and I was his moll. Luke had been the barman in a club we'd gone to and had tried to kiss me when Tony had been in the toilet. As much as I'd been enjoying the kiss, I was filled with panic that Tony would find out and I woke up sweating.

I sat up, my sleepy eyes searching round the room. Nope, no gangsters and certainly no Luke. I still had the memory of his kiss on my lips. My thoughts went to Tony and I became aware of the smell of coffee from the kitchen.

I swung my legs out of bed and slid on my slippers.

'I was just coming to wake you!' Tony entered, carrying two mugs. 'Thought you might fancy a bit of company before you got up.' He came over and sat beside me on the bed.

'Thanks.' I accepted the steaming mug of coffee.

'Well? Can a poor travel weary man get in and give you a morning cuddle?'

I glanced at my clock radio.

'Tony, I can't, I'm sorry. I need to get ready for work.' As I said that, my funky, purple clock radio pinged on as if to back me up.

'See!' I giggled.

He rolled his eyes.

'Bloody alarm. I should have reset it before you went to sleep and made you call in sick.'

'You were fast asleep on the sofa!' I complained.

'Sorry, it was a heck of a trip. I literally slept until about half an hour ago. Thanks for covering me up by the way.'

'Look it's a big day for me today,' I explained. 'I need to give Mr Welles my answer about the job.' I felt my body stiffen. It was a subject that hadn't been exactly comfortable the previous evening.

I saw Tony tense up too.

But whatever he was thinking, he let it drop.

'Nice coffee,' I said, changing the subject. 'It always tastes better when someone else makes it.' I took a sip, squinting through the steam.

'I'd better grab a shower before work.' I stood up and put my coffee on the side.

'Room for one more in there?' Tony took hold of my hand.

I really didn't need this. I wanted to clear my head and think about work. In bed the previous evening, in between thoughts of Luke's text, I'd had a bit of time to think about what my dream job might look like. Seeing as in a few hours I'd need to give them an answer at work, I wanted some headspace to consider what I'd come up with.

I tried to keep things light. 'Tony! You're incorrigible! Look, I know things didn't work out as we planned last night…'

'You're blowing me out. I get it,' he joked. 'I just wishing you were blowing me off!' and he pulled me back down on the bed and started kissing me. Not good first thing in the morning before toothpaste has been introduced.

I struggled and pushed him away, feeling quite queasy at his last comment. It sounded sordid.

'No! I need to go!' I laughed. 'Really!' I escaped and headed off to the shower.

'There'll be plenty of time for this, but not now.' I left him on the bed, frowning slightly.

I closed the door to the bathroom and locked it behind me. The last thing I wanted was Tony coming in while I was in the shower.

I let the water cascade over me and forced several unhelpful thoughts out of my head before focussing on work. Maybe I could accept the position and then see how it went; perhaps hand my notice in, in a few months, when something better came along? But, no, that wouldn't be fair to Mr Welles. And besides, if I thought there was something better out there, then wasn't that proof I had to turn the job down?

So far I'd decided that whatever I did next, I needed to get out and about more. On the road, driving. I generally loved driving and didn't get the chance to do it enough. I'd always fancied overseas travel too. Not being based abroad but the chance to travel with the job. Maybe like Tony did, international conferences; something like that. But I did love the research I'd been doing. I'd be very happy to do that sort of thing again. Location was important too. Very important. I could have done with more time, I thought as I rolled the different possibilities over in my mind. I should have been writing all this down, like Cat had suggested. Perhaps a clearer picture would have formed.

I dried myself off and put on my bathrobe. When I went out Tony was still on the bed. He looked at me strangely, his eyes narrowed thoughtfully. Suddenly I felt shy. Was he going to watch me dress? Or worse still, was he going to try and molest me again?

I must have given off some negative signals though as he stood up slowly, stretched, yawning noisily and headed off to the kitchen.

'More coffee needed. I'm still on New York time. Toast?' he offered.

'Lovely, thanks. I won't be long.'

I sat down on the bed to put on my tights and spotted my mobile on the bedside cabinet. Keen not to forget it, I picked it up. The screen immediately lit and suddenly Luke's message was on full display. *Oh no! Had Tony read it??*

I hastily got dressed and left my hair to dry naturally.

If Tony had seen the text, he didn't mention it and we actually had quite a laugh in the kitchen, mucking around like a pair of kids.

He drove me to work and kissed me goodbye as he dropped me off.

'See you very soon,' he said. 'I'll ring you at the weekend. Maybe we can get together?'

'That would be nice. I need to see Catherine though, she's off to Italy next weekend and I've hardly seen her lately. Perhaps we could all do something together?' I suggested.

'I'll call you then. Good luck today… whatever you decide.'

'Thanks.' I smiled and gave him a final kiss on the lips.

'Oh… Maggie?' he called, as I slammed the car door shut, the electric window whirring down as he spoke.

'Yes?'

'Did you remember your mobile?' His face remained neutral. 'Only I saw it on your bedside table. Just wanted to make sure you'd picked it up.'

'Um… yes, thanks.' I faltered, certain my face had turned beetroot. 'Best fly. See you soon.' I blew him a kiss and hurried off to the office.

Oh no!

Chapter Sixty

'Don't ask!' I instructed, as I entered the office, when Margot opened her mouth to speak.

I hurried past her, headed along the corridor and went quickly into my office closing the door behind me. My thoughts were racing.

What had he meant? He must have seen the text, surely. Why hadn't he said anything? Was he trying to catch me out? But then again, I hadn't done anything! Not unless you count lying about Luke being there on my birthday. Anyway, I hadn't really lied, just avoided the truth.

I needed to talk to Cat but she'd be working. I needed to talk to someone. Someone other than Margot though, she'd only end up reading my palm or, even worse, my mind.

Maureen! Suddenly, I wanted to talk to Maureen. In fact, I wanted to see all the old gang. To escape from where I was, to go back to before it had all started, all this stuff with Tony and Luke. I didn't even need to talk things through with anyone, not really. I just wanted to forget things.

I signed into Google mail and began to type an email.

Hi Mo!

How are you? How's everyone? Missing me I hope. I miss you! What are you up to tonight? Brickman's as usual? Can I join you? Pleeease! Need a girlie chat.

Lots of love Maggie.

XXX

I sent it and got on with my current project on prunes and possible investment opportunities. Apparently, prunes have one of the highest antioxidant ratings amongst fruit and vegetables and can help to slow down the ageing process. Perhaps I could start investing in a few myself? However, I think I'd rather have been doing research as to which chocolate tasted the best but had the least calories, or which alcohol gave you the least hangover. I hoped Mr Welles wouldn't pounce on me too quickly for an answer; I really didn't know whether I was coming or going that morning. I needn't have worried though; Margot came in shortly after with some news.

'Old Wellesy's off sick.' She came and sat down opposite.

'Really? How come?'

'His wife says it was something to do with an allergy to nettles. And you know what that means.'

'No. What?' I asked.

'Hangover. Too much nettle wine.'

I laughed. 'Do you reckon?'

'Deffo, he's been doing nothing else but brag about his wonderful nettle wine all week; serves him right if he's gone and overdosed on it.'

'Poor Mr Welles.'

'Never mind poor Mr Welles. He hasn't even brought us all a bottle in! You'd 'ave thought if he rated it that much he'd at least have shared it with us. Divine retribution, that's what it is. The Law of Cause and Effect.'

'Not another law!'

'Talking of which, how goes the love life?'

'Complicated.'

'Oh yeah?'

'Yeah.'

'Come on, tell Aunty Margot.' She put her elbows on the desk, resting her chin on her palms.

I sighed loudly.

'Luke's sent me a text and I think Tony might have read it. He hasn't said anything but I'm sure he has. Luke wants to talk and he wants me to stop seeing Tony and I don't know what to do. I lied about him being at my birthday bash and I'm sure Tony suspects. Then there was the card; that really confused me. He even put a kiss on it.'

'Who, Tony?' Margot interrupted my outpour.

'No, Luke. I don't know what he wants me to do. And then there's the matter of sex. We still haven't done it.'

'Who, you and Luke?'

'No, me and Tony!'

For once Margot looked confused.

'And Catherine's going away with Nico and I know it's to be expected, I mean they are getting married so they'll obviously spend lots of time together, but it's just that I miss her. And Tony's been kind of taking her place and now I don't know what to do, because I'm not so sure I like him as much anymore, and then there's Luke and it's all confusing and then I've got to make a decision on the job and, and… and…' I stopped and promptly burst into tears.

Margot calmly let me sob. She sat without speaking. Her only intervention was to pass me some tissues from up her sleeve, as I cried it all out.

I glanced down uncertainly at what appeared to be a screwed up ball of toilet paper.

'Don't worry, it's clean,' she said.

I attempted a smile through my tears.

'It's all such a mess!'

'What exactly is a mess?' Margot asked, remaining calm.

'Everything?'

'Let's get specific here,' Margot said wisely. 'Best thing to do is dissect it all, bit by bit. That's what we got taught at uni. Like how you eat an elephant.'

I looked blankly at her.

'Cut it up into little chunks.'

'Oh.' I sniffed.

'So, do you like this Tony bloke?' she asked.

'Ye-e-ss. Well I think I do, I did. But… it's all changed.'

'How so?' she asked.

'He's becoming so possessive! And I can't talk about things I want to talk about and he keeps asking me questions about what I do when I'm not with him. I feel like I'm suffocating.' I blew my nose.

She quizzed me further. 'And these things you want to talk about and caan't. What are they exactly? Or should I say who?'

I felt my face become hot.

'Thought as much.' Margot nodded.

'I never said anything!' I protested.

'Didn't 'ave to.'

I stared down at my lap.

'Seems like a pretty clear cut case to me,' Margot said.

'Oh yeah? You want to try being in my head for a change, instead of in your all-seeing, psychic, one.'

'I'm not all that psychic you know. If I had've been, I'd have realised that Darius had been 'avin it away with another bird for the last two weeks.'

My eyes widened in shock.

'What? Oh no! I'm so sorry.'

She brushed it off.

'Never liked him much anyway.'

I paused, then caught her eye and suddenly we both fell about laughing, knowing fine well she was lying through her back teeth.

'Seriously though,' she said, as we calmed down and she wiped mascara from under her black kohled eyes, 'you can't keep trying to fix stuff that isn't going to mend.' She stood up and turned to go, then looked back at me. 'And you can't keep covering up your feelings. Sooner or later they's gonna jump up and smack you round the face. Let's go out for lunch, my treat.' She gave me a Margot smile. Not a big beaming Catherine-type smile but just enough of one to show me that, for her, it meant the same thing. She cared.

I watched her walk away. Her little purple velvet miniskirt only just covering up her backside and the rip in her fishnet tights making her seem even more like a punk than usual. It was amazing; who'd have thought that someone who appeared so rebellious on the outside could be so smart and clued-up on the inside? 'Never judge a book by its cover', my dad always said. He was right.

My mobile rang then; it was Maureen. I was immensely pleased to hear her voice.

'Maggie! I can't believe you emailed me. We've been talking about you and were going to call you and find out how you were. What's going on? Are you OK? Are you having an awful time?'

'No, not awful,' I replied, 'but I'd so love to see you and catch up. I'm missing you all, even Craig!'

'Things must be bad if you're missing Craig!' she giggled.

Craig's voice sounded from the background.

'Hey, I heard that!'

'Shush, Craig we're talking *about* you, not *to* you!' Maureen said aloofly.

'He's sulking now, Mags.'

'Poor Craig. Tell him if he comes to the pub I'll buy him a big drink.'

She told him.

He called out from the background again.

'And tell her I'll give her a big snog, if she plays her cards right.'

I was cheering up already.

That evening as I walked in to the pub they all cheered loudly and most of the people in there turned round and stared. Craig leapt up and charged towards me, immediately cuddling me to him in a tight embrace, kissing my neck dramatically.

'Craig! Get off! People are staring.'

'I like an audience, me,' he said, doing it again.

'Come on.' He pulled me by the hand behind him and led me to where he and Maureen were sitting.

Bill was at the bar but came over and gave me a kiss.

'Ah the lovely Maggie. The place hasn't been the same without your pretty face smiling across the desk. We've missed you, you know.'

I smiled from the inside out.

'I've missed you all too.' I meant it more than ever.

Maureen threw her arms round me. 'It's so good to see you.'

I settled in while Bill got the drinks. It felt like coming home.

'Found yourself a bloke then? Craig asked. 'Or are you still hung up on me?'

'Always you, Craig, always you.' I accepted my drink from Bill who'd arrived with a tray full and I took a grateful gulp.

'So, how's the new job?' Maureen asked.

'So-so.'

'So-so good? Or so-so bad?' Bill chipped, in handing out drinks to the others.

'Bit of both. They've asked me if I want to join them full time.'

'How exciting!' Maureen bubbled. 'And, are you going to take it?'

'Not sure. I'm going to have a think this weekend. But listen, I've had enough of work to last me a lifetime. What's the goss? Tell me everything and leave nothing out.'

'Same old crap,' Craig said, 'only it's even more boring since you left, no one to flirt with. Sorry, Mo, apart from you that is.' He put his arm protectively round her shoulders.

'Go on with you. I'm far too old for you, Craig,' Maureen said seriously, albeit slightly hopefully. 'There's the temp though. She's quite attractive, if you like that sort of thing.' A brief moment passed then Maureen shot her hand up to her mouth.

'Ohhhh!' she wailed.

'What, ohhhh?' I asked, puzzled. 'What temp?'

'I told you not to say anything, Maureen!' Bill admonished.

'I'm sorry, it just slipped out.'

'So I've been replaced by a temp?'

'Only because Justin hadn't appreciated exactly how much work you actually did. It was only when you left he fully understood the capacity of your role,' Maureen dutifully explained.

I felt very put out.

'She's not a patch on you,' Maureen added.

'And you've got something she'll never have,' said Craig.

'Oh? What's that?'

'Tits!' Craig chuckled. 'She's flat as a pancake.'

I gave a watery smile back but they all looked a bit shifty.

'And is she… well is she any good?' I asked.

They talked over each other. 'Oh no, no, not at all, no, rubbish really, pretty crap.'

'We think Justin hired her because he likes her legs,' Bill said.

'You mean you like her legs, you old goat.' Craig slapped Bill on the back.

'I've never liked pancakes much,' Maureen said thoughtfully.

Despite their protestations, I felt miffed. Bloody Justin; the cheek of him. Maybe he just wanted shot of me and the company was really doing fine. Perhaps I could sue him for wrongful dismissal. That'd wipe the smug smile off his face. I considered the option briefly. Then again, I might get my old job back and despite how I was feeling, I really didn't want it. It would be like going backwards.

It went on to be a fun evening but CapiTel – moaning about CapiTel – became the main topic of conversation. How crap it was; how much of an arse Justin was, not getting paid on time… the usual stuff. I'd heard it all before. Contributed often enough! As I listened to them grumble, I was aware of what a lucky escape I'd had. It was funny; they all went on like they had no choice in the matter. They moaned and groaned but I didn't hear any of them talking about leaving. I'd been of the same mind; I was a fine one to talk. But at least I was out and I could make my choices from now on. As I listened, my mind went to my own situation and the choice that was facing me. It *was* a choice. I wasn't in a corner as I'd previously felt, more like a fork in the road. I had a decision to make, whether to go one way or the other. I didn't yet know which fork to take but I'd get there.

During the tequila slammers, I was suitably numbed to the point that life didn't seem so daunting. I thought about Tony but the pangs of fear and guilt had all but disappeared. Oh the wonders of tequila.

It wasn't as if I'd done anything wrong. Luke had texted *me*, not the other way round. I hadn't texted him back either. I could have done. I'd thought about it often enough the previous night, and all through that day, but I hadn't. I mean, what would have happened if I had? He would have sent one back to me and then me to him and then who knows what would have happened? Yes, I'd been very loyal and restrained, in fact positively angelic. Life in my tequila bubble was very safe and supportive.

It was my round and I was glad to stretch my legs and get some circulation back into my backside. All that time on a wooden bench was beginning to take its toll. I went up and stood at the bar, trying to get the barman's attention, which was almost impossible on a busy Friday night. Suddenly, someone came up behind me and whispered in my ear, making me jump.

'Hey, you, I'd forgotten how sexy you were.' It was Craig.

'You, Craig, are drunk!'

'Damn right I am. It's Friday night, why would I be anything else? And it's pay day!!'

he sang loudly, grabbing me round the waist and trying to jig about.

'Stop it! The barman's just walked straight past me. I've been trying to get his attention for ages and now you've mucked it all up!'

'Come on,' he said. 'It's useless here; the bar staff are all round the other side.'

He pulled me away, leading me by the hand for the second time that evening, in the direction of the larger bar. Only instead of stopping to get served, he swivelled his head round, winked at me and kept walking straight through between the crowded little tables and stools, right out the side entrance and into the cool night air.

It was dark by then, the chilly fresh air a welcome change from the heat of the pub. The bright orange streetlights glared down above us. A party of drunken revellers were noisily bouncing off each other on the other side of the road. Craig pulled me around the corner and spun me round, pinning me against the pub wall. He stood with his face just a few inches away from mine and smirked down at me, a familiar glint in his eyes. The revellers cheered loudly.

'Craig what exactly are you doing!?'

'Nothing yet...' He gave me a cheeky grin. 'Remember the Christmas party?'

Oh I remembered it all right, at least *parts* of it. Half a bottle of vodka and most of a bottle of white wine and, before I'd known what had hit me, Craig and I were playing tonsil hockey in the ladies' toilets at CapiTel.

'Ever wondered what it would've been like if we'd... you know?' he said.

'No,' I lied.

'Bet ya have.'

'Anyway, it would have been a disaster!'

'Oh yeah? How d'you reckon on that one?' he asked.

'Well, if we had, how would we have felt the next day, in the office?'

Craig looked thoughtful.

'Proud I reckon.'

I blushed.

'You're quite a catch, Maggie. And you've got a lovely arse,' he added.

I was a bit taken aback. It wasn't like Craig to pay people compliments.

'Come on, give us a snog, Mags. You know you want to. We've always had a bit of a thing between us.'

It was that 'thing' between us that I was worried about!

He went to kiss me but I put my hands up to his chest to stop him.

'Craig, I can't.'

He stood back and seemed slightly put out.

'What gives?'

'I'm sorry but... well... I'm seeing someone else,' I admitted, pulling a face. 'I'm really sorry, Craig,' I repeated.

'Oh... right.' He shifted back and straightened up his shoulders, squaring himself.

I stood away from the wall again and wondered what to say to make things OK.

'I'm very flattered, really I am, but I wouldn't want to do anything that might upset our friendship.'

He sniffed. 'No sweat. Just thought you might fancy a snog that's all,' he shrugged, attempting to mask his feelings with a macho face, and failing badly.

'Of course if things had been different,' I continued, 'and I'd been totally unattached, I'm sure I would have done. You're right, there has been a thing between us.' I figured I was safe to pay him a compliment. 'I do think you're very cute but I'm just not very good at being unfaithful that's all,' I explained

'Oh… right.' He looked a little happier then. 'Well, like I said, it was just a snog. No biggie, come on let's get a drink, your round.' He headed back into the pub, suitably appeased. And if I thought I needed any more proof that Craig was OK, barely two minutes had gone by when he spotted a couple of busty blondes and disappeared off to chat them up, leaving me at the bar.

Later, when we were all back at the table and Maureen and I were gossiping about Mandy and Justin, Bill cleared his throat and made a tinging sound on his pint glass with his pen to get our attention.

'I've got an announcement to make.' His face was red and shiny from drink.

The three of us turned expectantly to him, sitting proudly at the end of the table.

'I'm going to have a baby!'

There was a 'pregnant' pause as we all exchanged baffled looks.

I don't know who laughed first but, whoever it was, we all followed. Everyone apart from Bill was rolling around, tears in our eyes, giggling helplessly. Gradually though, we spotted the expression on Bill's face and one by one we stopped. He wasn't joking.

'You mean… you're not… serious, are you, mate?' Craig asked

'Completely!' Bill frowned.

'Gosh!' said Maureen.

'Wow,' I said.

'Only, of course, it's not me having it, it's my Tina.'

'Of course,' rippled quietly round the table.

'Sorry, Bill,' I said. 'I – we – thought you were having us on.'

Bill looked a little defeated.

'Gosh,' Maureen said again.

'I know you're probably wondering how on earth an old buffer like me could father a child but Tina's much younger than me and we've been trying for a while and it's finally happened!' His face broke into a wide smile. He was clearly as pleased as punch.

After the initial shock, we all congratulated him. Craig thwacked him on the back several times with laddish outbursts of 'sly old dog' and 'didn't know you had it in you' and 'glad to hear you can still let your snake out of the basket at your age!'. These were interspersed with Maureen insisting she visit

Tina to discuss her baby shower and suggesting various name options, and me sitting on Bill's lap cuddling him tightly, saying how much I loved him and Tina and that they had to come round for dinner. I never cooked anyone dinner, I was a rotten cook. I was very drunk.

It was during one of these hugs, that I noticed the pub door open and a familiar face walked in.

'Look!' I turned and hissed, nodding towards the door.

They all swivelled round. It was Mandy.

Mandy walked over to our table, making her way through the crowds. She looked upset. Maybe she'd got wind we were meeting and felt annoyed we'd left her out.

'What's *she* doing here?' Maureen whispered under her breath.

'Dunno but we're about to find out,' Craig said, as she reached the table.

'Hi, Mands, come to ruin...I mean join, the party?' Craig cheers'ed her with his pint.

Under her coat, Mandy had on a white mini dress and pink stilettos and, even though it was a bit tarty, the effect was pretty stunning.

'Show us your tits then, Mands,' Craig leered drunkenly at her.

She remained silent, her face blank. Then she plonked herself down unceremoniously beside Maureen, who was forced to shift up.

'Hello, Mandy,' I said, breaking an awkward moment. 'Long time no see.'

Her big, sad, eyes met mine. I saw her lip quiver and she promptly burst into tears. The rest of us exchanged puzzled glances as Mandy sobbed into her hands. Craig looked bemused and shrugged.

'Women!' he muttered to Bill.

Maureen tentatively put a hand on Mandy's shoulder, which made her sob even more!

'He's a bastard,' Mandy cried. 'I hate him!'

She rummaged around in her little white handbag and found a pink tissue. She blew her nose loudly and Craig pulled a disgusted face at me.

Maureen allowed her arm to go further round Mandy's shoulder and her face softened.

'There there, luvvy, who's a bastard?' she asked sweetly, sniffing a juicy story.

'Lemme guess. Justin?' Craig stated.

Mandy blinked up at him, seeming surprised.

'Yes,' she sniffed.

'What's he done, dear?' Bill enquired.

She looked round at us all in turn, as if to find out whether we were really being sympathetic. Then, seeing we were, she burst out into noisy sobs again.

'He'e'e'e's be'e'en ha'a'a'aving a a a an af'fai'ai'air', she wailed. Bill passed her a clean tissue from his jacket.

I refrained from saying that actually Justin was already having an affair… with her!

'How do you know?' Maureen asked rather too eagerly.

Mandy blew her nose again and straightened up a bit.

'First it was the mysterious phone calls in the office. He normally didn't care if I heard his phone calls, we didn't have any secrets, but then he started acting really cagey and sending me out on errands when I knew I didn't need to go on them, like he was hiding something. It was when you were still working there, Maggie, I remember because at one point I thought it might be you.'

'Me!' I cried in horror. 'Justin's the last person I'd…' I halted mid-sentence seeing the look on her face. 'Sorry, Mandy, I didn't mean…'

'No, it's OK. I know what you all must think. You probably reckon I've been really stupid but I fell for him. I couldn't help it,' she sniffed, tears filling her eyes again. Bill passed her another tissue.

'What sort of phone calls were they?' Maureen asked.

Mandy shook her head sadly.

'He'd lower his voice when I was around. And I pretended I wasn't interested but I'd spy on him without him realising. He used to get this soppy look on his face, like he was really into who he was talking to. Do you know what I mean? Like he was really in love. I know, cos he used to look at me like tha'a'a' t,' she broke down again. 'He's got so'o'o'me'o'one e'e'e'lse. He'e'e mu'u'u'u'st ha'a'a've.'

'So what made you realise it wasn't me?' I asked, still reeling from the thought of anyone thinking I could possibly be interested in a sleaze like Justin.

Mandy composed herself and her big moonlike eyes met mine. She gave me a watery, apologetic, smile.

'You see at first the phone calls came when you were out of the office, so I was certain that it was you. And then he kept telling you off in front of me and I was sure it was all a cover-up. That's why I kept giving you funny looks,' she admitted. 'But then the calls started coming while you were at your desk and you weren't on the phone, so I knew it couldn't have been you, it would have been impossible.'

'I'm so glad,' I deadpanned.

Bill disappeared up to the bar to buy Mandy a drink.

'He didn't go home last night,' she continued. 'I know cos his wife rang in this morning and asked what time he was back from his course. He hadn't been on a course! I book all his away-days and seminars and stuff and I nearly always go with him. I knew his every move; at least I thought I did.'

'He could just have been off sucking up to head office. You know what he's like,' I suggested.

'No, I'm sure I'm right. He just hasn't got the guts to tell me. Anyway, I've got proof!'

'Ooh, what proof?' Maureen would benefit from learning how to at least *sound* discreet.

'I got a call from his favourite jewellers on his direct line. I'm not supposed to answer his direct line. It goes onto his personal voicemail and it's the one thing he likes to keep private; but I had to know, I just had to,' she explained. 'They said his bracelet was ready for picking up. So, I said I was his PA and went to collect it.'

'You didn't!' Maureen cried.

Mandy nodded. 'It was the only way I'd know for sure.'

'But it could have been for his old bag of a wife,' Craig said, as Bill came back with Mandy's drink.

'Or for you even,' I added.

'I thought of that, and that's why I had to pick it up. I know his wife's taste. I would have known straight away if it was for her, or for me. Justin's bought me loads of stuff and he's had to buy his bitch-faced wife stuff to keep her off his back. I was always the one saddled with doing his dirty work and going to the jewellers. All the way down there I prayed it would be for one of us. I didn't even care if it was for her, I could've handled that, I know what he thinks about her.'

'So, what was it like?' Craig asked.

'Weird,' she said. 'I mean, it was OK but too chunky for my taste and it was silver. He'd never buy me or his wife anything silver; it was always gold.'

'Maybe he fancied a change for you and was going to surprise you,' Maureen suggested.

'But it had an inscription on the back.'

Maureen's eyes were out on stalks.

'It was a little heart with an arrow through it. You know, like you get carved on trees, with peoples initials either end of the arrow. It was quite an edgy design though; a sort of rock 'n' roll heart. I dunno, hard to explain.

'Gosh! And were there initials on it?' Maureen urged.

'Yes! One was J and the other was… S.' Mandy looked thoroughly forlorn.

'So, not for his wife then,' Craig said.

I frowned at him to be quiet.

'Exactly,' said Mandy, 'and it certainly wasn't M for Mandy, so there's someone else.'

'So who's this S then?' Bill puzzled.

'Maybe it's someone from that club thing he goes to?' I suggested.

'No, that's the Masons. They don't allow women.'

'Cheek!' Maureen said indignantly.

'Besides, he doesn't go much anymore. He's been spending all his spare time with me or at the golf club and just uses the Masons as an excuse to give his wife.'

'Could be anyone then; maybe someone linked to work?' Bill suggested.

Suddenly, like a bolt of lightning, realisation flooded through me.

'Of course, Bill's right. Think about it. Who do we know, initial S, who's linked to work; someone who suddenly disappeared off the face of the earth recently?'

Their expressions were blank. Then Bill twigged.

'You don't mean…'

'Exactly.'

'Sandra!' we chorused.

Craig pulled a revolted face.

'Justin and The Horse? Surely not, she's a dog; so to speak! Ha ha,' he laughed at his own joke.

'That would explain why we lost her as a client. I thought Justin was being pretty cloak and dagger about things,' I said.

Mandy looked horrified. 'It can't be her! She's awful; worse than his wife!'

'Her poor husband,' Maureen said wistfully. 'He's lovely, so gentle and kind.'

Craig got up and came round the other side of the table and squeezed in next to Mandy, giving her a cuddle. Maureen was now squashed up against the wall and got up crossly to squeeze her way out and go round and sit on Craig's stool.

'Chin up, girl. He's a wanker,' Craig comforted, 'you deserve someone loads better than that old git.'

'Bit odd though, don't you think?' Bill said. 'I mean surely if it was Sandra, wouldn't

Greenwich still be a client.'

'So maybe it's not her, after all!' Mandy looked relieved.

'Unless her husband found out and put the kibosh on CapiTel?' Bill added.

'Who cares?' Craig said, planting a kiss on Mandy's cheek. 'If it is Sandra, we'll know that Justin's got a screw loose. Anyone who dumps you to go out with *that* needs his head examined.'

Mandy managed a smile and snuggled slightly into Craig's arm.

So, it seemed Mandy was back in the crowd again and she was soon knocking back slammers with the rest of us. I have no idea how many we had but it was a lot. Enough to know I'd be murdering a large burger and chips on my way home. By the end of the night Mandy looked decidedly 'over' Justin and Craig had clearly helped the situation.

Finally, time was called and we piled out of the pub happily singing and giggling. Craig and Mandy announced they were going on to a club and did anyone want to

join them. We tactfully declined and, after hugging our goodbyes, watched them stumble off together with Craig's arm around Mandy, slipping down rather close to her backside.

Then it was Maureen's turn to make an announcement.

'I've got some news too!' she hiccupped, leaning, wobblingly, against the lamppost.

'Hooray!' Bill cheered. And, putting his arm around her, he 'mwaaa' kissed her on the cheek.

'I'm going travelling to the Himalayas with my best friend Marjory!' she proclaimed proudly.

'What?' I cried. 'When?'

'I don't know. I've only just decided,' she said happily. 'She asked me before and I said no but now I've changed my mind.'

'Hooray!' Bill said again, swaying about and looking like he might fall over.

'What made you change your mind?' I asked, leaning against the wall.

Maureen thought for a moment.

'I think it might be down to you.'

'Me? Why?'

'Because you escaped!' she giggled. 'You left the prison that is CapiTel.'

'Hooray!' Bill cheered rather more to himself than anyone else.

'I was sacked!'

'Made redundant,' she pointed out.

'Technically; but that still doesn't explain why you're going.'

She began twirling round and round in the street. 'Maybe...' she sang 'because I need to be freeeeee.' One more twirl and she was back to where she started. 'Ooh, I feel sick now.'

'It may just be the tequila,' I said feeling sick just watching her.

'No, I think it was the twirling round in circles,' she said.

'Not that, the travelling thing. It might be the drink talking.'

'I doubt it. I was thinking about it at work today as well but, seeing you, all ...unshackled, just put the icing on the cake. The cherry on the Bakewell, the missing piece in the puzzle, the...'

'OK, stop!' I held a wobbly hand up. 'But listen... you sure, Mo?'

'I think so! And who knows, I might bump into a munky hountaineer to carry my backpack!'

'A what?'

'A munky hount... no... no... I mean, a hunky mountaineer,' Maureen giggled.

'Where will you live?' Even from my drunken bubble, I was unable to imagine Maureen backpacking.

'A mud hut somewhere knowing my Marj'. She's been on and on about it for ages!' she sang happily. 'Getting away from this life and escaping the nine to five! Marjory wants us to lose ourselves in culture and spirituality,' she concluded dramatically. 'She's such an old hippy at heart. Gosh...' her eyes went wide and she looked very young all of a sudden, '...maybe I'll come back a hippy too!' Maureen seemed to consider this a marvellous idea and was about to start twirling again but I reached forward and grabbed hold of her arm, managing to stop her.

'We can escape and trek to our hearts content and live like nomads in the mountains with the goats.'

'Hooray for mountain goats!' Bill cried suddenly, punching the air before returning to his own little silent world.

Whatever next? Maybe Maureen would manage to find herself a native Himalayan along the path? Either that or she'd learn to speak 'Goat' and would come back a gibbering idiot. Regardless of the amount she'd drunk, though, she did seem happier than I'd seen her for ages. Justin wouldn't have any staff left if he wasn't careful.

Chapter Sixty-one

I woke with a throbbing head, a revolting taste in my mouth, an increasingly nauseous feeling and a dull, persistent, ache throughout my body. I felt terrible and I only just made it to the toilet to throw up the tequila and veggie burger from the previous night. The burger bar round the corner had been inexplicably shut and veggie burgers were the only things left in my freezer, so they'd had to do. I only remembered I'd eaten them when I saw the discarded packet on the armchair along with my mobile.

Feeling dreadful and silently vowing never to drink again, I dragged my duvet into the lounge and settled down on the sofa for a day of unwanted toxicity. I picked up the remote and was about to turn on the television when I had a sudden panicky flash of memory that blinded me with fear.

I got up again quickly, clutching my head and stomach, and grabbed my mobile from the chair.

Surely not. No.

Please, please, please let this not be a real memory. My battery had run down so I

found my charger, plugged it in and waited until the phone came to life, taking forever to load everything. All the while I pleaded with whoever would listen for it just to have been a bad dream or a fake memory my hangover was scaring me with. Finally, after what seemed like an eternity, I was able to access my messages.

Shit!

There it was as plain as day.

Bugger!

A text, from me... to Luke!

Shit, shit, shit!

Slowly, my brain pieced together what had happened. I read the text, feeling doubly dreadful as I did so.

Hey Lukey! What gives?

What gives? *What frickin' gives?* Who was I, some street kid from the Bronx? Some character from *The Jeremy Kyle Show?* And *Lukey*! Fuck, fuck, fuck, fuckety, fuck! *Lukey!!* I hadn't called him Lukey since we were kids! This was bad, worse than bad. What on earth was he going to make of it? He probably wouldn't even understand it, let alone want to reply to it.

I'd set my mobile up to send me delivery reports when someone received a text from me and so far nothing had come back from Luke. I prayed that, for some reason, he'd changed his number. Since Thursday night? *Get a grip, Maggie.*

I sat back down on the sofa and wrapped myself deep within the duvet, trying to shut out the world. The whole Luke/Tony thing crashed in on me then and without the security of my tequila bubble it was twice as bad as it had been the day before.

My cordless phone sounded loudly from the coffee table and groaningly I reached out and picked it up. Thank God for caller display. It was Tony.

I couldn't answer it, not then. I felt too guilty and embarrassed. It went on to answer phone and I sat cringing as Tony's voice filled the room.

'Wakey, wakey. Mags? Mags, you there? I can see your light on, I'm outside. Pick up, Mags.'

Outside? He was *outside!* And I was inside, hiding from him! I couldn't let him in. The light, left on from the previous night, would have to stay on all day now, in case he waited there. I wouldn't be able to go out anywhere, in case he stayed there spying on me. I didn't think I'd ever felt so bad! Tequila slammers had an awful lot to answer for. Never again, came the usual adage.

'OK, you're not there. Either that or you're still in bed. Ring me, yeah? Just wanted to find out how you got on at work. See ya, lots of love.'

I felt really guilty then. He was being nice. I knew how he'd felt about me taking the job but, by the tone of his message, he was genuinely interested in how things had gone. And here was I, a right mess, pretending I was out, having thrown my guts up from a serious session at the end of which I'd opened the communication lines with his brother. The one person he wanted me to keep away from. Poor Tony; I was a bad person.

I sat there like a rabbit caught in the headlights for nearly half an hour, before creeping over to the window to peer down through the blinds to the street below. Tony's car was nowhere to be seen. I relaxed a little.

At that point the phone rang; it was Catherine so I answered it.

'Hiya. How was last night?'

I groaned.

'Shall I bring the Nux Vomica round?'

'Please.'

'I thought we might catch a film later, what do you reckon?' she asked.

Relief flooded through me. This could be a chance to make things good with Tony.

'Could I...? I mean would you mind if Tony came along too?' I faltered. I knew Catherine had her reservations about him.

'Okaay,' she said slowly. 'You all right, Mags?'

'No, I'm horridly hungover. I'll tell you all about it later. Come round here before the film, I think I've just done something awful.'

'It's not that awful. It's only Luke for heaven's sake. He knows what you're like.'

Catherine handed me her little bottle of sanity and flicked the kettle on.

'He knew what I *used* to be like, past tense. He probably assumes I've grown up! And anyway, I'm supposed to be with Tony.'

She glanced in my direction.

'What?'

'Nothing.'

'You looked at me funny.'

'Did I?' she replied casually.

'Yes, you did.'

I watched her stir the coffees thoughtfully, tinking the teaspoon on the edge of a mug before setting it down on the kitchen counter.

She carried the mugs over and placed them on the kitchen table where I sat, still in my pyjamas. Scraping the chair back, hurting my head with the noise, she sat down and faced me.

'I think you just hit the nail on the head,' she said.

I stared blankly at her.

'When? How?'

'You said, "I'm *supposed* to be with Tony".'

'Yes, but... I... I just meant that I'm with Tony and I shouldn't have texted Luke... and...,' I paused then tutted, 'oh, I don't know.'

Catherine was watching me calmly.

'Look, just forget Luke at the moment.'

'I wish I could!'

'Seriously, just imagine he's not in the picture.'

'OK,' I said glumly.

'How do you feel about Tony?'

'In what way?'

'In any way; how do you feel about him? What do you think about him? Are you into him?'

I allowed my gaze to fall and rest on the salt pot, while I idly considered what she'd asked. I must have been silent for too long.

'Maggie, I may be wrong but if you really, *really*, liked Tony, I mean if you were sure about you and him, don't you think you'd have given me an answer a little quicker?'

'I was just trying to find the words.'

'And have you found them?'

I shrugged. 'Kind of.'

'OK, what are they... kind of?'

I was finding it difficult to put my feelings about Tony into words. It was like I had so many emotions all flying at me at once, I didn't know which one to pick. When it came to Tony, one emotion, one feeling, didn't sum up much at all.

'I feel a lot of different things,' I admitted.

'Such as?'

'Such as... well, such as... um...'

'OK, let's work it out shall we? Do you like him?'

I hesitated a second too long.

'Hmmm. OK... does he make you laugh?'

I perked up. 'Yes. Yes, he does... or at least he did.' I thought back to the reunion, the barbeque, the first date. He had made me laugh a lot on each of those occasions but... where had all that gone? Something about Tony had changed, I realised. Or was another side to him coming out that I previously hadn't seen?'

'So, do you fancy him?' Catherine asked.

'I think so.'

'Think so! Maggie, if you're in a relationship, especially at this stage, surely you should know whether you fancy someone.'

I hung my head, feeling like I was being told off.

I certainly *had* fancied him. The first time I'd seen him, I'd *really* fancied him. And I'd been looking forward to spending the night with him but it had all gone so weird and I didn't think we'd recovered after that fateful night when I'd cried out Luke's name. I told Catherine as much.

'So has that ruined things for the future then?' she asked. 'Because if it has, don't you think you'd better end it before you get hurt? Before you both get hurt.'

I didn't know for sure but right then I didn't feel able to make such a big decision. I felt desperately in need of consoling and emotional cuddling, not making life-changing decisions which could end up making me feel worse!

'Not tonight though, eh? I think I like him at the moment.'

'You mean you *need* him.'

I breathed a mournful sigh.

'Maggie, you've got a serious hangover, and you've done something you regret. I Certainly wouldn't be surprised if these were just feelings of need rather than want.'

I frowned.

'I'm sure they're not.'

'You don't have to convince me.' She stood up, went to the cupboard under the sink and got the biscuits out from my secret hiding place.

'And anyway,' I began, 'I need someone around right now because…' I hesitated, unsure if I should continue.

'Because what?'

'Well… because you've got Nico now. And, don't get me wrong, I'm really pleased for you but I miss you and I'll miss you even more when you get married and move in together. So, the idea of not having Tony around either isn't very appealing,' I admitted.

Catherine sat down again. This time she took both my hands in hers and I felt my eyes well up.

'Maggie, I'm still here. We're still best friends. I still love you.' A tear escaped from my eye and slid down my face.

'I don't want to be on my own,' I said, allowing a second and then a third tear to follow.

'And you won't be, not really. You and I will always have each other, even if sometimes we have to spend more time on the phone than in person.'

'I s'pose,' I sniffed.

'Listen, if Tony *is* right for you, then it'll all come good. But, when we're out tonight, have a good old think. In fact, *we'll* have a good old think, together. We'll both suss out whether he's right for you. OK?'

''K,' I agreed. 'Don't be too hard on him though. And don't bring out any self-help books and start citing them in front of him!' I giggled through my tears.

'Guides' honour,' she promised. 'Now go on, get showered and changed. He'll be here soon. We don't want him thinking you're a slovenly, hungover, couch potato, now do we?'

'But I am.'

'I know but if he is the one, my advice is to ease him into that side of you gently.'

''K,' I replied and headed off to try and wash away my persistent hangover.

The cinema was packed and stifling. Tony didn't look very happy and he hadn't fulfilled the consoling and emotional cuddling role too well so far. It was obvious, when he'd picked us up, that he didn't like my hungover appearance. The shower had done little to hide my piggy eyes, sallow skin and shaky hands. While Catherine had been in the loo, he'd quizzed me about the previous evening.

'So who was there?'

'Just the old work crowd. Maureen, Craig, Mandy, Bill and me of course.'

'How come you got so trashed?' There was an edge in his voice and I responded with one back.

'It was great to see them that's all. I wanted to let myself go… and I enjoyed myself!'

'Unlike the previous night?' he said sarcastically.

'No, it wasn't like that. I just wanted to unwind.' I'd started to feel even worse. He'd finally got round to asking me about the day at work.

'I didn't get to say anything,' I explained. 'Mr Welles was off sick.'

At least he hadn't mentioned the text from Luke and Lord knows I wasn't going to let him know I'd texted him back!

Tony had given me a cuddle then. 'Sorry if I seem like a bear with a sore head. It's been a heck of a week and I think I need a bit of TLC.'

The cinema seemed like the last place on earth he'd need then. A bunch of rowdy teenagers kept throwing sweets at each other in the queue and one hit Tony on the cheek. I thought he was about to explode and matters weren't helped by my catching Cat's eye and the two of us accidentally giggling.

When we finally got into the screen two, it was practically full. The only obvious three seats together were near the wall and people had to keep standing up to let us past.

'Sorry about this,' I said to Tony. 'I thought it might be quite relaxing.'

He gave me a stilted smile.

The film was awful too. Well actually, that's a lie. I thought it was funny and I know Catherine did, as she kept collapsing helplessly in the seat beside me. Tony on the other hand was a real killjoy and didn't laugh at all, so I felt unable to relax and laugh out loud.

Afterwards, we went for something to eat and finally Tony chilled out. He even made Catherine laugh on several occasions and I laughed with sheer relief that they might be starting to get on.

At the end of the evening, I was dying to get home and go to sleep. Tony and I still hadn't slept together properly and I guessed he'd probably want to but I really didn't. I just needed to sleep and I told him so after we'd dropped Catherine off.

'Anyone would think you didn't want to sleep with me, Maggie.'

'No, it's not that. I'm just really tired.'

'So I see.'

'Tony, don't be like this. I know things haven't exactly worked out on that front but…'

'And whose fault is that?' he snapped.

'Whaaaat?'

'You know what I mean.'

He hit a nerve.

'You can't keep bringing that up. It was one time; ONE TIME!' I raised my voice then felt weary.

We fell silent and I stared out the window at the streetlights swishing past above my head.

Was that the only reason we'd failed in that department, I wondered? I glanced across at Tony, his hands tense on the steering wheel. Did I fancy him? I tried to study his face without him noticing. He appeared hard and moody and I decided I didn't. Then he turned and caught me looking and his features relaxed. A big grin crossed his face and he shook his head. Suddenly, I did fancy him again. He looked lovely when he smiled. So handsome, so open, so safe, so gorgeous… so…so… oh no…! *Oh nooooo!* It was in that moment, in that smile, that wonderful, gorgeous, familiar smile, that I knew.

I knew for sure. The reason I'd been so besotted with Tony was nothing to do with him; not really anyway. It was because, when he smiled, he reminded me of Luke. I could see it clear as day now. That was the reason my stomach lurched every time I saw it. That was why I melted when he smiled and why everything else, all our problems, seemed to disappear. I couldn't believe I hadn't realised it before.

'We're mad, aren't we,' Tony's voice broke my thoughts, 'arguing, when we should be getting closer?'

'What...? Er... oh yes. Yes, mad...' I attempted a laugh as I stumbled over my words. The realisation had hit me hard.

'Tell you what, at Catherine's wedding, I'm going to make sure we have a fantastic time. I want to show you off to the whole world.'

His words jarred in my head.

'You mean...?'

'Exactly; I want people to see us together; everyone. I want people to see you're mine. This will be precisely the right opportunity to show them we're an item.'

It was almost as if Tony was talking to himself.

'... And we'll look great together, Maggie. Like a true couple. All this *silly stuff* between us will be sorted. Fear not.'

But I was fearing; I was fearing a lot.

Chapter Sixty-two

I had taken Monday off work to help Catherine hunt down the perfect wedding dress. I was due to be measured up for my bridesmaid dress while she was away so today was all about Catherine. And it wasn't, I decided, a day when I'd be discussing my realisation about Tony. That could wait.

Catherine had been poring over wedding magazines since Nico had proposed and she came round clutching a list of dress shops. She had earmarked her five favourites: Anna-Lisa Smythe, Every Little Girl's Dream, Joshua's of Chelsea, Magdalena's and White Angels.

Anna-Lisa Smythe appeared just as I had imagined; very upper class and immaculate but unfortunately, very snooty. She ran the shop herself along with the devoted assistance of a wispy-haired, podgy little girl called Betty, who did all the running around and had a tape measure constantly hanging around her neck. On closer inspection, I discovered that Betty had rather crossed eyes. I wasn't quite sure which one to look at and, so not to offend her, I kept flitting very quickly from one to the other just to make sure I got it right, smiling warmly so she wouldn't think I was being weird with her.

Catherine and Anna-Lisa-up-her-bottom-and-out-again-Smythe were flicking through silks and sashes and Catherine was quite breathless with awe. I wasn't so sure. Anna-Lisa kept saying things like, 'hmm, I don't believe we will be able to tailor this one to a larger size; we are somewhat limited, given your build', which I thought was awful! So, I whispered to a completely oblivious Catherine that we needed to check out the other shops too.

Betty, on the other hand, was lovely and when she saw my concern, whispered that Joshua's of Chelsea did a fabulous range in all sorts of shapes and sizes; she should know, she got hers there last year!

Every Little Girl's Dream was on the way but was inexplicably closed, which had Catherine assuming it wasn't meant to be so we headed to Chelsea where Joshua seemed to have the answer to all Catherine's needs. A bride's *dream*, Catherine said dramatically. I have to admit, the little bridal shop was full of gorgeous dresses and accessories and, as we crossed the threshold, the sun came out and shone through the window lighting up all the dresses on display.

'Oh, it's a sign, Maggie,' Catherine said excitedly.

Joshua was flamboyant, flattering and French. He looked a bit like Laurence Llewellyn Bowen, with billowing shirt sleeves and a green velvet waistcoat, only Joshua was about half the height and double the width. More like a squashed Louis XIV in fact.

'Arrr, zee figure of a Bottacelli Aangel,' he gushed, 'and a face to match.' He touched Catherine lightly on the cheek and she flushed.

'Come, come, please to follow me, I will show you material which will keess yourr skeen like seelken fezzers and tresses which will glide so smoothly and so lightly they will float above zee ground!'

Catherine and I followed obediently; Catherine, because she was dying to try on dresses that kissed her skin like silken feathers, and me, because I wanted to see a floating tress. I didn't even know what a tress was.

True to his word, Joshua (supplier and confidant to the Royals) was speedily coming up with dress after dress of admittedly heavenly material. It wasn't always possible to try the dresses on, as they had to be made in the right size, but there were a few larger sizes in styles that Catherine fell in love with, so she hurried into the changing room.

We both thought the first one was the most divine creation in the history of the universe until we saw the price tag and Catherine almost wept with grief.

'I'll never find anything so perfect!' she cried.

'You will, you will,' I soothed. 'Besides, it's not perfect because it's too expensive. Your perfect dress will be the perfect price too.'

She looked up at me with big watery eyes. 'You really think so?'

'I do.'

She giggled then.

'I'll be saying that when I walk up the aisle in a few weeks.'

She tried on another, which she couldn't get up above her thighs. She began hopping around in the changing room, getting redder and redder in the face, trying to coax the dress over her. Joshua must have heard the commotion, as he rushed in to stop her.

'Mais non, ma petite; it weel rrreeeep!'

He wrestled the dress off her, while Catherine did her best to cover her dignity.

I think she forgave his rushing in like that, though, because he'd called her 'ma petite'.

The third one she tried was very pretty and the right price but, when she'd got the zip up, she spilled out of the top so much we didn't think Nico, or the vicar come to that, would be able to concentrate on the service. So, she moved on through the selection.

Catherine was becoming more and more hot and sweaty.

'See, I told you. The first one was the best. I'll never find anything to compare.'

'We've some more to try and this is only the second shop we've been in!'

Joshua descended upon us again.

'You weeel trry zeees one; it eees special drress for you.' He held up a dress that was almost entirely covered by cellophane.

Catherine lifted up the covering and studied it on the hanger.

'I'm not sure,' she said sadly.

'Worth a try though, don't you think?' I urged.

'OK.' She glumly traipsed back to the cubicle and Joshua gave me a meaningful wink.

There followed the sound of cellophane being removed and several groans and huffs and puffs, while Catherine manoeuvred the dress on.

'Do you need a hand?' I called.

'No, I don't think so… oooh!' she exclaimed from the cubicle.

'Is that oooh good? Or oooh bad?'

She rustled her way out again, an expectant expression on her face.

'I think it might be an oooh good. What do you think?'

Definitely an oooh good.

It was beautiful. It looked nothing like it had on the hanger. The lack of cellophane had revealed a gorgeous, sleeveless, strapless dress with a sculpted, ivory bodice, embroidered with tiny pearls. The floor length skirt flowed, flatteringly, from a few inches below the fitted waist into layers and layers of rich ivory silk that sparkled with tiny diamante in the sunlight.

'What do you think?' she asked eagerly.

'What do *you* think?'

'Oh Maggie, I think I might have just found *The One*,' she said happily, twirling round and peering over her shoulder in the mirror to view the back.

From behind her, Joshua appeared with another mirror, which he set up so she could see every angle.

'I love it,' I said. 'You look breathtaking. Nico will cry.'

'He won't be the only one.'

'You like?' Joshua asked, smiling broadly.

'I like,' Catherine agreed.

He took his tape measure out and started to make a note on his pad.

'Now we measure,' he said.

'But can't I have this one?' Catherine asked frantically. 'It seems to fit OK!'

'"OK" ees not what we are wanting, Mademoiselle; "parfait" ees zee only word we weeel be using to describe your magneeeficente drress when it is made just for you.' And he bowed graciously before her.

Catherine curtseyed. And I just managed to stop myself.

'How long will it take?' Catherine asked from behind the curtain, as she took it off again.

'Maybe, we say, four weeks,' Joshua said.

'But that's too late!' Catherine squealed, poking her head through the curtain her eyes pleading at me for support. 'My wedding's in four weeks. I thought that would be plenty of time! What if there's a problem or something?' she wailed.

Joshua looked up at her thoughtfully and nodded solemnly.

'I weeel make zee phone call.' He picked up the phone on the table.

Within a few minutes, he seemed to have sorted out a queue jumping situation with Hetty the seamstress. Was the bridal industry overrun with Bettys and Hettys I wondered?

Catherine would be measured up now and the dress would be ready for her first fitting when she came back from Italy. There would be enough time for alterations the week before the big day.

Later, when we'd left the shop, Catherine started panicking.

'I am making the right choice, aren't I, Mags? We only did two shops after all. What if there was a better dress out there for me?'

'My Dad says there's always something better and something worse out there; it's about knowing *when* to make your choice.'

'Maybe he's right. It was lovely.'

'It was *sensational*, Cat! Besides, you said it was *The One*.'

'I did, didn't I.'

She paused thoughtfully.

'Not a patch on that pink bridesmaid dress in the magazine though.'

'Absolutely not.'

'There's still time to get that one instead, you know, Mags.'

'Thanks. I'll bear that in mind.'

Chapter Sixty-three

Mr Welles was still off sick when I went back in to work on Tuesday morning.

'Flu apparently,' Margot scoffed.

'You don't sound very convinced.'

'More like man flu, I reckon.'

'What's man flu?' I asked, puzzled.

'A cold,' she replied.

Mr Welles phoned in, shortly after I'd settled myself at my desk. He sounded like a bunged up tuba. Without referring to the job offer, he simply gave me a pile of work to do and I had to report to his partner Mr Mayer, who I generally hardly spoke to. I was completely snowed under and by the end of the day, I'd had little time to think about anything else so when the phone went at my desk and Margot announced that Pauline was on the line, I shot my hand up to my mouth in horror. I hadn't been in touch and suddenly felt dreadfully guilty.

'Pauline, hi! I'm so sorry I haven't rung. I've been seriously bogged down with work. I haven't even had a chance to breathe, let alone...'

'Maggie, stop, don't worry,' she interrupted. 'Listen, I need to talk to you. Can you come down at the weekend? It's important.'

'Of course. Are you all right?' She'd sounded serious.

'I will be. I just need to talk to you first.'

'Anything I need to be forewarned about?'

'No, I think it'll wait until I see you. Some things are better said face to face.'

'What on earth does that mean??'

She gave a slight chuckle. 'It's fine, Mags, really. I'll explain everything when we get together. Are you free Friday? You can stay over.'

'Yes, of course. I'm cat-sitting for Catherine though, so I'll need to feed Tom first but I can drive down after that? It might be eight thirty, nine o'clock. Is that still all right?'

'That's fine. Thanks. Terry's away for the weekend and I could do with the company.'

A worried feeling was mounting in the pit of my stomach.

'And put it this way,' she added, 'I think we're both going to need a drink, so it's best you stay.'

'Oh God! Is it bad news then? Please tell me.'

'Maggie, everything's OK. Trust me. I'll see you on Friday. And don't worry, there's no need.'

'But…'

'Look, Maggie, Terry's here and I need to talk to him before he goes out. Sorry to rush, see you Friday.'

And she hung up, leaving me staring open-mouthed at the receiver.

Despite her reassurances I was worried. I wondered if Timmy knew anything and toyed with the idea of calling him at his flat. But what if Pauline hadn't spoken to him, I could easily make him worry unnecessarily. I'd have to bide my time and leave it 'til Friday.

I was just sitting wondering if my own life was going to pick up again any time soon when I heard a familiar ting sound from my mobile; a ting that could only mean one thing – a delivery report. Someone had just received a message from me. And that someone was Luke.

I picked up my phone and sure enough, my message had just been delivered to Luke's number. I hadn't as yet stored his name in my phone, too risky; too uncomfortable for words. Once again, I replayed the text in my head.

'Hey Lukey, what gives?'

Ohhhh huuuge cringe!!

I tried to get on with my work but my mind was all over the place. Any second now my mobile was sure to bleep out a message. After all, I'd sent Luke a question, albeit a dumb one. What flaming well gives, indeed! A gun would have come in handy.

But the afternoon continued; half past five came, and nothing. And then the evening went past and still nothing. Maybe he'd decided I was a daft cow and that I should be left alone. I wasn't sure if that made me feel better or worse.

The silence continued through the rest of the week. Tony called a couple of times but I felt awkward talking to him, like I was hiding something from him. Trouble was I really didn't feel able to break it off with him. I still wasn't certain of my feelings towards him. After all, I'd reminded myself more than once, we had had some fun. The first date had been great. He'd made me laugh and… and… there had to be more to this than just a similarity to his brother. There *had* to be. I felt wretched all the time. Like a big dark shadow was looming over me and following me around everywhere I went.

Jenny had called on the Wednesday evening to say goodbye. She'd been full of her time in Edinburgh.

'I can talk Scottish,' she'd said proudly.

'Don't they talk English?'

'You'd think, wouldn't you? Oh no, there's a lot more to it. Morag says I've a natural talent. We sank half a bottle of Glenmorangie, each, and by the end of it, she was inviting me into their clan and everything; even threatening to measure me up for a tartan tunic!'

'She likes you then.'

'She *loves* me!' she said proudly. 'I'm like the daughter she hasnee haad.'

Jenny and John sounded so in love, I felt quite jealous at the thought. They'd soon be hiking through mountains and making love in caves and showering in waterfalls.

Catherine would be off for two weeks on Friday and although I was seeing Pauline at the weekend, overall, I felt alone. Tony was the only one left. Plus, I had to face the wrath that was Tom.

Letting myself into the flat on Thursday evening, the phone rang. It was Tony.

'I've been thinking,' he said happily.

'Oh yeah? About what?'

'You and me.'

I felt myself stiffen.

'Oh?'

'Yes. I've had a brainwave. I think we need to start over.'

Huh??

'I reckon we've had a bit of a rough deal, me being away, all the stuff with Laura, you know… everything. And now I've got to go away again. So it all points to one thing…'

'What do you mean you've got to go away again?' I couldn't help snapping.

'I'm truly sorry, Mags, it really can't be helped. It's a work thing again.

A major client in Geneva needs me over there to sort out a crisis.'

'I see. You're the only man for the job I suppose,' I said sarcastically.

'Something like that. Don't be mad at me. It's just business.'

I went silent, knowing I was acting like a petulant child.

'They do great chocolate in Switzerland you know,' he coaxed.

Despite myself, I immediately visualised a giant size bar of Milka and felt slightly appeased.

'And I'll be back for the wedding of course.'

The wedding; he'd be back for the wedding. Just in time to tell the world that we were an item. Great! And now I wouldn't get the chance to see him beforehand to suss out whether I actually *wanted* to try and work things out with him.

I sat playing with a loose bit of laminate peeling off the kitchen table.

'Maggie?'

'Yes, sorry, I'm still here.'

'I wouldn't go unless I had to.' He'd misread my silence.

'It's fine, Tony. You go.'

'I'm glad you understand. Now listen, I've got a plan,' he continued. 'I think we should treat the wedding as a sort of celebration. I'm going to book us into a suite at the hotel for the night of the big day. It'll be just like a first date. In fact, let's pretend it is.'

'I don't usually sleep with people on the first date.'

'I should hope not! This would be different though. Surely you could make an exception, seeing as it's me? Hmmm?'

'Maybe.'

'Come on. It's our big chance to announce to the world we're a couple.'

My stomach tightened up another notch.

'What's all this "showing the world" business? It wasn't so long ago we had to lie low.'

He hesitated.

'Don't know really, I've always enjoyed weddings and I think this one's going to be the perfect time for my family to see us together. Seems like a good opportunity to "kill two birds with one stone".'

'"*Kill two birds with one stone?*" That makes it sound like an ordeal. Anyway, who's the other bird?'

'It's just a figure of speech; Catherine's getting married and we're announcing we're together.'

I tried to buy some time.

'But it *is* Catherine and Nico's big day, Tony. We can't just steal their thunder.'

'We won't be stealing their thunder. I'm… I mean, we're allowed a little fun too, you know.'

My thoughts went unwittingly to Luke. He'd see Tony and me together; properly together. Of course, Luke knew Tony and I were seeing each other but to have him actually see us in the flesh, as a *couple*, that seemed a different matter; one that filled me with dread. My mind began to whirl round and round and I felt extremely hemmed in.

'I don't know, Tony. We've not exactly been close lately. I'd rather give it a bit more time before we announce anything to anyone.'

'You're not going cold on me now are you, Mags?'

'Noooo…'

'Well, then, it'll be fine, more than fine. It'll be perfect. I bet you're going to look damned horny in your bridesmaid's dress. Don't forget to wear your sexy undies. I'll be dying to rip them off you later with my teeth, then we can go out and I'll buy you some more.'

I felt sick.

'Tony, I'm really not…'

'Got to go, the other line's flashing. It's a conference call, must dash, babes. I'll call you before I go. Luv ya, kiddo.'

The phone went dead.

Don't love you, my mind echoed miserably.

Chapter Sixty-four

Friday night came and I found myself outside Catherine's front door, dreading going in. She and Nico had left that morning. Tom would be in there, with his smug look, his food intolerances and dubious sexuality, no doubt ready to pounce on me if I so much as went near him. I put the key in the lock and turned it warily, pushing open the door. Glancing around the flat I couldn't see him so I went to the kitchen to find his food. On the counter was an A4 sheet of paper headed up Tom's Diet and Routine.

I sighed.

I fixed the delicate cuisine, which I would have been quite happy to eat myself, and laid it out on the floor for Tom, making sure to replenish his water bowl… with Evian!

I decided to have a little nose around.

Catherine had photos all over the place; snaps of Nico and her together and happy, photos of me and the others. There was Pauline tanned and smiley from the holiday, Jenny when she was ten looking cute and funny. Oh and there was the gang, all together as teenagers. I smiled as I picked it up and realised, too late, that, in the background, as gorgeous as ever, was Luke. Damn that man, he was everywhere. I put the photo down quickly and picked up another photo of Nico. There was no doubt he was handsome; Cat was really lucky. She had been so excited to be going away on another holiday. It would still be very warm in Italy and they would be topping up their tans, which would hopefully hold out for the wedding. A romantic winter wedding; it sounded wonderful. I'd always day-dreamed of one myself, on a fresh, sunny, wintry day. Catherine and Nico were getting married in the pretty little church in Tillmouth. Once again, we'd all be back where we'd grown up. Mixed feelings of nostalgia and being left out welled up within me but I brushed them aside and went to find Tom.

I hunted around the flat but there was no sign of him anywhere. I started to panic. I couldn't have lost him already. Catherine would never forgive me.

He could have gone out the cat flap and down the fire escape but Catherine had said he was usually in at this time of day. He wasn't outside on the balcony, nor was he on his favourite chair. He wasn't under the bed, in any of the cupboards. He didn't seem to be anywhere! I knew there was a chance that a friend from the hospital where Catherine worked would pop in at some stage. Had she come in and accidentally let Tom out the front door? But Catherine had only just gone and the friend had known I'd be here this evening, so surely that wasn't likely... was it? I was really panicking now. Not even a day had gone by and already Tom was missing!

But as I passed Catherine's bedroom for the second time, I spied a rather suspicious looking lump behind the cushions on Catherine's bed. On closer inspection, I saw it was Tom. He had burrowed under Catherine's duvet and was now nestled up by her pillow.

I crept over and gently pulled the cover back a little. Tom opened his eyes sleepily and peered up at me. For a moment we stared at each other and I wondered if we were supposed to be staring each other out to decide who the boss was. But then Tom looked away as though he didn't care much for war. There was, in fact, no trace of malice in his eyes and it certainly didn't seem like he was about to get up and make his usual attempt to swipe at me. In fact, he looked (I can't believe I'm going to say this) sad; lonely even. My heart suddenly went out to him. He was missing Catherine. He knew she wasn't coming back for a while. Maybe he'd watched her pack. Poor Tom. I sat on the edge of the bed, put my hand down slowly and started stroking him, hesitantly at first, but, when he didn't seem to be putting up any fight, I made myself comfy, swinging my feet up on the bed and gave him a good old scritch behind the ears, which he seemed to enjoy. Before long, I was telling him that I would take care of him while Mummy (yes, I said Mummy!) was away and that we would be fine together, he'd see. At least no one could hear me.

Then Tom did something he'd never ever done in the history of my knowing him. He uncurled himself, left the confines of the duvet, stretched judderingly from head to toe, glanced up at me then proceeded to clamber up onto my lap, where he yawned, curled up again and settled back down to sleep, purring away happily. Amazingly, in the absence of Catherine, we'd finally called a truce and become friends.

502

I arrived at Pauline's at nine thirty precisely, later than I'd planned. Getting out the car, I extended my arms high above my head, linking my hands and stretching my body, first to one side then the other.

'Ahhh,' I released, out loud, breathing in the cool, crisp country night air.

Smells of bonfires and bracken pricked my nostrils. An owl hooted, making me jump. Apart from the odd sound from wildlife, it was so peaceful. The almost full moon shone brightly down from above me and, as I looked up, I saw a sky filled with stars; masses of them twinkling down. I couldn't remember the last time I'd seen a starry night. The bright lights of London hid them away. I allowed myself a few moments drinking in the sparkling sky, the country smells, the virtual silence, the cool fresh air, then I reached in and lifted my bag from the backseat and closed and locked the car.

I rang the doorbell, smiling at the empty milk bottles on the porch. I hadn't even realised milk bottles still existed!

To my amazement, Pauline quickly came to the door; still looking tired but very much on her feet again. She smiled and, for the first time in ages, her eyes smiled too.

'Pauline!' I cried, hugging her. 'You're walking about! Are you feeling better?'

'Sort of,' she replied, still smiling as she ushered me into the hallway. She took my coat and hung it up. 'Come on in, you must be knackered. Let's have a huge drink. You go through and make yourself comfy into the lounge, I won't be long.'

I went through to the large, peaceful room, the only sound being that of the impressive antique carriage clock on the mantelpiece. The walls were adorned with a delicately patterned, muted lilac wallpaper and the luxurious silvery blue carpet felt springy and expensive underfoot. Exquisitely furnished, it was such a comfy, inviting room. I sat down on one of the light blue, silk floral armchairs, sinking low and snuggling into a soft cushion. Sliding my shoes off I curled my feet underneath me, feeling myself physically relax.

It was good to get away, to be in someone else's life rather than my own. As I waited, I became aware of the stillness outside. Just the odd dog bark and owl hoot to break the silence. London was great but when I left it I could feel my whole body relax. I considered how wired up I often got living there. Busy people, busy subways, roads, shops, pubs; so much going on. A break from all that was just what the doctor ordered.

My mind went to Pauline and I started going over possibilities. What if she was just putting on a brave face? Could the news be serious? After all, she wouldn't have told me on the phone; she'd have known I'd only worry. Maybe she was just up and about because she was taking her last steps before the worst set in. Was this her final attempt to enjoy life before…

'Wine, beer, gin or whisky?' Pauline called from the kitchen, thankfully interrupting my bleak thoughts.

'God a whisky would be great….and any chance I could have a coffee to go with that?' I called. 'I'll come through and help you…'

'No, you won't; sit! Kettle's on; relax,' she ordered.

'OK!' I smiled to the empty room and shook my head. I was probably being silly. Pauline was going to be fine.

I could hear Ralfie barking in the garden. I stood and walked over to the French doors. There he was bounding around happily in the middle of the lawn, the moonlight and the light from the kitchen intermittently casting beams on him as he ran through the puddles of brightness. His shining eyes gleamed and his glistening, lolloping tongue bounced this way and that. He was going mad as two little foxes scurried off in opposite directions and Ralfie didn't seem to know which way to go. He finally circled round several times before stopping and flumping down in the middle of the lawn, panting heavily, his poor confused face looking one way then the other as he tried to work out where his playmates had gone.

Beyond Ralfie, large fir trees were silhouetted at the far end of the immaculate lawn and, above the tops of them, the moon sat smiling down at me from the night sky. Despite Ralfie's boisterous display it felt so calm. I sighed heavily.

I turned as Pauline came in with a tray of drinks.

'So, are you feeling better?' I asked, hopefully.

'Yes. I think I am.'

'That's amazing! How come?'

She put the tray down on the coffee table.

'All in good time. Let's have a drink first.'

I took one more long look at the garden again, then turned and walked over to sit back down.

'Nice here, isn't it?' she smiled, reading my mind. 'Don't know how you ever stick it living amongst all those tall buildings.'

'It's got its plus points, you know.'

'Yeah? Name me one,' she challenged, sitting opposite me on the large sofa.

'Restaurants galore?'

'You're always on a diet.'

'Shops which open late most nights, then.'

'Thought you were skint.'

'I am a bit,' I admitted. 'But that's beside the point. London's got clubs, pubs, restaurants, museums… um… theatres. You name it, London's got it.'

'When was the last time you went out to the theatre?' She raised one eyebrow.

'I can't remember. But the option's there should I want it. Besides, I like pubs and you can't beat a London pub.'

'Do you think of yourself as a city girl nowadays?' she asked, more seriously.

I thought for a moment.

'Maybe… partly, I guess; I do love the countryside though. I can think in the country and my roots are in Tilmouth.'

'Would you ever move back?'

I nodded without thinking. 'Probably. One day, anyway. Maybe when I find myself a rich husband to keep me in the manner to which I am going to become accustomed! How's Terry by the way?'

Pauline shrugged. 'He's had better days, I feel.' She passed a plate of sandwiches. 'I made these earlier. I didn't know whether you'd have eaten or not.'

'Not.' I gratefully piled several onto a little side plate as she poured out some fresh aromatic coffee to go with a huge malt whisky. She then settled herself back on the sofa and took a sip of her own whisky.

'When did Timmy go?' I asked.

'Sunday, although he's rung that often he might as well still be here.'

'He's only worried about you. We all are.'

Pauline shuffled her position and focussed on the floor.

'I'm glad you came down,' she said pensively, 'I needed to talk to you on your own.'

'So you said. You really freaked me out!'

'I'm sorry, that wasn't my intention. And you've to stop worrying right away. It's just… a little tricky.'

I said nothing.

She stood up and walked over to the window, cradling her whisky in both hands. She looked long and hard out at the sky and sighed deeply.

'It's such a beautiful night,' she said. 'I love it here so much but I don't think I'll be able to stay much longer.'

'Pauline, for goodness sake; I know you said not to worry but you're scaring me. What's going on?'

She took a huge gulp from her glass and turned back to face me.

'Maggie, I've got something to tell you and it's the hardest thing I think I've ever had to tell anyone ever. I don't really know where to start to make it any easier, so I'd better just get on with it.'

I braced myself for the worst.

Sometime later, I found myself out in the garden nursing my third whisky. If I had had a thousand guesses as to what Pauline was going to tell me, I'd never have got it. But it all made sense now. She was right, the news wasn't bad, thank God, but it was certainly unexpected. Pauline had come back and sat opposite me again, showing rare unease. She played with her glass, staring down into it, seemingly unable to meet my eyes.

'Wow,' she began, 'this is more difficult than I thought it was going to be. Now I'm here, I don't quite know how to say this.'

'Whatever it is, I'm here for you, hun.'

She smiled a wry, enigmatic, smile.

'You might not say that when you hear what I'm about to tell you.' She looked away from me. 'Although, I hope you will.'

I sat, my eyes fixed on her, completely perplexed. Time seemed to stand still, as I waited for her to speak. Silence hung in the air for what felt like an age.

'Maggie?' She finally broke it and glanced up at me.

'Yes…?'

'Oh God.' She put her head in her hands. 'I'm not sure I can do this.'

'Pauline, please. You've got to try. I'm thinking all sorts of awful things here. It can't be that bad, surely.'

She looked up at me again.

'Sometimes,' she began, 'sometimes people… might not be… well, they might not be what they seem. I mean, they are but perhaps things aren't quite what you thought they were.'

She sighed at my blank expression. 'I think the reason I've been so unwell… God it makes so much sense now,' she said more to herself than me, 'I think it's because I've been burying something. A secret.'

'Have you?'

'Not just any secret. Something I thought was…' She paused, searching for the word, '… wrong somehow.'

'You've lost me.'

'I know. I can't be making much sense.'

'Just tell me.'

Pauline took a deep breath. I'd never seen her so nervous.

'Oh Christ, shit, shit, shit.'

I was about to protest again, when she suddenly banged the cushion beside her hard with her fist.

'Oh, for goodness sakes this is ridiculous. The thing is, Maggie… the thing is… I'm… I'm gay, OK? That's the secret. I'm gay.'

My mouth fell open, as if with a will of its own. Even the carriage clock seemed to stop in its tracks. My eyes were wide as I stared at Pauline, who sat staring back, her expression waiting for mine. The large room now engulfed me and I felt like a little child on my best behaviour in my parent's sitting room when they had visitors; uncomfortable and not very sure what I was supposed to say. In my head, I played back the last thing she'd said.

Fuck! Did she say she was *gay*? As in *happy* perhaps?

'Wow,' I finally said. 'Are you sure?'

'Oh yes. I'm sure.' She laughed slightly, shaking her head as if in a private joke with herself.

'Oh.' I was actually lost for words.

Pauline's gaze was now permanently fixed on my face. 'What does "Oh" mean?'

'Are you OK?' I asked.

'It's not a disease, Maggie.'

'I didn't mean that! I meant, are you OK, emotionally?'

'Not really. Not quite anyway.'

'How do you mean?'

'Well, I need to know how my friends are taking the news,' she said pointedly.

I was very aware I hadn't reacted very positively at all. It just that I was stunned.

'I'm sorry, Pauline, but… this is a *huge* shock. I can't believe you're telling me this.'

I put my hand up to my temple, trying to work things out. Was I dreaming?

'So, why now? What's brought it all out?'

'The reason I wanted Timmy out the house was because I'd arranged for someone to come and see me. A friend of mine recommended her. She calls herself a life counsellor. I knew I needed to talk to someone. I had all these thoughts and feelings going on in my head and I'd got to the point where my head was so full up, I thought I'd explode if I didn't talk it all out. Anyway, to cut a long story short, I half-shared my thoughts with my friend; she made a call and along came Felix.'

'Felix? I thought you said it was a woman.'

Pauline shrugged. 'It was, she is, but her name's Felix. And before you ask, yes she is gay and no, she didn't convince me I was.'

'I wasn't going to say that.'

'Yes, but I bet you were thinking something along those lines.'

I went to protest but didn't.

'Anyway,' Pauline continued, 'we talked. I mean, *really* talked. I think it helped that she was gay. She must have known how to steer the conversation.'

I unconsciously poured out another whisky, offering her one at the same time. She nodded.

'So, one thing led to another, I ended up spilling out everything. Bit by bit the truth came out and I came out! The next thing I knew, I was standing in the middle of the room, this room, my arms outstretched, announcing to the world I was a lesbian!' She laughed.

I didn't join in, I couldn't. My mind was reeling. This was Pauline; Pauline who I'd known since we were kids. It didn't seem real somehow. Why hadn't I known before? Surely I would have suspected?

'I told her all about my health problems,' Pauline continued, 'but, d'you know, the funny thing was, I started feeling better the moment I got those words out. Amazing huh? Felix said that keeping such a huge secret in would have undoubtedly affected my health. She didn't seem surprised at all at how I'd been feeling. She even bet me that I'd get completely well again. And she was right. I'm feeling better all the time.'

'That's… great Pauline, really great… but… are you sure?' I blurted out. 'I mean how do you know for certain you're… gay?'

She smiled knowingly.

'I think, if I'm honest, I've probably always known, at least suspected, but I didn't want to admit it. I couldn't admit it. My whole life's been based on my being straight and I actually felt ashamed. Can you believe that?'

I vaguely shook my head.

'Frankly,' she went on, 'sex with men has never done much for me. I always felt so… so unlike the other girls and I just thought that was how I was, but when I did actually sleep with a woman, just the one time, it was different. Very different.' She must have seen my look of shock and added, 'Long story, Mags, probably not for now.'

I wasn't sure how ready I was to hear about how different it was sleeping with a woman.

'How different?' My mouth blurted without my permission.

She briefly studied my face, as if assessing whether to be honest.

'More me, that's all.'

'You've only slept with one woman then?'

'Yes. But before you try to convince me otherwise, I am gay, Maggie, and that's all there is to it.'

'Sorry, I didn't mean to...'

'I know,' she interjected.

'I should have faced things back then but I couldn't. I guess I wasn't ready to admit it, even to myself, so I buried it. I just wanted to be normal I suppose, other people's normal.'

'What about Terry? You married him.'

'Crazy, huh?'

'You seemed so well suited at the time.'

She smiled another wry smile.

'Oh we were suited all right. Back then at least. Stick us in front of a TV and ask us to play along with *University Challenge* and you'd never meet two people more alike. Send us off to another showing of *Madame Butterfly* and ask us to give an opinion on who played the better Pinkerton and you'd be on to a winner. But apart from our love of arts and culture, fine wines and a comfortable home, that, I'm afraid, is where the similarity ends.'

'Have you told him?'

'Are you kidding? I couldn't wait to get him out of my life!' she said. 'He's been having an affair with his partner for months.'

'Shit! How did you find out?'

'I've known for ages but, to tell you the truth, it was a blessing. The last thing I needed was him pawing at me all night.'

'Does Timmy know?'

'Yes, I told him earlier.'

'You see, I've always found women much more, well... comfortable I guess the word is. It's like I'm "coming home".'

I tried to ignore the double entendre that sprung to mind.

'I see.'

I knew I wasn't being very helpful.

She looked intently at me again and narrowed her eyes slightly.

'Maggie, you haven't said much. Please tell me what you're thinking.'

'I don't know,' I said honestly.

A thought crossed my mind.

'Why did you tell Timmy first?' I asked.

'I had to tell someone. Besides, I knew he wouldn't judge me,' she said, a slight edge to her voice.

'I'm not judging you!' I replied indignantly.

'Aren't you?'

Was she right? As pro-gay as I'd always been certain I was, I now found myself wondering whether I had only been pro-gay men without realising it. After all, they were safe. Fun. One of the girls. You could share secrets with gay men and discuss beauty stuff and jokingly bitch about people and you always knew they weren't going to make a move on you. I connected with gay men, felt comfy with them…but what the hell did I know about gay women? Had I even met a lesbian properly before and if not, why not? Did I feel threatened somehow? (Not a thought I was proud of) But, at that moment, at that point in time, I'm ashamed to admit I felt a little uncomfortable.

I allowed my thoughts to wash over me. And suddenly out of the blue, clarity hit me. This was utterly stupid. I couldn't believe what I was thinking. This was Pauline! My friend, my close, close friend Pauline. She must have been feeling awful, while I did a bigotry assessment of myself in her lounge! This was just a new experience, that's all. One that need simulating.

I saw that her eyes had welled up.

'Oh God, Pauline, I am sooo sorry,' I put my hands up to my face. 'It just took me by surprise. Of course it's OK. It's just not really the sort of thing one prepares oneself for in the morning. You know, get up, wash, eat breakfast, meet close friend for brunch, discuss the different functions of the clitoris and make plans to go to the West End showing of *The Vagina Monologues*.'

I realised a tear had escaped and was falling slowly down her left cheek.

'You don't approve then,' she stated rather than asked.

I felt really awful. I had covered my fear up with humour. Pauline had entrusted me with her innermost secret and all I could do was think of myself. I was a dreadful, insensitive, friend.

I leapt up and went over to sit beside her, putting my arm around her shoulder.

'Fuck. Just ignore me. It's just a bit surreal. I really am sorry. I don't know what comes over me sometimes. This must be so difficult for you. I'm a crap, idiotic friend. Of course I approve. I approve of you, whatever you do! I love you for goodness sake.'

I hugged her tight and it was then that she gave way in my arms and broke down in tears.

For some reason, I became aware of our knees touching and, inadvertently, I pulled mine away slightly. Pauline sounded like she was sobbing now but I realised, as she blew her nose, she'd actually started laughing!

'Don't worry, Mags.' She pulled away slightly and looked at me through her tears. 'If you're wondering whether I'm going to make a move on you – I'm not!'

'I wasn't!' I protested, shuffling in my seat beside her.

'Bet it crossed your mind,' she sniggered, straightening up. 'It's only natural, but don't worry, you're safe.'

'Oh. OK.' Something in me felt a little dejected.

Pauline reached out to the table and picked up her drink, gulping down the remains, as I sat with what she'd said.

She stood up then and stretched, before wandering over to the window again.

'Why am I safe?' I asked.

She turned.

'You're not my type!'

'Oh,' I said again.' And er… what is your type?' *Did I really want to know?*

She thought for a few moments.

'Perhaps quite reserved, even a little shy maybe, and… intellectual.' She came over and sat on the edge of one of the armchairs.

'Thanks! Nothing like me then.'

'Maggie, for goodness sake, you're my mate! One of my best mates! It would be like starting up an old car and expecting it to suddenly turn into a Porsche!'

'I think I'd rather be thought of as a Porsche than an old banger,' I said.

'You know what I mean though. Just take it from me. We're mates but that's all.

OK?'

'OK, but really I wasn't…'

'*OK?*' she insisted.

'OK, sorry!'

I had a flash of memory.

'So that was why you weren't all that fussed about Gorgeous Graham. Underneath, you didn't fancy him in the slightest.'

'Apparently so!'

I chuckled.

'Does Jenny know?'

'Not yet. Felix said I needed to tell people gradually and that it might be best not to tell her first.'

'You mean she thought you needed to practise on your slightly less fiery friends.' 'Precisely. God, Jen and I are so close and she's known me so long. I think she's going to be the most difficult person to tell.'

'Or she might be the easiest? You just don't know,' I said. 'Only one way to find out…'

Pauline pulled a face.

'I know. And I will, as soon as she comes back from Outer Mongolia or wherever she is.' She reached out and poured us both another drink. I could see she had visibly relaxed.

'You know, funnily enough, the thing I'm most dreading is Jen's reaction when she finds out she wasn't the first to know – again! She'll be fuming!' She laughed and I joined in.

We reached forward and cheersed our glasses together.

'Well done, Pauline,' I said.

'What for?'

'For sharing such a tough secret. I think you've been incredibly brave and I'm sorry you didn't feel able to share it sooner. We all love you, you know, whoever you are and whatever you do.'

I saw some private tears mount up in her eyes, so I tactfully took my leave. Standing and cradling my whisky, I made my way to the French windows, where I opened one of the doors and let myself out into the cool night air.

Chapter Sixty-five

'He's back,' mouthed Margot, referring to Mr Welles. She gave a sideways nod towards the meeting room. 'Asked if you were in yet.'

I shook my umbrella off then pretended to hang myself with an invisible rope. Margot sniggered.

I sneaked past the meeting room door hoping he wouldn't see me but a familiar voice boomed out.

'Ah, Maggie, the very girl. Got a mo?'

I raised my eyes to Margot and she did the hanging thing.

Back I went. Mr Welles was pulling down the projector screen, no doubt for the upcoming client meeting. From where I stood I could see he had lost some weight and I presumed that, unless he'd spent the week at a health farm, he must have really been ill the previous week.

'Morning,' I breezed. 'Are you better?'

'Much, thank you. Nothing like the wife's homemade apple pie and custard to speed up one's recovery, don't you know?'

I didn't but I suspected the lost weight would be found again before too long.

'Sit, sit.' He gestured to the long mahogany table.

I sat.

'Now then...' He came and perched up on the side of the long solid table along from me then gave me the benefit of his fatherly smile, '...I trust you've given my proposal some thought?'

I nodded.

'Well? Let's have it then. Are we going to enjoy the pleasure of your very pretty company for some years to come? Or has my offer been pipped at the post by some bounder in the competition?'

His eyes twinkled but I still found myself feeling uncomfortable. I hesitated, looking down and playing with the hem on my skirt. Like my own office, the only window in the meeting room was up high making the room appear gloomy, especially as it was teeming down outside. Nope, there were no streams of sunshine lighting up my decision. No last minute 'signs' indicating that this was the job of my dreams. Besides, I thought again, if I had to ask the question, 'is this the job of my dreams?', chances were it wasn't.

'It's actually neither of those options.'

He seemed puzzled. I cleared my throat.

'I'm sorry, Mr Welles, but even though I do really like it here, I don't think it's what I really want right now, not permanently anyway. The job's great and everyone's really friendly but I think I'd like to try and find something a little different. Give someone else a chance here. I hope you don't mind,' I added.

There I'd said it. And I'd meant it. I was going to hang on for what I really wanted. I wasn't sure what it was or where I was going to find it but I just hoped that a new person wouldn't join too quickly and I'd have a chance to at least look around before being unemployed and skint!

That evening, I lay in bed thinking about the day's big decision. Bob Welles had been disappointed but not surprised, which made me feel quite good about myself. He said 'he'd wondered as much' and that 'a girl like me was rather unlikely to stick with something she wasn't sure about'. At the time, I'd thought about Tony and had wished my personal life was as easy to figure out as my work life. Still, I had an increasing feeling I was really beginning to grow up. I knew this was the right thing to do. It felt right and I was going to trust my gut, my instincts. *And,* I had only had a mineral water with my pub lunch. Things were changing!

Chapter Sixty-six

A couple of days later, I had a dental appointment over in Wandsworth. It was a bit of an ordeal and the dentist kept 'hmmm'ing' and shaking his head.

'How long since you came to see a dentist, Miss Parsons?'

I thought about it.

'Too long probably,' I admitted. Actually, I said 'koo rrong hhorr hhorr rree' as I had his 'tools' in my mouth at the time.

He shook his head again.

'Hmmm.'

I was beginning to dislike him intensely. He sat back.

'Are you ready for the worst?'

'Not really.' I tensed. 'Can you say it really quickly and get it over with.'

He went back to my mouth and gave me another few prods with his weaponry.

'You need four fillings and a crown,' he said slowly.

'Huck,' I garbled, pleasantly.

Bastard. Didn't he know I was skint? And afraid of pain... and dentists?

Typically, his next appointment had cancelled and he decided we'd be as well to do one of the fillings and something called a 'crown prep' on the spot. It seemed to be a decision that had been made for me rather than an offer, so I endured tens of very stressful minutes of drilling and poking, along with several less pleasant 'hucks' while he was at it. Bloody dentists.

Having booked two more expensive appointments, I left the surgery with a swollen, numb face, feeling very disgruntled. I was busy wondering whether the other cavities could get better on their own and if a temporary crown could, in fact, miraculously last the rest of my life, when an unexpected sight caught my eye over by the town hall. It looked like a small wedding party as a photographer was throwing confetti then snapping away; but who wore a Stetson to a wedding?

I wandered across the road and saw that not only was it a wedding but it seemed to be a double wedding. Two grooms with huge Stetsons and rather odd suits and two brides wearing identical weddingy type dresses which would also have been quite in keeping in a wild west bar... and cowboy boots! They seemed to be taking it in turns to hold a big homemade sign saying 'Hitched and Happy...Yee Ha!!'

Oh well, it takes all sorts, I thought. One of the brides looked twice the age of her groom and, intrigued, I stood at the window of the nearby gym pretending to read the notice board, while I peered sideways to watch as the photographer snapped away and said helpful things like 'Say sex! Ha ha ha ha.' Both couples obeyed and said 'sex', while the photographer told them they were all naturals and that he wished all weddings were as easy as this one. There was something familiar about one of the young men in the Stetsons and, as he switched places with the other groom, I nearly had a heart attack! It was Charlie from the off licence!

It could only be the mother and daughter he'd talked about dating before. I stood there with my mouth open, no longer using the notice board as a cover up; too shocked to realise I was blatantly staring. Charlie must have felt my eyes boring into him as, without warning, he glanced sideways and caught me gawping. After a puzzled frown, recognition swept across his fake-tanned face and he waved.

'Hey there, Maggie!' he called, in a pseudo southern American accent.

Hey there?

'Come on and git!' he beckoned.

Git?

Grimacing and trying not to dribble, I went over and the photographer ogled me blatantly.

'Hey there, Maggie.' Charlie said again.

'I got me a braaad.' He nodded at his braaad, who howdyed at me warily. Her cowboy boots were lime green. Nice.

'Hi, Charlie. Congratulations,' I slavered, lisping badly and putting my hand up to cover my face. I had to ask. 'You been to America? Your accthenth kind of funny.'

Charlie grinned. 'We've been doing line dancing classes every Wednesday evening. Helps to get into the swing of things, you know?'

I didn't.

'We even got ourselves special names!'

He put his arm around the older of the two women.

'This is Marylou.'

I smiled uncertainly and shook hands with 'Marylou' who, on closer inspection, must have been at *least* twice Charlie's age. She had bleached blond hair with very black eye make-up coupled with shocking pink lipstick. She grinned, revealing that one of her front teeth was missing.

Nice.

'And this here's Tex and his new waaaf Jinny Lou.'

I giggled. 'Jinny Lou? Oooh, ith she any relation to…?' then I stopped myself, remembering that she was.

The next thing I knew, Charlie was insisting I have my photo taken with them all. Charlie (who the others referred to as Chili Bob) and Marylou were flanked by Jinny Lou and Tex. I stood like a lemon in the middle, my cheek swollen, work skirt and blouse totally out of keeping with the country and western style of the rest of them. I said as much, hoping they'd let me go back to the office, but it only encouraged Charlie, sorry Chili Bob, to plonk his Stetson on my head and insist the photographer (whose name was Steve, thankfully so) take lots more photos. Desperately trying hard not to dribble I managed a lopsided half smile, as only part of my mouth would move. I stood there feeling probably the most self-conscious I've ever felt, while Steve snapped away uttering encouraging anecdotes such as: 'make love to the camera darlin', 'You've done this before haven't you?' and the good old 'You're a natural. Ever thought of being a model?' Finally, Steve said he had enough photos. Small mercies and all that.

'It's like it was meant to be, Maggie!' Charlie/Chili Bob cried jubilantly, when I insisted I had to leave. 'Maybe we'll name our first born after you or something kerrazy like that!' And, with that, he thwacked me on the back, causing me to cough.

I guiltily wondered whether Marylou would still be able to mother a child at her age; perhaps IVF might be able to help?

'See yer round, Maggie!' they all called as I left, feeling like I'd just been in the Twilight Zone. At least they hadn't called me Maggie Lou.

The next day, my photo was splashed over the front cover of the local paper.

Margot was doubled over with mirth as she thwumped the folded newspaper onto my desk.

'Howdy, Maggie. That's a mighty faaan hat you gotta yourself into there.'

I took in the photo and pulled a face.

'It's a long story,' I said.

'Mr Welles wants to hear it. He thought you were at the dentist.'

'I was! And I've got to go for another two appointments,' I insisted. 'I can show him my filling if he wants to see it!'

The phone on my desk rang. Someone was calling my direct number.

'Hello?'

'So, moonlighting at weddings now are we? I must say you looked the part.'

'Hello, Tony. It's a long story.'

'I bet. Are you available for bar mitzvahs and funerals as well? Or is it just strange country and western weddings?'

'None of them, I just happened to be walking past. Charlie's someone I, um, know… sort of,' I faltered.

Tony sniggered.

'The strange and unravelling life of Maggie Parsons.'

I found myself blushing uneasily.

'Anyway, I just wanted to say 'au revoir'. I won't see you for a while. Not until our big day.'

'Catherine's big day!' I reminded him quickly.

'Same thing. Anyway, I hope you'll find time to miss me in between your other social functions.' He began laughing loudly then and I pulled the phone away from my ear, annoyed.

'I still can't get over you in that hat!'

'Ha bloody ha.'

'Aw, don't be like that, sweetie, you look adorable. But, I must say, for some reason, your face seems a bit of an odd shape.'

'Must be the angle it was taken at.' I couldn't be bothered to tell him about the dental work. It somehow felt like another failing.

'Well, be good and I'll give you a call when I get settled in. Or maybe we should just text until the wedding; you know, keep it low key and exciting.'

I knew I should be sharing in Tony's spirit of passion but I wasn't. I was feeling moody and offish.

'Anyway, babe, don't miss me too much.'

'I won't,' I said lightly.

As we ended the call, Margot, who was lounging with both elbows on my desk, chin in hands – and who had apparently caught most of the conversation from both ends – was on hand with her usual pearls of wisdom.

'Many a true word is spoken in jest.'

'Meaning?' I snapped.

'You won't miss him.'

I didn't have the strength or inclination to argue with her.

As if on cue my phone tinged a text; no doubt Tony adding some clever quip at my expense. Swiping angrily to my messages, I saw it wasn't from Tony after all. And this time I recognised the number. It was from Luke. He had texted me back. Finally.

I opened it.

'Are you still seeing him?'

'What's it say?' Margot asked, leaning over the desk for a look.

'You don't even know who it's from!'

'It's from Luke, stoopid! I knows thaat. One look at your reaction told me *thaat.'*

I scowled and swivelled the phone round to show her.

'Hmmm.'

'What does hmmm mean?'

She shrugged.

'What you gonna tell him then?'

A feeling of panic swept over me. Why was it that such an innocent question seemed so loaded? If I lied, I was certain Luke would see through me and accuse me of lying and if I told the truth, it was somehow worse. Mind you, what was the truth? I still hadn't worked that one out.

'Well?'

'I don't know!' I fretted. 'What do you think I should do?'

'Chuck him,' she said matter-of-factly.

'I'm not going out with him!'

'Not him, that Tony bloke. That way you can get yer rocks off with this Luke. That's how it's s'posed to be, you know?'

I didn't.

'That's all well and good but I've still got to answer his question,' I said.

'No, you don't. You can answer his question with another question.'

'Such as?'

'Such as "why d'you wanna know?"'

I liked that idea very much.

I quickly keyed the words into a message and sent it to him. A delivery report came almost immediately. Then we waited, and waited… and waited.

He didn't send a text through until later that afternoon, by which time I was like a cat on a hot tin roof. Any sound vaguely resembling a phone sent me panicking, eyes wide and heart pumping. When the text finally did arrive, I saw the number and couldn't bear to look at it.

'I can't face it! You'll have to read it!' I insisted, as I took the phone out to Margot in reception.

She took it from me.

'You sure? It might be private.'

'I don't care. I can't take any more of this suspense. At least this way you can soften the blow and read it nicely.'

''K,' she said, looking down at the message.

'It says "I think you know, Maggie".'

What did THAT mean?

That night in bed I considered the text every way possible. Was he talking about me going out with his brother and how he didn't like it? Was it that Tony wasn't right for me? Was it something else that I hadn't worked out? Or could it possibly mean… that he still cared for me? Could it? Is that what he thought I knew? Was it possible that Luke was jealous?

Chapter Sixty-seven

The weekend came and I hadn't texted Luke back. I couldn't think what to say. Anything I sent was bound to stir up a can of worms and what if I was wrong in my assumptions? Or what if I played dumb and then Luke came back and spelled it out for me; what then? No, best plan was to ignore it. Bury my head in the sand. It felt less painful somehow. All roads to Luke led to pain and I wasn't in the mood to handle that.

I took my solace with Tom. He and I were sharing a mutually beneficial relationship while Catherine was on holiday. I was even reading one of her cat books so as to become more knowledgeable on cat behaviour. Basically I became his surrogate mother and he became my replacement friend.

After feeding him on Saturday morning I headed for my bridesmaid dress fitting. While I was in there, standing up on a block, tape measures and pins everywhere, a text sounded from my bag. I apologised as the girl measuring me had to stop what she was doing and pass my bag up to me. Then I apologised again when I passed it back to her.

I jumped as I saw that the text was from Luke, and jumped again as I got a pin jabbed into my side. It was now the seamstress girl's turn to say sorry.

I read the text, my heart beating faster than was comfortable.

We need to talk. There's something you should know before the wedding. Luke.

I began shaking.

'Could you just stay a bit stiller for me for me, I don't want to stab you again,' the girl said.

'Sorry.'

I texted back with a trembling thumb.

What about?

After waiting for what seemed like ages my phone rang. I stared at it, as Luke's number flashed up at me from the screen. The girl looked up from her hemming wondering, no doubt, why I wasn't answering it.

I took a breath and pressed the green button.

'Hello?' I said.

'It's me – Luke.'

'Hello, Luke.' I could hear the strain in my voice. My hand was shaking badly.

'You haven't answered my question.'

'What question?' I decided to play dumb. Better than accusing him outright of fancying me then only to find out I was wrong. Oh, the shame of it!

'Don't play dumb, Maggie, it doesn't suit you.'

Shit.

'Are you still seeing my brother?'

I tried half-heartedly to take stock and physically moved my body into more of a position of power.

'What if I am, Luke? I don't see what it's to do with you.'

'Don't you?'

'No.'

There was a pause.

'OK, maybe you're right but I think you might thank me later.'

'Meaning?'

I heard Luke sigh, as if he was tired.

'Anyway, how's Sian? Taking care of her, are you?' I said, sarcastically then felt a bit guilty.

'What the hell's she got to do with anything? I'm not talking about Sian here; I'm talking about Tony.'

'Maybe I don't want to talk about Tony.'

He gave another heavy sigh.

'Maggie, don't be a fool. Just listen.'

A fool! Honestly, who did he think he was?

'Now hang on a minute, who are you calling a…?' I glanced down to find the girl eyeing me warily. I lowered my voice to a whisper.

'Who are you calling a fool? What gives you the right to phone me up and call me names?'

He tutted. 'I'm not calling you names; OK I am but I don't mean it like that. It's just… oh for heaven's sake, Maggie, you're too good for Tony. There are things you don't know. He's not treating you right.'

'And you know this for a fact do you?'

Luke paused again.

'See! You can't even give me a good enough reason to stop seeing him. You're just jealous!' I spat. 'You're jealous that Tony and I are together and you've got a messed-up life. It's history repeating itself, Luke.'

'*What?*' he replied incredulously. 'What are you talking about now?'

'I think you know.' I was aware I'd said the same words to Luke as he'd texted to me the previous day.

'This is ridiculous. Maggie, if you don't want to listen then I can't force you but I'll just say this one thing. You're a fool if you think Tony is going to make you happy. Has he told you about Laura?'

I felt myself freeze.

'What about Laura? That's all history.'

He laughed nastily.

'Yeah, I thought not. Ask him exactly how things ended with Laura, why don't you.

Go on, ask him. See what he has to say about it.'

'He's told me all about Laura.'

'Has he? And you believe him?'

'What do you mean?'

'Just ask him, Maggie. That's all you have to do.' Luke proceeded to end the call without another word. I stared at the silent phone, my mouth open.

What had he meant?

I let my arm slide down to my side, still in shock. The girl looked up.

'Shall I?' she offered, reaching up.

'Thanks,' I replied vaguely, passing her my phone.

'Men, huh?' she intoned happily. 'Can't live with 'em, can't live without 'em.'

I attempted a polite laugh but it got stuck in my dry throat.

What on earth was I going to do? If I spoke to Tony, he'd know I'd been talking to Luke and he'd be angry but I couldn't just leave it, could I? On the other hand, if I challenged Tony, that would mean I didn't trust him and that's no basis for a relationship... not that that prospect was particularly alluring right now.

Maybe something *had* happened when he and Laura had finished but did I have a right to know?

The seamstress had finished.

'There you go. You'll look lovely when it's all finished. Let's get you booked in for your final fitting.' She smiled pleasantly.

I went through the motions of making another appointment the following week, on the same day Catherine was coming in for her fitting, but my mind was hardly focussing so I gratefully accepted the little appointment reminder card the girl had written out for me, obviously realising I wasn't firing on all cylinders.

Afterwards, feeling anxious, I wandered aimlessly through the streets trying to make sense of things. My first thought was to phone Tony and hope I found the right words. My feelings of uncertainty around him were now mixed with a sickening need to know what was going on, but right then he'd be working. Besides, I knew I should really sleep on things or I'd just blurt out everything and, judging by experience, *I* might end up being the one in the wrong.

I forcibly pulled my mind back to the wedding and found a small amount of solace by focussing on how fab I was going to look and what fun the wedding would be. Perhaps I could give things with Tony a *little* longer. After all, he might be right. Maybe we could start over. I could ask him about Laura at the wedding. He'd tell me the truth and we could start from scratch with a clean slate. And Luke… well, Luke could go to hell. *Fool indeed.* He needed to go and sort things out with Sian and stop messing with my head.

That afternoon, a huge bunch of red roses arrived for me at the flat. They were from Tony. There was a card attached.

Darling Maggie.
Missing you! Can't wait to prove how much.
All my love, Tony XXX

You see, I scolded myself. Tony wanted me and he *was* a lovely guy… most of the time at least. I just needed to focus on the positive instead of the negative. Things were going to be fine, just fine. But, as hard as I tried to convince myself, I was finding it more and more difficult to push away the feelings of doubt.

During the evening, Pauline rang.

'I've lost Timmy,' she said.

'What...? How?'

'He's officially on the missing list. I've phoned his flat but it's permanently on answer phone and he's not picking up his mobile. He hasn't been for two days!'

'Have you left him a message?'

'Several and still nothing. I'm starting to wonder if he's more shocked about me "coming out" than he's letting on,' she said fretfully.

'He'll turn up. He's probably gone on some bender and will turn up with half the Arsenal Gay Football Association in tow.'

'Is there an Arsenal Gay Football Association?' asked Pauline.

'I'm not sure but if there is, Timmy will find it.'

She laughed.

'I suppose you're right. I'm probably worrying over nothing but, right now, everything seems to be worrying me. Are *you* OK?' she asked surreptitiously, 'about... things.'

We hadn't spoken since I'd heard her news.

'Of course! I'm absolutely fine, Pauline, honestly. It's all going to be fine. Don't worry about anything... it's not good for you! Anyway, how are you feeling, health wise I mean?'

'Much, much better. You wouldn't believe it.'

'But you were so ill.'

'Was, past tense. I can't quite believe it myself. Felix did say to expect miracles and she was right. Apparently, I'd been internalising so much stress trying to keep my secret safe, even from myself, that the whole thing was gradually dragging me further and further down and I became ill.'

'And you really are feeling that much better?'

'I feel stronger now than I can ever remember feeling; freer too. I can't believe I didn't face things sooner. I'd have saved myself a whole load of grief.'

'Um, Pauline...'

'Yes?'

'You know Jen's back later today.'

She laughed.

'Know? I've been crossing off the dates on my calendar for over a week. I can set my watch by the date, time and minute they'll be landing. As soon as she steps over her front door step, I'll be on the phone quicker than lightning. I need to get this over with. I think I'll leave you to tell Catherine though, you know how to handle her better than I do.'

I agreed.

'I'm looking forward to her wedding,' she went on.

'Me too,' I said, trying to ignore the pangs of anxiety in my stomach.

'Um, are you bringing anyone?' Pauline asked carefully.

'Er... no, just me.'

I suddenly realised what was coming.

'The thing is...'

'Yes...?'

'I was wondering... How do you think it would be if I brought someone to the wedding?'

I paused.

'Maggie...?'

'Sorry, I was just thinking.'

'About what?'

'About seeing you with a woman,' I replied honestly.

'And...? Are you cool about it?' she asked.

'Truthfully?'

'Truthfully.'

'Well, I'd be lying if I said it wouldn't be weird!' I laughed.

'One thing though,' I added, 'and please do take this the right way, Paul', have you thought about everyone else who'll be there? People are bound to be... surprised. Are you ready for people's reactions?'

'I'm not bothered about them really. It's the people close to me I'm concerned about. So, coming back to my question, I know it'll be weird but are you *OK* about it?'

I decided I was.

'Course I am, hun. Sorry if I seem a bit hesitant. It's just another step for me I guess. I mean, I've only just learned you're gay after knowing you for seventeen years; and now, here's a real live gay situation and I'm going to see you *being* gay!'

She laughed.

'Did you think I was going to be a celibate lesbian?'

'Possibly,' I admitted. Then I had a thought. 'Does this mean you'll hold hands like a couple?' I asked.

'Probably,' she said. 'I've even had my right ear pierced twice.'

'So you're dead set on this lesbian thing then?' I chuckled.

'No turning back now; my extra stud says it all.'

'What about your mum and Wally? Have you told them?'

'Yup. They've been fantastic. Mum actually said she'd suspected for years! I wish she'd bloody well told me. She could have saved me a whole load of stress!'

'Incidentally, who *will* you be bringing?'

'Her name's Sarah.'

I wondered idly if Sarah was a typical lesbian name. Then I wondered if there was such thing as a typical lesbian.

I had a lot to learn, I thought solemnly.

Chapter Sixty-eight

The next day in the office I decided I really ought to start job hunting. Mr Welles was advertising my position in the paper and, knowing my luck, the right candidate would waltz in off the street and I'd have a week's notice! I sat at my desk in my lunch hour and scoured the job pages. Margot came in with a doleful expression on her face.

'Wass'up?' I asked. 'You look like you've lost a tenner and found a pound as my dad always says.'

She shrugged and sat down opposite.

'Man trouble?'

She shook her head sadly.

'Margot?'

She shrugged again.

I closed the newspaper.

'Find anything?' she asked.

'No, nothing yet but I've got a couple of agency interviews on Thursday, so I'll get something. I can always do some more temping I guess, although, to be honest, I'd rather find something permanent. You know, something I can get my teeth into and not have to worry about when it's all going to end. Plus, I could do with some paid holidays and that way I can...'

Margot promptly burst into unexpected, noisy tears.

I rushed round the other side of the desk and put my arm around her shoulders.

'What on earth's the matter? Why are you crying?'

'I don't want you to go!' she sobbed. 'I don't wanna be 'ere on my own.'

I felt awful. I knew Margot had said she would leave if I did but I thought she was just being kind. I had no idea she felt so strongly.

'I'll come and visit. And we can still meet up and go out together.'

'It won't be the same,' she sniffed.

'Yes, it will! And besides, you might get a really nice girl to take my place.

She might be even nicer than me,' I added, hoping underneath that she wouldn't be.

'I don't want someone else!' Margot cried indignantly. 'I want *you* to stay.'

I was truly touched.

'I'm so sorry, Margot.'

I felt like I was deserting her. Each time I went past her desk, she gave me such a sad smile, I considered telling Mr Welles that I'd made a mistake and that I wanted the job after all.

But I didn't and on the Thursday I went off to sign back on with Eleanor at the recruitment agency who assured me of her best attention at all times. Then I went for an interview with Gerrard and Associates, an upmarket looking agency and head hunter that, according to the advertisement, handled finance, business administration, I.T. and marketing and had particular success in finding top-end positions in top-end companies. I wasn't sure I would fit in to a top-end anything but I went along anyway thinking I'd gained some good experience lately and it was about time I raised my game (an expression Jenny used a lot when she talked about work). I arrived at the large grand office building with glossy frontage and big silver signage and I swished my way through the heavy revolving glass door, announcing my arrival at reception. All in all, it was very plush indeed and I felt my heartbeat quicken nervously. As the building housed lots of different organisations, I was given directions to Gerrard and Associates and travelled up, via a glass lift, to the fourth floor. I wondered if anyone could see my knickers from the ground floor. The lift door opened and I was immediately met by Trudy; five foot nothing and dressed in a navy blue skirt and jacket, with her hair in a bun and who could easily have worked as an air hostess. She clutched her neat little hands in front of her and smiled a fixed Stepford Wife smile, before offering her tiny right hand to me for a lettuce leaf handshake; bluurrrrch.

'Welcome to Gerrard and Associates,' she sang in an American accent. 'I trust we can be of assistance to you.'

Any minute now I expected Trudy to burst into some sort of company song, soon to be joined, from the wings, by other similarly dressed minions chorusing out the joys of Gerrard's.

I was led to a (surprise, surprise) glass office and, sitting trussed up in my winter coat, I watched while dynamic looking men in suits, and young, neat, pretty girls in white blouses and pencil skirts, moved speedily round the office, clutching papers; the top halves of their bodies further in front than their bottom halves, so great was their need to get to their next point of call. I felt very small. I took in the smart grey and chrome office where I sat and, glancing up to the far corner, I found myself face to face with a security camera that (although I may have been a little paranoid) seemed to move as I did. Knowing my luck some jumped-up security guards were sitting having a good old laugh at my expense. Sniggering away because I thought I could get a job through an agency like this. Even worse, waiting to see if I'd steal anything! Although I have to admit the stapler was positively science fiction and would look rather good on my coffee table.

I was kept waiting twenty minutes and was beginning to perspire. Feeling self- conscious I took off my coat and hung it on the hook by the door. This time I was sure the camera moved. Honestly, what was I going to do, nick the bloody coat hook? As I sat down a young man who couldn't have been any older than me whooshed in, reeking of aftershave. He didn't meet my eye as he briefly shook my hand and immediately headed round the desk to the computer screen and started clicking away with the mouse before he'd even sat down.

'Maurice Goddard. Senior Consultant. Have they given you coffee?'

'No.'

'Fine,' he replied, obviously not paying attention in the slightest. Maybe he'd also been watching me via the security camera and had decided I wasn't worth interviewing, let alone giving coffee to.

He picked up the phone and buzzed through to someone.

'Hold my calls will you, Pen? What? …No, doubt it…' he glanced at me. '…Ten minutes tops.'

I felt myself blushing furiously.

Maurice had floppy, foppish sandy blond hair that fell over one eye. He kept flicking it back out again, reminding me of our old geography teacher Mr Trubshaw.

'We expect all our placements to dress very smartly,' he said pointedly. The resemblance to Tubby Trubshaw suddenly ended and I found myself inadvertently glancing down at my old suit. As Maurice clicked his way through various computer screens, I tried to scratch off a dried-on mark from my skirt with my nail.

'Sales?' he suddenly aimed at me.

'Er, sorry?' I spluttered.

'Can you sell?'

'Um, well… I don't know really. I've done some telemarketing.'

Maurice raised a quizzical, condescending eyebrow.

'Right.' He turned away and carried on clicking.

'Can you drive?'

'Yes.'

'Just as well,' he said without looking.

Would punching a recruitment consultant be considered a crime, I wondered? I thought not.

'Would you like my CV?' I offered.

'Huh? Oh yeah, sure.' He took the two-page CV and skimmed over it, mumbling to himself. 'OK. Sure. Mmm hmm. Right.' He put the CV down on the desk.

He swivelled round to face me, put his elbows on the desk, clasped his hands together and tilted his head slightly to one side, narrowing his eyes at me.

'OK, Maggie. Here's the deal.'

I sat up straight and tried to hold eye contact.

'Here at Gerrard and Associates, we deliver top quality personnel to top quality corporates. They expect the best, we give the best. Get it?'

I nodded.

'Now here's the question. Are you up for the challenge?'

I was completely taken off guard.

He continued.

'You see, I'm looking at you and thinking… let me see… air hostess, personnel… uhhh… maybe… yeah, maybe retail. I'm thinking neat suits, short skirts, high heels, name badges. Get where I'm going with this, Maggie?'

I nodded dumbly. I got it all right.

'So here's the deal.'

Again? Another deal. What was the first one anyway?

'We've got another division, just down the hall. I'm thinking more your style. More your angle. Get me?'

I half nodded, half shook my head. And before I had a chance to say anything, Maurice had risen from his seat and was already making his way round the desk, his arm outstretched.

'Come on then, up we get.' He guided his arm to my shoulder and began to help me up.

'But what about…' I began. Maurice looked at me, like I was a child trying to buy a car from him.

'Hmmm?' He smiled like a Stepford Husband.

It was awful so I changed what I was going to say.

'Er... my CV?' I nodded my head in the direction of the pitiful looking pages on the desk.

'Sure, I'm on it.' He reached for the CV and passed it to me, guiding me out through the tall glass door. Embarrassingly, I forgot my coat so I had to go back while Maurice, checking his watch, waited impatiently. Coat in hand he led me rather vigorously to the lift area. I almost broke into a run trying to keep up with him.

'Just down the corridor to your right. Name's on the door,' he said, shooting me a smile but already focussing his attention in to the main office and indicating to a tall man in a grey suit that he was just coming.

I was about to ask him what name was on the door but it came out as 'Where's the loo?'

He pointed in vague direction of the lift then disappeared.

I found the loos, rushed in and hid in a cubicle. Luckily the doors weren't glass but they were very tall with super stylish door handles and locks that clunked into perfect place. I sat down on the closed lid, once again feeling small. I had never felt so useless in all my life. He hadn't even interviewed me. He'd taken one look at me and my CV and decided I wasn't good enough for Gerrard and bloody Associates. I was absolutely not going to give Maurice bloody floppy fringe the satisfaction of going 'down the corridor' to some other snotty place to find out whether I may or may not be good enough for them.

Composing myself, I put on my coat again and, flushing the loo in case there were people outside, I headed back out. While I was checking myself in the mirror, a young girl came in crying.

'Oh, what's the matter? Are you OK?'

'Some snotty nosed woman just interviewed me and said I'm not up to the mark,' she sobbed indignantly, 'whatever that means! She's sent me down the corridor to some other crappy place.'

I guiltily felt marginally better that I wasn't the only one.

I said how sorry I was and when she'd calmed down I left her reapplying her makeup and headed back out to the lifts. Down I went, like my mood, to the reception. I thought I might as well go back to work and I grabbed a paper on the way. Thursday was jobs day. I sat down at the top of the double-decker and settled in with my paper for the journey back to Islington.

The thought of having no money and potentially having to tap my dad for cash again filled me with dread. My mother would no doubt be there waiting to dish the insults.

'Oh, Maggie, I keep *telling* you! When will you learn? If you just found yourself a decent young man to look after you then this wouldn't happen. Now, when I was your age... blah blah blah.' I shivered and turned to the recruitment pages. Glancing through, one of the jobs suddenly seemed to leap out the page at me.

Account Executive required for Central Herts-based financial services organisation. New company seeks loyal employees to muck in from the start. Account Management/Marketing background preferable. Duties to involve building client relationships, account management, corporate marketing, some PA work and customer service. Will be expected to travel. Company car included. Salary negotiable plus commission.

It sounded ideal! Financial Services – I'd worked successfully for Greenwich Finance; Account Management – well, I was certainly experienced in that; PA work – a new area but I was sure I could pick it up easily and, as for marketing, I'd done some at CapiTel and I could simply learn more about it... and travel! Just what I needed. A company car too! Central Hertfordshire wasn't far out at all. I could even drive to Tillmouth to see Mum and Dad after work sometimes and maybe stay over.

I knew I was being over-optimistic but I rang them immediately I got back to the office and emailed my – suitably edited for purpose – CV over.

As I was standing making the afternoon tea, Margot rushed into the kitchen, pretending to bite her knuckles.

'What? What's happening?'

She gave a sideways nod to Bob Welles's office.

''E's in there,' she whispered.

'Who's in there?'

'The man I'm gonna marry!'

'I thought you never going to get married,' I pointed out.

'A girl can change.'

I noticed Margot had touched up her make-up over lunch and had put on more eyeliner than usual, if that were possible. She'd even rolled her mini skirt up another couple of inches and she'd changed her stripy tights for some sheer black ones.

'Who is he?'

'His name's Barry. Shame but we can always change it. He's come for your job. He's been in there since before lunch. God, he's so hot, I might have to run in there in a minute and snog him to death. I'm just going in to aask if they'd like any more drinks. Hang on.'

And she disappeared off, only to reappear two minutes later, dramatically swooning around the kitchen door clutching her heart.

'To die for. No word of a lie.'

'Do you think he'll get it?' I asked.

'I'd bloody well give it to him.'

'Ha ha. Do you think he'll get the job?'

'Old Wellesy was just talking about Sunderland Footie club when I went in so they must be on good terms. He'd better bloody get it otherwise I might have to stalk him.'

Suddenly an extremely attractive, tall, guy with dark brown hair and eyes – probably in his early thirties – put his head round the door. I noticed he had a hole in one ear, where an earring usually went.

'Margot, isn't it?'

Margot nodded, speechless.

'I'm Baz. Looks like you and I'll be seeing a lot more of each other. I start next month.' He shot her, and then me, a dazzling smile. 'See you then.' And he was gone.

Margot waited until we heard the main front door close before reacting.

'Did you hear that? DID YOU HEAR THAT?' She grabbed hold of my lapels and shook me. 'He said we'd be seeing a lot more of each other!' And I watched as she staggered and swooned back out the door again, stumbled over Mr Welles, blurted out a vacant apology then skipped back off to her desk mumbling the name Baz.

I got an email from her half an hour later.

Been reading his CV He's a Scorpio, like me! I'm in big trouble! ;-)

I laughed to myself. It looked like Margot might not mind me going so much after all.

As I trudged up the stairs that evening (the lift was *still* broken), I saw a vaguely familiar, dishevelled heap outside my front door. It was snoring – loudly.

'Hello?' I ventured timidly. 'Who's that?'

The snoring faltered, then resumed.

'Hello?' I said again slightly louder.

This time, whoever it was pulled their coat further over them, displaying bright red jeans and a bare midriff.

I shook my head. I'd recognise those jeans anywhere.

'Oy, you. Wake up. It's the police. We've got you surrounded.'

A scruffy, blond-haired head shot up to vertical and a very dazed Timmy stared out from bleary, red, eyes.

'I didn't do it. It wasn't me!' he cried.

'Didn't do what, Timmy?' I crouched down beside him. 'Silly, it's only me. What are you doing outside my front door?'

'Waiting for you to come back; and don't do that police thing, I nearly shat myself!'

'Charming. Why exactly are you waiting for me? Did you know Pauline's sending out search parties for you?'

Timmy looked forlorn.

'Is she? She needn't be.' He stretched noisily. 'I'm officially found now and in the possession of a very sensible Maggie Parsons, who will take care of me and see me right. Or so I'm hoping?' He looked at me anxiously.

'Hmmm, before I decide how sensible and accommodating I'm going to be, you'd better come in and tell me everything.'

I stood up and taking Timmy's hand I pulled him up beside me. He promptly bent over again, clutching his head in his hands.

'Head spin,' he groaned to the floor.

I noticed his creased top and caught a slight whiff of BO.

'You need a shower.'

'I know,' he agreed despondently.

Then I spotted some ominous looking black bags in the corner.

'Timmy…why've you got three bin liners with you!? Please tell me you're on the way to the launderette.'

'Kind of. Maybe we could go inside now and I could sit down for a little while, before you bite my head off. You might need a drink.'

I sighed.

'Sounds like it. Come on then; hurry up, before I change my mind.'

Timmy followed me into the flat, dragging his bin liners. I closed the door behind him.

'You'd better ring Pauline. She'll be worried.'

He pulled a face.

'Couldn't you do it?'

'Why?'

'She'll only want me to explain in detail where I've been and I don't think I'm quite up to that yet.'

'So you want me to lie for you.'

'Please.'

'Timmy, I wasn't serious!'

'No. Sorry, of course not. Well not lie exactly, just tell her I'm fine and she's not to worry and that I'll call her in a couple of days. I need to get my head straight. Pleeease, Mags.'

I hesitated so he tried a different tack.

'Actually…' he frowned purposefully, 'you could always think of it as payback for fibbing about that Jye bloke coming over to visit me.'

Then, softening again, he stuck out his bottom lip, reached over and began pawing me.

I tutted. 'I'll think about it. You know she's worried that you've gone AWOL because of her.'

'What? Why?'

'You know, her being gay and all that.'

'So, she did tell you. She said she was going to but I thought she might think twice.'

'Oh? How come?'

Timmy shrugged.

'Not the sort of thing you go round telling everyone.'

I started to feel a bit paranoid.

'I'm not exactly anyone though, am I?'

'No, that's what I told her. I told her you'd be cool about things.'

'Good. Well… that's good then.'

Going into the kitchen I began to uncork some wine. Timmy followed me in, still dragging his bin liners.

'I suppose you'll be eating and drinking me out of house and home then.'

'Probably,' Timmy admitted. 'But I'll be very good. I'll even tell you you're a fantastic cook if you like.'

'Don't push your luck. Now then, where exactly have you been over the last few days? I hope you're not in any trouble.'

Timmy went silent.

'Timmy…?'

'I think I need a drink.'

'Sounds like I'll need one too.' I poured out two large glasses.

I made him put the bin liners in the corner of the hall because they smelt too, then, taking the bottle with us, we sat down on my comfy sofa and Timmy gratefully guzzled some wine before filling his glass up again.

'Thirsty?'

'It's been a very long few days.'

'Where have you been?'

'Oh, here and there.'

'Here and there, *where* exactly?'

'Don't be mad at me, Mags?' He looked pleadingly into my eyes, picked up my Snoopy cushion and cuddled it to him.

'You'd better tell me quickly then, so I can't interrupt.'

'OK. I've been sleeping rough, under the arches. Bit like Phil Mitchell! "Gaan daan The Arches"' he mimicked, attempting to appear hard.

'Oh, Timmy, no! What happened? What about your flat?'

'Slight problem. The landlord's kicked me out.'

'Why?'

'A small matter of rent arrears.'

'How small exactly.'

'Small enough. Couple of months. Maybe three.'

'Three months! Timmy, no wonder he kicked you out.'

'He's a she. And she's a bitch.'

'I think I'd be a bitch if someone owed me that much rent.' I took a sip of my wine, then another.

I had a thought.

'But you could have come straight round here. I certainly wouldn't have seen you sleeping on the streets, had I known.'

'Sorry.'

'Was it awful?'

'Double awful. You don't want to know what people do when they need to go to the toilet. I thought I'd seen it all.'

I shuddered.

'At least I had a sleeping bag. Some people just sleep under sheets of cardboard. I felt really bad for one guy, he didn't have any shoes on.'

'How the other half live,' I said solemnly.

'And then some,' Timmy said.

'I suppose your sleeping bag needs a wash then?'

'No. I left it for the guy with no shoes; gave him a pair of my old trainers too.'

'You always were a soft touch for the underprivileged.'

'You're a fine one to talk. Saving little flies if they fly into your bath.'

He paused. 'Still do that?'

I nodded. 'You?'

He nodded.

We sat in mutually connected, comfy silence for a few moments, sipping away at our wine.

'You'd better tell me everything before I phone Pauline. First though, go and have a shower. Snoopy looks like he's about to faint from the smell!'

An hour later, Timmy was back on the sofa, clean in crumpled tracksuit bottoms and one of my old oversized tee shirts. He smelt of Miss Dior Silky Shower Gel.

'Come on, talk to me then. Why are you so destitute, hun?' I asked.

He shrugged, hugging Snoopy back into position.

'Timmy?' I said slowly.

'Yes?'

'I'm worried about you.'

'That makes two of us,' he admitted.

His face was pale and drawn, his eyes heavy and tired.

'Timmy, how long have I known you?'

'Um… about sixteen years, I guess.'

'And do you trust me?'

'Ye-e-s,' he replied warily.

'And you know that anything I say to you will be because I care about you and not because I'm interfering in your life.'

'I guess,' he said shiftily, pulling his knees up and sticking his finger inside a hole in his sock.

'In that case I am going to say something that's been on my mind for a while now.'

He dropped his gaze to the ground as if he knew what was coming.

'Honey, I'm sorry but I think you're taking too many drugs.'

'I…' he began.

'Please, just let me finish.'

'Now, I don't know too much about them. Goodness, I've only ever taken stuff three times in my life, but two of those times have been because of you.'

'I didn't make you take them!'

'No, I know that, perhaps that's not fair but, if it hadn't been for you, I wouldn't have been able to take them. Anyway, never mind that; that's not what I'm saying. I'm saying that, with my limited experience, I think that you're doing a lot more than any of us know. You look terrible, Timmy. And now you're overdue on your rent and sleeping rough for goodness sake! What's going on?'

He was silent.

'Are you in trouble?' I asked carefully.

'No.' His lip trembled.

'Then what? Please, Timmy, I want to help.'

He turned away from me.

'Timmy?'

'It's not… oh I don't know; I just feel…'

He gulped some more wine and the room fell silent for a few moments.

'Hun, if you can just get things out in the open, you're going to feel better.' My thoughts went to Pauline.

'But I don't know what's happening to me, Mags. I feel crap. My life is a complete mess. Nothing's going right for me and I don't know who to turn to.'

'You can turn to me,' I said, squeezing his hand beside me on the sofa.

'I don't think you'll be able to help me.'

'I can try.'

A tear suddenly sprung in the corner of his eye but he wiped it away.

'I'm a mess, Mags. There are no two ways about it. I'm a failure and an idiot.'

'No, you're not!'

'I am. You don't know the half of it. You think I do too many drugs? Define too many. I'll tell you what I'm doing, shall I? I'm doing stuff whenever I have the money to do it.'

'How often is that?'

'It used to be a doddle. I used to have money, so it was whenever really; all the time.

But then I lost my job at the club and it got more difficult.'

'What have you been taking?'

'Coke mainly.'

'But why?'

He shrugged.

'It always felt so... easy, I guess. It kinda protected me. I mean, all my life I've felt different, an outsider, like I didn't belong. I've never felt like anyone really understood me; or got me.'

'I did!'

'I know you did, babes. You were one of the very small minority but I hardly ever see you. No, I mean people generally. Being gay hasn't helped. And coke's acted like a shield, so nothing could get me at me. Plus, you know, it sorted my head out. It's always seemed like there were two people inside me, two personalities.'

'How do you mean?'

'This is going to sound weird but... I get this internal battle going on all the time in my head. Everything I do, I find I'm judging myself and arguing with myself. Trying to be perfect all the time but always finding something else to find fault with. I feel like there are two clear personalities in one and they're always fighting! On the one hand I'm shy and reserved, I know that sounds unlikely but it's true, and on the other I'm the confident guy, everyone's friend, the joker. That's the side people expect. And the drugs, the coke, the E, alcohol, well, they level me out. Help me to live in that side of me... so that people accept me, I guess.

'But surely it's best to respect all your personality, Timmy, all of *you* – instead of just one half. I know you've got your shy side; I love you for it. It makes you more accessible somehow, more real. People who know you and love you want the real you. In fact, I bet pretty much everyone prefers a person to be themselves. Are you sure that the Mr Confident is the real you? Cos I'm not.'

'I don't know, Mags. One minute I think it is but then I get so burned out being *up* all the time. Coke helps me be up; blimey there's nothing like it, but...' He stared out of the window and went quiet.

'But what...?'

'The comedowns are so awful; dreadful. Talk about demons.'

'Are you... I mean, what about now? Is this a come down?'

'Every day seems to be one at the moment,' he said.

'Are you actually taking drugs every day?' I asked, shocked.

'Pretty much but I haven't had anything today.'

'Oh, Timmy, you must stop, please. I can't bear the thought of you hurting yourself like this.'

'I don't know how to stop though. It's a vicious circle.'

'Why?'

'If I carry on I get to feel half normal but I'm broke all the time and, if I stop, then I feel crap; so crap.'

'How do you afford it though; I mean with no job?'

He turned his head away from me then and his whole body tensed up.

'Timmy?'

'I can't tell you, Mags.'

'You can. You can tell me anything, I won't judge you I promise.'

'It's too awful,' he said, picking at his fingernails and cleaning the dirt out of them, one by one.

'Nothing's that awful, surely.'

He put his head in his hands.

'I'm so ashamed.'

I leant across and rested my hand comfortingly on his shoulder. He started crying quietly.

We sat for a while like that, neither of us talking. As Timmy cried, it was like he was living some internal realisation. He kept shaking his head and saying things like 'I've been so stupid' and 'What have I done?' and just when I thought he'd calmed down more tears came. After a while though, he stopped suddenly. He swivelled round and looked directly at me then, his face strewn with tears and his eyes red.

'If I tell you something, you must promise never ever to tell anyone,' he sniffed, wiping his face on his arm.

'I promise.'

Timmy took a breath and exhaled fast.

'I met this guy in a club, an Arab. Ahmed his name was. We hit it off. He was good to me; quite a bit older, but kind.' He laughed. 'Or so I thought.'

'What do you mean?'

'The reason he was so kind was that he wanted me to work for him. He knew I was down on my luck. After all, that's pretty much all I could talk about. How I'd lost my job, how stupid I'd been and how my life was a mess.'

'OK, so what did he want you to do?'

'I didn't mean to get involved but he was so, like I said, kind. He made it sound like it was all OK. That I was OK.'

An awful feeling of knowing was creeping over me.

'He was a pimp, Maggie, a lousy fat arse of a pimp.' Timmy started to cry again.

'Did he make you do things?'

'He didn't have to. By the time I'd heard him out about how I was a good person and I would just be doing it to get in some extra money, money I needed to get me on my feet again, I was sold. I chose to do it. It was all down to me.' Timmy looked ashamed.

'So what happened?'

'I ended up sleeping with a load of different guys, mainly wayward Arabs, who would come over on business from Saudi and places like that. At first I got a bit of a kick out of it. There were some nice guys actually. And very rich!' He perked up slightly and gave me a watery grin, wiping his face again. 'It was big bucks and the tips were amazing. I started living really well, if you can say that. But then it began to get heavy.'

I felt sick.

'How...?'

'Ahmed wanted a piece of me all the time. Every time I thought I'd come to the end of a night, someone else would need me, even ask for me by name. I think that was what kept me going, you know, thinking that someone actually wanted me personally. I felt... special. God I was working all the hours ...and then one day...' He trailed off.

I squeezed Timmy's hand and waited.

'... this guy got heavy with me. He started hitting me while we were doing it in his hotel room. He wouldn't stop. He kept whacking me, like he was getting some sort of a kick out of it.'

'That's horrid.'

'Tell me about it. He wasn't a big guy but, let me tell you, he had muscles like a boxer and I couldn't fight him off. He pinned me down on the bed and wouldn't let me up. I was trapped. Then he pulled some rope out from under the bed and started tying my wrists to the bedpost. I couldn't breathe with him on top of me, crushing me. I was so scared. I remember thinking that I could die in that room. He could suffocate me or beat me up so badly that I would just die there. I didn't know if anyone would care. I remember my life kinda flashing before my eyes. They say that happens and it does! I thought about my life and it seemed so shit and, you know, right then, I wasn't even sure if I cared.'

'Oh Timmy, you poor, poor, thing; we would have cared.'

'I know,' he said sadly.

'Never mind that now. You're safe and that's the main thing. Tell me what happened, how did you get out?'

'That was the ironic thing really, I was busy struggling under this guy and there was a knock at the door. It was Ahmed. I guess we must have run over time or something, because when he didn't get an answer he started knocking really hard and raising his voice in Arabic. The guy I was with jumped off me and looked pretty alarmed, so I managed to get myself up and pull one of my wrists free which gave me a free hand to untie the other one. That one was really tight, I wasn't sure I could undo it. The guy put a bathrobe on and answered the door and the two of them began yelling at each other. I panicked.'

'What did you do?'

'I called out for Ahmed and, for once, the guy was there when I needed him. He must have heard the panic in my voice, because he came in and took one look at me with my cuts and bruises, trying to get myself free, and really laid into the other guy. I finally got the rope undone and managed to get my things together and get half-dressed while they were arguing, then I legged it. I never went back, I never even got paid for it but I'm glad. I don't want to be paid for sex anymore and I certainly didn't want to be paid for being beaten up and raped.'

'When did all this happen?' I asked.

'I stopped doing it about six weeks before our holiday. I didn't have a job but I had a fair bit of money, so at least I wasn't out on the street. I was in such a mess though. A couple of my gay mates took me in hand but I think they got a bit sick of me being down all the time. That's when I met that Brazilian guy, Fabio, I told you about. He was a doll; so dreamy. I really fell for him and, even after everything that had happened, it felt like life might get back to normal. I was still doing drugs, mainly in secret, but I felt more in control of things. Then Fabio broke up with me, because he found out what I was doing and didn't approve. And my world fell apart. I know we hadn't been seeing each other for long but I guess I'd pinned all my hopes on him, thinking he was the answer to all my problems. I thought he was the guy who was finally going to save me. He didn't of course. He couldn't. That was... *is*, down to me.'

Timmy sighed heavily.

'Anyway, then you guys called about the holiday and I decided to spend the last of my money on that and a load of coke and E to take with me. I figured I could leave everything behind me, you know, all my problems, and somehow, after Spain, everything would miraculously change for the better. Only it didn't.'

Oh, I knew all about that.

'So here I am. No money. A drug habit I can't afford to keep and a flat in London I can't afford to rent, with all my things in it! I have no way of sorting this out. I don't know what to do.'

I sat, thoughtfully digesting everything Timmy had told me.

'Are you prepared to get help? With the drugs I mean?'

Timmy stared at the floor for a few moments.

'I don't know if I can stop.'

'Do you want to?'

'Honestly?'

'Yes.'

'I can't imagine life without drugs. Coke especially.' He paused. 'But I guess if someone showed me a way to give it up and get my life back on track and start feeling normal… yeah, I'd give it up. I'd get help.'

'Good. That's a start. God I feel terrible that you went through all this on your own. What did you think we'd do; abandon you?'

'I was ashamed, Mags. I didn't want to get anyone involved, especially those close to me. I didn't want you knowing what I'd done. I couldn't have faced it if you'd found out and not wanted to know me anymore.'

I shook my head and felt tears well up in my eyes.

'I'd never have turned my back on you.' Tears edged their way down my cheek.

Timmy noticed.

'God, Mags. I'm so sorry. I never meant for you to get hurt.'

I sniffed. 'Well, you'd better promise you'll let me help you now… otherwise, there'll be big trouble!'

We sat and cuddled each other, connecting and sniffing quietly.

Then I straightened up suddenly, a solution forming swiftly in my mind.

'You can move in here with me.'

He glanced at his bin liners still sitting in the hallway.

'Properly I mean. We can get your stuff from the flat and sort out your rent somehow. We'll all club together.' I thought about my own job situation, grimaced internally, then pushed the thoughts aside. 'We'll find a way.'

Timmy looked panicked.

'But that means telling the others. I don't think I could face that.'

'How do you think they'd feel if they found out you'd kept on hiding all this from them?' I recalled the similar the conversation I'd had with Pauline in Spain.

'I don't know.'

'Well, I can tell you. They'd feel terrible; just like I do.'

Timmy's faced was crestfallen again, so I took on a gentler tone.

'OK, let's forget about that for now. We'll sort this out bit by bit. You can take the sofa here, until we work out what to do for the best.'

'I feel like a waste of space,' Timmy said.

'Well, don't. You're not. You just need help.' I had a thought. 'Maybe you could have a chat with Felix.'

Timmy's eyes widened.

'What, that lezzer bird that Pauline saw?'

I laughed.

'She's supposed to be very good.'

He shrugged.

'Well then. That's sorted.' I handed him the phone.

'What's this for?'

'You're going to phone Pauline and tell her you're safe. She's worried sick that you've turned your back on her. Don't you think you owe her an explanation?'

'Do you think she'll be cross with me?'

'Probably.'

He pulled a face. 'Fancy Pauline being a lezzer!'

I couldn't help but smile.

'Yes. Funny how it's the people you think you know the best, who come up with the most unexpected surprises,' I said pointedly.

Chapter Sixty-nine

Finally, Catherine was back and I couldn't wait to see her.

She arrived at my door the following evening, her face bronzed and beamy and her chubby arms showing off a deep tan.

'Look at my white bits,' she said proudly, pulling her top to one side and displaying a white line at the edge of her bra. 'I had to keep moving the straps on my swimming costume down cos I didn't want strap marks showing above my wedding dress.'

'Why have you got bin liners in your hall?' she puzzled.

'Timmy's here. He's staying for a while.'

Timmy had in fact nipped out for a bit so I went on to explain his plight.

Catherine was completely shocked and tears mounted in her eyes.

'Poor darling Timmy, what he must have gone through. Some people need their bits lopping off! Thank God he's here and safe now away from those awful people.'

We agreed that as soon as the wedding celebrations were over we'd talk things through with the others then do something special for Timmy. We'd make sure he knew we were there for him, no matter what.

'I went out with a man once who said he'd like to tie me up,' Catherine said thoughtfully.

'Really? I don't remember you telling me that.'

'I'd forgotten all about it until now.'

'What did you say?'

'No, of course!'

'But how did you… approach it?'

'I said I was saving myself for the man I married. That's enough to scare any man off but I think I also told him I had a rope allergy,' she giggled. 'How's Pauline?'

Having already talked her through Timmy's problems, I then began the rather difficult task of explaining that one of our best friends was now batting for the other side.

Catherine was astounded.

'I can't believe it! How long has she known?'

'She's suspected for ages but didn't want to admit it, apparently.'

'Gosh, poor Pauline; to be alone with something so big. That Felix woman was right. No wonder she was ill.'

'She'll be glad you see it that way. She's been worried about how we'll all take it.

I busied myself with opening a bottle of wine. I could hear Catherine's mind ticking over as she sat at the kitchen table.

'Does that mean she'll wear dungarees now and have her hair cut even shorter?'

I laughed. 'I don't know about dungarees but she's had her ear pierced twice.'

'She's really serious about it then.'

'That's what I said.'

'I wonder how you can tell if you're a lesbian or not.'

I frowned quizzically.

'I mean, you would have thought you'd know pretty much straight away, like when you were really young. But people seem to take ages to suss it all out, don't you think? Can't see the attraction myself. Not that I have any objections you understand,' she added.

'I just couldn't imagine not having anything to… you know, play with.'

'Does that mean…?'

'No, still a virgin. But a girl can tell what she's going to like and what's not for her.'

'So how was it then? The holiday. How were his parents?'

'Bliss… and fat! In that order!' she said gleefully.

'What…?'

'That didn't come out quite right; but they are! Bigger than me! His mum is anyway. Isn't that wonderful?'

I nodded, wondering if it was.

'Oh, they're so lovely! His mum treated me like her long lost daughter and his father gave me some homemade cheese.'

'Ri-i-ight,' I said slowly.

'It smelt really awful but I took it anyway. My suitcase stinks now. I'll have to wash all my clothes. Oh that reminds me, I've bought you a present.'

She went out to the hallway and brought in a carrier bag covered in Italian writing.

'*Et voilà.*'

'That's French.'

'Yes, but I can't remember what the Italian is for "here you are".'

I opened the bag.

'A straw donkey!' I exclaimed.

'Not just any donkey. It's a good luck donkey. The woman in the shop said it was also a symbol of virility. She spoke very good English. Anyhow, I thought you could use some good luck in that department.'

'Thanks! Um… nice saddle blanket,' I added, trying to be diplomatic.

'Poor thing would be roasting if he wore that in Italy. I wonder if it comes off.' With that, Catherine reached over and extricated the blanket from the donkey. We both shrieked. Underneath the blanket was a huge penis!

When I'd stopped laughing I managed to speak.

'No wonder she said it was a symbol of virility. Look at it! It's almost life size! Put the blanket back on! Hurry up! Timmy'll steal if it we're not careful.'

'I'm so sorry. I just thought he was so cute and would be company for Mobear and that other one you've got in there.'

I wondered if I was imagining the slight edge to Catherine's voice.

'I bought you these too.' She handed me a long flat packet.

'Italian… joss sticks. Um, thank you.'

'You're welcome. The woman said you burn them to attract the perfect partner. Go on, light one up. See what they smell like.'

So I did.

Thirty seconds later…

'Quick!' Catherine cried. 'For goodness sake put it out. It's horrible!'

I sat observing the now wet-ended smelly joss stick and the phallic donkey.

'Thanks, they're… lovely.'

'Sorry!' Catherine giggled. 'Oh well, at least we had a laugh.'

The front door opened and Timmy wandered in.

'Hiya. Welcome home. How was Italy?' he asked Catherine.

'Hot. How was sleeping rough?'

'Cold,' Timmy admitted.

Chapter Seventy

The big day was looming. Catherine and I had been to have the final alterations done to our dresses but despite everything fitting perfectly, and Catherine's dress looking even more divine than ever, she was in tatters. Later we'd be making the journey up to Tillmouth then heading to the little church to have the wedding rehearsal and she couldn't concentrate on anything else.

'What if I forget my lines?' she fretted on the way home.

'They're not lines, they're vows. Besides, who cares? It'll only be a few of us tonight. You've still got a few days to practise for the real thing.'

'Will you help me rehearse them?' she asked, as we wobbled around like a couple of teenagers right at the front of the top deck of the bus. We had decided to avoid the underground as it was such a lovely fresh sunny day.

'Only if you promise to throw me the bouquet.'

She glanced sideways at me.

'Who's the lucky man – Tony?'

I shrugged, pretending to be engrossed in the views below.

The bus drew up to a stop and I stared out into the windows of the shops. My attention was drawn to a busy cafe, with tables and chairs still out on the pavement capturing the bright sunshine. People were wrapped up in jumpers and coats but it was sunny enough to enjoy the outdoors still and eat al fresco.

Suddenly, my heart jumped as a couple at the far table caught my eye. The woman had her back to me and looked familiar but it was the man who I recognised immediately. There was no mistaking the stunning blond hair still streaked from the summer sun; the tanned skin, strong jaw line and even from this distance, I could feel the depth of those vivid blue eyes.

Luke.

Luke and another woman.

My stomach lurched and I began to feel sick. Who was she? I strained to see but it was difficult from the angle. The bus started ambling away and I felt a panic that I might not get to know. But as we began to pick up speed, the woman turned slightly in our direction and I got a clear view of her face.

I felt the colour drain from me. Laura.

Shock shot through my body. I quickly faced forwards again and sat staring straight ahead of me, not knowing whether to say anything to Catherine. But the feelings were so strong I had to let them out.

'Did you see them?' I blurted.

'Who?'

'Down there in the cafe.' I pulled on Catherine's arm and pointed.

'Who...? Where...?'

'It was Luke. And Laura! Oh my God, what are they doing together?' My mind was racing and I just knew something wasn't right.

'Probably just catching up; they went to uni together after all. Doesn't seem that odd that they'd be together, surely?' Catherine said.

I could feel my face, cold and white. That morning's coffee and croissant were churning around in my stomach and threatening to come back up again.

'Maggie? You OK?'

'Yes,' I said quietly.

'Well, in that case, how come you look like your whole world's just been turned upside down?'

How come indeed?

The rehearsal went well and Catherine finally relaxed when she finished reading her vows without a single mistake. Both sets of our parents were there and Catherine's two little nieces, the other two bridesmaids. While the parents hadn't really been needed both our mums had insisted on being the ones to bring and look after the two little girls and they were so excited you'd have thought it was them getting married! Poor Nico was incredibly nervous and kept fluffing his words and blushing madly. He'd only met Catherine's mum and dad the once and was clearly very anxious to get things right in front of them.

As chief bridesmaid, I knew I wasn't really doing my duty. All I could think of was why Luke had been with Laura. What had she been doing in London anyway? Was she coming to see Tony? And Luke, why was he there? Had he been working? Had he got a job in London? There were so many possibilities, but something wasn't right. I recalled Luke's words from our phone call:

There are things you don't know…
Ask him exactly how things ended with Laura…

My mind spun with possibilities. Maybe… oh God, please no… but maybe something awful had happened between Tony and Laura and she'd run to confide in Luke and they'd ended up together! Or perhaps that's why Tony and Laura had really split up because she and Luke had fallen in love? Was that what Luke wanted to tell me before the wedding, so I wouldn't be shocked when I saw them as a couple. But… then again, Luke had talked like he wanted to warn me off Tony so there must have been more to it. Tony had to be involved, didn't he? And surely… I mean… Luke had been angry about me being with Tony. Why, if all along he'd fallen for Laura? It didn't make sense, any of it. I tried and tried to fathom things out, my head pounding with a stress headache.

That night I stayed at Mum and Dad's and, back in my old single bed, I found myself remembering the time I'd lost my virginity to Luke. How vulnerable I'd felt afterwards. How alone.

I allowed my mind to travel freely over the ten years that had gone by since that night. How I'd changed. All the things I'd done, the jobs I'd had, the flats, the friends, the relationships. My life and how it had played out without Luke in it. How petrified I'd felt when I'd thought I was going to see him at the reunion and then how devastated I'd been when he hadn't shown up. And of course the things that Tony had told me about why Luke had run out on me all those years ago.

Old memories surfaced, leaping and flitting from one to the next then on to the next in a torrent of video footage, and lying there curled up on my bed I began to allow the hurt and pain of the past to fully surface. It had waited so patiently and, finally, I let it in. The pain came in great waves washing over and over me time and time again. Round and round it went as I relived all the hurtful memories that came to me, wounding me like history repeating itself. Instead of trying to escape the memories and bury them, I let them in, for once allowing myself to feel the true extent of what had happened. The pressure in my head grew and grew until I was doubled up on the bed wondering how on earth I was going to make it stop. Then suddenly, quite suddenly, it lifted; gone. It was like I'd walked into a clearing in my mind. The pain disappeared, the memories cleared and I felt like I'd come out the other side of something. My mind was calm, free, at peace. I opened my scrunched-up eyes, feeling shell-shocked, and it was then, only having gone through what I'd previously tried to suppress, that I started to see the true reality; the feelings I'd had when I'd actually seen Luke. The way he'd taken my breath away when I'd bumped into him on the stairs at the farm. That feeling of knowing he was there, without even seeing him; the undeniable connection that still existed between us. The emotions I'd experienced when he'd sent me the birthday card. The real, true feelings I'd felt underneath the surface that were only now allowing themselves to be revealed. Despite all the logical thoughts I had about him and Sian, here, in my old room, it was as if the past hadn't happened. It was like I could scrape all the years off leaving just the foundations, just the truth; the illogical truth. I knew, lying there, that there was no point in denying it. My feelings on the bus had jolted me to the core and I couldn't ignore them. Seeing Luke, Luke with another woman, for whatever reason, had been like a kick in the stomach. The news of Sian had come as a nasty shock that I'd somehow managed to bury but this time, I'd *seen* him with Laura. This was different. The very thought that he might be seeing her had shaken me so deeply I could hardly breathe when I thought of them together. It was no use. I had to face up to it. These emotions bubbling up inside me were far from the hatred I'd tried to believe they were at Mr H's party. The feelings coursing through me were ones I'd felt before; deep intense feelings. Now all I had to do was figure out a way to stop them surfacing and ruining my life all over again.

Chapter Seventy-one

I trudged through the following week, the run up to the wedding, trying to act positive. Everything felt so out of control. Part of me wanted to ring Tony, to try and snap out of my feelings for Luke and stop all the nonsense going round my head.

True to his word, Tony had been texting me from Geneva but, unlike our previous text fest, full of innuendos and suggestions, each time I answered, I had to wrack my brains to think of a suitable response. One that wouldn't commit me to anything but that wouldn't end our relationship either.

I stayed as 'up' as I could, mainly for Catherine's sake. This was her time and I didn't want to ruin anything. Besides, with Timmy hanging round the place in search of salvation, I had to stay strong for him too.

However, out of the gloom came a welcome spark. I received a reply from my job application. I had an interview.

I rang and arranged a suitable date for after the wedding and as I put the phone down, I knew I'd done the right thing handing in my notice. Mr Welles had told me formally that Baz, Margot's future husband, was starting. I had precisely three weeks to get a job. Even if this new company wasn't for me, I'd find something. I was sure of it.

On the Thursday evening, I went round to Catherine's flat. She had collected her dress and was dying to try it on again. She was a little stressed, because she was convinced she'd put on weight since the fitting and was worried about getting into the dress again. So I had brought round my own scales and, with a bit of surreptitious fiddling with the dial, she had in fact lost two pounds, the dress had fitted her perfectly and all was well in Camp Wedding.

In just twenty-four hours, we would be heading up to the Hillside Grange Hotel where the reception was being held and where I was spending one night with Catherine and supposedly a second night with Tony. It was a gorgeous country hotel, about ten miles outside Tillmouth. Old beams and open fires, silver service and four-poster beds. Nico's family were incredibly wealthy and had insisted on paying for the hotel accommodation along with most of the day. There had been talk of going to the Tillmouth Manor, but Nico wanted to get away from work, besides he was concerned he'd start clearing up tables after the meal.

Catherine and I were due to leave the following afternoon, to get to the hotel in plenty of time for some pampering beauty treatments in the spa then we'd have our hair and makeup done on Saturday morning, the morning of the wedding, along with the other bridesmaids, Catherine's two little nieces.

I'd avoided calling Tony all week but he had called me from Geneva just as I was leaving work earlier that evening. He was full of the joys of spring.

'I know it's cheating, but I had to call. Guess what?'

'What?' My voice was flat.

'The hotel room I booked for Saturday night has got a Jacuzzi.'

I knew, at that point, I should have said something. Something like, 'Er sorry, Tony, but I can't go through with it; I'm having weird feelings about your brother, see?' or, 'Why don't you stay in Switzerland for another week, we can manage here, it's only a wedding for goodness sake,' or even, 'Sorry matey, I've spontaneously combusted and you're talking to my long lost twin sister.' Something. Anything! But I didn't. I just made the right noises and let the moment pass. I even said 'Me too' when Tony said 'Luv ya' before we hung up. How silly is that? Why do we do these things? Talk about covering up your true feelings.

And so now here I was living a lie. Poor Tony was going to think all was well and that we were going to have a night of unbridled passion, when all I could think about was his bloody brother who, for all I knew, was off in the land of love with Tony's ex bloody fiancée Laura!

I managed to break away from my thoughts and smiled as I watched Catherine glowing at the sight of her reflection in the mirror above the fireplace. She was standing on top of the coffee table to get a good look as the mirror had the most flattering lighting in her flat. Tom eyed her suspiciously from her armchair. For his part in the celebrations, he had been given a bow tie, bought from Joshua's at an incredibly hefty price. Catherine said that Nico could always wear it afterwards. I momentarily wondered whether Tom was actually going to *be* at the wedding but Catherine went on to say he would be wearing it in their honour back at the flat and it would be just like he was there with them. I wrestled with a picture of Tom seated at the top table with his bow tie and top hat, eating with a knife and fork and meowing his distaste at being offered bread; as if the staff hadn't been told enough times of his delicate stomach. But as Tom dismounted the armchair and headed over to slither round my ankles, I remembered that I was actually rather fond of him and he could have a bow tie and a wheat intolerance if he wanted to.

Catherine looked down at me gleefully.

'It's finally happening, Mags. Can you believe it?'

'I know; this time on Saturday, you'll be Mrs, Mrs, what's his name again?'

'Oh, Maggie, what are you like, it's Moretti,' she admonished.

'Mrs Catherine Moretti. It sounds like a film star's name.'

'Do you think so?' She was clearly pleased.

'Or a Mafia boss's wife,' I chuckled. 'Have you checked out his family history?'

Catherine looked genuinely concerned so I changed the subject.

'Are you going to learn Italian?'

'Yes, most definitely. Nico's already begun teaching me a few words and I've bought an Italian dictionary.' She pointed over to her table in the window, where it lay open beside her Cedric the Pig mug.

'I've even started practising some words so I can greet his parents properly when I see them again. I keep getting a bit lost though. So many of the words seem the same and I get muddled up.'

'You'll be fine. They already think you're lovely. And Mr Moretti gave you that smelly cheese. I think that says it all. Don't you?'

I had brought a bottle of champagne round as a little celebration. So I popped the cork and poured each of us a glass. I sat watching her glowing at her own reflection. She was unmistakably happy.

'Cat?'

'Yes?'

'Do you think things will be the same when you're married?'

'No, I won't be a virgin anymore!' she cried happily.

'I didn't mean that, I meant...'

'What?'

'Well, we'll still be best friends won't we?' I could feel a lump in my throat.

Catherine stepped down, a bit inelegantly, from the coffee table and came and sat next to me on the edge of the sofa. She took my hand and gave it a squeeze.

'Maggie, you will *always* be my best friend; always. And just because I'm getting married and moving away, doesn't mean…' she trailed off.

She paused, her eyes widened as she clearly realised what she'd said.

'Moving away!? MOVING AWAY!?' I cried. 'Where??'

'Um, well, Tillmouth of course. I thought you might realise?' she said very unconvincingly.

'No! I didn't realise!' I was near to tears. 'I just assumed you'd be here in this flat, the two of you.'

'Oh, Maggie, I've been trying to find a way to tell you but I didn't know how. And now I've blurted it out like this. I'm so sorry. Please don't be too upset.'

'But when? When are you leaving?'

'Not for a while yet; I still have to sort things out with the landlord here and Nico is going to stay on at the hotel for a bit longer while I work my contract out at the hospital. But then we'll…' She stopped for a moment. 'Oh heck, I was going to save it as a surprise announcement at the wedding but I might as well tell you now.'

'Tell me what?' My voice was high and anxious.

'Nico's parents have offered to buy us a house in Tillmouth. Can you believe it? I didn't realise how wealthy they were! I was completely overwhelmed when they told us.'

'A whole house!'

'Yes, all we have to do is find one.'

'What a chore,' I said sulkily. I knew I was being childish and churlish but I couldn't help it.

Catherine rubbed my hand like I *was* a child.

'I'm sorry it's come out like this. I'm going to miss you dreadfully. Promise me you'll come and stay.'

I looked across at her and wondered how I would cope when she was gone. Tears filled my eyes.

'I'll miss you so much,' I choked, feeling physically sick at my imminent loss.

She leant over and hugged me, the two of us tearfully sniffling over each other's shoulders.

'I want my own room!' I half cried, half laughed, holding on to her tightly but pushing my grief back down and forcibly stopping the tears that still wanted to fall.

We pulled away and Catherine took a couple of tissues from a box on the table, passing me one. We wiped our eyes.

'So you will visit then?'

'Of course I'll come and visit! I'm not joking about the room; I'll be up so often you won't be able to get rid of me.'

I paused, more tears escaping of their own accord.

'But I really don't want you to leave!'

'It won't be so bad.' Catherine soothed. 'It's not that far away. Maybe you and Tony can get married and move in next door?' she said, very half-heartedly.

I studied her face carefully and she looked away.

'You don't like him do you?' I said, finally facing up to what I'd suspected for a while.

She sighed.

'It's not that I don't like him, it's just...'

'What...?'

'Well, I don't really trust him.'

My eyes widened.

'I'm sorry, Mags, I don't mean to be horrid but I am your best friend and I think you'd always want me to be honest with you, wouldn't you?'

I nodded glumly.

'Don't get me wrong,' she continued, 'I don't dislike him; in fact, he's been very charming and funny most of the time and we did kind of grow up with him... in the background anyway, but... oh I don't know, maybe I'm imagining things and being overly protective of my best buddy but there's something I can't quite put my finger on.'

'You could try?'

Catherine hesitated.

'I suppose it's more of a feeling I get, women's intuition perhaps? Although there is one thing.'

'Oh?'

'I keep thinking about that note Nico delivered to Tony at the farm, when he couldn't get in touch with me on holiday. What if Tony did get it and decided not to respond? I got the impression he didn't like Nico when he met him at Mr H's barbeque. I haven't had the guts to ask Tony, though.'

I could feel my heart growing heavier by the second.

'And there's something else too,' Catherine continued.

'I thought there might be.'

She squeezed my hand. 'I'm sorry but I have to say this, Mags. I don't think he treats you very well, not really. Not like you deserve to be treated anyway.'

I shrugged sulkily, feeling unable and unwilling to argue in Tony's defence.

Part of me wanted to tell Catherine how I felt about Luke and about all my issues with Tony and my fear of being left alone but I didn't want her to feel responsible for me, so I kept quiet.

'I just want you to be happy, Mags. You don't look it you know. I couldn't bear it if you got hurt.'

I saw the worry in her face and suddenly felt selfish. This wasn't the time or place to be talking about me and my stuff.

I straightened up and passed her her glass.

'Now listen you, don't worry about me, I know how to handle Tony Henderson. Come on, get that champagne down you and let's concentrate on getting you ready for the big day.' I hoped I sounded braver than I felt.

Later that evening Catherine and I began packing her things. There were clothes and make-up everywhere and her dress hung in cellophane on the back of her bedroom door.

'I'm worried I might forget it if we leave it there.'

'Fear not,' I said, 'I've already put a Post-it note on the front door. Oh, and before I forget, I've brought you something for Saturday.' I picked up my handbag and took out a little box I'd wrapped earlier.

'A present! What is it?'

'Open it and find out.' I handed her the small package and she sat down on her dressing table stool.

She unwrapped the paper and opened the little box, revealing a pair of intricately- crafted, dangly pearl earrings to match her dress and her grandmother's antique necklace.

'Oh Maggie, they're absolutely beautiful!' she exclaimed.

'I didn't think you were that keen on the ones you had, so I thought these might be better. I hope you like them.'

'They're adorable!' Turning to her reflection in the dressing table mirror, she put them on.

'They're perfect, just perfect. Thank you so much.' She came over and hugged me tightly.

'They can be your "something new".'

'Yes! And my grandmother's necklace is my something old. I've got a lacy blue garter for "something blue".' She picked it up from the side, and twirled it round her finger.

'And then for my something borrowed, Pauline's lending me…' Catherine shot her hand up to her mouth. 'Oh no, Pauline's bracelet; what with everything going on, I forgot all about it! How am I going to get it?' she cried.

'It's fine, Cat. I'll call Pauline and get her to drop it in to the hotel room. Don't worry.'

'Yes, but what if it's an omen?? I've got to have everything in place, Mags, otherwise something's bound to go wrong,' she wailed. 'Ohhhh, and I didn't want anyone to see me before the church.'

'Then she can hand it over to me. Relax! You and your bloody omens.'

We headed for bed at ten o'clock and I brought us both a cosy mug of milky hot chocolate for sound sleeping purposes. I sat on Catherine's big bed as she climbed in and snuggled up under her quilt. Passing her a mug, we began sipping earnestly.

'I can't believe you're getting married. My best friend is getting married.' I smiled a little dolefully at her.

Catherine, my oldest and closest friend was about to be whisked off into the world of marriage. And all of a sudden, as if they had been waiting for permission which had just been given, my real tears came. Catherine reached across and took my drink from me, placing both mugs on the bedside table, then she leant over and cuddled me tightly and let me cry. Just like she had all those years ago after I'd been with Luke. Only this time she couldn't promise to look out for me and be my bestest buddy in the world and always be there for me, because now she wouldn't be. Not in the same way. Things would change, they had to now. And despite my brave face earlier, I was sad; really, really sad.

'Maggie. It will be OK you know, truly it will. You'll see. I know that, right now, it doesn't seem that way but we'll never be apart, not really.'

'But you'll be so far away. What am I going to do without you?' I sobbed.

'You can come and stay, whenever you like and for as long as you like. And if you don't get a job in London, you can move in with us and get a job there instead then find a flat nearby and it'll be just like the old days.' She passed me a tissue.

I blew hard.

'Do you really think so?' I sniffed.

'Yes, really. You can do whatever you want with your life, hun. You don't have to stay in London if you don't want to. The world's your oyster. You've just got to know what you want and then follow your heart,' she said, quoting wisely from her 'bibles'.

'I suppose so.' I dried my eyes on my sleeve.

'I'm sorry. I'm supposed to be looking after you!' I laughed, sniffing noisily.

With my tears cried, I felt a little clearer in my head and we sat and finished our drinks then I tucked her in.

'My last but one night as single woman.'

'Your last but one night of sleeping alone!'

'Goodbye, virginity!' she hugged herself.

Goodbye, Catherine, I thought to myself.

Chapter Seventy-two

I woke up to find the sun streaming through the cracks in the curtains. I was sleepily considering the day ahead when the door swung open with great gusto, banging loudly against the wall and making me jump.

'Oh my God, oh my God, it's tomorrow!' Catherine burst in, exclaiming loudly to the air. 'I'm nowhere near ready, I'm sure I've forgotten something. Where are my shoes?' Without waiting for a reply, she whooshed back out again, flapping noisily.

I remained snuggled under my duvet, in relative calmness, wondering whether half a bottle of rescue remedy would be dangerous in Buck's Fizz the following morning. Today would no doubt be nothing by comparison. Catherine had already made me promise to get up at seven thirty the next day, and the wedding wasn't even until two!

Later that morning, when we were packing the car up, Catherine was uncharacteristically barking orders, but I gracefully allowed myself to be cautioned, reprimanded and admonished, while trying to make sure everything was packed into my newly cleaned car. Considering the circumstances, I decided she was allowed the odd personality defect.

With the car all packed, we did a final, final, FINAL check of our luggage and then Catherine almost had a heart attack as Tom poked his head out from behind my legs. He had obviously followed me down in the lift and didn't look like he had any intention of going anywhere but into the car with us. I winked at him and he nudged my calf.

Once Tom was safely secured back in the flat and his babysitter had been called – again – and arrangements had been double-checked, we were off.

After several minutes of trying to find a route B, in case our normal route had been subjected to a freak accident or an earthquake or something like that, then another ten minutes of Catherine mentally rechecking that all had been packed, and then another ten of going over the plans for the wedding, she finally fell asleep. Not before pointing out that it would be her final car journey as a single woman. Which had gone with previous expressions like 'the second to to last breakfast I'll have as a single woman' and 'the last time I'll be in my flat as a single woman', which then encouraged thoughts that it won't be if Nico bottles out and changes his mind, and 'what if he has? Then what?' Or 'What if his parents have decided they don't like me after all? Will they still buy us the cottage?' And so on. Even asleep, she looked fretful.

The peace and quiet gave me some breathing space and time to piece together the enormity of what would be occurring the following day. Not just to Catherine but to me. I was currently trying to convince myself that Luke was actually a really bad person who didn't deserve my constant stomach swooning whenever I thought about him and that Tony was in fact a really good person who did. Why was life always so complicated?

We finally arrived at the hotel and drove up the long winding drive.

Catherine stirred at the sound of gravel under the tyres. She opened her eyes flickeringly and rubbed them awake, before bolting upright.

'We're here!' she shrieked. 'Oh God, Maggie, we're really here!'

'We are,' I said calmly.

'You know, I'm arriving here as a single woman and...' she paused, her voice deepening, 'I'll be leaving as Mrs Catherine Lucy Moretti, wife of Nico Alessandro Moretti.'

'Do you think you'll feel like a different person?' I asked as I parked the car in the car park to the rear. I switched off the engine and turned to see Catherine deep in thought.

'I think I might you know. I think I might feel more... grown up. Yes, more of an adult.'

'You'll have to practise writing your new name,' I said.

'You mean like this?' Catherine whipped out her address book, turned to the back note pages and revealed several pages of Mrs Catherine Moretti scrawled in big loopy letters across them. 'Nothing like being prepared, that's what I say.' She grinned.

We carefully unloaded our dresses which Catherine clutched protectively to her as I hauled out our cases then we locked up and made our way across the gravelled car park and round to the front of the hotel.

Catherine and I stood back and stared at the facade. It was stunning. A huge white palatial building with white pillars flanking wide steps up to the largest front door I think I'd ever seen. More steps to the side of the hotel went down to huge lawns and an ornate fountain spouted around the Venus de Milo *with* arms. So not *the* Venus de Milo at all really, maybe a distant relative. Perhaps even a sister, or maybe…

'Maggie! Stop daydreaming, I need you with me!' Catherine's voice interrupted Venus's family tree.

Having checked in at the huge ebony reception desk surrounded by cream marble flooring, a couple of bellboys took our luggage and we were pointed in the direction of the swooshing-doored, silently moving lifts. Once up on our floor, we padded along the silent, lushly carpeted corridors, marvelling at the silk wallpaper and gilt-edged pictures of landscapes and country scenes that adorned the walls. We found our room entitled 'Willow' at the end of a spacious but short corridor with no other rooms off it. Amazingly, 'Willow' turned out to be a suite. It was huge! Catherine's parents had paid for tonight's and the following night's accommodation when Nico would be joining Catherine for their first night together. I tried not to dwell on the following night. A night I was supposed to be spending in a room with Tony.

Catherine burst in excitedly. 'My God, it's almost as big as my flat! I had no idea Mum and Dad were booking a suite!'

We marvelled at the mini bar, which was actually more like a real bar. There were even two bar stools and a cocktail shaker.

Catherine picked up a note from the coffee table, pinned down by an expensive looking bottle of bubbly. It read:

To our darling daughter and of course our wonderful new son-in-law.
We wanted you to celebrate in style.
All our love Mum and Dad XXX

Catherine kissed the note and hugged it to her.

'Oh bless them!' she cried, happily.

'Look at your bed! It's huge!' I shrieked, running through some double doors, which led to what appeared to be the main bedroom. After a hunt round, opening various doors, I discovered a second, smaller bedroom off the main living area and sat down then lay back on the ample, firm, bed, swishing my arms around like I was making a snow angel, marvelling at the grandness of the suite. Catherine had headed out through the French windows to check out the wide balcony.

'I feel like royalty,' she called. 'Come and see this view!'

I joined her and the two of us stood side by side, leaning over the ornate black railings, marvelling at the beautifully kept lawns surrounded by silvery winter borders. Giant oaks and towering silver birches flanked the edges and a low mist hung over the patchwork fields moulding the sumptuous curves of the land as far as the eye could see. Crows called impatiently from branches and a wood pigeon, calm by comparison, sounded in the distance. Apart from the cries of the birds, the only sound was the constant cascade of water from the fountain. The sun was hidden and the damp chilly air caused me to pull my jacket around me.

Catherine pointed to our left where a cordoned-off area housed an unlit bonfire in its centre.

'That must be where the fireworks are going to be tomorrow night. I wonder if they'll put bride and groom guys on top of the bonfire.'

A wooden construction that looked like it was set up, aptly enough, for Catherine Wheels, had been erected to one side and a pile of colourful outside lights and decorations were strewn across a groundsheet ready to enhance the celebrations.

'God, I'll be wetting my knickers tomorrow I'll be so nervous.'

'Don't worry. I'll be plying you with Buck's Fizz as soon as I can.'

'In that case I'll be wetting my knickers with Buck's Fizz.' Catherine moved back into

the room and sat down on a chaise longue.

'Poor Nico will be stuck in his bedsit tonight,' I pointed out. You gonna call him?'

'No! It might be bad luck to talk to the groom before the big day. She slid her shoes off, tucked her feet up underneath her and picked up the leather-bound room menus from the low coffee table. 'Anyway, he'll be fine. And so will we!' she sang happily.

I went through and checked out the bathroom, which had a massive wet area with a Jacuzzi and the biggest taps I had ever seen. The walls and ceiling were mirrored, which was a little disconcerting as I went to the loo. Face to face with my own reflection I could almost see the butterflies in my stomach growing larger and larger. I could feel a mini-bar moment coming on.

I went back in and saw Catherine had seemingly read my mind having poured out two whiskies.

'I thought these might prepare us for our spa treatments... plus get rid of my nerves!'

We had arranged the works for that evening: massages, manicures, pedicures, body scrubs, all sorts. We both agreed Catherine would need something relaxing to take her mind off the following day… in fact we both would.

Sure enough, the treatments did the trick. I don't think either of us had been more blissfully chilled in our lives. Having had our hands and feet 'icured, our thighs pummelled, and our scalps Indian head massaged, it was the Japanese hot stone, cold ice thingamajig massage that finally left us so zoned out we could hardly walk, let alone string sentences together. From the spa, we bumped our way sleepily along corridor after corridor unable to find our room, until we realised we were on completely the wrong floor, but we finally reached our suite and collapsed onto my bed, heavy with sighs and moans.

'That was awesome.' Catherine sounded like a hippy.

'Totally.' I joined her.

'Do you think that's where the expression getting stoned comes from?' she asked, referring to our incredible Japanese hot stone massages.

'Probably.'

'Heaven.'

'Definitely.'

'Do you think, on our salaries, we could warrant a session like that every week?'

Catherine asked hopefully.

'Definitely not.'

'Shame.'

'Totally.'

'We could always head down to Brighton beach and pick up a few stones then stick them in the oven for half an hour.'

'Or the microwave.'

'Good idea. Even quicker.'

'Probably a bit too hot though. We'd end up with great welts on our backs.'

'Shame.'

There was no way we were going to the restaurant that night, we felt too out of it. So I, being the non-bride, had the job of ordering room service.

'Was I OK?' I asked Catherine as I replaced the receiver. 'I can't really remember what I ordered.'

'You were fine until you called the waiter darling,' she said lazily.

'Did I?'

'No,' she giggled.

I half-heartedly tried to lift my arm up and hit her with a cushion, without much success.

Two house salads and two glasses of 'just the one – strictly for medicinal purposes' champagne arrived half an hour later and we ate without saying much, hungry after our treatments. Afterwards, feeling a little more awake, we lay on the bed, propped up by pillows, sipping our drinks in comfy silence. Catherine was the first to speak.

'Do you still think about Luke?'

I hoped I didn't look as startled as I felt.

'Why do you ask that?'

'Just a feeling I get sometimes.'

'What kind of a feeling?'

'A feeling that… maybe the two of you might have gone well together, that's all,' she said, burping champagne as confirmation.

'I thought you said before that some things were better left in the past and that I should accept we weren't meant to be.'

She shrugged.

'I know; I did say that didn't I.'

'Yes. You did.'

'It's just that… well, if I'm honest…'

'Weren't you being honest before then?' I interrupted.

'Yeah, yeah I was,' she said sleepily, 'but… it seemed more relevant then. I can't remember why.' She sighed.

'But, I guess I always thought that you and Luke were… you know… good together. I kind of hoped you might end up as a couple.'

I fell silent.

'So, do you?' she asked.

'Do I what?'

'Think of him.'

'Sometimes,' I admitted.

'Sometimes a little, or sometimes a lot?'

I said nothing.

'Thought so. I saw the way you were when we saw him with Laura.'

I looked down and pretended to examine my newly manicured nails. Then I spoke, quietly. Truthfully.

'I'm not sure I can forgive him for what he did to Sian. He left her high

566

and dry with a baby on the way. How could he do that?' It was the one shred of doubt I was managing to cling on to, to stop myself going insane with desire.

'Is that the real reason? Or has it got something to do with what happened when… you slept with him?' she asked carefully.

'What do you mean?'

'Well, you now know he thought you were pregnant back then and that's why he didn't call you, right?'

'So?'

'So, isn't this the same pattern repeated? Maybe it's not the Sian thing that's annoyed you, maybe it's really that?'

I sighed.

'Imagine being left on your own with a baby,' I said distantly.

'I'm right aren't I? That's just it. You feel for her because you can imagine how you would have felt,' she said calmly.

I felt my stomach and throat tighten.

'You know, Mags, he was ever so young. You both were. I bet Luke was so scared that he didn't dare get in touch. He probably thought everyone would be out to get him.'

'Why are you sticking up for him?' I asked, grumpily.

'I don't know.' She paused. 'I suppose I don't like to see any of the gang falling out that's all. Besides, there are two sides to every story and…' she trailed off.

'What?' I urged accusingly.

'Look, don't have a go at me for saying this but I think Luke was really brave to approach you at his dad's party. He must have felt awful, especially when you wouldn't talk to him.'

I felt myself blushing hotly.

'Whose side are you on?'

'I know it might be hard but couldn't you just try and talk to him? Let him explain? It might make things easier all round tomorrow.'

'But what if I had been pregnant, what then?' I tried to fight back the tears that were already pricking at my eyes.

'He would probably have been even more scared but I should think, knowing Luke, he would have done the right thing. Scared or not, he's not one to turn his back on people.'

'He's turning his back on Sian,' I said huffily.

'Yes, but we don't know what's gone on between them, we've never even met her. Maybe she's really awful and perhaps she doesn't want Luke involved, or maybe... well anything could have happened. Don't you think you might be judging him a bit harshly?'

A ball of anxiety was mounting in my stomach. I wondered what I was most afraid of. Forgiving Luke? Or the fact that, if I did, I would have to admit that I was finding it more and more difficult to use Sian and the past as an excuse anymore.

Chapter Seventy-three

The alarms (four of them) had been set for seven thirty and I woke up with a horrific jolt from such a deep sleep, my heart pounding ten to the dozen. Two of the alarms were across the other side of the room, so I groggily threw back the covers, swung my legs over the side of the bed and, after a few of moments of semi-conscious blurriness, made my way grudgingly over to turn them off. There was no question of staying in bed. I had to be in charge today. Catherine would be a wreck.

I knocked quietly on her door to wake her up gently.

'Come in!' Catherine's voice shrilled anxiously.

I entered to find her sitting bolt upright, her eyes wide and fixated.

I sat down on the edge of her bed, breaking her trance.

'What's wrong, hun?'

It transpired she had woken at six and hadn't been able to get back to sleep. She was panicking about her eye bags.

'I'm going to look like a panda!' she cried hysterically, waving her handbag mirror at me. I wondered whether it was too early for Buck's Fizz.

'Sit down and breathe slowly,' I said calmly, getting up and going to the fridge for the little Tupperware pot of cucumber slices I had packed the previous day.

'What made you bring that??' she asked incredulously.

'I wanted to be prepared in case something like this happened!' I grinned and went to put the kettle on.

Having been to the loo (and got the shock of my life when I realised that my new baby doll nightie, instead of making me look cute, in fact made me resemble a giant toddler) I came out and found Catherine cradling her knees and rocking herself gently on her bed.

I sat down beside her again.

'It'll be OK you know.'

She turned to me, her face scared.

'Will it? How do you know? I mean, what if it's too soon? What if I've made a mistake? What if we aren't right for each other and we have too many language problems and what if…?'

'Cat, sweetie, where's all this come from? You've been over the moon about getting married. What's changed?'

'I don't know… really.'

'Come on, what is it?'

'I'm probably just being silly.'

'About what?'

Her lip started quivering and I thought her face was about to crumple.

'What if he takes one look at my body and hates it? What if he thinks I'm ugly?'

'What? What are you talking about? He thinks you're beautiful. And you are!'

'I don't feel very beautiful.'

'Well you are, trust me. You wait 'til you get your dress on later.'

'But that's just it. I'll be clothed; hidden!'

'Nico saw you on holiday in a swim suit didn't he?'

'Yes, but I always wore a sarong over it so he never really saw me properly.'

'OK, but what about at the reunion and then after Mr Henderson's party. You shared a bed for goodness sake!'

'I know. But it was dark and I had most of my clothes on, so that doesn't count.'

'OK, well…' *Think, Maggie, think…*

A sudden memory punched its way into my consciousness.

Of course!!!

'Cat, listen, you told me he loved your body.'

'When?'

'The morning after the reunion. You said he hated skinny women and loved how comfy you were. He said you made him feel safe.'

'Did he?'

'*Yes!* You came in and told me the next day, I promise you. I can't believe you've forgotten that. I thought at the time what a lovely thing it was to say.'

Tears pricked at Catherine's eyes. 'Maybe.'

'Maybe nothing. Come on, you must remember.'

'Kind of.'

'It may not have been those exact words but I absolutely promise you it was near enough.'

Her forehead furrowed and I watched as she dug deep into her memory.

'You know I think he might have done. I remember something about it because... yes, because I was wondering, at the time, if it was true that Italian men liked their wives to look like their mothers – and she is big; very big.'

'See!'

'Oh, Mags I think you're right. I do remember.' She lit up like a chandelier. 'So he really does love me as I am.'

'Totally.'

She looked relieved but her face quickly fell again.

'He still hasn't seen me without clothes though.'

'I'm pretty sure that if he loves your body with clothes on, he's liable to love it even more with clothes off, don't you think?'

Catherine still seemed worried.

'That's not all though.'

'Go on...?'

'I know I'm being silly but I'm so nervous about tonight. It's my first time with a man, properly with a man. I'm not sure what to expect. I've only ever seen one real penis and that was by accident. Unless you count all those photos in that copy of *Playgirl* we found in your mum's bedroom when we were young, and they made me feel ill just looking at them!'

'I still can't believe my mum read *Playgirl*,' I said, thinking back.

'What if it's too small?'

'Or too big!' I suggested.

'I don't think that would worry me as much?'

'No, fair enough.'

'I think it's probably a bit late to worry now. You love each other, that's what counts; and you'll make it work, yeah?'

She nodded then she smiled.

'Perhaps you could phone me tonight and give me instructions as we go along?'

'I could draw you a map and some diagrams if you like. Mind you, after my last attempt in bed with a man, I think it might be me that needs help!'

The morning whizzed past after that. We showered and washed our hair, oiled and powdered and pampered ourselves until we were gleaming, then donned our bathrobes.

The hairdressers came at eleven. There were two, one for Catherine and me and one for Catherine's little nieces, who'd arrived shortly beforehand with their father Mike, Catherine's brother-in-law. Mike was a broad northern 'I speak as I find' bloke, under strict instruction to leave his wife Clare, Catherine's sister, in peace to get ready. Obligingly, he'd delivered the girls but on seeing all the girlie underwear and products around the suite, he'd blushed and bolted off to the hotel gym.

Catherine had her hair subtly streaked with a lighter blonde to show off her tanned skin, she was then blow-dried and her hair beautifully pinned up before pearly flowers and sparkling diamante were threaded in and out. Finally, a delicate tiara of twinkling stars was added. She looked gorgeous.

The hairdresser somehow convinced me to go curly! I was horrified at first but she came across so kind and trustworthy and assured me it would be really special so, with some of Catherine's rescue remedy, I was chilled enough to let her do her thing. When she'd finished I was almost as much in shock as I had been when I'd straightened it for the first time. Instead of the usual frizzy mass, she'd somehow managed to coax the curls into glossy spirals that cascaded dramatically around my shoulders. She'd used a curling tool that had created the most perfect corkscrew ringlets, now framing my face, and she'd put on a special light serum making my gypsy-like hair shine like never before. Sparkling red and clear stones were strategically threaded through my masses of dark locks, which reflected and gleamed in the light when I moved. She finished off with a flourishing spray of ultrafine glitter that twinkled like tiny little fairy lights. I felt like a model!

'Gosh! I think that's even better than straight, Mags!' Catherine marvelled as I paraded in front of her in my underwear and new hairstyle. 'That must be the most amazing I've ever seen you look!'

I was completed chuffed and blown away with my new style.

'I can't believe I've gone all his time and not known it was possible to avoid the frizzy bush look. What a waste of twenty-eight years of hairstyles. I actually like it curly!'

Jasmine and Kate, the little ones, were like perfect dolls. They had put their little red dresses on first and, once their hair was piled up and positioned in place, they were walking around like they had books balanced on their heads and didn't dare move in case they fell off. They, too, had been sprayed with hair glitter, which they thought was very exciting and kept admiring themselves in the wardrobe mirror and turning their heads to catch the light. To keep them warm, they wore little white fur shawls around their shoulders. They'd have miniature red and white posies when they walked up the aisle and what with the red and white flowers that would, by now, be adorning the church in Tillmouth, we'd all complement each other perfectly in the red and white theme of the day.

The make-up lady arrived at midday and I felt this was perfect timing to crack the champagne open and sort out the Buck's Fizz. I even gave the make-up lady a glass and prayed silently that she wouldn't get too flamboyant with the blusher. I needn't have worried though; when she'd finished, Catherine and I looked like we had just stepped off a film set. She'd worked miracles and made us utterly glamorous with colour palettes to suit our skin tones and complement our dresses. Catherine had a subtler look with browns and mauves complemented by some delicate false lashes – just perfect for making her eyes huge and clear but still allowing her dress to be the shining star, whereas I was given a smokier more dramatic look and smouldered with smudged greys and black.

Kindly, she offered to look after the girls for a while, so we could finish getting ready. Time for the dresses.

I closed the doors to the main bedroom behind us and leant on them, pulling a face at Catherine.

'Here we go!'

Butterflies mounted in my stomach as I stepped into my lovely red dress, and Catherine helped me up with my zip and whistled at my reflection in the mirrors on the front of the fitted wardrobes. 'You'll look better than me!'

I wouldn't and I didn't want to, but I was secretly very pleased with my appearance. Then it was Catherine's turn. She needed a bit of help with doing up the intricate, pearled bodice and as she stood straight, I arranged the masses of rich ivory silk of her skirt so it flowed evenly around her. The tiny shining diamante, through the layers, picked out and matched her sparkling hair so she glimmered in the sun that had just come out and lit up the bedroom in beams of light through the window. I carefully dusted some delicate glitter shimmer over her bare flesh then gently positioned a silken shawl around her shoulders. Once she'd put on the necklace and earrings, I took a step back, shaking my head in wonder.

'You look so beautiful.' I felt tears mount in my eyes.

'Don't cry, your mascara will run.'

I blinked the tears away and took both Catherine's hands.

'Love you.' I bit my lip.

'Love you too.' She smiled and we hugged tentatively, not wanting to ruffle each other up.

We turned back and admired ourselves in the mirror.

'This is it then, Cat. Your big day.'

'And night.'

'And life!'

'I feel like this is all a dream.'

I pinched her.

'Ouch! What was that for?'

'Just wanted to prove it was real.'

'OK, I got the message.' She frowned, rubbing her arm.

Out in the main part of the suite, the girls were getting very excited. They had cajoled the make-up girl into putting some light nail varnish on their fingernails and were busy admiring their little hands.

Running later than planned and on their way to change in Catherine's sister's room, Pauline and Jenny turned up briefly with the 'something borrowed' bracelet for Catherine who insisted on hiding in the bathroom until they'd gone so they wouldn't see her until the church.

When the girls were showing Pauline the balcony and the place where the fireworks would be that evening, Jenny and I were left alone.

'Can't believe you got to hear the fucking news first again,' she said crossly.
'Sorry.'

She shrugged. 'S'OK I s'pose.'

'How was the holiday?' I asked.

'Yeah, *seriously* great thanks.'

'You'll have to tell me all about it later.'

I paused, wondering how to say what I needed to say.

'Um…you OK… about… things? I mean… Pauline,' I ventured.

Jenny shrugged again.

'Yeah. Whatever floats her boat.'

'I'm sure she's relieved you don't mind.'

'She's still my bezzie mate. Ha! Now she's my lezzie mate too!' Jenny grinned then hushed her voice. 'She's meeting some bird in a bit.'

'I know.'

'You fucking would,' she snorted, rolling her eyes. 'She keeps telling me off for calling her a lezzer.'

I laughed.

'Can't call her a dyke either. Dunno what I'm supposed to call her.'

'Gay?' I suggested.

Jenny thought for a moment.

'Or just Paul' I s'pose. It's always worked before.'

They left, wishing us luck and, almost immediately, there was another knock at the door. In came the best man – Nico's cousin Matteo – with a handheld video camera. He had the task of filming the day and his first job was to get the all the girls in their splendour before the big event. Catherine introduced us all but Matteo only appeared to have eyes for the volume of Catherine's breasts which I guessed would be featuring quite heavily on camera.

Finally, video taken, Buck's Fizz downed and teeth re-cleaned, we were ready to go. We were just about to call reception to check on the cars, when there was another knock.

'Who on earth is that?' Catherine said, worriedly. 'It had better not be Nico. He knows he can't see me before the church.'

She picked up her skirts and rustled out of sight but it was her dad with the bouquets. In he came, smiling around the room. Catherine poked her head round the door then, seeing who it was, blushed and came into view. With such an intense look of paternal love, her father gazed at his daughter. Standing there in his top hat and tails, I don't think I'd ever seen anyone look so handsome and proud. I saw his eyes fill and he walked over and took Catherine by the hands taking in her appearance.

'You're like a princess.'

He stood back a little, still holding her hands and shook his head.

'I can't believe my little girl's getting married.' He kissed her lightly on the forehead and squeezed her hands. 'Good luck, sweetheart. Go and make your young man happy.'

The phone rang.

The cars had arrived.

The watery winter sun shone determinedly in the hazy blue sky and looked set to stay for the day. I headed off for the church with the bridesmaids leaving Catherine behind in the hotel lobby with her father.

We were driven along in a classic white Rolls Royce and the girls giggled and chattered excitedly beside me in the back seat. Our dresses rustled when we moved and our flowers smelled sweet and fresh. On my lap my elegant posy was larger than the girls'; a simple arrangement of deep scarlet and dazzling white roses. I lifted it to my nose and inhaled the exquisite fragrance. The butterflies in my stomach were growing in size and anyone would have thought it was me getting married. After what seemed like just a few nerve-wracking minutes, we arrived at the little church and the driver parked up, got out, circled round the back of the car and opened my door. Holding out his arm, I leaned forward and held onto it for safety as I carefully stepped out of the car. The girls followed and one by one, taking my hand, jumped down the high step from the car doorway, landing on the crunchy gravel. All giggles had stopped. It was almost show time.

Despite the sunshine it was very chilly. You could see our breath in the air but it made it all the more magical. The day was perfect for a wedding.

The promised red and white flowers, matching the bouquets, had been arranged in pots at the front gates to the church and around the entrance. Up ahead, the vicar was waiting to greet us all. I guided the little bridesmaids and we walked up the drive together and through the big old oak doors that led into the church, smiling and whispering our hellos to him.

The smell of old wood and incense, mixed with more flowers, filled my nostrils and the dulcet tones of the church organ reached my ears. I could see it was being played by one of the old school dinner ladies who had been there when we were at school. The girls and I stood to one side, behind a curtain that cordoned off a little vestibule. There we stayed, waiting, while the last guests arrived. The ushers were in the inner doorway, pointing people to their pews and, as I peered through the curtain, I could see that the church was full.

As the final few guests hurried through the main doors, on the ushers' instruction we came out and waited nervously between the inner and outer doors and I watched while they settled down in their places. People chatted excitedly to their neighbours, clearly buoyed up with expectant excitement as the time neared for the bride to walk down the aisle to meet her groom.

Up at the top of the church on the right hand side, Nico stood, hopping nervously from foot to foot, his hands in his pockets. Every now and then he turned round to check the doors, no doubt for signs of Catherine.

His parents, his skinny sisters and his brother sat in the front row and an array of Italian family members and friends took up the next few rows. I thought how great it was for Nico that they'd all flown over for the wedding.

Behind them was a collection of friends, most likely from the UK, including what appeared to be half the staff from the Tillmouth Manor Hotel.

I watched Nico's flamboyantly dressed mother for a few moments. Catherine had been right; in the nicest possible way, she was huge!

I could see my mother, sitting with Catherine's, at the front to the left, with the pew clear beside them for us to join them for the ceremony. I was now feeling very anxious. I would soon have to walk down the aisle in front of all those people. It was almost as nerve wracking as I imagined getting married myself would feel like. I hoped Catherine's cleavage would take the focus away from me. I quickly scanned the church. Tony would be there by now... so would Luke.

I watched Nico panicking as Matteo, who had joined him, was frantically feeling all his pockets and looking very worried. Then, laughing loud enough for me to hear him from where I stood, Matteo revealed the rings, safe and sound, from his trouser pocket and laughed even louder when Nico punched him, rather hard it seemed, on the arm.

The girls and I stood nervously waiting.

Then from behind me, I heard a car drive slowly on to the gravel outside. The vicar poked his head round.

'She's arrived,' he whispered.

The ushers were given the nod and hurried up the aisle to their places. I felt sick with anticipation.

I went to the outer door and watched as the white – this time vintage – Rolls Royce, drew up. Catherine was helped out of the wedding car by her father. She stepped down, righted her dress and, lifting it slightly from the ground, took his arm. The two of them moved gracefully up to the church entrance. In they came and stood beside us in the cold stone-floored entrance hall between the two sets of doors, just out of sight of the people in the church. The girls and I arranged Catherine's skirts again and trailed her train behind her. She looked at me and grimaced. I squeezed her spare hand and grimaced back. She took a couple more steps up to the inner doors and her father, beside her, gave her a last sideways glance and winked.

'Here we go, girl. Deep breath.' He smiled proudly at his daughter and took a deep breath himself.

The vicar squeezed passed us, wished Catherine good luck then walked quickly into the main church and up to the front by the altar. The organist was given the signal.

Pum pa pa pa pum pum puuuuum. Pum pa pa pa pum pum puuuuum.

Everyone in the church swivelled round in their seats to take their first peek at the bride. Women took out their hankies and men straightened their ties. We were off.

The *Wedding March* sounded out through the church. Ta tum ta tum, ta tum ta tuuum.

Catherine bit her lip and met my eyes for the last time as a single woman then, arm in arm with her father, began to walk slowly up the aisle.

Then it was our turn. I checked the girls, making sure they were close behind me, took my own calmative deep breath and began to walk slowly forwards, following Catherine and her father up the aisle.

We glided in our practised steps in time to the music, smiling at the guests as we went. I couldn't tell you who I smiled at, they were all a sea of hats and suits and colours. Nor could I tell you how long it took us, though it seemed like an eternity. But finally the eternity ended and we reached the front of the church where the vicar stood happily waiting to begin the ceremony.

My stomach was in my mouth as Catherine and Nico came to stand together and Catherine smiled coyly at her husband to be. Nico stood tall and proud like a love-struck teenager spilling over with emotion.

The vicar smiled warmly at them both and nodded at us to take our positions in the front pew.

Relieved, I settled myself and the girls in beside Catherine's and my parents, glancing along and whispering hushed hellos.

'Dearly beloved,' the vicar began, 'we are gathered here today…'

'You look utterly gorgeous,' a voice whispered from behind me. I turned round to see Tony leaning forward from the pew directly behind mine. I felt myself tense but smiled briefly, before quickly turning back to watch the ceremony.

Where was Luke?

Soon it was time for a hymn and, as we stood, I felt a hard jab in the back. With a good excuse to turn round and inspect the guests, I saw Jenny two rows back, leaning forward to get my attention. She shone, as pleased punch in an elegant fifties style skirt suit with black gloves and a black pillbox hat. A handsome, proud, John stood suited and booted to her left, and winked at me. A happy and healthy looking Pauline was to the right of Jenny and she gave a slight sideways nod to the young woman beside her who was small with a sweet face. She had short straight mid brown hair, little wire-rimmed glasses and piercing green eyes. I smiled.

'Sarah,' Pauline mouthed.

'Hello, Sarah,' I mouthed, giving her little wave before swivelling away again.

When Catherine and Nico got to the vows, I reached across to accept a tissue from Mum. As I did so, I heard a cough from somewhere not far behind me. Something about that cough made me turn round and I found myself staring straight at Luke, just a few rows back, looking as stunningly gorgeous as I had ever seen him look. The effect of the petrol blue suit against his blond hair and his bluer than blue eyes, brought out by the colour, was breath-taking. He stared back at me for a moment that was longer than comfortable with such intensity I forgot to breathe, and my mouth fell open. I willed myself to turn back to the front but the pull was almost too much. Luckily, Catherine's voice caught my attention as she repeated her vows after the vicar and I managed to turn to the front again, my heart beating wildly. But it was at that moment, that very moment that I knew for sure. Despite everything, despite the past and the way things had been between us over the last few months, I was every bit as in love with Luke now as I had ever been.

The service was beautiful but as the vicar said 'I now pronounce you man and wife' my recent fears were compounded. That was it. In some way, Catherine had gone from me. It didn't feel as though things would ever be quite the same again.

Later, as I watched the happy couple together I wondered when my turn would come. *If* my time would come.

We were shortly to assemble in the grounds for some outdoor photos. Even in winter the gardens were so pretty. The tall prominent trees stood majestically as a dramatic backdrop and the silvers, reds and greens of the shiny evergreens blindingly reflected the rays of the winter sun. After the outside shots, the bride and groom and close friends and family would go back inside to the lounge area for photos on the wide red-carpeted stairs next to the huge roaring open fire.

Where we stood, you could see everyone's breath meandering outwards and upwards in great streams of white and people were huddling together and rubbing their arms to keep warm. The photographer was happily busying himself moving this way and that, smiling and laughing effortlessly to keep everyone's spirits up as he arranged them to make his shots perfect. It was a far cry from the last wedding photographs I'd been snapped in. Thankfully, not a Stetson nor a 'yee ha' in sight.

Up I shivered for the bride and groom and bridesmaids shot, then up again for close family and bridesmaids. And again when he called 'friends of the bride'.

Like a jolt it hit me. Friends of the bride meant both Tony and Luke would be up there too. As I began to walk to the group, Tony slipped in step beside me and confidently slid his arm into mine before kissing me on the cheek. I inadvertently pulled away.

'Watch the make-up!' I tried to make a joke of it.

He narrowed his eyes a little but said nothing and we walked up to get into place. As we did so, I saw Luke watching us but, as he caught my eye, he looked away with a face like thunder. I grew distinctly uneasy.

When we were in place I glanced along the row at him and my nerves were replaced by a longing to run up to him and kiss him so hard and tell him that it was him I really wanted, not Tony. The moment we'd shared in the church had gone straight to the core of my hidden desires for Luke and whipped them up into a frenzy of lust and love. I now candidly remembered the ecstasy all those years ago of just knowing he had been in the same room as me. I remembered his touch, his smell, his face, his body, oh God, his body. I ached inside, I felt physically sick with longing. This was the feeling I had always had for Luke. The reason I'd had such intense anticipation about going to the reunion. The reason I'd felt the electricity at Pauline's when our hands had accidentally touched and the reason I knew I was completely and utterly in love with him. Whatever had happened in the past, these feelings were far too strong to ignore.

Tony's arm weighed heavily on mine in the middle row and, were it not for the fact that the photographer ordered us all to our different places which split Tony and me up, I would have felt compelled to move away from him anyway. He winked at me as we parted; 'later', he mouthed smiling seductively as if to him everything was fine. His life was sorted out, so it was only left for me to fall happily into his arms. But things had changed. I had changed. I couldn't do it anymore. In fact, I doubted whether I ever could have.

Then, as if things weren't getting uncomfortable enough, as we settled into the photographer's arrangement, Luke was positioned right behind me! The back of my head felt like it was on fire.

Timmy stood beside me and linked my arm, making me feel only marginally better. Jenny stood in front of me and belched.

Several frowning faces turned and looked at me! I nudged her hard in the back and heard her chuckle.

The photographer called for another helping of cheese and sex then more people were swapped around to be snapped and flashed. Everyone shivered through the photos, eager to move into the warmth of the reception and start on the champagne and canapés.

For just a minute or so, I was out on a limb on my own not needed in any of the shots. Once again, I felt him before I saw him. The surge of energy up the back of my right side sent me off balance and I knew, before he spoke, that he was there. Luke's warm, firm body smothered the air beside me. I could hardly breathe.

I almost melted as I stared up in to his blue, blue eyes. His blond hair was ruffled by the light breeze. I saw the way the cream shirt hugged his broad beautiful chest and set off the brown of his still-tanned skin. The skin on his neck inviting my touch. His wide full mouth begging to be kissed. I longed to run my hands through his hair and smell his familiar smell. Ten years was nothing. I could remember it all like it was yesterday.

His voice wakened my dreaming.

'So, you're continuing with this madness then?' he said, his tone flat, emotionless.

With a sudden shot of pain, so strong, surging through my body I realised then that it was too late. No matter what I felt for Luke, I saw in his face that he must have hated me for being with Tony. I'd let him down. I had to try and explain.

'It's not like that, Luke.'

'It is from where I'm standing.' It would have appeared to everyone else that nothing was wrong but close up his angry blue eyes were cold and hard and his voice was full of bitterness.

We stood in silence for a few moments.

'Why are you so angry, Luke?' I felt the need to at least keep him talking.

'Laura doesn't deserve all this. She hasn't taken it well.'

'What do you mean? That's not what she said in her letter.'

'What letter?' he frowned.

'The one she sent after Tony finished with her.'

Luke looked down at me with an odd expression on his face. He was about to say something, when the photographer called again.

'Men only please.'

'Just like a strip club!' some smart alec called from the crowd, making people laugh.

Luke turned and strode off to join them, glancing briefly over his shoulder at me, his brow furrowed into a perplexed frown.

I didn't see him outside again after that and finally it was time to go back into the hotel. The key members of the wedding party warmed up by the fire and more photos were taken on the stairs. Most people were in the lounge bar but once everyone was back inside and the photos had finished, we were called through to the main function suite. It was beautifully laid out. One wall was all glass with French doors to the gardens, flooding in great beams of bright yellow sunlight across the floor and tables. A huge chandelier hung from the centre of the room catching the light and twinkling, bringing what seemed like hundreds of tiny crystals to life. From the ceiling an array of sparkling decorations hung, with silver balloons and red and white ribbons. Two walls were strewn with soft white drapes from ceiling to floor and slashes of red silk had been draped over the tops in swags and tails especially for the occasion. Most of the main room had tables set out with flamboyantly creative red and white centrepieces, and little shiny red heart shapes were scattered like confetti across the cloths. The top table had matching balloons and streamers and the stunning wedding cake was set on a table to one side. Crystal champagne flutes glistened and sparkled as the sun, streaming through the windows, caught them. Another smaller bar with an ebony black bar-top was near the arched entrance and two small alcoves with cosy seats in nestled to one side, offering some escape from the main room. Then to the other side, there was a large area without tables and chairs, for people to stand and chat, with a dance floor right in the middle for later.

Catherine and Nico stood side by side near the main archway, flanked by two sets of proud parents, greeting people as they came in and smiling radiantly. Guests milled around with champagne and canapés, smiling and laughing. I loved weddings. I loved all the relations and friends together in their finery glowing and gushing over the bride and groom, and feeling gorgeous and attractive in their own wedding outfits. I loved the feeling of togetherness, the feeling of family; the atmosphere and the infectious laughter. It somehow made me forget everything else in life, just for that day, like it was a world of its own and nothing outside mattered. I wished I could have been with Luke together as a couple; sadly, though, I knew it wasn't to be. I glanced round anxiously searching for him and my eyes fell on my parents. They were heading towards me through the guests and, by the expression on Mum's face, she had something on her mind. She bustled up, immaculate in a two-piece lilac suit, followed by Dad who had been forced to buy a new suit and appeared to be hating every minute of being trussed up in it. When they finally reached me, Mum tugged at my arm and led me off to one side. Dad hung back, pulling a warning face.

'Maggie,' she whispered curtly. 'I need to talk to you.'

'What's wrong Mum?'

'What's wrong? I'll tell you what's wrong. I've just heard that your friend Pauline is…' she paused, glancing around quickly to see if anyone was listening, '… a lesbian!' she finished with a hiss.

I raised my eyes to the ceiling.

'And…?'

'What do you mean, "and"?'

'And what, Mum? What's your point?'

'Well, it's, it's not right. I mean she's a married woman. She can't just expect to up and change sides when the mood takes her. Her poor husband.' I looked at Dad and knew what she meant.

'"Her poor husband" has been having it away with his partner for months,' I retaliated and she blushed angrily.

'Listen, Mum, Pauline hasn't just done this on a whim. It's taken a lot of courage to come out like this. She's gay and that's that. You'd better get used to it.'

'People can't keep changing their minds when the going gets tough. All this talk of gay and straight, it didn't used to be like this. Men and women just got married and got on with it.'

'You know, our generation didn't invent being gay, Mum.'

'Well, it seems like they did.'

'You're just mad because you found out Louis Walsh was gay.'

Her lips pursed. 'That was a vicious rumour.'

'Whatever.'

'Next thing I know you'll be telling me you've followed suit,' she said, sniffily.

I paused. 'Oh so thaaat's it.'

'What? What's it?' She flushed.

'You're worried that it might be catching. It's not a disease, Mother!'

'I know that.'

'And you're quite safe, I'm still batting for the same side.'

'Maggie! Don't use those expressions.'

'I could use a lot worse!'

She was clearly quite worried, so I softened a little. Mum wasn't anti-gay, she really wasn't, but she was set in her rather old-fashioned ways and always seemed to feel that things like this, things close to home, would somehow reflect on her. That the neighbours wouldn't approve.

'Look, Mum, try not to think about labels. Pauline's Pauline and she's exactly the same person as she was before you found out.'

Mum hmmphed.

'Douglas, I need another glass of bubbly.' She waved her empty flute unseeingly in Dad's direction. I grinned at him as he flourishingly bowed behind her back then stepped forward with a wink in my direction, took her glass and headed off to find a waiter.

I spotted a friend of Mum's coming over so I took my chance for a quick exit.

'Must go, Mum. Stop worrying, yeah? It's the way of the world. Best to go with it rather than fight it.' I gave her a kiss and headed off for the loos.

I imagined her telling Dad that Pauline's new-found sexuality had obviously somehow had an unfavourable effect on me.

In the toilets I discovered Jenny, Pauline, Sarah and, bizarrely, Timmy, all having a good laugh about Catherine's cousin Robert, whose wandering hands had become a bit of a standing joke amongst the women. Jenny had apparently been about to black his eye but Pauline had stepped in and stopped her.

'I think even I'd draw the line at that little oik,' Timmy camped. 'Have you seen the *size* of that hideous ring!?'

'Well, he hasn't touched me.' I wondered if I should be put out.

'I shouldn't think he'd dare when you look like that,' Jenny said. 'Cool bridesmaid dress and the hair is *amazing*, Mags. Where've you been hiding that?!'

I laughed.

I caught Sarah's eye and she smiled.

'Hello,' she said tentatively.

'Hi.' I reached out to shake her hand but she leaned up from her short height and kissed me on the cheek.

'Pauline's told me all about you.'

'Oh dear,' I said.

Sarah nodded in agreement.

'Pretty much!'

A welcomed chuckle rippled through our group and I felt like a little hurdle had been successfully jumped.

I went to the loo and when I came out of the cubicle the others had gone and Catherine had come in and was at the mirror, reapplying her lipstick.

'Hello, Mrs Moretti.' I gave her a big hug. It was our first time alone since the hotel room.

She beamed at me in the mirror.

'I can't believe I'm married; it feels so surreal.'

'Happy?' I asked, washing my hands beside her.

'Delirious! I'm having such a perfect day. It's like something out of Mills and Boon. Apart from the fact I think I've just accidentally called Nico's mum a goat in Italian!'

I laughed.

'And look', she held up her left hand. 'It's official; I've got both rings to prove it.' The diamond engagement ring had been joined by a gold band with tiny diamonds in one single row along the middle of it.

'You've done it then. No turning back.'

'I'll let you know in the morning. The wedding's nothing compared to the wedding night. I'll have to pace myself or he'll be making love to me while I'm crashed out on the floor! How are things on the Henderson front? Any developments?'

'Well, I guess if you count realising I'm in love with Luke a development, then yes I suppose there has been one.'

Catherine eyes grew wide with shock.

'What? Really? Since when?'

'Oh, probably since the age of ten.'

'What on earth are you going to do?'

'Dunno. Nothing I guess. He's made it pretty clear he hates me for being with Tony and I can't say I blame him really.'

'Maybe I could say something,' she suggested.

'No! Don't tell him! I couldn't bear him knowing. I'm just going to have to end it with Tony somehow and then forget all about the Henderson brothers.'

'Poor you.'

'Oy, stop worrying about me. You've got a wedding reception to enjoy.' I linked my arm through hers and we headed back out. I hoped I'd sounded cool and casual enough to Catherine. I didn't want to ruin her wedding day with my tales of woe even though, underneath my façade, the pain of Luke being there was crucifying me.

Over at the little bar Catherine introduced me to the frightfully well-spoken and well-heeled Robert, her cousin with the roaming hands.

I needn't have worried about being left out of his fondlings. He soon made up for it and kept nudging my breast accidentally on purpose as he reached for his drink. Catherine had to disappear as more and more people wanted to congratulate her. So unfortunately I was left to fend for myself.

Robert's short podgy arms led down to short podgy hands and fingers where he sported a large, gaudy, gold ring set with a square black stone, flanked with what appeared to be diamonds. I could smell he'd been smoking a cigar and my stomach turned over.

'So, Magsie...' he began.

'Um, it's Maggie actually.'

'Of course it is. Huge apols! Huge apols!'

I sighed inwardly.

'So... *Maggie*, fwhah fwhah fwhah...' he chortled loudly, coughing splutteringly as he did so, causing me to cover my mouth, 'what does a ravishing young woman like you do on your days orf?' He licked his lips.

I did nothing to hide my distaste.

'Oh you know... the usual, nothing special.'

'Come on, come on. You'll need to give me a bit more than that, if I'm going to be able to chat you up properly, what!' His smarmy grin showed off somewhat yellow teeth, and his no-doubt expensive suit was far too big for him and made him look like he was auditioning for a position with the Mafia.

'I tend to stay in a lot, on my own, and read; very boring really.' I smiled sweetly.

'Well, in that case, you must allow me to take you out sometime. We can't have a gorgeous young filly like you staying in and being boring now, can we? What! I'd better take your number right away.' He reached inside his jacket pocket for his phone and began to swipe to his contacts.

A deep voice sounded from behind us. 'Maybe Maggie is perfectly happy just as she is.' For once, with impeccable timing, Tony had appeared. I felt almost relieved. Robert's face scowled momentarily on Tony's arrival but he graciously tipped his head at the competition and scanned the room for some other breast to rub. 'What!'

Tony led me away into one of the two unoccupied alcoves. Once we were on our own, he stood beside me and, as if he specifically intended people to notice, he proceeded to drape his arm loosely round my shoulders.

'Everyone will see us!' I complained.

'They'll know soon enough.'

I felt my whole body tense up. Here I was with Tony Henderson and I hadn't even told my friends we were seeing each other. Jenny would be so mad with me for not telling her and now I wanted out and didn't even want her to know!

We stood there in an uncomfortable silence staring out towards the crowd like a couple of ordinary onlookers watching the world go by. But I could feel the tension emanating from Tony and I could smell heavy alcohol fumes on his breath.

'I was beginning to think you were avoiding me.' He spoke without moving. His gaze still fixed on the room.

My breath caught painfully in my chest.

'No, it's just… I've been talking to people and looking after Catherine, that's all.' I knew I should have been asking him how his trip went and catching up on all the news but it felt all wrong.

'She doesn't appear to needs looking after now.' Tony nodded over to where Catherine and Nico were smiling into each other's eyes.

At that moment Luke crossed our path and, as if on cue, Tony leaned closer to me. Burying his face in my neck, he kissed it and breathed in heavily.

'You smell gorgeous, I can't wait for later,' he said loudly.

I wriggled uncomfortably beside him and managed to pull away but not before Luke's eyes bore into mine. His attention flickered on to his brother, then without a word he walked off. It was like their father's seventieth all over again, only this time the person I was desperate to escape from was Tony.

'Wonder what his problem is?' Tony said, downing the last of a large glass of whisky I suddenly saw he had in his right hand, and placing it on a nearby table.

'So, when are you going to make me the happiest man in the room then, Miss Parsons?'

He pulled me back towards him again and I moved my face away from the smell of his breath.

'Tony.' I struggled. 'It's Catherine's wedding, I can't just disappear.' I broke free a second time wishing he'd get the hint.

'That's a shame.' Yet again he pulled me back to him, more aggressively this time. I was desperate to be somewhere else, anywhere but there, but I was frightened to cause a scene. Danger seemed to be seeping from Tony's every pore.

He studied me carefully. 'Not going cold on me are you?'

'No, I'm... look, just not here, OK?' I pulled away and stayed away, straightening myself beside him.

'Why not here...?' His eyes had taken on an angry glint.

'Because it's Catherine's wedding, I told you that.' I adjusted the little red and white button hole I'd carefully pinned to my dress. Tony had managed to squash it when he'd pulled me against him.

He stood back, tilting his head thoughtfully to one side.

'It appears the lovely Maggie has turned into the ice maiden.'

Unnerved, I dropped my focus to the ground.

'And we wouldn't want that, would we?' he went on.

With an unconscious response, I shook my head, just a little, but seemingly enough to give Tony the impression that things were under control, his control.

'Good. Because when I start announcing that you're with me, it would be nice to know you're in agreement.'

This was awful, I had to do something.

'Tony, I think we should wait,' I said quickly.

'And why's that?' he was watching me quizzically.

'This is Catherine's time, not ours. Let's just let Catherine and Nico have their day and then we can think about what to do next.'

'What do you mean, think about what to do next? I thought we'd agreed.'

'No, you agreed. It was your idea, Tony.'

'Meaning...?'

I really didn't want this conversation right then.

'Tony, please, not today. Let's just enjoy the reception. We can talk about this afterwards.'

'What's wrong, Maggie?' He placed his large hand firmly on my shoulder. 'You're backing out on me, I can feel it.' His face took on the angry expression I hated.

'I... listen, not now, OK?'

'Something's happened to change your mind hasn't it? Or should I say some*one's* happened.'

I turned to face him.

'What do you mean?'

'It's that fucking brother of mine isn't it? He's said something.'

'Luke? No. Why? What would Luke say?'

He shrugged and fell silent.

Tony stepped forward and grabbed a glass of champagne from a nearby waiter, not even offering me one. Agitation was oozing from him.

Fuck him! I thought, suddenly beginning to hate him. *What had I ever seen in him?* I stared angrily out from the alcove scanning the main room for friendly, familiar, faces but, momentarily, couldn't see any so I was stuck in this limbo land, just Tony and me. It felt like we were on a desert island with everyone else blurred around us on distant shores. I didn't want to be anywhere near him but my legs and arms felt heavy and restricted. We stood in silence for what felt like an age. I was busy planning my escape, when Tony put down his glass and reached out to me turning me to face him. He lifted my chin up towards him.

'I'm sorry, Maggie, let's not fight.'

I sighed and tugged my face away from him. Here we go again. We'd been here before. There was nothing left for me to say but the inevitable. This was all wrong. I had to tell him how I felt. But before I could decide how to do just that, from across the far end of the room a face caught my attention. A face I recognised. A woman was coming through the crowds her gaze flicking one way and then the other, scouring the room. Suddenly her eyes fixed on her target and her expression changed. She strode forward, moving pointedly through groups of people, excusing herself assertively as she went. She now had a hard, unchanging appearance to her face and clearly knew exactly where she was going and what she wanted. She was heading towards our little alcove; towards us. Her eyes were trained very definitely on Tony and me. Cold, enraged eyes.

Laura.

As she came forward, pushing people out of the way now, there was no mistaking she was angry; very angry. Unease seeped through my body. Any minute now she would be upon us.

I stood rooted to the spot. To go now would have felt like a weak thing to do so I stayed put, praying for some sort of divine intervention. As she came nearer, and people in our eyeline moved out the way, I became aware of something about Laura that I hadn't noticed when she'd walked in. Something that only became apparent as she got closer.

I couldn't believe it. It couldn't be? Oh my God!

Laura… was well and truly pregnant!

Laura reached us and stood there smouldering.

'You bastard!' she spat at Tony – a far cry from the simpering, polite Laura I'd met before.

She turned to me.

'And you, you bitch.'

I looked down at her bump. Yup, definitely pregnant.

I was dumbstruck. So many things were going through my head. How, when, whose was it? Tony's I presumed. And judging by the size of the bump, he would have to have known about it.

Tony was glaring at Laura.

'I thought I told you to stay put,' he hissed.

'Oh yes, you told me all right. And now I can see why?' She tossed her head in my direction. 'Trying to get all cosy with this little whore I suppose, you bastard.'

My face registered shock but I said nothing.

'Tony, what's going on?' I asked, finally.

People had begun to stop around us and have a good nose.

'What's going on? *What's going on?*' Laura raised her voice and more people looked over.

'I'll damn well tell you what's going on, your fucking boyfriend has been cheating on you with his fiancée – get it?' she said sarcastically.

Fiancée? This couldn't be happening. I'd had no idea and I had to make her see that.

'But, Laura… I thought you'd split up and I certainly didn't know you were, well, you know…'

Laura scoffed. 'Pregnant, I think is the word you're after. With child. Up the duff.'

I attempted to piece things together in my head. Laura was clearly several months pregnant so… had she conceived when they were still together? Or even… when she *believed* they were together and Tony had assured me they weren't? Was that it? Had they been a couple all along? Could Tony really have been lying to me from the start?

My mind swirled round and round trying to work things out but whatever was going on, I sincerely wished I wasn't a part of it. What must people think? My mother was going to have kittens.

Seemingly out of nowhere, Luke appeared and walked up to stand in front of Tony.

'It was only a matter of time, Tony. You know that. You may be my brother but I couldn't let this go on any longer.' Luke had a bitter expression on his face.

Oh God, he must have known. Why the hell couldn't he have warned me…or is that what he'd been trying to do?

'Piss off, Luke. This has got nothing to do with you.' Tony said, angrily.

Laura fumed. 'You leave him alone. If it hadn't been for Luke, I wouldn't have known anything about your sordid affair.'

So it was true, Tony had been having the affair with me. Luke had known all along and he'd told Laura. He must really hate me. I felt sick.

'I don't get it,' I began. 'I thought you were cool with all this. When I read your letter I…'

'Letter…?' Laura spat, 'What letter. To who…?'

'To me,' I said, puzzled. 'The letter you sent saying that I was welcome to him.' Laura's gaze went from me to a very uncomfortable looking Tony. An expression of sarcastic satisfaction spread across her face.

'Is that right? she said smugly. 'Well, how interesting. Why don't you tell us all about this letter, Tony? My memory seems to be a little fuzzy and I'd so love you to remind me exactly what I wrote.'

Tony went white.

'Tony?' My voice came out quietly. 'It *was* Laura who wrote me that letter, wasn't it?'

Laura's voicing was mocking. 'Oh sure, I'm really likely to send a letter to my fiancé's bit on the side, aren't I?'

I felt ashamed.

'And what did that letter say exactly? Hmmm?'

'That… that, you were OK with Tony and me being…' I hesitated, stealing a glance at Luke's cold expression '… together. That we wouldn't see you again and you wished us luck.'

Laura laughed loudly, viciously. 'Oh, you'd need luck all right, trying to work out what was true and what was a lie every time this bastard opened his mouth! I think you've been had, Maggie. In fact,' she laughed nastily, 'we've both been had.'

Tony was seething like he was ready to explode.

A crowd had formed and was staring at us now and I could see Pauline close by, clearly wondering whether to intervene.

Laura shook her head in Tony's direction. 'I don't know what you're looking so pissed off about, just because you've been caught. It's me who deserves to be pissed off. Thankfully, there's someone who cares about my welfare a darn sight more than you do. And thanks to him, I find out today that it would be in my interest to show up to this bloody wedding. It's just as well I did by the looks of things.'

Tony scowled at Luke before turning away and stepping forward towards Laura.

'Laura, just leave it! You're causing a scene and making a fool of yourself. We'll talk outside.' He reached to grab her by the shoulder.

'Not so fast!' She jerked away.

Then Laura's face became incredulous. With the flat of her hand she banged her own forehead.

'This is all making sense now. No wonder you tried to keep me away and keep everything so secret with this baby. And you told me it was all because of Jenny.'

'Me?' Suddenly Jenny emerged and rushed forward, glaring angrily from me to Tony to Laura. 'What the hell's going on? What's this got to do with me?' she cried.

'Your darling brother seems to think that, because you lost a baby, I'm not supposed to show myself in case you get upset. But that's rubbish isn't it, Tony dearest. That was just an excuse to keep me out the way.'

Jenny flushed crimson, her eyes wide with shock. John appeared beside her and put his hand on her shoulder. Had she told him? I wondered.

Tony stepped in again. 'Just shut up, Laura, you're causing trouble. This is a wedding.

Have the respect to keep this out of such a special day.'

Through the onlookers I could see my mother approaching, her lips mouthing something fast and inaudible to my father.

'Respect? RESPECT?' Laura yelled. 'Don't you talk to me about respect after what you've done. I'm having your baby and you're having an affair.' Laura's sarcasm was palpable. She paused and a smirk crossed her face. 'And, of course, let's not forget one thing…'

Tony glared at her.

'You knew that if I was around there was more chance of your little secret getting out.'

'What's she talking about?' Jenny's voice rose angrily.

Rex Henderson had arrived beside us and I bit my lip with shame. I hated the idea of anyone thinking I'd known Laura was pregnant, but particularly Mr H.

Luke intervened again. 'Why don't you tell us, Tony? Tell us what Laura's talking about.' Tony squared himself angrily to his brother. 'Just leave it. She's talking rubbish.'

'Tony?' I questioned, finding my voice.

'She's mad,' he replied. 'She doesn't know what the fuck she's talking about.

Come on, Maggie, let's get you out of here.' He pulled me forward.

'No, Tony, stop. I want to hear what Laura has to say,' I was defiant. I caught Luke's eye but looked away immediately.

'I've told you she's mad, she's...'

'Don't give me that,' Laura spat. 'It's you who's mad, my darling fiancé. Huh! Fiancé! That's a joke. The only mad thing I've ever done is to get involved with you and let you talk me into having your baby!'

Laura saw my expression change.

'Yes, that's right. Your doting boyfriend has been on at me for ages for a son and heir, someone to inherit all his worldly goods. And now here I am, pregnant. And guess what? He wants to keep me hidden! Afraid of me finding out about you and, apparently, you finding out about me! And of course, the main thing being, if I turn up I might spill the beans.'

'Leave it, Laura.' Tony reached forward to stop her speaking, but Luke stepped in and pushed him out of the way.

Laura continued. 'I'll tell you what he's really hiding, shall I?'

I nodded, painfully aware by now that the whole room seemed to have fallen silent.

'Mr Perfect here has been trying to manipulate the farm out of his dad,' she said, a look of satisfaction crossing her face.

There were breaths drawn all around us and I turned quickly to see the colour drain from Mr H's face.

Jenny stormed forward again.

'What the fuck are you talking about?' she demanded.

'Jenny!' said her father. 'Remember where you are.'

'No, Dad, not this time. I want to know exactly what she means.'

Laura shrugged. 'Exactly what I said. He's been spending months, years even, trying to win his dad's approval and affection. Taking off at every given moment to "*help out*",' she emphasised sarcastically. 'To go and dig some fields, mow the lawns, mend the sink, you name it, our Tony was daddy's little helper. Only it was all a con and I knew it and *that's* why our wonderful Tony didn't want me around; because every time we had a row, I swore I'd let the cat out of the bag and ruin his little plan.'

Luke was furious. 'This had better not be true, Tony? This had better be one hell of an ugly mistake.' He pushed hard at Tony's shoulder so Tony fell backwards into the alcove, knocking me off balance in the process and causing me to stumble. For a moment I thought I saw anguish in Luke's face.

Tony righted himself and stepped forward again trying to defend himself to Luke.

'You're just worried about your inheritance going to me. Anyway, it's not true. Why on earth would I want to do that? I love my Dad.'

Laura replied, 'Oh yes, you love him so much, you want to make him think you're the perfect son, the most capable one, and the one who's best suited to running the farm just so he leaves it to you to run after he's gone. And of course with a baby on the way, well, all the more reason. I'm surprised you managed to keep it a secret for so long. All because of her I suppose.' She pointed at me again and I blushed fiercely.

'You son of a bitch!' Luke swung at Tony, landing a punch straight to the left side of his face, sending Tony crashing backwards into a table and onto the floor, smashing several glasses.

'Let me at him!' Jenny yelled. 'You bastard! How could you?' She flew forward and tried to grab Tony's hair but Luke caught her arm and manhandled her out the way.

'Leave it, Jen, he's not worth it,' Luke said.

Mr H looked like the wind had been knocked completely out of his sails. Tony clambered up again.

'Dad, please, it's not like that. Don't listen to her.'

His father seemed to study Tony with an expression I couldn't read and Jenny rushed to him hugging him tightly.

'Don't worry, Dad, we'll sort this, I'm here for you. We all are.'

Jenny's eyes were filled with tears. 'How could you, Tony? How could you?'
Finally, Tony's fuse broke and he shot forward to Laura.

'See what you've done, you bitch! This is all your fault.' His hands went
for her neck. Men from all directions ran forward to pull him off Laura, who
lost her balance and tumbled to the floor; people rushed to her assistance –
including Luke. Tony was dragged away from her and I inadvertently moved
forward to help then stopped myself. I was feeling too ashamed.

'Leave me alone. Get off me,' Tony shouted to those attempting to hold
him back. He managed to pull his arms free with such a force that, as he did
so, the back of his hand hit me hard smack in the face and I too fell backwards
to the floor, completely stunned.

'Oh no!' he groaned. 'For God's sake!' Tony cried out into the air, putting
his hands to his face and dragging them roughly back through his hair.

Blood poured from my nose and my mother rushed forward to my rescue,
helping me up with the aid of Catherine's dad. Someone handed me some
tissues, which I held up to stop the bleeding.

Tony was obviously stunned, like a rabbit caught in the headlights. His
anxious eyes flitted nervously first to Laura then to me.

'I'm sorry, Maggie. I didn't mean…' He took a step forward.

'You beast; you brute; get away from her.' Mum staved him off with her
Luis Vuitton handbag. 'Someone call the police. My baby's been hurt.'

'Don't, Mum, it's OK.'

I felt shocked, hurt and ashamed as she ushered me to a nearby chair but I
needed to know how Laura was.

'Mum, please, is Laura OK?'

Laura had been helped to a chair close by, surrounded by people. Her face
was white. She was visibly shaken.

Catherine and Nico now stood gobsmacked beside Jenny.

I felt dreadful. Poor Laura. But I still had to know. I had to know why
Tony had got me involved in it all. He didn't even appear to particularly care
about me. I looked up at him where he stood, defeated, wrecked.

'Why, Tony? Why all this, and why did you get me involved?'

'You wouldn't understand,' he said dismissively.

'Just tell me,' I said.

'Yes, Tony, why don't you?' Laura shouted over.

I met Luke's eyes but I had to turn away again. I was so embarrassed.

'I think I can answer that.' A voice came from behind me. It was Mr H.

He stood calmly staring at Tony. There was no denying the pity he felt for his son.

Mr H was about to say something but then seemed to take in the crowd. He cleared his throat and spoke slowly and evenly.

'I wonder if you kind people would mind giving me a few moments alone with my family and their loved ones; I think a little privacy may go a long way.' He smiled slightly. 'And please, Catherine, Nico, accept my humble apologies. I aim to clear this up as quickly as I can, so your wonderful reception may continue without any more interruptions.' A slow mumble grew from the spectators and gradually they dispersed in different directions.

With the rest of us left alone, Mr H put his hand on my shoulder.

'I'm sorry you had to be dragged into all this, Maggie, I have a feeling none of it was down to you. I don't think Tony really wanted to hurt me either. Did you Tony?'

Tony cast his gaze downwards and shook his head.

Jenny still clutched her father's arm, protectively. 'What do you mean, Dad?'

'I think this has more to do with Luke.'

'*Me?*' Luke was incredulous.

'I'm afraid so, son. I believe we are dealing with a rather nasty case of jealously here.' Luke was clearly bewildered. 'Jealousy? Who's jealous of who?'

'I'm right, aren't I, son?' Mr H said sadly to Tony, whose shamefaced expression fell to the floor.

Mr H continued. 'For some reason I believe Tony thinks you are my favourite son, Luke. He's said as much in a joking aside but I fear that many a true word is spoken in jest.'

'I'm correct aren't I, Tony,' he said softly. 'And I believe he saw young Maggie here as a way to get back at Luke.'

Tony stood quivering, near to tears. I actually felt sorry for him.

Luke looked quizzically at his brother, then at me, then back at Tony.

'Tony? What's Dad talking about?'

Tony's eyes sprung with tears. 'This is all your fault,' he shouted at Luke.

'None of this would have happened if it hadn't been for you!' He let out a pitiful sob. 'It was always you. You were the golden boy. You were the one who could do nothing wrong. You were the one people said was cute and funny. No one gave a damn about me. None of you!' he shouted.

'That's not true, son,' his father said quietly.

'Yes, it damn well is. He got everything; everything! I didn't want him to get the farm too. That's why I wanted to take it. I knew you'd leave it to him. He's the oldest. Huh, get that, the oldest *and* the favourite. I had no chance. I thought if you saw me doing a good job, a really good job, you'd give it to me. I just wanted to make you proud.'

An angry Jenny launched in again. 'No, you didn't. You wanted to trick him.'

'I didn't!' Tony cried. 'Jen, please believe me, I didn't mean it to be like this, any of it. It just got out of hand.'

'The farm is left equally to all three of you,' their father answered gently. 'I love you all equally.'

'Well, it didn't feel like that,' Tony said, taking a handkerchief out of his pocket and blowing his nose loudly. He sat down dejectedly on a nearby chair.

Rex Henderson walked over to him and put his hand on his son's shoulder.

'Perhaps you can explain to Maggie why you involved her, Tony.' I couldn't believe how calm he was being.

Tony started shaking his head. He glared up at Luke with a mixture of anger and defeat in his eyes. 'You had everything. The looks, the charm, that "little boy lost" appeal that everyone seemed to dote on. You got the best toys and all the attention and then...' his voice cracked, '... then you even took my mother.'

Luke was stunned.

'Mum?!'

'Yes, Mum. If it hadn't been for you she'd still be here. If you hadn't gone on about ice- cream, if you hadn't made her go out in the car, she'd still be alive.' Tony put his head in his hands. His shoulders shook. He sobbed noisily.

Luke's expression was one of puzzlement; his eyes were flicking from side to side, as if he was trying to recall the past.

'But, Tony, it wasn't like that. I didn't...' Luke stopped suddenly, his mouth fell open. 'Shit.'

My mind was working overtime and memories of the past sprung up. *But... that wasn't how it had happened.* I clearly remembered Luke telling me the whole story. It had been a very young Tony begging for the ice cream that day, not Luke.

Luke remained silent. He must have realised Tony's mistake but said nothing. He was bound to be feeling terrible.

Tony looked up, wiping his tear-streaked face on his sleeve.

'So, now it was my turn,' he continued. 'I wanted to take the one thing… the one person…' he nodded over to where I was sitting, '… you wanted more than anything.'

I froze with shock.

Catherine came up behind me and put her hand on my shoulder.

Luke rubbed his brow then ran his fingers through his soft blond hair. He suddenly looked overwhelmingly tired and tears filled his eyes.

'No, Tony,' he said quietly, his voice breaking with emotion. 'You got it wrong, bro. You got it so very wrong.'

With that, Luke walked away from the alcove, squeezed Laura on the shoulder giving her a reassuring smile, then made his way out in the direction of the main doors. My heart left me for a moment and I desperately wanted to reach out to him, to take his pain away.

Mr H stepped forward to Tony. 'I think you and I need a little talk, don't you, son?' He took Tony's arm and helped him up then led him gently away.

Soon after, Laura stood up to go too. While I was relieved she seemed OK, I hated myself for wondering if she'd be following Luke. After all, she'd said he cared about her far more than Tony did and that had been clear today. I felt an urge to say something to her but what could I say? How could I possibly make this situation any better? As she left, she looked over at me and we held eye contact for a second or two. Then she shook her head, as if with pity, and walked away.

Mum helped me to the toilets to be cleaned up and, for once, she didn't have any cutting remarks.

She fetched two lots of toilet roll from one of the cubicles, wet them slightly under the warm tap then dabbed the first over my bloody nose and the other gently around my eye. I really hoped I wasn't going to have another shiner.

'My poor baby,' she soothed as she dabbed.

Actually, I felt a bit like a poor baby right then. I felt a fool, a stupid fool. I had been completely taken in by Tony. All that time he'd made me think he was with me. All those occasions he'd said he was trying to make things right between us. I realised, suddenly, that he'd probably not been working away at all, maybe he'd never even been to Paris or New York or Geneva; they'd likely just been smokescreens. The gifts he'd supposedly brought me back could have come from anywhere. Had he, in reality, been leading a 'normal' everyday life with Laura? No wonder he hadn't wanted me to come to his

London flat. He and Laura probably spent a lot of their time there. That would have accounted for why I'd seen Laura in London, with Luke. I could have kicked myself for being so naïve. Tony had used me to get at Luke and I'd fallen for it. Tony's words to Luke rang in my head:

'I wanted to take the one thing, the one person, I knew you wanted more than anything else'

For a few moments when he'd spoken, I'd had hope. Hope that Tony was right and that Luke still wanted me, but then when Luke told Tony he'd got things so very wrong, my hopes had been crushed. I could have handled a black eye, two black eyes. I could have handled all of it, if it had been true. If Tony had been right. But like Luke said, he'd got it all wrong. Tony had simply been caught up in the past. I knew what that felt like.

Mum put her hand on my arm. 'Would you like to stay with us tonight... for a few days even, until you feel a bit better?' she asked kindly.

'Maybe,' I replied.

'You can stay for as long as you like.'

Somehow things got back to normal and the reception continued. Once people had said their piece to those concerned, offering sympathy and understanding, the wedding quite simply picked itself up again. Music started and the mood was lifted. There were so many people who hadn't been involved in the fracas that, amazingly, it seemed quite easy to carry on and the upheaval was all but forgotten.

Catherine and Nico were full of smiles again and the smell of food was coming through the double doors from the kitchens.

Had it not been my best friend's wedding I would have made my excuses and left but I put on my bravest face ever and carried on with the day.

I scanned the room for Luke but he was nowhere to be seen. He'd probably gone home to escape the crowds. A big part of me wished I could have gone with him, talked to him; but to say what? It would have been embarrassing for us both. He'd said everything I needed to hear. It was painful but I had to accept it. I wished I could have just switched off my feelings but there was no denying it, I still loved him so much.

It wasn't long before we were called for the meal. The food looked delicious, it was a shame I wasn't really hungry. Silver platters came out carried by young and attractive waiting staff, all smiles and good manners. In a break with tradition the oblong top table consisted purely of the bride and groom and their parents. I sat on a round table close by with little Jasmine and Kate to my left, and making up the rest of the table were Jenny, John, Timmy, Pauline, and finally Sarah, who sat to my right.

'You OK?' she asked kindly.

'I'll live,' I said. 'Thanks for asking.'

I surreptitiously watched Jenny, I was sure she would still be upset. I hoped she wouldn't blame me. But I needn't have worried. She must have felt me watching her because she looked up and her eyes became kind as she gave me a resigned smile. No doubt there would be time for us to talk.

As we were eating our dessert – tiny chocolate logs with little sparklers in them for fireworks night – the waiting staff came round with champagne and we settled in, ready for the speeches. Matteo as the best man spoke first with thick, accented but very good English and had us in stitches as he told and acted out the story of how Nico had been caught trying to steal a pig when he was a young boy and how his parents had been called to the police station and had to make out they were really cross, when all they could think of was how they could have fed the family for weeks! Apparently they used to be poor.

Catherine's father stood up and made us all cry, talking about how happy he was that his little girl had turned out so lovely and pretty and clever and how much he was looking forward to getting to know his new son-in-law and his family. He also hinted at the possibility of a grandchild which made Nico blush and he and Catherine had a little cuddle. We all said 'Ahhh' then.

Nico's mother stood up and spoke in amazingly clear English, on behalf of her and her husband who didn't speak it quite so well. We watched as she squeezed Catherine's hand and told her how happy she was to welcome her into the family.

Nico finally stood and made us all cry again as he told everyone how it would be impossible to love anyone more than he loved Catherine.

It wouldn't be long before they left to start their new life in Tillmouth. London wouldn't be the same without Catherine and thinking of it then, on top of everything else, made me feel even more lonely and bleak. Soon I wouldn't have a job, Catherine would be gone and I'd have to temp again.

I thought about Mum's offer of staying with her and Dad for a while but I knew now that wouldn't work. I'd stay tonight, but that would be enough. Luke was here, Laura was here. There was no place for me. With a sudden pang of intense jealously, I wondered if Luke and Laura might actually get together. After all, regardless of anything that may or may not have happened before, there was nothing to stop them now. I screwed up my eyes at the vision that had come into my mind. Luke and Laura and more little Henderson babies.

I needed to get this day and night over and done with. I had to head back to London before anyone could make me feel any worse than I already did.

Jasmine tugged at my arm interrupting my thoughts.

'Why has your nose all got blood in it?'

'It's a long story.'

'Like a bedtime story.'

'No, not really.'

'I like stories,' she said thoughtfully.

'Do you?'

'So you can tell me if you like.'

I smiled, despite myself.

'I banged my head on a table,' I lied.

'That wasn't a very long story.'

'No, it wasn't was it. Never mind, maybe I'll read you a bedtime story the next time we both go and stay with Aunty Catherine.'

She seemed suitably appeased.

'Have you been to our house before?' she asked.

'No, I don't think I have.'

'We've got a sandpit,' she announced proudly.

'That sounds fun. Do you like playing in it and making sand castles?'

'Sometimes,' she said, 'but once I did and Daddy made me go and wash my hands cos they got all mucky.'

I paused.

'Uh huh.'

'Do you know Tom?' We'd apparently moved on.

'Tom who?'

'Tom the cat! Aunty Catherine's cat.' Jasmine frowned at my ignorance.

'Yes, I know Tom.'

'Well Aunty Catherine brought him over one day and he pooed in our sandpit,' she said seriously.

'Ah,' I realised the significance. 'Is that why you had to wash your hands?'

'Yes. My daddy said I had to use the nailbrush too, 'cos it was all under my nails.' She studied her nails carefully.

'Well, I'm sure Tom didn't realise it was your sandpit.'

'No, he probably didn't.'

'I licked my finger and Daddy told me off,' Jasmine continued, obviously not finished with the subject.

I looked down at the remains of my chocolate log, which seemed to have lost its appeal.

It was dark outside now and the room had been gently lit giving a warm ambience to the occasion.

We had coffee and before long the tables were cleared and the band members were setting up on the stage. Not long after, the main lights were turned right down, the stage and dance floor were lit up, and the band began. It was, of course, time for the bride and groom to take their turn on the dance floor for the first dance. A spotlight had been rigged up, which followed them around the floor as they held each other close. Sitting watching them, it struck me I'd never had the chance to have a love like that; an equal, reciprocal love. The only person I'd ever really loved didn't love me back. I saw that now. Had Luke ever loved me?

From behind me, Cousin Robert's chubby hand appeared on my shoulder, making me jump. He leant down and spoke in my ear.

'I say, seems like there might be a bit of an opening don't you think? What!'

'Sorry?'

'Well, your chap's buggered orf so you'll be needing a partner. What!' Unfortunately, I couldn't think of a suitable rebuff so, before I knew it, as the music changed and more couples joined Catherine and Nico, I was pulled up too and was soon being twirled and whirled boisterously around the dance floor. Every now and then, I caught sight of Sarah, Pauline and Timmy giggling in my direction. Jenny, who had apparently gotten over the events of earlier, had her back to me and was going totally over the top and pretending to snog the air while groping her own shoulders, back and bum as if she was in a clinch with someone. John was trying half-heartedly to make her stop but couldn't keep from laughing.

Holding on for dear life, Robert was sweating profusely, which was very off-putting as the quicker we twirled, the more the beads of sweat sprayed off in various directions, including mine. The music changed again but, despite my protestations, he wouldn't let me go! This was much to the continued amusement of the table. Finally, at the end of the song, I managed to make my excuses but not before Robert had whipped out his phone again and was insisting I gave him my number. I could hear Jenny howling mercilessly and I thought about giving Robert her number instead but decided it might not be such a good idea in the long run. So, I gave him Pauline's and hoped she wouldn't be too mad with me when I explained later.

Escaping, I moved out the way of the bright lights of the dance floor and, feeling the need for some well-earned time out, slipped round the back of the tables and out through some double doors, one of which had been opened a little to let in some cool night air.

Outside, the large lit terrace was free of people apart from one of the hotel staff who was lighting the upright gas heaters around the tables. I walked through the blanket of heat they gave off and out to the relative darkness on the other side. Right then it was cool fresh air I needed to clear my head. Later, when the fireworks started, everyone would be heading out in droves to watch them light up the night sky but for now, thankfully, I was on my own. I was glad to finally have some space. Usually I would have felt excited and lifted up into the spirit of the moment with the possibility of fireworks; I'd always loved them. But I just felt sad.

The young guy finished lighting the last patio heater and as he disappeared inside I wandered further across the terrace to where it ended and a slope down to the lawns began. Leaning over the stone wall surround, I breathed in the night air and watched as it escaped through my mouth, turning a ghostly white in the cold air.

A sudden voice behind me startled me.

'The last time I saw you on a hotel terrace, you were kissing another man.'

A second passed before I turned, my heart in my mouth, only to see the face that I knew belonged to the voice.

Luke.

He stood just a few feet away from me, the moonlight behind him casting his face in shadow so I couldn't see his expression. The music swirled from inside and I glanced past him, through the glass doors, to see people hurling themselves around the dance floor safely out of earshot.

In my confusion, I found my voice and, from somewhere deep inside me, I spoke.

'What hotel? Who was I… kissing?'

'The reunion. You were outside with that Elvis guy from your year.'

I thought back.

'But… you weren't at the reunion.' I still couldn't see his face.

'Yes, I was. Just briefly.'

I was completely taken aback.

'Jenny said you were working!'

'That's what I told her. I didn't want anyone to know I was over. I didn't know if I'd have the courage to turn up that night.'

Confused thoughts whirled around my mind, colliding with each other.

'But you did come…'

A brief silence passed.

'Let's just say, in the end, I couldn't keep away.'

'I didn't see you…'

'Nobody did. I stayed on the edge – on the edge of the terrace to be precise.'

He'd moved forward slightly and I saw a trace of a smile cross his lips.

I suddenly felt sick. Had Luke been the person I'd heard while Elvis and I were having that kiss? Had he really seen us?

Embarrassed, I looked down to the ground.

'But you didn't go in; why?'

His deep, assured voice caressed the air. 'Don't you know?'

I shook my head.

'Well, let me see now. My school reunion, my perfect girl; you'd think I'd have wanted to come in, wouldn't you?'

I said nothing. Unable to allow myself to believe he could have been talking about me.

'And then, there she was with some idiot from school, who really didn't deserve to be anywhere near her, let alone kiss her. I realised then that I'd probably lost her, so I left. I went back to my mate's house. I hadn't told anyone I was going, probably because I didn't know myself if I could face her.'

I couldn't take this in. *Perfect girl? Lost her?*

'Her?' I faltered.

'You, Maggie.'

He moved a step closer and then another and my heart caught in my throat.

'Tony was right about one thing,' he said slowly.

'Was he?' My voice squeaked. My eyes had grown wide.

He took another step and I could feel the energy sparking between us.

'He was taking the one person in the world I wanted.'

Then with one more step, he was there. Directly in front of me, so close, so very, very close. I almost lost my balance, my feelings were so strong.

Luke reached forward and touched my cheek and I thought I'd pass out.

'It's always been you, Maggie. Always. Don't you know that?' he said hoarsely.

I shook my head, dumfounded.

'Ever since you knocked around with my kid sister, I thought you were adorable. Ever since we got together all those years ago, I've known. I don't think I've ever forgiven myself for treating you the way I did.'

Catherine's words came flooding back to me and I managed to find my voice.

'You were young, Luke, we both were. It was a long time ago. It doesn't matter now.'

His anxious eyes sought mine. His gaze was intense. 'What do you mean it doesn't matter?'

'I don't mind anymore.'

When Luke spoke again, there was panic in his voice.

'Maggie, please tell me exactly what you mean. Are you saying...' he took a breath then exhaled slowly. '...are you saying you don't care about me?'

I looked at him, up close now. I could see his face, the moonlight picking out his strong jaw darkened with a five o'clock shadow. His straight nose, his smooth skin, his deep blue eyes fixed on me, searching, desperate, passionate. There was no mistaking it. Luke was scared I might not feel the same way.

'Luke, I... I just meant... it's the past. What happened, happened. I don't blame you anymore. It... well, it hurt that's all. So much...' I trailed off.

He ran his hand through his hair and sighed, shaking his head, clearly ashamed.

'I was such an idiot. I should have come back from uni. I *wanted* to come back. You have to believe me, Maggie.'

'Then what stopped you?'

He was silent for a few moments.

'Tony, I guess. If he hadn't warned me to stay away, I would have been back like a shot to see for myself that you were OK. But even then it was touch and go. I still thought about coming back but, when you didn't answer my letter...' his voice trailed off.

It seemed to be the time for confusion.

'What letter? And what do you mean Tony warned you to stay away. When? Why?'

'He told me you were pregnant and that you wanted nothing to do with me, ever. I wouldn't have it at first. I was determined to see you... nothing could have stopped me... except when Tony drummed into me all the things you'd said about me, how much you hated me and how I'd ruined your life, finally he managed to convince me I was the last person you wanted around and it was best for you that I respected that. So I did, I stayed put. I guess I really didn't want to hurt you any more than I had.'

I couldn't believe what I'd heard. This was a completely different version of events to the one Tony had given me.

'And the letter?' I asked.

Luke frowned.

'You didn't get the letter?'

I shook my head and he sniffed a laugh.

'I remember it well. Heartache, poured over pages and pages. Explanations, apologies, you name it, it went in the letter. But I don't get it. I gave it to Tony to...,' he paused, '... shit. He didn't give it to you, did he?'

'No, he didn't give me any letter, Luke. Tony's been lying to you. He's been lying to all of us. I wasn't pregnant. I wasn't even *nearly* pregnant. At your Dad's seventieth, Tony told me that all those years ago, after we... well, you know... you'd old him that the condom broke and you were scared in case I was pregnant and that's why you stayed away.'

'What? But... yeah, sure that bit about the condom was true. And I *was* scared. I admit that and I did confide in Tony that I was worried I might have got you pregnant, that's why I didn't write straight away, I needed to get my head straight... but you being pregnant wouldn't have kept me away. Not on your life! God, I can't believe he convinced you I'd do that.' Luke looked crestfallen.

'Tony called me at the digs,' he continued, 'and said he had to see me. He came up to uni one lunchtime. I remember it like it was yesterday. He sat me down on a bench in the grounds and told me you were pregnant; that you were going to get rid of it.'

I shook my head. 'It wasn't true, Luke. Tony said he tried to convince you to come back to Tillmouth and make things right but that you refused.'

'I don't believe it!' He turned away angrily. 'I even emigrated to Sweden to try and get over you. He's completely screwed things up for us.'

A moment's silence passed between us, then I reached forward and tentatively took Luke's hand.

'Has he?'

His head swivelled back and his big blue eyes stared questioningly into mine.

'We're here now,' I said quietly.

Luke reached up once again to touch my cheek, smoothing a lock of hair behind my ear.

I breathed in the familiar and erotic aroma of Luke's skin as his fingers touched my cold face. I'd never forgotten the scent of him. It had always seemed so… right. I felt tears mount in my eyes. My emotions were running over. I suddenly felt myself hurting again, a bittersweet pain. I loved him so much. The feelings were as strong now as they had ever been.

Luke broke the tension gently stroking my spiralled hair.

'I've missed those sexy curls of yours. I've missed *you*, Maggie. Everything about you.'

I looked down blinking back the tears, not wanting him to see me blush.

'So, has Tony won?' he asked.

I looked up. 'What do you mean?'

'Did he … get you, like he planned?'

I paused.

No, Luke, Tony never got me. He played a good game of trying to win me and, for a while, I thought it might work but he wasn't y…' I stopped myself quickly.

'He wasn't what? What, Maggie?' He searched my face, urgently, taking both my shoulders in his hands.

I felt shy and uncertain. I'd been so hurt. So many years of pain. I couldn't go through that again.

'Luke, I don't know if this is right… I…'

'Maggie, please. What were you going to say?'

'No, stop, I'm not sure about this, about any of it.'

I tried to compose myself. Warning bells were sounding in my head.

'What about Sian?' I blurted out.

Luke looked puzzled.

'What about her?'

'Haven't you got some unfinished business?'

He shook his head, perplexed.

'Sian's history. We should never have been together for so long.'

'But…' this was it; this was the moment '… the baby. What about the baby?' Luke's look of surprise was genuine.

'What baby?'

'Yours and Sian's baby.'

'Maggie, you've lost me.'

I thought back.

'I heard you on the phone at the farm. I heard you talking about her being pregnant. You sounded so angry.'

His face seemed to be searching for the memory.

'Wait a minute...' he said. 'That wasn't Sian on the phone that was Laura! She called me, one of the many times she called me about Tony, in a right state about the way he was acting. And she just blurted it out.'

I started piecing things together.

'But...I heard you call her Sian.'

Luke looked bemused then realization crossed his face along with a broadening smile.

'You're right! I did! I *did* call her Sian. It was by accident though. I just came out with the wrong name in the heat of the moment.'

'So... Sian's not pregnant then?' I stammered.

'No! No, she's not. Oh my God, I can't believe this. What a mess.' He was shaking his head now but with an incredulous grin on his face. 'What an absolute mess. You know the crazy thing is Sian *thought* she was pregnant, a little while back. That's probably why I used her name on the phone, instead of Laura's. That's why we got engaged. That's why I was going to marry her. I guess I thought I'd run out on one pregnancy, I sure as hell wasn't going to do it again. But it was a false alarm, thankfully. She'd been on these antibiotics at the time and the test showed positive but, when it came to it, she wasn't. The doctors said these things happen sometimes, drugs interfering with tests, you know...?' He was talking fast now but trailed off again, as he realised I'd been staring at him.

He smiled.

I smiled back.

'So before...?' he began, questioningly, 'When you didn't finish what you were saying...?'

Again, I looked down, my cheeks growing warm.

'Is there any chance you might have been about to say, what I think you might have been about to say?' He tilted his head on one side. He was teasing me now.

I looked up at him and so desperately wanted to kiss him.

'That depends on what you thought I was going to say, doesn't it,' I said tilting my head to the opposite side, my smile widening.

He dug me in the ribs.

'Ouch!' I dug him back and he began to tickle me, just like he'd done in the past.

I squirmed and started to giggle, then he started too and we writhed around together like a couple of teenagers. But after a little while, we both stopped suddenly and once again our gaze locked.

'I was going to say, he wasn't you,' I finally finished.

Luke's eyes were misty. 'Maggie, do you know how long I've wanted you? Do you know how many nights I have lain awake thinking about you? It was always you, Maggie, always. I…' He stopped, hesitating as his words left him. He gently drew me towards him then held my face tenderly in his strong hands, before reaching down and kissing me very softly. I melted into him, my eyes closed in ecstasy. After a while he broke away and smiled lovingly at me.

'I love you, Maggie Parsons, I completely and utterly love you,' he said.

'I love you too, Luke.'

'Peanuts and Eggcups,' he said softly.

'Huh?'

'Remember the game.'

'Of course!' I answered, my heart smiling.

'We were the only ones to ever get the peanut in the eggcup, remember?'

'I remember.'

'Against all odds. Even though everyone said we couldn't do it, we didn't give up. We just kept on going for it, until we made it happen.'

He squeezed me to him and I squeezed him back.

We stood like that in each other's arms for what felt like ages, rocking gently to the music in the background.

Suddenly, the doors across the terrace crashed open loudly and people began spilling out on to the terrace.

'The fireworks are about to begin,' my dad called breathlessly, rushing in our direction, closely followed by Mum. Dad appeared to take in Luke and me together and he smiled knowingly at us both. His white shirt was open and his tie had obviously been banished to his pocket. He looked hot from dancing and his eyes were alive as he pulled my mother behind him, her face flushed, seemingly quite happy to be pulled. Mum threw back her head, laughing as they ran off down the bank towards the men standing with torches ready for the start.

Other people followed. Among them Jenny, who, at first, frowned quizzically, then rolled her eyes and tutted before heading off. I heard her indignantly say to someone… 'Honestly, I'm always the last one to know anything around here!'

Another load of guests came out then and Catherine and Nico were in the centre of them. Catherine caught my eye, glanced at Luke then smiled happily at the two of us.

We watched as everyone joyfully made their way down to the bonfire.

Then Luke looked back at me and grabbed my hand.

'Come on then, you, let's go and watch these fireworks.'

Closing his hand tightly around mine, he pulled me with him and we ran down the grassy bank, following the others, laughing as we went.

'And then who knows…' Luke called out, panting breathlessly beside me, '… later, we might just make some fireworks of our own.'

I laughed recklessly beside him.

'Oh by the way,' he added… 'these Sting tickets of yours…'

*

A few moments ago I had a call on my mobile from, get this, The Horse! Sandra, my old CapiTel client. Amazingly, the job I applied for is with her new company! She and Alexander have apparently split up. He'd been having an affair… and here's the bizarre bit… he was having an affair… with Justin! Can you believe it!?

When I heard the news, I immediately thought about the inscription on the bracelet that Mandy had talked about. We'd all thought it was S for Sandra. I couldn't work it out at first but then Sandra referred to Alexander as Sandy. Of course! He's Scottish and Alexander often gets shortened to Sandy in Scotland! Wonders will never cease.

Anyway, Sandra is thrilled about the interview and says it's only red tape. What with all my experience and her knowing me and all that, she really wants me to join the firm and, do you know… so do I. It sounds pretty much perfect, for now anyway. I'm so glad I held out for something better.

I'm on my way to Tillmouth in a little while, to the farm. Luke and I are going to be staying there for a bit while we look around for our own place.

Somewhere close by, near our real homes and near Catherine. Luke and I both love the country, unlike Tony who'd only pretended to love it as part of his little charade.

The good thing is, Tony is getting help and he and his dad are sorting things out together and, bit by bit, I think the family will be OK.

I'm just packing up my things. Timmy's taking over my flat. He moved in after the wedding and he's going to take on the tenancy when I leave. It's all worked out really well, because he's managed to land himself a job at the off licence of all places. Charlie's emigrated to Texas with Marylou, Jinny Lou and Tex. Before he left he put in a good word (seeing as I'd always been such a good customer) and managed to swing Timmy the job. The weird thing is that when Timmy and I were hauling his things up the stairs (the lift's still broken), we bumped into Pip. He explained that Andrew had moved out. He couldn't handle Pip's somewhat scattered approach to life. And Pip had never really forgiven him for the Leo business. Anyway, let's put it this way, by the look in Timmy's eye and the way Pip blushed when Timmy winked at him, I wouldn't be surprised if it was a bit more than a cup of sugar Timmy would be after from his new neighbour.

So, like I said before, sometimes things are just meant to be. If you'd have asked me nine months ago whether I believed in fate I'd have answered, only the village one where still, to this day, I clutch my sides giggling helplessly about a particularly hilarious incident involving my mother, a pint of scrumpy and a large drunk dairy cow. I never did tell you that story did I? Never mind, another day, perhaps.

The thing is... thinking about those last nine months and everything that's happened, I reckon Cat was definitely onto something. Visualising and focussing on what you want seemed to work for both of us very successfully. And Margot's Law of Attraction, well that seemed to be working whether I liked it or not! Probably worth looking into that a little more in the future. So, the question is, do I believe in fate?

Well, Luke and I finally found our way back to each other even in the face of adversity. Like it was meant to happen... so perhaps I do. I find it rather comforting to think that there's a helping hand somewhere, guiding us to the paths we've chosen, or that are best for us... so perhaps fate, destiny, is all a part of that.

In the end though, it seems that whatever roads we choose, whatever decisions we make and whatever life throws at us along the way... things have a habit of working out for the best. Life's funny like that, don't you think? Ultimately, we arrive at the right places, with the right people... and perhaps most importantly, at the right time... and, however that happens, I'm extremely grateful.

The End.

Lightning Source UK Ltd.
Milton Keynes UK
UKOW02f0142040716

277647UK00001B/1/P